Four Leaf Cross

Alex Goble
Jacob Converse

For Gary and Becky Heimark

Without them, there would be no Glen Dale

Preface

I was twelve years old, in the sixth grade, sitting at the kitchen counter, talking to my mom about my day at school while she washed dishes. The phone started ringing, and I could see the Caller ID from where I was sitting. I wasn't expecting a call, but I knew it was for me.

"Hello?"

"Goble!" the voice of my best friend Erik exclaimed through the speaker. "You busy this weekend?"

I paused briefly to think before answering, "No, what's up?"

"You want to come over this weekend and fight gunnysacks?"

"Fight...gunnysacks?" Did I hear him right?

"Yeah!" he answered, as if he'd proposed something as normal as a game of kickball. "I put a bunch of gunnysacks on fence posts out in the woods and my dad's been making wooden swords for me! I've got shields, too, and a bow we can shoot arrows with if we're careful."

Oh. *Now* it made more sense. Erik and I had spent years playing in the woods with sticks pretending to defend the realm against ogres and trolls. It still sounded a bit strange to me, beating up on empty feed sacks from their farm, but I really wanted to use one of those wooden swords, and I agreed to go.

That weekend marked the very first Gunnysack War on the Heimark farm, and I'd never had so much fun in my life. We didn't have a grand story or our own defined characters back then. Erik, his sister, myself, and a couple other friends decked ourselves out in peasant's flannel and stormed the colored autumn wilderness with our wooden weaponry, vanquishing our feed sack foes as we slipped through the mud of the previous night's rain. We had a campfire with a kettle full of stew, served in wooden bowls with a side of Tolkien-inspired lembas bread, both made by Erik's mom Becky, who we still to this day affectionately call "The Missus."

When the day was done and the battle was won, we all agreed that we needed to have another Gunnysack War. Over the course of that winter, when we would visit the Heimark farm, we would "forge" weapons and armor in the basement, using Erik's Lord of the Rings encyclopedia as our guide. The next spring, we gathered once again for another Gunnysack War. This time, we constructed characters and stories for ourselves. We gave ourselves a king named Bartholomew to fight for, in the land of the Glen Dale. The gunnysacks became more than just outlaws and rogues, but bloodthirsty orcs with a warchief threatening to conquer our kingdom and all of its commonfolk.

A second Gunnysack War turned into a third, and then more after that, our stories and our characters growing each time we rallied at the Heimark farm to defend the Glen Dale. We always had a basic idea as to who we were waging war against, but for the most part, we allowed the story to develop organically rather than follow a specific script. We'd relive the tale we'd spun later that night and excitedly conjure stories for our next campaign.

At first, the Gunnysack Wars were our closely kept secret. In a small town high school, everyone knows your name, and for most of us, it's a daily battle to fit in, to seem like an acceptable human being amongst your peers. Some of us were varsity football players. Others were stars in the prestigious production that was the high school musical. One of us would even be crowned Homecoming King our senior year. In the early days of our secondary educations, the thought of everyone knowing about our annual tromps in the woods wearing bright costumes and wielding wooden weaponry seemed like social suicide.

In the twilight of our senior year, we were still getting together at least twice a year to defend the Glen Dale against evil. We even brought in more friends to share the experience. We began to realize that most of us didn't care quite so much anymore if others found out about our unique hobby. And, to our surprise, most that did find out weren't appalled or even judgmental. To this day, as a grown adult, I've revealed the secret of the Gunnysack Wars to new friends, and nobody seems to even bat an eye at the idea. I feel very fortunate to live in an era where being such a nerd isn't considered outrageously taboo.

As we got older, we'd often ask ourselves if we'd ever grow out of the Gunnysack Wars. Some of us did, and that's all right. As in any tale of adventure, friends and allies come and go, even when their impact resonates thousands of pages later. Most of us, however, continued to gather for our adventures, even through college. It was difficult, of course, because we had to plan around more than just our summer jobs. We were all growing up, and it sometimes required months of planning to tab a weekend that suited everyone. Two or three Gunnysack Wars a year wasn't realistic anymore. To keep our story growing, we began to write short stories to share with one another.

Real life happened. We graduated college, and we moved on to find our own paths. While we hoped to continue our Gunnysack tradition, we knew our opportunities would be few and far between. We had pictures, memories, and a collection of short stories to hold on to. I decided that wasn't enough for me. The tales of the Glen Dale needed to be written in book form, from the beginning, and words can't describe how happy I am to have the first completed.

I have a few thank-yous to get to, but I first wanted to address you, dear reader, for as you turn the pages of Four Leaf Cross, you're likely going to notice some themes you recognize from other books or otherwise, especially if you're from my generation. I want to reiterate that the Gunnysack Wars is a collaborative effort, and when we crafted our tales so many years ago, most of our young minds were inspired by literary icons like Tolkien, Weis, and Hickman. I believe that our story has matured and grown an identity of its own, but I'm not the least bit embarrassed to admit that many seeds were sown to grow the garden. I've spent a great deal of time debating on whether or not to arbitrarily change the names of races, people, and even some elements of spellcraft in order to disguise those inspirations. In the end, I decided against it. I consider these similarities a tribute to the stories we all enjoyed. Without them, we would have never donned any cloaks or strapped any swords to our belts.

I cannot share this book without first thanking my dear friend, the previously mentioned Erik Heimark. While my specialty is the quill and the ink, the most inspiring and creative person among us is undoubtedly him. The weaponry and armor he was able to create was nothing short of astounding, and I can't tell you how many selfless hours that man has spent crafting amazing costumes and props for his friends. He's a brilliant storyteller as well, and while I was always quick to inject our tales with grandiose magic and thundering dragons, he was the one who could dream up realistic and intriguing cultures, using both true historical references and the exciting elements of fantasy to give our tales the lifeblood they needed. He was also the one that was awake at dawn for every Gunnysack War to prepare the fields of battle, and though we all helped pick up the "bodies" at the end of the day, I know how much time he spent cleaning up our mess when we all left to return to reality. Thank you, Heimark, for your inspirations, your patience, and for your unconditional friendship since second grade. None of this would have happened without you.

I also have to thank one of my best friends and co-author, Jacob Converse. He moved to our town in my freshman year of high school, where I first met him at football practice. It didn't take long for us to become friends, and we invited him to attend the Gunnysack Wars a year later. Since then, he's been one of our most stalwart members, and as of this writing, is the only one among us to boast a tattoo depicting an Aariad crest. He's spent countless hours cataloging our stories, chronologically arranging them, and editing the abundance of mistakes we all leave behind. He's been my greatest supporter in this endeavor, and holds the Gunnysack Wars to as high of a standard as I do, if not more so. When I finished the first draft of this book, he wasn't afraid to tell me that he thought it could be better, and he was right. We've been on a lot of battlefields together, in the Gunnysack Wars and in real life, and I know I can always count on him. Thank you, Converse, for your hard work, your never-ending support, and for all our talks around the campfire.

Thank you also to my good friend and fellow author Chase Potter for all of his guidance on self-publishing. There's a lot more work that goes into this than I thought there would be, and it would have been far more difficult without his help. He's saved me hours of turmoil and frustration.

Thank you to my cousin Rachel for the beautiful cover portrait. It's an absolutely stunning job from a supremely talented artist.

Lastly, I want to thank everyone else who was a part of the Gunnysack Wars growing up, whether they're still involved or have said farewell. This project, both in writing and in-person, has been one of the most memorable and happiest experiences in my life. Thank you for everything.

And with that, I'm proud to present the first book in The Gunnysack Wars, Four Leaf Cross. It's my sincerest hope that you'll enjoy reading it half as much as I enjoyed writing it.

Long live the Glen Dale.

Prologue

The Forging of the World

In the beginning, there was nothing. And from nothing, Beginning was born. From the bleak eternal space, a great and terrible being manifested, surrounded by emptiness. What emerged from the void has many different faces, the shape and colors decided by those that tell the tale. The elves speak of this titan as Y'nashtas of All Colors, the Grendosians across the sea refer to him as Chaos, the sworn enemy of order and discipline, and the dwarves of Dur'Imoir go so far as to say that The First Forger, as they call him, was born in the image of a great dwarf with a flaming beard and a hammer of pure diamond.

Whichever interpretation is true, all agree that Beginning was both lonely and baffled by his own spontaneous existence. The creation of his children, the Four Forgers, was an accident and a miracle, and when the first god saw what he had given life to, he only further descended into madness, bewildered by his own unbridled power. His children, alarmed by the enraged entity, subdued Beginning, both pitying his confusion and fearing what he might further unleash. The one who would become known as Gapinon created the first world, a prison for Beginning. They locked the mad god within that world, where he yet resides today.

That task complete, the four remaining gods looked upon one another. The shared experience created a bond between them, a comfort in the face of the great challenge that laid before them: what would they do with the great oblivion that surrounded them?

"Can you make more of those?" the one who would be called Kaijaras asked to Gapinon, referring to the world he had forged for their chaotic father.

"Let us see!" Gapinon responded enthusiastically. And make more of them he did, his hands molding great existences in the vast space of darkness. When there were half a dozen before the four of them, they looked upon them and saw empty canvasses, simple color splotches against the void.

"We should fill them with something!" the goddess named Essence proclaimed. The others agreed, even Kagothai, who was most shy and timid of the Four Forgers. And so Gapinon took hammer and chisel and carved out beautiful mountains, valleys, oceans and rivers, all the beautiful sights one can see when traveling across the lands.

"They need something more," Kaijaras proclaimed, rubbing his chin thoughtfully. What were their worlds missing? Then it came to him. Their father's world was occupied by the great thundering lord. Their new worlds needed inhabitants! Sensing the gift that Beginning had unwittingly bestowed upon him, Kaijaras began to create life before their very eyes. Just as Gapinon had forged the worlds, the Lifegiver, as he would soon also be known as, gave breath to those that would roam them.

He began creating those that shared his likeness, the humans. Giddy with his wondrous creations, he began to stir in variations to their appearances. Shaping more slender creatures and decorating them with pointed ears, similar to his sister Essence's, he also fashioned the elves. Essence rejoiced at the sight of them, declaring them her favored choice.

The next day, the Lifegiver was in a particularly mischievous mood. He then gave life to short men with naturally thick beards, bulbous noses, and beady eyes, also giving them thunderously loud voices, finding the booming shouts coming from the miniature men quite humorous. (It should be noted that the mountain dwarves of Dur'Imoir hotly contest this part of the legend, insisting that their ancestors were reverently created in the image of Beginning)

It wasn't long before the first men began to grow hungry. Essence filled the world with all varieties of plants and designed beasts of countless kinds, needing only Kaijaras's blessing to bring them all to life. Soon after, the gods began to witness their creations performing an unusual behavior: they were using both plant and animal hide to craft homes for themselves!

"We should have our own homes as well!" Kaijaras proclaimed, turning to his brother Gapinon. "Can you forge homes just for us, dear brother?" Diligent as ever, Gapinon took up his forging hammer and set to work, creating realms for all of his siblings as well as himself.

For many decades, life in the newborn world was astoundingly peaceful and simple. The gods watched over their creations as they cooperatively flourished in the lands crafted just for them, giving birth to children of their own. It was a wondrous thing to behold. But as you may have guessed, the time came when the first men began to succumb to old age.

It was a tragedy to witness. When he had first given life to his creations, Kaijaras hadn't the slightest idea that their mortal forms would perish. In an effort to help his brother make sense of all this, Gapinon brought the Lifegiver down into the world, upon the shores of the ocean. He pointed to the pebbles, round and smooth from the constant washing of the waves.

"Their bodies are like all things, Kaijaras," Gapinon explained. "They are not like us. Time washes over them, and time is a far greater force than the caress of these ocean waves."

The Lifegiver was fully prepared to mourn the loss of each of his creations when something strange happened. He saw them reappear, their images lifting from their own bodies. Touched by the hands of the gods, the mortals possessed what we call a soul. Kaijaras felt delight at first, but it was soon followed with dismay, when he realized that the wandering souls could not be heard by the living loved ones they had left behind. Wandering aimlessly, the departed lamented and reached for those that could not hear them.

Something had to be done. Kaijaras called for his brother, Kagothai. The Lifegiver knew that the soft-spoken god wished to have a part to play in the grand scheme of the universe. Explaining the phenomenon of death to his brother, Kaijaras persuaded Kagothai to watch over the souls of the dead and to harbor them safely in his home world. Kagothai, who had felt the cold touch of loneliness for many years, found comfort in greeting the souls who had found their way to the afterlife. Legends told by the Kantos tribe describe a union of souls who offered to guard the ethereal side of the world and aid the fallen in finding their way to the hands of the Death Shepherd, and these ancestral souls have become the focal point of worship for those tribesmen.

This is where the trouble began, and also where the tale reaches a fork. The Sandspeakers of the desert city Chai'Rin tell tales of Essence's loneliness, being the only goddess among her male counterparts. They say that the goddess fashioned her own companion, a being formed of raw energy, something mystical and wild to behold. Chai'Rin calls this being *Ran'allakah*, roughly translated in Commonspeak as "The Fury". The native desert morphs believe that Essence is the only true goddess, the other three Forgers being great spirits on a lesser level, and that the *Ran'allakah* is to be both feared and respected, as she is the lifeblood that gives the morphs, both of sand and water, their core of existence.

The majority of historical scholars instead believe that Essence looked upon the dying mortals with empathy. It didn't take long for old age to share its place as a cause of death. Other factors came into play, such as the winter elements, and poisonous berries that had begun to naturally grow in the forests she had helped create. The mortals also discovered the harrowing touch of disease. To aid them in their toils, Essence created the mortals' greatest boon: magic. Hand selecting her favorite mortals, the goddess spoke to them in their dreams, instructing them on the delicate balance of using it. Only a few days later, she also introduced the world to the idea of flight, scattering thousands of birds from the heavens into the world, from the smallest chickadee to the proud eagle. Lastly, Essence brought the mighty dragons into the world, declaring that the creatures would watch over and protect her mortal children. Legends say that Xavier, the first born dragon, had enchanted scales that could cure the diseases that were beginning to surface in the world of men with the touch of a hand.

Kaijaras, whose pride had swelled with all of his great accomplishments, resented both Essence's magic and creations. He did not become immediately hostile, instead choosing to offer his own gifts, as the goddess had done. Speaking through the dreams of his favored mortals, men and women with the ability to mend cuts, bruises, and disease began to emerge in the tribes. Their gratitude sated the Lifegiver for a short while, but ultimately, Essence's gifts of magic were far more intriguing than what Kaijaras had to offer. He demanded that Essence pull her gifts from the world of mortals.

The tale the Sandspeakers tell varies here as well. According to Chai'Rin legend, Kaijaras had grown jealous of the *Ran'allakah*, whom Essence regarded as her lover. The Lifegiver first imbued some of his chosen mortals with healing abilities, not to gain favor with the mortals, but to attract the attention of his divine sister. When she remained infatuated with her created companion, Kaijaras's envy transformed into anger, and the jealous god attacked the *Ran'allakah*.

More popular lore suggests that Kaijaras instead attacked Essence herself, who refused to relinquish the gifts she had bestowed upon the mortals. To protect herself from the wrath of the Lifegiver, the goddess retreated into her home world, erecting an enchanted barrier to keep her brother out of her domain. Kaijaras, full of vindictive anger, would not be deterred so easily. Calling upon the aid of his brother Gapinon, the Lifegiver set out to demolish the shield that surrounded Essence's home.

It must be understood that in the earliest days of the world, the thrones that the gods sat upon were much closer to the home of their created mortals, visible high in the sky even to the naked eye. And so when Kaijaras began to rain down blows on the enchanted shield with his sword, and Gapinon smashed against it with his colossal hammer, the mortals below witnessed all of this. The very idea of violence and warfare was unknown to the first men, but with an example provided to them by their creators, the seeds were planted. And as Kaijaras and Gapinon pummeled Essence's arcane shield, it began to fracture and break, the shards tumbling down to the world of men.

In place of a broken magical shield, Chai'Rin legend says that Kaijaras slashed at the *Ran'allakah*, wounding the creature of magic and causing her blood to fall from the heavens, spattering the world below. Whichever tale is true, the result was the same. The arcane remnants fallen from the heavens shattered upon the earth's ground, their power releasing and spreading like fungal spores. Corrupted by the rage of the gods, the enchanted shards did not transform most of those affected in a pleasant manner.

A group of elves were the first victims of the exposure. Their bodies shrank, their backs became hunched, and their skin turned an assortment of bruise-like greens and pale greys. These were the world's first goblins, a mutated mockery of their former selves.

The dwarves were most fortunate of those transformed. Those in proximity of the fallen shard visibly shrank, but instead of evolving into something akin to the goblin, both the gnome and the kender were born that day. The gnomes were smaller, weaker, and beardless, but their attitudes were immediately and significantly cheerier than their dwarven brethren, boasting even larger noses and bright, bulbous eyes. The kender were smaller, but their noses shrank, their beards disappearing as well. They were even more sprightly than the gnomes, causing quite the chagrin among the testier dwarves. It didn't take long to discover the primary trait of the newly born kender. The belongings of all of those surrounding them began to mysteriously disappear. The kender seemed to oblivious to their own thievery, however, insisting that those around them had merely lost their possessions. You can imagine the outrage this must have spurned among the dwarves, who so covet what belongs to them.

The affected humans, the most adventurous of the original three races, were spread far across the land, and were therefore the most affected by the volatile shard magic. Among the plains, they grew over half their original size, creating the world's first ogre tribe. Even more fearsome than the ogre, the mountain men mutated into thundering trolls, with beady red eyes and yellowing tusks. Perhaps the most humorous of transformations, though you may not think so if you've ever had the displeasure of meeting the result, were the cow herders that were nearby when an ill-placed shard crashed to the earth. In a most unfortunate manner, the humans and their cattle merged into ill-tempered, violent beasts, with hooves, horns, and twitching black snouts. The birth of the minotaur had just taken place.

The actual number of those affected by the broken shield of Essence is still disputed to this day. There are many tales from sailors upon the sea that depict terrifying creatures rising from the deep to swallow entire ships. These legends, whether or not they are true, are a primary reason for the Aariad's limited naval ventures.

Perhaps the greatest beneficiaries of the shard chaos were the elves, disregarding those that fell to the goblin curse, of course. A group who were living in what is now known as Ashtalath witnessed such a shard falling from the sky, traveling in the direction it would have landed. When they came across it, it remained unbroken, nestled in a bed of peat that had softened its fall. Curious, the elves took the relic back to their encampment, and though the shard slowly shrank over time until it was nothing more than dust, it still evolved those that surrounded it. Over time, the elves transformed into what we now call the night elves, or the *kaldorei,* in their tongue. They soon found themselves naturally attuned to the darkness, some of them developing strong druidic powers.

The creation of the morphs of Chai'Rin must not be forgotten, though the details of their genesis are a well-kept secret. The most the Sandspeakers have divulged to curious scholars is that blood that had touched the *Ran'allakah's* heart before departing the body fell upon the desert sands, its power potent enough to create life of its own. Though their people will not absolutely confirm this, it is widely believed that the laws of Chai'Rin forbidding the spilling of blood upon the earth are directly correlated to the *Ran'allakah's* wounding and miraculous creation from its occurrence.

The elves weren't the only ones who coveted the unbroken shards of the shield. Gapinon was the first to break open a fissure wide enough for he and his brother to enter their sister's home world. In his haste for retribution, however, Kaijaras forcibly shoved his brother out of the way. He was so hurried, in fact, that as he pushed himself through the rift, his sword fumbled from his grasp, falling at Gapinon's feet as the Lifegiver rushed in to subdue his sister. Perhaps Kaijaras believed that his brother would carry his sword in for him. He was sorely mistaken. The forger of worlds was already brewing with emotions of dejection and resentment, for though he had crafted the lands that the mortals lived on, it was Kaijaras and Essence that they favored most. There were days he wondered if the world of men even remembered he existed. His proud brother taking his help for granted was the last straw for the Creator. Instead of carrying the Lifegiver's sword beyond the shield, in his rage he hurled it towards the world of mortals. He tied his hammer to his belt and knelt down, gingerly collecting a few of the splintered shards for himself before disappearing to his own world.

The mortal world began to boil over. The Lifegiver's sword, heaved from the heavens by Gapinon, struck the first dragon Xavier, piercing him between the scales and sinking into his flesh. Roaring in pain and panic, the great creature took flight in desperation, retreating to Mount Fangfire, the very one just outside the proud Kingsbanesin of today. He was never seen again, rumored to have burrowed his way under the colossal bluff to die in peace. One of the most popular Kingsbanesin prophecies is that of the spirit of Xavier, lingering under Mount Fangfire, biding his time til he may return to the world in a great vengeful fury alongside the one bold enough to seek him out. To this day, many have tried, only to find the deepest tunnels impassable.

Throughout history, mankind has needed little more reason to go to war than harboring differences with others. This was true even for the first Great War. Influenced by Kaijaras and Essence, who had engaged in a brutal struggle high above, the mortals' distrust for their newest mutated cousins evolved into violence. The trade of armor and weapon forging took several quick strides ahead of their time to meet the need for bloodshed. Carnage reigned supreme in the world of men.

While mortals require sleep and rest, the wrath of the gods can burn brightly for much longer before fading. Kaijaras and Essence dueled for the entire span of a moon, completely oblivious to their brothers' activities. Kagothai, who had seen countless resting bodies and the souls that matched them, had never laid eyes upon a mutilated corpse desecrated by war, or the livid souls that clawed out of them hungry for revenge. The exposure began to warp the Death Shepherd's mind, corrupting him with a morbid madness. As he shrouded himself with darkness, his home of souls quickly transformed into a haven of nightmares, a dread place fit for a harbinger of wickedness.

Gapinon, who was falling prey to his own malice, called out to the Death Shepherd. "Our vain brother and sister hold no regard for us, Kagothai. Help me, so that we may solidify an alliance that shall be feared by both gods and men!"

Kagothai, who still harbored great loneliness under the insanity he enshrouded himself in, agreed without hesitation. While Kaijaras and Essence fiercely fought above, Kagothai and Gapinon reached out with grasping hands into the world, seizing handfuls of mortal men and dragging them into Gapinon's lair.

He would not hold such a title for long, but the Creator had one last forging to complete. Using the shards he had collected from Essence's shield, he created a great and terrible forge of cruel, twisted metal and unholy heat. Using the kidnapped men he and the Death Shepherd had gathered as his forging material, he began to mold his own mortal race that would worship him as the others did his siblings. Their tortured screams filled his world as his wicked smith's hammer beat down upon them, shaping them into his grand design. The heat from the forges began to consume his realm, and as it intensified, it twisted the Creator's own visage. The first race he perfected were the orcs, but the glimpses of himself that he caught in the reflection of his cooling trench inspired him to create his master work: the demon. From the hulking red-skinned brute to the cunning pale fiend, Gapinon created a legion who would kneel down to worship him.

It was not his creations for which he wished to be worshiped for any longer, however. With the aid of Kagothai, Gapinon opened a rift into the world of men, pouring his legions into the lands to destroy everything that men had taken for granted. Just as the orcs and demons had been born, the rise of what we now know as the Destroyer came upon that terrible day.

The demonic legions set fire to the grass and to the trees. The warring tribes paused in their fighting in the face of the new threat. Some of the races were inspired by the havoc of the Destroyer's army, mainly the goblins, trolls, and ogres, and swore fealty to the brutish onslaught. Recognizing the need to unite if they were to survive, the other races forged their own alliance to fight back against the dark tides.

Finally realizing what was unfolding in the world of men, Kaijaras and Essence ceased their fighting to gaze upon the carnage below. Smoke was billowing to the sky, stinging their noses. At first, they wished to descend to the mortals' world to aid in their plight, and they called upon their brothers to join them in their defense. They were greeted only with threats and calls for war from both the Destroyer and the Death Shepherd. Seeing what Gapinon had transformed into, they then understood who had unleashed the foul creatures on their precious lands. Kagothai, too, was a pale, miserable shadow of his former self, and Kaijaras's heart twisted in guilt and remorse at the sight of him. The Lifegiver begged his brother to return to his side, but like Gapinon, Kagothai had grown spiteful as the mortals had grown fonder of Kaijaras and Essence's followings. His answer was both cruel and obscene: he began to reanimate the bodies of the fallen on the world of men. The first risen dead began to blossom on the battlefields like cancerous growths, striking fear into the hearts of the mortals before they fell upon them.

The brother and sister deities could no longer afford to squabble over the use of magic in the world. With the lives of all mortals at stake, they combined their efforts to bolster the power of those fighting the armies of evil. The joint powers of both Essence's first mages and Kaijaras's holy fighters proved to be a deciding factor in the mighty clash. Though the word 'paladin' was not yet a recognized term in the earliest days, a fearsome barbarian infused with the Lifegiver's augments by the name of Odo Saarian acted the part, his blessed axes laying waste to countless of the hungering undead upon the field of battle. Alongside Odo, there was a woman especially favored by Essence, whose true name was not known but was commonly referred to as the Blue Witch. Some legends speak of the Blue Witch gaining unnaturally long life following the goddess's touch. Others say that when her time comes to die, her spirit inhabits the body of a lesser mage to live another lifetime. Whatever the truth of it is, the Blue Witch, her entire body dyed in light navy tones, was told to have immolated two dozen orcs in the spell of a single breath, sending them scattering and howling in agony. Her renowned power played just as crucial of a role as Odo's, if not more so.

When it was abundantly clear that the Destroyer's armies had lost the battle, the Forger sought to withdraw his forces back into his home world. Favoring the demons, he opened a portal for them first, commanding them to return to his side. By the time they had retreated, however, the forces of men had closed in upon the rallying orc forces and those that had taken their side. Fearing that the armies may follow the demons through the portal, Gapinon opted on the side of prudence and closed it, wishing to fight another day. It should be noted that while there is little known about orcish lore, a single story transcribed from the tellings of a Hordelands warlock says that the orcs do not believe that the Destroyer abandoned them on that fateful day. Rather, they believe that Gapinon could only maintain the portal for so long, and asked his favored subjects for the selfless service of defending it while the demons fled. When the portal closed, the greenskins and their allies scattered, fleeing the battlefield to reunite elsewhere. The majority of them congregated where few humans cared to travel, in what we now refer to as the Hordelands.

As the dust from the Great War settled, Kaijaras and Essence came to terms. If for no other reason, the Lifegiver deemed that magic could be allowed to exist to combat the evil forces that their brothers had set loose upon the world. He warned of the dangers of magical abuse, however, and this dogma has been carried down from cathedral to cathedral all the way to present day. Essence vowed to assume the role of a balancing factor for both the world and the heavens, and though this is open to speculation, many believe that the universe naturally aligned itself to make it so.

The mortals of the world never again wholly united after that. They separated into tribal factions, many of them traveling great distances to establish flourishing kingdoms, the most noteworthy of these being the first Kingsbanesin empire, first of the mortals to tame Essence's dragons. They continued on with their own lives, and while they never forgot the gods that created them, their attentions were shared with life's countless other adventures. As the gods grew further from their thoughts, the realms of the deities began to push away from the world of mortals until they could no longer be seen watching over them from the sky. The druids of the White Forest have been known to believe that the moon was created by Essence, to serve as a reminder of the days when the Four Forgers were much closer to the world of men.

There are many stories of lesser gods to be found in the libraries of mortals, as well as told in tales by tavern patrons, ranging from the goddess of wind Ninta to the parasite god of death, Beruv. The validity of these tales is a prize sought after by many scholars, and perhaps one day, our children will add ink to these pages to credit them as fact. For now, though, I can only tell of the forging of our world and the first hands that crafted it. Such history should never be forgotten, lest we be doomed once again by power and pride.

Written and interpreted by Iuvas Ulaeron

Kingsbanesin Archives: Section B, 1239

Chapter One

A trickle of sweat formed on Deltore Ulaeron's brow, trailing down his temple before falling from his cheek, plummeting to the cluster of tall, imposing buildings below. If it wasn't the hottest day of summer yet, it had to be pretty damned close. He brushed a knuckle against his forehead as another droplet began to form, then once more to brush away a long strand of hair the color of stained hickory. The wings of his dragon, Kirwedax, beat lazily in slow rhythms as he circled the city of Kingsbanesin. He was on his scheduled patrol, and wouldn't be relieved for another long hour under the overbearing sun in the cloudless sky. Wistfully, he wished for a rogue breeze to cut through the stale air. Not the faintest gust would come, however, and he couldn't bring himself to coax Kirwedax into a faster flight just for his own relief. He could tell that she was weary of the dreary heat as well, and dragons were far more resilient in such conditions. No, he would just have to soldier on. He wished he could at least peel off his scale armor, though. But he wasn't about to break protocol, not when the punishment might very well be an additional shift in this stifling air.

His duties wouldn't end after his shift was up, either. Tonight was the gathering of the Dragonrider's Guild, and the garrison in which they conducted their meetings was warm and inviting in the winter, but almost unbearably stuffy in the humid summer days. The Dragonrider's Guild was the most esteemed organization in all of Kingsbanesin, and it met twice a month. On the seventh calendar day, they met with the young Governor Galdoys Veriknock and his council. Their discussions were almost always the same, involving two key topics: the movements of their neighbors, the Sherinalu elves, and whether or not they could begin to outright ignore the Gunnysack Treaty. On the twenty-first day, the Dragonriders met independently, in their cramped garrison with the stagnant air and conspiratorially lit candles in their iron chandeliers. Likewise, those meetings typically involved two topics: the upkeep of their dragons and their necessary equipment, and whether or not they should abandon their traditional purposes and wholeheartedly align themselves with their ambitious budding leader.

It had not always been this way. Deltore had heard the stories countless times by his father Iuvas's fireplace. Iuvas Ulaeron had once been a dragonrider as well, but had found himself captivated by the stories of the past, and had retired at an early age to become one of Kingsbanesin's most respected historians. Deltore remembered his father sitting in his chair, puffing on a hand-carved tobacco pipe, telling his tales with both an air of enlightenment and forewarning. *History should never be forgotten, lest we be doomed by it*, he would say ominously.

In the earliest days of the land of Aariad, kingdoms were little more than masses of traveling tribesmen and nomads. It was Saragocx, or "Golden-Eyes", that first learned how to tame the mighty beast known as the dragon. This led to the most powerful and enduring dynasty in all the land, the city of Kingsbanesin imposing its will on every other kingdom with the display of the ferocious creatures. There were no governors, no councilors, there were only the monarchs of the Kingsbanesin Empire, and their word was law. They collected taxes all across the land and drafted the firstborns of every mother they could find into their army, their strength flourishing year after year.

It remained this way for many ages, and Kingsbanesin grew comfortable high upon its perch. As with all reigning powers, however, it was not fated to last. Lord Garan Haymirk of the Glen Bailey, along with his general Arden Halderstadt, rallied a number of other kingdoms to begin a bloody revolution known as the Gunnysack Wars. The hard-earned victory had required the effort of every peasant, whether they were man, woman, or child. As Kingsbanesin's dragons had swooped across their fields, scorching their crops with their flaming breath, masses of ordinary civilians smothered the flames with empty gunnysacks soaked with water. Their presence became more notable than even the united armed forces led by Garan and Arden, and the name was coined before the ashes of war had a chance to settle.

After many years of bloodshed and hardship, the rebellion finally pushed back the empirical forces of Kingsbanesin, cornering them in their own city. Arden Halderstadt rode forward through the streets, to the royal palace of King Sylvester Iubach, flanked by his soldiers, and demanded the sovereign's surrender.

Sylvester Iubach was not the proudest name in Kingsbanesin history, for he became increasingly mad the closer he came to defeat. Instead of accepting the terms offered to him, Iubach threatened to unleash what remained of his dragons upon his own people, pushing the deaths of the innocent onto the consciences of the rebellion's leaders. Not wishing for more unneeded slaughter, and possessing a desire to remain above Iubach's standard of honor, General Halderstadt entered negotiations with the desperate king. It was then that the Dragonrider's Guild was formed, or at least the rough idea was introduced, and the Gunnysack Treaty was written. The Guild, its members handpicked by the leaders of the rebellion, was to remain in control of the surviving dragon brood, allowing Kingsbanesin to preserve its heritage but removing the threat of retaliation from Iubach. The Treaty ordered strict regulations on Kingsbanesin's trade and military development, and the title of 'king' was to be dissolved, the position of 'governor' taking its place. A senate committee was formed (many of its members from the rebelling kingdoms, though a select few Kingsbanesin natives were named as well) to keep a healthy checks-and-balances system in place alongside the watchful eye of the Dragonrider's Guild.

Iubach agreed to all of these terms. Unfortunately for the former king, the people of Kingsbanesin did not forgive his threats. A fearsome mob formed shortly after the announcement of surrender, and Sylvester Iubach was beheaded on the streets. The leader of the insurrection, Raul Grantson, took Iubach's place as Kingsbanesin's new governor. Rumors of Raul being placed upon the seat by the Glen Bailey were abundant, but never proven. And from that day on, the former empire of Kingsbanesin began to rebuild both its structures and its dignity. The Aariad enjoyed a long age of peace and prosperity as the former empire of dragons remained under careful supervision through both the Senate and the Guild.

But just as empires crumble, so do treaties that preserve peace. As time moved on, the senators and dragonriders that kept the balance in check passed away, and so did their children, as did their children after them. The Gunnysack Wars became a legend, the reality of the brutal revolution lost to those who the tale was passed down to. As the decades turned into a century, the Kingsbanesin senators, who had much to gain from the resurrection of the old empire, began to whisper in the shadows among one another, careful at first, but increasingly bold as the years went on, until finally all realized that their unity could mean great prosperity for all of them. Their dialogues with the Kingsbanesin governor no longer challenged his views, but instead added to them with encouragement.

The Dragonriders, who cared less for riches and more for the honor of their positions, remained a challenging voice in Kingsbanesin for many years after the senators, but they too lost their enthusiasm for a system put in place by strangers from past legends. They were, after all, the most skilled riders of the scaled beasts in all of the Aariad. Why shouldn't their kingdom reign supreme? Still, they did not trust the senators or the governor to truly respect the security they brought to Kingsbanesin, and it wasn't until the rise of their most recent leader, Galdoys Veriknock, that the discussions of merging their cause to the Senate became serious. Worse, the talks were polarizing. Some of the members, particularly those who were older, held nothing but disdain for the young firebrand. Many of the younger members were incited by his personality, however, and insisted that they abandon their archaic resistance to the political branch of their kingdom.

As Kirwedax circled in another languid loop around the city gates, Deltore mulled over his thoughts on Galdoys. Regardless of opinions among the Dragonrider's Guild, they could all agree on one thing: the governor was going to break the Gunnysack Treaty in his lifetime, with or without their approval. His first act following his induction was to ban every other race from Kingsbanesin aside from humans and a handful of resident dwarves from Dur'Imoir, for which the fruits of their labors would be sorely missed were they not permitted in the city gates.

No eradication of elves was necessary upon the announcement, for none stayed in Kingsbanesin longer than half a day. Shortly after the Gunnysack Treaty had been signed, the Sherinalu Vale stopped permitting their neighbor to harvest lumber from their forests, something they had been forced to endure for ages. Under the scrutiny of the successful rebellion, Kingsbanesin had no choice but to accept that the land was no longer accessible to them. But festering within that acceptance was an animosity towards the elves, and as is often the case with prejudice, it mutated into a distrust for all those that were not strictly human. Elves that dared to spend the night in the city often never awoke. The murders could never be directly linked to the Senate, however, and so the only remaining solution was for those of Sherinalu blood to keep their business within the city brief.

It was a poorly kept secret in Kingsbanesin that children would occasionally dare each other to approach the border of the Sherinalu, where young elves on the other side would gather to do the same. They rarely ventured to the other side, mostly resorting to taunts and teasing, but physical scuffles were not unheard of. It was also well-known that Galdoys had been part of a particularly humiliating tussle in his youth, one that had fostered a grudge that had only grown with age. That was the part that concerned Deltore. He was fiercely proud of his Kingsbanesin heritage, and shared no love for their snide elven neighbors, but he knew when he was being played for a pawn, and he resented being used as one to settle the debts of a childhood quarrel.

Regardless of the motive, the move by Galdoys came dangerously close to open defiance of the Gunnysack Treaty. The restriction of the elves, as well as the recent imprisonment of a group of Sherinalu that had ventured too close for comfort, were practically inviting intervention from the empire's neighbors. The Senate had already been contacted about the disappearance, but Galdoys had returned the correspondence, dismissing the "unfortunate event" as the act of miscreant bandits. Nobody believed the governor's claim, but the fascinating part was that no army had showed up at their gates. The growing belief among all of Kingsbanesin was that no army would come, that the outside world feared the might of the dragon empire once again. Towering above his city upon the back of a dragon, it was easy for Deltore to believe the truth of that.

He glanced over his shoulder as Kirwedax turned again with a beat of leathery wings, something in the distance catching his eye. They were far away, too far to reach the sky over Kingsbanesin before his shift would end, but there were storm clouds on the horizon. He uttered a silent prayer of thanks to the Lifegiver. When his shift was over, he would bring Kirwedax to Mount Fangfire, the towering earthen dragon stable that loomed over the city's northern wall. Hot and sticking with a layer of dried sweat, Deltore decided that if the rain came in a timely enough manner, he would walk from the mountain roost to the Dragon's Guild garrison in nothing but his skivvies, and to hell with what any gawkers might think. This heat was miserable, and he would welcome a shower.

He was so absorbed in his fantasy that he almost missed the moving figure outside the city wall, making its way to the sewer grate on the southeastern end. The figure was cloaked in dark brown, its face concealed by a hood as it approached. Deltore feigned ignorance at first, though he gave Kirwedax a quick double-tap against her left flank, a signal for her to be ready to dive. As she glided in another arc, the dragonrider watched the intruder from the corner of his eye. The stranger was indeed examining the sewer grate, but they would find no entrance there. Deltore saw a tethered hook appear in the cloaked one's hands. As he and his dragon began to fly over the intruder's location, he kicked at Kirwedax's flanks with both feet. With a short, eager screech, the dragon plummeted down towards the invader with a thunderous flap of her wings. Deltore reached into the saddle bag next to his thigh, pulling a snare net from the pouch as they descended.

The figure below looked up with alarm. Deltore saw his hand dip into the folds of his cloak, drawing something that shimmered in the intruder's palm. It soared upwards, directly towards Kirwedax's maw, and Deltore pulled on her reins, easing her back with a corrective buffet of her wings. The shimmering object did not collide with the dragon, however, but instead hovered around her reptilian eyes, darting back and forth like a curious insect. And then, with a quiet whine like a steaming kettle, it began to flare with intermittent flashes of bright light, darting back and forth across the dragon's vision.

Kirwedax screeched, clawing at the blinding miniscule pest and snapping at it with her jaw, but it evaded every attempt to swat it away, continuously flashing with the blazing white light. Deltore shouted, trying to calm the beast, but her head was already thrashing about like a berserk ogre. Whipping her skull from side-to-side, Kirwedax dove at the ground below, towards the brown-cloaked figure that had turned to escape back into the forest surrounding the city. It was a jarring landing as the dragon touched down, her claws digging into the soil as she continued to screech and toss her head to and fro as the orb relentlessly flashed. Falling from his saddle, Deltore collapsed to the ground, the wind leaving his lungs in a rush as he landed. In a helpless fury, Kirwedax lifted off once more without her rider, flying in the direction of Mount Fangfire. Deltore cursed, calling out to his winged steed, but he quickly abandoned the lost cause and drew the sword that was sheathed to his belt, charging into the wilderness in pursuit of the stranger that had both wounded his pride and threatened to breach his city's walls.

He caught sight of him as he charged through the forest, weaving between brush and trees as he followed in hot pursuit. He was fast on his feet and gaining on his prey. As they both bolted down a hill, dodging the maple trees that silently stood watch, Deltore began to close in. As a patch of giant ferns approached, he reached out and grasped the cloaked intruder's shoulder, spinning him around as he tackled him into the thick vegetation. They landed on the ground in a tangle, but Deltore was on top. He drew his blade, pointing the tip down at his quarry. "By order of Galdoys Veriknock and the city of Kingsbanesin, I-"

He paused as he looked down at the face of the accused, surprise halting his tongue mid-monologue. It was not a man he had chased down into the forests. It was a woman with pale skin, bright blue eyes, and beautiful thick ebony locks that tumbled out from her hood as she peered up at him. Deltore shook his head and lowered the point of his blade, using his other hand to brush sweat from his brow. "What in the hell-"

"Go on," the stranger said in a measured tone, her voice shallow with the effort of regaining her breath. "I'd like to hear the formalities."

"What did you even hope to accomplish by-"

"So because I am a woman, you won't give me the standard rhetoric?" the stranger interjected, her brow lofted challengingly.

Sometimes, the gods fate us to the strangest circumstances. There, tangled in the bed of ferns, the two strangers locked gazes, the air around them brimming with fierce energy. Deltore became suddenly aware of the compromising way he was positioned on top of her, and to his despair, he felt an urging resistance against the front of his trousers. He did not know it, but below him, the stranger was hinging on a curious excitement, for in the life in which she was known by name, her role required a display of chastity, and as it often does, the sworn virtue had created in her a longing that had an aching to be satisfied. And with Deltore looming over her, the muscles standing out in his neck and his hair falling across his face, the primal side of her that she had suppressed for so long threatened to unleash itself upon the man. It all balanced on what he would do next, for if he dared to try forcing himself upon her, her lust would curdle into a violent opposition, and she was far from defenseless.

"Well?" she insisted when the dragon rider remained silent. "Will you not arrest me, then?"

Deltore sighed and sheathed his sword, lifting himself up on one hand. "No," he said gruffly, "just get up and get out of-"

That was all it took. Before he could react, the stranger reached around his head, grabbing him by the back of his hair as she lifted herself to press her mouth eagerly against his. Deltore froze, overcome by a brief stupor, but it was short-lived. He kissed her back hungrily, pushing her back down against the ground. Like a spark to a dry field, their passions ignited as they grasped one another, abandoning all inhibition as their bodies moved against each other. Their breathing heavy from the summer humidity and the rush of desire, they both worked to free Deltore from his armor. When it lay in a heap next to them, they both unlaced their trousers. Deltore slid his hand up her stomach to cup her breast, drawing a gasp from the stranger. He moved to pull her cloak away, but she impatiently snatched his hand, and with the other, guided him inside of her. He worked with a steady, pronounced rhythm as she grasped at his back, her fingernails digging into the flesh glistening with sweat. Her release came quickly, as did his half a moment later.

Releasing a trembling breath, Deltore rolled off of the cloaked woman, collapsing onto the soil with his bare back, staring up at the sky through the treetops. The clouds he had spotted while atop Kir-wedax were beginning to encroach, their bodies dark and menacing against the sphere of blue. The dragonrider turned to look at his spontaneous partner, who was murmuring softly under her breath as she stared up at the same sky. He listened a moment and realized she was praying.

"What did you come here for?" Deltore asked in a murmur. Insisting upon the role of the imposing patroller seemed pointless now. The stranger looked back at him, then returned her gaze to the sky, her eyes following the swiftly rolling clouds.

"I came to steal from the treasury of the wealthy nation of Kingsbanesin," she replied softly, the vindictive edge to her voice that Deltore had heard earlier entirely absent.

"What was that trickery you used upon my dragon? Where did you get it?" he asked, sitting up onto his elbows now. The cloaked woman remained where she was, folding her hands across her stomach.

"It is known as an *amra*. I stole it," she answered simply.

"Must have been a stroke of luck for you, then," Deltore said. "I don't know how you thought you'd get in without being seen. Your best bet would have been to pose as a merchant or something and come right through the front gate."

"I shall keep that in mind," the woman said curtly as she laced her trousers back up and got to her feet, smoothing out her clothing. "If you aren't going to arrest me, sir, I will be on my way."

Deltore got to his feet as well, glancing over her as she adjusted herself. Already, desire was burning at his loins again. The stranger was tantalizing, and though he knew it was clouding his judgment, he couldn't bear to simply allow her to disappear. "Can I see you again?" he asked as he pulled his undershirt back over his head.

The woman pursed her lips, staring back at him, saying nothing for a moment. She examined him, almost in a shy manner at first, but soon deciding that it wasn't worth the effort to try fooling herself. She admired his entire form, as if she were gauging the worthiness of such a risky rendezvous on his physique alone. "Yes," she said, and though a touch of guilt could be heard in her words, the thrill of it overpowered any hesitation.

"I have the same shift tomorrow," Deltore said, taking a step towards her. "Meet here at this time?"

"I'll signal you once with the *amra*. Don't miss it," the woman replied. Deltore grinned and leaned in for a kiss, but the cloaked stranger turned away, walking through the thicket of giant ferns, the hem of her cloak catching against their stems and sending them springing backwards as they passed over.

"Wait!" Deltore called out, taking a single step in her direction. "You didn't tell me your name." The stranger paused in her stride. In the distance, the sound of a croaking frog came from a nearby pond, followed by another as the two began what would soon be a loud chorus of mating calls. Finally, the cloaked woman turned her head, calling out over her shoulder.

"Melaitha. My name is Melaitha," she said. Deltore smiled and opened his mouth to tell her his own name, but she was already gone, disappearing into the wilderness beyond. The dragonrider watched her go, and as she vanished from sight, a rumble of thunder rolled across the sky. The faint pattering of raindrops against tree leaves began to sing a hushed song above.

They met the next day, and the day after that. Deltore brought a blanket with to avoid the unpleasantness of bare skin against soil, roots, and thorns, but beyond that, their reunions were much the same. Their passions only grew more heated with every meeting, their lovemaking fierce and eager under the cover of the ferns. Their conversations were brief when they were finished, but each time, they learned a little more about one another. Or, rather, Melaitha learned more of Deltore, who was far more willing to share his life's details with his new lover. Melaitha, on the other hand, was much more reserved. Her mysterious nature made her all the more desirable to Deltore, however, for he longed to know what secrets she kept. She prayed after their every copulation, and though she was fiery when they joined, she was strangely timid with the prospect of nudity, doing her best to keep her hood over her head each time. It would fall occasionally, and each time she would interrupt whatever they were doing as she scrambled to pull it back over her head. Between the prayers and the peculiar modesty, Deltore suspected that she was a woman of faith, but beyond that, he could only speculate as to where she came from or who she truly was.

His patience could only carry him so far, however. A few weeks into their affair, as they lay between the ferns with laboring breaths from their rutting, Deltore looked over at Melaitha, who was fidgeting with her hood and using the end of her cloak to dab at the sweat that streaked across her flushed face.

"Come live with me," Deltore said.

Melaitha froze. Slowly, she lowered the corner of her cloak and looked back at him with wide eyes, her shoulders still rising and falling with her heavy breath. "What?" she asked in a whisper.

"Why not?" Deltore replied, sitting up on an elbow. "Are we just going to keep meeting in the woods until winter comes? I wake up every morning, and the first thing I think of is you, and when I go to sleep at night, it takes everything in me to silence those same thoughts just so I can drift away into slumber. Why lead such a life of risk, feeding yourself through thievery, when I can give you a roof over your head and the security of a home?"

Melaitha sat in silence, clinging to the corner of her cloak as she considered Deltore's offer. She pursed her lips, looked back over at him, and finally allowed a smile to break. "Yes," she answered.

And so the peculiar situation became even stranger as the thief moved in to the dragonrider's home. Deltore had little difficulty getting Melaitha into the city. Members of the Dragonrider's Guild were rarely questioned by the gate guards, and affairs involving a new mistress were no exception. For the next couple weeks, they carried on as they had since the day they met, only now, they did not have to part ways when they were through with their coupling. Even though Melaitha's mysteries remained undiscovered, their relationship grew into something more than just a physical affair. Their interactions grew affectionate and tender. Deltore had a multitude of questions for his lover, but for the moment, he was content to simply enjoy the dream he had found himself in.

And then one night, when the heat wave had come to an abrupt halt, inviting a brisk cold front that trailed the streets like a wandering specter, everything changed. The moon was shining in the night sky, its pale light flooding their bedroom, and in the latest hour, Melaitha quietly slipped from underneath the covers, dressing herself as silently as she could by the bedside. Her sudden absence stirred Deltore from his slumber, and his first reaction was to ask her if everything was all right, but a nagging instinct told him to feign sleep. And so he lay there, watching her through a single squinted eye as she daintily dressed herself in trousers and tunic before wrapping her cloak around herself, glancing down at the bed warily every couple moments. Deltore's heart began to race as he saw her take the sheathed sword he had laid across his cabinet drawer, but she did not turn upon him. Rather, she clasped the belt around her waist, glancing once more over at him. Deltore quickly shut his eye as she looked over, wondering if she could hear his heart hammering in his chest the way he could. He slowly released a measured exhale as he heard her carefully open the bedroom door and sneak out into the hallway.

He waited, unmoving, as he listened to her footsteps quietly tread through the house towards the front door. When the faint creak of it opening reached his ears, he threw the covers off of himself and swung his legs off the edge, his bare feet touching the wooden panels below. He tugged on his boots in a hurry, snatching his own cloak, black-threaded with the Kingsbanesin dragon embroidered below the shoulder blades. He moved swiftly but with care as he ventured out from his home into the night. He glanced towards the east, and then to the west, spotting a shifting shape under the moonlight, hurrying down the street. He frowned with befuddlement. What in the gods was she up to? He kept close to the side of the street as he followed her, his eyes quickly adapting to the darkness as he pursued Melaitha.

She continued westward through the city, but eventually veered towards the south. She would occasionally pause, glancing at her surroundings, causing Deltore to press his back against the nearest building and hold his breath until she continued onward. He noticed that she was looking for landmarks as she hurried into the heart of the city. Had she been plotting this out while he had been patrolling?

At one point, a cloaked stranger passing Melaitha by paused to leer at her. Deltore held his breath as he froze, silently commanding the man to leave her be. He couldn't just let the stranger harass her, or worse, assault her, but in coming to her rescue, he was sure he wouldn't discover what she was up to. Fortunately, Melaitha grabbed hold of the stolen sword's hilt and stared at the man challengingly. The stranger, deciding she would not be easy prey, cursed at her and went his own way into the night. Deltore released a trembling sigh of relief, his heart still thundering in his chest as he followed her.

She finally led him to her destination. Deltore frowned in confusion as Melaitha crossed the cobblestone street to the doors of the Kingsbanesin dungeon. He saw her hand reach into a pocket and pull out a round object. It began to glow with a soft white light in her palm, and he realized that it was the *amra* she had unleashed upon Kirwedax.

Realization struck him like a splash of ice-cold water. The *amra*. Something like that hadn't been crafted just anywhere. He was no expert in magical artifacts, but he would have bet his favorite dragon saddle that what Melaitha carried was elf-glass. It all fell into place. She wasn't just some traveling thief. She'd come from the Sherinalu Vale. She couldn't go through the front gates, because she would have been turned away. And when Deltore had chased her down, she had decided to seduce him into smuggling her inside. His heart dropped into his stomach as anger surged into his neck, flushing his face. He knew the real reason she had insisted on keeping her hood over her head, even in the throes of passion. There was only one way to be sure.

He bolted across the street, the sting of betrayal fueling his speed as he closed in on Melaitha, who was carefully prying open the front door to the dungeon. She winced as she heard the sound of swiftly approaching boot falls and turned around, unsheathing the sword at her belt, but Deltore was already upon her. He snatched her wrist and pinned it against the dungeon door. Melaitha released a cry of surprise, dropping the *amra* from her hand. It fell to the ground and bounced away in a manner that no natural glass could, making soft clinking noises as it descended the stone steps to the door and rolled out into the street, its pale light dimming as it escaped.

"Deltore, what-" she exclaimed, but the dragon rider didn't wait to exchange words. With his free hand, he reached up and pulled back her hood. In a panic, she clawed at his hand with the one that wasn't holding the sword, but it was too late. Deltore pushed back the hair that covered her left ear. What he saw confirmed his suspicions. It was a broad point, indicating some other lineage, but there was no doubting the elven blood in Melaitha.

"What's going on out there!?" a voice barked from inside the dungeon.

"It's over, Mel," Deltore said grimly. "Let go of the sword."

"Deltore, please, I-"

"*Let it go,*" the dragon rider commanded. Melaitha's expression was crestfallen. Defeatedly, she loosened her grasp on the sword's hilt. It fell with a clatter to the stone carved steps. Deltore took hold of her shoulders and pulled her away from the front door just as it opened. Peering out at the commotion was the warden, Jeffrey Emmerson, as well as three prison guards that had hurried to see what the fuss was about.

"Deltore?" Jeffrey asked with puzzled eyes. He had receding dark red hair that came up in a tuff in the middle of his scalp as well as a doughy, gentle face. He was by far the least intimidating prison warden Deltore had ever seen, at least upon his first impression. It took a great deal to rile up Warden Jeffrey, but if you made the mistake, you had one angry bear on your hands. "What's going on?"

"I'm placing this woman under arrest," Deltore said, his tone withered with scorn. "She's an elf that weaseled her way into the city with lies and trickery. She came here armed with intent to free the elven prisoners."

An awkward pause filled the air as Jeffrey stared at the upset man. Deltore had all but confessed to an outsider that Kingsbanesin was indeed holding the elves in captivity. Deltore felt foolish at first, but it quickly dissolved into impatience. What the hell did it matter? She was only going to join them.

Jeffrey took a few steps out, pushing back Melaitha's hair as she stood with defiant silence. The warden murmured, glancing at Deltore before releasing a weary sigh. He stepped back into the dungeon's entrance, calling for manacles. Melaitha's determined expression faltered as the guards approached her, placing the irons on her wrists as they began to lead her inside.

"Wait," Melaitha cried out as they ushered her inside. "*Wait! Deltore!*" She craned her head to shout in his direction. Jeffrey gave a stiff nod to the guards, causing them to pause, allowing her to speak as Deltore glared at her reproachfully.

"You lied to me, Mel. This whole damned time, I thought I was in love. That woman doesn't even exist," Deltore said bitterly.

"No, Deltore," she pleaded, trying to pull closer to the dragonrider, but the guards held her firmly in place. "I *do* love you, I'm sorry, I just...I had to do this, please understand..."

"Take her away," Deltore growled as he started to turn away.

"I'm with *child!*" Melaitha cried out as the guards began pushing her again towards the descending stairs. They paused once more at her proclamation, however, as did Deltore. He abruptly turned around, the color draining from his face.

"What?" he said in a weak voice.

"I am," Melaitha answered in a voice that warned of coming tears. "My moon blood should have come and gone weeks ago, Deltore. It's yours. There's been no one else."

The silence was agonizing. Not a single foot moved, and for what seemed like an eternity, nobody spoke. Deltore could only stare at Melaitha with a dumbfounded, vacant expression. The warden Jeffrey finally broke the stillness in the air. "It's your call, Ulaeron," he said softly.

A heartbeat passed, and then another. Finally, Deltore shook his head as he turned and disappeared from the front entrance, closing the door behind him. Fresh tears began to leak from the corners of Melaitha's eyes. Jeffrey shook his head sadly, but gave the signal nevertheless. The guards escorted the elf down into the dungeon depths below.

Chapter Two

Melaitha's capture soon led to a war between Kingsbanesin and the Sherinalu Vale. Not a war fought with blade and blood, but with quill and ink. Soon after the elf woman's imprisonment, letters began to arrive at Governor Galdoys's palace by the wings of a raven, demanding her release, as well as the other prisoners that were surely held in the empire's custody.

A great deal was learned about their prisoner through the letters. Her full name was Melaitha Riverwen, and unlike most of the elven priestesses of the Sherinalu, who were devoted to the goddess Essence, Melaitha's worship belonged to the Lifegiver, Kaijaras. As was suspected, she was only partially elven, perhaps as little as a sixteenth of the heritage in her blood, but her charitable and compassionate spirit had earned her a place in the forest city's temples.

The Sherinalu Vale admitted that Melaitha was sent to scout for the missing elves, but were adamant that she was invited into Kingsbanesin by one of its own dragonriders. They further claimed that she had reported her activities to the council, and there could be no doubt that she was being held in custody by the empire, and that if she had witnessed the sight of the other elven prisoners, that would be proof enough of Kingsbanesin's guilt. Much to Galdoys's outrage, Melaitha had indeed seen the other captives as she had been escorted to her cell. If her imprisonment had been the elves' plan all along, they had executed it flawlessly.

Unlike the battle of the sword and shield, the war won with words was often a prolonged and patient siege. The two cities exchanged letters back and forth, playing a careful game of politics with one another. Behind closed doors, Galdoys lobbied for true combat, calling for the unleashing of their dragons. The Senate agreed, but the Dragonrider's Guild, which was in all reality the more important party, did not see the same way. While some of the younger riders were eager to test their training, the guild's chief officer, Mekoda Sanreaux, vehemently dismissed the notion of breaking the Gunnysack Treaty for "a squabble over pointy-eared troublemakers." The debates were long and heated, but in the end, the Dragonrider's Guild sided with Mekoda, leaving Galdoys to fight his battle with quill alone.

Dragons or no dragons, the Sherinalu Vale began to make accusations of Treaty violations. When they could not extract their kin from Galdoys's grasp, they brought the Glen Bailey into the fold of their argument, and the process began anew. As this was transpiring, however, a prisoner in the dungeons of Kingsbanesin grew heavier with child. On the same day that King Bartholomew of the Glen Dale (the territory occupied by the Glen Bailey) flew out on the back of a gryphon to mediate the conflict in person, Melaitha Riverwen went into labor.

A dungeon is no place to bring a child into the world, and a prison warden is certainly no substitute for a midwife, but despite her condition, Melaitha had not been permitted a leave of absence from her captivity. Jeffrey Emmerson had two choices as the priestess's labor began: leave her fate in the hands of the gods, or help her deliver her baby. For the gentle bear of a man, the choice was simple.

He did his best to make Melaitha comfortable, providing as many towels and blankets as he could find. He found the cleanest wash basin he could, setting it near the cell cot, and began his vigil as Melaitha cried and pushed with all her might. The cell block was a chaotic mix of noise, a blend of the mother's cries of labor pains, Jeffrey's vocal encouragement, and the constant roar of the neighboring prisoners, bellowing for her to bite down on a rag and let them sleep. But despite all their howling, the labor went on for hours.

Finally, when it seemed Melaitha had taxed all of her strength, she gave birth to a squalling baby boy. The infant slid into the arms of the warden, who cradled him for a brief moment as the reality of what he had helped accomplish sunk in. Melaitha's weary moan woke him from his stupor, however, and he carefully severed the umbilical cord and washed away the film of afterbirth in the basin. The child properly cleaned, Jeffrey carried him gingerly back over to his exhausted mother, who took him with trembling arms.

"Thank you, Jeffrey," she said in a raspy whisper as she cradled her newborn. Her words were sincere, too. It had been a long eight months in captivity, and it was an awful place to endure a pregnancy, but the warden had extended every courtesy he could afford, including this last service. She had no doubt that he risked certain punishments for allowing her special treatment.

"He's a beautiful boy, m'lady," Jeffrey said softly as he washed his hands in a separate pail of soapy water. "What will you name him?"

"I have no idea," Melaitha murmured as she smiled down at her infant son. "All this time in here, you'd think I would have come up with something."

Jeffrey patted a towel against his hands and forearms, pursing his lips in a tired smile. "When I still lived in Gohand with my folks, Pa would always tell me stories at night about a knight without a kingdom to claim him that would ride from village to village, helping the farm folk, the traders, the hunters, y'know, all of them that lieges tend to forget about, even when they're getting fat off their taxes. His name was Cadohaden, and I always thought that if I ever had a son, I'd name him after the traveling knight in Pa's stories."

"Cadohaden..." Melaitha murmured, testing the name on her tongue. "What does it mean?"

"It means *forever enduring*, unless that part was just Pa telling his stories as well, which I'll warn ya is a fair possibility, m'lady," Jeffrey answered.

"I like it. *Cadohaden*," she repeated, gently rocking her son in her arms. She paused before looking back up at the warden. "But if you were going to name your son that..."

"My lady," Jeffrey said, shaking his head as he tossed the towel into the bucket. "I'm gettin' old, and I don't meet many nice girls working in a place like this. If you like the name, give it to him. He'll be a strong lad someday, worthy of it, I'm sure."

"Lifegiver bless you, Jeffrey Emmerson," Melaitha said before looking back down at the baby. "Cadohaden..." She paused as she recited his name. Was it to be Ulaeron, or Riverwen?

Suddenly, a high-pitched grating noise came from behind the warden as the cell door opened behind him. Deltore Ulaeron came stumbling into the cell. His face was drawn and shadowed, and a patchy beard that hadn't been the least bit trimmed or groomed was stuck to his face like a batch of assorted hair clippings. The smell of rye whiskey filled the room as he approached Melaitha, who held little Cadohaden protectively against her chest.

"Heard I was gonna be a father," Deltore mumbled with a booze-addled tongue. His bloodshot eyes were having trouble focusing, but it was clear he was leering at something in particular. It was the child's ears. They were almost completely rounded, the sliver of elven heritage disguised behind the human characteristics.

"That's your son, Ulaeron," Jeffrey said as he took a cautious step towards the dragonrider. "Got nothin' more than a thimble of Sherinalu blood in him, I'd say. Nobody will know the difference."

"Everyone...everybody *already* knows the difference, you ogre," Deltore growled. He turned away from the mother and child, walking away in a daze towards the cell door. "That's no son of mine," he mumbled as he departed.

Melaitha held the child tightly to her breast as his father lurched away. Jeffrey shook his head slowly as he looked down at the two. "Sorry, m'lady," he said quietly.

"You needn't be, Jeffrey. Thank you for everything you've done," Melaitha said, her eyelids drooping as she muttered. "Forgive me, but I need rest."

"O'course, m'lady," Jeffrey said. He picked up the basin and the bucket and left the cell. He knew there was nothing he could do, but it gnawed at his very soul to think that newborn Cadohaden would spend his first night in this beautiful world locked up in the dreary dungeon of Kingsbanesin.

* *

King Bartholomew Celandine of the Glen Dale walked a thin line upon arriving in Kingsbanesin. His wife, Queen Meredith, had died giving birth to their daughter Aven less than a year before, and he was still struggling to find ways to cope with her passing. The first and most frequent was by drink, but he hadn't completely succumbed to the will of the bottle. His other method was to busy himself with proj-

29

ects, and a resolution between the dragon empire and his elven allies was an undertaking that he had chosen to commit all of his energy to. He would not return home without a solution.

It would have been the king's folly to try bullying Galdoys Veriknock into surrendering, however. Even under the Gunnysack Treaty, Bartholomew himself was aware of how strained the agreements on that document were. He knew that if any situation were allowed to boil over, there would be a catastrophic war that would cost many lives all across the Aariad. He and his councilors would speak with hushed voices as to what the solution may be, but as of now, nobody was quite certain of a peaceful plan to disarm Kingsbanesin. So for now, he simply had to tread lightly on the issue of the squabble over the elven prisoners.

Fortunately, Galdoys was not quite as bold as he would have liked to be without the full support of the Dragonrider's Guild. He had no shortage of snide remarks and insults directed at the Sherinalu Vale during Bartholomew's visit, but in the end, he was cooperative. Bartholomew did not make threats, but instead made it clear that such a fuss over people Galdoys thought so low of did not reflect well on an empire that boasted such strength. The petty, backhanded flattery worked as desired, and the governor agreed to release the Sherinalu prisoners, as well as Melaitha Riverwen, in exchange for Bartholomew's promise that he would discourage the elves from trespassing on Kingsbanesin territory. "The Treaty explicitly states, Bartholomew, that in exchange for the empire's cooperation, we are allowed to remain a nation under our own control! And *that* means we are allowed to enforce the borders of our domain, even against those that helped your ancestors usurp mine oh so long ago! So I'll let that riff-raff go, but you tell them to stay in their forests that they care so much for!"

It was hardly the respect that Galdoys owed Bartholomew, but the Glen Bailey's king was not going to risk open war over the governor's tone of voice. And so the deal was struck, though the issue of the child born of the Sherinalu priestess and the Kingsbanesin dragonrider remained unsolved.

"Troublesome little bastard, isn't he?" Bartholomew joked, implying, of course, the child's siring as opposed to an inclination.

"He's a boy, the son of a dragonrider, no less," Galdoys answered. "He'll never be one himself, not with that tramp's dirty blood in him, but he'll stay in Kingsbanesin. We'll make a soldier out of him, or at the very least, a blacksmith's gopher."

Bartholomew's face darkened at this. It was no slight against his late wife, but perhaps there was a vicarious sympathy for a mother his daughter would never have. "Kingsbanesin can remain the boy's home, but you must allow him to see Melaitha. Whether she has to come here, or he is permitted to visit her, it matters not, but she endured nearly her entire childbearing behind iron bars. This will help atone for that crime."

Galdoys's face pinched in a bitter glare at this, and with that simple command, peace hung precariously in the balance. Finally, the governor waved his hand dismissively, snorting with derision. "Fine. He can go visit the long-eared succubus. Do you have any other demands while you're here, O Great King?"

"That will be all, Galdoys," Bartholomew answered. "Do take care, and maybe send us a letter now and again. I like to keep up with old friends."

Such correspondence never occurred, of course, but for the time being, the matter was settled. Deltore Ulaeron was given the majority of custody over his son, though he hadn't even declared his desire for such. Melaitha Riverwen and the other elven captives were released to the Sherinalu Vale, and the Kingsbanesin Senate appointed a nanny to care for the newborn Cadohaden, a servant of the court named Henrietta Yorel.

It took Deltore many months after that to overcome both the guilt of his actions and the heartache of Melaitha's deception, but when he finally came to terms with what had happened, he grew to love his son after all. He saw much of himself reflected in the boy, save for the rich blue eyes he'd inherited from his mother.

As soon as Cadohaden could hold a sword, Deltore placed one in his grasp. It was only swordplay at first, but the boy's father had a knack for teaching, and before long, he began to see the beginnings of a true warrior in his son. Nothing made his chest swell more with pride than the day Cadohaden successfully parried one of his father's attacks, deflected the wooden blade, and poised the tip of his own against Deltore's abdomen. That was the day they moved on to blunted steel weaponry.

That was not the only teaching Cadohaden received growing up, however. As promised, Galdoys allowed the boy to travel to see his mother, with Henrietta and usually a Kingsbanesin guard to escort him to the Sherinalu Vale. As the years passed, Galdoys finally grew tired of organizing the escorts, and gave Melaitha exclusive permission to enter the city to come visit Cadohaden (though she chose her visits carefully planned according to Deltore's dragonrider duties). If Deltore was the boy's sword, Melaitha was his faith. She taught him all the lessons of the Four Forgers, especially about the Lifegiver. She instructed him in both the virtues of prayer and honest character. For many years, Cadohaden enjoyed both the attention and important lessons from each of his parents.

As he grew from boyhood to adolescence, however, all of that changed. Childhood only lasted so long in the world, and at a certain age, everyone was supposed to become something, a contribution to the society that they had grown up in. He had never been exempt from chores, of course, both in Kingsbanesin and his mother's home in the Sherinalu Vale, but as he drew nearer to manhood, it was expected that he would assume a formal role. Deltore and Melaitha, who had only spoken sparingly with one another in all of their son's life, now needed to speak in great length, face-to-face, about the future of their son.

Deltore was insistent that Cadohaden join the Kingsbanesin army, pointing out his prowess with all the weaponry he had trained him to use. Melaitha, on the other hand, wished for him to join the Cathedral and become a cleric, away from the front lines of battle in an army that he would never be considered an equal in.

They both knew it would be a bitter and arduous battle over the fate of their son. What they didn't know is that they would unite once more before Cadohaden Ulaeron found his destiny.

Chapter Three

The wooden steps creaked as he made his way down from the upstairs of Deltore's home. Mumbling, Cadohaden pushed away the strands of dark blonde hair that were plastered against his face. He hadn't slept well the night before. He rarely did when he knew Melaitha was coming to visit.

The staircase descended to the home's entrance room, which had two doors leading to adjacent rooms on either side as well as the front door leading into the streets of Kingsbanesin. Around the staircase, however, accessible from both sides, was Deltore's kitchen. Cadohaden rounded the corner, his socks silent against the floorboards as he made his way into his father's kitchen. He could see the heat glowing from the stove that sat in the corner. On the nearest counter sat a tin plate with three strips of fried bacon as well as a serving of eggs. A block of cheese had been placed along the edge as well, and there was a half loaf of bread sitting next to a knife. Atop the stove sat a steaming pot of water, and nearby was Deltore's red tin that he kept his ground roasted beans that he used for his morning drink. It was a bitter brew known as "coffee", and the beans were a delicacy import from the southern nation of Gohand. It was popular in the Dragonrider's Guild, at least, in the morning. Rye whiskey and ale were the drinks of choice for the after-shift hours. Cadohaden didn't like the taste of coffee, despite his father's insistence that he would acquire a liking for it.

A pail of water sat on the other side of the kitchen. Cadohaden opted for a tin cup of that instead of his father's coffee as he carried his plate away from the counter. A door waited in the back of the kitchen that lead out onto a balcony. Deltore's home sat near the city wall, but it also sat on an earthen rise that elevated it enough to see over the ramparts, out into the forest beyond. The homes of the dragonriders were not what anyone would call elegant, at least not compared to the nobles or the senators, but they enjoyed a few comforts that came with the position. Deltore's was that balcony that stood watch by the wilderness. Mount Fangfire was a magnificent sight from anywhere in Kingsbanesin, but Cadohaden especially liked the view from his father's perch. This day was no exception. As he stepped out into the fresh morning air, the rays glanced off the mountain in ways that made it seem blessed by Kaijaras himself. He saw a dragon lift off from the open-faced landing perch near the upper levels of the mountain, the beast descending upon the city to begin the dragonrider's rotation.

"You slept in too late," his father remarked from a cedar-carved chair a few feet away. A short table sat next to him with a tin plate, miniscule crumbs revealing that Deltore had already eaten his breakfast. Cadohaden sat down in the empty chair next to him, biting into a strip of bacon.

"You could have woken me up," his son answered between mouthfuls of his breakfast.

"You're eighteen years old, Cadohaden," Deltore said sternly, glancing over at him briefly before returning his gaze to the mountain beyond. "You're a man now, and more importantly, you're a warrior. You have to learn to rely on your own instincts, not mine. Most of your peers enlisted two years ago. It's time to grow up."

Cadohaden frowned as he picked up bits of egg from his plate. "So you and Mother made a decision, then?" He knew that no such conclusion had been reached already. Deltore's expression curdled, his jaw setting.

"She'll be here later today. But that's what the decision will be. You're a man of Kingsbanesin, and you're damn good with any weapon I put in your hand. I won't have that talent wasted with you spending the rest of your life dusting temple pews and lighting candles," Deltore said.

"You were saying that two years ago," Cadohaden said as he took a drink of water.

"All the more reason for you to be taking it seriously!" Deltore said, looking back over at his son with a hard expression. "Being in the Kingsbanesin army is an honor, son. You've been using your mother's interference as an excuse to drag your feet for too long now."

"What if I wanted to join the Dragonrider's Guild?" Cadohaden countered, setting his cup down next to his chair. There was nothing quite like arguing with his father to wake him up in the morning. "Mekoda Sanreaux has been showing me how to handle the dragons. I'd be good at it. I'm just another grunt with a shield if I join the legions."

"The man's got a soft spot for you, but he shouldn't be giving you false hope," Deltore said with a quick shake of his head. "You know you can't join the Guild, Cadohaden. There's no point in arguing about it."

"But why?" his son protested anyway. "The Dragonrider's Guild is supposed to keep the governor in check. So why do we follow his rules for who gets to be in it?"

"Because that's *just the way it is*, son," Deltore said with an impatient sigh. "There's plenty of honor being in the army, and you've got what it takes to make a name for yourself in it."

"I hate when you two fight about it," Cadohaden said, frustration bleeding into his voice as he folded his arms. "Sometimes I think you're both just looking for a reason to fight, and I'm the most convenient excuse you have. Why do you two get to make the decision anyway? What if I wanted to do something else?"

"And what will you do?" Deltore snapped. He whirled around in his chair, facing Cadohaden with a strict glare. "Do you know how to forge armor? Do you plant crops? Bake bread? Butcher cattle? If you want to make the decision for yourself, then go on, go find yourself a master to apprentice for. Explain to them what you'd like to do with your life. Know what they'll ask you? They'll ask you what you already know how to do. And when you tell them 'nothing', they'll tell you to be on your way. You want to know why? Because *they* have sons that *they* taught to do what *their* fathers taught *them*. That's the way it works, Cadohaden. I taught you to be a great warrior, and so that is the service you will bring to Kingsbanesin, and I expect you to make me proud while you do it. There is no more room for stalling, son. The governor himself told me that it's time for a decision to be made about you. Frankly, he doesn't care if you carry a sword or a dish rag, but for the life of me, Cadohaden, don't shame me by doing something other than what you were destined to do. All right?"

"But Grandfather was a historian-" Cadohaden began.

"But he was a warrior first," Deltore interrupted. "And if you live to serve your kingdom until you reach the same age, then by all means, lay down your weapon and take up the quill. Until then, I'll hear no more nonsense about running around a temple in robes, from you or your mother."

Cadohaden, his face flushed with indignation, got to his feet, gathering his plate. "I'm going into the city," he said brazenly.

"As you wish," Deltore said, not moving in the slightest to stop his son. "Enjoy your last couple days of boyhood, Cadohaden, for they are coming to an end. Stay busy until sundown, if you would. The Dragonrider's Guild is meeting here in the evening, after I've spoken to Melaitha. We've found an inside source from the Senate that's willing to tell us what Galdoys has been up to in his meetings that don't involve us. And keep that to yourself."

Cadohaden briefly forgot his anger towards his father in his surprise. The Ulaeron house had never hosted a Guild meeting, official or otherwise. At first he wondered if perhaps Deltore was up for a promotion, but then remembered how their home was in a quiet part of Kingsbanesin, and realized that was probably the motive for the location. He found his temper once more and muttered bitterly, "Fine." He didn't really have any friends to confess the secret to anyway.

He stalked back into the kitchen, closing the door behind him, taking care not to slam it. Even when his fiery adolescent temperament ignited, Deltore had taught him long ago to shut the doors of his home with care, and even when he was angry, his instincts prevailed. He hurriedly scrubbed his plate in the kitchen wash basin before making his way to the front door. His sheathed sword was still leaning against the wall from where he'd last left it. Pulling on his boots and buckling the belt attached to the sheath, he plucked his light blue half-cape from a hook next to the door frame. It didn't really match his tan trousers and white linen shirt, but it was a gift from his mother, and he'd never taken too much time to appear fashionable for peers that didn't associate with him anyway. He opened the front door and marched out into the gravel street in front of his father's home.

Kingsbanesin was not the cleanest city in the Aariad. As busy as it was, Galdoys and almost every governor before him prided themselves in fueling the construction and expansion of the buildings within its walls. Many of the homes were stacked, and most other buildings reached to the sky with spires like stone fingers. The wind would carry dirt from Mount Fangfire and ash from the dragons it hosted, and over time, the sediment collected against the walls of the buildings. Cadohaden peered up at one of the guard towers as he passed it by, wondering if the color of the stonework was true, or if grime had given it the illusion of some other shade.

Despite the lack of beautification, Cadohaden was proud of his home city, even if it wasn't proud of him. It boasted an impressive number of employed citizens. Almost everyone had a role in the resurrection of the old empire. Its people kept their chins up and their voices proud, which wasn't difficult when your city was the only one to have the privilege of owning a legion of dragons and trained riders, even after the infamous Gunnysack Wars. The stories weren't told quite the same to Kingsbanesin children as they were to the others of the Aariad, of course. In the retold versions, Sylvester Iubach was further villainized, portrayed as a great traitor that Kingsbanesin cooperatively helped overthrow alongside the rebelling nations.

Most people were well fed, which made for a content populace. During its empirical reign, Kingsbanesin had secured a great deal of farm territory and quickly established relationships with the farmers that tended to their animals and crops. Some of the farms grew into their own miniature townsteads, the most recognizable names being Sheephold and the Sugarmaple Belt. Most often, these booming farm lands would fall into the possession of Kingsbanesin itself, as the city would recommend upgrades and luxuries that few farmers could resist, but could scarcely afford. The empire would then offer them loans with substantial interest, and without fail, the farmers would fall into debt that they could not pay back, and end up surrendering their prized estates to Kingsbanesin to even the collectors' scales. It was a cunning and vicious strategy, but with the farms in the empire's control, the food was theirs to distribute at prices that would sate their people. More than once, this control had quelled potential uprisings before they could become dangerous.

It wasn't food that interested Cadohaden on that late morning, however. As he wound his way through the city streets as they turned from gravel to cobblestone, he made his way to the Creator's Terrace. The name often confused visiting traders, who assumed that it implied a corner of the city designated for worship, even though Kaijaras had never held such a title. It was not a place for temples and monks, however, but for the shops of tradesmen making a living. It was not the home of the city's most esteemed crafters, who owned shops closer to the royal palace, but for those who crafted for ordinary citizens. Cadohaden's destination was the smithy of the disgraced Gus Anthony.

Gus Anthony was a blacksmith with an ample gut and a blonde beard. He could forge all sorts of things from iron, but his specialty was the crafting of tools. A great number of Kingsbanesin tradesmen came to Gus to have new tools made or existing ones repaired. Unfortunately, the blacksmith's humble success gave him a hunger for more coin. Years ago, he'd begun to smuggle out his tools to Kingsbanesin's southern neighbor, Wardrin.

Kingsbanesin was not strictly an isolationist empire, but all trade outside of the city walls was by law managed and conducted by the Senate. Gus's clientele did not help his case, either. Wardrin was not officially an enemy of the empire, but there was no doubt who Galdoys would target after the Sherinalu Vale if he decided to break the Gunnysack Treaty. The blacksmith's penalty would surely have been severe, but before a verdict was even handed down, Gus Anthony pleaded for the Rite of Atonement.

The Rite of Atonement was an ancient Kingsbanesin law most often called for by men who would otherwise be sentenced to exile, a lifetime imprisonment, or death. It gave the accused the right to accept a task from the Senate and the governor that would redeem them for their crimes. The harsher the sentence, the more impossible the assigned task usually was for the guilty. It was uncommon, but not unheard of for the tasks to be a sure death sentence on their own, such as an order to enter an ogre's cave and slay the family within without assistance. It would still offer them a chance at survival, however slim, and be a far more honorable death than the noose or beheading.

Gus's task was ongoing and likely would be for the rest of his life. Galdoys Veriknock offered his atonement in the form of crafted weaponry. He commanded the blacksmith to forge a sword for every single soldier enlisted in the Kingsbanesin army. The empire would provide the materials but he would not be paid for his hours of labor. Gus pleaded with the governor, beseeching him to allow him to craft hammers or picks instead, but Galdoys was not interested in the tools of trade. He wanted a blade for every soldier, and so the matter was settled. Gus began his assigned work. It was a slow process, being so out of his element, and he still needed to fill orders for tools to support his family. More soldiers continued to enlist in the army as well, and Galdoys informed Gus that he would be in charge of providing for them all until each one was equipped, sealing the hopelessness of his assignment.

Cadohaden pushed open the door to Gus's smithy, stepping inside. There were buckets lining the walls filled with assorted tools; some were crafted for customers, others were the blacksmith's own. A smoothly sanded counter was anchored to the wall with a variety of tools laid across it for display. Cadohaden could hear the sounds of hammer beating against iron, and knew he would find Gus in the room beyond, which had an open-faced wall for ventilation. He ventured deeper into the shop to find the blacksmith working the billows, flaring the coals of his furnace.

Gus's hair was sweaty and stringy, face red with the exertion of his craft. He had a thick leather apron over his front that was covered in black smudges and oil stains. Wiping the back of his hand across his brow, he looked at Cadohaden with wide-eyed wariness. For such a burly man, he could be a nervous fellow. "Master Cadohaden! What can I do for you today, son?"

"I was just passing through, Gus," Cadohaden said, trying to be nonchalant. "Mother's supposed to be coming around today. Father says I'm going to be in the army, whether or not she or I like it."

"Oh," the blacksmith answered. He reached behind his head and scratched his neck with a gloved hand. "You're not here for your sword, are you? I mean, I'll get to it, son, but I've got a back order list longer'n a dragon's...well...y'know," Gus said uncomfortably.

"No, really, I didn't come here for a weapon," Cadohaden said, tapping the short sword that was already sheathed at his hip, ignoring the blacksmith's awkward abandonment of his joke. "I was actually wondering if maybe I could come work for you, Gus. As an apprentice."

If Gus had looked uncomfortable before, it was nothing compared to the distress that settled over him at Cadohaden's inquiry. He set his hammer down next to his forge and wiped his brow again. "Gods, is it hotter'n a dragon's fire gland," the blacksmith muttered as he grasped for something else to say. "Well, whaddya know how to do, son?"

"Nothing," Cadohaden admitted, but spoke up again before Gus could say anything more. "But I'm a hard worker, Gus, I am! I can lift things for you, I can deliver your orders, I can stand on the street and call in customers! Whatever you need me to do!"

"Look, Ulaeron, I'm sorry," Gus said, fidgeting with his apron. Every time his gaze met Cadohaden's, he immediately redirected it elsewhere. "I'm sure you're a good worker and all. But I already got three sons that do all that for me, and they can all make horseshoes. Davey's well on his way to takin' over the shop, really. I'd love to put you to work, but I'm afraid I just don't have enough to pay you anything. I'm not even sure I'd have the time to teach you anything even if I didn't *have* to pay you. These swords I'm throwing together for the soldiers, they take up all my free time. I just don't know how I'd do it, son."

Cadohaden's shoulders slumped as he stared down at the soot-smeared floor. He hadn't really been sure that Gus would have accepted his offer, but he had been hoping for at least a 'maybe'. He just wanted some small measure of control over his own fate. "Okay...I understand, Gus," he mumbled in reply.

"What do you want to be a smith for, anyway?" Gus asked as he grasped his hammer once more. "Deltore's raised you to be a fine warrior, son. You've been great in all the youngling melees. That Cassim Uthaireaux always gives you a run for your gold, but I think he's a year or two older than you anyway. The point is, men that my sons will grow up to be live to make weapons for men that *you* will grow up to be, so why in the Lifegiver's name would you want to trade places?"

Cadohaded frowned. He was beginning to feel irritated. Perhaps it was the mention of Cassim, or maybe it was the way that Gus had indirectly called him a boy, comparing him to his sons of which the oldest was at least five years younger than him. Maybe it was just the sweltering heat of the forge. Whatever it was, he no longer wanted to be here. "I don't know, Gus. I think I'll be on my way. Lifegiver bless you." His mother had taught him the courtesy of departing blessings when he was a small child.

He departed the blacksmith's shop, leaving Gus to watch him trot away with a baffled expression. He marched back into the street, his sheathed sword clapping against his leg as he made his way north once more. He didn't want to be in the city anymore. He was sure he'd be seeing plenty of it on his rotations when his father finally conscripted him into the empire's army.

He made his way back in the direction of Deltore's home, but that was not quite his destination. About a quarter mile northward, along the city wall, there was a fissure in the stonework wide enough for a person to squeeze through if they shuffled sideways. The fracture had begun to form a few years back, and with the intermittent freezing and thawing of spring, a significant crevice had opened. Such disrepair was rarely ignored in Kingsbanesin, as the royal court had a team of masons suited for such tasks, but season after season, the hole remained. There were rumors that Galdoys wanted to tear a large section out from the barrier and construct an imitation of the peculiarly named western coast city of Eastfen's Titan's Wall (*Eastfen in the west,* Melaitha would always repeat cheerfully during his geography lessons), which was an engineering miracle that used a massive slab of stone as a gate, and was lifted and lowered with a series of sturdy cogs and chains. Others said that the governor was simply pocketing the gold that was supposed to be used for the repairs so that he could indulge his appetite for wine and whores. Whatever the reason, the rift in the perimeter only grew taller and wider. A haphazard array of scrap boards had been nailed across it, but everyone who had a childhood in Kingsbanesin knew that the center plank's nails sat loosely in the mortar, and could be pried away far enough to slip through.

He did just that, and stole away from the city with the sooty buildings and towering spires. He disappeared into the thick of tall field grass that surrounded the wall before evolving into the forest that bordered both Mount Fangfire and the elven lands, the Sherinalu Vale. He didn't know exactly where he would go, but the wilderness always seemed to bring him a sense of peace, regardless of where he was. He ventured beyond the forest line, into the shade of the oaks and maples. He swatted at his cheek as a whining mosquito landed on his skin. He looked forward to autumn, when the colors of the trees would turn into a beautiful flourish and the pestering insects would vanish.

The occasional leaf crunched and rogue twig snapped under his feet as he decided to make his way to the southeast. He remembered stories that his grandfather Iuvas would tell about a silent ranger of old that could creep through the forests and kill five ogres without a single one of them realizing his presence before it was too late. The tales had fascinated him as a child, but as he grew older, he began to doubt the truth of them. Try as he might, in any given season, he could not wander through the woods and remain silent. As carefully as he moved, there was simply no way to travel further than a dozen feet and not betray your location to listening ears.

He walked through the trees, pausing occasionally to admire an animal track or the rubbing of a deer's antlers on a sapling. Eventually, his wandering feet brought him to a modest stretch of a cedar swamp. Near the bend of a creek that trickled through, a broad cedar guardian lay at an angle, its twisting roots exposed above the bed of peat it lay upon. This was Cadohaden's favorite spot in all the wilderness he had explored beyond Kingsbanesin. There was a gap between the nest of roots that he could sit in comfortably, and the leaning cedar behind him provided an ample backrest. He could sit in that nature-made chair for hours listening to the gurgle of the creek nearby. He drew in a deep breath through his nose and folded his hands against his abdomen, letting his eyelids drift shut. He could feel the warmth of the sun rays that filtered through the treetops. A dark violet hue bloomed under his eyelids from the light that reached his face. The stream chirped away happily as water rolled over the roots of the army of cedars. Cadohaden drew in another breath, and then another, and soon enough, he fell into a dreamless afternoon slumber.

He laid there until the forest began to grow dark as the sun sank further towards the west. He awoke with a start to the sound of shouts in the distance. Blinking away the fog of his nap, he rose to his feet as a feminine shriek soon followed. He tripped over the roots of the cedar on his first step, falling face-first into the surrounding peat. He pushed himself up again, a smatter of swamp soil clinging to his front. Checking his footing this time, he bolted in the direction of the chaotic noise. He churned his legs as he ran, careful to bound over the roots that lifted up from the soil bed below.

When he discovered the source of the shriek, it was clear enough that those who had caused the shouting were long gone. As Cadohaden pushed away a wayward thorn branch that was reaching out to snag at his cloak, he saw two figures before an oak tree, a young male and female. The former was sitting on the ground, his back against the tree behind him, and a cut just above the corner of his eye was leaking blood down his cheek in a steady stream. There was a bruise blooming at the hinge of his jaw, which was unusually square for someone with elven ears. As Cadohaden examined the stranger, he noticed the broad shoulders, curling brown hair, and the faint crop of adolescent stubble across his cheeks. There was no denying his elven qualities, but Cadohaden would have bet a shining coin or two that one of his parents was of human blood. It was hard to tell when elven heritage played a part, but he looked to be only a few years older than Cadohaden.

The young woman was an elf, to be sure, and her flowing brown hair and hazel eyes were enough to quicken Cadohaden's pulse. He'd followed other children out to the border before to shout taunts at the elves in the forest, but he'd never actually seen one up this close. She was leaning over the elf-human, her rune-etched blue cloak puddling against the forest floor, and was dabbing at the wound with a white cloth that was quickly becoming saturated with red. Her eyes flicked toward him in a snap as Cadohaden cleared his throat, approaching tentatively.

He didn't know what to say. He wasn't even sure what he would do. Kingsbanesin and the Sherinalu Vale weren't officially at-war, but that didn't change the empire's attitude toward the elves. Was there some way he was supposed to be behaving here? Was he even in Kingsbanesin territory anymore, or had he crossed the border into the Sherinalu? All at once, Cadohaden realized the awkward position he was in. All he could spit out was, "Uhm...I, ah, is he all right? What happened to him?"

"Does he *look* all right?" the elf woman snapped in reply, Commonspeak rolling off her tongue fluently. "He was beaten by his own kin."

"Which one?" Cadohaden asked without thinking. Realizing the blunt stupidity of his question, he felt his neck flush with embarrassment as the elf's glare sharpened.

"Is there something you wanted, human? Or are you just here to point and laugh?" she quipped as she wiped another trail of blood from the other's cheek.

"No, not at all," Cadohaden found himself saying. "Is there anything I can do to help?"

"I've got it under control. Be on your way."

Cadohaden pursed his lips, glancing between the two. He didn't want to go. An immediate attraction had blossomed the moment he had seen the elf, but it was more than that. He was beginning to realize just how lonely he was. There wasn't any real reason for him to become acquainted with these two, but maybe if he could help patch the stranger's wounds, he would have one. Neither of them knew about the shred of elven blood his mother had passed on to him, and so they could not judge him for it. Would they even if they did know? He wanted to find out, but a second glare from the elf indicated he might not get that chance. He began to turn away when the sitting stranger spoke up in a rasping voice that indicated he'd received a swift punch to the throat.

"What is your name, *den'loier?*"

Cadohaden halted and looked back over his shoulder. The young man was looking up at him, and the woman tending to him had a look of both surprise and exasperation. What had he called him? The term was familiar, and certainly elvish. He knew that his mother had taught him at some point, but he couldn't remember what it meant.

"Apologies," the stranger rasped when Cadohaden remained silent, placing his palms against the dirt and pushing himself forward a little. "Just a habit. *Den'loier* means 'friend' in Sherinalu. I am Eliliweth Heraketh, or sometimes 'Half-Elf', if you ask my, ah...friends that just left. My true friend here is Elunamara Shadowsong."

"Just Elune," the elf said guardedly, her expression remaining distrustful.

Cadohaden's heart quickened eagerly again in his chest. It didn't seem so hopeless after all. "I am Cadohaden Ulaeron, son of Deltore Ulaeron and Melaitha Riverwen." The other two both blinked in surprise at the announcement of his mother's name. Elune's expression softened considerably.

"Your mother is Melaitha?" she asked.

"I, ah...yes," Cadohaden said warily.

"I see," Elune said quietly. "She teaches from the Lifegiver's Codex at our temples. She's a good...person," she finished with an awkward stammer as she struggled to classify Melaitha.

"Are you sure you two don't need some help?" Cadohaden asked cautiously.

"Well, if you insist," Elune said, turning her gaze away as she produced a pouch from underneath her cloak. "Hold that cloth against the wound and put pressure on it while I wrap it."

Cadohaden hurried over to comply with the instructions, kneeling before Eliliweth and taking the cloth from Elune, his heart quickening once more as his fingertips grazed her knuckles. He pressed it against the half-elf's forehead as she began to pull bandages from her pouch. "Why did they hurt you?" he asked.

"Because my father was human," Eliliweth answered, as simply as if he were discussing why the ground is wet after a rainstorm.

"That's all?" Cadohaden said with a frown as Elune began to wrap the bandages carefully around the half-elf's head.

"They've never needed any more reason than that," she quipped as she worked.

"Just a troublesome few," Eliliweth said dismissively. "I don't want to give you the idea that the Sherinalu Vale is full of the likes of them. Besides, I'm sure with Melaitha Riverwen being your mother, this can't be all that unfamiliar to you. You *do* come from Kingsbanesin, right?"

"Well...yeah," Cadohaden admitted vaguely. "But I've never been... *beaten* or anything. My father is pureblood human, though, and my mother is just barely elven. If you didn't know my parents, you wouldn't even know I had any in me."

"But that doesn't stop them, does it?" Eliliweth said with a faint, knowing smile. Being so close, there was no doubt that the half-elf was young, but his voice had an air of wisdom to it all the same. Before Cadohaden could answer, Elune pulled away from the half-elf, studying her work. Silently deeming it satisfactory, she packed the remaining length of bandage back into her pouch before tying it back to her belt. Cadohaden moved back a few paces but remained kneeling before them.

"So, are you two...together?" Cadohaden heard the words fall from his mouth before he could rein them in. His neck turned dark crimson once more. What the hell was wrong with him?

Elune turned red as well, shooting a glare in his direction before busying herself with her pouch again. A weary smiled emerged on Eliliweth's face before he shook his head. "No. Elune is one of my closest friends, but that is all. What are you doing out here, Sir Cadohaden?" he asked, abruptly changing the subject, much to Cadohaden's relief.

"I was just relaxing in the cedars to the west," he said, jerking his head in the rough direction of where he came from. "I'm to be enlisted in the Kingsbanesin army soon, so I thought it best to enjoy it while I could." Elune's expression darkened once more, but Eliliweth's only grew curious.

"I've overheard young Kingsbanesin men boast about joining the army. You don't sound nearly as excited as they did," the half-elf remarked.

"I want to serve," Cadohaden said, choosing his words with calculation as he dragged the tip of his pointer finger against the ground near his foot idly. "It's just that I always thought I would join the Dragonrider's Guild, like my father did. I'm not allowed to because of who my mother is, and she'd prefer I sit in a temple all day reading from the Codex."

"That's unfairly simplifying a cleric's duties," Elune pointed out quickly.

"It is," Eliliweth said in agreement. He adjusted his position against the tree once more with a wince and a grunt. "But I understand your frustration. It's hard to compromise when it comes to the role you want to fulfill."

"I want to honor them both," Cadohaden confessed. He'd never had anyone to express all of this to. It felt good, even in these odd circumstances. "My parents, I mean. They haven't been in agreement over a damn thing since I can remember, but they've both given a lot for me. Father could have left me out here in the woods in a cradle and nobody in Kingsbanesin would have blamed him. And I know that Mother risks her own safety to come see me. But they can't find any common ground on what I'm to do with the rest of my life."

"Why is that any of their business?" Elune interjected. The guarded edge in her voice had retreated once more. She almost sounded genuinely curious.

"That's just how it is in Kingsbanesin," Cadohaden answered. "Your parents raise you to do something, and when you're old enough to do it on your own, that's what you do. Isn't that how it is in the Sherinalu?"

"It is not," Elune answered with a perplexed frown. "Nobody is an exact replica of their parents. Why would anyone restrict themselves to what their elders know when there's a chance you could do something that would contribute so much more?"

"Have you considered joining a paladin order?" Eliliweth said, dousing what was threatening to become a heated debate.

"A what?" Cadohaden asked.

"Kingsbanesin doesn't have one yet? Well, if they have followers of Kaijaras, I'm sure they'll have paladins soon enough," the half-elf said. "Have you heard of Kaijar Keep, Cadohaden?"

"I've heard the name, but I don't really know what it is," Cadohaden admitted.

"It's a holy citadel far to the south of the Aariad," Eliliweth explained. "With vast lands, filled with people that swear fealty to the Grand Bishop. Nearly their entire populace is completely devoted to the Lifegiver. They keep to themselves, mostly. Their concerns lie mainly with the mage island Novinar. They keep each other in a healthy balance of power.

"Anyway, the idea of putting priests in armor and giving them weapons originated in Kaijar Keep. I don't know who decided so many years ago that holy men need to stay in their robes when they're on the field of battle, and apparently, neither does Kaijar Keep, because they've begun training what they call paladins."

"Wearing heavy armor is exerting. It's hard to channel any kind of magic with that kind of burden," Elune pointed out.

"Well, yes, there's a trade-off, I suppose," Eliliweth admitted. "But from what I understand, they train you to adapt to fatigue, or at least to work some simple blessings while in combat. I don't think you'd see one exorcising a demon while fending off an angry troll or anything, but even healing a man's wound while still having the protection of armor would be a great boon, or so I would think."

"How far south is Kaijar Keep?" Cadohaden asked dubiously.

"Oh, Kaijar Keep would be a grueling journey on your own," Eliliweth said. "But the idea of paladin orders has spread north. You've heard of the Glen Bailey, right?"

"Of course," Cadohaden answered. Everyone in Kingsbanesin knew of the kingdom that had conquered them in the Gunnysack Wars.

"They've begun training paladins at their Monastery," Eliliweth said. "It's being spearheaded by a man named Crusader Nevic Baltwin. If you don't think you'll get a fair opportunity in Kingsbanesin, and you really want to honor both of your parents, think about visiting the Glen Bailey."

Cadohaden considered the half-elf's words. He was sure that such a 'visit' would not be as simple as Eliliweth had put it. Galdoys Veriknock would doubtlessly be displeased to hear that a man overdue for enlisting in his army was journeying to the Glen Dale to inquire about joining another order. Still, what Eliliweth said made sense. If there *was* a way to honor both his mother and father, this sounded like the best way to do so. "How do you know so much about the Glen Bailey, anyway?" he asked.

"I go there often," Eliliweth said, a subtle yearning coloring his words. "It's like a second home to me." Judging by his tone, Cadohaden wondered which of the half-elf's homes was truly secondary.

"I'll think about it," he promised.

"We should be going," Elune said, wrapping her arm underneath Eliliweth's and assisting him onto his feet. "It isn't safe so far out here after dark."

Cadohaden knew it was true, but his heart sank nonetheless. There was a contented fire burning happily in his chest at his new-found chance for real friendship. "Will I...ah, see you two around?" It sounded absurd, asking his elven neighbors such a thing, but he couldn't leave without asking.

"Perhaps," Eliliweth said as took a few steps away from the tree, wincing at some hidden pain. "Elune and I come out here to hunt for truffles. If you find the time, you might find us out here in the late afternoons. Otherwise...maybe we shall meet again at the Glen Bailey?"

Cadohaden smiled and nodded. "Perhaps, yes!" It was a promise he knew he shouldn't be making, but saying it made him feel more in control.

"It was good to meet you," Elune said with a measured voice. "And if you see Melaitha, tell her to travel with care. I think the Sherinalu Vale needs her more than most of us know."

"I will!" Cadohaden said, almost too eagerly, and he felt his skin turn crimson once more. Elune's smile was subtle, but genuine, and it only made him flush a deeper red as she and Eliliweth disappeared into the wilderness, back to the Sherinalu Vale. He watched them go, and then turned in the opposite direction, back towards the stretch of cedar trees.

Chapter Four

"Here's one," Eliliweth murmured as he knelt down before a mossy patch under a towering oak. The half-elf dug his fingers into the soil as he procured a black, warty truffle, brushing the dirt away from it with one hand as he held it in the palm of the other.

"Good find," Elune answered admiringly as she looked over his shoulder at the delicacy he held. She angled her gaze over her own shoulder as Eliliweth gave the truffle a quick brushing, trying to judge the distance they'd covered since parting ways with the young Kingsbanesin man. They'd been moving at a slow pace, but had still been traveling for over an hour. She was still both irritated and a little disturbed that the elven ruffians had tracked them so far just to rough up Eliliweth. That persistence crossed the line of just bullying; it was a brooding prejudice that made her worry what else her own kin might be capable of, despite her half-elf friend's constant assurances that it was all just the troublemaking of youngsters. She knew that many of the Sherinalu's adults had no qualms with the constant harassment.

She dismissed the troubles from her mind before they could fester into deeper resentment. She looked back at Eliliweth and asked, "Are you still doing all right? Do you want to stop for a bit?"

"By the Goddess, Elune, I'm fine. Promise," Eliliweth insisted as he stood up, though she could tell how much effort he was putting into disguising a wince of discomfort.

"Something has to be done, Eliliweth," she said softly, her head shaking side-to-side. "It isn't just children being children anymore. The ones who attacked you this time, they're old enough to know better. We're *elves*, we're *supposed* to be better than that, even in our youth."

"Who would...who would we go to?" Eliliweth asked, having to pause once as his voice caught, still raspy from being struck in the throat. His words were patient, not out of anger, but somber nonetheless. "And what would they do? I can't have an armed escort everywhere I go, friend. That would only encourage the others to carry weapons as well. I don't wish to see these little scuffles escalate."

"They're not just 'scuffles' anymore, Eliliweth," Elune insisted. "I had to bandage your head today. What will it be next? Stitches?"

"If Cadohaden Ulaeron is around to give you a hand, I'd say the two of you could patch up anything," the half-elf said with a faint grin. "I think he fancied you, Elune."

"What?" Elune said with a faint scoff, shaking her head again. "He's a Kingsbanesin boy, Eliliweth, don't be ridiculous. And don't change the subject, either, I'm quite serious. If we're going to be followed all the way out here by little vagabonds that will go so far as to split your scalp open, where do we expect it stop? If we bring this up to the Tribunal-"

"Elune," Eliliweth interrupted, taking a step towards her. "I'll be all right. Really. There isn't anything the Tribunal will do that will make it worth our while. If everything goes as I think it will over the next couple weeks, it won't matter anyway. Sometimes the best way to win a battle is to not fight it." The half-elf didn't wait for a retort this time, but turned around and continued his way towards the Sherinalu Vale.

Elune frowned impatiently as she followed alongside him. Her friend had a great wealth of proverbs that she often found inspiring, but in this case, it felt like a poor rationalization. He had piqued her curiosity, however. "Things are going well with King Bartholomew, then? You make it sound like you won't be a citizen of the Vale much longer."

"I don't want to prematurely get my hopes up, but I think he wishes to have me as a member of his court," Eliliweth said with an excited smile on his face. "You remember all the time I spent away in the spring? I was visiting the swamp kingdom of York on his behalf, learning more about their ways of life. I discovered things that I think will actually benefit the Glen Dale as well, and Bartholomew agrees. I'm supposed to meet with his council during the Solstice festival."

"That's wonderful to hear, my friend," Elune said with a smile, temporarily forgetting about the beating as he spoke of the positive news. "Would you be required to surrender your citizenship in the Sherinalu Vale if you took such a position?"

"I don't know," Eliliweth admitted quietly. "But I don't know if it would sway me either way. I love the Vale. But I don't know if I could make a difference there. I believe I would have plenty of opportunity in the Glen Dale."

Elune's smile widened as she listened. They walked in silence for a while, their boots crunching against the leaves and pine needles beneath them. She couldn't help but feel a bit envious, however, for she had both similar yearnings and doubts about how she would fulfill them while remaining in the Sherinalu Vale. The elves weren't strictly isolationists, but they devoted little attention to the outside world, and their culture was deeply rooted in tradition and habit. As mystical and complicated as elves were fabled to be, her brethren were usually as predictable as the countryside farmers. She'd ventured to the Glen Bailey with Eliliweth before, and the city was both intriguing and comforting. She did not possess the favor of King Bartholomew the way Eliliweth did, however, and so she had little hopes for any claim to citizenship. The Princess Aven had promised to ask about an ambassador's position for her, but Elune knew better than to count any chickens before they'd hatched. Either way, the Sherinalu elders were not about to encourage such notions, and worse, she felt as though her parents were dangerously close to forbidding it. She was not obligated to obey their commands, but elven families were traditionally very close, cooperation integral to the success of the Vale as a whole. A fracturing between her and her parents would make life very difficult.

Her thoughts were interrupted as she heard a crunching noise up ahead, coming from the opposite direction. Eliliweth did as well, for he stopped in his tracks as he squinted into the wilderness. Elune could see a figure moving between the trees, and she reached out for the half-elf's shoulder, ready to pull him into hiding in case the Sherinalu youth had decided to come hassle him once more.

It turned out not to be any of the ruffians they'd encountered before, however. As the figure approached, Elune began to recognize him as Faltorim Veayu. With a set of wide shoulders and square jaw, at least by elven standards, Faltorim was the youngest member of the Sherinalu elder council. He routinely performed menial services for the Vale, such as daily distribution of food and water, but also had a more distinguished role: he was the creator of homes for its residents. Upon reaching adulthood, every member of the Sherinalu society was grant-ed their own home, though it was not constructed in the traditional manner used by their human neighbors. Rather, elven mages such as Faltorim would find a great forest tree and proceed to bend and warp its image until it became a small treetop cottage. Nearly all elven res-idents lived in such crafted homes, and Elune had been granted her own only a few years past by Faltorim Veayu himself.

"Faltorim!" Elune said in surprise, frowning at the elder with curi-osity. "What are you doing all the way out here?"

"*Alu'nadoe*, Elunamara Shadowsong," Faltorim said with a bright smile, forest-green irises glimmering with his demeanor. He nodded his head briefly at Eliliweth and murmured his name in greetings as well, though he barely registered the half-elf's presence before fixating on Elune once again. "Lady Sinomeluna was concerned with your ab-sence. She asked that I seek you out."

Elune released an irritated sigh through her nose, brow furrowing as Faltorim explained his presence. "My mother needn't worry herself. I usually spend most of the day away from the Vale when gathering truffles. I've told her as much."

Faltorim shrugged his shoulders and pressed his palms together in front of his stomach. "I thought that was the case, but she seemed distressed, and I had finished with my duties for the day, so I told her I would come."

I think it's fair to say that she had other motives, Faltorim, but per-haps you knew that as well, Elune thought to herself in brooding si-lence.

"Everything's all right, Faltorim, I can assure you," Eliliweth said politely.

Faltorim finally looked upon the half-elf with true observation, the elf's face pinching in what may have been an attempt at concern but came across more like annoyance. "You say that, Eliliweth Hera-keth, but I see a bandage wrapped around your head with a spot of red. Just what happened to you?"

"Just a tussle with some of the Sherinalu's younglings, is all. Noth-ing serious," Eliliweth said in a tone that was more assertive than the words he'd chosen.

"You're picking fights with elves younger than you?" Faltorim responded dubiously.

"He was absolutely not," Elune interrupted, taking a step towards the elder with a frown. She was typically known for having an abundance of patience, but she could not stand there any longer while Faltorim tried to unfairly shift the blame over to Eliliweth. "There were three of them, Faltorim Veayu, and though Eliliweth had every right to break each of their arms, and I assure you that he could if he wished to, he did little more than shove them away until he had no other choice than to fight back. By the Goddess, Faltorim, those little bastards could have *killed* him, and this isn't the first time this has happened. You're an elder; can't you bring this up to the Tribunal and have some punishment handed down? I'm appalled that this kind of behavior is just ignored in a place like the Sherinalu Vale! There *are* others who know that this has been going on!"

Both Faltorim and Eliliweth stared at Elune in stunned silence as the woman who was usually so softspoken scolded the young elder, her pointed ears turning red as she continued to lecture him. As she fell silent, she almost looked sheepish for a brief moment before reasserting her irritated demeanor. Between the young Kingsbanesin man and now Faltorim, she was more flustered than she'd been in quite some time.

Faltorim cleared his throat awkwardly and lifted one of his hands, sliding his fingertips along his right ear as he said, "Apologies, Elunamara. I didn't intend any disrespect."

"I prefer Elune, and it's not me you should be apologizing to," she answered curtly.

"Of course, sorry," Faltorim said, dipping a stiff nod at Eliliweth, though he didn't quite meet the half-elf's gaze. "I apologize, Eliliweth. I was not aware that this was a recurring issue. I'm not sure, ah... 'scuffles' fall into the category of issues that the Tribunal reviews, but I will have words with a few people and get this mess sorted out."

Eliliweth glanced over at Elune with a grim smile that silently said *I told you so* before turning his gaze back to Faltorim with the same tight-lipped grin. "I would just like to be able to come pick truffles without being assaulted, is all. There's no need to get the Tribunal involved."

"Excellent," Faltorim answered, looking clearly relieved by Eliliweth's assurance. "Well, if that's settled, should we make our way back, then?"

With the matter 'settled', the three of them continued the return journey to the Sherinalu Vale. Elune kept relatively quiet as they made their way back, despite Faltorim clearly having a stronger interest in conversing with her over Eliliweth. She found herself feeling weary and impatient with his passes. It was no secret that he fancied her, much to her parents' delight. She'd heard on more than one occasion why she should be leaping at the opportunity to be courted by an elf with such a solidified role in the Vale and even brighter potential in his future. She'd be lying if she said that she'd never considered entertaining Faltorim's interests. He was good looking, well-groomed, and wore a pleasant scent that she still hadn't been able to pinpoint. He was well-established, to be sure, and in most situations he was considerate and polite. But Faltorim, as well as other suitors that had attempted to win her over, could not seem to interact with Eliliweth without letting their scorn for the half-elf slip through their flowery speech. She wasn't sure if he or the others were actually that perturbed by Eliliweth's half-blooded nature or if they were simply jealous of her friendship with him, but whatever the reason, it was not a compromise she was willing to make.

With the discomfort of having Faltorim as an escort, the way back seemed to take twice as long. Eventually, however, they approached the city of the Sherinalu Vale, the treetop buildings visible from the ground, rope bridges strung from one to the other in a network of roads similar to that of a human city. There were buildings on the ground as well, but most were either crafted from the guided growth of massive tree roots or assembled with brilliant white marble, primarily the sanctuaries of worship. Elune could see sentinel archers posted in the trees along the city's perimeter, ever watchful for threats that may deem the elven city easy enough prey.

"Well, here we are, safe and sound," Faltorim said matter-of-factly as they crossed over into the Vale. The sun was nearly tucked under the horizon, the crimson rays filtering in through the treetops giving the forest city a dim glow. "Can I walk you back to your abode, Elune?"

"I can manage on my own," Elune said, her tone not quite as sharp as it had been during her tirade back in the wilderness, but still firm.

"Ah," Faltorim said with a faint crease in his brow, his hands folding in front of his waist. The elder stood there awkwardly for a moment in silence, glancing between the two of them before adding, "Could I perhaps have a moment alone, then?"

"Is it really something you can't say in front of Eliliweth?" Elune countered. She knew she was bordering on harsh, but Faltorim's insistence on scooting her friend away from her was beginning to thoroughly annoy her.

"Well," Faltorim said, looking over at Eliliweth, who only peered back in wait. The elder finally sighed and shrugged a shoulder. "I suppose not. I just wanted to ask you, Elune, if you already had a partner for the Solstice Ball this week." His eyes darted back over to Eliliweth meaningfully.

Elune sighed inwardly. No, she didn't have a partner for the Solstice Ball. Had Faltorim asked her the day before, or taken her request for Tribunal involvement with Eliliweth's troubles more seriously, she might have accepted. Not that she had any feelings for Faltorim, but it was a societal norm for everyone to attend with a date, and she was confident that she could enjoy the evening with him. Skipping the event entirely was always an option, but was just as frowned upon as going stag, and she didn't need lectures from her mother or father about her presence in the community. All of this considered, she was simply too offended by Faltorim's behavior around Eliliweth to accept his invitation.

"I'm sorry, Faltorim," Elune said, her words woodenly formal. "I have an obligation already."

"I see," Faltorim said, the disappointment plainly evident in his voice. His lip pursed resentfully as he flicked his gaze in Eliliweth's direction once more before. "Do have a good night, then."

Faltorim turned away from the two, his gait brisk as he disappeared into the Vale. Elune watched him go with a faint pang of guilt that only vexed her more, for she knew she didn't require any obligations to turn the elder down. Her own disinterest should have been reason enough. Eliliweth watched her with a curiosity for a moment before asking, "You truly have plans for the Solstice Ball?"

"No," Elune said a bit more curtly than she intended. "It just sounded more polite than saying I've had quite enough of Faltorim Veayu for one evening."

"I thought that might be the case," Eliliweth said with a thin, apologetic smile. "You don't have to spurn potential dates to the Ball on my account, Elune."

"I don't want dates that treat my good friends like second class citizens," Elune said with insistence.

"I appreciate it, friend," Eliliweth said as he lifted his hand, placing it on her shoulder briefly with a gentle squeeze. "I just don't want to cause you any trouble, is all. Though I'm sure there are elven gentlemen in the Vale that can tolerate our friendship."

"I'm sure there are," Elune said quietly as she folded her arms across her chest. "I'm not sure it's worth the trouble yet, anyway."

"What do you mean?" Eliliweth asked, letting his hand fall back to his side as he frowned in puzzlement.

"I mean…" Elune began, twisting her mouth a bit as she searched for the words. "Even if there is someone in the Vale that I might be interested in, I'm past the age now where I can just have a romantic interest. What I mean is…well, you know. For all the progress we've made as a society, with all the wisdom and knowledge we seek for our records and our understanding of the world beyond our borders, there's still this expectation here that at a certain age, you just…you just *accept* a spouse, whether or not you wish to be married. You have a duty in the Sherinalu Vale to begin a family as soon as you're able. We live longer than perhaps any other race across the Aariad, but we're in this tremendous hurry to settle down with someone so that elves like Faltorim can grow us a new home with enough space to accommodate children. There's no time to truly get to know your partner, or experience new things, or just anything that doesn't involve an immense amount of pressure. Does any of that make sense?"

"It does," Eliliweth replied thoughtfully. "I hadn't really thought of that until now, but now that you say it, that seems to be a recurring theme."

"It isn't just a theme, it's…it's our way of life," Elune said with frustration. "Would I like to go to the Solstice Ball? Of course. It's a wonderful time. But if I go with someone who could be seen as my mate, like Faltorim, it won't just be the partygoers or my parents that will assume I'm ready to be wed. My date will probably infer the same, and who could blame him? Half of the maidens there who aren't betrothed will be before winter arrives. It's just what happens."

"Come to the Glen Bailey with me, then," Eliliweth said. "They celebrate the Solstice as well, but in a different way. It's a city-wide festival, full of music, drink, and cheer. I was extended an invitation by King Bartholomew himself, and I was told to bring a guest. There won't be any presumptions or intrusive questions."

Elune studied Eliliweth curiously as he made his proposal. She could tell that there was no romantic inclination to his invitation, to her relief. She and her half-elven friend had briefly explored the possibility of a relationship ages ago, only to quickly realize that while their bond was strong, it was one of sibling-like nature. Even though she knew that Eliliweth would someday make a magnificent life partner for someone, she couldn't imagine there being anything more than a friendship between them. "They'll still talk. Everyone here, I mean," she said, though she was unable to contain her smile. Another adventure to the Glen Dale was just what she needed.

"Then let them talk," Eliliweth said with a shrug of his shoulders. "It wouldn't stop them, anyway. Besides, before I last left the Glen Bailey, Princess Aven told me that she hoped you'd accompany me again the next time I returned. You may have more friends there than you do here, if you don't mind me saying."

"I don't, actually," Elune answered as her smile broadened, forgetting her previous irritations as she considered the idea. "I think you're right, friend. I'd be happy to come along."

"Wonderful," the half-elf answered. "We'll leave at first light."

Chapter Five

He decided that he had wandered far enough southward to head towards Kingsbanesin's southern entrance. Under the cover of tree-tops, the brooding red light of the sun was just barely penetrating the canopies, and though he didn't fear the forest in the darkness, he knew better than to test the whim of fate. There were more than just wild animals that crept into the forests at night.

He finally broke the forest line and cut his way through the tall field grass towards the road leading to the southern gate. There were dewdrops clinging to the blades, collecting against his half-cape and boots as he parted through them. He approached the gate and noticed with dismay that the portcullis was closed.

"Who goes there?" a voice shouted from above the ramparts. A silhouette leaned over the stone barrier with a torch in his hand. It was one of the watchmen; Cadohaden was pretty sure his name was Tagart.

"It's Cadohaden Ulaeron," he shouted back. "I'm returning from business."

"Business!?" Tagart guffawed from above. "Sure you did!"

"You let me out through here yesterday."

"I did bloody not!"

"Well, it was you, or someone that sounded a hell of a lot like you," Cadohaden challenged.

"Well you aren't bringin' back any goods, so you must have been sellin'!" Tagart bellowed from above. "So let's see the coin you got!"

"Oh for dragon's blasting bowels," another voice shouted out from above. Cadohaden didn't recognize the new one. "He doesn't have any coin, dimwit, he was just out dawdling in the woods.

"You!" the unknown guard's voice shouted down at him. "I know you crawled out of that hole on the northern end! You stay the hell away from there, or next time you can camp out here at the gate til Daddy comes to get you! Open the damned thing up for him, Tags."

Cadohaden bristled indignantly at the chiding, but he didn't know what else to say, and unless he actually wanted to spend the night outside the city, he knew it was best to just keep his mouth shut. A few seconds later the portcullis began to lift, coming to a stop only four feet above the ground. He rolled his eyes and ducked underneath, just barely getting across before it began to lower once more. It touched back down with a solid *clank* as he stepped back into Kingsbanesin. He paused, a faint frown crossing his brow. Everything seemed strangely quiet.

In a harsh booming blast, the sound of an explosion came from the north. Cadohaden froze, squinting against the dim light of the late evening sky. Suddenly, he could hear the muffled sounds of distant screams coming from the same direction. Trepidation crawled up from his toes, dancing up and across his spine, and for a moment, he couldn't seem to move. The shouts from the rampart guards awoke him from his stupor, and he bolted into the heart of the city, towards the northern wall.

His heart hammered in his chest. The noise had come from the north. But how far north? Close to Deltore's home? He told himself that it couldn't be, that it must have been an accident at a smithy, or an alchemist's shop, anything that made a lick of sense. He told himself he was right, that it had to be something like that, but it didn't stop his feet from pounding forward with an urgent sense of dread. More screams reached his ears as he sprinted tirelessly across Kingsbanesin, dodging market tents, assorted barrels of goods, and the waves of citizens that had stopped to stare off in the direction of the commotion. Cadohaden didn't bother to apologize as his shoulders bumped and even knocked over some of the gawkers, even as they shouted after him while they struggled to get back to their feet.

Finally, his feet brought him to Deltore's home. For a brief moment, he was relieved to see that it looked to be unharmed, but the feeling was quickly smothered with another bout of anxiety as he saw the smoke rising behind it, a sinister omen in the background. The screams were louder now, accompanied with violent bellows and snarls. He could hear the clash of steel against steel, and with a trembling hand, he unsheathed the blade at his hip before running closer to the chaos.

The smoke was coming from the city wall, or what remained of it. Flames licked the jagged rubble that formed a maw-like opening where the fracture he had departed from had been only hours ago. Something had exploded where the rift had been, and it had collapsed the wall for no less than thirty yards in both directions. Brutish creatures were pouring in from the outside, dressed in scraps of fur and mismatched patches of armor. Their weapons were an assortment of barbaric creations and clearly stolen armaments from civilized places. Many had painted faces, an array of blacks, blues, and reds, but Cadohaden could see the skin tone underneath, a variety of mottled gray to deep forest greens. He had never seen one before, but his father had told him countless tales. Orcs were storming Kingsbanesin.

Everything was moving so quickly. He could sense his vision beginning to tunnel as he gazed out across the field of battle. He recognized almost everyone in the resistance. They were all Dragonriders, his father included, and they were desperately trying to form a shield wall in front of the breach, though many of them were still in casual dress, lacking anything resembling armor. The weaponry they held seemed improvised as well. Cadohaden saw one of the men wielding a lantern post like a spear, furiously jabbing it at the greenskins that were threatening to push into the city.

He turned his gaze back to Deltore. He seemed more prepared, adorned in his scalemail and wielding a double-bladed battle axe. His father had shuffled towards the shield wall's flank, swinging the axe in furious arcs, repelling the orcs as they threatened to swarm the defending dragonriders. Orcish blood coated both his weapon and his person, his hair plastered against his cheek with the violet-red substance.

To his horror, he caught sight of Melaitha as well. She was moving back and forth behind the shield wall. Men would stumble backwards after an orc would land a blow. The priestess rushed over to them, kneeling before them to try to heal their wounds. Some of them got back to their feet. Others remained sprawled on the ground, clutching at their afflictions. Occasionally, Melaitha would get to her feet, look out over the chaos, and scream a prayer with outstretched hands. Following the direction of her outcries, Cadohaden spotted a hunched orc with a tattered robe and a gnarled root staff standing in the middle of the opened rift, and he quickly understood. The orcs had brought a warlock with them, and the priestess was trying to keep his malefic curses at bay as well as heal the wounded.

He told himself to charge forward, to join the fray, but his legs would no longer obey. His gaze darted back to Deltore and remained fixated in despair as he saw his father furiously cut his way into the orcish mob. Cadohaden found his voice and called out to him, but it was no use. Consumed with battle lust, his father was burrowing his way right into the pack of marauding orcs.

His feet found their freedom once more. Cadohaden charged towards his father, shouting for him to pull back, but Deltore was disappearing into the greenskinned fray. A strangled cry escaped him as his father vanished into the violent mob. He saw the nearby orcs' attentions divert towards the rampaging human that was mushrooming himself into their ranks. They turned their weapons towards him and collapsed upon the dragon rider. Cadohaden released one more defeated cry of anguish before helplessly turning his fevered gaze to the shield wall, looking for his mother.

Like a flood breaking through a dam, the orcish tide burst through the shield wall, sending the dragonriders sprawling as the swarm charged through. Cadohaden ran towards Melaitha, but stumbled backwards as a tumbling dragonrider barreled into him. He craned his neck, desperately trying to find her once more, and there she was, on the ground and frantically trying to get back to her feet.

Time slowed to a crawl as Cadohaden looked on in horror. He tried to wade his way through the chaos towards his mother, but he couldn't make himself push through as fast as he was commanding his body. He heard the blare of brass horns somewhere off in the distance, but it was only a dim noise as the uproar of violence became a muffled drone in his mind. He watched, destitute, as an orc with a tattered leather kilt and exposed torso took a calculated step towards his mother. Cadohaden screamed, but never heard the sound as the brute lifted a broad claymore over his head with two massive hands. Melaitha lifted her arms, as if she might deflect the blow, but it would not save her. The gleaming blade fell in a menacing arc, burying its edge into her shoulder, just below the neck. Her head jerked backwards, her mouth falling open in a ghastly gape as a ribbon of blood trickled out from her lip. The orc grinned savagely, placed a hide-bound foot against her chest, and pushed her off of his blade, leaving her to collapse against the ground lifelessly.

The uncertainty began to melt away. Cadohaden felt something dark and violent surge in his chest. He could hear shouts coming from the ramparts, but it was far away and unimportant now. He locked his gaze on the fiend that had killed his mother. Blood surged in his neck with insistent pulses, and he gripped the hilt on his sword with unbridled rage. This beast would die. If it was the last thing he ever did, he would kill this invader. He stormed forward. He collided with another orc, knocking the brute over, but he leaped over him and kept going. The one with the claymore needed to die. He would be the first.

The brute's head turned as Cadohaden charged forward, but he couldn't react in time. Swiping away the claymore's blade, he reversed the swing in a furious motion, slashing open the orc's throat. The greenskin's eyes widened in surprise as he stumbled, dropping his weapon and lifting his bulky hand to his neck, but the young warrior was relentless. With a howl of abandonment, he swung back and forth, over and over, mincing the brute's face with murderous attacks. The bloodied corpse of the orc fell to the ground, and Cadohaden heard heavy steps thundering behind him. He turned to face another as it lunged towards him with a club of steel prongs. He charged towards the orc, burying his already bloodied blade into his exposed abdomen. The orc gurgled in his face, dropping his weapon as the steel sunk into his gut. Cadohaden snarled in response and threw himself forward with a vicious headbutt, knocking the invader over as he pulled back his sword.

He stumbled backwards as the orc fell to the ground. Purple smudges blossomed in his vision and he was instantly sure he hadn't executed the headbutt correctly. He stared in dazed confusion around him as he noticed the number of orcs had greatly thinned. Were those Kingsbanesin soldiers around him? As he peered at his surroundings, the smeared stars gradually fading from his sight, he saw not only that a brigade of Kingsbanesin infantry had arrived, but two teams of archers had collapsed on the scene, lining the ramparts from both sides of the charred opening. In his blood fury, Cadohaden hadn't even noticed the barrage of arrows raining down on the orcs from above. On the other side of the barrier, he could see the surviving invaders retreating back into the wilderness. Some of the infantry soldiers lined up, closing off the gaping hole in the stone wall, but most of them were bending over to examine the fallen dragonriders. Cadohaden couldn't see a single one stirring from where they lay.

He didn't know where to go first. His vicious anger quickly soured into a heart-wrenching grief. Trudging forward, he approached his mother's body. Her glossy eyes stared sightlessly at the sky above. Falling to his knees, he lifted her upper body onto his lap, a choked sob catching in his throat as he dragged his fingertips over her eyelids, carefully pushing them shut. Her still-warm body lay limp in his arms as he trembled, the blood from her gaping wound warming his leg as it puddled under his knee. He brushed a strand of hair out of her face as he gently rocked her back and forth. "Mother," he said weakly. "Mother, I'm so sorry, I'm so sorry, I'm so sorry…"

A quiet whine of grief escaped his throat as he cradled her. Nothing seemed real. It was only hours ago that he had walked through this same place, the worst of his worries being his parents' feuding and what would become of his life when he enlisted in the army. All that seemed so insignificant now as he held his mother's lifeless form. He looked over with dread to where Deltore had fallen and cringed at the sight of the crumpled body laying in a pool of blood, his visible wounds like open mouths shouting accusations at him as they drooled crimson saliva. Cadohaden clenched his jaw and looked away, shaking his head. Could he dare to think that this was all a dream?

A harsh grunt interrupted his hypnotizing grief. Warily, he looked up at one of the strewn bodies. It was Mekoda, the leader of the Dragonrider's Guild. One of his eyes was hemorrhaging blood, and with a gloved hand, he was holding back his innards as they threatened to spill from a gaping gut wound, but he was yet alive. In an agonized whisper, he croaked, "Ulaeron. Come…come here." Cadohaden gently set Melaitha back down upon the ground, looking up at the Kingsbanesin soldiers as they examined the other bodies. "No," Mekoda snapped in a hollow grunt. "Before they see."

Cadohaden lifted himself to his feet and walked over to the dying dragonrider, kneeling before him gingerly. "Sir," was all he could think to say.

"Listen to me," Mekoda rasped with a cringe. "Listen…to me. This was no…this was no goddamned accident."

"What?" Cadohaden said, too loudly. He glanced fervently over at the Kingsbanesin soldiers, assuring that he hadn't drawn any of their attentions before looking back down at Mekoda. "What do you mean?"

"Exactly what I said," Mekoda grunted. "Our insider never...ungh... never showed up. It was a set up. Galdoys...made a deal with the orcs. I'm sure of it."

Cadohaden's eyes widened. It was no secret that Galdoys would be remembered as one of Kingsbanesin's most ruthless governors, but would even he go that far? "That can't be true," Cadohaden said in hushed tones. "Why would he betray his own dragonriders?"

Mekoda turned his head, looking at the inspecting soldiers that were slowly making their way towards them. He looked back at Cadohaden and reached out with the hand that wasn't holding in his stomach contents and gripped his ankle insistently. "Because we're not... all...here, Ulaeron. Do you see Curtis Zeffitir among the dead? Do you see Blaine Iuvaq? All the young pups that...rrrngh...that were pullin' for that mad bastard...they didn't show up either. Galdoys is fillin' the Guild with men that...that won't say no to him. I'm telling you...this was no accident."

"How can you be sure?" Cadohaden asked. There could have been any number of reasons that some of the dragonriders weren't there.

"Don't be a damned fool, boy," Mekoda said. He released his grip on Cadohaden's ankle and jerked his thumb towards the looming northern mountain. "Mount Fangfire is *right there*. You're telling me that...that they didn't see all that in time to send down a dragon?"

Cadohaden looked up at the vigilant mountain. All of a sudden, it seemed less like a proud landmark and more of a monolithic traitor. Harsh reality struck him like a marksman's arrow. Mekoda was right. The mountain roost was never unattended. From such an elevated view, there was no way they wouldn't have seen the orcish attack. Galdoys was never hesitant to employ the use of Kingsbanesin's dragons. Cadohaden looked to the sky. Someone should have been patrolling, but not a single winged beast roamed above. Galdoys had forbidden the intervention.

"Good," Mekoda grunted. "You understand. Deltore was a good man, Cadohaden. Your mother...I didn't know your mother, but she was your mother all the same. They both died here. Don't let that go unanswered. Now...there's a mercy blade in my boot sheath. Put me... put me out of my goddamned misery."

Cadohaden looked down at Mekoda's boot. Sure enough, the handle of a long dagger could be seen sitting in the dragonrider's boot sheath. Hesitantly, he reached down and pulled it from its leather fold. He turned it over in his hand. It had a thin, sharp blade and a deadly point.

"It's getting dark out," one of the soldiers called out from nearby. "Somebody round up some damned torches so we can get this sorted out."

"Slide it right through the armpit. Right...right into the heart," Mekoda wheezed through his teeth. Cadohaden had been so enthralled with the conspiratorial discovery that he had forgotten how much agony the man was in. "Go on, boy, do it."

He looked down at the mercy blade, then back at Mekoda. He had just killed for the first time, but this was different. Even if the dragonrider was pleading for it, he was no orc. He had perhaps been the closest thing to a friend Cadohaden had. He felt his jaw beginning to quiver.

"It's time to grow up, Ulaeron," Mekoda murmured impatiently. "Don't get soft on me. Your folks are gone, boy. The choice...the choice is out of your hands now. Prove to yourself that...that you're a man now. Put. Me. Down."

Cadohaden swallowed and blinked away the tears stinging the corners of his eyes. Mekoda was right. His parents were gone. It didn't feel real yet, and he knew it would come down hard on him when it did, but life would never be the same again, and he couldn't afford to pretend that it would be. He gently lifted Mekoda's arm and tucked the blade underneath, the point pressing against the dragonrider's armpit.

"Swift and...steady, Ulaeron," Mekoda said in a pained whisper. "Make it quick."

Cadohaden wet his lips, looking up at the soldiers that were closing in. He looked back down at Mekoda, focusing on the good eye. The dragonrider nodded grimly. Clenching his teeth, Cadohaden thrusted the mercy blade through. He cringed as blood frothed from Mekoda's lips, but the dragonrider's hand clasped his shoulder reassuringly before falling still.

He furiously fought back the threat of tears. He could not fall apart. It was time to grow up. Mekoda was right. He would not let this go unanswered. A few of the soldiers were coming towards him with puzzled frowns, but he had no time to speak to them, nor did he truly trust them. How many of them knew of Galdoys's treachery? He got to his feet and ran back towards the heart of the city. He didn't think he could bear to look at the bodies of his parents anyway. He had to focus on his task. He heard shouts behind him, but no pursuing footsteps as he sprinted through the gravel streets.

Adrenaline coursed through him. He was numbly aware of the exhaustion that would grip him sooner or later, but a volatile blend of anguish and anger fueled his strides as he ventured deeper into Kingsbanesin. He spotted a man in a violet robe rounding a street corner and came to a stop in front of him, his face flushed with exertion. He didn't recognize the stranger, who had accentuated crow's feet and was mostly bald save for a pair of unkempt sideburns, but most men who wore robes in Kingsbanesin were members of the Senate.

"Where is the governor?" Cadohaden said between heavy breaths. "Where is Galdoys Veriknock?"

The robed stranger grinned and steepled his fingers in front of his chest. "He is in the Hall of Feasts, young man, celebrating this great victory over the savage orcs!"

"The blood hasn't even dried yet!" Cadohaden shouted. "How could they already be celebrating?"

"Victory is like fire, and the smoke can be seen from afar," the stranger said cryptically, his smile widening.

Rage rose in Cadohaden's throat like bile, and he suddenly wanted to strangle the grinning fool in front of him, but he knew he could not waste time. He pushed off on his back foot, sprinting further into the city. His chest grew tight with the exertion, but he could not stop.

The Hall of Feasts was one of Kingsbanesin's oldest structures, originally constructed to host celebrations whenever the empire successfully subjugated another nation. It was not the largest or even the most formidable building in the city, but it was the most treasured and meticulously cared for, not only by Kingsbanesin's nobility, but the general public, for its doors were open to all. Antiques and heirlooms from past wars decorated the walls, giving visitors a sense of pride in their heritage.

Cadohaden slowed as he reached the Hall's doors. Two guards looked him over. The one on the left said flatly, "State your business."

"Is the governor inside?" Cadohaden asked between drawn breaths.

"State your business," the guard repeated firmly.

"My father perished fighting the orcs," Cadohaden answered. "He cherished Galdoys's leadership, and it was his dying wish that I tell him so."

The guards looked at each other, then back at the young warrior. Last wishes were sacred in nearly all cultures across the Aariad. After a brief pause, the guard that had spoken nodded, and the two opened the twin doors they stood in front of, allowing him inside. His heart slamming against his chest, Cadohaden did his best to appear composed as he marched inside.

Torches lined the long hallway that led to the feasting chamber, their flames crackling like beacons of glory as Cadohaden passed under them. His footfalls echoed against the stone floor below as he approached the inner doors. He grasped both of the bronze handles and hoisted the doors open himself, the light from the inner chamber pouring into the entrance hall as he did so.

Were it not for the anguish gripping his heart, Cadohaden would have marvelled at the inner chamber, even though he had already seen it before, when he was a child. Great braziers lined the walls, the torches even larger than the ones in the entrance hall. Below them, tall pewter candlestick holders stood like palace stewards. At least a dozen chandeliers hung from the ceiling, an arrangement of candles sitting in them as well. And in the center of the chamber, a great stone hearth sat. The proud fireplace was in the image of a dragon, crafted by the legendary sculptor Viqorin Baracuriad in the days of old. Under both of the stone creature's unfurled wings, stacked lumber sat upon mortar platforms. In place of a scaled stomach was the hearth's hollow, the logs and glowing coals burning inside. The dragon's head was pointed triumphantly towards the ceiling. The stonework ended at its maw, where a steel stovepipe protruded from its throat and reached all the way to an opening in the ceiling, an escape for the smoke. Bronze adornments were wrapped around the pipe in the shape of wreaths of flame.

Around the draconian hearth, wide tables and sturdy chairs were aligned on both sides. Unlike the palace, there were no decorative tablecloths or folded napkins, for this was a house inspired not by the comforts of luxury, but by the glories of combat. Trophy weapons lined the walls underneath the blazing torches. Most had a brass plaque underneath, detailing what battle they were used in, and if it was known, which soldier had carried it. The entire chamber was a testament to the mightiest empire the Aariad had ever known.

The hall was filled with mostly nobles and their servant escorts, but a few high-ranking officials from the army were present as well. Cadohaden scanned the tables. Most of the guests looked as though they had just settled in, but as he circumvented the great dragon hearth, he spotted a group that looked as though they had been mingling for quite a bit longer. A furious darkness within him reared its head as he laid his eyes upon Galdoys Veriknock, who was sipping something from a silver chalice. His general, Cedrinn Kalsonstad, sat to his right, and to his left, Blaine Iuvaq of the Dragonrider's Guild chewed at a half-eaten turkey leg. These men were here to celebrate a victory, but it was clear they had arrived well before the dust had settled at the northern wall.

Cadohaden unsheathed his sword, the cords in his neck thrumming with his beating heart as he stalked towards the governor. Distantly, he could sense voices hushing around him as he marched forward. Finally, as he neared the governor's table, someone shouted a warning. The governor looked up from his chalice as Cadohaden drew nearer. He had olive-blonde hair that fell past his jaw, watchful avian eyes, and a small patch of hair under his lower lip. As another shout called out from behind Cadohaden, the governor set down his chalice calmly and lifted his hand, palm facing outward.

It felt as though an invisible man had shoved him squarely in the chest. Cadohaden's sword fell from his grasp as he tumbled backwards in surprise, landing on his back and driving the vindictive air from his lungs. Was that magic Galdoys had cast upon him? How could he have forgotten that the governor was a mage? As he tried to collect himself, a figure rose up over him, the sound of steel leaving its sheath singing through the silence that had settled over the chamber. Blaine Iuvaq stood over him with a contemptuous glare, his sword point pressed against Cadohaden's neck.

Cadohaden remained still, his chest rising and falling with his weary breathing, his fatigue finally catching up to him. Every eye in the chamber watched as Galdoys Veriknock rose from his seat, clasping his hands behind his back as he rounded the table to approach his would-be assailant. He was wearing dark scarlet robes and a gold fleece mantle that had dragon wing embroidery stitched into the shoulders. He looked down at Cadohaden, the bridge of his nose scrunched with snide scrutiny.

"Well well," the governor said with a mocking smile. "It's the Troublesome Bastard himself. What brings you to the Hall of Feasts, boy, on this glorious evening of Kingsbanesin triumph?"

"That sham was no triumph!" Cadohaden shouted from his place on the floor. Iuvaq pressed the tip of his blade a little harder against the young man's skin in a warning gesture.

"At ease, Blaine," Galdoys instructed with a wave of his hand. "The boy is no threat to me." Iuvaq sneered down at Cadohaden before pulling back his sword, returning it to its sheath. The dragonrider took a step back, but he kept a watchful glare trained on the young warrior. Cadohaden rose to his feet and pointed a finger at the governor, shouting for all to hear within the feasting chamber,

"Galdoys Veriknock is a traitor and a fraud!" he shouted. The Hall of Feasts was aglow with the warm, triumphant light of the torches, candles, and sculpted hearth. It casted vindictive shadows across the young man's face as he made his declarations. "He intentionally left a fracture in the city wall to allow the orcs inside, and planted the Dragonriders Guild where they would be left to defend the city alone!"

"You're accusing me of persuading orcs to invade my own city?" Galdoys said with a patronizing chuckle. The governor lifted his hand, pulling at the patch of hair under his lip with a thumb and forefinger. "I knew I was a stellar diplomat, but I think the Hordelands are beyond even my reach, no?"

A rumble of low laughter echoed through the chamber at the governor's jest. Cadohaden's nostrils flared indignantly as he lifted his arm, flourishing his pointed finger out at the governor again as he shouted above the murmured noise, "It's true! All of the dragonriders that were opposed to Galdoys's way of doing things were gathered at my father's home, just outside where the orcs attacked! Not a single dragon descended upon the battle, and reinforcements didn't arrive until *after* they all lay dead!"

"Interesting," Galdoys countered. "Very astute of you, young Ulaeron. It seems like a wildly clever plan. I only have one question. How in the Lifegiver's name did I gather all of the dragonriders that I wanted eliminated at your father's home? I don't believe I called for a gathering. It would have been recorded in the archives. Prestor?"

"The last sanctioned meeting with the Dragonriders Guild was just under three weeks ago," the man named Prestor spoke up from his chair. The hunched man had been an apprentice historian when

Cadohaden's grandfather Iuvas had yet lived. "I was not informed of any gathering at Deltore Ulaeron's residence, my lord."

"One of your senators betrayed them!" Cadohaden shouted, his face flushing red once more. "He was supposed to inform them of your behaviors, but instead he…" He trailed off, the words disintegrating on his tongue. They left a bitter flavor as he realized how Galdoys had talked him into tying his own noose.

"I see," Galdoys said, the faintest hints of a smile tugging at the corners of his lips. "So the Dragonriders were attempting to recruit a spy, despite the open dialogues we have each and every month, and *I* am the villain here?"

"You left them to die!" Cadohaden shouted in frustration. He was floundering now, but he didn't know how to stop.

"General, what is standard protocol for surprise invasions upon the city?" Galdoys asked, keeping his eyes focused on Cadohaden as he inquired. They glinted auspiciously as he spoke.

"When the alarm is sounded, we make sure our gates are secure and our walls appropriately stationed," Cedrinn said, loudly enough for the entire hall to hear. "We cannot ignore the risk of falling for a diversion. We organize a resistance force, of course, to respond as quickly as possible, but it can take time to assemble, and we cannot send our reinforcements into battle in small groups. They would be butchered. It is every soldier's duty, dragonrider or footman, to be aware of this and to defend as steadfastly as possible until aid can arrive. This is understood by all who enlist." The general stared at Cadohaden meaningfully.

"Blaine," Galdoys said when the general had finished. "You are in charge of the air patrol schedules, are you not?"

"I do not write the schedules, my lord, but I do distribute them," Blaine Iuvaq replied.

"And who was scheduled to patrol the skies when the orcs attacked?" the governor asked.

"Deltore Ulaeron, sir," Blaine answered, narrowing his eyes at Cadohaden in a challenging leer. A buzzing noise arose in the chamber as noblemen murmured with excitement to one another, their voices igniting with the thrill of the scandal.

"I see. Thank you, Blaine, General," Galdoys said. He then rose his voice to the level of announcement.

"My lords and ladies, we were nearly the victims of a heinous conspiracy, it seems, at the hands of the Dragonrider seniority. This is certainly a tragedy, for the Guild is a proud order. But I have faith that the surviving youth will cleanse it of its corruption and restore it to its former glory.

"It gives me great sadness to think that men I called friends could betray me as they did, but let us not remember them with scorn, for most of them served the empire dutifully for many years. It took a terrible event for them to remember their honor, but in the end, they still defended those they had sworn to. Let us remember them in that light. To the Dragonriders!" The governor reached across the table and grabbed his silver chalice, hoisting it to the air in a toast. The chamber hall echoed the sentiment and they all drank in unison to the memories of the fallen. After taking a long drink, the governor sat the chalice back upon the table and turned to Cadohaden with the sad frown of a man who knew how to feign pity when he needed to.

"And as for you," Galdoys said, his voice growing hushed. He took a few steps towards Cadohaden, lifting his hand once more. Cadohaden felt unseen pressure at his back, preventing him from retreating. The governor was a dangerous enough man without the ability to wield magic. "You are guilty of treason on two counts. One, for intention to harm your governor. And two, for association with the conspiring dragonriders, possessing knowledge of their schemes without bringing the information to the proper authorities. The punishment for such crimes is execution.

"But I shall spare you the noose," Galdoys said, lifting his voice so that the entire chamber could hear the proclamation. A hushed gasp circled the hall. "For it was your father that poisoned your mind. You are young and naïve, with impure blood. Only so much can be expected of you. So I will show mercy. You have an hour to leave this great kingdom, and you will not return. If you are seen leaving the gates any later than that, the sentries will be instructed to fire at your back."

The room grew hushed once more as Galdoys stood in front of Cadohaden, lifting his hand. The young warrior felt his face burn with resentment as the governor reached out with his pointer finger, placing it on the upper corner of Cadohaden's pectoral. In two slashing motions, Galdoys drew an invisible 'X' on his chest. It was an old Kingsbanesin gesture that originated in the early days of the empire, when the city would hold grand melee tournaments. Competitors wishing to insult their opponents would slash the end of their swords in a quick crisscross pattern against their tabards. Over time, the flourish developed a double meaning, and became used with a finger more often than a blade. It usually meant the traditional insult, but could also be used to illustrate a man's dishonor, often performed during the sentencing of a crime, just like the one handed down to Cadohaden. He could see the impish smirk threatening to break free on the governor's face, however, and he knew which interpretation Galdoys had intended for him. He grinded his teeth together in his fury.

"Now remove yourself from honorable company," Galdoys said, turning away from him. With a snarl, Cadohaden lunged at the governor. The chamber hall gasped again, but Galdoys was ready. He turned around and extended his palm again, sending the young man tumbling backwards with a poltergeist's shove. "...Before I change my mind," Galdoys sneered.

Cadohaden pursed his lips together as he scrambled back to his feet. His heart was heavy with grief, and his face still burned with seething anger. But the military officials were beginning to rise out of their seats, their hands reaching for their weapons, and Blaine Iuvaq looked as though he would like nothing better than his own chance at apprehending the intruder. Realizing the futility, Cadohaden turned and sprinted out of the Hall of Feasts, back into the darkened streets of Kingsbanesin.

Time seemed to lose meaning as he ran through the streets once more. The structures on each side of him became a blur, meaningless visual noise surrounding him from every angle. His chest felt tight as he choked back the sobs that wanted to escape. It wasn't fair. None of this was fair.

He stopped at his father's home before he left the city. He almost announced his arrival out of habit, but bit down on his tongue before he could do so. If the words had left his mouth, he would have collapsed right there on the entrance room floor. He could barely stand to be in there, but he had something to do. He took the stairs two at a time and rushed into Deltore's room. He began pulling at dresser drawers and cabinets until he found what he was looking for: his father's stash of spending coins, a pouch filled with coppers, silvers, and even a small handful of gold coins. The act made him feel like he was robbing his father's grave, and it pinched at the inside of his stomach, but he knew that if he did not take it, it would fall into the hands of the Kingsbanesin soldiers that would surely search Deltore's home. That, and it would buy him an ample amount of time to lurk in the taverns that held vigil over the travelers' roads.

He tried to think of anything else he should take with him. He thought about his father's collection of weapons, but he already had his sword, and if he was to wander about like a gypsy, he could only carry so much on him at once. The idea of searching through his father's belongings began to overwhelm him, and so he left, hurrying into his own room to find his pack and whatever clothes he could stuff inside. With that finished, he hurried down the stairs and ran out of the front door, leaving it wide open as he left without looking back.

He ran towards the southern gate. He wanted to be far away from the tragedy at the northern wall. He wanted to say goodbye to his parents once more, but he knew he was running out of time. His survival instincts were guiding him now, and they lead him southward. He could hear the guards murmuring about him as they lifted the portcullis below, allowing him to leave. He ran underneath and kept going. The muscles in his legs were cramping, his knees were sore and swollen, and there were fresh blisters forming at the bottoms of his feet. He ignored them, though, and kept running as far as he could, leaving Kingsbanesin behind. He veered off the road, into the wilderness beyond the wall. He knew where he wanted to be.

Branches struck him in the face and thorns snagged at his trousers, but he barely felt them as hot tears began to pool in his eyes. His heart felt physically pained, like it was cracking open in his chest. He finally reached the cedar swamp and took a misguided step, his leg sinking into a soft spot in the peat. Releasing a sob of grief and frustration, he pulled his muddy boot out of the muck. He finally slowed down to a trudging walk, looking desperately for his favorite leaning tree. He blinked away the tears a few times, scanning the moonlit swamp. He wandered for only a few minutes before he came upon it, its nest of coiling roots looking more inviting than they ever had before.

He dropped his pack to the ground and unbuckled the belt that held his sheathed sword, letting it fall as well with the metallic clink of the clasp. He knelt down in the hollow of the roots, curling into a ball. He rested his head upon one arm and wrapped his other around his head, his forearm resting against the side of his skull. His shoulders began to heave, a husky whine hitching in his throat as he laid there helplessly. He didn't know if the cedars were in Kingsbanesin territory or not, but he no longer cared.

It's time to grow up, Ulaeron. Don't get soft on me. Your folks are gone, boy. It's time to grow up, Mekoda's voice echoed in his head. Cadohaden knew it was true. Every word was true. But he couldn't grow up right now. He didn't have the strength. Not yet.

Holding his arms tighter against his head, he surrendered himself to the grief and the pain as he laid there below the cedar trees and cried.

Chapter Six

The air was still in the world of Nollofolith, as it always was. The skies above were a torrential maelstrom of burning comets and suspended flame, but the atmosphere of Daemonaar's single moon was tranquil, a perpetual eye of the storm. It was rare for one of the Destroyer's minions to be given such a coveted gift as a personal world of their own, even one as small as Nollofolith, but Kavagor Ulgeroy was no mere minion.

Long ago, when Gapinon and Kagothai had first forged their alliance against their siblings, Kaijaras and Essence, the two dread deities had sealed their cooperation with the birth of the sinister apparition. The Destroyer gathered the ashes left in the wake of forging his proud creations, the demons and the orcs. Kagothai harnessed the souls of the first orcs that had fallen in battle against humanity in the world of mortals. Together, they manifested a terrible specter. The floating ash of its form somewhat resembled a human body, twin violet beacons levitating where its eyes should have been. The only true corporeal part of the apparition, however, was its pair of floating hands. Though the flesh was gray and mottled, it was difficult to decipher their true color, for the hands were eternally bleeding, an unending fount for the corrupt magic it would wield. They named the horrible creation Kavagor Ulgeroy, and though it is difficult to directly translate the violent language of Demonic, the closest Commonspeak interpretation would be "Blood Ash". Kavagor was given a single purpose: to train demons and prepare them for the conquest of the world of mortals.

It should be understood that not all of the Destroyer's spawn are created alike. Typically, demonkin can be classified in three different species. The first, and easily the lesser of the three, are the *gordorn*, which are shriveled whelp-like forms of their greater cousins and primarily serve as Daemonaar's drudges. The second are the *barshkor*, the hulking red-skinned brutes that are the muscle of Gapinon's demonic army. While Kavagor held responsibility for the *barshkor*, his role was typically a distant oversight, an authority for the demon lieutenants to report to.

The ash mentor's primary focus, however, were the *roaq* demons. The *roaq* were much smaller than the *barshkor*, slender in frame, pale-skinned with horns that just barely protruded from the skull, but they were by far the most dangerous of the Destroyer's demonkin, for they were cunning, manipulative, and above all, born with a natural affinity for the most unholy of blood magic. These were the charges that Kavagor prided himself in developing. These were the agents that would someday issue in the horrific cataclysm that the Destroyer hungered for. So great was his purpose that Kavagor had been given his own personal world, Nollofolith, away from the burning hell of Daemonaar, so that he could instruct the *roaq* that would carry out Gapinon's will.

This day was one of great importance, for Kavagor had been instructed to select one of his *roaq* pupils to enter the mortal world. This was no minor event, for creating passage into the world of mortals required a complex ritualistic sacrifice from a warlock on the other side. The Destroyer had spent months now whispering into the mind of a mortal, coaxing him into researching the ghastly task, and the man was nearly ready to perform the summoning.

Such opportunities could not be wasted on inadequate demons, especially among the *roaq*. It was possible for Gapinon to transport his spawn to the world of mortals himself, but it required a strenuous amount of effort, and each of the Four Forgers coveted their own strength, hoarding it in paranoia, for each of them were constantly watching the others, waiting for signs of weakness. It was the same for all the gods, and the neutrality was enforced by Essence. Direct intervention in the world of mortals was no longer the trivial task that it was in the earliest days of existence. Pushing the scales with their own hands was a risky endeavor, one that none of them had taken in ages.

Instead, they relied on the wills and the ambitions of their worshipers to influence the world. And if Symon Blacknail, the mortal sworn to perform the summoning, was willing to sacrifice a few friends in order to summon a *roaq* demon, it would greatly please the Destroyer.

Kavagor had selected four demons to compete for the rare opportunity. They sat cross-legged in a semi-circle around the ash wraith, their knees just outside an illuminated rune that had been etched upon the stone platform they sat upon. Three of them were male, and the remaining was female. This was usually how Kavagor picked his classes, for it indulged a strange fantasy of his, where he felt like the original god, Beginning, creating his own Forgers that he would unleash upon the world.

To the wraith's left sat Deveguill Sever, a thin demon even by *roaq* standards, his cheekbones like blades threatening to puncture his pale skin. Next to him sat Krizzick Darksoul, with glinting eyes of cunning and a wash of faded violet hair that fell past his chest and shoulder blades. Lak'shii, the demon temptress, sat next to Krizzick, her voluptuous and exaggerated curves just barely covered with translucent scarves of silk. Her hair was like long strands of flesh that simply continued on from her scalp, a nest of faceless pale snakes that descended halfway down her back. And next to Lak'shii, to Kavagor's right, sat Terodar Soulrender, a demon that possessed a secret unknown even to himself. Terodar's rise to power had intrigued both Kavagor and the demon lord Gapinon. They were both eager to see how his tale would unfold.

An uneasy feeling was twisting in Terodar's stomach as he sat cross-legged around the rune, his pointed chin lifted in his best display of confidence. He had spent countless hours studying and training for this day. He was through with Nollofolith. He was ready to carry out Gapinon's will in the world of mortals. Still, he couldn't help but feel the pinch of discomfort when Kavagor's haunting eyes passed over him. It always seemed to him as though his mentor's gaze lingered on him longer than they did his peers. Was it his dedication to mastering his natural talent for blood magic? Was that enough to garner attention from the Blood Ash?

"Rise, students," Kavagor commanded in a hiss. Even to his demon pupils, the wraith's words seemed to singe their ears as they entered. Nevertheless, each of them rose obediently. The circular rune at their feet began to glow with a greater intensity, as if it had anticipated this moment as well.

"The day has come. The mortal worm is nearly ready to grant one of you passage to his world. We will see which of you is worthy of the privilege.

"Each of you knows what is at stake. There will come a day when our burning lord will enter the world of mortals himself, to cleanse it of the corruption that Kaijaras indulgently stains it with. He bides his time, waiting for the right opportunity. What role do you play in this?"

"We must prepare for his entrance," Krizzick said quickly with an eager hitch to his voice. "We must gather followers, soldiers, warlocks. We must eliminate those that would threaten his fiery arrival," he finished with a flourish and a proud smirk. Terodar couldn't resist rolling his eyes. No doubt Krizzick had been poised and ready to answer any question Kavagor could conjure. Obedience was a requirement of those that served the Destroyer. Bootlicking was not.

"Darksoul speaks the truth," Kavagor hissed, much to Krizzick's beaming delight. "Lord Gapinon will not take the world of mortals unchallenged. His siblings will see to that. Even the Death Shepherd, who we speak of as our ally, would not allow the Destroyer to reign unopposed. You must prepare not just for the arrival of our burning lord, but for the interference of the other Forgers. When the time comes, my children, we will need an army that will give the Destroyer the precious time he needs to see the world turned to ash.

"You will use the gifts that you were born with," Kavagor continued, casting his ghostly eyes in Terodar's direction for a brief moment, much to the demon's confusion. "Blood magic will pave the way for you, but it will not be your sole savior. It is attuned here, in the Destroyer's world, but you will find it dampened in the world of mortals. You will need your cunning and your ruthlessness to prevail. Have I made myself clear?"

"Yes, *en'sa*," the four answered in unison, speaking the demonic word for 'mentor'.

"Then your test begins now," Kavagor's voice rattled. His violet eyes flared, and slowly, one of his disembodied hands departed from the floating ash of his spectral form. With its pointer finger outstretched, the ever-bleeding appendage hovered over to Deveguill. The demon pursed his lips shut as the hand approached. The fingertip pressed against the middle of his forehead, leaving a crimson mark where it made contact, and at once, Deveguill's eyelids drooped shut, his head falling forward. Terodar watched as the levitating hand trailed over to Krizzick, once again pressing its pointer finger against the demon's forehead, and then over to Lak'shii, both of them closing their eyes upon its contact, their heads falling forward like limp dolls.

Terodar's heartbeat grew more urgent as Kavagor's hand hovered over towards him. This was it. All of his study, his commitment to his training, came to a pivotal fork here with the wraith's test. He furiously searched his mind for any last-second pointers he could conjure, but the bloodied finger was upon him, pressing against his forehead. Nollofolith faded into darkness as the feeling of plummeting descent overtook the demon.

He awoke in a room that he did not recognize. As he sat up, he realized with curiosity that he was laying under silken sheets upon a cushioned mattress. He pushed the sheets off of himself as he stared in awe at the object he lay upon. It felt as though he had spent the night upon a cloud. They did not have such luxuries in Daemonaar, for Kavagor believed that an abundance of comfort created complacence, of which he would have none in his *roaq* students.

He lifted his legs and swung them over the side of the bed, his hooves touching down on the floor. The walls were crimson, glowing with a sensual light that came from a glimmering chandelier, decorated with silver trim and embedded diamonds that glinted against the light from the candles fixed upon the holders. Two large velvet cushions sat in the room's corner, one on each side of a strange bowl-like apparatus with hoses attached to the stem. Terodar had read of such mechanisms before. Mortals would pack flavored tobacco into the bowl, ignite it, and pull its smoke in from the hoses. If you had the coin to afford it, you could instead use tincture grass, a wondrous opiate that would make all of your troubles vanish for a few hours of tranquility.

Just as the thought crossed his mind, he saw that the bowl had mysteriously filled with a squarely woven pack of green grass. Spontaneously, the weave ignited, and though there was nobody on either end of the hoses, smoke began to stream out from the ends, as though invisible poltergeists were breathing in from the stems. The room began to fill with the intoxicating vapor, and Terodar could feel his senses beginning to dull with the ecstasy of the drug. His eyes widened, his serpentine pupils flaring as three figures began to press themselves into the room from each wall, as though they were departing paint transforming into life forms as they peeled away. The demon blinked, and suddenly the strange manifestations were a trio of enchanting elven women. They were entirely naked, save for a transparent cloth that hugged their torsos, glimmering gems embedded in the material. They approached him, reaching out with their hands. The one in the middle smiled with gorgeous full lips, her voice filling his head like the soft chimes of a bell. "You needn't carry on any further, Terodar. We are in your castle, and you are king. We can't wait to show you all that is yours. But first…" She reached down, her fingertips tracing along the outside of his ebon robe, feeling the outline of his member. Terodar swallowed, an electric sensation dancing up his spine at the feel of her hand. Soft mattresses weren't the only comforts strictly regulated by Kavagor. Something murmured to him, however, deep in the back of his mind, even as the three naked elves traced their hands along him.

You must never settle for paltry victories or hollow trophies, for though they may satisfy a dullard's dreams, it will coax you into an indulgent laziness. An act of such sloth will invite those more ambitious than you to take what it was you settled for. It was from the fifth chapter of Kavagor's educational tome, and Terodar knew it well. These women and this castle were no consolation prize. His drug-induced mind desperately wanted it to be true, but he knew that it could not be. Forcing himself to focus, he put his tongue between his pointed teeth and bit down until he could taste the coppery tang of his blood. *Your power is fueled by blood, and you must never hesitate to draw your own first.* The first chapter, third paragraph.

The elf who had spoken to him was on her knees, lifting up his robe with sensual murmurs of promised pleasure. Without hesitation, Terodar grabbed her by both sides of the head, twisting it with a violent jerk. She croaked as her neck snapped, and her two companions recoiled. In an instant, their entire appearances mutated, their faces becoming reptilian, their spines protruding as they hunched, their exotic curves becoming sinewy muscle as their fingernails grew into graying talons. Shrieking, they both lunged at the demon, but Terodar was ready. He pushed off on his hoof, lunging backwards, and hissed a demonic spell, bringing his hands up towards both of their heads. As he swung his palms together, clapping them against one another, the creatures' skulls collided, guided by an unseen force. The loud cracking noise of their fracturing skulls accompanied the visceral pop of their necks breaking, and they collapsed to the floor on top of the third seductress.

He drew in a trembling breath, the blood pooling from their mouths sending a tremor of ecstasy across his skin. His eyes darted back and forth across the room, desperately searching for another foe to vanquish. The rush of blood magic was tantalizing, clearing the clouds enveloping his mind. He wanted more. Suddenly, at the far wall of the enchanted room, a door materialized. It creaked as it began to open, and Terodar stepped forward eagerly, an incantation already upon his tongue.

It was not an enemy that greeted him at the door, however. Deveguill stood on the other side, staring at him with those sunken eyes. Even though it denied him another opportunity to indulge his craving, his student peer was a welcome sight among all the confusion. It would have been a stretch to call Deveguill his friend; demons aren't known for classifying their brethren as such. But among Kavagor's four pupils, Deveguill was the only one Terodar would call an ally. Their shared enmity towards Krizzick and their indifference to the seductress Lak'shii had forged a natural bond between the two.

"Quite the elaborate trap Kavagor set for us, isn't it?" Deveguill mused with a thin-lipped grin.

"I expected as much from him," Terodar said as he stepped out into the hallway alongside the other demon. He looked over his shoulder to see the door he had stepped through fade into a blank wall slate. He turned back to face Deveguill. "Did the whores speak the truth? Are we in a castle?"

"Of some fashion," Deveguill responded, looking both ways down the hall. "I know not if it is a dream or reality, but it's part of the test either way, I'm sure."

"My lords!" a voice called out from further down the hall. They could only see darkness towards the end, as if they were in a dimly lit cavern tunnel, but a human with servant's garb materialized from the shadows, bustling towards them with a panicked expression. Terodar couldn't help but feel amused by the idea that Kavagor had granted them a fantasy of mortal kingship. "The dragon men are here, my lords! They're on the castle roof! Come quick!" the servant shouted anxiously before disappearing back into the depths of the hallway.

Deveguill turned and grinned at Terodar once more. "Best not keep the dragon men waiting, then. Let's be on our guard." Terodar nodded in agreement, half a dozen different spells already in the back of his mind as they proceeded guardedly down the hallway. The light seemed to follow them as they made their way through the corridor, though there were no torches, candlesticks, or chandeliers to be seen. The stone walls were decorated only with blank canvas portraits. As they ventured further, Terodar began to see shapes forming on the portraits. They were black at first, but began to change to a violet hue. Terodar realized that they were Kavagor's eyes, following them through the canvas as they walked past.

The hallway finally came to an end, revealing a spiraling wooden plank staircase that ascended to the castle roof. Terodar didn't hesitate to step onto it first, Deveguill following behind him. They carried themselves upward, and as they looked below them, they saw that the steps underneath were disintegrating into embers and ash, scattering to the shadows underneath. Terodar peeled his gaze away, turning his eyes towards their destination. He could see an open doorway above, and a faint blood-red sky beyond it.

They pulled themselves up through the roof door, Deveguill scrambling up just as the steps burned away below his hooves. The door fell shut and faded from sight, melding into the plank castle roof. The sky was a dark crimson, like coagulating blood, the thin fingers of clouds stretched across the sky like lichen-covered digit bones. The servant that had summoned them was nowhere to be seen, but a legion of armored men stood, each equipped with a sword and a square tower shield, a dragon emblem painted across the front of each. A screech sounded out from above, and the two demons looked up to see a red-scaled winged beast swooping around the castle roof, the billow of its wings booming down upon them. Terodar frowned as he studied the circling serpent. The great beast had a rider.

"Is that Krizzick?" he asked Deveguill.

"Perhaps. Lak'shii is among the men," Deveguill answered, pointing a bony finger towards the assembled soldiers. Terodar's frown deepened as he saw the seductress, sitting naked upon a pavilion lifted on the shoulders of the soldiers with a delicate crown upon her head.

"Warriors of Kingsbanesin, these creatures come to threaten your queen!" Lak'shii shouted from her perch, pointing a finger back at the two. "Kill them! Kill them now!"

With a unanimous grunt, the soldiers lifted their tower shields and began to charge across the rooftop. Neither Terodar nor Deveguill hesitated to pull their ceremonial knives from their belt sheaths, dragging the blade edges against the inside of their forearms. As the cuts bloomed red, the two began to hiss demonic incantations.

The soldiers approached just as the sound of warping wood creaked below. Suddenly, the platforms began to splinter in a straight line, the wooden shards lifting like a jagged row of teeth in front of the soldiers. The armored men began to trip over the knee-high blockade. Some of them suddenly tumbled forward, their legs falling through the openings rendered in the roof as the wood formed its line of siege-breaking spikes. The soldiers began to climb over one another as Lak'shii screamed for their heads, but the two demons were ready. Directly behind the line of splintered wood, flames suddenly leaped up from the broken planks, the soldiers crying out as the fiery tongues lapped at the faces of the ones that had fallen forward.

"Quickly! Onto the terrace!" Terodar shouted as the flames began to spread with unnatural speed, eating at the rooftop hungrily. He and Deveguill bolted back towards the stone terrace surrounding the roof, both of them scurrying onto one of the pillars that lined the castle's edge. Turning back to the swarm of soldiers still closing in on them, they called for more fire, their spells fueled by the blood of the men that had been punctured or trampled by the others.

Lak'shii's screams could be heard over the howls of pain from her men, but her threats were futile. Nearly an entire half of the roof was engulfed in flames, and the soldiers were no longer barreling forward, but retreating back towards their queen. The planks groaned under the weight as the flame ate away at support beams underneath. It would all come crashing down back into the castle soon enough, but they could not let themselves fall prey to distraction. *Even in glorious victory, you remain surrounded by unseen threats. Never let down your guard.* The seventh chapter, Terodar recalled, and the threat that still lurked was far from unseen. Krizzick was guiding his dragon back around in the sky, turning it towards the demons.

Terodar could hear the roof nearby giving way with a groan of surrender, and the panicked screams of the doomed soldiers gave him a tantalizing satisfaction, but he remained focused on the looming dragon. He lifted his hands, palms outstretched, and snarled a string of demonic chants.

The dragon grew closer, and for a brief moment, he feared he had uttered something wrong. And then it happened. Holes suddenly began to bloom in the dragon's wings, small at first, but they quickly began to expand, like flame eating away at the center of a parchment scroll. The dragon shrieked in pain, flapping its tremendous wings in futility as Krizzick shouted at it from his saddle. It was a hopeless cause, for the dragon's wings had nearly whittled away to the bone frame.

"Look out!" Deveguill hissed. Terodar suddenly realized that despite its crippled wings, the dragon was still plummeting directly towards them. The two leaped from their pillar, dancing carefully across the ridge towards the next as the last few soldiers clinging to the remnants of the roof finally fell into the castle depths. The two demons jumped onto the castle pillar, clinging to it fiercely as Krizzick and his dragon slammed into the pillar they had been standing on only seconds before. The roof trembled as the pillar collapsed under the weight of the collision, sending a scattering of stones hurtling to the ground far below, the dragon and its rider soon following, twisting as they tumbled towards the earth.

Terodar and Deveguill carefully sat up upon their perch, looking over their shoulders at the gaping fracture the dragon had left in the castle wall. Their gazes turned towards the remnants of the roof, which was little more than a few burning boards clinging to the stone sides. Deveguill cackled and turned over, sitting on the edge of the pillar, overlooking the strange crimson landscape they had been summoned to.

"Well well, look at us, kings of the castle," he chuckled.

"Indeed," Terodar replied, pushing himself up into a kneeling position, looking out into the mirage world as well. "Do you think this is the works of Kavagor's thoughts, or ours?"

"Hard to say," Deveguill answered. His voice was becoming curiously cold. "I've only read about the castles of mortals, myself."

"As have I," Terodar said, angling a questioning glance at the other demon. No steps had appeared in the roof hollow to escort them elsewhere, nor had any flying beasts descended upon them to take them to safety. They remained isolated on the edge of the castle roof. "Are we to simply wait, then?"

"No," Deveguill answered in a flat tone. "Only one of us can be summoned, Soulrender. Two of us remain."

Terodar's brow furrowed as he glanced back out towards the red horizon. He tapped his fingertips against his kneecap, then glanced over his shoulder once more, perhaps in vain hope that a staircase would yet appear. When nothing of the sort happened, he looked back at Deveguill. "So...what? We're to fight to the death on this pillar we barely both fit on? That seems almost insulting."

"*The road to triumph rarely appears as you would imagine,*" Deveguill quoted from their tome. "I would not expect it to end like this, and yet it must."

Terodar stared hard at his fellow student. His entire body was tensed, ready for the slightest movement, but none came. Deveguill simply stared forward, his legs dangling over the stone pillar. Finally, the demon spoke, "Terodar."

"I'm listening."

"Give me the victory."

"What?" Terodar hissed incredulously, eyes narrowing.

"Look," Deveguill said with a voice oddly empathetic for one of demon blood, "I didn't wish to tell you this. I couldn't imagine it would come to this. But you and I, Terodar, we don't fight for our own victory. We fight for the triumph of the Destroyer. That is our purpose. And though we nearly stand as equals, I'm afraid I simply have the greater chance of success."

"Speak plainly, Deveguill," Terodar growled.

"Your blood is weak, Terodar," Deveguill answered. "I do not know why. But I have overheard Kavagor speaking to his lieutenants about you. He is intrigued by your ascent, but is convinced nonetheless that you will ultimately fail. I can only guess as to what your flaw is. All I know is that it exists, and though I wish there was another way, it is your duty to do what is best for our lord Gapinon. *Your purpose, your very existence, it belongs to the fiery hand of the Destroyer.*"

Terodar looked down over the wall's edge, at the ground so far below. He swallowed. He knew that there was a secret that Kavagor kept from him. He couldn't imagine what it was, but nonetheless, Deveguill had addressed it. The demon drew a deep sigh and bowed his head.

"End it quickly, Sever, if that is what you must do," he said with a subdued voice.

"You honor me, and you honor our lord Gapinon," Deveguill said softly as he lifted himself up, standing over the kneeling Terodar. He gripped his ceremonial dagger and lifted it above his head, focusing on the back of Terodar's neck.

In a rush, Terodar pushed himself back away from the pillar's edge, swinging his arm at Deveguill's knees. The demon balked, eyes wide in surprise as Terodar's arm swept his legs out from under him. Losing grip on his dagger, Deveguill tumbled down upon the pillar as Terodar pushed himself up. There was no hesitation. As Deveguill's dagger clattered against the pillar and disappeared off of the edge, Terodar kicked his fellow student with his hoof, rolling him over towards the pillar's edge. With a panicked cry, Deveguill grasped the edge as his body dangled from the side.

"No!" Deveguill cried out, scrambling to reaffirm his grip on the pillar. "No, Terodar, you can't! You know what I say is true!"

"*When your foe cannot win with sword or with spell, they shall instead fight with word and with wit. You must be prepared to fight in the same manner,*" Terodar recited as he stepped over to the ledge, glaring at Deveguill with harsh, glinting eyes. "You truly believed I would simply lay down and accept defeat, Sever? I thought better of you."

Deveguill opened his mouth to plead, but Terodar was finished wasting time with idle banter. With two swift kicks of his hoof, he pried the demon's fingers away from the edge. With a howl of despair, Deveguill fell to his doom, his robes whipping in the wind as he descended.

Terodar fell to a knee once more, watching his fellow student fall. Only when Deveguill's body landed with a grotesque thud against the ground far below did he peel his gaze away, finally feeling safe to do so. He looked around, wondering how he himself was going to get down, when a bright white light began to flood his vision, a high-pitched tone piercing his mind as he began to lose feeling. He numbly clutched at the pillar, embracing it as though it would anchor his consciousness, but only seconds later, the world was a blank slate to him.

He couldn't say how long the comatose state lasted, but he finally began to sense feeling in his body once more, his legs first. He could feel his eyelids moving and something hard beneath his legs. The overbearing white was beginning to clear, his vision slowly returning to him. He was back in Nollofolith, sitting in the semi-circle around Kavagor, the glowing rune below him. As his sight recovered, he noticed with surprise that the other three pupils were not dead after all, but still sitting in the same positions they had been before Kavagor's disembodied hand had dismissed them into the strange dream. He wondered if they had all shared the same hallucination, or if each of them had been given their own separate test. He saw their smoldering glares trained on him and thought he knew the answer already.

"You continue to fascinate me, Terodar Soulrender," Kavagor's voice hissed from his ethereal form. "Composure, finesse...and cunning. All of these attributes saw you through the test, and I deem you the one worthy of the summoning. The rest of you...well, we've certainly all learned something from this experience, haven't we?"

"Yes, Master Kavagor," Krizzick spoke immediately. Terodar was feeling far too accomplished to be bothered by Krizzick's simpering mannerisms, however.

"Gather your things, Soulrender," Kavagor said, turning his haunting eyes back to Terodar. "The preparations have begun. The mortal worm only waits for the Destroyer's command."

* *

It was a quick process, gathering his belongings, for demons of all kinds in the realm of the Destroyer had little need for possessions. Subtlety would be necessary in the world of mortals, however, and so Terodar packed four hooded cloaks, a small variety of ceremonial garb, his ritual dagger, and of course, the tome that Kavagor had given him on his first day of training. He met with the horrifying specter outside a temple in Nollofolith. Its walls were constructed of a strange dark blue crystal that was supposed to heighten the powers of a *roaq* demon. It was normally intended to give initiates a feel for the power they possessed, but on this day, it was where Kavagor would call upon the portal that would take Terodar to the world of mortals, and to the destiny that awaited him.

The portal was only a frame now, standing eerily along the back wall of the temple. It was constructed of fused demon bones, several joints visible along its bow, the occasional barb protruding outward. Deveguill, Krizzick, and Lak'shii all knelt on the far side of the temple, watching. Kavagor stood before the empty space of the dormant portal. His mastery of blood magic, augmented by the crystalline temple, would be more than sufficient to open the gateway from Nollofolith. It was their mortal warlock on the other side that would require a great deal of sacrifice to summon something as powerful as a *roaq* demon.

"Are you ready, Soulrender?" Kavagor hissed, his levitating hands flexing in anticipation of the spell he was prepared to cast.

"I believe so, Master Kavagor," Terodar said with the faintest hint of hesitancy. Nothing was too subtle for the dread mentor, however.

"Are you not committed to such a task?" his haunting voice rasped.

"No, Master," Terodar insisted, shaking his head. "I would only ask what it is that you speak to the others about. The ones that our lord Gapinon commands. What is it that makes my blood weak? Why is it such a surprise that I was the one to emerge victorious from the test?"

Kavagor's violet eyes narrowed, his clenching hands pausing in their movement as he stared at Terodar. The demon swallowed, feeling as though the specter's gaze was burning through him, but he could not afford to look weak now.

"Were I to tell you," the wraith hissed, "it would only weaken your resolve. Content yourself with the knowledge that you have surpassed the expectations of even our lord Gapinon, Soulrender. Perhaps one day it will no longer matter. But for now, you will carry out the Destroyer's will with no more questions."

It was the most elaborate answer Terodar knew he could hope for. He bowed his head obediently. He supposed it truly didn't matter. He had passed the test, not the others, and it was he that would venture into the world of mortals. "I am ready, Master Kavagor," he said as he lifted his gaze to meet the haunting visage of the apparition.

"Good," Kavagor answered, his eyes turning to face the empty portal frame. The temple grew quiet as his disembodied hands slowly rose, palms upturned towards the ceiling as blood drained between his fingers. A sound like howling wind suddenly penetrated the still air, edged with the harsh whispers of Kavagor. Terodar shifted his weight from one hoof to another. The wraith was communing with the chosen warlock, instructing him to begin the ritual.

Several minutes passed as the sound of hissing wind carried through the temple. Nothing seemed to happen at first, and Terodar felt himself growing uneasy. What was taking so long? Had the mortal begun to second guess himself? His worries faded, however, as a low growl escaped his mentor, and suddenly the demonbone portal began to glow a faint eerie blue inside the arc. He could see the energy twisting into oblivion, the bending light inviting him inside. Kavagor's eyes did not turn, but his hissing voice spoke,

"Enter, Terodar Soulrender. Remember all that I have taught you."

The demon drew in a deep breath, gritted his teeth, and marched forward towards the portal. Stepping through the blue light, he faded from sight, the swirling portal closing behind him as he crossed over.

Chapter Seven

The early morning air was not yet hot, but it held the promise of a sweltering afternoon. Sir Strigson Ganisalp could see the sleep-deprived fatigue in the eyes of the soldiers who were most accustomed to the afternoon training rotations, but the Glen Bailey's general was confident that by the time late afternoon rolled around, they would be grateful for the daybreak training that safeguarded them from the sun's most beating rays.

He walked among the ranks as captains called out their cadences, each soldier responding in unison as their blunted blades jabbed and swept. Their shields lifted and pressed, arced and tilted with every issued command. The training grounds were tightly packed with the abundance of participants, but their disciplined movements kept them from striking one another's elbows and shins even as they stood mere inches apart. Normally, there would be ample space between each practicing soldier, as a typical day called for varying rotations to the training schedule. Today, however, was the Summer Solstice, and while most of his men would have the pleasure of enjoying the festivities later that day, nobody under his command was exempt from training on any given day, even a holiday such as this. And so that morning, with the rising sun, he'd lined up as many of them as he could inside the Glen Bailey's training grounds, next to the barracks. There wasn't enough space for everybody; the greener recruits had been taken outside the city walls for standard conditioning. There wasn't a soul in armor that didn't despise the general's exercise regimen, but to be a member of his army, a recruit's physical form had to be up to par before even a wooden blade would be placed in their palm. *Those are the rules, boys.*

Strigson Ganisalp was a tall man with closely cropped chestnut hair and a meticulously trimmed beard that gave his chiseled face the faintest of an auburn shadow. While clean-shaven faces were often mandatory for soldiers, men in positions of authority were allowed thin beards if they were willing to keep them neat. The rules were relaxed in the winter months, when a thick beard could help prevent frostbite and dried, cracking cheeks, but in the heat of summer, men in Ganisalp's army learned to wield a razor just as well as they did a sword.

One of his lieutenants, a man by the name of Mekudii, called for a brief rest as they finished another circuit. Strigson approached him as the soldiers surrounding them took their respite, extending his left hand. "Your sword, Lieutenant," he said with authority.

"Sir," was all Mekudii answered with as he handed his general his blade, placing the handle in Ganisalp's. Strigson curled his thumb and pointer finger around it, the remainder of his digits pressing awkwardly against it as he adjusted his grip. The remaining three fingers on his left hand were slightly disfigured, curled inward like an eagle's talons. He'd suffered an injury to his forearm years ago, when Queen Meredith was still alive, though she would not have lived a day longer had it not been for Ganisalp. Two arrows had pierced right through his armor and torn into the muscle beneath the flesh during an ambush. King Bartholomew's healers had successfully mended the wound, but the feeling in those three fingers had never returned. Each morning, after he'd finished his breakfast, Strigson would massage the deadened digits in an attempt to hold their form, but it wasn't enough to keep them from gradually mutating with lack of use.

His nose wrinkled in impatience as he rolled his thumb once again, trying to get the blasted fingers to settle around the sword's handle. They finally yielded to his demands, coiling loosely around the leather binding. He often offered his crippled hand when demanding a sword. He wanted his soldiers to see him do it, to ensure they had no excuses for a lack of a trained grip. But he also did it with the faintest of hopes that at some point, he would feel the sensation against one of the numbed fingers. King Bartholomew often asked if any feeling had returned. The general hoped that one day he would feel as optimistic about the crippled fingers as he pretended to be for His Majesty. They were both a blessing and a curse to Strigson. There was no greater honor than making such a sacrifice to save the life of one he was sworn to protect. And he knew that his wounding had been a great boon to his promotion to general. But at the same time, he resented the feeling that his trophy injury had placed him in his position. He was still young for a general; he'd never led his army against another of equal size. And without the full use of his left hand, he wasn't the soldier he used to be.

He murmured a soft chiding to himself as he passed the sword handle from his left hand to his fully functional right. He was allowing himself to become distracted in front of the vast majority of his soldiers. It was an unsettling lack of discipline. He drew a breath of air into his chest before calling out loudly enough for the entire training field to hear, "We spent a lot of time last week working on using your shield as a weapon, not just something to hold in front of yourself while you let your enemy batter it to bits. I've seen improvement since then. Most of you remember now that whatever you hold in your hand is a weapon, regardless of what shape it is.

"I've started to see something *else*, though, and I think too many of you are concentrating on swinging your shields around to remember that the pointed steel you hold in your other hand is used for attacking as well. In too many drills, I'm seeing soldiers intentionally chop at their sparring partner's blade, like you're just trying to force an opening for all of these fancy shield maneuvers we've been working on.

"Ready yourself, Gettles," the general said to the closest soldier nearby. The man barked a crisp 'yes sir' and lowered himself into a defensive stance, sword and shield at the ready. Strigson advanced, jabbing the point end of his borrowed blade at Gettles' armored chest. The soldier swiped the jab away with his shield before offering an exchanging strike at the general. Strigson swept his free arm in front of himself, the bracer protecting his forearm acting as a shield on its own as he swatted it against the flat of Gettles' blade. He stepped in immediately, lifting his sword hand above his head before bringing the pommel end down towards the soldier's skull, stopping with just a fingernail's width of space between. He nodded and patted Gettles' shoulder, murmuring a command for him to stand down as he backed away to address his army once more,

"We're not playing patty-cake here, boys," Ganisalp called out even as he matched the gaze of one of his lieutenants, a woman named Mya Ness. Women who had the grit to serve in the Glen Bailey's army had been welcome to do so for decades, even if the training field terminology hadn't changed. "There's a time and place to parry with your sword and to block with the shield, but make no mistake, even when you're on the defensive, every move you make should be an effort to bring yourself closer to a successful strike. Never, *ever* waste precious seconds and energy fixating on breaking your foe's blade. If their sword happens to snap on collision, great, but as I just showed you, an enemy will find a way to improvise when their life depends on it.

"I want one-on-ones, now, and this time, use those swords as they were intended," Ganisalp ordered, and following his command, lieutenants and captains began to echo the orders, herding soldiers into sparring pairs as they broke ranks. Just as with their circuit drills before, there was barely enough room in the packed grounds for such an exercise, but that was all right with Strigson. There was rarely any more room on a battlefield in times of war, and it wasn't often these numbers could be simulated in practice situations.

He handed Mekudii's blade back to the lieutenant before the general folded his hands behind his back, his right fingers curling around the unfeeling digits of his left with an idle stroking of his thumb against the deadened joints. He paced slowly from left to right as he watched the sparring, pausing intermittently to correct or praise. Many of the men he reviewed were several seasons older than him, and though he occasionally received a begrudging glare from a veteran with iron whiskers, the overwhelming majority regarded him with the respect that his position demanded. He knew there were generals in the armies of neighboring kingdoms that would never tolerate contempt from any soldier, green or gray, but Strigson had studied enough military history to know how mutiny could boil over from the fissures of spiteful retaliation. He was confident enough that any conspiratorial whispers would be silenced by the men that believed in his leadership. As long as they obeyed his commands, they could glower all they wanted.

A figure caught his eye as he turned on his heel, coming from the direction of the training ground gates. A small smile emerged on the general's face as he recognized the approaching individual. The dark red hair blowing about her shoulders with occasional strands stuck to her forehead with perspiration from the day's heat could belong to none other than Princess Aven, who wore a casual light green split tunic and dark leather boots that cuffed underneath her knees. Unlike most royalty, or even the magistrates of King Bartholomew's court, she did not travel with any escorts, chin held proud and high as she marched forward, more independent than any heir to the throne in all of the Aariad. Granted, this was in part due to her talents as a mage, but even so, Strigson had always been impressed with her willingness to forego the armed entourages she was entitled to. She was not particularly tall and had a lithe frame, but she was nonetheless one of the more imposing figures on the training grounds.

"Sir Ganisalp," Aven said with a formal air and a smile as she approached him. "You're aware that today is the Summer Solstice, correct?"

"Your Grace," Ganisalp answered using the proper title for an heir to the throne. He allowed himself a smile as well, though he took care to keep his demeanor professional. "I am, and that is why your soldiers will be given a half-day off to enjoy the celebrations." The clacking and clanging sounds of colliding practice weapons carried on behind him, each soldier disciplined enough to continue in their training even in the presence of royalty. Upon orders to cease, they would each immediately drop to a knee. Salutes were always delayed during battle training, as Ganisalp had insisted upon his promotion. *If our troops are trained to stop and salute even in the heat of battle, it will be the last thing they ever do,* he'd insisted to Bartholomew.

"What of the ones who will be on patrol during the festivities?" Aven asked curiously, turning to peer out at the swarm of sparring soldiers. The soldiers and the city guards were technically two separate entities, but many of them belonged to both factions, particularly the lower ranking troops.

"Even the ones on rotation tonight should have at least two hours of relief," Ganisalp said assuredly, following her gaze back to the training. "For those scheduled, Bartholomew has purchased a big bag full of wooden tokens from the Dur'Imoirian dwarves that will be handed out among them. They can be exchanged for free mugs of ale. Do you find that satisfactory, Your Grace?"

"I do," Aven said, her smile widening a bit as she glanced back at the general. "Morale is important, Strigson. We want the Solstice to be a happy occasion for everyone."

"Understood, Your Grace," the general answered, though he had to tear his gaze away from his king's daughter. By the gods, he was being threatened with countless distractions this morning. He silently blamed it on the excitement of the upcoming festivities, even though he knew that wasn't a sufficient excuse.

In truth, Strigson had harbored an infatuation for the princess for many years. Her smile was enough to give his chest a stir and his knees tingling sensations. He'd been tempted to ask for her courtship before. Aven seemed to enjoy his company, and he was well liked by her father. While the political implications as a whole could certainly get a bit complicated, it wouldn't be even close to the most scandalous pairing in the history of royal Aariad couples.

What kept the general from voicing his affections was a man named Captain Wyatt Darjin. While still whispered as a secret within the Glen Bailey, it was common knowledge that Aven was romantically involved with the young soldier, who had no medals for heroism or noble bloodlines that would justify such a marriage between the two. Word traveled of the affair, as it always does, and when King Bartholomew caught wind of the rumors, he had promptly "promoted" Wyatt to a position at Arden's Watch, an outpost owned by the Glen Bailey that was conveniently leagues away from the city. That move had doubtlessly put a timetable on the forbidden romance, but Aven Celandine was a strong woman, and Strigson continued to hear mutterings from the patrol guards that she was still departing on a saddled horse in the dead of night towards the north. It couldn't last, but for now, it was enough to keep the general silent.

"Soldiers! The Princess Aven Celandine!" Sir Ganisalp called out, facing the crowded ranks before him. At the indirect command, the ranks immediately turned and dipped to one knee like clockwork.

"At ease, soldiers," Aven said with a rising open-palmed gesture. The troops rose just as uniformly as they had knelt, each firing off a salute before standing at attention, awaiting further orders.

"Good work today," Strigson said as the training fields fell silent. "But keep in mind not just today's practices, but the ones from yesterday, and the day before. I don't want to see lax technique with your boards the next time we gather because you're all too focused on your swords again. I've said it before and I'll say it again: the soldier that lives to see the next fight is the soldier that has the most developed form. Berserkers and brutes might land a lucky strike here and there, but they all die within minutes by the blade of a disciplined soldier. The taverns may be full of stories about titanic men that sever an enemy's limb with one swipe, but it's the well-rounded fighter that will tell them of how he felled the fearsome foe shortly after.

"Those of you scheduled for rotations may now report for duty. Speak to your supervisors about a gift from the crown when you arrive. The rest of you...enjoy the celebrations, but drink your fair share of water. I don't need men passing out during drills tomorrow. Other than that, have a happy Solstice. Dismissed."

The soldiers broke ranks, filing out towards the water barrels that were stationed near the training ground exits. They were visibly weary from the warm exercises, faces sheened with sweat, the skin red from exertion, but each of them seemed to have a light step and a glimmer in their eye in anticipation of the festivities. Even those that were scheduled to patrol seemed cheerier than usual. They'd all been promised gifts from the crown, of course, but each of them knew that the music from the streets would reach their ears even up on the wall's sentinel towers. It would be a welcome break from the usual monotony of their patrols.

Strigson watched his departing soldiers for a moment before turning his attention back to the princess, curiosity etched across his face. "Was it the soldiers' compensation that brought you here this morning, Your Grace?" he asked.

"No," Aven admitted, folding her hands in front of herself as she looked back at the general. "I just came by for some practice, in truth. Some sparring if I can find a willing partner. If not I'll make do with the archery targets."

"I'll need to check in on my captains to ensure all the patrols are accounted for in a little while, but I have some time to help if you'll accept it," Strigson replied.

"Why wouldn't I accept help from the Glen Bailey's general?" Aven answered with a shrewd smile. "Do you think I fear that you will humiliate me, Strigson Ganisalp? We've sparred before, if I recall correctly."

"Of course not, Your Grace," he answered. Their verbal contest didn't fray his nerves. This was normal banter from Aven. He was quite accustomed to the steps in this dance. "I simply didn't wish to impose, is all."

"Anxious doesn't look good on you, Strigson," Aven challenged as she folded her arms, though her analytical smile persisted. "Would you mind staves today? I'd prefer to avoid any knicks. Not that they bother *me*, but if I have to endure disapproving glares at a bandage from my father's magistrates today I just might throw a wine goblet at someone."

Strigson considered reminding the princess that the training grounds was full of blunted swords, but she always insisted on using true blades during their private duels. He doubted she'd make an exception this time. "Wouldn't mind at all," he answered, the formality in his voice beginning to wane as the last few straggling soldiers began to filter out through the gate, well out of earshot. "This way, then. You're meeting with the magistrates during the Solstice?"

"You and your soldiers aren't the only ones who work during a holiday, Strigson," Aven said as they made their way across the grounds towards a rack suspended on a barracks wall with a collection of staves nestled between wooden pegs, assorted in order of height. "Father always addresses the public during the Summer Solstice, you know that."

"I do," Strigson answered as they approached the rack, his hand reaching for one of the wooden poles as he lifted it off its resting place. He tested his grip on it quickly as he continued, "But I always thought he kind of...well, you know. Just winged it. It's usually the same time thing every year. 'May our crops grow high and our health remain sound.'"

"It's true," Aven answered as she plucked her own staff from the rack, gauging its length and weight with both hands before determining it satisfactory. Nodding at the general, they both broke away from the barracks wall, marching over to a ring of raked dirt that would serve as their sparring grounds. "This year's different, though. Eliliweth has been studying some farming methods over at York that he thinks we can introduce here, or at least on *our* portion of swampland. He's shown me the details and I don't see any reason it shouldn't be successful."

As they got into their respective positions, Strigson pulled out a single glove that he kept tucked into his belt during training and slid it over his crippled hand. The middle, ring, and pinky finger were all crafted with hardened leather that helped keep his contorted fingers from bending awkwardly as he handled a staff. The smooth patch over the palm helped him adjust quickly if his grip happened to falter. "Well, at least it should be an idea that the magistrates approve of, right?"

"At first, absolutely," Aven said with a coy smile. "Until they hear his plans for distribution. I think they're going to be dismayed at how many pockets other than their own are going to be filled with his plan. I'm anticipating a lot of nasally whining all throughout the afternoon."

Strigson craned his head upward, taking a quick peek at the sun that was beginning to unleash a more vengeful heat from above. "I know how bloody hot it gets in those chambers. Better hope that's all that's on the agenda today."

"I don't think it is," Aven said, a thoughtful frown crossing her brow. "Father made it sound like he had something to address as well. I think it's about Eliliweth, and I would imagine he's about to announce some kind of formal position for him. Probably a diplomat of some sort, maybe for the Sherinalu Vale. I'm hoping I can pry it out of him before the meeting."

"I knew he'd be something special when he got that promotion to be the Ashlands captain a few years back," Strigson said, turning the bottom end of his staff back and forth against the dirt, creating small circular divots with each rotation. "Not just anyone can hold that position. Lot of different personalities and egos in that unit. He handled it like a real leader. If he didn't have such a knack for politics I'd worry about him coming for my seat."

Aven clicked her tongue against the roof of her mouth and shook her head. "You're being modest, Strigson," she chided him as her fingertips tapped against the staff in her hand. "But he'll do well with whatever Father appoints him to. Selfishly, I only hope he doesn't become so occupied that he doesn't have time for me. I don't mean to sound as though I'm a child losing her playmate. I only mean that there are only so many people I can truly *talk* to, or at least ones that will speak with me honestly. The maids are suitable if I'm looking for someone who will agree with me unconditionally, but I prefer more sincerity than that. Elune can provide that as well - the elf woman from the Sherinalu, I'm sure you remember - but she's there more often than she's here, and unless I can convince Father to give *her* a position as well…" She trailed off, jaw working slowly as she mulled over her thoughts.

"You're the *princess*, Aven," Strigson said assuredly, shifting his weight from one foot to the other as he felt sweat begin to blossom between his shoulder blades. By the gods, it was getting hotter by the minute. "I'm sure Eliliweth will make time for you."

All at once, Aven seemed to recognize the vulnerability she'd exposed to the general, and her posture stiffened immediately, a flush forming in her face that Strigson suspected had nothing to do with the heat. It was easily the most personal confession she'd ever given the general, and he could tell that she was unsettled by the allowance. He was sure she was more comfortable sharing such insecurities with Wyatt Darjin, but then, the Arden's Watch captain wasn't here, was he? Was that Strigson's fault? *Careful, son,* he thought to himself in a tone that sounded strikingly like his late father's. *You know the rules about this. Just because you can doesn't mean you should.*

"Yes, well…" Aven said as she briskly cleared her throat, her hands lifting the staff off of its resting position, angled defensively across her chest. "Shall we, then?"

Their conversation came to an end as Strigson obliged, closing the distance between the two as he lifted his staff as well, holding it a bit off-center to compensate for the lack of strength in his left hand. While it inevitably compromised his technique, he'd learned to adapt long ago, and could still wield a polearm effectively enough to present a challenge to the princess.

Back and forth the staves swung, their ends clacking together as they lifted and dipped, offering strikes and parries as they dueled. They maneuvered in a slow circle as they sparred, both attempting to lure the other off-balance. The general would occasionally press forward, thrusting the center of his weapon against Aven's in an attempt to overwhelm her. She was as agile as she looked, however, and simply used his aggression against him as she wheeled around him at an angle, swiping the end towards his hip as she rounded him, forcing him into a defensive posture. Strigson gave his best effort in the duel. He'd learned his lesson long ago not to grant the princess any leniency. The first time she had requested a spar, he'd allowed her to win, not bothering to break a sweat in the process. With her powers as a mage, she'd lit small plumes of fire under his boots until he moved them with the intensity he was capable of.

Sweat began to course down their faces, stinging their eyes as it slid into their corners. Their knuckles began to throb from the collisions with the other's staff. Dust kicked up around them as they danced, the clacking of the poles increasing in tempo as the princess began to grow impatient. It didn't take long after that for Strigson to find the weakness he'd been searching for. Catching her off-balance, he locked the center of his staff against hers and gave her a shove as her feet were crossed in a stagger.

She collapsed in the dirt with a grunt, landing square on her bottom as her staff fell from her grasp with a clatter and rolled away from her. Slowly, Strigson approached her, ready to offer his good hand to help her up, but to his surprise, Aven snarled and clawed her way up from the dirt, charging the general. He lifted his staff again defensively as she coiled her fingers around it, a hiss escaping her as she tried to wrench it from his grip. His instincts told him to ease up, but he reminded himself of the consequences before twirling her around in the exact direction she was pulling. As she swung, however, she thrusted her boot between his ankles, hooking her foot around his as she tumbled, jarring him just enough to get him to stumble forward, the staff coming loose in his addled hand as it too landed in the dirt.

He wasn't certain how it happened, but not a breath later, he found himself tumbled over the princess, his hands reaching out to try to balance his weight. His knees just barely missed bashing against hers, thumping against the dirt with a dull pain. As he lifted his head from the ground, he felt with both excitement and horror as his thin beard bristled against the line of her jaw. Fully realizing the compromising position they had managed to collapse into, he hurriedly pushed himself up onto his knees, hoisting himself back up as he reached his hand down to her. "Your Grace," he murmured with embarrassment. "I'm sorry, I didn't-"

"Don't apologize, Strigson, by the gods," Aven said in an attempt at sounding casual, though she was clearly just as rattled by their fall as he was. She accepted his offer with as much grace as she could manage, however. "You know that I don't want my duels to be half-hearted. Things happen."

"Yes, well…" Strigson said as he took in a few bracing breaths, brushing some dirt off of himself after Aven had stabilized herself. "I didn't expect you to try snatching my staff away."

"Well, if I get knocked down in battle, there's no way in hell I'm going to just lie there and let someone bludgeon me to death," Aven answered as she brushed dirt off of her tunic as well before drawing her knuckles across her forehead, pulling strands of her hair away from her eyes. "Thank you, though. I think that was exactly what I needed to keep my wits about me today when those plump magistrates start wailing about tax percentages."

"Preemptive release, huh?" Strigson asked with a quick chuckle as he plucked his staff up out of the dirt.

"Exactly," Aven said after a heavy breath passed between her lips. She grabbed her staff as well before extending it towards the general. "Would you mind putting that back up for me? It looks as though I'll have to get myself cleaned up before the meeting, and I don't have much time left."

"Of course, Your Grace," Strigson answered as he reached out with the gloved hand, grasping the staff between his pointer finger and thumb. He held both of them at his sides, looking as though he were about to use them as stilts.

"All right then," Aven said, giving her tunic another brushing for good measure before offering the general a weary smile. "Thank you again, Sir Ganisalp. I appreciate you taking time out of your busy day, even on the Solstice, for my sake."

"You need only ask," Strigson answered. "Best of luck in there today, Your Grace. I pray that your brush with bureaucracy today is short-lived."

"As do I," Aven said. She turned away, beginning to march towards the training grounds' exit. Strigson pursed his lips, weighing a decision in his mind quickly before calling out,

"Aven."

She paused, looking back over her shoulder with lifted eyebrows. "Yes?"

"Ah, look," the general said, tapping the staff in his right hand against the ground a few times before continuing, "I know that what we do isn't quite the same thing, but...if you do find that your friend Eliliweth becomes too tied up in the future, you can always come talk about things with me. I think you'd be surprised at the similarities our positions share."

She watched the general scrutinizingly for a moment, her expression unreadable. Strigson had squared off against brutish men with biceps the size of coconuts before, but it was the princess's gaze now that made him the most nervous. He was beginning to regret his offer when a faint smile crossed Aven's face. She replied, "Actually, I don't think I'd be surprised at all. I'll keep that in mind, Strigson. Thank you."

She turned and marched away, all the way out of the training grounds this time. Strigson allowed himself to watch her go for a brief minute before forcing himself to turn around back in the direction of the staves' rack. A grin was widening across his face, and he couldn't hope to contain it. Despite that, however, a familiar voice murmured in the back of his mind.

Careful, son.

Chapter Eight

Tranquility is not in the nature of a demon. And yet, as Terodar traveled through the portal from Nollofolith to the world of mortals, he felt a strange calm as he passed timelessly through the folds of existence. His mind began to wander, and he thought back to the secret that Kavagor wouldn't reveal to him. Something began to whisper at the back of his mind, urging him to remember a concealed secret, and for a brief moment, he thought he might pull it from the soil it was buried under.

Just like a dream that ends too quickly, however, Terodar awoke once more in a world much different than Daemonaar or Nollofolith. Eyes wide in temporary shock, the demon blinked as his vision began to adapt to the strange sunlight of the mortal world. He looked down at his hooves to see that he was standing on a rock that was spattered with blood. Turning his head in a slow swivel, he saw that he was perched upon the center of what was known as a Stone Circle, one of many ancient ritual sites used by the first mortals to wield magic. The stones were placed intermittently in the direction of a compass, aligned in just such a way that allowed the arcane currents to flow with greater ease. Beyond the Circle, they were surrounded by trees. They seemed familiar to the demon, but that couldn't have been possible, for there were no plants in Daemonaar that stood taller than his knees. The mention of them in his studies must have painted a vivid picture in his mind.

He began to notice the bodies that were strewn around where he stood. There were at least a half a dozen men and women, their eyes wide and glossed over, trails of blood drying against their chins. Each of their throats had been cut, but Terodar suspected that they hadn't been bled until after they had perished, for the bodies harbored no signs of struggle. Looking up further, he finally noticed a single man standing a few paces away, eyes wide with greedy awe. His hair was unwashed and slicked back against his scalp, and Terodar found himself comparing him to a rat with a hint of annoyance.

"Symon Blacknail, I assume?" Terodar growled lowly.

"It worked!" the warlock cried out in a shrill pitch, a look of relief and excitement washing over the rodent-like man's face. "By the Destroyer's burning fist, it worked! I knew it would, of course! But of course I did!"

Terodar scowled, only further annoyed by the sound of Symon's voice. He looked once more at the bodies surrounding him. "They weren't aware how much they would be sacrificing, were they?"

"Oh no," Symon said with a mischievous smirk. "A cup of silverfang tea, passed around the circle, that made the job much easier, haha!"

"Cunning, but cowardly," Terodar remarked as he stepped off the stained stone, standing a good foot taller than the human warlock. "Blood magic is most potent when it is drawn through a struggle. Or were you not aware?"

"Well I managed to bring you here, didn't I?" Symon snapped, his nose twitching with his words in the most infuriating manner. "Now I command you to be silent! What should I have you do first? Oh, the possibilities are endless!"

Terodar's face darkened at the worm's order. His lip curled and he approached the warlock menacingly. Symon Blacknail's face paled as the demon approached, and he took a wary step backwards before reasserting himself, jabbing a finger in Terodar's direction. "Stop! I command you to stop!" the warlock cried.

Terodar lunged forward and seized Symon by the throat just as the warlock had begun to call upon his gift of blood magic. Hissing through gritted, pointed teeth, the demon growled, "Perhaps you misunderstood your place, worm. You did not summon me to rule over me. *You* do not command *me*. You brought me here as a service to your lord Gapinon. *His* success is *your* reward, and I find your stupidity and arrogance insulting. I have little patience for those that insult me. Do you understand?"

Symon's eyes were bulging, his pale face turning tomato red as Terodar squeezed his throat. Desperately, the warlock bobbed his head, gasping for breath as the demon's fingers sunk into his neck. "Good," Terodar snarled before releasing him. The warlock collapsed to the ground on his knees in a coughing fit, one hand reaching up to caress the bruised marks left by the demon's grip.

"Now," Terodar said as he walked away from the gasping warlock, "on to your question as to what we shall do first. Before anything, we shall-"

His speech was interrupted as a shout came from beyond the Stone Circle, from the surrounding trees. The demon scowled as he glared in the direction it had come from, but his annoyance was quickly replaced with surprise as an arrow came hissing through the brush, nipping at the corner of his robe and just barely missing Symon as it buried itself into the soil nearby. Crouching down, Terodar hurried over to the warlock as another barrage of arrows came sailing across, disappearing into the other side of the wilderness.

"Make yourself useful, worm!" Terodar hissed as figures began to emerge from the forest line. Squinting, the demon could only make out the weapons that they carried, and the wooden shields on their arms. Whoever they were, Terodar doubted the fired arrows were a misunderstanding.

"Help!" Symon cried out, scurrying away from Terodar with flailing arms as he approached the armed strangers. "There's a demon here! He's trying to-" The warlock gasped as one of the approaching men drove his notched blade through his stomach. Blacknail sputtered as the stranger pulled the blade out and smashed his fist against his rodent face. Terodar gnashed his teeth as he watched the warlock tumble to the ground. This was all wrong. He had been expecting a powerful and cunning summoner, not a coward thriving on good luck. Regardless, Symon Blacknail's luck had run out, and the ambushers were closing in on Terodar.

"By the bloody hells, the simpering twit was right," the man with the now-stained blade said. He was wearing cracked, mismatched leather armor, and had a scrap of burlap tied around his face as a mask. "At least I think he was. That *is* a demon, ain't it?"

"Looks like one if I've ever saw one," the man next to him said, tapping a blackjack club against his own knee and shifting the weight of his shield on his arm.

"A'rright then," the one who had killed Symon chuckled. "There's two ways we can do this, demon. You can let us tie yer hands and gag you, and we can go find ourselves a buyer for your pale hide. *Or*, we can just lop your horned head off your shoulders and sell that as a bounty. I think yer worth more alive, but we'll have buyers for both, and I got no problem doin' this the easy way, which is carryin' your head in a bag and not worryin' about you misbehavin'. So which is it gonna be?"

Terodar grinned. As the fool had been jabbering, his followers had all walked into the Stone Circle. There was more than enough blood coating the ground to cast the spell he had in mind. He didn't waste any time with pointless dialogue. Lifting his palms, he hissed, "*Ix'ral tonokiir!*"

The ground below the armed men suddenly began to burst at the soil, pillars of flame surging upward towards their faces. Three of the men had arrows pointed at Terodar, but the flash of scalding fire startled each of them enough to send their arrows astray. The man with the notched blade howled and cursed as he furiously beat at his eyebrows with his forearm, trying to snuff out the embers that had formed at the hairs. The blasting flames hadn't killed any of the men, but the demon wasn't finished yet.

"*Norros'i,*" he hissed, clenching his open fists as the mercenaries finally began to recollect themselves. The corpses strewn around the center stone suddenly began to swell, their skin flushing with the purple of drowned bodies. One of the men stepped on a bloated carcass as he took an angry step forward. The body's flesh burst, spattering the man with steaming blood that hissed as it began to eat through his clothing like acid.

One by one, the other bodies, including Symon Blacknail's, all began to explode around the encroaching bounty hunters. They screamed as they tried to wipe away the corrosive substance, but they only succeeded in spreading it to other parts of themselves. They wailed and convulsed as the blood burned away at their flesh, rapidly creating blistering wounds as it chewed through their skin.

Terodar grinned as he stepped forward, unclasping his hands as the rush of the corrupted magic coursed through his body. Such a grisly scene was euphoria to his senses as the virulent substance drew even more blood. Emboldened by the Stone Circle, it gave the demon a high he hadn't experienced in ages.

The feeling of ecstasy came to a halt as he realized his mistake. Caught up in the rush of what he had done, he had pulled his attention away from the threat of danger. Most of the men were kneeling now, sobbing hysterically as they begged for the pain to stop. Some had fallen silent, finally embraced by the cold hands of death. One of the archers, however, down on one knee, was staring Terodar down, an arrow drawn and aimed at the demon. Hissing blood was eating away at the man's shoulder, but the malice in the mercenary's eyes said that he would take the demon down with him. Time slowed down as Terodar fumbled for a spell to protect himself. He suddenly couldn't focus. How had he been so foolish, so arrogant, only moments after crossing over into the world of mortals?

A battle cry came from the archer's direction, and Terodar braced himself for the bite of the arrow, but it never came. Confusion settled over the demon as a figure he hadn't spotted before came sprinting towards the kneeling archer, a blue half-cape fluttering behind him, long dirty blonde hair vaulting with the stranger's every footstep. A flash of steel glinted in the air as the young man lifted a sword, swinging it down on the mercenary, whose eyes grew wide with shock a mere heartbeat before the blade buried itself into his neck. Twitching, the archer released the arrow, sending it sailing five paces shy of the demon.

"No," Terodar whispered, his voice low with despair and desperate denial. "No, no, no…"

The young man looked over the dead archer, his face painted with a streak of blood that had splattered from his victim's neck. He walked around the body, frowning curiously at the hissing violet blood that was still eating away at the skin of the mercenaries. He came upon one of the men who was still crying in pain, swiping his hands at his trousers in vain.

"Who are you? Who do you serve?" the young man in the blue half-cape demanded. "Tell me and I'll put you out of your misery." He lowered his sword point to the mercenary's chest.

"Aaaahaah!" the mercenary cried before gibbering, "We're jus' hired men, is all! Makin' our way south for a job! We just…*nnnnngh,* we just stopped 'cause we saw the demon! Eastfen Trading Commission pays a good bounty for the heads, worth twice their weight in gold! *Ohhh, PLEASE* m'lord, it hurts so bad!"

"What job to the south?" the young man demanded. The mercenary answered no more questions, though. Reaching up, he grabbed the sword by the blade, drawing blood onto his hands as he pulled the tip down between his solar plexus, granting his own execution. The young man cursed himself for letting his guard down before pulling back the blade. He finally approached Terodar, wiping the blood from his sword off on the shin of his trousers.

"I saw those thugs rob a village north of here, I've been following them since-" the young man paused, his jaw dropping in surprise as he finally got a good look at who he had saved. "What...what *are* you?!"

"I'm a *demon*, you fool, were you not listening to that blubbering dolt!?" Terodar snarled at the stranger. He was bent over now, kneeling on the ground. Kavagor's tome was sitting on the soil in front of him, open-faced with its pages turning of their own accord.

"I thought...I didn't think he was being literal, is all," the stranger answered. The confidence and vindication he had worn when charging into the fray had evaporated now, replaced with confusion and doubt. His blue eyes looked down at the book, its pages still turning over without assistance. "What's happening?" he asked warily.

Terodar did not answer. He only bowed his head in shame as the pages of his tome finally ceased their turning. The ink on the paper began to glow, and a scathing, hissing voice began to speak from the book itself,

"The offspring of Lord Gapinon are the highest and most powerful blood of all the races that infest the mortal world and any other known to the Forgers. Therefore, it is of paramount importance that a demon be self-sufficient and completely independent from the lesser races.

"Shall any blood of Gapinon, slave or champion, have their life safeguarded by an insect of lesser breed, they shall be collared by their own pact that binds them. They shall serve the larva that saved them so that they may know just why the breed of Gapinon is the vast superior in any world. They shall remain chained to their new master until the Lord Gapinon himself decides that they are worthy of once again being called his child."

The words spoken, the illuminated glow upon the ink faded, the book turning over and slamming shut with a condemning clap. The young man's brow furrowed even deeper as he slowly turned his gaze back to Terodar. "What?" he asked incredulously.

"Did you not hear what it said, or are you just soft-headed!?" Terodar snapped, his fingernails digging into the soil as he curled his digits. "It is an ancient demon law. If the lives of any of my kind are directly saved by...well, *yours*, then I am bound to your will until the Lord Gapinon deems me fit to return to his service. I could have survived the arrow, you know. His aim didn't look to be all that terrific, but of course, you had to so *valiantly* come to my aid, didn't you? Are you always so meddling, or is this just my cursed luck!?"

"Look, I didn't know what you...what you *were*," the young man said, lifting a hand to scratch at the back of his head, his face still scrunched in puzzlement. "And I didn't know anything about 'ancient demon laws', I had only been tailing this lot since they looted that village, and I saw a chance to bring them to justice."

"Ah," Terodar quipped snidely. "Your idea of justice is to wait until your victims are screaming for the release of death, and to interrogate them until they carve up their own hands to end their own misery?"

"Shut up!" the stranger snapped, his neck turning a flustered red. Terodar opened his mouth to retort, but found that his tongue would suddenly no longer obey him. Each time he tried to speak, a painful cramp twisted through it that kept him silent. The blonde-haired one stared at him in wonderment for a moment before shaking his head. "I'm sorry, I...you can speak. I'm just trying to make sense of this."

"I think I've laid it out pretty clearly," Terodar said curtly, finding himself able to speak once more. Gathering the broken shards of his pride, the demon picked up his tome and rose to his full height, looking down at the mortal with undisguised contempt. "My name is Terodar Soulrender. Like it or not, I am bound to your will, human, and will remain so until my god releases me. There are countless mortals who would sacrifice a great deal for such a service - that worm lying dead among his cult, for example - but all you had to do was pretend to be a hero. If you find that inconvenient, you are certainly welcome to spare me the humiliation and order me to drop dead. That is within your power."

The young man stared at the demon searchingly with his pale blue eyes. Lifting a sleeved arm, he wiped away the blood streaked across his face. Terodar could see the thoughts warring in the mortal's mind.

"Have you done anything to deserve death?" he asked carefully.

"A question requiring some perspective," Terodar said. "But even by the lofty standards I suspect you hold, I have done nothing more in your world than emerge and defend myself against a rabble of would-be assassins. The other bodies you see here were slain by hands not my own."

"I see," the stranger said, his expression not relieved in the slightest. "What did you come here for?"

"To conquer this world in the name of the Destroyer," the demon answered plainly. He could have lied to the human. He was skilled in the art of deception. But he had spent less than an hour on the most privileged of tasks he could have asked for, and he had already disgraced himself in the most demeaning of ways. He was ashamed of himself, and at the same time, he was furious that such a law even existed in a culture that encouraged using lesser beings for personal gain. He remembered asking Kavagor about the strange law, and when the Blood Ash would not divulge any explanation, Terodar had whispered the questions instead to Deveguill. *It was written very early on, during the age of the first men,* Deveguill had answered. *Our Lord Gapinon was still very bitter over the worship of his siblings, and wrote The Pact in a jealous rage. I think perhaps he became aware of the, ah...conflicting nature later on, but his pride would not allow him to admit that it was a mistake.* For Terodar, death truly felt like the better alternative in comparison to serving this human whelp, and so he would not bother to mince words with him.

"I...I see," the young man answered, scratching at the back of his head again. The fidgeting gestures were beginning to aggravate Terodar. "I...I'm not sure what to do about this. I'm a follower of Kaijaras, you see, and-"

"I care not what paltry god you worship, human," Terodar interrupted impatiently.

"Let me finish," the mortal said, and the demon found his tongue to be uncooperative once more. "Obviously, I've heard things about demons. Mother told me about them, and your god, Gapinon. I know that you are evil." Terodar rolled his eyes. He'd heard that mortals were simple creatures. He hadn't known their perspectives were much the same.

"But...Mother also taught me that nobody is beyond redemption," the young man continued. "That none of us ever reach a point where we cannot turn back to the Lifegiver and redeem ourselves. I've never read anything that says demons are exempt from that law. Perhaps...

perhaps your code will let my code help you find redemption? I can show you. I can help you. I'm supposed to. Those who follow the Life-giver are supposed to help those that need it."

It was the most putrid, abhorrent idea Terodar had ever heard. His lip curled in displeasure. He wanted nothing more than to choke the life out of this starry-eyed runt. Something murmured to him, however, deep in the back of his mind, and despite his violent desires, he listened to that distant intuition. He studied the young man. His youth spoke of an innocence, and yet, there was a fresh wound somewhere in his soul. He remembered a passage from his tome. It was simple, but powerful. *Victory at any cost.* Was there a victory to be had here? Could he crush that innocence, mutate it into something terrible and malefic? Could he salt that wound until something sinister surfaced? His anger began to ebb as he considered the possibilities. The mortal would be his master, but there was more to ruling than just issuing commands. You had to nurture loyalty and influence, give life to the bond between lord and servant. Empires were never built on orders alone. The ones that lasted won the hearts of their people. Could Terodar's empire begin with this fledgling, even under the pretense of reversed roles? He despised this position he had found himself in, but maybe all was not lost.

"Perhaps," Terodar said, ensuring that his voice held the begrudging tone he was sure the young man would expect.

"A willingness to try is all I ask," the young man said.

"Very well," Terodar snipped, folding his arms across his chest. "I will play your game, human, though I don't think you understand just how dangerous it will be."

"I understand more than you may know," he answered. The young man approached Terodar and extended his hand towards him. "My name is Cadohaden Ulaeron, son of Deltore Ulaeron and Melaitha Riverwen." Terodar narrowed his eyes at the offered hand, as though he were being shown something distasteful. The one named Cadohaden frowned and motioned his hand insistently. "Shake," he commanded.

Terodar tried once more to ignore the will of his new master, but he was quickly reminded of the painful consequence. The muscles in his arm began to cramp and protest acutely, drawing a wince from the demon until he finally submitted, curling his slender fingers around Cadohaden's hand, returning the shake. *What an utterly idiotic gesture,* he thought to himself.

"Well," Cadohaden said, releasing the demon's hand and nodding his head towards the south. "We should get moving, then. The sky won't stay lit forever."

I suppose he finds his chatter clever, Terodar thought. "And where are we going, Master Ulaeron? If I might be so bold, of course," the demon inquired with a hint of mockery.

To Terodar's surprise, the human willingly and almost eagerly re-told the story of his past. He spoke of his father, his mother, and even his own conception, which his father had supposedly recounted in un-comfortable detail after a night of too many cups of wine. He spoke of Kingsbanesin, of the Dragonrider's Guild, of Galdoys Veriknock and Mekoda Sanreaux. Terodar watched Cadohaden's face pinch with grief as he told him about the night he met Eliliweth and Elune, the orcish invasion that had occurred upon his return, and what Mekoda had told him with his few final breaths before Cadohaden put him out of his misery. He told him everything about his encounter with the gov-ernor in the Hall of Feasts, and his exile that followed. Terodar did his best to appear stoic and intent as he listened, but on the inside, he was grinning. His instincts had been right about Cadohaden. It was written all over the young man. There was both innocence and trauma, anger and altruism. But most importantly, he harbored both loneliness and the perfect amount of naïvety. Terodar had emerged from the burning worlds of Gapinon only a few hours past, and the attention-starved whelp was divulging all of his life's secrets to a spawn of the Destroyer. All was not lost, indeed.

"And so," Cadohaden said as they carefully toed their way down a steep trail descending into a mossy lowland at the edge of the for-est they had been weaving through, "we are going to the Glen Bailey. Mother and Father aren't here anymore to fight over what my future will become, and so the choice is up to me. If the half-elf spoke the truth, I can learn how to become a paladin from Crusader Nevic. I can carry on with the rest of my life not feeling as though I chose one parent over the other."

"Will the girl be there?" Terodar asked carefully. "Elunamara?"

"She goes by Elune," Cadohaden answered quickly. His face turned a faint crimson at his immediate response. Terodar restrained a smile and told himself to remember that reaction. "And I'm not sure if she will be. I don't even know if Eliliweth will."

"I see," the demon answered. "And will this Crusader Nevic train you, with a demon at your beck and call?"

"I don't know," Cadohaden answered, his brow furrowing thoughtfully. "You may have to wear a hood or something. I don't think warlocks are forbidden within the Glen Bailey, but I'm not sure about demons."

Delightful, Terodar thought. *He's already willing to lie on my behalf.* "How fortunate that the standard garb from the Destroyer's burning world is a hooded cloak," he said with an appropriate lick of mockery.

The further they traveled towards the Glen Bailey, the more confident Terodar grew that he could turn this situation in his favor. They set up camp that night under a starlit sky, and Cadohaden slept soundly only a few feet away from the demon, who watched him as he slumbered. Not once did the young man roll over to peer at his new companion suspiciously. The demon suspected that it was Cadohaden's hope that this newly found forced friendship could steer his thoughts away from the demise of his parents and his exile from Kingsbanesin. He was quite certain that was why the young man had tailed the mercenaries that had robbed the village. Instead of spending his time reflecting on the wounds of the past, he had immersed himself in his own quest for personal heroism, intent on scrubbing away any shame he might have felt, despite the corruption of Galdoys Veriknock.

They departed again in the morning. Cadohaden followed a similar routine of polite talk and friendly gestures, beginning his day by wishing his demonic companion a 'good morning' with a bright grin. As much as the young man's eagerness pleased the demon, Terodar didn't have to put any effort into appearing agitated by his chipper demeanor.

The air was still hot under the sun of high noon, but a cooling breeze surrounded them as the walls of the Glen Bailey began to appear on the horizon. Cadohaden broke into a grin at the sight of the standard flags whipping against the wind upon the ramparts. A cart could be seen further south, nearing the gates, looking to be carrying a wagon full of potatoes. Terodar frowned as they closed in on the city. "What the hell is that noise?" he snipped.

Cadohaden looked over at him with a quizzical frown, then laughed and shook his head, carrying on with a lingering chuckle, as if the demon had uttered some jolly jest. Terodar's expression curdled as he hissed, "Don't patronize me; what is that sound?"

Cadohaden's expression flattened as he looked back at Terodar. He blinked a couple times in a naïve fashion before replying, "Oh! Oh, I'm sorry, I didn't think you were being serious. That's music, Terodar. Sounds like it's coming from a lute, a flute, and maybe a string of bells. They don't have music in Daemonaar?"

Terodar glared at him with a smoldering gaze. "Why, of course, Master Ulaeron. In the world of the Destroyer, we busy ourselves with trivial nonsense like the sounds of glorified racket. No, we don't have music on Daemonaar. We commit ourselves to snuffing out worlds that practice such inane foolery."

"You could have just said 'no,'" Cadohaden murmured, his expression souring. Terodar allowed himself a half-hidden grin of satisfaction. He'd had his fair share of bright-and-cheery from the young fool, and it was pleasing to see that attitude doused.

"It really is loud, though," Cadohaden remarked as the gate sentries came into sight. "There must be a festival happening! Is it the Summer Solstice? I'd bet they're celebrating the Summer Solstice!" Terodar's lip curled. He already had his doubts about venturing into the thick of the city. If there was a celebration going on, there would only be more mortal urchins to bump into, with their intrusive curiosity and their ale-bolstered antics.

When they finally reached the gates, the sentries were opening the massive oak doors to allow the potato cart passage inside. They promptly shut them closed as the trader disappeared into the depths, and the guard's attentions turned back to the two approaching.

"Who goes there?" one of the armored men called out. His hair was jet black and braided over each side of the mantle of his chainmail coif. His emerald eyes were friendly, but guarded.

"My name is Cadohaden Ulaeron," the young man answered. "And my companion goes by Terodar Soulrender." *You couldn't be bothered to invent a less incriminating name?* the demon thought as he scowled under his hood.

"State your business," the guard commanded.

"I'm seeking someone by the name of Eliliweth Heraketh. Is he here?"

"He's here," the guard confirmed. "But I doubt that he's got the time to entertain visitors. Was he expecting you two?"

"Not...necessarily," Cadohaden admitted slowly. "But I'd also like an audience with Crusader Nevic. Will you let us in?"

"Didn't get any word about the Monastery expecting guests neither," the guard answered, folding his arms across his chest. "What about your cloaked friend, there? Does he have an important visit scheduled? If there's a coven of warlocks gettin' together, I'd sure like to know about it."

"My friend...is a warlock," Cadohaden answered with as much authority as he could muster. Terodar rolled his eyes under the cover of his hood. "But he is only here as my protector, not to meet anyone else of his kind. I've heard word that even disciples of Gapinon are welcome in the Glen Bailey. Was that a lie?"

The guard's eyes narrowed in a testy temperament. "It's true enough. But he'll be watched closely. And at the first sign of trouble, he *will* be detained. With as much force as is necessary, I should add.

"I can let you two in on the premise of attending the Solstice festival. Maybe you find who you're looking for, maybe you don't. If both Eliliweth and Crusader Nevic are too busy enjoying themselves to entertain the likes of you, then you'll be asked to leave when the festival is over. We don't need loitering warlocks in our streets."

"Fair enough," Cadohaden answered with a polite nod of his head. "Thank you, sir."

"It's Lieutenant Mekudii," the guard answered before gesturing for the gates to be opened. "And it's considered bad manners for a visitor to attend a festival and not spend any coin, mind you."

"That won't be a problem," the young man replied cheerily with a quick pat of his coin pouch. Terodar couldn't help but shake his head and glance around warily for eavesdropping pickpockets. Cadohaden's misfortune might be amusing, but to be completely bereft of coin would be more than inconvenient for the both of them.

The doors shut behind them, and Cadohaden's gaze immediately lifted towards the sky. Terodar looked over and realized that the young man was surveying the tops of the buildings. "It's not as big as I thought it would be," Cadohaden said. It was the first mortal city Terodar had witnessed, but even to him, the Glen Bailey seemed to be of humble stature. The structures looked as though they were sturdy and built with fine materials, and the streets were certainly winding their way towards a wide expanse of them, but there were very few that rose above the ramparts that protectively surrounded the Glen Bailey. There were two exceptions: what Terodar assumed was the royalty's castle, and what he could sense was the Monastery that the lieutenant had referred to. Judging by Cadohaden's shrewd frown, however, neither of them were the massive structures he had dreamed of in his quest southward.

What they lacked for in empirical show, however, the Glen Bailey amended with the festive colors of the Solstice. Ropes were strung from across the streets every which way, greens and ambers and gold cloth draped from above, billowing proudly in the summer breeze. The demon began to see the same emblem stitched upon many of the banners: a sigil with a closed wooden cross and four different leaves on opposite ends. It was no doubt the symbol of the Glen Bailey.

As they drew nearer to the center of the city, Terodar spotted a canal that bisected the city, a bridge crossing over a hundred paces or so in front of them. There were children laughing and chasing each other near its bank, a few elderly women watching over them, away from the bustle of laughter and music coming from further within the Bailey. As the two of them crossed over the bridge, Terodar's eyes followed the river as far as they could, wondering where it came from. His distraction nearly led him to bump right into a pair of fairly inebriated men swaggering happily towards them. The demon expected drunken curses and taunts, but the men only laughed and cheerily apologized before continuing on their way.

"It's so…modest," Cadohaden finally said, breaking the silence between the two as a cheer erupted in the distance as a song concluded. "Some of our guard garrisons in Kingsbanesin stand as tall as their royal keep."

Terodar felt a strange sensation itching behind his ear. He followed the instinctive cue and looked over his shoulder. The guard was far behind them, well out of earshot, but the lieutenant hadn't been bluffing when he told them that they would be watched. He turned his head back around, annoyed. "And yet, humble as it is, they led a successful mutiny against Kingsbanesin. And it's not 'yours' anymore, Cadohaden. You were exiled."

The words clearly stung the young man, who bristled at their speaking, but he did not challenge them. "I realize that. I just have to wonder how they managed to do it."

"Well," Terodar answered coyly, "we're in the right place to find out."

Chapter Nine

"Outside, the ale flows like rivers into the mugs of the masses," Magistrate Bertram Archibaum complained, his delicate fingertips tapping against the window pane as he looked outside. "And here we sit, cramped in this chamber hall, sweating like pigs."

Eliliweth Heraketh brushed a knuckle against his temple, dabbing at a bead of sweat that had begun to gather. He silently remarked that if Archibaum knew anything about pigs, he would know that they didn't actually sweat, but he knew it would be a poor choice to vocalize his thoughts. It *was* stiflingly hot in the keep's council chamber, however, and Archibaum wasn't the only magistrate that was quickly growing hot and irritated. Even Bartholomew's daughter, Princess Aven, who took pride in her disciplined and collected appearance, was fanning herself with a folded sheet of parchment, her face flushed from the heat.

"Aw, quit your whimpering, Bertram," King Bartholomew Celandine growled, though he dabbed his forehead with a handkerchief as he did so. "Everyone in this bloody room knows you don't like ale anyhow."

"Well, *I* like ale, and I'm up here," the plump magistrate named Wallace Tibault grumbled, pulling on the front of his nobleman's robe to air out his chest. "This can't wait til tomorrow, Bartholomew?"

"Everyone here would rather be down there drinking, I know!"

Bartholomew snapped impatiently. His Majesty wasn't known for having unlimited patience, and the humidity was not extending it. "But we've had two days for indulgence now, and on the third day of the Solstice festival, we must make our appropriate announcements to the people! Most importantly, how we're going to survive as a kingdom for another year, so that we may celebrate the Solstice once again!"

"So let's tell the simpletons that the autumn harvest will be bountiful, the cows will be fat, and the barley rich! It's all formality anyway, everyone knows that," Magistrate Dirk Wellingson sneered, his eyebrows bowing in their notorious caterpillar-like manner.

"Those 'simpletons' all work hard to keep this kingdom's coffers full, Wellingson," the half-elf finally spoke. His voice was quiet, but firm. He had to tread carefully with the magistrates. King Bartholomew liked him, but the collective council could make life very difficult for those they did not care for. He could not simply sit and let this noble insult the common folk, however. "And we have allies attending the festival as well, and they should be reassured that the Glen Bailey is as strong as ever."

Magistrate Arnold Seasar snorted from his seat. He was bulkier than even Wallace Tibault, and was no doubt hungering for a generous sample of every food being marketed down at the festival. "Tell me that you did not bring us up here simply to be lectured by this outsider, Bartholomew," the magistrate grunted.

"The boy has more than practiced promises to give to the people," His Majesty said, giving his beard a quick tug, as he often did when complimenting someone. He nodded in Eliliweth's direction. "He has ideas, and prosperous ones at that! Tell them, Eliliweth."

"Very well, your Majesty," the half-elf said, leaning forward in his chair and folding his hands on the table in front of himself. "As many of you know, the Glen Dale shares a border with the swamp kingdom of York. Near that border, however, we own swamp land that we aren't putting to use."

"That's because it's swamp land," the old and withered magistrate Edward Carson rasped with a sour glare. "We aren't putting it to use because it is useless."

"Why have we assumed that for so long?" Eliliweth questioned, taking care not to allow his voice to express the true impatience he felt with these old stubborn nobles. "York has survived for longer than even the Glen Bailey, and yet, we have never taken the time to question how it is so! And so His Majesty sent me as an ambassador to the swamp kingdom to discover the answer."

The grumbling response was immediate, the heads of the nobles shaking, many of their chins wagging as they did so.

"An awfully official errand for a boy with no title!" Wellingson remarked with a scowl.

"We weren't consulted about this!" Archibaum whined.

"I am your king, and I do not need to consult the lot of you about whether or not I send someone to visit with a trusted ally!" King Bartholomew barked, clapping his fist on the table.

"Gentlemen! Father!" the princess Aven said, brushing a strand of dark red hair out of her eyes. "Let Eliliweth finish. The sooner we are finished, the sooner we can get out of this sweltering keep!"

The king's expression softened at Aven's interruption. There wasn't a soul in the Glen Bailey who could get away with the same. His temper had not always been so heated. The day Queen Meredith had passed away, the same day she had given birth to their only daughter, was the day that Bartholomew's temperament changed. The princess, so much like the mother she had never met, was the only one who could call forth the Bartholomew from so long ago. "Right," Bartholomew muttered. "We're getting ourselves off track. Please continue, Eliliweth."

"As I was saying," the half-elf said, looking at the magistrates with a measured glance. "The York natives showed me how they feed themselves using the swamp lands. They cultivate wild rice and grow cattail leeks, and store so much of it that it feeds them almost all throughout the winter! We *own* land that can be used for the same! How many years now have the farmers of the Glen Dale been bickering over cramped farm fields and coming to this court to verify the property lines of their farmsteads? Let us find a few farmers who are down on their luck and offer them this land! We show them how to grow these crops, we collect a small portion for the crown, we collect our taxes when they sell their share at the market, and each farmer has a little more land to work with. Everybody will benefit from this."

The transformation of every magistrate's expression was almost instantaneous. The glint of greed shone in every eye as they glanced at one another with smirks that only emerged with the promise of more gold in their pockets. King Bartholomew crossed his arms across his chest, a proud grin on his bearded face. "Did I not tell you? The boy is a genius!"

"Your Majesty," Eliliweth spoke up over the excited murmur that had quickly blossomed in the chamber room, "I would also suggest that half of the share we collect for the Glen Bailey should be given to the people of York."

The room fell to an abrupt silence once more, the coinlusting expressions reversing once again to the skeptical scowls of disapproval. All at once, the room filled with agitated grumbling. King Bartholomew pounded his fist against the table, glaring at the magistrates before turning his gaze back upon the half-elf. "And pray tell, Eliliweth, why would we give half of the crops we harvested to York?"

"With respect, Your Majesty, the farmers will harvest them. The Glen Bailey will simply collect them," Eliliweth answered. It was a bold move, correcting the king in such a manner, but it was crucial to making his point, and he did not lower his gaze when Bartholomew's bushy eyebrows furrowed. "The people of York gave their time freely to teach the ways of swamp farming to us. It would only be appropriate that we return the gesture with the same level of generosity. Historically, farming on territorial borders has been perhaps the most common cause of conflict across the Aariad. A fair, even split in the city's yield would ensure that such tensions never rise."

"York has always been the Glen Bailey's most staunch ally," Archibaum said with a wrinkled nose and a prominent scowl. He pulled a small bottle from his pocket containing green liquid, popping the cork and tapping the vessel's bottom over his tongue. Bertram was known for his periodic consumption of plantain extract, to ease the arthritic pain in his joints.

"All the more reason to carry on with Eliliweth's plan," Princess Aven challenged, folding her arms across her chest. "We must never take our allies for granted, Lord Archibaum. First and foremost, because that would not be the right thing to do. And if you insist on finding some sort of practical reason, we should keep in mind that the hunters of York fend off the minotaurs of the Sunrise Knolls almost every other day. The minotaurs do not cross directly through the swamps of York, I will remind you. The hunters go out of their way to dissuade the beasts from using the Spruce Ridge as a road *directly* into the Glen Dale. We do not ask them to do this, and they do not demand anything in return, but it is a kindness that we have complacently accepted for many years now. This is a perfect way to demonstrate our goodwill."

The chamber room fell quiet once more as the king and his magistrates mulled their words over. Aven glanced over at Eliliweth. She did not smile, but the corners of her lips twitched in just a manner that told him that she was on his side. With the most subtle of nods, the half-elf acknowledged his understanding and fought to keep a business-like expression. The two of them had not always cooperated so well. When Bartholomew had first taken the half-elf under his wing, the princess had seen him as nothing more than a nuisance that complicated her influence over her father. It had taken them very little time to realize that while they did not always see things eye-to-eye, their vision of the Glen Bailey's future was much the same.

"Bah," King Bartholomew said, dabbing his forehead with his sleeve. "And once more, the wisdom of youth makes us all look to be very old fools. Put this proposal in writing, Pleatus."

"At once, sir," a man with bulbous eyes and a velvet cap said from a desk huddled away from the table in the corner of the room. Pleatus Leland was the crown's royal scribe, though Eliliweth had seen him in the wine cellars with Bartholomew, boasting of his vast knowledge of grapes. The half-elf wasn't sure what he thought of the scribe yet. He seemed to be the type that wore a different face when there weren't any men with titles present in the room. Eliliweth hadn't yet met a man of that nature who had any sense of honor.

"Now," Bartholomew said, silencing the grumbles from the magistrates that were beginning to surface once again, "there is something else we must discuss before we venture out into the festival.

"I believe this decision is long overdue. The boy has more than proven his worth in counsel. His rare combination of youth and perception will serve this kingdom well, beyond my days of walking this world, and perhaps even beyond those where my daughter will rule. Today, lords and lady, I am going to announce to the people of my official intention to appoint Eliliweth Heraketh as my Chief Advisor. We shall hold his inauguration one week from now. It will be the perfect excuse to extend the Solstice festival for another couple of days, hah!"

The princess could no longer contain her smile. She looked over at Eliliweth with a bright grin. The half-elf felt his face flush as the eye of every magistrate turned once more to stare at him with glassy surprise. His heart was hammering in his chest. Truly? He was to be the king's Chief Advisor? It was no secret that Bartholomew wished to give him a position of political power in his court. As the king had stated, he *was* a voice of perception, something that was difficult to find in a room full of elderly nobles. But Eliliweth had also known that Bartholomew had taken him under his wing in hopes of earning the favor of the elves of the Sherinalu Vale, as well as the secluded night elves of Ashtalath. Such a prominent promotion was more than simple pandering. This was a stunning decision.

"Chief Advisor?!" Edward Carson rasped, his withered jaw quivering as he spoke. "By the gods, your Majesty, it's one thing to have the boy in your court, but the notion of giving him such a title is...it's lunacy!"

"We weren't consulted about this!" Arnold Seasar bellowed, his jowls quaking with the outburst.

"*Enough!*" Bartholomew roared back, pounding his fist against the table. His face had turned nearly purple with anger. "How many times must I repeat myself? *I am the king.* This decision is mine to make. *Your* roles are to *advise* me, and to be quite frank, your collective advice has been short-sighted and lacking for many years now! If I have found someone who can better fill that role, I do not need to *consult* any of you to act upon it!"

A tense, uncomfortable silence filled the room as the magistrates' chattering subsided, their demeanors settling into brooding resentment. Eliliweth shifted in his chair. Should he say something? Should he assure the magistrates that he would do his very best to better the kingdom they called home? Did he even owe them that kind of sentiment? They certainly had not been supportive of his presence in the crown's discussions, even without an official title.

"Your Majesty," Bertram Archibaum finally spoke as he steepled his fingers, breaking the strained silence. His voice was calm and collected, but his eyes betrayed his true agitation. "You are right. The decision to appoint your advisors is yours alone. However, I must remind you that we of your council do not sit here by chance alone. We are the Glen Bailey's investors. It is not only the coin of the kingdom's coffers that gives it life. Each of us contribute in our own way, from our own pockets, to ensure that everyone and everything under your reign flourishes.

"Each of us knows that Eliliweth is a fine young man, and can serve the Glen Bailey well. However, as the kingdom's most prominent investors, we only ask that our voices be heard in regards to his... promotion. The boy does not own any lands, nor does he employ any workers. Would such a position be appropriate for someone so inexperienced, Your Majesty? Perhaps, perhaps not. We would only like the opportunity to discuss this with you. I'm quite certain we could reach a fair conclusion after some open dialogue."

Bartholomew's eyes were narrowed, his mouth puckered indignantly. It was evident that the king was not interested in engaging in any dialogue with the magistrates, but Eliliweth knew that his Majesty could not openly disregard their request. Whether or not they had any power to overrule Bartholomew's decision, they were all in control of a substantial portion of the kingdom's flow of coin. The half-elf was certain that the magistrates benefited from the Glen Bailey far more than the city benefited from them, but if they were to relocate to the wealthy kingdom of Eastfen, it would be more than just an inconvenience for the realm. If they wanted to have words about Eliliweth's promotion, it would be unwise for the king to simply dismiss them.

"Very well," the king conceded. "The lot of you may have your say. But I warn you, the decision is still my own, whether or not you all approve."

"Your Majesty," the scribe Pleatus piped up from the corner of the room, "in the interest of having a *true* discussion about the half-elf's role in your court, perhaps it would be best if he were not present? It would be uncomfortable for the magistrates to express their true feelings on the matter, or so I would think." Eliliweth restrained himself from glaring at the simpering scribe, but he realized at that moment that he did not care for Pleatus Leland.

"The scribe speaks out of turn," Magistrate Wellingson remarked, "but he's got the right of it. We can't be expected to have an honest discussion about this with the boy sitting right there. Perhaps the princess should take him to the festivities? The Solstice Festival is enjoyed most by the young. It's an awful shame to keep them both cooped up in here with us stuffy old men." The magistrate nodded pointedly at Aven, whose jaw flexed as her face turned red with indignation.

"I assure you, Lord Wellingson, that I have my own input as to-" she began.

"He is right," Bartholomew said, interrupting his daughter with an air of weariness. "Aven, escort Eliliweth to the festival outside. You two should be enjoying this blessed day."

"But Father, I-"

"That was not a request, Aven," the king iterated with a softer tone than what he had used with the magistrates, but none less firm.

"Very well," the princess said sharply, standing up from her chair and sliding it under the table with a vindictive thump. She lifted her chin up in a snap, nodding stiffly at Eliliweth. "Come, Eliliweth. Let us go occupy our feeble, childish minds with the festival parlour tricks and the overwhelming array of colors. We mustn't bother the wise old men with our frivolous input. Come now."

Bartholomew sighed openly at his daughter's jaded retort as Eliliweth obediently rose out of his chair, sliding his under the table. He nodded at the magistrates with a polite 'good day' and followed the princess out of the chamber hall. He knew nothing good could come from the magistrates having the private ear of the king, but Bartholomew had given his command, and not even his own daughter disobeyed Her Majesty. The princess and the half-elf closed the chamber doors behind them and walked down the hallway. Aven's gait was brisk and irritable.

"I am sorry, Princess," Eliliweth said as they walked side-by-side. "That was insulting of them to ask for your dismissal on my behalf."

"Not as insulting as it was for them to imply that you are not capable of finding your way out of the castle on your own," Aven quipped. "Besides, we both know why they truly sent me away. Those bloated ticks never pass up an opportunity to badger Father about which of their fat, spoiled sons will take my hand in marriage." The princess turned her palm over face-up, and with an uttered incantation, a small wreath of flame leaped up from her hand before she snuffed it out with a grasp of curled fingers.

Eliliweth looked over his shoulder down the hallway and was relieved to see nobody. The princess's spell, however briefly cast, spoke volumes about her agitation. She used it in the open so little that it was easy to forget that she had the gift of magic. She was the first in the Celandine bloodline to have a talent for the arcane in many generations, almost as far back as the Gunnysack Wars. When her gift had been discovered, it had been nurtured immediately. Four times now, Aven had visited the mage island of Novinar to spend months learning in their university. Archmage Cadrinn himself had written to King Bartholomew, expressing his enthusiasm for Aven's affinity for her talent.

In the same way that magic was not forbidden in the Glen Bailey, however, it was not celebrated either. The head of the kingdom's Mage

Unit, Benton Cusair, was a humble man of magic, and insisted that the arcane must never become the focal point of interest for the Glen Bailey, for it was far too susceptible to corruption. Others whispered that the Monastery, primarily Priestess Ecila, had a hand in enforcing that cultural aspect. Whatever the reason, magic was not a celebrated facet of Glen Bailey culture, used solely as a means to an end, and so for Aven to risk someone seeing her use hers in anger was surprising indeed.

"His Majesty won't truly give you away to one of *their* sons, would he?" Eliliweth asked. There was no jealousy in his question. Though a marriage between himself and the princess was an interesting concept, Bartholomew had made it fairly clear that while the Sherinalu Vale would no doubt praise such a union, it would not garner significant enough reward. Eliliweth held no true sway in the decisions of the Sherinalu Vale. His pending position as advisor would lead to warmer relations, but the Sherinalu elves would have no obligations to the Glen Bailey if the half-elf married the princess. The mixed blood of their children would have been an entirely different controversy on its own. Besides, the half-elf would never be able to truly devote his heart to the princess. Like his elven friend Elune Shadowsong, he had formed a sibling-like bond to Aven Celandine. Even a political marriage would feel unbearably strange.

"He will not," Aven said with conviction as they began descending the stairs to the lower level of the keep. "But for the sake of courtesy, he must listen to their offers. I know he would like to wed me off to King Rhone of Eastfen's son, Micah, but the boy is hardly old enough to lift a sword, much less sire a child."

"Do you even want children, Aven?" the half-elf asked. Her studies in Novinar would surely end with the birth of a child.

"We all have our duties, Eliliweth," the princess answered quietly. There was more than one meaning to her answer. The half-elf chewed on his tongue as he debated his next question. As they reached the ground level, he worked up the courage to ask,

"There is no hope for marrying Wyatt?" he asked quietly after making sure nobody was within earshot. He expected a glare, or perhaps even a slap on the chest for broaching the subject of one of the kingdom's worst-kept secrets. Wyatt Darjin was a soldier in the Glen Bailey army that had captured the princess's heart. The two had ignited a fiery romance, one they had tried to keep discrete, but in a humble kingdom like the Glen Bailey, it was most difficult to keep any relationship hidden from discovery. When word reached the king about the recurring trysts, Wyatt was "promoted" to the position of captain at the outpost known as Arden's Watch, leagues away from the Glen Bailey. Named after the Glen Bailey's general during the Gunnysack Wars, Arden's Watch had once been a rendezvous point and barracks for the allied forces that watched over the defeated Kingsbanesin empire. It was now more prominently used as a bastion for Glen Dale troops patrolling the outlying villages and farms for raiders and orcs, and it was the perfect location for a protective father to transfer a soldier that threatened the honor of his only daughter. Aven was far too determined to let her father quash the relationship completely, of course. Eliliweth himself had offered an alibi for her absence on more than one occasion. He knew as well as she did, however, that a marriage to another would be the dagger to deliver the final blow to the romance. There would simply be far too much at stake if it evolved into infidelity.

"There is not," Aven said as they reached the towering keep doors. Though there were guards on either side, waiting to open them for the two, the princess's voice did not shy in volume. "As royalty, I have had many privileges that the common folk do not have. Marrying someone of my choice is not one of them. I have a responsibility to this kingdom and its people, those who have worked hard to keep the lifeblood flowing through its veins. I have come to terms with this." Her voice was level and collected, but Eliliweth could sense the pain in her words, as well as an unusual disquiet. He noticed that she did not mention whether or not the relationship was continuing in the meantime, but he knew that he had pressed his luck already.

They walked down the stone stairs to the cobblestone street awaiting them, circumventing the raised platform that had been temporarily constructed for the king's future announcement to the public. Eliliweth smiled as the sounds of music reached his ears. He loved the Solstice festival. There was so much abundant life in the Glen Bailey during it, in all forms. The color, the music, the visitors from other kingdoms, the farmers who had allowed themselves a day for leisure in what would perhaps be the only time that season. They didn't have to venture far before they saw a half dozen dwarves from Dur'Imoir lounging around a number of branded casks. They were handing frothing mugs to an assortment of men and women gathered around their roughly hewn table, and laughing uproariously between swigs of ale.

"A dwarf's laugh is perhaps the most abrasive noise that actually warms the heart," Aven remarked with a faint grin as they made their way over to the bearded visitors. She would not let thoughts of her inevitable marriage or the conniving antics of the magistrates douse her spirit on this festive day.

"Oi!" one of the dwarves bellowed from the table as he spotted Aven. He hoisted a mug over his head with so much enthusiasm that foam sloshed over the rim, spattering his brow and bushy black beard. "Princess Aven Celandine finally comes outta tha' castle to grace us with 'er beautiful self! I've got an ale with yer name on it, Yer Grace!"

"Daros Flint," the princess replied as the two approached. Those gathered around the dwarves turned their heads, and upon seeing the king's daughter, immediately knelt down before her. "Oh, stand, stand!" Aven insisted. "We are all here to celebrate, not to trouble ourselves with formalities. Just half a mug, please, Daros." It was poor manners to turn down a dwarf's offering of drink, but it was acceptable to ask for a smaller portion, as wasted ale was an even more grievous insult.

"If'n yer sure, Yer Grace!" Daros answered with a guffaw before pouring half of the mug into an empty one sitting on a stool nearby. The dwarf hoisted it to his lips, downed the split portion, and then turned to hand the other to Aven with another laugh. "And *THIS*...this must be th' half-elf that everyone an' their bloody mother keep jabberin' about! *HAH!* My question for ya, boy, is whether'n ya can hold yer ale like a *man*, or a bloody *elf!*" Daros didn't wait for an answer from Eliliweth before he began pouring another mug for the half-elf. Aven looked over at him with quirked eyebrows and a small smile. Dwarven courtesies were not for the faint of heart.

"My thanks," Eliliweth said as he accepted the outstretched mug. He held it in his hands, taking small whiffs of the scent rolling off of the foamy head.

"Well don' jus' bloody stand there *sniffin'* it, *drink* the damn thing!" Daros bellowed with a slap of his own stomach. Accepting the challenge wholeheartedly, Eliliweth tilted the mug to his lips and craned his head back, letting the pungent liquid spill into the back of his throat. He was sure that if he took his time, the flavor would be enjoyable, but as he worked his way to the bottom of the mug, all he could think about was the room in his stomach that was rapidly disappearing. Daros and his flock of dwarves began pounding on the table, bellowing *DRINK! DRINK! DRINK!* as the half-elf kicked back the ale.

Just when he thought that he couldn't take another gulp, the frothy remainder of the last swallow pooled over his tongue. He slammed the mug down on the dwarves' table, wiped away the foamy head from his upper lip, and released a powerful belch. At once, the dwarves broke into an uproarious cheer, clunking their mugs against one another and taking long swigs of their own in salute. Even the citizens that had gathered around the kiosk began to cheer and clap at the demonstration, intoxicated in both the ale and sense of camaraderie. Daros took the empty mug, filled it again, and handed it over to Eliliweth. "Yer all right, half-elf, yer all right!" the dwarf laughed. "Ya can take yer time on that one...*OR NOT!*" Daros burst into another round of deep-bellied laughs, as did the other dwarves around him. Eliliweth and Aven nodded and gave their thanks before walking away to find something else of interest. The half-elf was full and a bit dizzy, but his chest was warm with pleasure.

It was only moments later that they came across his dear friend Elune Shadowsong, wearing a summer dress of green and violet, her hair bound in a single braid between her shoulderblades. She weaved her way through the gathered people and embraced both Eliliweth and Aven. She had come with him instead of attending the Solstice Ball in the Sherinalu Vale, but had spent the last couple days in the Glen Bailey by herself. She'd possessed a desire for time on her own as long as Eliliweth could remember.

"What did King Bartholomew wish to discuss?" she inquired, glancing at both Eliliweth and Aven, imposing the question upon both of them.

"Ah, well, a few things," Eliliweth said vaguely as Aven looked to him for whatever response he wished to give. "He likes the idea of planting the swamp crops. A few other things...we'll have to wait and see what comes of it." Elune gave him an odd glance, but didn't press the issue.

"I've spoken at length with my father, Elune," Aven said, guiding the subject elsewhere. "With the blessing of the Sherinalu Vale, we would be honored to have you as their ambassador."

"The honor would be all mine," Elune replied with wide eyes of surprise, clearly taken aback by the princess's announcement. "I'm afraid that I haven't yet sold the idea to the Sherinalu council yet. They would prefer someone of greater age, I think."

"But none of greater age have stepped forward," the princess said with lofted eyebrows.

"So I've said to them," Elune said with a knit of frustration in her brow.

"Well, when they change their minds, we'd love to have you," Aven said. Her tone was more business than personal, even though she and Elune both considered themselves friends. It was a matter of the state, however, and the princess sometimes had difficulty transitioning between the two.

As they made their way further into the city, mugs in hand, someone else caught Eliliweth's eye as he and the other two drew nearer to the source of the joyous music. The familiar figure turned to look at him with blue eyes, face framed by a crop of blonde hair. The half-elf recognized him as the young man from the borderland wilderness, who had found Elune dressing his wounds. Smiling, the pleasant buzz of the dwarven ale still running through his blood, Eliliweth pressed through the crowd to offer a hand to Cadohaden Ulaeron.

"It looks as though you took my advice, friend! Welcome to the Glen Bailey!" Eliliweth said with a beaming grin as Elune and Aven followed behind him.

"Glad to see you well," Cadohaden responded with a smile of his own, shaking the half-elf's hand fervently. It was clear that the young man was a bit flustered with his new surroundings, paired with the influx of festival goers. "And lucky as well, I imagine. The guards at the gate told me you'd be busy."

"They were fair to warn you," Eliliweth said before turning around. "You've met Elune already-"

"Yeah!" Cadohaden answered a bit too quickly, flushing a bit red as the elf lifted her eyebrows in response.

"And this," the half-elf continued, missing the awkward response as he trailed his open hand towards the princess. "Is Princess Aven Celandine of the Glen Bailey. Your Grace, this is Cadohaden Ulaeron, son of Deltore Ulaeron and Melaitha Riverwen, of Kingsbanesin."

"Ah, well...formerly of Kingsbanesin," Cadohaden replied with a clearing of his throat. He bowed to the princess nonetheless, even though Eliliweth had turned a curious gaze upon him. The half-elf looked back behind him, however, as he noticed Cadohaden's perplexed expression. Glancing over his shoulder, Eliliweth saw the guarded glare of the princess. It wasn't at Cadohaden, however, but behind him. Following her stare, the half-elf finally noticed the hooded figure in the black cloak standing behind the young man. He'd seen the figure earlier, but hadn't realized before that the tall, mysterious person was waiting behind Cadohaden.

"That man is a warlock," Aven said with an accusatory edge to her voice.

"And it was my understanding that warlocks were not forbidden in the Glen Bailey," the cloaked figure answered coolly.

"Forbidden, no. Frowned upon, yes," the princess answered back unabashedly.

"With all due respect, Your Grace, I have endured worse than the frowns of human women, even royal mage women," the warlock replied without skipping a beat. Aven bristled, her lip curling, but Eliliweth lifted his arms with open palms.

"All right, let's all calm down a bit," he said. "Is the warlock a companion of yours, Cadohaden?" he asked, looking at the young man with a measured stare. Cadohaden looked uncomfortable under the trio of scrutinous gazes, but he answered nonetheless,

"Yes. His name is Terodar Soulrender, and he is traveling with me. It's...it's kind of a story that would probably be told best around a table. Maybe with a drink. Or two drinks. But I promise that he will do no harm."

"Are you in a position to make that promise, Cadohaden Ulaeron?" Aven asked with a piercing gaze.

"I am," Cadohaden replied immediately. "Look, we're not here to stir up trouble, Your Grace. I was actually hoping to visit with a Nevic Baltwin, if-"

"You plan on visiting the Monastery with a warlock at your side?" Aven interrupted sharply.

"Your Grace," Eliliweth said patiently, taking care to use the appropriate public title. "He's trying to explain himself."

"Look, I really think that perhaps we should-" Cadohaden began, but he was interrupted once more as the blaring sounds of trumpets came thundering from behind them, coming from the direction of the keep. All heads turned at the sound, and the chiming of the music halted at the sound of declaration. A hushed murmur swept over the gathered crowd as they began to filter towards the keep.

"That was a quick decision," Eliliweth said with a puzzled frown. His stomach was beginning to twist in anticipation, the ale he had quaffed suddenly feeling like an unwelcome guest in his gut.

"Let's go," Aven commanded. She glanced back at Cadohaden and pointed at him and the cloaked figure with spread fingers. "You two. Follow us. We're going to have a talk when the declarations are over."

Cadohaden looked to Eliliweth questioningly, and the half-elf jerked his head vaguely in a follow-us gesture. Aven's brow furrowed at the young man's questioning, but she said no more as she guided the five of them towards the platform, which was quickly filling up with the magistrates, Pleatus, and then a man in decorated armor, a horsehead emblem etched onto his breastplate. The Glen Bailey's current general, Sir Strigson Ganisalp, stood with his hands folded below his waist on the far end of the platform, eyes scanning the crowd for potential threats. The half-elf saw Ganisalp's gaze linger on the cloaked warlock for a few extra seconds before moving on to others in the gathered crowd.

"Are you going to go up there, Princess?" Elune asked as they approached the platform.

"I was not included in any final decisions, so no, I will watch and listen with the rest of my people," Aven said briskly. her wounded pride as obvious as an infected blister.

Finally, when all of the magistrates had seated themselves at the platform, King Bartholomew emerged from the keep, to the cheers of the gathered public. He smiled through his beard and approached the decorated pedestal that must have been placed only moments before the declaration. His Majesty lifted his arms to quiet his people before he spoke with a deep projection,

"Good people of the Glen Bailey! Visitors from other kingdoms! Friends and strangers! It is my pleasure to welcome you to our fine city on this blessed Summer Solstice! Are we enjoying the festivities?" The crowd answered with an eager roar of approval, especially the drunken dwarves of Dur'Imoir, their ale sloshing over their mugs as they lifted them to the sky.

"Most excellent!" his Majesty answered as the crowd began to hush. "I want to thank everyone who brought goods from their homes to share with the people of the Glen Bailey! Our alliances keep us strong! Our friendships forge a future of security that will last for ages!" The crowd roared back once more in reply, and Bartholomew's smile grew wider through his beard. Once the noise had subsided, the king continued in his speech.

He addressed the plans for the swamp farming on the border-lands of York. He explained what could be grown there, and how the York farmers had done so for ages. When he announced that lands would be freely given to farmers that would be willing to participate, an excited murmur passed through the gathered crowd. Bartholomew followed with more traditional rhetoric, mostly of unity, growth, and the promise of tomorrow. All the while, Eliliweth's stomach turned over inside of him. He realized that his throat was as dry as a dirt road. He scanned the expressions of the magistrates seated behind the king. They didn't look terribly displeased. Was that an ill omen? He suddenly found himself wishing that Bartholomew hadn't made the announcement of his official promotion during that meeting. The sensation of his hopes being choked was a miserable feeling.

"Lastly," King Bartholomew finally said from his pedestal. Eliliweth could feel his heart slamming against his chest, his knees trembling with anxiety. "It is well known to all of you that in the past few months, I have taken an honored guest at the keep's court. He is a unique young man, hailing from another kingdom, and a unique bloodline.

"What some might consider weaknesses, however, this young man uses as rare strengths, strengths that are very hard to come by in this day and age. His insight is both brave and refreshing. He does not heel like a dog; rather, he gives me honesty without fear, even when he knows I will not approve of what he has to say.

"Eliliweth Heraketh of the Sherinalu Vale is the type of advisor I need at my right hand. I have no doubt that if given the opportunity, he will help lead the Glen Dale into a golden age that will be told in legends for centuries to come. It would not surprise me in the least bit if his influence extended beyond our borders."

Eliliweth shifted his weight at the ample serving of praise the king was delivering. He didn't feel worthy of the boasts Bartholomew was making. People nearby were beginning to notice that he stood among them, and he felt as though more gazes were upon him than the king himself. Bartholomew wasn't finished, however.

"Despite my assurances that Eliliweth is prepared for an official seat in my court, your magistrates remain unconvinced that he is ready for such a task. We stand at an impasse. Perhaps this is a blessing, how-ever, for though your nobles force my hand, I suspect that my charge for Eliliweth Heraketh will be something he has dreamed of for years now. I can think of no one more worthy of undergoing the endeavor.

"Good people and friends of the Glen Bailey, to prove that Eliliweth is prepared for the position of Chief Advisor to the Crown, I hereby declare him for the Trials of the White Forest!"

Stunned silence settled over the crowd. Eliliweth's mouth opened in a soundless gape. Suddenly, the crowd of onlookers burst into uproarious applause, throwing their fists into the air. Even more eyes turned to stare at the half-elf as he stared dumbly at King Bartholomew, whose eyes met his. A bright grin emerged on the king's face, and Eliliweth realized that his Majesty had known it would come to this for some time now.

"My good people, we'll have much more to celebrate in the weeks to come! Now, let us return to our drinks and our dances!" Bartholomew shouted to another wave of cheers.

"By the Goddess," Eliliweth finally murmured.

"What are the Trials of the White Forest?" Cadohaden asked with a befuddled frown.

"Eliliweth," Princess Aven said, her voice stern even though her eyes were glinting with mirth. The half-elf was sure that the king had shared this with her beforehand. "We must go elsewhere before you are admired to death. Bring your...your friends. I am not quite ready to let them out of my sight."

"Congratulations, Eliliweth," Elune said warmly, pulling the half-elf into a quick embrace before Aven began to steer them away from the commotion.

"Let's go," the princess said with authority. She guided them through the throng of revelers, away from the chaotic joy.

Chapter Ten

They ventured through the Glen Bailey, through the hordes of people waving their foaming mugs. Men and women bowed as they recognized Princess Aven, and as they stood to their feet, they gave Eliliweth a clap on the shoulder as he walked past. Cadohaden took in all the sights as they made their way through the streets, but truly, he was only half paying attention. His mind was occupied with worry. Had bringing Terodar into the city cost him his chance at meeting with Crusader Nevic? Or was it even worse than that? Would he find himself in a jail cell before the night was over?

The place the princess led them to didn't seem like a prison, however. It was larger than most of the city homes they had wandered past, but smaller than the occasional mansion that had emerged among them. It looked to stand three floors above ground, the siding eggshell white and the roof tiles a royal blue. Aven rapped her knuckles against the door. Moments later, it opened, revealing a woman who stood a couple inches taller than the princess, wearing what looked to be the robe of a mage.

"Hello, Leora," Aven said in a businesslike tone. "Is Benton available?"

"Greetings, Princess," the woman replied. "And I'm afraid Benton is out enjoying the festivities. Is there something I can do for you?"

"There is, Leora," Aven answered. "I have with me a visitor from

Kingsbanesin, and with him, a companion that favors blood magic. I have a few questions for the two, and if you would be so kind as to supervise the discussion, I would most appreciate it."

The mage woman studied Cadohaden for a brief moment, but her attention was truly grasped by the hooded Terodar. Her eyes narrowed as she quietly scrutinized him, no doubt sensing for his aura of power. What she discovered seemed to disquiet her, as she murmured, "Would you like me to go seek out Benton? Or Krendrick?"

"I think the two of us will suffice," Aven said confidently, glancing once over her shoulder in what Cadohaden was sure was a 'just try to make trouble for us' look. "Eliliweth and Elune should be able to help us if the discussion goes sour. Eliliweth will undergo the Trials of the White Forest, if you hadn't heard already, Leora."

"I had not!" the mage woman said with an instant smile. "Congratulations, Eliliweth!"

"Thank you, Leora," the half-elf answered. He still seemed to be in a state of mild shock. Cadohaden's brow furrowed as his curiosity arose once more. What in the gods were these Trials that everyone found so exciting?

"Shall we?" the princess said in a way that was more of a command than a question. Cadohaden glanced back at Terodar once, but the demon's face was still shrouded by his hood, and he gave nothing that resembled a comforting gesture in return. Taking a deep breath through his nose, Cadohaden followed the princess and the others in through the door, Terodar bringing up the rear.

It didn't take Cadohaden long to confirm that this building was a house for the magi of the Glen Bailey. The first floor looked normal enough; there was a room with couches and chairs, and on the other side, past the wide hallway with bedroom doors, a quaint kitchenette could be seen. Next to the assortment of couches, however, there was a staircase, to which Aven led them up with Leora following behind the cloaked demon.

The second floor was clearly the mages' library, though Cadohaden was surprised at how humble it was. He had never stepped foot into a mage's study before, but his grandfather Iuvas had told him many stories in his childhood about the wizard towers of Novinar with their grand archives of magical texts, about Kingsbanesin's own arcane library, and even tales about underground vaults of old, libraries buried by the world's first mages to contain enchanted secrets that could be disastrous if fallen into the wrong hands. Given all of the legends Iuvas had told him, the library of the Glen Bailey's mage house seemed underwhelming by comparison. Terodar confirmed Cadohaden's suspicions as he growled, "Are you hiding the rest of your texts elsewhere?"

"No," Aven snapped as she turned around and folded her arms across her chest in front of one of the few bookcases. "What you see here, warlock, is a respect for the gift of magic. At the Glen Bailey, we do our due diligence to understand the basics of the arcane. Benton takes great care to ensure that magic never becomes a danger to the good people of this kingdom, and if that means he must keep his own talents in check, he is more than happy to do so. I would not expect a warlock to understand."

"Fire can consume an entire city, but do you restrict your people to flint and candles?" the demon drawled.

"Terodar, stop," Cadohaden said as Aven's face flickered with vindictive anger. He could sense the demon's body tensing indignantly, but his tongue halted obediently nonetheless.

"You are guests in this kingdom, and hardly in a position to question our customs," Aven said with a fiery energy. "Now, I want to know: what is it you wish to find at our Monastery that you cannot find at the Kingsbanesin Cathedral, and what made you think that recruiting a warlock would be wise, given your goal in the Glen Bailey?"

"I don't belong to Kingsbanesin," Cadohaden said, his voice barely loud enough to hear.

"That doesn't answer my question," the princess retorted.

"Your Grace," Eliliweth interrupted, taking a step towards the two. "Cadohaden came to my aid in the borderland forests after I was assaulted by own kin. Elune can attest to that. I sensed then that he was a man of honor, and I still do. Let's take a breath here and allow him to explain himself. Cadohaden?"

Cadohaden peered at Eliliweth gratefully. It was a generous statement, saying that Cadohaden came to the half-elf's aid, for he had done little more than press a cloth against a wound while Elune had bandaged him up. When the Glen Bailey's king had announced that he wished to make the young half-elf his official advisor, Cadohaden had thought he had misheard at first. Such a thing would have never happened at Kingsbanesin. For someone as young as Eliliweth was, his elevated view in the eyes of King Bartholomew didn't seem to bury his humility.

And so Cadohaden recounted his tale for the princess, beginning all the way with the unique story of his birth. He told her about Deltore, about Melaitha, and Galdoys's treachery at the fractured Kingsbanesin wall that led to both of their deaths. He told her of Mekoda, the leader of the Dragonrider's Guild. He told her how he put the man out of his misery with the mercy blade. It made him nauseous to describe it. He had pushed the memory from his mind since the day it happened, but he couldn't ignore the fact that the first life he had ever taken was a friend of his. Even the blood of the slain orcs unsettled his conscience. He knew that day had changed him. He just didn't want to admit or even realize how much it had.

He then spoke of the village that the raiders had plundered, and how he had followed them to the Stone Circle where the warlocks had finished their ritual. He told Aven how he saved Terodar's life, binding him to his service. It occurred to him far too late that he had left a gaping hole in that story, and the princess was much too perceptive to overlook it.

"I've studied a great deal about warlocks and their magic, and I've never heard of such a law. What ritual were the warlocks performing? Why was Terodar the only one to survive? None of this makes sense," Aven asked in a scrutinizing barrage of questions. Eliliweth did not interrupt her this time. He only watched Cadohaden with a quizzical frown, his gaze moving over apprehensively to Terodar every few seconds.

"Well, he's…" Cadohaden began, wetting his lips as he considered his words. He looked back to the hooded demon. Terodar only stood stiffly where he was, the light from the nearest window washing over his black cowl. Cadohaden looked back at Aven, who stared back at him unflinchingly, her eyebrows lifted in expectation. He knew there wasn't any way for him to dance around the truth of the matter. Besides, he owed his honesty to Eliliweth, who had thrown him his support without question. "They were summoning Terodar," he finally said. "He was the ritual they were performing. He's a demon."

The silence was tense and brief. All at once, Aven's hands were outstretched, as were Leora's, as their palms pooled with summoned magic. Elune drew both of her blades from their sheaths, twin sabres with moon etchings upon the hilts. Eliliweth was the only one who did not draw a defensive position, but the half-elf took a protective step backward, eyeing Terodar with guarded suspicion.

"You come as a guest to the Glen Bailey and bring one of the Destroyer's spawn in with you!?" Aven said in an accusatory hiss.

"He *is* bound to my will!" Cadohaden insisted, lifting his hands as he took a step back towards Terodar, as if he could hope to shield the demon from their menacing glares. "And I spared his life so that he might seek redemption!"

"You cannot cure a demon's nature!" Leora shouted from behind Terodar, who still had not moved since Cadohaden's confession.

"The Lifegiver's Codex says that nobody is beyond atonement!" Cadohaden answered quickly.

"I know the passage that you speak of, Cadohaden," Eliliweth said. "*There is no man or woman so shadowed in disgrace that they cannot be touched by the light of Kaijaras.* I just don't know if it was meant to include demonkin. Are they truly men, after all?"

"Who are we to say?" Cadohaden answered defensively. "If you ask any teacher of the Lifegiver, they will tell you that Kaijaras's grace is absolute! If the Lifegiver's power can cleanse a corrupted soul or mend wounded flesh, why can't it save a demon willing to repent?"

"Is he willing to repent?" Aven asked suspiciously, her glare focused on Terodar. The demon stood quietly as the room fell silent. And then, he lifted his hand to his hood, pulling it away from his head, revealing his pale skin, his serpentine eyes, his small horns protruding from his skull. With a thin smile, he answered,

"The boy commands, and I obey. It doesn't matter whether or not I wish for redemption. It is his will."

"This is a matter that extends beyond the will of the crown," Aven said. "We must speak with Priestess Ecila. You wanted to visit the Monastery, Cadohaden Ulaeron? You're going to get the chance. My question is this: do I need to call the guards to escort you two?"

"That...that won't be necessary," Cadohaden said. He could feel his skin flushing hot around his neck. This wasn't going as well as he'd hoped it would. *I suppose I should just be happy I'm not in chains*, he thought to himself miserably.

"See that it isn't," Aven said with authority. She glanced over at the half-elf. "Eliliweth, I feel as though we should summon my father for this. He should be aware of our unique visitor."

"Very well, Your Grace," Eliliweth answered quietly. He stole a glance at Cadohaden, his expression troubled. He said nothing more, however, as he departed the mages' library, descending the stairs back down to the first floor.

"Leora, Elune, if you two would be so kind as to follow behind us," Aven said, her tone indicating that it was more of a command than a request. "Come along, Cadohaden...Terodar. We shall see what the seeress thinks of your schemes for the demon's redemption." The demon leered at the princess and pulled his cowl back over his head, but followed obediently when Cadohaden complied.

On their way to the Monastery, the festive colors no longer seemed so vibrant to Cadohaden as he and Terodar tailed the princess, Elune and Leora behind them to suppress any urges to flee. The merrymaking of the citizens no longer seemed so joyful. Each inebriated eye that fell on them as they proceeded through the city seemed to carry the harsh glint of judgment. He told himself that it was all in his imagination, but he couldn't suppress the dreadful knot in his stomach as they drew nearer to the place of the Lifegiver's worship. Had this all been a mistake?

The Monastery was made of dark gray stone and mortar, the roof accentuated with a cylindrical bell tower that sat in solemn silence. A collection of moss and vines crept up the sides, though it was clear that careful hands had trimmed and shaped them. It was an oddly druidic celebration of life for a temple devoted to the Lifegiver. It was different in almost every aspect from the towering cathedral of Kingsbanesin, whose acolytes were constantly on cleaning rotations for both the inside and out, the impeccable stone surfaces free from the slightest smattering of dust. The brass fixture on the cedar doors was the wing-and-shield symbol of Kaijaras, but the slightest tarnished detail coloring it almost made it seem more ancient and wise. The Monastery itself was an entity of faith, and despite its humble size, Cadohaden suddenly felt very small standing in front of it.

Aven glanced to her left, and then to her right before turning around to face her two questionable visitors. "I will go inside and find the priestess. You two wait out here. And believe me when I say that there are enough guards about that you will not escape should Elune or Leora call for help."

Cadohaden nodded stiffly in response, unsure of what else he could possibly say in reply. He looked over at Terodar as the princess disappeared into the Monastery. The demon's posture was tense, his pale hands curling into fists and unclenching in a nervous manner. "What's wrong?" Cadohaden murmured.

"What do you think?" Terodar snapped back in a strained voice. "We're standing in front of holy ground. I'd be more comfortable standing in a fire."

Cadohaden wasn't sure just how literal the demon's words were, but Terodar didn't sound like he was in any mood to elaborate. He simply looked back at the Monastery doors, sucking his lip over his bottom row of teeth and grinding on it with the upper set. Neither Elune nor Leora spoke a word as they watched over the two. Cadohaden could feel the onlookers beginning to pause in their celebrations to peer curiously at the peculiar scene in front of the holy house.

Several tense minutes stretched by before Cadohaden suddenly heard the blare of a trumpet behind them, as well as the rhythmic clomping of boots that were getting closer with each militant step. Looking over his shoulder, he saw Eliliweth approaching once more, only this time, King Bartholomew himself marched alongside him, surrounded by an armed escort, each one carrying a halberd or spear. Cadohaden recognized a few of the men behind Bartholomew as the magistrates that were seated upon the platform during the public address.

"I should have an ale in my hand and music in my ears, but instead I am called to this spectacle," Bartholomew grumbled impatiently as he and his entourage came to a halt before the gathered four. "Now what it is so damned important that my celebrations should be interrupted?"

"Father," the princess's voice called out from the Monastery doors. Cadohaden turned around in surprise. He hadn't heard the doors open as the king had approached. Standing next to the princess was another woman in white robes, a thin shawl wrapped around brown hair that curled with the humidity of the air. Her skin was pale and her mouth was thin, but the most noticeable feature of Priestess Ecila were her clouded, teal-green eyes. She was doubtlessly blind. So how was it that she seemed to stare back directly into his soul as he looked at her?

"The young man that stands before you is Cadohaden Ulaeron of Kingsbanesin, son of Deltore Ulaeron and Melaitha Riverwen," the princess continued. "His presence is one I wouldn't have assumed suspicious, if not for the companion that he brought in to our city. Terodar Soulrender, remove your hood."

The demon stood unmoving at the princess's command. Only when Cadohaden muttered the words "do it" did Terodar finally comply, lifting his arms in slow, stubborn fashion as he pulled his hood back over his head, revealing his horns to the king and the crowd, who broke into gasps at the sight of them. Most immediately began whispering. Some began calling for his execution on the spot.

"Silence!" the king bellowed, and the crowd quieted dutifully. Bartholomew squinted suspiciously as he turned his gaze upon Cadohaden. "Cadohaden Ulaeron. I remember you. You were but a squawling babe last time I laid eyes upon you. I fought for you, boy. I stuck my neck out, and the Glen Bailey's, when I got involved with Kingsbanesin's handling of your custody. So choose your words carefully and tell me why you would bring a spawn of the Destroyer into my kingdom."

Once more, Cadohaden pleaded his case, revealing the story of his exile from Kingsbanesin, his desire to join the paladin order of the Glen Bailey, and recounting the odd circumstances that had landed him a demonic servant. The crowd muttered bitterly at the story of Galdoys Veriknock's treachery, and then grew hushed as they listened to the strange tale of Terodar's summoning and the invoking of the ancient Daemonaar law. They looked at one another thoughtfully as the young man spoke of his hope to redeem Terodar's soul, reciting the passage from the Lifegiver's Codex that deemed such a task possible. As he spoke, another voice in his head warned him that he was the only one who knew what would end the demon's service to him. He knew he should divulge that detail, how the decision was ultimately in the hands of the Destroyer himself. But as strongly as his conscience commanded it, the words did not cross his tongue. They would never let Terodar live knowing that truth. But would Gapinon ever consider Terodar worthy of release if Cadohaden could bring him even a half step closer to devotion to Kaijaras? No, of course not. And so he decided it was something that need not be shared, and hoped that nobody would ask the question.

Bartholomew stroked his beard as he listened to the story. He glanced over at Eliliweth as Cadohaden concluded. "You were right to bring this to my attention. Apologies for my, ah...my gruff response." The king cast his gaze upon Cadohaden once more, and then to Terodar, sizing up the demon, who only stared back with undisguised contempt.

"In all my years as king of this land, I have never encountered such a bizarre situation," Bartholomew confessed. "I require your wisdom,

Priestess Ecila. Is this all but a fool's errand?"

Ecila did not respond right away, her blind eyes studying the demon in a haunting stare. Cadohaden was amazed to see Terodar finally fidget under her eerie scrutiny. Finally, the priestess spoke. "I know every word of the Codex, inspired by the Lifegiver, and while there are many verses warning of the evil nature of demonkin, there is nothing that specifically states that their corrupted souls cannot be cleansed by the light of Kaijaras.

"We mustn't forget, however," Ecila said in her voice that sounded of ghostly chimes as she began to descend the Monastery's stone steps, "that demons are creatures that speak lies and embellishments with great fluency. Terodar obeys your commands, Cadohaden Ulaeron, but have you truly tested the worth of his words?"

"Of course I have," Cadohaden immediately answered, but as the priestess's blind eyes turned towards his voice, doubt suddenly began to spread through him like ink through water. He frowned, looked over at Terodar, and then back at Ecila. "I mean...I've *seen* his body force him. You can tell that he doesn't want to obey, but he must."

"Sweet child," Ecila answered, "lies are not woven from word alone. How are you so sure that the demon does not feign these reactions in order to gain your trust? Do you not see what he could accomplish by doing so?"

"He told me that I could order him dead if I wished," Cadohaden protested.

"And what better way to win over a young heart than to offer his own life as proof?" the priestess answered, shaking her head. "I ask you again, Cadohaden, have you truly tested the weight of this demon's promise?"

Cadohaden swallowed, glancing over at Terodar with pursed lips. The gathered crowd waited in silence, their eyes wide in anticipation. The demon only stared back with a smoldering glare. Finally, the young man slowly shook his head. "No...I have not," he admitted in a defeated mutter.

"I did not think so," Ecila said. That blind stare was terribly unnerving. Cadohaden was certain that she saw *something* in those around her. The priestess took a step backward, giving the two a wider berth as she lifted a finger towards the Monastery door. "For the safety of our people, we must know for certain that the demon's will is truly bound to you, if we are to consider any option other than death. Order

Terodar to place his hand upon the brass symbol on the door."

"No," the demon immediately hissed. "I cannot."

"He can," Ecila insisted, her finger still pointing towards the door. "It will be excruciating, but we must know the truth. Order him to do it, Cadohaden, or we will be left with no other choice."

"Cadohaden," Terodar said in a voice that betrayed the panic fluttering in the demon's chest. "Don't."

"I'm sorry, Terodar," Cadohaden said quietly, his jaw flexing as he lifted a hand that mirrored the priestess's. "I have to do this. I order you to touch the brass symbol upon the Monastery door."

"No, *no!*" Terodar shrieked in response, but the demon's hooves began trudging forward, his legs lifting woodenly as he slowly approached the Monastery. Princess Aven descended the stairs as well, moving away from the door as Terodar lurched towards it.

A groan of pain escaped the demon as he began to encroach upon the holy ground. Curses flew from his lips as his hooves carried him onward. As he drew within inches of the stone steps, his groans became howls as smoke began to curl from his pale flesh, lifting towards the sky in thin tendrils as his skin started to blister. With a blood-curdling shriek, Terodar resolved himself to finishing the task quickly, charging up the steps towards the Monastery door, the stench of his burning flesh sweeping across the crowd. As he pushed his palm against the Lifegiver's symbol, Terodar's head jerked back as an agonized scream escaped him in tortured harmony with the hissing noise of his searing palm.

"Come back!" Cadohaden shouted as he stepped forward, his face stricken with the magnitude of Terodar's pain. "I order you to come back!" Terodar immediately lurched backwards, tripping over himself as he pushed away from the door. He howled and cried out as he tumbled towards the ground, the stinking vapors following him all the way down. As he rolled onto the soil below, he desperately scrambled back away from the Monastery, his nails digging into the dirt as he clawed his way forward.

He finally returned to Cadohaden's feet. In a display of pain and humiliation, Terodar curled into a ball, steam still rising from his black robes as he linked his fingers behind his horned head. Gritting his pointed teeth, quiet whimpers escaped the demon as he twitched and trembled on the ground.

"Are you satisfied?" Cadohaden asked the priestess, unable to suppress the accusatory tone in his voice.

"I am," Ecila answered, her expression flat and emotionless. "But there is a lesson to be learned here, Cadohaden, and for all of you gathered. There is always a price to pay when you dabble in evil. Whatever you may gain from it, there will always be a painful consequence to bear in return."

"So he truly obeys the boy's orders," Bartholomew said as he folded his arms across his chest. "Where does that leave us, then? If Nevic agrees to train Cadohaden as a paladin, the demon clearly can't enter the Monastery with him. Are we to allow him to wander the streets at his own whim?"

The crowd began to murmur as the king's question hung in the air. A few seconds passed, and a tall, thin man in a gray robe with long brown hair and a hook nose emerged from the throng. "If there is a place for one such as Terodar, it is in the Mage Unit. As much as Cadohaden may wish it, the demon cannot find salvation through Kaijaras. I think that much is obvious. He is a *roaq* demon, however, and that means he has at the very least an adequate grasp of basic magic. With time and nurturing, I believe I can show him to use his gifts for the greater good, without the barbaric behaviors of a warlock. This is also a great opportunity for us to better understand the world of Daemonaar, if he will tell me what he knows. Let me give this demon purpose."

Cadohaden turned to look at the stranger that had spoken, doing his best to ignore the acrid stench of Terodar's burned and blistered skin. This had to be the mage Aven had requested when they had ventured across the city, Benton.

"That would seem a heavy burden for you, Benton Cusair," King Bartholomew rumbled. "Are you sure of this?"

"I am, Your Majesty," Benton answered. His voice was soft, like one accustomed to the quiet of a library, but not subdued. "I don't believe there has ever been a chance to study demons in such a safe manner."

"If I may, Your Majesty," Ecila countered, the faintest of frowns crossing her delicate brow. "Regardless of the demon's display of obedience, I think it is a far cry to call any study of this creature 'safe'. Nothing good can come of this."

"How can we be so certain, Priestess?" the mage Benton answered. "We know very little of demonkin save for what the Codex tells us, which is thin in terms of studied fact, and decorated with generalized denouncements of all things evil. And as I have said before, we are not a kingdom of policies based off of the Lifegiver's word."

"They are direct descendants of the Destroyer!" Ecila said, her voice rising for the first time since she'd emerged from the cedar doors.

"Who was once known as the Creator," Benton challenged, lifting his nose ever-so-slightly. "You have your views, Priestess, and I respect them, but I just don't see this as such a clear decision. I have no records of anyone successfully invoking such a pact. This is...this is a historic opportunity!"

"This is quite unlike you, Benton," Ecila said. "I thought we had an understanding as to what priority magic - particularly such dangerous magic - had in our kingdom."

"Whether the demon lives or dies, I will carry out my duties," Benton answered. "I don't feel strongly one way or the other. But I don't believe we should pass this up based purely on fear of what the demon is. We may never get another chance at this. If we could perhaps save lives in the future by learning from Terodar, then it would be irresponsible to act rashly."

"And just how would he save lives?" Ecila began, her volume rising as her expression began to betray her impatience. "You speak of acting rashly, I can't think of anything that might-"

"Enough," Bartholomew said stoutly, drawing silence from both the mage and the priestess. "Benton, are you certain that you can learn a substantial deal from tutoring this demon?"

"Nothing is certain, Your Majesty, but he is a *roaq* demon. If there is knowledge to be gained, it would come from his type, and if I can get him to open up to me, I am confident that it will be substantial."

"Your Majesty, I really must-" Ecila began.

"I am sorry, Priestess. Your input is appreciated, but this...Terodar has passed your test, and from the looks of it, it was quite torturous. I will not have him punished for seeing it through," Bartholomew said sternly.

"I hereby declare that Terodar Soulrender will begin training under the tutelage of Benton Cusair. You're on a short leash, demon. At the first sign of trouble, you will be hastily executed. Have I made myself clear?" the king asked. The demon, still smoldering in a literal and figurative fashion, slowly lifted himself up on an elbow to glare furiously at Bartholomew, his skin shining with a sheen of sweat and fluid from his many burns.

"Answer him," Cadohaden ordered in a murmur.

"I understand," Terodar growled, his words sounding as though they were being pulled from his mouth by a thick rope.

"Most excellent," Benton answered, taking a few steps towards them until he was standing over the demon. He looked even taller up close, his head blocking the sun from Terodar's face. "If you would, Cadohaden, order a safeguard for me?"

Cadohaden blinked in response. "A safeguard?" Benton pursed his lips, his nostrils flaring with the faintest hint of impatience.

"If you could order Terodar to obey my commands as well, I feel as though that would ensure both my safety and his," the mage answered.

"Oh! Oh, right…" Cadohaden said, clearing his throat and scratching the back of his head. The heavy weight of guilt in his chest felt conflicting and strange. Terodar was a demon, capable of all types of cruelty, but this public example had been a humiliating ordeal. He couldn't help but feel ashamed as he looked down at Terodar, who glared resolutely at the soil below him.

"Terodar, I command you to obey Benton Cusair's commands as though they were my own," he said quietly. Though the demon did not move, Cadohaden could sense an added invisible weight to Terodar's shoulders. The demon's wounded pride was palpable in the air around him.

"Most excellent," Benton repeated, pressing his palms against each other in front of his chest. "Come with me, Terodar Soulrender. We have much to do."

"What are you going to do to him?" Cadohaden asked with a suspicious frown. "He's done everything you've all asked for. You can't torture him!"

"We wouldn't do anything so barbaric, Cadohaden, I assure you," Benton said as Terodar begrudgingly lifted himself up, wincing as he made his way over to the mage. "I won't spend a minute today studying him. His burns need to be treated, and he needs a space to call his own in the Mage House. You may come visit him tomorrow if it would ease your worries."

"I will," Cadohaden promised, trying to meet the demon's eyes with a look of encouragement, but Terodar only stared beyond the mage that had commanded him with unforgiving surliness, his every step a rigid movement that split one of his many burn blisters. Wasting no more time, Benton bid his king a farewell and began guiding the demon back to the Mage House, the heads of every onlooker following the two as they disappeared from the scene.

"We will regret this," Priestess Ecila said softly.

"I have faith that Benton will recognize the danger, if it happens to surface," the king said with conviction. "At the first sign of trouble, Ecila, he will face the chopping block. As for Cadohaden, see to it that he gets his visit with the Crusader."

Ecila's blind eyes moved vaguely in Cadohaden's direction. "I know not where Nevic Baltwin is," she said woodenly. "You will have to come back tomorrow, young man. We shall see if he thinks you worthy of joining the Monastery's holy order. Myself, I will have to sleep on it."

"Thank you, Priestess," was all Cadohaden could think to say. Everything was happening so quickly.

"Now then," Bartholomew said with a bit of a huff, "if all these distractions have come to an end, I have some celebrating to catch up on!" And with that proclamation, the king began marching back into the thick of the city to the jubilant cheers of the eager crowd. The magistrates that had followed immediately tried to draw His Majesty's attention, but Bartholomew ignored them, the call of the ale much more enticing than the worried words of noblemen. The crowd began to disperse as Bartholomew departed. Priestess Ecila dipped her head with a courteous goodbye, her tone not quite matching her words. She effortlessly climbed the Monastery steps and disappeared inside.

"I'm sorry that had to happen," Eliliweth said with a faint frown as he approached Cadohaden. "I do think it was necessary. But it was hard to watch nonetheless."

"Yeah…" Cadohaden said as he scratched the back of his neck once more. He was finding himself increasingly unable to find appropriate responses to anything being said to him. "I know he would have done the same in my position. Without a second thought."

"I hope you're aware of how serious my father's promise is, Cadohaden," Aven said as she approached the group as well. "If the demon causes any trouble, he'll be put down, and there will be no debating it."

"I know," Cadohaden replied in a subdued tone.

"Look," Eliliweth said calmly, "it's been an exciting day, to say the least, and all of these festivities are maybe a bit much right now. Shall we find our way back to the keep? Bartholomew gifted me with a bottle of Gohandian mead just last week to celebrate the Solstice. Perhaps we could all enjoy it and ease our nerves a bit."

"Perhaps later, Eliliweth," Aven said. "You should return to the Mage House and find some study material for your upcoming Trials. I'm sorry I didn't suggest it earlier - we were a bit preoccupied."

"Ah, yes," Eliliweth answered. At first, he looked disappointed at the idea of relaxation away from the hustle and bustle, but eager fire quickly sprang back into his eyes as he remembered Bartholomew's announcement. He smiled cheerily and said, "I have so much work to do. Do you know when I am to depart?"

"Not yet, no," Aven replied. "But I can go with you and help you find the reading that will help you most. I think it's safe to say that I've read most of the material regarding the White Forest."

Eliliweth agreed enthusiastically, and almost turned on his heel to hurry back in the direction of the Mage House, but stopped as he saw the lost expression on Cadohaden's face. He looked like an uncomfortable scarecrow, his shoulders slumped, hands held open and loose at his sides, his eyes full of uncertainty.

"Oh!" Eliliweth said, waving his hand as though it would banish the discomfort. "I'm sorry, Cadohaden, I didn't mean to be rude. You don't have anywhere to go here, do you?"

"Well, an inn would suit me just fine, if you could just point out-" Cadohaden began.

"Nonsense!" Eliliweth said insistently. "We have guest rooms at the keep, and I know there is at least one that is vacant. I'm not mistaken, am I, Your Grace?"

Aven's gaze was a bit frosty, as if she thought that the half-elf may have overstepped the authority he did not yet possess, but she nodded regardless, saying, "Yes. Pleatus was given a permanent residency within the Keep, so his guest room is now open. It is on the third floor, Cadohaden, and there is a hook on the outside of the door. Hang a belonging of yours on it to show that it is claimed for the moment." Her last few words were pointed and carried no apology.

"Can you find your way there?" Eliliweth asked.

"I...think so," Cadohaden answered, glancing at the figure of the keep in the distance. Finding his way back there would be easy enough. He wasn't so sure about the inside, or if he would be questioned by anyone after entering. Eliliweth spotted his hesitation and shook his head.

"I'm sorry, I assume too much," the half-elf said quickly. "Let me bring you back, Cadohaden, I will show you."

"I can take him," Elune's voice interrupted. "I would like to go back and write a letter to my parents in the Sherinalu before the courier leaves in the morning anyway." Cadohaden felt his skin flush as she spoke. He pursed his lips in irritation with himself as he felt the heat, which only made it darker.

"Of course! That would work just fine," Eliliweth said brightly, oblivious to Cadohaden's embarrassment. "I will see all of you later to share that mead, if not tonight, then tomorrow. If all goes well with Crusader Nevic, then we'll have all the more reason for a drink. Make yourself comfortable, Cadohaden. Shall we, Your Grace?"

The princess nodded and moved to the half-elf's side, but not before casting an admonishing gaze in Cadohaden's direction. The message was so clear that she may as well have spoken it. Terodar wasn't the only one who would be watched carefully during their visit.

"Follow me, Cadohaden," Elune said in a tone that he couldn't clearly decipher. It wasn't cold, but he was fairly certain that the elf hadn't yet decided what she thought of him. He was sure that his flustered responses to every interaction he had with her weren't aiding his cause. And so he made a conscious effort to appear collected as he followed beside her back in the direction of the Keep.

They were uncomfortably quiet for several moments as they weaved their way around drunken revelers and one particularly animated fire dancer that nearly dropped one of his roaring torches upon Cadohaden's shoulder. As they entered a less clustered pocket of people, however, Cadohaden finally broke the silence. "So...what is the White Forest? And what are the Trials?"

Elune lifted her eyebrows as she looked back at him. "You really don't know? The legend of the White Forest isn't specific to the Glen Dale. We speak of it even in the Sherinalu Vale. I thought everyone knew of it."

Cadohaden felt his neck turn hot again. So much for appearing casual. "If anyone has ever told me of it, I don't remember it."

"Oh," Elune answered softly. "I didn't mean to be rude. It's just surprising, is all. The White Forest lies within the Glen Dale, not far from the patrol routes of the Bailey guards, but still a respectful distance. It is home to the wisest men in all the Aariad, perhaps even the world. Do you know of The Binding?"

"Yes," Cadohaden answered as they circumvented a cloister of drunken men that were laughing merrily and shoving one another with just as much enthusiasm. His grandfather had told him those tales. "It was a group ritual performed by the Aariad's first magi. They buried and locked away artifacts of great power and books of ancient knowledge to prevent...to prevent, I don't know. A magical disaster."

"It was a mutual disarmament for each practice," Elune gently corrected. "Unchecked, magic could have torn this land apart. Enough magi came to their senses, fortunately, and recognized that danger. The Druids of the White Forest are descendants of those very men. Their wisdom has attracted numerous wonders that most of us can only speculate about. Above all, though, they recognize the need for balance. They have great power and a mastery of the gift of magic that would shame even the archmages of Novinar, but they rarely use it, because they know what would become of any abuse."

"So they worship the goddess Essence?" Cadohaden asked curiously.

"In a way," Elune said after a brief pause for thought. "The Goddess aligns with most of their philosophies. But they see beyond the worship of Essence. Balance requires a knowledge of everything in this world, and that includes the other Forgers and whatever deities have been lost to history. It also demands a grasp of things beyond magic and the worship of gods. You could not approach the Druids of the White Forest and ask to look into a crystal ball, for they would instead show you a crystal with a thousand facets, each reflecting a different perspective."

"Did you just come up with that on your own?" Cadohaden asked in awe.

"It's a common expression," Elune explained quickly, a faint flush blooming in her cheeks. "I don't just practice pretty phrases in private to impress others."

"You really are good with words, though," Cadohaden complimented her, only to internally cringe at how simplistic he knew he sounded.

"Linguistics are an important practice in the Sherinalu Vale, but this kingdom has helped as well," she answered. "If you spend enough time here, you will be surprised at how many of the common folk know how to read. That is the Monastery's doing. Ecila's clerics pay visits to both the children and their parents for basic lessons, and a handful of those who learn will visit the Monastery on their own for more advanced teaching. If enough of us are educated, it begins to affect us all."

For the second time that day, Cadohaden approached the stone steps to the Glen Bailey Keep. He silently wondered how it was that Elune so readily identified with a kingdom to which she was not native, but he had other questions for her already, and he did not want to overwhelm her with a barrage of inquiries about herself. "So the White Forest is home to the wisest druids in all the land. What are the Trials, then?"

"It's difficult to say, specifically," Elune said as they began to ascend the steps. "In recorded history, there are few who have endured them, and even fewer who have been willing to tell their tales to a scribe. Details are few and far between. But it is understood that the Trials are a glimpse into the purest enlightenment a mortal can behold. The true test is whether or not the subject can recognize it."

"That's it? The Trials are simply a lecture from the druids?" Cadohaden asked as the doors to the keep were opened. Elune's brow knitted as they entered the castle.

"I would not put it so simply. Anyone can enter the White Forest to hear a 'lecture', as you said. Most do not, for many reasons. It may be a harsh thing to say, but the reality is that most common folk live their lives in devotion to a trade, to an army, to their family, to a god, or some combination of those. As much as they respect and admire the legend of the White Forest, they do not have the luxury of leaving their homesteads and families in pursuit of enlightenment.

"Those with the power and privilege for such endeavors rarely take the opportunity, for kings and nobles are proud, and to learn from someone else is to express humility. By asking for someone else's wisdom, you acknowledge that you yourself don't already possess it. I know that King Bartholomew has visited to hear the druids' counsel. I believe King Rhone of Eastfen has as well, and though it has been some time, elven elders from the Sherinalu and Ashtalath have entered the White Forest in hopes of advice or perspective.

"The Trials, however, measure a soul. More than anything, they present a reflection of those undergoing them. A long time ago, esteemed men would storm into the White Forest and demand the chance to endure the Trials, as if it were some game in a gladiator's arena. The druids would grant them the opportunity, but it did nothing to bolster their pride. Most of them saw their own shortcomings, their greed, their cruelty, their many deceits. It turned them into either angered tyrants or depressed husks of their former selves. They would leave the White Forest and spread lies about the druids, that they were charlatans, gypsies, mad fools camping in the wilderness. They would not conquer the druids, however. Though they made every excuse for why it wasn't worth the time, the truth of the matter is that they were all afraid of men who could show them their true selves.

"That is why it is such an honor to participate in the Trials. The highest royalty will not for fear of what it will show them, and even though the druids would never turn them away, the simplest farmer will not offer himself, for it would be seen as disrespectful by his neighbors, even if not by those of the White Forest. It takes the command of a king for someone to be judged worthy. And there are few kings in this world who are humble enough to deem someone below them worthy of a task they will not embark on themselves. Does all of that make sense?"

They were ascending the spiraling staircase to the upper floors as she asked him that question. Yes, it did make sense to Cadohaden, and he couldn't help but think of King Bartholomew in a new light. As the monarch of a kingdom that had led a rebellion against his homeland of Kingsbanesin, he'd had difficulty viewing the bearded man as anything but a grouchy aristocrat, despite Eliliweth's praises for the kingdom he commanded. And the more Elune told him of these Trials, the less surprised he was that he'd never heard of the White Forest. Her descriptions of the proud nobles that would not heed the druids' advice sounded just like the men who ruled the Kingsbanesin Senate under Galdoys Veriknock. For all Cadohaden knew, tales of the White Forest may have been outlawed in his home kingdom. Why else would Iuvas have never mentioned it to him?

"So who decides whether or not he passes the Trials?" Cadohaden asked as they began making their way down the hallway of guest bedrooms.

"I'm not certain, to be honest," Elune admitted. "I don't think there's any official declaration from the druids on who passes or fails. If Eliliweth fails, he himself will know, and he could not hide that disappointment even if he tried."

Cadohaden contemplated this as they passed door after door, assorted belongings hanging from the hooks to signify their owner. "Do you think he will pass?"

"Yes," Elune said without a breath of hesitation.

"You two are close, aren't you?" Cadohaden asked, taking care to make the question sound more curious than envious.

"We are," she answered. "I helped him through some difficult years in the Sherinalu Vale. In turn, he showed me everything the Glen Bailey had to offer when Bartholomew took him under his wing. He is one of my best friends. The king could not ask for a better advisor."

They walked in silence for a few moments as they continued down the hall. Cadohaden noticed that their strides had both slowed, the doors passing them by languidly as they trudged forward. Finally, however, they came to a door with a bare hook, looking lonely among the rows of those with sentimental trophies. He wet his lips as he realized he didn't have anything from home that he could use. All he had taken in his haste to leave Kingsbanesin was his sword, some clothes, and some coin.

As he averted his gaze from the waiting hook, however, something caught his eye: a loose thread from his teal blue half-cape, hanging from the corner. He lowered his hand and grasped the end, pulling on it gently before pinching it with his other hand at palm-length. With a quick tug, he broke the string. He lifted the thread to the hook and tied it around carefully, admiring it solemnly as he thought of the day Melaitha gave him that gift. He shifted his weight from one foot to the other awkwardly as he remembered Elune standing behind him.

"I was sorry to hear about your mother," she said quietly. "I meant it when I said she was a good person, Cadohaden. She deserves more than to be remembered through an interrogation before a crowd of strangers."

Cadohaden swallowed as he stared at the blue thread on the hook. The death of his parents was something he knew he still had to come to terms with, but since his banishment from Kingsbanesin, everything had just moved too quickly for him to truly reflect on it. He'd forced it out of his mind time and time again. It felt to him less like they had perished and more like he was simply traveling on his own, away from them, and would someday return to find them exactly as they were before. Over time, he found himself almost believing that comforting lie. He knew he couldn't allow himself to be swallowed by his own desperate deception, but he wasn't sure he was ready to stare reality in the face just yet.

"Thank you," was all he could muster up in a quiet murmur.

"Do you..." Elune began, pausing to avert her eyes, as if she were considering her familiarity with him. "Do you want to talk about it?"

Cadohaden finally looked away from the thread and over his shoulder at the elf standing behind him. He found himself transfixed by her chestnut brown hair and hazel eyes, only this time, there was no embarrassed flush burning at his skin. Somehow, in that moment, they'd found a comfortable middle ground, and it felt right. And yes, by the gods, he wanted to talk about it. He knew he needed to. But a nagging voice deep in the back of his mind held him back. He wasn't sure he *could* talk to Elune about it without completely breaking down before her, and he wasn't ready for her to see that part of him yet. He wanted to be strong for once that day, and not just for her sake, but for his own. He'd allowed both himself and Terodar to be tugged around obediently all day on invisible leashes, submitting to the whim of anyone who held even a minor title. He wanted to feel strong and capable again, and it needed to start at that moment.

"I'll be all right. For now," he said. "But I may take you up on that another time." Elune smiled in response with a look of sincerity and empathy.

"Another time, then," she said. "I will let you get settled into your room. I expect I'll see you again, Cadohaden." She turned away from him, striding in the direction they had come down the hallway. He watched her go, part of him wanting to call for her to return, but the steadfast half of him prevailed. He took the handle of the door and pressed down on the lever above it with his thumb, opening it with a creak of the hinges.

As he stepped through the door, he saw a modest room with simple furnishings, but it seemed more like home than anything he'd resided in since leaving Kingsbanesin. A narrow bed was tucked against the corner, a small table sitting next to it with a stubby candle sitting in a rounded plate, wax drippings almost pooling over the curved edges. There were ink smudges left on the table. Whoever Pleatus was, he'd certainly spent many nights writing letters by candlelight.

There was a miniature pine dresser on the adjacent side from the bed, a mirror sitting on top of it with the faintest coating of dust, a small square window above it to its right, allowing a narrow ray of natural light inside. Cadohaden slumped his pack off of his shoulder and rested it against the leg of the dresser, setting his sheathed sword down and leaning it against his belongings. He untied his cape and draped it across the dresser before shuffling over to the bed. He collapsed against its stiff surface.

He didn't intend for it to happen, but exhaustion coaxed sleep into his mind nonetheless, his boots still on his feet. He dreamed of dragons, death, and disaster.

Chapter Eleven

"This one...and maybe this one, too, at least the first few chapters," Aven said, gently pulling books out from the shelves by their spines before handing them off to Eliliweth, who already had several cradled in the crook of his arm. "And I think that should get you started."

"Thank you, Aven. I really do appreciate it," the half-elf answered. As they stood in the Mage House's library, his eager smile began to dwindle. The sounds of an angry demon hissing could be heard even from two floors above. Benton was no doubt applying a salve to Terodar's many burn wounds, and the demon sounded none too pleased.

"I'm sorry about all of that, Eliliweth," the princess said quietly, folding her arms across her upper abdomen. "None of that could have been easy for you." Any excitement on the half-elf's face vanished, replaced with a drawn look of sadness. He had only been a baby at the time of his parents' deaths, and it had been at the hands of a vengeful demon. It had only been a few years since the half-elf's caretaker, an elven elder named Marian, had finally told him the truth of their demise, but Aven knew the wound had left a scar. She also knew that some part of Eliliweth wanted to blame himself for their deaths, even though he had been powerless to stop it.

"It wasn't easy," the half-elf conceded. "But I suppose I can't hold this Terodar accountable for the actions of some other demonkin."

"You might," Aven said with a frown. "Demons aren't like us, Eliliweth. Ecila was right to be cautious. There has never once in recorded history been an example of a demon acting in a way that was pure of heart. If Benton can somehow extract useful information from him, then perhaps this is a risk worth taking, but at the first sign of trouble, I promise you that the threat will be swiftly eliminated."

"I trust Benton," Eliliweth answered quietly, shifting the books in his arms. "He will do the right thing."

"For a man with half-elven blood, you are very trusting," Aven said. Her voice carried no condemnation, only a humbled admiration.

"If none of us were given a chance, we would never progress," Eliliweth answered before quickly deflecting the praise in a change of subject. "I hope you don't resent me, Aven. I know how captured you were with the legends of the White Forest."

"Only a little," the princess admitted. She wasn't one to sugarcoat the truth, even to spare a friend's feelings. "But there is no use dwelling on it. Father would not permit me to go while he is still on this earth. He worries that it might affect my ability to rule in his stead. Perhaps someday, when I have an heir to the throne, I will take the Trials. Until then, I have my studies in Novinar, and those have been an adventure in their own right. Besides, it's not as though I've never visited the druids with Father. The White Forest is beautiful, Eliliweth. I'm happy you get to see it."

"If there is anyone deserving of taking the Trials, it's you, Aven," Eliliweth said.

"Now you're just flattering me," Aven said with a dismissive flick of her hand. "Come. I don't want to hear the demon shrieking any longer, and you have studying to do."

They left the Mage House, returning to the streets of the Glen Bailey as they ventured back towards the keep. Their conversation became more casual after that, putting the whirlwind of events that had transpired into the back of their minds. They spoke of the festival, of the coming fall harvest, of Aven's return to Novinar in a few months, and traded jokes about the king's magistrates. They had done so many times since Eliliweth had been brought into the Glen Bailey. He was the brother Aven never had, and she fervently hoped that the half-elf could pass the Trials and become an official advisor. One day, she would wear the kingdom's crown, and she knew it would be a far easier task with a friend such as Eliliweth at her side.

"What do you think of Cadohaden?" the half-elf abruptly asked as they passed a man creaking away at the rope of a water well. Aven pursed her lips at the question, pondering a moment before answering,

"He seems a bit troubled, and I know a brash type when I see one. Bringing a disguised demon into the walls of our kingdom doesn't make the greatest first impression, but he came seeking the Monastery, I suppose. Maybe there's hope for him."

"I think so," Eliliweth replied. "I think he and I could become good friends, if he's given the opportunity to stay here. His heart's in the right place." Aven gave the half-elf a slanted glance before turning her gaze forward once more. She knew that Eliliweth hadn't had many male friends his age growing up. Elune had been there, of course, and the princess herself had certainly been a friend to him, but his stocky nature and strange heritage had made him more of a target in the Sherinalu Vale than a peer. Though Eliliweth was many years older than Cadohaden given his elven blood, in the age of spirit, they were much the same. She only hoped that the young man wasn't duping her dear friend.

"I'm sure it will work out for the best," the princess replied vaguely. They continued to walk in silence from that point on, absently admiring the continuing celebrations of the Solstice as they approached the doors to the Glen Bailey Keep. When they finally arrived at the stone steps, she turned and smiled at the half-elf brightly. "I'm very happy for you, my friend. I think we should part ways now. You have some studying to do, and I think I could use a hot bath. This muggy air leaves an unpleasant sheen of sweat across the skin."

"Thank you, Your Grace. Your blessing means the world to me," the half-elf replied, and for a moment, it looked as though he intended to embrace her. The public view demanded a level of dignified composure, however, and he had an armful of books regardless. And so they parted ways with exchanged polite nods and smiles before they entered the city's castle once more.

Aven strode towards the north end of the keep, where a single staircase could be found leading to an area that was not necessarily private, but treated with vigilant respect, as royalty and their guests would roam between dressing and bathing rooms. Adjacent to those was a room with a flat stove, a great cauldron sitting on top of it. Buckets of water were poured in and brought back out with hot vapor coiling from the contents to fill the baths in the rooms nearby.

Her skin *was* feeling sticky from the day's humidity, but in truth, Aven needed some time to silently sulk, as selfish as it made it her feel. Eliliweth hadn't been wrong when he said how he knew she had been captivated by the White Forest's legends. Though she knew it was unlikely, she had secretly hoped for some time that her father would task her with the undergoing of the druids' Trials. She really was happy for Eliliweth. But today was a holiday, and if she wished to use some of it to brood in a tub of hot water, she didn't think that was unreasonable.

And there was the matter of her stiff hands and forearm muscles from the staff sparring with Sir Ganisalp earlier that day. She pressed her fingertips together and flexed her joints as she pushed her palms towards each other, trying to ease the lingering aches. She had nobody to blame but herself for his full engagement in the duel. She'd insisted on it every time in the past. Her mind briefly trailed to the moment he had tumbled over her, as well as the brush of his trimmed whiskers against her jawline. She shook her head, swiftly banishing the memory from the front of her mind. The contact was purely incidental, of course, and she had no reason to feel as though she'd betrayed Wyatt in any way. But her reaction at the recalling was just enough to give her heart the faintest tug of guilt. Strigson was a handsome man, after all.

She frowned as she entered the dressing room with the many robes hung from wooden pegs along the wall, a basket of washcloths and a tray of soaps set in front of a pedestal mirror. Usually, there was a servant of the Keep waiting at the door that led to the stove room to ask if visitors would like a bath poured. Perhaps they were tending to the fire underneath the cauldron now. As Aven neared the other side of the room, though, she heard more than one voice in the room beyond. That was odd; if conversations were ever carried on, they were typically in the room with the bathtubs. She pressed her fingertips against the wooden paneling of the door and gave it a firm push, stepping into the stove room.

She paused mid-stride as she entered the near-unbearably hot room. Embers were glowing happily behind the grates of the stove, steam rising from the black cauldron that was set on top of it, but there were no servants within. Instead, what looked to be the entire gaggle of Bartholomew's magistrates were gathered in a circle around the cauldron, as though they were acolytes tending to a great iron altar. Each one had cherry-red cheeks from the heat, sweat glistening on their skin, dark blossoms on their royal clothing where it had soaked through.

"What's going on here, gentlemen?" Aven asked suspiciously with a frown to match her tone.

"What does it look like we're doing?" the large Arnold Seasar grunted as he wiped a sleeve across his gleaming brow. "We're getting ready for a bath."

"All five of you? I know there are two tubs in there, but that still seems like a bit of a squeeze to me," Aven remarked, giving Seasar's bulky form a meaningful up-and-down glance that suggested the quantity of men wasn't the only issue with his claim.

"I beg your pardon!?" Seasar barked, a droplet of sweat dripping from the end of his nose.

"And I beg yours," Aven snapped back without hesitation. "I care not what businesses you own in the kingdom, Arnold Seasar, you will address me as 'Your Grace', and you will drop the flippant tone from your voice. If the five of you find pleasure in each other's bathtime company, it's no concern of mine, though my father might find it all to be a bit conflicting in the royal court. Either way, I would only like to know how long you will be, so that I may take a dip myself...after the tubs have been drained and scrubbed, I mean."

"By the gods, we aren't here for...for *that*," the withered Edward Carson croaked at her, adding a half-hearted 'Your Grace' after a strained pause.

"No?" Aven asked as she folded her arms. She could feel her own perspiration beginning to bloom against her skin. The heat was oppressive. "Surely you're all aware that the servants will scrub your back with a brush if you're unable to reach between your shoulder blades."

"Your Grace," Bertram Archibaum said hastily as he snaked his way around Wallace Tibault and Dirk Wellingson to approach the princess. He steepled his fingers in front of his chest as he offered her a smile. "Might you and I speak in private for a moment?"

"Is there something you must say that cannot be said in front of your fellow lords?" Aven said challengingly.

"Please, Your Grace," Archibaum insisted. "Only a moment of your time, I promise." The princess scowled suspiciously at him, then at the other magistrates mopping their brows around the stove. She looked back at Archibaum and gave him a curt nod.

"Make it a quick moment, Lord Archibaum."

They excused themselves from the stove room, shutting the door behind them. Aven immediately turned to confront Archibaum, but the magistrate shook his head insistently and beckoned with his hand, guiding her out of the dressing room and back into the short hallway that led back to the staircase. Once they were on the other side of the dressing room, he leaned towards the door, pressing his ear against it. Satisfied, he nodded quickly and turned towards Aven. His voice was low and hushed,

"This is what I will tell them when I return, Your Grace. I will tell them that I discussed Lord Wellingson with you, about a rash on Dirk's nether regions that did not come from his wife. He wanted assistance in concocting a believable alibi, and was too ashamed to admit it to you in person."

"What do you mean, 'that is what you will tell them'?" Aven hissed.

"Because that's not what is truly being discussed, Your Grace," Archibaum whispered back, his wide eyes a grave omen. "Words of treason are being spoken in there. But they must not know that *you* know. That is why I will tell them this little lie."

"*What!?*" Aven snapped back through gritted teeth. "*Treason!?* If you speak the truth, Archibaum, then I will call the guards and have them arrested for conspiracy!"

"No! No no no!" Archibaum murmured fervently, lifting his hands with open palms. "Evidence has already been planted, Your Grace, and if they know they have been discovered, someone else will take the fall. That someone is Eliliweth Heraketh, Your Grace. No, they must be caught in the act if they are to face justice, or they will slip through the cracks. If they are imprisoned without probable reason, they have lesser nobles that will incite their workers into riots at best, and a civil war at worst."

"And so what, I am to simply sit on my hands until treason is committed?" the princess growled lowly.

"No, Your Grace. I have a plan. But I don't have the time to tell you now. They will grow suspicious if I speak to you much longer, and if that happens, they will surely excommunicate me, if not outright kill me. But we must speak again, Your Grace, away from where we might be heard, and soon. I wanted to send word to you sooner, but I do not know if there are any servants I can trust. Will you meet me at the Ogre Pint at sundown tomorrow?"

"You don't think we'll be heard in a tavern?" Aven asked dubiously. "Can we afford to wait that long?"

"Most of the drunkards are out in the streets during the Solstice festival, and His Majesty extended the celebrations by announcing Eliliweth's Trials," Archibaum murmured. "We can hide in plain sight in a tavern. Come wearing a cloak. And yes, we have time. This is a delicate matter, and the pieces are being laid out with patience and precision. I have to keep close to their plot if I have any hope of foiling it. But I need your help, Princess."

Aven narrowed her eyes at Archibaum, studying his deep black pupils. "Give me one reason why I should trust you, Bertram," she muttered through her teeth.

"Your Grace, I'm a greedy old miser. I will be the first to admit it," the magistrate said hurriedly, his head swiveling around to glance with worry at the door behind them. "I enjoy the privileges that come with being a magistrate. But I am *no traitor*. The Glen Bailey has given me everything. *Your father* has given me everything. I would not stab my king in the back. But if I had protested their ideas from the beginning, they wouldn't have breathed another word in my direction of their intentions, and I would simply be another head on a pike when it was all said and done.

"Besides, Princess, if I were truly conspiring against the crown, I would have led you out here and told you that we were only giving Wellingson advice on the rash he picked up from a gypsy whore, and that the man was too sensitive to admit it in front of you."

Aven stared hard at Bertram Archibaum, her jaw flexing as she ground her teeth. The magistrate wet his lips and glanced over his shoulder nervously once more before turning back to gaze at her with pleading eyes. A moment of silence passed before the princess finally hissed,

"Fine. Ogre Pint. Sunset tomorrow. But if I get the slightest sense of trouble, Bertram, I will bury you and those other noble fools in this."

"That won't be necessary, Your Grace," Archibaum murmured. "I must go. I have been gone too long already. Be there tomorrow. It is of utmost importance." The magistrate turned away before Aven could respond, hurrying into the dressing room, his slippers softly tapping against the floor with every stride.

The princess watched him go. Treason. The word alone made her skin flush with anger. She turned away and stormed back towards the staircase. Her speculations would haunt her all through the night. She wanted to tell someone of Archibaum's revelation, but she knew could not. Not before she knew the details, and how much danger both her father and Eliliweth were in. She couldn't risk anyone else going to Bartholomew, for nothing would stop him from imprisoning the magistrates if these rumors reached his ears. It was a delicate situation indeed.

Chapter Twelve

Demons do not sleep as most mortals do. Whether you walk through the halls of a *roaq* training school in Daemonaar's late hours, or brave the bloodspattered barracks of the brutish *barshkor*, you will find that though they may have their eyelids closed, their bodies still appear alert, even tense. They may even open their eyes as you walk past, as though they were expecting your arrival all along. Their version of sleep is more of a meditation, a time to refocus their unholy energies.

That night, sheer exhaustion brought Terodar Soulrender closer to true sleep than he ever could remember. He thought that the sting of the many burns would keep him from any form of rest, but the salve that Benton had applied to each one had a soothing effect, and the spoonful of the thick clear liquid the mage had commanded him to swallow had numbed every nerve in his body. He hadn't been given any sort of bed that resembled comfort. He hadn't even been given a room that resembled comfort.

When he'd first arrived at the Mage House after a humiliating, agonizing shuffle across the Glen Bailey, Benton had allowed him to lay upon one of the couches on the first floor. And as he had begun to apply the salve to the demon's burn wounds, he commanded one of the other mages that he called Krendrick to prepare a room for their newest guest. As Terodar had hissed and threatened, he'd heard in the basement level the sounds of clinking jars and clattering cans, followed by the scrape of wooden legs against a stone surface.

When they had finally aided Terodar down the basement steps, guiding him to his newest domain, he had discovered with resentful disdain that Krendrick had cleared out a cannery room for the demon's abode. There was a deerskin cot tucked in the corner, a couple dusty wooden shelves against the opposite wall with rows of clean circular marks where the jars had been removed, and between the two, a short, three-legged stool with a leg that was visibly prying away from the base of the seat. The two mages brought Terodar to the cot, set him down upon it, and then gave hurried promises that they would return shortly. Benton went so far as to order the demon to remain in the room until told otherwise, as if Terodar were in any condition to escape.

He'd been grateful for the brief moment alone, however. As soon as the two mages were out of sight, the demon had hoisted himself to his hooves, gritting his teeth against the splitting pain lancing across his pale flesh. He'd tucked his hand into his robes, clasping the demonic tome he had carried from the world of Daemonaar. Benton had not yet stripped him down to tend to the burns on his torso or his thighs, thankfully. Had he discovered the tome, he would have no doubt taken it away and stored it among the unworthy books on the second floor library. Terodar could have survived without Kavagor's tome, but if he stopped ritually devoting himself to studying it, he knew he would begin to lose his iron grip over his blood magic talent. And with Benton no doubt intending to snuff it out, he had to hide his only treasure. But where?

His gaze had darted from corner to corner of the room. There was nowhere to hide it. He'd thought his best bet would be to tuck it in the back corner under the canning shelf, maybe wedge it under the back leg if he could lift it up without screaming. He began to shuffle over to the shelf when something else caught his eye. He'd lifted his head, staring at the ceiling above. Two hulking wooden beams crossed over the ceiling of his improvised bedroom. Along the beam that was closest to the wall furthest away from the door, a hollow strip ran across like a freshly opened wound. It had appeared as though it had once been an imperfection, a gnarled knot in the tree, but had either fallen out over time or been removed.

As fast as he could shuffle, gritting his teeth against the pain skittering across his flesh, Terodar had lurched over to the shifty-looking stool and picked it up as carefully as he could, setting it underneath the flawed beam. He'd clamped his teeth together once more as he carefully scurried onto the stool's seat, watching with trepidation as the suspect leg began to droop inward. He froze, his back hunched and his flesh burning with pain. The leg finally ceased its dangerous bend. Licking his cracked lips, Terodar had begun to stand, holding out his arms to balance, silently commanding himself to ignore the lancing sensations across his burns and blisters. Gripping the tome by its spine, he took in a shaking, bracing breath. Sucking in air through his teeth, he stretched himself towards the ceiling, extending his arm as far as he could, the whole limb shaking with the weight of the book and the torment of the burns. He had desperately tried to push the edge into the beam's crevice, but he'd been just shy of the opening. Biting down on his tongue, he'd pushed himself up on the tip of his hoof, his knee quaking underneath him. He had felt the blisters along his stomach opening and draining fluid as he pulled them taut. His vision had begun to close in as his muscles and flesh angrily protested.

Finally, he'd felt the tome slide into the flaw. He had released a trembling breath of relief before lifting his gaze. It was resting within the crevice, but nearly a third of the book still hung out from the beam, the spine exposed. He'd pushed up on his hoof once more, lifting his hand to swat it further into the flaw when he had heard a snapping sound underneath him.

The seat of the stool gave way underneath him as the leg buckled. His arms had pinwheeled as he went flailing to the floor with a crumpling thud. Terodar gasped soundlessly as pain wrapped around his body like constricting barbed wire. A quiet, agonized croak had rattled in his throat as he tried to blink away the purple smudges flooding his vision. It had taken all of his effort to redirect his gaze back to the pillar above, where his demonic spell book was still hanging traitorously from the wooden beam. His ears had perked as he'd heard footsteps coming back down the stairs.

He'd bitten down on his tongue again as he desperately clawed himself onto all fours. He knew he had to move the broken stool away from the beam, or Benton would surely turn his gaze upward. Furiously, he'd pushed the wooden remnants towards the front door, sliding them across the hard surface of the floor as the sounds of the mage's footsteps drew even nearer. With the broken pieces in front of the door, the demon had scurried back to the deerskin cot, clambering into it as his blisters pulled open with his efforts. Rolling himself onto his back, he'd taken in labored breaths as he stared at the ceiling. He was coated in sweat, his chest rising and falling from the task. He'd suddenly become aware of the dull throbbing in his shoulder where he'd clumsily landed against the floor.

The door had opened, revealing Benton with a concerned frown, a jar of salve in one hand, and a smaller capped bottle in the other containing a clear liquid. The mage had stared down his hook nose at the splintered remains of the stool, pushed aside by the opening of the cannery room door. "What's all of this?" he'd asked slowly.

"I was testing...testing its sturdiness," Terodar had said with his best attempt at a sneer. He had barely the energy for his usual snide attitude, but he couldn't make it seem as though he had been exerting himself in another manner.

"Testing its sturdiness," Benton had replied flatly. "And so you smashed it against the floor?"

"It...it failed the test," Terodar had answered with a dry chuckle. "Best find another one if you want to...to mother me, Cusair." He'd watched the mage's eyes, looking for the quickest glance towards the ceiling. The mage had only shaken his head with an exasperated sigh, however, and called out over his shoulder,

"Krendrick! If you would be so kind as to find me a chair? It seems I will need another one."

Benton's assistant had brought down a new chair, this one with four legs and a sturdy backrest, and for the rest of the night, the mage had tended to the demon's wounds before administering him with the nerve-numbing substance. If anyone saw Terodar's tome hanging from the beam's hollow, they did not say so. After every burn had salve applied to it, Benton had left the room, letting the medication take over from there.

That had all been the night before. Morning had come, though the demon couldn't tell the difference. He normally had a keen sense of time, but the dose of numbing liquid Benton had given him the previous night still lingered within him, keeping his mind faintly fuddled. He could hear footsteps coming down the stairs, though, and guessed that a new day had arrived, and with it, the questions that the mage was dying to ask him.

It was indeed Benton that opened the door, a candle tray held in his hand, the flickering flare of the squat wax candle seated upon it giving Terodar's cannery cell a faint glow of illumination. The mage had a friendly smile on his thin face that irritated the demon. Then he noticed a round wooden plate held in Benton's other hand, a collection of fruit and nuts arranged on it.

"How are you feeling this fine morning? Care for some breakfast?" Benton asked amiably.

"I feel like an overcooked tenderloin," the demon snapped back. "And speaking of meat, would it have been too taxing for you to bring some down for me?"

"We mages have to be conscious of what we eat," Benton said as he held the wooden plate out for Terodar to help himself. "We spend a great deal of time studying, and so we must avoid large portions of fatty meat. A soft body makes a slow mind, or so they say."

"Tell that to your fat magistrates, they're only advising the king, after all," Terodar sneered before wincing at the painful peeling of a blister on his abdomen. "And don't say 'we' like I'm one of your pigeon-headed mages."

"Not yet," Benton replied with a quaint smile, only further aggravating the demon. He lowered himself into the chair that Krendrick had brought down the night before and set the candle down on the floor between himself and Terodar. "But with any luck, we'll make you a pigeon-head yet. A few grapes, perhaps?"

"I'm not hungry," Terodar snapped. His stomach immediately groaned in protest, only widening Benton's smile. The demon's expression curdled venomously, but he finally conceded, plucking a few grapes from the plate and shoveling them into his mouth. They were on the sour side, at least. He had no taste for sweets.

"Shall I have Leora fetch you some water?" Benton asked courteously.

"No," Terodar quipped. "Whatever the hell it is you came down here for, Cusair, get on with it, so you can sooner see yourself out."

"Very well," Benton said, setting the plate down in his lap. "Though I should warn you that nothing we do will be abbreviated. This isn't a semester of schooling, Terodar, nor will it be a few afternoons of idle questions. Your presence has been accepted in the Glen Bailey under the condition that you will be rehabilitated. I will benefit from any knowledge you might have, given your identity, but our ultimate goal here is to have you be a contributing member of this kingdom."

"Contributing member," Terodar snorted. "I can see that you're a man who doesn't mind sprinkling his words with a pinch of sugar."

"You are a demon," Benton said firmly. "You will never be given free reign within the city. Over time, however, and with the right amount of effort, we can give you a longer leash."

"A longer leash!" the demon replied mockingly. "How pleasant! Will I have to endure a monthly trial-by-fire at the steps your lovely Monastery, or have I been sufficiently tortured enough for passing through the gates?"

"That will no longer be necessary," Benton said assuredly. "We have no doubts as to your obedience. I don't, at least, and my opinion is what matters."

"Your opinion surprises me," Terodar answered, shifting a little on his cot and drawing a wince from the stretching of his blisters. "With that paltry collection of books up there on the second floor, I wouldn't have bet a toenail clipping that you'd be willing to risk my head soundly on my shoulders for 'knowledge', as you say."

"Ecila was not wrong," Benton answered, plucking a walnut from the tray and crunching it between his teeth before continuing, "You are a dangerous creature, and I am a cautious man. The mastery of magic is a dangerous concept, for it is power. Every man knows that power leads to the temptation of more power. Such struggles are common for Novinar, but they have no place in the Glen Bailey.

"Your captivity, however, is not about learning how to use the power that demons command. There's no secret there. It uses the barbaric method of blood magic. But given your compliance, we can study things that may one day protect our people. We can observe your tendencies, your weaknesses, your strengths. Opportunities like this are rare, and so despite my cautionary methods, I would be foolish to pass on a chance to keep my people safe."

"So you will keep me locked away in the basement of this pitiful excuse for a mage study to poke, prod, and ask incessant questions for the rest of eternity. And you call blood magic barbaric?" Terodar sneered.

"That's not what I meant by you being a contributing member of the Glen Bailey," Benton said between the delicate placement of individual grapes upon his tongue. His calculated precision in this minute task was infuriating. "Every warlock has the capability of commanding magic without the use of demonic or blood energies. This is an accepted fact among the most ancient wizards of Novinar. I have no reason to believe that you are an exception. We will teach you to wield magic in its purest form, from the Goddess herself, and you will be a true member of our Mage Unit."

Terodar scoffed, "I'd rather you choke the life out of me, if your spindly fingers could handle such a feat. Krendrick looked like he might have enough muscle for it, why don't you call him down?"

Benton smiled, but it was a thin, strained expression. The demon was finally getting under his skin. "You won't get such a wish granted, I'm afraid. I have the power to force you to do my bidding, Terodar Soulrender, but I would prefer that I did not have to. Life will just be more pleasant for the both of us if you cooperate."

Terodar rolled his eyes and leaned his head back on his cot. In his peripheral vision, he could still see the tome jutting from the flawed beam. He didn't dare look at it directly, and the more time he spent bickering with Benton, the higher the chance the mage would discover it before the demon had a chance to more aptly hide it. "I think you and I have different views on what 'pleasant' is, mage. Regardless, I'm growing tired of this nonsense. Can we get your quota of questions for the day out of the way so that I may sit here and heal in peace?"

"So glad we could come to an understanding," Benton said, his smile widening. He leaned over in the chair, setting the wooden plate down on the floor before righting himself again, folding his hands in his lap, as if he were a school teacher displaying patience for an unruly child. "What can you tell me of the sand city of Chai'Rin, and the morph people that dwell within it?"

Terodar frowned at the mage incredulously. "You spend all this time prattling on about the opportunity to learn all you can about demonkin, and the first question you ask me is about a city and race entirely unrelated to anything about me? Are you drunk?"

"The issue is of topical importance," Benton answered patiently, his tone bordering so close to condescending that it made Terodar grit his teeth in annoyance. "No kingdom or cause has ever successfully allied with the desert city, and King Bartholomew is interested in ending that drought. We've sent messengers and ravens in hopes of establishing a mutual foundation, but thus far all of our attempts have been fruitless. Any knowledge you might have could be the answer to opening communication with the Sandspeakers."

"Has it occurred to you, Benton, that maybe not every man, woman, and child wants to be associated with the glorious Glen Bailey? That perhaps you and your superiors might come off as a bit pretentious?" the demon said mockingly.

"Tell me what you know about Chai'Rin, Terodar, and speak truthfully," Benton said, the patience in his voice finally fading.

"Very well," Terodar answered, the direct command from the mage compelling the words from his mouth. "Though I suspect I will have little more knowledge than you already do. The Destroyer has ways of seeing things, of knowing things, but that does not mean he shares all of these answers with every one of his underlings. He gives orders and information to his appropriate generals, and they pass down what is necessary to those below them.

"I can tell you that Chai'Rin may be one of the most ancient cities in all of the Aariad, born around the same time as magic was introduced to the world. There are two different morph creatures that inhabit the city; one of sand, and one of water. They believe that magic is not just a manifestation of Essence, but a goddess of her own, the *Ran'allakah*, Essence's lover, even. They don't even call her by Essence. Translated into Commonspeak, she is 'The Mother Earth.' There's plenty of frivolous nonsense about what 'Mother Earth' does for the land, but I can't tell you truthfully what it all is. I only suspect that most of it is rubbish."

"You're aware of Chai'Rin's origins, but so are we," Benton said, unfolding his hands and placing his palms upon his knees. "We're more interested in cultural aspects and distinctions, what we could do to appear more relatable to them."

Terodar narrowed his eyes, his words laced with snide mocking as he answered, "Cusair, when the Destroyer sets his eyes upon someone, he has only one thing in mind: *conquering* them. He is not interested in learning about their dinner etiquette or their style of dress. I do know that in times of war, their goal is to kill without spilling blood on the earth, as a sign of respect for the *Ran'allakah,* who was wounded by the Lifegiver in the earliest times, her own blood giving birth to their people. Other than that, no, I have no 'cultural' tips for you. Historically, the morphs of Chai'Rin have been an isolated and self-sustaining city. If you want to seem 'relatable' to them, your best bet is probably to leave them the hell alone."

Benton's nostrils flared as his fingertips began fluttering against his knees. Just as the mage looked as though he had conjured a retort, however, the sounds of footsteps came from the stairs outside Terodar's room. Benton turned to look over his shoulder as a knock came at the door. "Yes?" he asked.

"My lord, there's a visitor here, a young man that wishes to see the demon," Krendrick's voice came from behind the closed door. "Should I let him in?"

"Ah, that must be Sir Cadohaden from Kingsbanesin," Benton said, lifting himself onto his feet. "Go ahead, Krendrick, I am done conferencing with Terodar."

"*Conferencing?*" Terodar scoffed. "You know, Benton, between your flowery words and your distaste for your own talents, you should have just pursued the life of a diplomat. You would have to drop that ever-present air of superiority, of course, but I suppose more outrageous things have happened."

Ignoring the quip, Benton looked down at the bedridden demon and said, "I will return in the late afternoon to check on your health and ask you more questions. As soon as you are mobile, we will begin your retraining." The mage didn't wait for a snarky response. He pushed open the door and departed, leaving Terodar to await his visitor.

Moments later, another set of footsteps came trotting down the stairs, and soon after, the door opened once more. Just as Benton had predicted, Cadohaden Ulaeron stood in the doorway, squinting at his companion on the cot. "How are you doing?" he asked as he made his way into the cannery room, the young man's eyes scanning the surroundings dubiously.

"Oh, fine, just fine," Terodar quipped. "I'm layered in burns and blisters, have been given a canning room as a place to call my own, and have been bombarded with inane questions since I awoke."

"I'm sorry about yesterday," Cadohaden said quietly as he settled down into the same chair that Benton had been in only minutes before.

"Sorry? You're *sorry!?*" Terodar snapped back. A shiver of pain coiled through his flesh as he raised his voice. "You ordered me to perform a *trick* for those simpletons yesterday, a trick that *made my flesh split open!* And you're *sorry!?*"

Cadohaden's eyes widened at the demon's outburst, his mouth hanging open in surprise as the words lashed at him from Terodar's tongue. "I just came to see if you were doing better," he finally managed to say.

"Oh, well, *praise* to the Lifegiver, then, for your concern!" Terodar hissed. "I can already feel my wounds closing with all of your well-wishes!"

They sat in uncomfortable silence for a few moments as the demon brooded and Cadohaden shifted himself on the chair awkwardly. Terodar could feel his heart racing as the blood churned furiously through the veins in his neck. He knew he needed to befriend the Kingsbanesin whelp if he were to have any chance at shirking his way out of his Pact. He knew his rage would do him no good, but he couldn't help himself from unleashing his anger. Cadohaden had paraded him around like an animal the day before. All demons endure some form of punishment through humiliation during their training, *roaq* or *barshkor*, but Terodar had never experienced such disgrace in his entire life. He would not simply pass that off as a rite of trust.

After several moments, a flush began to color Cadohaden's face. His brow furrowed as he scowled down at the demon from his chair, his lip pursing before he finally spoke, "You know what, demon? I'm not sorry. I'm not sorry at all. You know what happens when cities of men catch spies and infiltrators in their kingdom? They imprison them. Sometimes they torture them. Because they're a threat. It's not the right or wrong thing to do, it's the *necessary* thing to do, and you, Terodar, are an infiltrator, a threat against not just this kingdom, but the whole Aariad! You admitted that much to me when I saved your life. You didn't come to this world to sightsee, you came to conquer. And guess what? You. Got. Caught.

"I tried my best, Terodar. I didn't want to see that happen to you. But don't you sit here and pout at me. Aren't demons supposed to be smart? You knew what you were getting yourself into. You knew the risks. I might have control over you, but that doesn't change how you got here in the first place. I think you can still do some good in this world, and I want you to help me, but if you can't take a beating without becoming a miserable wreck, then I'm just wasting my time."

Terodar looked back in surprise at the fuming young man. There it was: that spark, that fire that could be harnessed. It was still there after all, even after the multitude of orders he'd followed from every man and woman that wagged a finger at him the day before. He wanted to answer with another helping of snark, but that fierce resistance gave him pause, and more importantly, it gave him reason to reach out once more.

"Fine," the demon conceded. "You've made your point. But you'll forgive me if I'm a bit testy, as breathing alone gives me the feeling of a switch being slapped against my skin."

"They use switches in Daemonaar?" Cadohaden asked in surprise. Terodar frowned at his own analogy. No, they didn't use switches in Daemonaar. The *barshkor* had all varieties of whips and clubs used as disciplinary tools for training, but the *roaq* were typically subjected to more psychological punishment. So why did the sting of a switch seem so familiar to him?

"No, they do not, but I know what a damned switch is. It's fairly common knowledge, Ulaeron," Terodar answered.

"Right," Cadohaden answered, though his puzzled frown persisted on his face. "Anyway, I wanted to tell you that I'm going to the Monastery today to speak with Crusader Nevic. I'm guessing we'll have a better idea of whether or not we're staying here after that."

"Let's hope it goes well," the demon said dryly. "I don't see them letting you just walk back through the gate with me in tow."

"Maybe not," Cadohaden admitted. "But we'll worry about that if it gets to that point. I talked with Eliliweth this morning before leaving the keep. If I become a citizen of the Glen Bailey, I'll be able to escort you to places within the city. You won't have to stay locked up here all day and night."

"How wonderful," Terodar said. He tried his best to sound genuinely pleased, but it was just too damned hard for him.

"Well, I can't stay," Cadohaden said as he lifted himself from the chair. "The Crusader is expecting me, and it probably wouldn't look all that good for me to keep him waiting. I will visit you again tomorrow and let you know what happened." The angry fire Terodar had seen in the young man's eyes was gone now, hidden away, replaced by an upbeat and optimistic demeanor.

"Very well," the demon answered. "I have some laying down and doing nothing to get done, anyway." He wasn't sure what reaction that would invoke, but Cadohaden allowed himself a quick grin at the half-hearted attempt at a joke.

"Benton asked if I'd take this upstairs with me," Cadohaden said with a puzzled frown, lifting the chair he'd been sitting on, gripping it by the top of the backrest. "Said something about you smashing all the furniture they give you."

Terodar gritted his teeth, his lips pursing into a thin line as he watched Cadohaden lift the chair's legs up off of the floor. It would have been the ideal boost to completely conceal his tome in the flaw of the ceiling beam, but he wasn't sure what he could say to have him leave it there without raising suspicions. He didn't have any possessions to set on it like a makeshift table, and he wasn't going to be doing any sitting in the near future.

"You aren't obligated to do Benton's bidding," Terodar said, trying to disguise his intentions with exasperation.

"I'm already pushing my luck, Terodar. I'm not going to get into any fights over a chair."

"Fine, take it then," Terodar sneered. "Run along. Didn't I tell you that I have plenty of being useless to get to?"

"I'll leave you to it, then" Cadohaden said with a subtle shake of his head as he turned away, heading towards the door with the chair in tow.

"...Best of luck, Ulaeron," Terodar found himself saying to his own surprise. Cadohaden looked just as taken aback, glancing over his shoulder with lifted eyebrows, but he nodded and lifted his hand in a farewell gesture.

"Thanks."

Terodar waited as he listened to Cadohaden's footsteps travel to the staircase, up to the next floor, and then all the way out of the front door of the Mage House. He silently listened for someone else to descend the stairs. He could hear the occasional creak of the floor as either Benton or Krendrick moved about, but nothing seemed to indicate another impending visitor. Bracing himself once more, the demon rolled out of his cot. Crouching down, he grabbed it with both hands and began to tug it closer to the center of the room, underneath the hollow of the support beam.

Inch by inch, he scooted the legs of the cot further away from the wall, taking care not to create too loud of a disturbance. Benton had believed his lie about shattering the ill-repaired stool out of spite, but Terodar wasn't sure what excuse he could concoct for moving his bed without drawing attention to the tome. Finally, he managed to set it directly underneath the beam.

He climbed onto the cot, the hide material swaying treacherously underneath him as he tried to maintain his balance, all the while ignoring the pain of his burns. He lifted his gaze, holding out his arms to steady himself, focusing on the exposed spine of the book. His cot didn't have as much height as the crooked stool had offered. He had only one option. He steadied himself, bent down at the knees, and took a deep breath before lifting his hooves off of the cot in a cautious jump.

Lifting his hand, he gave the book another firm swat as he hung suspended in mid-air. With a triumphant rush, he felt it give a significant slide into the beam. He fell back down upon the cot, immediately losing his balance as the hide turned over like a ship in a tumultuous sea, and once more he tumbled to the floor, pain wracking his entire body as he collapsed against the solid surface below.

He gritted his teeth to avoid making a sound and listened once more for curious footsteps. He took slow, steady breaths through his teeth, silently commanding his heart to slow to a normal pace. The floorboards creaked above in one direction, then lazily meandered in another. He remained motionless for several more moments, listening, but no footsteps came stomping down the basement stairs.

Finally convinced that he was safe, he rolled back over and looked up at the shadowed ceiling, barely illuminated by the candle that Benton had left behind. He could still see the book, but it was well concealed in the dim light, and was now at least flush with the surface of the beam. Rattling off a relieved sigh, the demon painstakingly rose to his hooves once more. Just as carefully as he had moved it away from the wall, he began the slow and steady process of scooting the cot back where it had been.

He was exhausted, and his skin was burning with insistent protests by the time he had the cot back in place. Quietly groaning to himself, Terodar rolled back onto it, letting his head swivel loosely to the side as he once again tried to steady his breathing. At some point, he would have to invoke some sort of cloaking spell over the demonic tome. The mages here were not yet fully attuned to the sense of his energies, but they would be soon, and when that time came, they would detect another presence coming from the ceiling of his room. It would have to wait, however. He didn't have the strength to call forth a wisp of smoke, much less a protective enchantment.

His eyelids fell shut with weariness, but a faint smile crossed his face. Hiding the book was a small victory, but it was a victory nonetheless. He knew those would be few and far between in the days to come.

Chapter Thirteen

"How is he?" Eliliweth asked as Cadohaden opened the door to the Mage House, stepping back into the streets of the Glen Bailey. The half-elf had dark smudges under his eyes from a night of fervent studying.

"He resents me," Cadohaden answered with a slight shrug as they began walking in the direction of the Monastery. "But I think he'll come around. Thanks again for coming with me to see the Crusader. I know you have a lot of work to do before your Trials."

"I still have some time, I'm sure," Eliliweth said with a knowing smile. "I don't know if you've noticed, but our good king enjoys his celebrations. He will continue to use his announcement as an excuse until the people grow drink-weary and impatient. Besides, I thought you might need some support in case Ecila decides to add her own input to your request."

"What's with her eyes?" Cadohaden asked, immediately looking embarrassed at the bold approach to his question, stealing a few glances around each shoulder to ensure that the priestess was not mysteriously hidden in the shadows. "I mean...what caused her blindness? Has she been that way all of her life?"

"I don't know," Eliliweth answered with a curious frown of his own. "She was here before I became involved with the Glen Bailey. I've asked Aven about her. I am told that she has the gift of sight, but not in the way that you and I do. She can see the souls of mortals, and their struggle between purity and corruption. Apparently she approached the gates many years ago, and would only say that she wished to serve the Monastery of the Lifegiver. She would not answer questions as to her origins or intentions. She would only repeat that she wanted to serve Kaijaras. And, well, the Monastery rarely turns down offers like that. And so she began serving as an acolyte. It didn't take long for her wisdom and insight, not to mention her steadfast faith, to become recognized, and as the Monastery's elders passed away of old age, she quickly rose to the position she holds now."

"Hm," was all Cadohaden could respond with at first as he circumvented a pile of horse leavings on the cobblestone. "And what of Crusader Nevic? What's his story?"

"Nevic Baltwin came to us from Kaijar Keep, actually," Eliliweth explained. "Every once in a while, the holy city's Grand Bishop sends us a gesture of good faith, though I think they do so more out of moral obligation than necessity, if you know what I mean. The last time they did so, Nevic arrived, pledging his service to the Glen Dale if we would accept it. It didn't take him long to receive Ecila's blessing, and that was all the convincing Bartholomew needed."

"They just...sent one of their paladins here to serve Bartholomew?" Cadohaden asked in a puzzled tone.

"To serve the Monastery," Eliliweth gently corrected. "To Kaijar Keep, faith knows no borders. As to why Nevic was chosen, he says that the sun glares harshly in the south, and so he volunteered for an assignment that would bring him to cloudier skies."

"Why would sunlight be a deciding factor for such a man?" Cadohaden asked, only looking more confused as Eliliweth elaborated.

"You'll see when we get there," the half-elf said with a grin and a wink. Cadohaden opened his mouth to protest the half-elf's dodge, but he drew it to a swift close as a looming shadow passed over both of them. Instinctively, his hand went to the hilt of his sword as the figure passed by overhead. Had Kingsbanesin come with dragons to claim their runaway?

His hastily invented fantasy vanished as he saw that the winged beast overhead bore feathers instead of scales, a proud avian head attached to a lion's body. His skin flushed as he silently reprimanded himself for such a foolish notion. The Gunnysack Treaty wouldn't be broken over a bastard exile. "I didn't know the Glen Bailey owned gryphons," he remarked as he cleared his throat. He could tell that the half-elf was doing his best to courteously avoid laughing at his panic.

"Their roost is that way," Eliliweth said, turning his body to point in the southeastern direction of the city, where a circular stone tower sat nestled near the corner of the Bailey's wall. "We don't actually own the gryphons, though. They're...borrowed, I guess is the best way to put it. From Kaijar Keep. They know all the secrets to raising the winged beasts, and they have the only hatchery known to exist in the Aariad. They actually have a rotation between us, Eastfen, Munite, and Wardrin during the fall, spring, and summer. They're all sent back to Kaijar Keep during the winter to avoid harsh weather and to breed."

"And what do they get in return for the use of their gryphons?" Cadohaden asked, his eyes on the quickly vanishing form of the gryphon heading in the direction of Eastfen.

"From us, large sacks of seeds," Eliliweth explained. "The land by Kaijar Keep is not nearly as fertile as it is in the Glen Dale. They have to plant a great deal of crops to feed their population, as nearly half of their harvest usually fails."

"Why not move further north?" Cadohaden asked. "Or just trade for grown crops?"

"Pride," Eliliweth said simply. As they passed through the Market Square, a man selling apples shouted for their attention. The half-elf smiled in return and lifted a hand in a grateful gesture, but the two continued past without browsing the vendor's fruit. "They preach against it, but it's by far the most abundant sin in Kaijar Keep. They want to feel independent, and so they buy seeds to grow on their own, instead of crops already harvested by others. As far as the location goes, well, it's a city almost as large as Kingsbanesin. They can't just pick up and move it all."

"But it had to be founded at some point," Cadohaden countered. "Was the land more fertile back then?"

"Maybe," Eliliweth said. "But legend has it that the city's first Grand Bishop, a man named Paul Crossmon, was guided southward by Kaijaras himself. Some think Crossmon was just suffering from severe dehydration, but nobody knows for sure. More importantly, it isn't a disputed point in Kaijar Keep, and so the land will forever be sacred to them."

"Which of your warriors get to ride them?" Cadohaden asked, the excitement clearly heard in his voice.

"They're not used for combat," Eliliweth answered quickly. "It's part of our agreement with Kaijar Keep. They're fierce beasts, but vulnerable to a volley of arrows. If they don't have enough to breed, they no longer have anything to offer us. They're sometimes used to deliver goods, but they're most often ridden by ambassadors on assignment. Bartholomew has ridden them on a handful of occasions."

"Oh," Cadohaden said, his voice dampened with disappointment. "So maybe the Crusader wasn't just a gift of well-wishes after all?"

"Perhaps not," Eliliweth said with a small smile and a 'you-got-it' nod. "His arrival really was a greater gesture than we anticipated from them, but I don't think it's unfair to say that there was a motive. They rely on our trade, and I'm grateful for it. For our sakes and theirs. I don't wish to see what lengths they would go to to maintain their illusion of independence."

They continued to walk in silence for a few minutes as Cadohaden contemplated all of what the half-elf had told him. He had only spent a couple days in the Glen Bailey, and already he had learned so much more of the world around him than he had known while living in Kingsbanesin. He was quickly beginning to realize how much knowledge was withheld from the proud empire's people. Was it any wonder why his grandfather had elected to become a historian?

They finally reached the Monastery, pausing in their strides to admire its exterior as they stood near the same places they had the day before with the crowd of onlookers gathered to witness the scrutiny of the outsider and his demon companion. Cadohaden wet his lips as he stared at the brass fixture on the Monastery's doors. He couldn't shake the feeling that he would somehow get scorched in the same manner as Terodar had if he ventured any further.

"Let's go," Eliliweth said, shaking Cadohaden from his stupor. Silently bracing himself as they approached the cedar doors, he released a breath of relief as he passed through them unharmed. His reprieve was fleeting, however, for as they entered the main chamber of the Monastery, he began to feel the smothering sensation of unworthiness.

What the Glen Bailey's Monastery lacked for in glistening ornaments and bright treasures displayed in the name of faith, it grandly compensated with an array of tall pewter candle holders, impeccably preserved paintings, and polished wooden decorations. Alongside the entrance to the sanctuary, two wooden shields were fastened to the stone walls, each featuring an intricately carved depiction of the Lifegiver. On the left, it showed the holy god looming over a blazing sun horizon, the souls of countless rising from a field of battle, ascending to the heavens. On the right, Kaijaras was kneeling alongside what appeared to be the Glen Bailey's river canal, a gaggle of children surrounding the deity to stare at him with admiring gazes.

Eliliweth led him into the sanctuary, where the number of lit candles grew dramatically in comparison to the entrance room. A crimson carpet was laid out across the center of the room of worship, and on each side, meticulously crafted wooden pews sat in rows towards the center, where an altar stood with green and white cloth adornments hanging over the edges. Proud pewter pillars formed ranks on the outsides of the pews in support of the roof. A few rays of light penetrated the dusky air from above through the bell tower, illuminating the top of the altar and glistening off the ceremonial chalice that was placed near the center. Behind the altar, a statue of Kaijaras stood, chin tilted proudly upward. He carried no weapon, but nestled in his left hand was a shield. The sculptor had magnificently recreated the flowing weaves of the deity's cloak behind him, and the stone of the armor had been so carefully polished that it seemed to shine like true steel in the candlelight.

Standing before the altar was Priestess Ecila, her white robes glowing in the dim light of the Monastery's interior. A robed acolyte was also standing in the shadows with a taper candle, tending to the unlit wicks. She paid no attention to the visitors as they walked towards the altar, diligent in her sacred duties. Ecila, however, turned around to peer at them with those strange eyes that seemed to have a haunting glimmer to them in the safety of the Monastery.

"Hello, Eliliweth Heraketh. Hello, Cadohaden Ulaeron," she said in her voice of specter chimes. Cadohaden felt a shiver run down his spine. Either the priestess was acutely aware of their individual scents, or the half-elf had spoken the truth. She could identify them through their souls, visible to those peculiar blind eyes.

"Good morning, Priestess," Eliliweth answered politely. "Cadohaden is here to visit with Sir Nevic Baltwin. Is he up?"

"Everyone that tends to the Monastery is up with the sun's first light, Eliliweth," Ecila said gently. She turned her gaze upon Cadohaden, who swallowed under the scrutiny. "You still wish to pursue this, then? To join the Glen Bailey's order of paladins? It *is* an odd desire, given the company you keep."

"Priestess, I don't want to sound rude, but I already stated my case regarding Terodar before you and a good deal of strangers," Cadohaden answered. His voice was measured but firm. "I believe that I can help the demon find redemption, especially if I can learn the ways of the paladin."

Ecila's lips narrowed to a thin line, but she nodded her head before answering, "As you say. I would normally not bless such a dangerous notion, but I think Nevic's judgment in this particular case would be more...perceptive. Amalia, dear, would you fetch him for me?"

The acolyte straightened her posture and gave the priestess a quick nod followed by a soft affirmation before treading quietly into the Monastery's eastern wing. A few moments later, she reemerged with a tall, imposing figure flanking her right side.

Crusader Nevic Baltwin was almost a comical looking figure in his white cleric's robes. Complementing his height, his shoulders were broad, the curve of his muscles visible against the clothing's fabric. His wide feet looked as though they could physically crush the sandals under them into a fine powder. And as Nevic drew nearer to the altar, Cadohaden began to understand Eliliweth's jest about the glaring sunshine of the south. His skin was porcelain white, his irises a stark pink. Cadohaden had never seen an albino before, but his grandfather Iuvas had told him stories of "colorless" people that some nomadic tribes feared to be halfbreed demonic humans. He might have laughed, but there was no mistaking the nature of Nevic's stride: underneath the robes of a holy man walked a skilled soldier.

"So this is the Kingsbanesin exile I've had so many people come chatter to me about," Nevic Baltwin said in a rumbling low baritone.

"Crusader Nevic, allow me to introduce Cadohaden Ulaeron," Eliliweth said.

"I hear you brought a demon into this city," Nevic rumbled without missing a beat.

Gods, he cut right to the chase, didn't he? Cadohaden thought to himself. "I did, Sir Nevic. He is bound to my will, and I believe his soul can be redeemed. He proved his obedience yesterday by touching the brass symbol on the Monastery's door. I don't think it's an exaggeration to say that it nearly killed him."

"And yet, you did not surrender him to the many voices that called for his death," Nevic said, folding his bulky arms across his chest.

"I couldn't," Cadohaden answered with a faint frown. "I couldn't just...hand him over. He hadn't *done* anything. And nobody could say for certain whether or not his soul *was* beyond redemption."

To Cadohaden's surprise, Nevic nodded at him and offered a tight-lipped smile. "Then you displayed compassion, courage, and conviction all in one act, virtues I look for in paladin recruits. Did you show a capacity for wisdom? Perhaps not. Don't think I'm giving this demon my blessing, Ulaeron, but any coward fearing for his life would have gladly gave him over to the guillotine or the noose. If there is a place for the creature, it is in the Mage House, though I trust you understand how short of a leash he is on."

He would have felt weariness at yet another reminder of how dangerous his companion was, and even felt a pinch of indignation at Nevic's labeling of Terodar as a 'creature', but his heart had swelled with the albino crusader's praise. And so he simply nodded and offered a grim smile. "Yes, Crusader," he replied.

"Are you devoted to the Lifegiver?" Nevic asked, his pink eyes scanning him unflinchingly. "Is it your wish to bear the standard of Kaijaras alongside that of the Glen Bailey? Because if you are not, Sir Strigson Ganisalp is always recruiting for his army."

"No, Crusader, I am...I *am* devoted to the Lifegiver," Cadohaden stammered.

"You seem hesitant," Nevic challenged immediately.

"No, Crusader," Cadohaden answered quickly. "It's just that my father was one of Kingsbanesin's dragonriders, and wished for me to be a soldier. My mother, though, she was a priestess of the Lifegiver. They both died during an orcish siege on the city wall. I wish to honor both of them with the path I walk through life. I thought this would be the best way to do that."

Nevic exchanged a glance with Ecila before training his gaze on Cadohaden once more. "So, in truth, it is the memory of your mother that you are devoted to, not the Lifegiver," he said. There was no accusation in his tone, only observation.

"No," Cadohaden insisted. "My mother raised me to be a man of Kaijaras. I truly am devoted to the Lifegiver. I had spoken to Eliliweth about pursuing this before their deaths; he can speak for me on that."

Nevic glanced over at the half-elf, who only nodded in affirmation. The pale crusader's eyes turned back to Cadohaden. "How often do you pray?" he asked.

"What?" he answered with a frown.

"How often do you pray?" Nevic questioned once more, slowly. Cadohaden wet his lips, trying to think back to the last time he prayed. Was it the night of his parents' deaths, curled up under the cedar trees in the border swamp? Before that?

"Once a week, mostly," Cadohaden admitted, feeling a flush creep into his skin. He knew that wasn't as often as Nevic was expecting. The pale man stared at him in silence for a moment, his expression unreadable. Finally, he said,

"Your honesty is appreciated. Yet another virtue I seek among recruits. But I'm not impressed with your devotion, Ulaeron. If I am to take you on as a student of the Monastery, as a warrior of the Lifegiver, that will have to change. You should be practicing your devotions at least twice a day, if not more."

Cadohaden blinked. "Are you saying you're accepting me?" Nevic turned to glance over at Ecila once more. The priestess only stared back with her thin line of a lip, her expression impassive.

"Well, Priestess Ecila has not expressly forbidden it, so I am considering doing so," he answered. He walked up to Cadohaden, standing only a foot away. "Draw your sword," he commanded.

"Crusader?" Cadohaden asked with a frown.

"I thought your father was a warrior," Nevic said with a hint of impatience. "Did he not teach you his ways? If you wish to join the order I oversee, Ulaeron, I would advise that you stop second-guessing my every command. Draw your sword."

There was no hesitation this time. With a practiced grace, Cadohaden pulled his sword from its sheath, holding it comfortably in his palm as he stared at Nevic, awaiting further instruction. "Hold out your other hand palm-up and lay the blade across it," he ordered.

Instinctively, Cadohaden nearly asked for elaboration, but closed his teeth around his tongue before the question could leave his lips. Turning the sword over sideways, he outstretched his opposite arm and cradled the flat of the blade against his palm. Nevic waited, folding his arms across his chest. A very pregnant pause passed as the crusader watched Cadohaden. With sword in hand, the young man stood unmoving, certain that the examination was only a test of his patience.

Finally, Nevic broke his statue-like pose and closed the distance between the two. He placed both of his broad hands on Cadohaden's shoulders. His fingers had a solid grip. The crusader closed his eyes, and Cadohaden once more fought the urge to ask what exactly was happening. And then he realized that Nevic's lips were moving, a silent chant passing over them as he held his shoulders.

To Cadohaden's surprise, the blade held before him gradually began to glow with a faint golden light, starting at the center in a thin line before washing over the entire face of the steel. It bloomed brighter and brighter, a beacon among the candlelit sanctuary, illuminating Nevic's face, strained with concentration. With the added light, Cadohaden could see the faint marks of age across his visage. The defined lines beginning to perk at the corners of his lips, the faded battle scar across one translucent eyebrow, the slightest relaxation of the skin across the jaw line, all indicating an age beyond what his true time in this world actually was.

Eventually, Cadohaden's blade stopped growing brighter, the radiance diminishing like a candle flame with a glass jar placed over it. Nevic opened his eyes, glancing over the light of the sword, but his expression indicated that he had felt what he was looking for without the need to see it. "You have the ability to wield the Lifegiver's light, Ulaeron," he said. "Revealing that in you didn't come easy for me, and it won't for you, but if you're set on this, you have the capability."

"I am, Crusader," Cadohaden answered confidently. "I want to join your order."

"Very well, then," Nevic answered. The crusader looked at Eliliweth. "Stay here, Heraketh. I'll have a use for you soon. Cadohaden, come with me. I have need of my armor." Cadohaden frowned, but this time, restrained himself from asking any questions. Nevic saw his curiosity, however, and rewarded his silence with an explanation. "You don't just join the paladin order and become a knight, Ulaeron. Do you have a squire's humility? Come along, now."

Nevic's quarters were only a door down in the eastern wing of the Monastery. The room had a surprising scent of dried rose petals, and as Cadohaden observed his surroundings, he saw the flowers suspended from the ceiling in the left-hand corner. His assistance in buckling on the formed leather armor turned out to be more of a formality than an actual need, as the crusader equipped most of it as effortlessly as he had surely done for the cleric robes earlier that day. With a no-nonsense impatience, the crusader instructed Cadohaden in the buckling of the straps that held the shoulderguards in place, as well as the bindings above the waist that fastened the molded breastplate. Cadohaden admired the iron studs embedded in the leather. Someone had given this piece added attention during its creation. When they were finished attending to Nevic's armor, the pale crusader lifted a two-handed broadsword from a weapon rack hanging near the door frame. There was also a strangely cut white cloth hanging from an adjacent peg. Nevic grabbed it between his fingertips and tucked it under the collar of his breastplate before leading Cadohaden back out into the hall.

The crusader didn't stop for any more formalities as they emerged once more into the sanctuary. He only gave Ecila another nod, the priestess responding with a stiff tilt of her head. Nevic beckoned Eliliweth, who was still standing patiently near the edge of a pew. "Let's go," the crusader commanded.

"Where are we headed?" Cadohaden asked as they followed the hulk of a man down the crimson carpet. He felt more assured in asking a question that didn't directly challenge an order.

"It takes more than just an ability to wield the Lifegiver's gift to become a paladin, Ulaeron," Nevic explained as they walked out through the front doors of the Monastery, into the late morning sunshine of the Glen Bailey's streets. "Most of our acolytes are capable of that. Us paladins, we wield sword and shield in harmony with our faith. We will see how well your father trained you in the art of combat." With that, the crusader pulled the cut cloth from his breastplate and pulled it across his face, covering everything save for two thin openings across the eyes. It was a mask to cover his face from the sunlight, Cadohaden realized. Nevic reached his arms back and pulled an attached hood from his undershirt out from behind the leather armor, draping it over his head. It made him seem like some sort of bizarre muscular ghost.

Cadohaden felt a stir of excitement in his chest as he once again began a trek across the city. Finally, he could showcase his talents in a manner he felt comfortable with. The entirety of what Deltore had prepared him for in life was a matter of debate, but one thing was certain: he had shown him the ways of the warrior.

The Solstice celebrations were still happening across the city, even the day after, though most of the revelers that were out in the streets that morning were moving slowly, their minds hazy from the festivities of the day before. Every gaze that fell upon the three of them, however, incited a murmur of excited whispers. Cadohaden heard all varieties of gossip fragments, from the Trials to demons to Nevic's own name. Word had seemingly spread quickly about this outsider's appointment with the crusader.

They neared the keep, but instead of approaching it, Nevic steered them southward before guiding them down a westward street. Cadohaden looked up to see a garrison within the walls, reinforced pole fencing surrounding the entrance. Around fifty yards alongside the perimeter, he spotted another garrison-like structure posted inside the grounds. It was undoubtedly a soldier's barracks. He glanced to his right, scanning the fence perimeter and saw a near identical structure, only a bit taller. The latter had flags with the Glen Bailey sigil stitched across them, flaring triumphantly in the gentle morning breeze. Atop the garrison, a guard looked down at the incoming visitors. Recognizing Nevic, he lifted a gauntleted hand and called out orders to the men below on the opposite side of the oak doors. With a creak, they opened to admit the three inside. They passed through the garrison to the other side, exiting another door to find themselves in the soldiers' training grounds.

Cadohaden squinted against the sun as his eyes peered across the open grounds. On the opposite end of the enclosed training fields, nestled against the city wall, was a well-maintained stable, though only three horses were in their pens at that moment. Pressing the tip of his tongue against the inside of his cheek, Cadohaden studied the recruits that were training on the wooden dummies, clacking their replica weapons against the limbs and hoisting their shields in rhythmic defensive positions. At the far northwest corner of the grounds, he could see a thin oval-shaped rut where cavalrymen had practiced their jousting. Two men were atop saddled horses presently, though their training movements were slow and calculated, clearly at work on their form rather than agility.

On the opposite corner, next to the southern barracks and behind the wooden training dummies, Cadohaden spotted an alignment of archery butts, and immediately recognized Elune standing at a mark several paces away, peppering her targets with impressive precision. He'd always heard about the astonishing accuracy of elvenkind. It didn't look like a myth to him. He cleared his throat and shifted his weight from one foot to the other. He wasn't sure whether or not he wanted her to notice his arrival. The thought of both outcomes gave him a lingering knot of dread in his stomach. He couldn't afford to be distracted right now, but a part of him wanted her to see him display the skills Deltore had taught him. Would she be impressed? Indifferent? *Get it together, you fool,* he thought to himself in irritation.

"There aren't as many soldiers here as I thought there would be," Cadohaden remarked. There couldn't have been more than fifty men across the field.

"These are the newest recruits," a commanding voice said from Cadohaden's left, taking him by surprise. He turned to look in the direction of the outspoken voice and immediately recognized him. With short-cropped chestnut hair, a face full of trimmed stubble, and the armor with a horse's head emblazoned across the heart on the breastplate, there was no mistaking the Glen Bailey's general, Sir Strigson Ganisalp. He continued, "Some of our others are out with the lieutenants for field training. Others are filling in the gaps in our guard schedules. But most of them are out in the Glen Dale, patrolling our roads and safeguarding our farms and villages, using Arden's Watch as a headquarters. No other kingdom in the Aariad grants more protection to the common folk living outside its walls than the Glen Bailey. That's what makes us the greatest kingdom in all the land, Cadohaden of Kingsbanesin. We preserve both the goods that keep our economy alive and the loyalty of our people. Our structures may not be as dazzling. Our nobles may not wander the streets with shimmering gems reflecting off every inch of their doughy bodies. But make no mistake, we are the strongest kingdom in all the land."

"Well said, Sir Ganisalp," Nevic said with a proud air of approval, and Eliliweth murmured his agreement with a beaming smile.

"If all of your men are patrolling the countryside, though, doesn't that leave your city exposed?" Cadohaden asked curiously. The recruits at the training dummies were beginning to take notice of the visitors. A warning glare from Ganisalp reasserted their discipline, however, and sent them back to their routines.

"Every detachment, from the proudest legion to the smallest scouting troop, has a bullhorn on at least one of the soldiers," Ganisalp boasted as he looked back at Cadohaden. "We've devised patrols in such a way that if one of these bullhorns is sounded, another patrol is sure to hear them. Each soldier is taught a signal code that will help others determine where they need to move in order to assemble defenses. This goes for all sides of the compass. If they spy a dangerous enough threat to warrant a call to arms in the Glen Bailey, there is an alarm for that as well. If that is sounded, our soldiers will begin evacuating the farms and villages and rally here at home. That's a last resort. Our goal is always to defend the land from being pillaged, and our soldiers are not afraid to meet the enemy on the open field."

"I've never heard of such a tactic," Cadohaden admitted. He wasn't sure what response the general was seeking, and so he decided to keep his answers simple for the moment.

"The swamp kingdom of York uses it," Ganisalp answered. "As do the elves of both the Sherinalu and Ashtalath, to a point. Eastfen has a similar strategy, though they're more quick to scurry back behind their Titan's Wall for protection. I hear they have one hell of a food hoard hidden under their keep."

"Cadohaden, this is Sir Strigson Ganisalp, General of the Glen Bailey," Nevic said. "If you join the order of our paladins, you'll typically answer to the Monastery's leadership, but in a combat situation, his word is as good as law."

"Good to meet you, Sir Ganisalp," Cadohaden said.

"I wouldn't make that claim too hastily," Ganisalp said with a hard smile. "Paladins are required to report to training duty here, just like the other soldiers, and nobody leaves here with soft hands. But I think Nevic here is interested in seeing whether or not we can skip your puke phase."

"Puke phase?" Cadohaden asked with a bewildered frown.

"You've never heard that term before?" Ganisalp said with a dubious squint. "It's what we call the first few weeks of training for raw recruits. Before we even bother with lessons on weapons and armor, we put them through workouts like they're the Destroyer's own army of chore donkeys. Then, after they've all spilled their stomachs onto the soil a few times, we put wooden swords in their hand. Do we need to do that with you, Kingsbanesin?" The empire-derived nickname rolled off the general's tongue like residue from a bitter herb.

"I'm not soft, sir," Cadohaden said confidently, straightening his spine as he saw Elune making her way across the training field. Ganisalp noticed his averted gaze, following it to the approaching elf. He looked back at Cadohaden and snorted quietly through his nostrils.

"Drevor!" the general called out. A young man overseeing the recruits at the wooden dummies turned around at the call before jogging over, approaching just as Elune came to a stop outside the circle, a curious look on her face. The man called Drevor was just as muscular as Nevic, with a mop of dark brown hair and a chin that was too round to match his fit form. He was wearing battered practice armor, not an inch across it that wasn't marred by a dent or scratch.

"Sir Ganisalp?" Drevor asked with a crisp salute.

"Cadohaden, Drevor Angson here is one of Nevic's most promising paladins. You'd do well to follow his example," Ganisalp boasted, glancing at the crusader, who nodded his own confirmation to the general's statement. "Drevor, grab some practice swords. The blunted ones."

"At once, sir!" Drevor said before hurrying away to the barrel sitting next to the herd of wooden dummies. He came back with two single-handed blades, their edges broad and dull for the purpose of training. The paladin marched up to Cadohaden, handing one of them over. He took a step back as Cadohaden accepted and adjusted his grip on the hilt of the other, bending his knees in a combat-ready position.

"Give the other to Eliliweth, Drevor," Ganisalp commanded. Both Drevor and Cadohaden looked up at the general in surprise. Cadohaden swiveled his head over to peer at the half-elf, who was nodding his head slowly, as though he had expected this. A mild pout crossed Drevor's face, but he obediently walked over to Eliliweth and handed him the blunted blade.

"Give him hell, Mad Rabbit," Drevor said to the half-elf. Eliliweth responded with a tight smile of familiarity as Cadohaden looked between the two in confusion. He hadn't heard anyone else call the half-elf by 'Mad Rabbit'. Had Eliliweth served in the army as well?

"Show us your Kingsbanesin prowess, Ulaeron," Ganisalp ordered, folding his arms across his breastplate. "Begin."

The cue was all he needed. The adrenaline of battle bloomed in Cadohaden's chest, giving him the odd sensation inside the elbows that seemed to waver between tense strength and tingling weakness. He feigned a lunge forward at Eliliweth, gauging the half-elf's reaction. He was calm and collected in response, positioning his feet shoulder-length apart and turning his body sideways, narrowing the target.

They strafed in a slow circle for the first moment, getting a feel for the other's poise. Cadohaden searched the half-elf's gaze for a hint at his next move, but Eliliweth's eyes betrayed nothing of his plan. Whether or not he had served in the Glen Bailey's army, he was no greenhorn soldier. They stepped in to each other, trading quick blows, each parried with the other's blade, the sounds ringing across the training field.

Finally, Cadohaden broke the stalemate. He pressed in aggressively, churning his arms in a furious series of swings. The half-elf parried each, but his posture began to shrink as Cadohaden started to overpower him. The rush of triumph swelled in his chest and he moved in, aiming a jab at Eliliweth's abdomen.

Suddenly, the half-elf reversed his momentum, digging in with his heels and launching himself forward. Before Cadohaden could reposition the angle of his strike, Eliliweth drove his shoulder into his solar plexus, driving the air from his lungs as he toppled backward. He landed on his buttocks in the grass, nearly losing the grip on his sword's hilt. Eliliweth charged forward for a finishing blow, but Cadohaden reasserted his grip and blocked the downward jab with a cross-parry, pushing the tip away wide of his left shoulder. He curled up onto his back, lifted his legs, and planted his feet against the half-elf's stomach. With a grunt and a heave, he kicked his legs outward, shoving Eliliweth back to the grass in the same fashion he had barreled Cadohaden over.

They both scrambled to their feet, chests heaving with adrenaline and exertion. Distantly, Cadohaden could hear a few clapping hands around them, but he kept his focus trained on Eliliweth. Suddenly, Ganisalp's voice called out from behind him. "We got ourselves a couple of scrappers, then! Someone grab a pair of boards. I want this to get physical."

They stared each other down as Drevor rushed to grab shields, returning to them hastily and handing each of the sparrers a barrier with faded and chipped paint that had most likely bore the colors of the Glen Bailey in their earlier days. They each tucked the handle into their grasps and the strap over their forearms before encroaching on one another again, bodies crouched into combat stances.

It was as before: they circled each other for a few moments, searching for a betrayal of movement. When neither would yield a tell, Cadohaden pressed in, jabbing forward with his shield arm, bashing it against Eliliweth's. With twin grunts, they pushed their weight against each other, and Cadohaden felt a faint release in the pressure as the half-elf tried to swipe his blade underneath the blockades at his opponent's knees. With a hiss of air exhaling between his teeth, Cadohaden arced his sword underneath as well, colliding it with Eliliweth's, stopping it just short of his outer thigh.

He felt his chest begin to burn as he dragged in staggered breaths, locked in position with both shield and sword, a fierce growl escaping the half-elf as he pushed back. Finally, Cadohaden drew in a bracing breath and gathered his strength, surging forward as he marched Eli-liweth backwards, breaking their shield hold at the center. He swung with the blade once, twice, three times against the half-elf's blockade, the dull edge barking against its face. He swiped once with the edge of his shield, clipping it across Eliliweth's, and brought his sword down once more in a strong arc.

Suddenly, Eliliweth crouched down, nearly lowering himself to a knee as he lifted his shield up to his eye level. Surprised, Cadohaden stutter-stepped, his balance wavering as the half-elf rushed forward, the center of his shield colliding with Cadohaden's upper abdomen. He felt his diaphragm cramp once more with the impact, and suddenly Eliliweth was driving him backwards. His feet abruptly left the ground and before he knew what was happening, he was sprawled on his back, his sword loosened from his grip. He grunted as he simultaneously tried to draw air back into his lungs and get to his feet, but a blunted steel point was resting against his throat as Eliliweth stood over him, shoulders rising and falling with every heavy breath. Cadohaden pursed his lips and punched his shield against the ground below him in frustration. Every move he'd made suddenly began replaying in his head, his mind already pointing out every imperfection in his memory.

"At ease, Eliliweth," Ganisalp said, his hands still clapping together, as were those of a few other soldiers that had gathered to watch the spectacle. "Not bad, Ulaeron. But you're not in warrior shape yet. You got tired halfway through, and that's when you started getting reckless, hoping you could finish it off quickly."

Eliliweth dropped the blunted sword to the ground and offered his hand. The sting of the loss was still sharp, but Cadohaden accepted the gesture and allowed the half-elf to hoist him back to his feet. As his breath returned to normal, he swiped a lock of hair out of his face with his forearm. He turned his gaze to the gathered onlookers, scanning the faces of Ganisalp, Nevic, Elune, Drevor, and the other assorted soldiers that were still strangers to him.

"It's your call, Baltwin," the general said, eyes still summarizing the potential recruit. "He's better than most of the fresh meat that get dumped in here. Still softer than he admits, but I could change that."

Cadohaden knew he was in no position to argue the general's claim. He wouldn't have been even if he had beaten Eliliweth in combat. He turned his gaze to the masked cleric in leather armor with a hopeful expression, trying to read the man's thoughts behind the slit holes in the white material.

"It is not a leisurely path, Ulaeron," Nevic warned. "Most of your days will be divided between the Monastery and the training field. And I should tell you now that as a servant of the Monastery, your duties go beyond the sanctuary. You will be expected to give your time and energy to the common folk of the Glen Bailey. The Lifegiver watches over his children, and we must be the vessels that make it so."

"I understand, Crusader," Cadohaden said, his breath finally returning to normal. "This is what I want."

"As you wish," Nevic answered. "Come with me, then, to the Monastery. Your training will begin today. I hope you weren't expecting a grand induction ceremony; there are no such accolades for my paladin recruits. And Eliliweth, thank you for your assistance. That was the challenge I needed to see."

"Of course, Crusader," Eliliweth answered. Cadohaden stared at the half-elf, still flabbergasted by his performance. Eliliweth turned and gave him a humble smile. "When you are finished for the day, Cadohaden, you should seek Elune and I out at the keep. I still have that promise to fulfill."

The Gohandian mead, Cadohaden remembered. He glanced over quickly at Elune, who mirrored Eliliweth's smile in his direction. There was no haughty judgment in her eyes over his loss to her friend. He didn't know why he'd feared the idea. It seemed ridiculous now that everything had settled down.

"Come along, then," Nevic said, gesturing for his newest recruit to follow him. Cadohaden handed off his practice sword and shield to Drevor, who gave him a quick wink as he accepted them. Sir Ganisalp called out to him as he followed Nevic out of the training grounds,

"See you tomorrow, Ulaeron. Be ready."

Chapter Fourteen

As the sun began to set, the citizens of the Glen Bailey began to numb their hangovers with the same method that had brought them about: the ale flowed freely from the kegs, wine sloshed over the rims of goblets, and mead was passed around circles of laughing revelers. Nobody was sure if they were celebrating the Solstice or the announcement of Eliliweth's Trials. All they knew was that they were still celebrating.

It made it easy for a cloaked princess to slip through the crowds without detection. She simply carried a wooden mug in her hand and walked with the slightest stagger, lifting her drink in cheers to the inebriated folks who saluted her with thick speech and lazy smiles.

The further she strayed into the city, the heavier her heart grew. All night and all day, she had wrestled with Archibaum's warning against going to her father. She didn't doubt that Bartholomew would arrest the magistrates immediately. What she wasn't so certain of was Bertram's assurance that without being caught in the act, the arrests would breed chaos and riots bordering on civil war. How sure could Archibaum be that her father was in no danger for the moment? Did he have that much control over the other nobles, or was it all a fearful bluff? For all she knew, the man was just scared witless over being discovered by either side of the conspiracy. If her father's life was in danger, then she was doubtlessly committing treason by withholding information.

Aven tried her best to put her concerns to the back of her mind as she began to vanish from the light of the many torches and bonfires littering the market square, casting shadows on the buildings around them as the merrymaking carried on around them. Mug still in hand, she ventured deeper into the shadows of Hennessen Alley. The cobblestone ended and turned to gravel as she made her way towards the Ogre Pint Tavern.

"'Ey, you," a disjointed grunt came from between two buildings, a shadow shuffling towards her with a drunken stagger. "Ya got some coin to buy me a drink? I'm starrin' to sober up an' I don' like it much." The inebriated man stumbled up to her with a leer. She could smell the brew on his breath.

"Can't help you," she said quietly as she tried to veer around him.

"Bullshet, ya can't," the stranger grunted as he got in close enough to press his chest brutishly against her shoulder. "Wait...wait...yer a woman, aren't ya? A'rright, why don't ya jus-"

Whispering the spell under her breath, Aven stepped into the drunk, her slender fingers clasping around his throat. "*Sanu,*" she murmured, and the man's body twitched and jittered as electrical current flowed from the tips of her fingertips over his neck. At a loss for breath, the stranger collapsed to the gravel with silent croaking gasps, clutching at his throat, his body still twitching from the shock.

"You accost me or any other woman in this city ever again, thug, you won't survive to try it a third time," the princess warned, keeping her voice low and muffled but harsh with conviction. The man couldn't answer, still clasping at his throat as he laid on the ground. Aven wasted no more time with him, marching onward towards her destination. She wasn't worried what he might say if he had recognized her. She was fairly certain he wouldn't remember their encounter the next day, and even if he did, nobody would believe his tale after seeing the evidence on his face of his drinking the night before.

She strode down the alley without any further interruption, her feet carrying her to the roofed porch of the Ogre Pint Tavern. The structure looked more like many of the homes within the city than it did a pub, but it had a reputation as being one of the more rowdy establishments in the southern half of the Glen Bailey, so much that the king had decreed a year before that during the evening hours, two city guards be present inside to supervise the debauchery. She had checked the guard's schedule before leaving, however, to be sure that tonight would be an exception, given that most of the Pint's clientele were roaming the streets quaffing imported dwarven ale. Her suspicions had been correct. There wouldn't be any guards here to question the motives of either her or Lord Archibaum.

Her brow knit in a faint frown as she approached the door. The Tavern's most recognized icon hung suspended from a chain latched to the top of the porch roof. It was a bleached ogre skull, the upper cranium sawed off. An iron handle was hooked at the sheared top and under one side of the jaw, giving it the look of a macabre tavern mug. It was a barbaric ornament, but all complaints requesting to have it removed had been deflected by Bartholomew, who secretly found the hanging mug amusing. Aven shook her head and walked through the tavern's door, closing it quietly behind her as she entered.

The entrance opened up to a large dining hall, with tables and chairs aligned in rows in front of a bar that stood in the back. Two more ogre skulls were seated on opposite sides of the bottle rack behind the server, and on each side of the tavern, a staircase led up to an inner balcony that hugged the walls on each side, wide enough for tables to be placed with an aisle along the edge for a waitress to walk through. The soft, pulsating glow of the candles placed on the tables could be seen from the lower level, but not much else. Aven spotted a shadowy figure hunched over one of the tables on the loft level. She had no doubt that it was Bertram Archibaum. She turned her hooded gaze back to the dining hall in front of her, looking for patrons. The magistrate was right. Most of the riffraff that congregated here were out in the city streets. Only one stranger was seated at a table on the lower level, a thin elderly man with a drooping face and a head that was almost bald save for a dozen or so hairs sticking almost straight up from his scalp. His eyes were lost and glazed as he held his mug apathetically in his hands. She wouldn't have to worry about him eavesdropping. He was clearly only here to drown his own sorrows.

She gave the hood of her cloak a quick tug further over her face and walked across the room to the other end, where the barkeep tapped his fingertips against the counter impatiently. He was clearly in a sour mood, likely from all of his lost business due to the Solstice celebrations. "What can I getcha," he said flatly, staring at her with eyes reddened from weariness and a drinking habit. The evidence of broken capillaries could be seen in his face from the faint crimson blotches on his cheeks.

Aven didn't use her voice. She couldn't afford to have the barkeep recognize it, but she needed to buy a drink to avoid getting hassled or being asked to leave. Silently, she pointed a finger at a clear bottle of hazy golden ale and set her mug down on the counter. The barkeep lifted her selection from the rack. She could see stark fingerprints over the collected dust on the glass as he turned it over, filling up her offered mug. "Five silvers," he grunted. It was an expensive price for an ale she guessed had been hastily brewed with half the necessary ingredients, but she wasn't here to sample fine drink. She laid an entire gold coin on the counter with a meaningful nod. The barkeep didn't have to ask what the generous tip was for. Whatever she was here for, he was to keep his nose out of her business. He picked it up, examined it, and then nodded as well, pocketing the coin before deliberately turning away from her, busying himself with rearranging the bottles on the rack.

Taking the filled mug, Aven walked back to the staircase right of the entrance door, rounding the corner as she began to ascend to the balcony level. She glanced over once at the drunken old man sitting at the table, but his sorrowful gaze hadn't drifted at all. Satisfied, she hastened her stride a bit, stepping onto the upper balcony and moving through the shadows towards the dimly lit table. The hooded Archibaum was waiting, a wine glass with smears from a dirty rag sitting in front of him, two inches of a white wine sitting inside. *By the gods, Bertram, could you make yourself look more conspicuous? Nobody comes here to enjoy wine,* she thought as she shook her head. She settled down into the chair across from the magistrate, lifting her mug into the depths of her hood as she sipped at the ale. It tasted like brewed cabbage. Patrons came here for the atmosphere, not the quality of the drinks.

"Were you followed?" Archibaum's voice said in a low, nervous mumble from across the table.

"I wouldn't have entered if I was," Aven answered as she set her mug back down.

"Of course, of course," Archibaum murmured, tapping his fingertips lightly against the side of his glass. His other hand reached into his cloak, procuring his bottle of plantain extract and pulling off the cork. He tapped a few drops onto his tongue before capping it again, his eyes darting back and forth nervously as he slid the miniature bottle back into his cloak.

"Calm down. You'll draw attention to yourself," the princess warned despite the abundant vacancy in the tavern. "Let's get down to business. My father is in danger, and you're aware of the plot against him. What is to happen, and how soon?"

"Not so...not so fast," Archibaum murmured. Aven could hear the man grappling for his courage. She hadn't expected him to be so fretful. The Ogre Pint was not a glamorous establishment, but there were worse in the Glen Bailey, even during the busy evenings. "If I am to tell you everything, I need the promise of immunity. I don't want to go to the dreaded dungeons, Your Grace."

"If you yourself have not directly endangered the king, then I can see to it that you come out of this a free man, Bertram. Your innocence depends on what actions you've taken, and whether or not you tell me the truth this night," Aven said lowly.

"I have plotted, I have schemed, but I haven't shaken any hands, Your Grace," Archibaum answered, wringing his own hands as though he might wash the proverbial blood from them. "The contracts were written and signed mostly by Carson, though Tibault has moved most of the gold. I have only listened, nodded my head, and spoken when the time seemed appropriate. It's a delicate matter, Your Grace. I couldn't seem hesitant."

"Contracts? Gold?" Aven hissed, drawing a panicked *sh sh sh!* from Archibaum, whose hooded head swiveled over to look down to the lower level. The drunk hadn't moved a bit, and the barkeep was lazily swabbing a cloth around the counter. The princess shook her head impatiently and glared at the magistrate. "You speak of assassins, don't you?"

"Yes...I..well, in a way," Archibaum stammered, drumming his fingertips together quickly before lifting his wine glass, draining the remainder of whatever qualified as wine in the Ogre Pint down his throat. "At first, we planned to use...conventional methods. We hired some men that claimed to be from the Hand of Draqin. Our plan was to move them into the city, enlist them in the army, and bribe, trick, or threaten the right men to promote them into positions that would be close enough to Bartholomew to finish the job."

"Are they in the kingdom now?" Aven asked in murmured alarm.

"No, no," the magistrate answered. "They never made it. Their bodies were found near a Stone Circle in the northern Glen Dale, Your Grace. I'm not even quite certain they were true members of the

Hand. But either way, we were hesitant to approach anyone else for fear that we may be blamed for putting them in an unfamiliar situation, whatever that was. So we considered a...an alternative measure," Archibaum said softly, letting his voice trail off.

"We don't have time for your cryptic nonsense, Bertram, what alternative measure?" Aven pressed.

"Orcs, Your Grace," Archibaum whispered, his head swiveling once more to look for eavesdroppers below. Seeing none, he looked back at the stricken face of the princess. "The Kingsbanesin boy spoke the truth. Someone hired a clan of orcs from the Hordelands to assault the empire's wall. The brutes confirmed it to us when we, ah...conferenced with them. They offered to do the same, if we would only ensure that they had a quick route to the king."

"You..." was all the princess could hiss for a moment as she restrained the anger threatening to loosen her tongue into a fit of furious screaming. "You conspired to have *orcs* invade my kingdom and murder the king?"

"Not...not invade, Your Grace," Archibaum whispered swiftly, his voice catching nervously as Aven's fingernails dug into the surface of the table. "Infiltrate. They were told to limit the casualties, if at all possible, that Bartholomew was the only desired target, I-"

"You are *not* doing yourself any favors, Bertram," Aven growled, her jaw set as her nails scratched lines into the table. "How could you? How could you be so damned spineless, so bottom-feeding desperate that you would hire Hordeland brutes to murder your king, at the risk of so many lives? Are you magistrates all empty-headed fools? Do you really think the orcs would take any care whatsoever to spare anyone's lives? And what would you do if they decided not to heed your preferences, Bertram? *Arrest them?* Tell me, Lord Archibaum, do you have a *single* honorable bone in your body, or are your muscles held together with a collection of twigs and tree sap!?"

"*Your Grace,*" Archibaum murmured frantically as he once again looked around for eavesdroppers. Frazzled, he looked back at the princess. She saw his lower lip trembling and realized that he was on the verge of tears. He pleaded, "I did not...I did not get to where I am today by being courageous, Your Grace. My talents lie in smart investments and coy words. *I am not a brave man.* When the other lords began to whisper of these plans, I...I didn't know what to do, Your Grace. I didn't want them to kill me out of fear. *I* was afraid, Your Grace. I still am. That is why I confronted you outside of the bathing room. That is why I invited you here. I'm not proud of my behavior, Your Grace, but I want to make it right. Please. Please help me."

"You want to make it right, but be spared the punishment of imprisonment," Aven scoffed. "I'll tell you how that will happen, Archibaum. You will come with me to the royal court and confess this treason to His Majesty. The Glen Bailey is in greater danger than I thought."

"No!" Archibaum squeaked, lifting his hands and waving them back and forth in protest. "Your Grace! They have a scheme already in place in the event that they are discovered. By the gods, they almost set it in motion when you discovered our meeting!"

"Speak of it," Aven hissed through her teeth threateningly, already half out of her chair, "and quickly." Archibaum nodded hurriedly, his hands twitching like he was searching for hidden notes on the table.

"Over the past few months, each of us magistrates have, ah... skimmed a bit of pay for all of the tradesmen that work for us. Small amounts, but enough to make a significant sum over a period of time. During that time, we forged communications between the king and the half-elf, detailing plans of a frivolous tax that would fatten their pockets. If the artisans were to discover the documents, the numbers in the taxes would match their total earnings. The documents are hidden in a stack of business correspondence, designed to appear as though they had accidentally fallen into the mix.

"Should the original plan be discovered, a few whispers in the right ears will put these documents into the hands of the artisans. With the right words spoken by the magistrates when these are uncovered, there will be enough outrage from every cobbler, carpenter, and blacksmith under our employment to incite a riot chaotic enough to require the Glen Bailey army. And when the army is distracted, we anticipate there will be an opportunity to end Bartholomew's life even with our own hands. The act could easily be blamed on an angry rioter lucky enough to make his way to the king.

"They don't want to take that course of action, Your Grace, because they want to assume control over the kingdom with as little cleanup as possible. Our artisans make us a healthy sum of coin; we don't want to see them dead. But I had to do a great deal of convincing to keep them from setting it in motion after you came upon us in the stove room, Your Grace. Do you see why this is a delicate matter? If you accuse the magistrates of hiring orcish assassins after they present evidence of the crown pilfering their coin, it will look like a claim of desperation, not of vindication."

"We wouldn't need to resort to exposing the assassination plot," Aven retorted indignantly.

"Are you so sure, Your Grace?" Archibaum asked. "The mind of a slighted laborer doesn't often follow a clear path of logic. Can you afford such a risk, gambling against the chances of a full-scale riot?"

"And what else are we to do, Bertram?" the princess asked impatiently, her voice rising once more. "Wait for the orcs to arrive and act surprised when they disappear into the shadows with my father laying in a pool of his own blood?"

"No, Your Grace," Archibaum answered as he wrung his hands once more. "We only have to catch them in the act. Leave no question for the common folk as to what they were up to."

"I'm not waiting for the orcs to show up at our walls just to show proof of their treason," Aven snipped. "We'll put our soldiers' lives at risk for nothing."

"We don't have to wait for the orcs, Your Grace. The day the savages are to infiltrate our walls, the magistrates have a messenger prepared to fly out on gryphonback to signal the greenskins to advance. He's an opportunistic, coin-grubbing dwarf, here from Dur'Imoir for the Solstice celebrations. Question him now, and he'll deny it all, but if we can catch them in their rendezvous at the aviary, I promise you, he'll sing like a trained canary. We need only wait for the meeting to take place. I will be alerted the day before. Plenty of time for you to organize a sting, Your Grace."

"How long before they act?" she pressed.

"They wish to wait for the half-elf's Trials," Archibaum conceded. "They believe the most lively celebrations will be held during that time, and they can proceed with their plan without Eliliweth's watchful eyes upon them. They hope the people will be too damned drunk to even realize what has happened before it is too late."

Aven stared hard at the magistrate across the table from her, her mouth pursed into a thin line. She could feel the anger throbbing at her temples. She wouldn't have known about this plot were it not for Lord Archibaum, but she couldn't help wanting to choke the man for allowing this treason to continue. Bertram's eyes danced away from her stare, his gaze averting to the shadows under the intense scrutiny. His lower lip was beginning to tremble again. If she hadn't been so bloated with rage, she would have pitied him. How could a man with such standing, wealth, and esteem lower himself to such a feeble showing?

"You keep a watchful eye on your fellow magistrates, Bertram," she said with a growl of severity. "And you keep me informed of every hair that's out of place on their sweaty scalps. You play your part well and keep the situation under control, because if I get the faintest idea that things are getting out of hand, I will have those jesters arrested, riot schemes or not. Let me assure you that your freedom *and* your survival hinge on the well-being of the Glen Bailey's people. You will answer for any bloodshed with days in the dungeon for every drop, or perhaps even your own head. Have I made myself abundantly clear, Lord Archibaum?"

The magistrate's face had paled with every spoken word, but he nodded in understanding, mumbling a soft, "Yes, Your Grace."

"Good. Then I will hear from you soon, I expect," the princess said, and finally, she hoisted herself up, sliding her chair under the table with a vindictive wooden screech under the legs. Grabbing her mug, still mostly full with the unpleasant ale, she gave her hood a quick tug over her face as she stalked down the stairs to the lower level. She didn't bother to look at the drunk or the barkeep as she stormed out of the door.

Anger surged through her as she closed the Ogre Pint's front door behind her. Scathingly, she glared at the skull ornament hanging from the porch roof and splashed the entirety of her ale all over the bone trophy. Shaking every last drop from the vessel, she walked into the darkness of night once more, her knuckles white on the handle of her mug.

How had this come to be? In years past, her father had been meticulously cautious about choosing his appointed council. Had he grown complacent? Apathetic? Or had their promises of returned investments swayed him into turning a blind eye to their corruption? Could she contain herself long enough to see Archibaum's plan through? She knew that part of the game of politics was a mastery of utmost patience, but she despised it. This wasn't just politics. This was the safety of the people she would one day rule over. How could she look at the serpents that were threatening that safety with anything but eyes filled with fury? How far could she take this before she was no better than that worm Bertram?

However she proceeded, she had to do it with care. She didn't doubt the sincerity of Archibaum's warnings regarding the forged documents. The magistrates had risen to power chiefly by the skill of persuasion. Whatever scheme they had concocted for their laborers, she was sure it was nothing short of a mastery of cunning.

Subterfuge was the magistrates' game, not hers. But she was going to have to beat them at it. And she would have to do it with the strength to carry the guilt that was already weighing on her heart.

Chapter Fifteen

The sun was long gone from the horizon as Cadohaden returned to the keep that evening, finished with his first day of initiate duties at the Monastery. As Nevic had warned him, there were no accolades or celebrations for his induction. He had been given a thorough tour of the Glen Bailey's holy house, received some rudimentary quizzes on the Lifegiver's Codex, and consulted with Priestess Ecila, whose sightless gaze strangely seemed to rest colder on him than it did on Nevic or the various acolytes tending to the house of worship. He knew that his acceptance into the paladin order did not please the seeress. He could only hope to win her over with time.

The keep guards stared at him vigilantly as he entered the castle, but most of them recognized him as Eliliweth's honored guest by now, tilting their heads stiffly in affirmation as he wandered past, climbing the spiral staircase to the half-elf's quarters. He had shown him the way earlier that morning, before they had departed to the Mage House. Cadohaden needed only to trust his memory to bring his feet to the right location.

As he approached Eliliweth's quarters, he saw that both the half-elf and Elune were already waiting outside of the door with excited smiles. Held in one hand, Eliliweth carried a clear bottle filled with a honey-colored liquid, the hammer-and-horns sigil of Gohand etched into the glass just below the neck. The contents sloshed around the empty space below the cork as the half-elf lifted it in a cheer. "Cadohaden! We were just about to come looking for you," Eliliweth exclaimed.

"Fear not, I'm here," Cadohaden replied with a tired grin. "Where are we going?"

"Have you been on the roof of the keep before?" Elune asked.

"No," he answered. "Can we get up there?"

"With the right key, we might," Eliliweth said with a wink, and with his other hand, he lifted an iron ring that was strung to his belt, and with deft fingers, revealed a hefty looking skeleton key. "Let's go," he said eagerly as he began to lead the other two further down the hallway.

They reached the corner of the hallway, approaching a narrow wooden door with rusted hinges. Eliliweth slid the skeleton key into the lock below the handle, the mechanical series of clicks leading to a quiet creak as he pulled it open with a gentle tug.

"I thought this was only a broom closet when I saw it last," Cadohaden confessed as he peered into the musty opening.

"Well, there are brooms in there," Eliliweth said with a chuckle as he passed through the door frame. "But beyond them is another set of stairs that will bring us a better view of the night sky."

The closet was narrow, and Cadohaden managed to kick over a broom that was leaning against the wall instead of hanging on its rack. He muttered a quiet apology and righted it. Elune turned around and pointed meaningfully at the door. He closed it behind him as they moved through the narrow space. As Eliliweth had promised, a staircase awaited them at the back end of the closet, just as narrow, the stairs unpolished with a tall space between each step. Cadohaden pressed his palms against the walls as he followed Eliliweth and Elune, only to quickly withdraw them as he felt the layer of dust clinging to the wood. He wiped them off on his trousers and opted to instead trust his own balance as he trailed his two friends.

It was a dark ascension, but finally, Cadohaden heard a creak from above, and in contrast to the darkness in the staircase, the night sky poured in rays of moonlight as the door panel was lifted by the half-elf's hand. Each of them stepped out onto the roof, their eyes lifting to the starry sphere of the summer night sky. The moon was not quite full, but shone with a bright pale gibbous, illuminating the vast top level of the Glen Bailey's keep. The only points that stood higher than the roof were the turret towers on each corner, a dim glow in each of the windows from lit lanterns within, but otherwise seemed unmanned.

"No guards?" Cadohaden asked, frowning curiously at the stone sentries surrounding them.

"Not at this hour," Eliliweth answered. "Usually one rotates between each of them during the day, but at night, it's too dark to see anything below when you're so high up. They man the guard towers below on the ramparts at night, and only are assigned duties here during emergencies."

Cadohaden nodded, studying the rest of the keep's roof. There was both a weapon and archery rack sitting in the center, as well as a few empty cauldrons that were undoubtedly to be filled with hot oil if the keep ever came under siege. Beyond that, however, there was little to be seen, aside from the occasional splotches of dried bird droppings across the planking. He saw the shadows of three figures as he turned his head, however, lined up alongside the short battlement. There, a trio of wooden chairs sat, turned to face the northeast, overlooking the fields of the Glen Dale instead of the swarm of the city. Eliliweth began to lead the three of them over, pulling the cork from the bottle with a definitive *pop!*

"Looks like this isn't the first time you've all gathered up here," Cadohaden mused.

"Yes," Elune answered wistfully. "Eliliweth, Aven, and I have spent a few summer nights up here. Where is the princess?" she asked, looking pointedly at the half-elf.

"She said she couldn't come along tonight," Eliliweth said with a faint frown as he sniffed the bottom end of the cork. "She looked troubled when I asked her. Said she was just tired, though. It's not like her to disguise her irritations. I hope she hasn't grown sour over the thoughts of my Trials." His brow knit with worry as he wondered out loud.

"Aven is very happy for you, Eliliweth," Elune said kindly but firmly as the two of them settled into the chairs, the half-elf on the left, Elune in the center. Eliliweth gestured to the one on the right.

"Have a seat, Cadohaden," he said as he gave the bottle of mead a quick swirl. Cadohaden obliged, lowering himself onto the seat. It wasn't the most comfortable chair he'd ever placed himself into, but after such a long day, just being off his feet seemed like a blessing. He traced his fingers over his diaphragm, remembering where Eliliweth's shield had slammed into him earlier that day. He wondered to himself if his presence had persuaded Aven to remain absent for the night. He hoped not. He relished his newfound friendships, but he would feel perpetual guilt if he discovered that he was creating a rift between any of them.

"Guest drinks first," Eliliweth said cheerily, handing the bottle off to Elune, who passed it to Cadohaden. "Though I suppose it isn't appropriate to call you a guest anymore, if you're now officially a member of the Glen Bailey's paladin order!"

"Maybe," Cadohaden said as he accepted the bottle from Elune. "I still feel like a guest, though." He lifted the mouth of the bottle up to his nose, taking a tentative sniff. He could smell how sweet it was without even tasting it, along with the mildest hint of clover. He lifted the bottle to his own lips, tilting it back as the contents washed over his tongue and pooled down his throat. It was indeed sweet, but the strength of the alcohol balanced it into a smooth pull. He lowered the bottle, rolling the remainder of the liquid across his tongue, and handed it back over to Elune. "It's good," was all he could think to say.

"The Lakafra family in Gohand knows their drink," Eliliweth said with a chuckle. "It won't be long, Ulaeron, before you'll feel right at home. I'm glad you decided to come here. It may end up being one of the best decisions you'll make in life."

Cadohaden smiled, but otherwise remained silent, folding his hands in his lap as he stared out over the battlement wall and out into the moonlit fields of the Glen Dale. From the corner of his eye, he could see Elune take a swift, polite sip of the offered bottle before handing it over to Eliliweth. The half-elf took a heartier swig before setting the bottle down on his knee, savoring the flavor in the same way Cadohaden had. The paladin recruit glanced over to his left, studying Eliliweth for a moment before working up the courage to ask, "How'd you earn the name 'Mad Rabbit'? Or better yet, where did you learn to fight like that?"

Eliliweth took another quick sip of the Gohandian mead, handing the bottle back to Elune before answering. "You know where the Ashlands are, Ulaeron?" he asked as Elune took another diplomatic sip from the bottle before handing it off to her right.

"Yeah," Cadohaden answered as he accepted the bottle again, bringing it to his lips for another drink before elaborating. "It's along the northern border of the Glen Dale. It's where the rebel forces clashed with the Kingsbanesin empire during the earliest days of the Gunnysack Wars. Kingsbanesin won that battle, forcing the rebels into retreat, their dragons scorching the soil for distances leagues wide."

"The land never recovered," Elune interjected as the bottle was passed to her again.

"Hence, the name Ashlands," Eliliweth said with a nod. "It isn't easy to travel across, but still easier than cutting through the lands of our neighboring kingdoms, or at least it was for raiders and orcs, when the Bloodpike Clan was fighting for territory along the border. Anyway, it demanded a vigilant patrol, not only for the Glen Bailey, but for the Sherinalu Vale as well. I was part of a cooperative unit between the two kingdoms. That's how King Bartholomew caught notice of me." He took another drink of mead as he paused.

"So that's where 'Mad Rabbit' came from," Cadohaden surmised.

"Yes," Eliliweth said as he handed the bottle off again. "I'm young, Cadohaden, but I used to be younger, and I had more of a temper. I wasn't very well liked among my peers. Some of them never grew out of that resentment, as you saw when we first met. When they pushed, I'd push back. I carried that aggression into my service in the Ashlands. That's where the 'Mad' part comes from. The other is just, well... Heraketh. It starts with 'Hare'. You know what I mean."

"Oh...oh, yeah, that makes sense," Cadohaden replied, feeling a bit sheepish as he accepted the bottle again. He supposed that shouldn't have been too difficult to decipher on his own. He took another swig of the mead, noting the warm sensation beginning to bloom in his cheeks as the alcohol began to settle in. He handed it off once more, and noticed that this time, Elune passed it on to Eliliweth without taking a sip. The half-elf didn't look surprised by this, taking another drink before resting it once more on his knee. Cadohaden spoke up again, feeling a little more bold with the aid of the mead in his blood. "Maybe this is a foolish question, but was it just more - I don't know - comfortable being in a patrol of both elves and humans?"

"In some ways," Eliliweth said, rolling the mead around in the bottle lazily, his gaze out towards the open Glen Dale. "It was never the Sherinalu Vale I was uncomfortable with, though. It's a beautiful place. I feel at home there, too, in the right company. I volunteered for the Ashland campaign for a different reason."

"What reason was that?" Cadohaden asked. For a while, Eliliweth said nothing, only rotating the bottle on his knee, swirling the liquid inside. Cadohaden saw Elune fidget in her chair and suddenly feared that he'd overstepped his familiarity with the half-elf. Finally, however, Eliliweth said,

"You sought to join the paladin order to honor your late parents, right?"

"Yes," Cadohaden answered, the memories returning to him as a pang of grief squeezed at his heart. The numbing effects of the mead did not shelter him from it; rather, they made him feel all the more exposed to the anguish he'd been fighting since leaving Kingsbanesin.

"Then you'd understand if I told you that I, too, chose a path that would honor their memory," Eliliweth answered, lifting the bottle to his lips again before handing it off to Elune. She took a small sip this time before passing it to Cadohaden. The half-elf continued, "My father was from the Glen Bailey, my mother from the Sherinalu. They met in the Ashland patrol, fell in love, wed, and gave life to a half-blooded child before leaving this world."

Cadohaden took another drink from the bottle. The sweet taste of the mead was beginning to feel gritty on his teeth. He rested the bottom against his thigh and looked back over at Eliliweth, who had grown silent. "You don't have to tell me what happened if you don't wish to," he said quietly. The half-elf looked back over at him.

"I consider you a friend, Cadohaden. Do you want to know what happened to them?"

"I do," he answered honestly, handing the bottle back to Elune. Eliliweth nodded and continued with his tale,

"Before I was born, there was a summer month known as the Hell-dawn. Legends say that the stars and the world were in near-perfect alignment to provide the ideal conditions for summoning demons. Even the most novice warlock gypsies tried their hand at calling forth the Destroyer's spawn. Many failed, at great consequence, but just as many succeeded. Reports and rumors began to trickle in from all directions of the compass of demon sightings, particularly around the Ashlands, where the orcish Bloodpike Clan was known to be. Word began to spread of a demon that was issuing orders for his brethren, a thin *roaq* demon whose skin had strange color patterns. He was red-fleshed instead of pale, and the skin on his nose was black as charcoal. They called him the Cardinal.

"My parents' patrol was the first to successfully track down the Cardinal, who was leading a pack of Bloodpike orcs and a few other summoned demons. They put each of the greenskins down and fought a fierce battle with the Destroyer's spawn. Each of the demons fell, save for the one with the red skin and the black nose. The Cardinal fled to safety, and wasn't seen again by any patrols.

"Some time after, my mother discovered that she was with child. Both of my parents decided that Arden's Watch was no place to bring someone into the world. And so my father built a house for his family, on the border of the Ashlands. He said that he wanted a quiet home away from the hustle and bustle of the city or the patrols, but I suspect his pride got the best of him, that his home doubled as a personal outpost so that he could watch for the return of the Cardinal and take the demon's head."

Cadohaden listened intently, his eyes widening as the tale carried on. He watched Eliliweth swirl the mead in the bottle a little more, take a sip, and then hand it off to his right. Elune looked over at him as she offered the bottle again. Their eyes met. He couldn't discern what was behind her hazel irises. Was it sorrow, sympathy, or just an acknowledgement that he was a true friend now, sharing their secrets? He peeled his gaze away from her as he gingerly accepted the bottle and looked back at Eliliweth. "The Cardinal returned, didn't he?"

"He did," Eliliweth said with a nod, his voice low. "It was after my mother had given birth to me. I was only a baby. If my father was indeed waiting for the demon, his senses failed him that night, as the Cardinal broke down the front door. My mother heard the hellion before he entered the home, and hid me underneath the bed as my father scrambled for his sword.

"My father paid the price for his pride. He and my mother were no match for the demon. He bound her to the bed, a curse knotting her muscles and rendering her immobile as she lay helpless. The Cardinal incapacitated my father and laid him out on the kitchen table. He began a torturous ritual, mutilating him as he still lived, using dark magic to keep his soul entrenched in his body longer than it ever should have as he sliced flesh and cracked bones. It wasn't only his mouth that screamed, but his spirit as well."

"How didn't the screams wake you?" Cadohaden asked in a stricken whisper.

"My mother," Eliliweth said quietly. "Or at least, that's what I was told most likely happened. She was magically gifted, Cadohaden. As soon as the demon bound her, she began to pry apart the curses with her mind, releasing her muscles from paralysis. As she did this, she channeled a soothing spell to numb my senses and shield my ears from the horrors in our home, and to disguise my presence from the Cardinal."

"All the while watching the demon butcher your father," Cadohaden murmured, shaking his head. "That sounds awful."

"I dream of it sometimes," the half-elf answered distantly. "Though I don't think my invented memories would ever come close to the true horrors. When my father's soul finally detached itself from his body, the Cardinal began to dissect him, separating his limbs like an animal in a slaughterhouse, hanging them from the ceiling in a circular pattern. It was likely that he was trying to open a portal to Daemonaar, to send my mother to the Destroyer's world to serve as a slave.

"As the demon began the ritual, however, my mother finally released herself from her paralysis. With my father's sword on the other end of the cottage, she grabbed the closest weapon she could: his rib, laying on the floor next to the table where the Cardinal had mutilated him. She drove the fractured end into the demon's neck as he chanted his unholy incantations. It would kill the demon, but not before he attacked her in a rage, his nails shredding her skin like blades over parchment. They both bled out on the floor of the cottage, surrounded by the suspended body parts of my father."

They sat in silence for a moment as Cadohaden reflected on the horrific tale. The night sky didn't seem so peaceful anymore. The stars looked ominous, even threatening, glinting promises of the cruelty that the world was capable of. He didn't know what to say. It was Eliliweth that spoke next, however, after drawing a long breath,

"My mother dead, I soon woke up from the enchanted slumber, and began to bawl. I was fortunate enough that a patrol was passing by my parents' home the next morning, or else I might have starved, hiding underneath the bed. My parents were given a proper funeral, and the Cardinal's body was burned with the blessing of the Monastery. I was returned to the Sherinalu Vale, and placed in the care of one of my mother's closest friends: Marian, an elven elder of the Vale's council.

"Marian raised me as his own. He was also how I came to know Elune, for he was her father's brother. For many years, I didn't know what had become of my parents. When I asked, Marian would only tell me that it was a tragic accident, and that I would learn the truth when I was older. The older I grew, the more I insisted that he tell me, until finally, he could no longer bring himself to deny me. He told me every last gruesome detail.

"Marian saw my potential as a diplomat, given my mixed blood, and had spent most of my childhood teaching me how to be one. But when he told me the tale of my parents, the very next day I traveled to Arden's Watch to speak with the recruiter about patrolling the Ashlands. I would never meet them, but I had to know their travels. I thought that if I walked their path, I would somehow feel their presence."

"Did you?" Cadohaden asked when the half-elf paused.

"At first, no," Eliliweth said, reaching his hand out in a silent request for the mead. It was handed back to him, and he took another drink before continuing. "Looking back on it, I think that's where I truly earned the name 'Mad Rabbit'. I was frustrated and bitter that I couldn't even find a connection to the parents I had never met by taking up the same banner they had represented.

"And then one day, Marian visited my patrol on the back of a horse. He asked my sergeant's permission to take me on a recess for the day. Together, we rode to the Ashland's border to find the remains of an old cottage home. I had ridden past it many times before, but the home had sat where the grass still grew, and so tall vegetation and a collection of boulders had hidden it from view.

"There wasn't much to see. After determining what had happened, both the Glen Bailey and the Sherinalu looked at the cottage home with a great deal of superstition. The only solution was to burn away the wicked aura still clinging to it. And so I turned over a few charred and rotten beams before kneeling down in the waste. A wind picked up across the plain, rolling over my shoulders, and I finally felt their presence. The moment I did, something began to irritate my right knee. I lifted it out of the ash to find a rusted spoon buried underneath. It was the only keepsake I came away with that day, but it gave me some peace. Marian brought me to my parents' graves before we returned to the patrol. I had been there many times before, but it was different this time. Every time before, I felt only bitterness and resentment for their absence, towards demonkin, the gods, even my own foolish father for building that damned home so far away from anyone else, exposed and vulnerable. But with that spoon in my hand, I finally let myself feel grief for what had happened, for never knowing who they were.

"My patrol tour ended soon after that. I wasn't quite ready to return to the Sherinalu just yet. I felt as though I owed my full focus to the patrol for at least another campaign. Well...one campaign turned into another, and after that, a vacancy opened up at the captain's spot. I was given the promotion. It wasn't always easy. Cooperative efforts between men and elves don't always come without a hitch, but I found I was pretty good at keeping tensions from boiling over into anything serious. I stayed for another year and a half before I felt the urge to pursue something beyond a soldier's calling, and when my rotation was finished, I relinquished my post and returned home to the Sherinalu Vale. I received a letter from King Bartholomew only a few days later, inviting me to the royal court to discuss matters of state. And so... here I am."

Silence prevailed once more as Cadohaden let the tale soak into his mind. He felt sorrow for Eliliweth's loss, and while their shared burden of deceased parents gave him some sense of bonding towards the half-elf, he couldn't help but feel a bit guilty, knowing that before Deltore and Melaitha had died, he'd had many years of growing up with both of them as his mentors and guardians.

"I'm sorry," Eliliweth murmured a moment later, finally breaking the silence. "I didn't mean for this night to be so heavy-hearted."

"Don't apologize," Cadohaden said with a quick shake of his head. "Thanks for sharing that with me. I'm sure it isn't easy to relive that."

"It isn't," Eliliweth admitted. "But it gets a little easier every time."

They sat in silence once more, only this time, it was a comfortable quiet. The stars in the sky didn't seem so maleficent anymore. They were only twinkling sentinels, a symbol of timeless wisdom, detached from the frustrations and pains of the mortal soul. Cadohaden wasn't sure how long they sat there, but eventually, Eliliweth calmly stood from his chair, looking down at the two of them. "I think it's time that I found my bed."

"You're probably right," Cadohaden said as he began to rise out of his own chair.

"Wait," Elune said to Cadohaden's surprise, looking directly at him. "Will you stay a moment longer?"

"I-" Cadohaden began, his heart taking a small leap in his chest. "Sure. I can stay."

Eliliweth looked from Cadohaden to Elune curiously, a puzzled frown on his brow. When the elf revealed nothing more to him, he lowered himself in a quick bow and a weary, half-inebriated smile. "I'll bid you both a good night, then. We should do this again, sometime. Just...perhaps with happier tales next time."

"That would be great," Cadohaden said with a warm smile, his heart still churning anxiously from Elune's request. He tried to look casual as she bid Eliliweth a good night as well before the half-elf walked away from the alignment of chairs, disappearing below the rooftop with a squeak of the door's hinges. Cadohaden cleared his throat, trying to wipe his palms off on the knees of his trousers with some measure of subtlety before looking over at Elune. "What is it?" he asked.

"I...have something for you," Elune answered hesitantly. She pushed away her cloak and opened the pouch at her belt. From within, she revealed something wrapped in a light silk cloth. "I hope I don't assume too much with these. I didn't ask Eliliweth to stay, because I didn't want to put you in an uncomfortable position. If this is too familiar a gesture, just tell me, I promise I won't be offended."

She handed him the silk cloth gingerly, placing it in his open palm. With a curious frown, Cadohaden began to unfold the ends that were tucked over the neatly bound parcel. As the corners fell to each side, he saw two small, oval-shaped translucent figurines nestled upon the cloth. He opened his mouth to ask what they were, but snapped it shut with surprise as suddenly, the figurines illuminated with a soft golden glow. He vigorously fought the reflex to toss them out of his hand as the strange crystalline shapes began to move. His eyes opened wide in wonderment as he saw what the figurines were: two glass butterflies, their legs stretching as their wings unfolded, gently flexing as though they had freshly emerged from their cocoons.

"What are they?" Cadohaden asked quietly.

"They're made from elfglass," Elune murmured. "Enchanted by the magi of the Sherinalu Vale. I...the way you told the story, it didn't sound as though you were ever given the chance to give your parents a ceremony of passing. When we lose a loved one in the Sherinalu, we first bury the dead and commit them to the earth. Then...we climb the tallest tree in the forest, the *Lumshura'alu*, the 'Spirit Watch', in the darkest hour of night. From the perch of the *Lumshura'alu*, we release one of these *hym'cleur*, one for every departed soul, and as they vanish into the night, we accept that their spirits have moved on from this world.

"I...I don't mean to presume anything. It is not my place to tell you when it is time to accept the passing of your parents, or to tell you how their memories should be celebrated. But I think it would ease Melaitha's spirit...and perhaps it would for your father as well. If you don't wish for this, I can take them back."

Cadohaden stared at the two *hym'cleurs* in his palm. They did not move, save for the faint flexing of their wings as they sat glowing upon the silk cloth. His chest was full of emotion, so much that he wasn't sure which of the many were dominating. Without looking up, he asked softly, "What becomes of them? The figurines, I mean."

"They fly for some time. Eventually, they dissolve into dust, usually well after they've vanished from sight," Elune explained. "They are enchanted to behave that way by the magi that craft them."

Cadohaden nodded, staring at them for another moment before turning his gaze slowly up to Elune, who stared back at him with uncertain eyes. A sad but appreciative smile crossed his face as he said, "Thank you, Elune. This is the kindest thing anyone has ever done for me." It was true, by leaps and bounds. A relieved smile formed on the elf's lips, the glow from the figurines reflecting in her eyes.

"Are you ready to let them go?" she asked in a voice barely above a whisper.

Cadohaden looked back down at the *hym'cleurs*. He knew that she meant more than just the crystal figurines. What exactly did that mean, letting them go? To forget what happened to them? To let go of the vengeful desire deep down in his heart, a furious need to see Galdoys Veriknock pay for their deaths? Or was it just to know that they were gone now, that they couldn't come back to guide him anymore, that if he wished to honor their memories, he couldn't allow himself to sulk over their absence? He thought he could do that. He knew he needed to. He finally nodded in response, standing up from his chair, all the while staring at the glass butterflies in his palm.

Elune stood up as well, guiding him over to the edge of the battlement wall. They stared off into the night sky together, the *hym'cleurs* glowing in Cadohaden's grasp. She looked down at his hand, then up to his face before murmuring, "When you're ready, gently release them into the air."

He nodded as he looked down at their golden wings, lazily flexing up and down as they waited. A lump began to form in his throat as hot tears stung the corners of his eyes. Growing up with Deltore and Melaitha as his parents had been anything but easy. But they had both been there for him. They had laid the foundation for who he was today. They both knew and had cared for him, something he hadn't realized how much he had taken for granted until Eliliweth had told him his tale. There wasn't any way to go back and change what had happened. But at that moment, he knew he could go forward honoring their memories instead of struggling against it.

With a gentle lift of his arm, he hoisted the *hym'cleurs* into the night sky, the silk cloth fluttering and twisting as it fell slowly towards the ground below. The golden elfglass figurines, however, suddenly became lively with animation, their wings beating enthusiastically as they glided away, sailing towards the open fields of the Glen Dale. His vision began to blur over as their images grew smaller, like lazily floating stars shimmering across the sky.

He didn't realize how hard his hands were gripping the edge of the battlement until a soft touch grazed his knuckles. He took in a shaking breath as he looked down to see Elune's fingertips tracing over the back of his hand. He took her hand in his, intertwining their fingers before looking back out to the fading lights of the released memories. His skin did not flush, nor did his palm become clammy with fringed nerves. He only stood in silence, holding Elune's hand, as he watched the *hym'cleurs* vanish into the night.

Chapter Sixteen

In the stifling days of summer, the only place filled with a more oppressive heat than the Hordelands was the desert city of Chai'Rin. That thought was small comfort to Grathul Heavyhand, however, as he knelt in his hide tent, the sweat collecting in beads across his shaved scalp, trailing down his broad cheekbones, over his chiseled jaw, and soaking into the black snarls of his full coarse beard. The black braid that was woven at the back of his skull, below the shaved portion, clinked as the iron weights woven into the hair knocked against one another as he shifted his weight. With one of his massive, blocky hands, the chieftain of the Goreknuckle Clan held a yearling goat firmly in place. In his other hand was a ceremonial knife belonging to his master warlock, Gragnath Fire-Eyes, who watched in a crouched position next to the chieftain's cot. Standing on the other side of the cot, musclebound arms folded across his chest, his younger brother Razuk Heavyhand observed silently.

"The Destroyer compels you to make this sacrifice in his name, *ursh'kanra*," Gragnath rasped the word for 'chieftain' in the orcish tongue. Though the warlock had stripped himself of most of the black tatters for robes that he usually wore, he was still adorned with a long black cloth that was wrapped around his head like a shawl, the material clinging to his skin in dark patches of sweat. He was smaller than the other two, but still admirably sized for an orc, his muscles lean and sinewy. "Take this goat's life, that our lord Gapinon will bless you and grant you strength to aid you in the task at hand."

Grathul displayed no hesitation. Curling his arm around the goat, the animal released a single panicked bleat before the edge of the blade tore open his throat, spilling blood onto the ground before him. The goat kicked and thrashed as it emitted terrible strangled noises, desperately choking for air that would not find its lungs. The chieftain eased the creature down onto its side as its struggles became weak and fruitless, the crimson life still emptying from its wound in draining pulses. With a low mumble that hinged on a cruel chuckle, Gragnath lurched forward, maintaining his kneeling level as he scooted forward to the sacrificed goat. Leaning over, the warlock pressed his hands into the pooled blood, murmuring dark incantations as his eyelids fluttered shut.

Grathul watched as Gragnath performed his ritual. Nearly every chieftain in each of the Hordeland clans kept a gifted warlock in their service as a high-ranking member of the tribe. They advised their leader, trained their acolytes, and though they rarely took the mantle of "chieftain", they were feared and respected with just as much magnitude, if for vastly different reasons. It was well-known in the Hordelands that the Goreknuckle Clan had the greatest warlock of all the tribes in Gragnath Fire-Eyes. Grathul was a proud chieftain, and worshiped the Destroyer's strength more than his gift of unholy magic, but he knew he was fortunate to have the elder Fire-Eyes in his clan.

"Close your eyes, Chieftain, and feel the strength of the Destroyer wash over you as I decorate you with the blood of your gift to him," Gragnath growled ceremoniously. Grathul obliged, closing his eyelids. He flexed his neck, keeping his head still as Gragnath's palms pressed against his cheeks and slid up over his closed eyes and across his scalp. The blood of the goat was yet warm. It felt sticky against his sheened skin, but as the warlock performed his blessing, the chieftain could feel his chest swell with the exhilaration of the dark magic he was performing. His heart began to beat with a strong urgency, but he remained calm, walking the thin line between intense focus and frenzied battle-lust. It was important that he maintained this balance, at least until his task was complete.

"Open your eyes," Gragnath commanded. The chieftain obeyed, feeling the goat's blood against his eyelids as they pushed back up towards his brows. He remained kneeling patiently, knowing that the ritual was not yet over. The warlock held out his hand for the knife. Grathul placed it in his palm, and Gragnath began to cut open the goat's stomach, pushing away folds of furry hide as his hand disappeared into the corpse with a series of grotesque suctioned sounds as his fingers weaved through the organs. A grim smile passed over the warlock's face as he gripped what he was searching for, and with a grit of his jaw and a steady pull, he tore the heart out from the body's opening. His forearm shining with fresh blood, Gragnath handed the raw muscle over to Grathul. "Consume it all, Chieftain, to give you a small taste of the victories that are to come."

Raw heart did not vex Grathul. He had endured this ritual many times before. He began to devour the organ, his teeth shredding the slick flesh as he worked it down his throat hungrily, the blood blessing granting him a morbid enthusiasm for the barbaric liturgy. When his bloodied palm was finally empty, he felt his body become emboldened with newfound strength. It became more difficult to maintain his balance of composure, but he reigned in his primal desires, watching Gragnath for a sign to stand.

"Rise, Grathul Heavyhand, servant of the Destroyer," Gragnath rasped as he got to his own feet, lifting his red-stained hands upward. "Embrace the burning spirit of the Destroyer, and carry out his will."

"I shall," Grathul rumbled as he got to his feet. His nostrils flared as he filled his chest with the tent's pungent air, thick with the coppery stench of blood. He looked to Razuk, still standing next to the cot with his arms folded. "Are they gathering?" he asked his brother. He had been inside his tent most of the morning, allowing Gragnath to guide him through a pre-ritual meditation.

"They are," Razuk answered. "When last I checked, there was no sign of the Pillage Lords. But they will show." Grathul nodded, his teeth grinding against each other as the blessing of blood continued to surge through his veins. The Pillage Lords were a clan led by the orc known as Ganshu'Dai. To earn the right to rally each of the clans, Grathul had visited with every leader, demanding their attendance. If the chieftain did not willingly abide, they were bound by honor to present themselves if either the challenger or one of their champions bested the other in single combat. Grathul Heavyhand's reputation was renowned in the Hordelands, and so there was little opposition to his summoning, but Ganshu'Dai was one who initially refused. Razuk had fought as Grathul's champion for the right to demand the presence of the Pillage

Lords, killing one of Ganshu'Dai's followers, an unusually hairy orc that was simply known as 'The Beast.'

"Then I will prepare for your heralding, Chieftain," Master Gragnath said with a cracked-lipped smile. "If you have no more need of me, that is."

"No, that will be all, Master Gragnath," Grathul answered. He was the warlock's superior, but addressing him with the title that his acolytes used was a gesture of respect for his talent and power. He was the only one who was ever afforded such a courtesy. "You honor me with your blessing."

"The Destroyer honors you," Gragnath corrected, his smile widening. "I am but an instrument for his fiery hands." The warlock shuffled his way out of the tent, sunlight bursting forth from the open flap for a brief second before it fell shut once more with a flutter.

Grathul and Razuk stood in silence for a moment, the only sound coming from the open wound of the sacrificed goat, small drops of blood landing in a puddle with a quiet *plink, plink, plink.* The younger brother was the first to speak up again as he unfolded his arms from his chest. "Do you think he will challenge you once more?"

"Ganshu'Dai?" Grathul said in a measured voice, still focused on maintaining the delicate balance in his mind and spirit. "I have no doubt. It is no small thing, to call every clan together. If he will fight me on that, he will oppose what I will demand next. And this time, he will name himself as his champion."

"You need only say the word," Razuk grunted, "and I will fight for you once more."

Grathul looked to his brother with pride. It was no small offer that Razuk made. Next to Grathul, Ganshu'Dai was one of the fiercest warriors in all of the Hordelands. The younger Heavyhand was no true match for the Pillage Lords' chieftain, and he was smart enough to see through his pride and know the truth of it.

Brotherly bonds like Grathul and Razuk's were not common in orcish culture. The traditions of family that were often practiced with humankind and their cousin kin were not recognized in Hordeland clans. Their tribes were the only family that most would acknowledge. Lifelong mates were a rarity. Most orcs mated based on each other's physical attributes, aiming to give life to strong warriors that would bolster the might of their clans. An orcish childhood was similar to that of a wild beast. The mother would raise it until it was strong enough to fend for itself, or rather, for as long as the mother felt was an appropriate amount of time to reach such an age, whether they were ready or not. They would then detach themselves from their child's dependency, placing their survival in their own hands.

After the matronly bond was severed, the orcish adolescent would make a new life for themselves. Oftentimes, they would surrender their sire's surname, embarking on conquests to earn one of their own. If their father had an exceptionally proud heritage, sometimes they would fight to retain their name. Grathul and Razuk's father, Vokarr Heavyhand, was such an example, and both of them had earned the right to bear his name at early ages, continuing the glorious legacy. Gragnath's son, Gorogis, had also taken the last name of his illustrious father after displaying a great aptitude for blood magic. The warlock's other son was a rare exception. Jukah Fire-Eyes had been born with a soft mind, ill-fit to care for himself. Such failed specimens were usually put out of their misery, but Gragnath pitied his addle-minded son, even if he would never admit it, and took him in as a personal grunt. Usually, this would have garnered a great deal of scorn and open shaming from his greenskinned kin, but it was a foolhardy thing to cast grief upon the most gifted warlock in all of the Hordelands.

As was the case with parenthood, sibling relationships were never assumed. If they occurred, it was most often a bond of warrior brotherhood, not blood obligation. Both Grathul and Razuk had come to respect their pedigrees, each of them choosing to remain with the Goreknuckle Clan, as had their father Vokarr. At exceptionally young ages, they both fought an ascending battle to the position of the clan's *ursh'kanra* when their father had perished from infection, a tragic end for a warrior with dreams of dying in bloody battle. It ended with a trial by combat between the two of them, and when Razuk had fallen to the ground with an assortment of blade wounds and the edge of an axe at his throat, he did not ask for surrender, but instead glared defiantly up at Grathul, facing his execution with fearless resolution. Instead of killing him, however, Grathul helped him to his feet, naming Razuk *tok'rekha*. It meant 'blood brother' in orcish, and though they were already so by literal definition, to be given the ceremonial name was a far greater honor. Their friendship was as strong as forged iron from that day forward.

"Not this time, *tok'rekha*," Grathul answered. "With what I plan to demand of my kin, I cannot ask for a champion to fight in my stead. I must be willing to seize this with my own hands."

"I thought you'd say that," Razuk muttered, walking over to the goat's corpse and hoisting it up by one of its lifeless legs. Dragging the animal to the tent flap, he looked over his shoulder at Grathul. "Are you ready?"

The chieftain took in a deep breath through both nostrils. His cheeks were tingling warmly, like he'd taken a few pulls from a bottle of rum, but his mind was sharp with focused clarity. "I am," he rumbled confidently. The brothers in blood left the tent, striding out to meet the vindictive sun that beat harsh light down upon them.

Thrum, thrum, thrum, the drumbeats sounded as Grathul emerged from his tent. Before him was a platform-like boulder, protruding from the ground like a fractured bone from skin. His tribesmen were on either side of the lifted stone rise, and at his appearance, half a dozen of them began clubbing their cured hide instruments with leather-capped batons in a foreboding staccato. Every other member of the Goreknuckle Clan not tending to a drum turned and pounded their curled fists against their chests in salute. The chieftain acknowledged his clansmen with a stiff nod of his head as he began to ascend the rock that looked out over the vast plains of the Hordelands. What greeted his eyes was a fearsome sight to behold.

As far as his eyes could see, there were gathered orcish clans, shoulder-to-shoulder as they begrudgingly waited to hear from the chieftain that had summoned them through the ancient rites. It was a myriad of greens, mottled grays, and olive-tan skin, all awaiting his announcement. Like waves upon an ocean, the gathered mob rippled back and forth as the ill-tempered brutes fought irritably for adequate space. Grathul could hear the grunts and bellows of skirmishing orcs as fights broke out among the masses. This was no cause for alarm. It was expected, almost traditional during any large gathering of their kind for brawls to occur over the slightest insults. If any of them ended in fatalities, not a single one would blink an eye in surprise.

There weren't only orcs gathered to hear his statement, either. Though they were the majority by far, the Hordelands was also home to the hunched, lithe goblins, with their wide bulbous eyes and bean-stalk noses. A dozen trolls could be seen as well, looming over the orcs at three times their size, most carrying bulky bludgeons in the form of massive tree trunks. What was truly amazing was that these trolls were the runts of their litters, escaped from the northern mountains south of Annon, choosing instead to live where they were more dominant by comparison. Three of the gathered trolls belonged to the Goreknuckle Clan, and Grathul had made use of their brawn on more than one occasion. They were dim-witted, but obedient and easy to please.

The ogres, on the other hand, were more unpredictable and quick to anger, but still followed the orders of their orcish chieftains, for most of them knew of crueler masters on the northwestern point of the Hordelands, the province uncleverly named the Hornlands by its denizens. Minotaurs ruled those prairie lands, and were far smarter and more ferocious than their ogres, who they treated as second-class clansmen. Once in almost every decade, the ogres would try to revolt, and the outcome was never in their favor. Because of this, many fled southward to swear allegiance to an orcish chieftain, where they were protected if they were not caught attempting to escape their bull-men masters.

Grathul's eyes trailed over the mass of gathered tribesmen, scanning the crowd for a particular face. He spotted the one he sought. Pressing their way through the mob, the clan known as the Pillage Lords had arrived, as their honor dictated, and their chieftain Ganshu'Dai led the way, his braided topknot swaying with every stride, a bulking war axe draped over his shoulder. The *ursh'kanra's* nose wrinkled as he met Grathul's gaze. Satisfied with the attendance, the elder Heavyhand spread his arms, bellowing out to those gathered before him,

"*Brothers! Sisters!*" the chieftain bellowed. "I have visited each of your leaders in their territories, asking for your audience on this day! And for those of you who refused it, I earned the right by combat!" A low mumble passed through the crowd, accompanied by a few selective cheers from those of the Goreknuckle Clan. Grathul took in another deep breath. The thrill of commanding their collective attentions threatened to overcome him, paired with Gragnath's blood blessing. He took a few seconds to regain his composure before he continued,

"These past few moons, brothers and sisters of the Hordelands, I have heard whispers reach my ears through trusted allies, from the Goreknuckles *and* beyond. Rumors that turn the stomach and set my heart on fire with anger. Tell me truly, my brothers and sisters in blood: have any of you taken payment from human worms to perform tasks that they have no spine to do on their own?!"

The murmur of the crowd quickly fell to a hush as orcish eyes turned to one another. There wasn't a soul that was gathered that didn't know of whom Grathul spoke of. Finally, after a few tense moments, a figure began to push through the crowd. He pressed through the front row, tall by orc standards, angular patterns cut into the stubbled crop of hair on his scalp. "I, Sankor Bladebreaker, *Ursh'kanra* of the Boneguards, speak on behalf of my tribe. We took payment in blade and leather from the humans of Kingsbanesin, it's true. But we *killed humans* doing it. What honor is there to be lost in taking the lives of the pink-skinned wretches?"

"What honor is there to be gained by doing the bidding of a human wretch!?" Grathul bellowed, the cords bulging in his neck as the adrenaline surged through him. "It matters not if it calls itself noble or peasant, anything *you* want from the human, you *take* it, and its life as well if you so desire! And if they outnumber you, you die a glorious death by taking as many to the afterlife with you as you can!"

"Piss on that!" Sankor shouted back, drawing murmurs from the crowd once more. "The Kingsbanesin humans have *dragons*, Heavyhand, and there is no honor being torched alive by their flaming breath like ants under a match!"

"The dragons are kept in check by the humans' overlord neighbors," Grathul growled in return. "Kingsbanesin is subservient to its kin. You choose to be hired peons for inferiors that answer to many masters!"

"Their place on the food chain means nothing to the Boneguards," Sankor snapped back indignantly. "We are to do the same for a few robed pigs of the Glen Bailey, one of the masters that you speak of. Their position means nothing."

Grathul stared at Sankor from atop his stone perch. The gathered mob suddenly fell into stunned silence as the other members of the Boneguard Clan began to shift nervously. A vein began to bulge from the chieftain's scalp as he glared seethingly down at Sankor. "You mean to tell me," he breathed in angered huffs, "that you sold your dignity not to *one* pack of human rats, but to another as well!? What is left of your spine, Bladebreaker?! Anything? Or did you have your clansmen craft one from forest saplings!? Would you get on your hands and knees and offer yourself to a swamp gnome in exchange for a bronze belt buckle!?"

"You cannot-" Sankor began to call out, but Grathul cut him off, bellowing,

"*Be silent, you miserable cur!* Your frailty flecks off your lips like spit with every word, and I can feel it against my hide even from up here! Brothers and sisters," he continued, lifting his arms once more to the gathered legions, "*this* is why I have gathered you here today, why I have risked the life of my own and the life of my *tok'rekha* to bring us here!

"Do you not see what we have become? We are orcs! We are the Destroyer's chosen! But what has time made us? No longer do we raid and pillage! These villages and fishing wharfs that we pride ourselves on ravaging are weak, near defenseless, and at the first sign of humans with a scrap of armor across their chests, we flee back to our homeland, so that we can glare at one another from the boundaries of our territories! We tell ourselves that we are strong, that we could crush anyone that crosses us, but how can we say that when it is easier to fight one another instead of the moles that claim ownership of nearly all the Aariad!

"And now, brothers and sisters, we are reduced to this! To running errands for these pinkskins in hopes of a pat on the head! Are you dogs, wagging your tails in hopes of approval from your masters? I see some of you out there, shaking your heads, insisting that you are not as cowed as I say, but *true* orcish warriors would not allow even their neighbors to commit such cowardice! We should be *united*, to display orcish strength to all of the Aariad, against all our enemies! Humans! Elves! Even the minotaur tribes, who hold claim to land in *our* home, we have passed off as a simple nuisance, as though it does not stain our honor by fearing the point of their horns, or the edge of their axes!

"Tell me, Sankor Bladebreaker!" Grathul snarled, pointing a finger down at the Boneguard chieftain. "What did your pinkskin masters ask of you?" Sankor wrinkled his nose, saying nothing at first. Then, he looked to his left and right, seeing only expectant and grim faces from his kin. Begrudgingly, he replied,

"They asked for the same as the dragon men. They wanted us to get through their walls and kill off a few troublesome gnats. They said they would create an opening for us."

"Ah," Grathul grunted. "*They* would create an opening for *you*. What does that sound like to you, brothers and sisters!?" His question was met with a flurry of angry responses, few of them discernible to the chieftain's ears, but the feeling was just right: pure outrage.

"Then here is what I say we do!" he bellowed, slamming his curled fists against both sides of his chest. "For the first time in far too long, we stand as *one!* We *end* this subservience and march upon the Glen Bailey! We will meet these robed pigs, butcher them, and toss their limbs over the walls, so that their people will tremble in fear of what is to come! And we will not be *given* an opening, fed by the palm of the human wretches! We will *break it open ourselves!* Now tell me, brothers and sisters! *Who will join me, as one clan, to restore honor to our people!?*"

The response was electric. Grathul could feel his heart swell in his chest as the Hordelands seemed to cry its support in one singular triumphant roar. Weapons were lifted into the air, shoving pits beginning to open up in the crowd in aggressive celebration of his proclamation. There was one clan, however, that was not partaking in the wild, contagious enthusiasm. Ganshu'Dai and his Pillage Lords stood stoically, the chieftain's arms folded across his chest. The jubilee continued until finally, Ganshu'Dai took hold of a leather cord hung over his shoulder and across his torso, lifting a curled battle horn off of his body and placing the mouthpiece against his lips. A drawled rumble reverberated across the plains, dampening the roar of the crowd as curious eyes turned to the chieftain of the Pillage Lords.

"Grathul Heavyhand speaks the truth," he called out as he handed the battle horn off to one of his clansmen. "We have strayed from the path of our ancestors, from the path of the Destroyer!

"But," he continued pointedly, turning and lifting his chin to peer at Grathul, "the chieftain of the Goreknuckle Clan earned the right to gather us here. Not to lead us as an army. Your clever tongue does not earn you any other titles, *ursh'kanra*. Let an orc who has the strength and the spirit to command do so."

Grathul glared down at Ganshu'Dai. Razuk had foreseen it like a prophet. Ever proud, the Pillage Lords' leader would not take orders from him just because he was told to. He would have to earn this right as well, this time with his own hands. That suited Grathul just fine. He could beat Ganshu'Dai in combat. And if he would not surrender, an execution here in front of all of his kin would only reinforce his claim as this great army's general. He jumped from the edge of his stone perch, landing on the soil below with a graceful bend of his knees. "Someone fetch my axes," he growled, eyes never leaving Ganshu'Dai's as the Pillage Lords' chieftain rolled his bulky war axe off of his shoulder.

A young orc named Veshkrim emerged from the gathered Gore-knuckles, both of his chieftain's hand axes at the ready. Holding them by the end of the handles, he delivered Grathul's weapons to him. The chieftain took in a deep breath as he examined them and tested his grip on the leather bindings wound around the handles. The blades glistened against the afternoon sun. Anticipating such a challenge, he'd spent extra time ensuring that they would cleave through flesh like wet parchment. He tapped the back end of one against the other. Satisfied with the solid sound of the tap, he turned to face Ganshu'Dai, who had marched forward, away from his gathered clansmen, standing in the center of the open space that had quickly cleared out.

"Stand down now," the Pillage Lords' chieftain growled. "And I will let you live, Heavyhand. I will need lieutenants of your strength when we conquer the pinkskins."

Grathul spread his arms, the toned muscle of his torso rippling against his flesh as he lowered himself into an aggressive stance. He opened his mouth, ready to shame the usurper with a retort, when a thumping sound came from behind. Seeing Ganshu'Dai's brow dip in puzzlement, Grathul turned cautiously to look across his shoulder.

The most massive of the gathered trolls was lumbering his way through the crowd, impatiently swiping away those that did not move fast enough. Grathul recognized him by the dragon skull that was tied over his head as a crude helmet. It was Bolg, the largest of the Hordeland trolls, and a member of the Boneguard Clan. Bolg was notorious not only for his size, but for his far-fetched tale of slaying a dragon with only his bare hands and taking the head as a trophy before decorating his own with the skull. Most suspected that Bolg stole the skull from one of his mountain cousins before fleeing for the Hordelands, but it was hard to argue with someone who was three times your size and had arms wider than your torso. An assortment of different bones were tied around the troll's chest with no evident pattern, the remains of great beasts occasionally clacking together as he lurched forward towards the scene of the duel.

"Little orcs," Bolg thundered as he approached the two chieftains, his speech choppy and rudimentary even in the orcish tongue. "Little orcs fight to lead against pink pigs in Bailey. The Heavyhand talk down to every other here. Maybe Bolg tired of orders from them smaller than him! Bolg crush *both* of you at same time, and then Bolg lead us to kill all humans!"

Both Grathul and Ganshu'Dai stared at the hulking troll incredulously. Trolls demanded a certain level of respect based on their sheer brawn, but ages had past since the last one had demanded any kind of leadership role, much less the privilege of commanding an entire Hordeland army. The two chieftains turned to face Bolg when a voice snarled from the crowd, Sankor stepping forward angrily, barking, "Bolg, you incompetent oaf! Shut your wagging maw and get yourself back to-"

If such aggressive orders had worked for the leader of the Boneguard Clan before, they failed Sankor Bladebreaker that day. With a brutish roar, Bolg spun himself around and swiped a massive arm at his chieftain, his entire fist closing around the orc's neck. Sankor's shout of surprise caught in his throat as Bolg tightened his grip, lifting him off of the ground and pulling him closer to his skull-adorned face. "The Heavyhand was right," Bolg breathed menacingly. "You are worm. No spine in little worm." Before the chieftain could protest, the massive troll squeezed his brutish hand around Sankor's neck. The orc's eyes quickly turned bloodshot red, his face purpling as his neck snapped under the pressure.

Bolg gave the orc's neck another firm squeeze, pushing a rope of saliva and blood from Sankor's open mouth, and then dropped him to the ground with a limp thud. A rolling grumble rumbled in the troll's throat as he stared challengingly at the gathered crowd, eyes wide in shock at what he had just dared to do. When nobody spoke, Bolg turned once more to face Grathul and Ganshu'Dai. "You follow Bolg now," he rumbled, "or Bolg will crush you both at same time. Bolg not scared of big talker little orcs."

Grathul released an irritated sigh through his nostrils. They shouldn't have to duel a beast of a troll to earn the right to lead their brethren into battle. It was understood, even among most trolls, that the orcish intellect placed them in positions of leadership. Unfortunately, Bolg was a physically gifted behemoth, and apparently too dim-witted to understand that concept. Despite the unfair odds, with so much at stake, Grathul could not back down from the troll's challenge. His gaze slid over to Ganshu'Dai, who held his war axe at the ready, silently waiting for Grathul's agreement. He had to admire his rival's good sense. Though they were at odds only moments ago, Bolg's challenge gave them common cause, and without hesitation, he was ready to fight at Grathul's side. That was the spirit the Hordelands that had been lacking for so long now.

Unfortunately, their combined efforts, even in victory, would only be in vain, leaving them in the same position they had been prior to Bolg's weighted challenge. Grathul could leave no questions as to who would reign as the alpha wolf in the pack that would conquer humanity. "You have gravely forgotten your place, you inane, empty-skulled fool," he growled at the troll. "I will remind you where you stand, and I don't need the Pillage Lords' *ursh'kanra* to do so. Veshkrim! Take this," he commanded, holding out one of his axes as his clansmen rushed forward to take it from him, a confused frown on his face.

Ganshu'Dai squinted suspiciously at him, lowering his weapon in his hands. He snorted at Grathul and shook his head. "You will damn us with this foolishness," he growled, but he slung the handle of his axe back over his shoulder and marched towards the perimeter of the gathered orcs, turning around to observe the one-on-one duel. A wide, stupid grin broke out on Bolg's face as he took a few steps towards Grathul, staring down at him.

"One not as fun," the troll boasted, "but I make you die slow enough for both." His mighty fist gripped the massive tree limb that he used for a bludgeon. There were scuff marks, patches of stripped bark, and brown splotches of dried blood littering the improvised club. Grathul did not dignify the taunt with a verbal retort. He only wrinkled his nose, drew a line of phlegm in the back of his throat, and spit it at Bolg's hairy, calloused feet.

It incurred the desired effect. With an indignant bellow, Bolg stormed forward, lifting his club over his head menacingly as the gathered onlookers began to chant in a rhythmic pattern. *Ruh! Ruh! Ruh!* they sounded as Grathul charged forward, his arms churning as he sprinted at the troll's legs. Despite what it seemed, he hadn't surrendered one of his axes as a show of arrogance. He needed to be light on his feet to bring down the hulking brute. As Bolg dropped the tree limb down in a wicked arc, Grathul leaped forward, hugging the handle of his hand axe against his chest as he dove for the ground between the troll's feet.

He rolled as he landed, feeling the faint ripple of air left in the wake of Bolg's meaty fist as the troll tried to snatch him with his opposite hand. Grathul hoisted himself back up to his feet in a graceful move for an orc of his size. He readied himself to reposition away from the troll's swinging arms, but Bolg had a leg in the air as he attempted to stomp on the orc. Grathul lifted his hand axe, strafed two strides to his left, and swung, cutting into the troll's thick hide and severing the hamstring underneath.

The chants grew louder as Bolg bellowed in pain, bending over as his leg buckled underneath him. The behemoth of a troll dropped his tree limb weapon and fell to the knee of his good leg, using it as a swivel to turn around. Grathul was two steps ahead of him. He tossed his axe to his left, in front of Bolg as the troll swung an arm at him like he would an insect. Jumping, the orc chieftain tapped his palms against the troll's forearm as it hurled towards him, vaulting over it as it came across. The tops of his feet caught the arm as it moved across, sending him tumbling forward into the dirt, but he scrambled back up to his feet quickly, grabbing the axe he had thrown only seconds before. Standing in front of the hunched, raging troll, he charged forward and buried the axe's edge into Bolg's inner elbow, cutting the ligament. Bolg howled once more, lifting his other arm up to slam down on his foe, but Grathul hadn't quit. Pulling the axe from the fresh wound, he wound up once more and buried it into the oblique muscles alongside the abdomen, between two of the troll's decorative bone adornments. Bolg groaned, tilting to his side awkwardly as his arm dropped in response.

Grathul took three steps backward as the stunned troll swayed on his feet. Hunching over, the orc chieftain charged forward, lowering his shoulder as he slammed into Bolg's lower abdomen. Colliding against the bones strapped to the troll sent a painful jolt through him, promising an ugly bruise against the skin, but Grathul's surging adrenaline numbed the sensation. Pride swelled in his pounding heart as Bolg tumbled backwards against the impact, landing with a heavy thud against the dirt below. *Rah! Rah! Rah!* the crowd cheered uproariously as the chieftain turned away from his foe, marching back to Veshkrim and extending his hand. The young orc grinned and handed him the axe he had left behind before beginning combat with the bold troll. Grathul took the axe and marched back to Bolg, who had turned over onto his stomach before the rabid onlookers.

He walked between the troll's spread legs, the left bleeding profusely above the knee where Grathul had split the hamstring. The chieftain lifted his leg onto Bolg's upper thigh, pushing himself up onto the troll's buttocks. His eyes narrowed as he walked across the brute's spine, glaring at the back of his head as Bolg began to push himself up in vain. Stepping onto the troll's shoulders, Grathul snarled and brought down the axe's edge upon the ornament dragon skull. It released a sharp crack as a fissure split down the middle of the cranium. Bolg's head sagged forward, dizzied from blood loss and the impact of the blade. Relentlessly, bolstered by the encouragement of the gathered crowd, Grathul rained blows down upon the skull until it finally split, hanging lopsidedly on both sides of the troll's head. With each of his feet, Grathul kicked the shards off of Bolg's head, the bleached remnants tumbling down to the ground, landing next to the puddle of vomit that the troll had voided after several bludgeonings. The chieftain lifted his chin triumphantly and spread his arms, bellowing to the gathered in a voice laced with a rush of bloodthirst,

"Which of you disputes my leadership now!?" he roared. "Which of you will challenge me, standing upon the shoulders of the Hordeland's mightiest troll, conquered alone, by my choice! Tell me, brothers and sisters! Do you find me fit to lead you into glorious battle!?"

The response was overwhelming. Grathul could feel the sheer volume of the bellows pressing against his chest. He grinned maliciously as he scanned the fevered crowd. Even Ganshu'Dai and his Pillage Lords applauded his victory. The chieftain had no choice. After Grathul had willingly fought against Bolg on his own and won, it would look petty and weak for him to challenge his authority once more. Grathul could see it in Ganshu'Dai's stern expression. It was not the outcome the Pillage Lord's chieftain had hoped for, but it had earned his begrudging respect.

His battlecry pierced the air as he lifted the hand axe once more, swinging it in a vicious arc upon Bolg's exposed head, burying it above his eyes. The troll shuddered, a spasmodic twitch shivering down his hulking body before it collapsed to the ground, blood and bits of brain matter pooling from the fresh wound. Every sense ignited with fervor, Grathul roared to the gathered once more, "Follow me, my brothers and sisters! Follow me as your warchief, as your *ursh'kinta*, and we shall restore the honor that our names have not known for too long! Let us conquer the humans together! The Glen Bailey wants us to kill for them!? We shall *bathe their city in blood!*

"But first," the warchief called out as the orcs bellowed their approval, "there is an infection among us, my warriors. A weakness that we can tolerate no longer. For us to be strong, it must be cut out." Stepping towards the perimeter of the crowd, Grathul narrowed his eyes and pointed, turning the heads of onlookers as they stared. The remainder of the Boneguard Clan were shuffling nervously, trying to filter out of the crowd without notice. They froze momentarily as Grathul directed the attention towards them. Then, in a heartbeat, they turned, each of them trying to scramble their way out of the mob.

"We cannot tolerate such cowardice!" Grathul shouted. "*Put the mongrels down!*"

Sunlight glinted off the edges of the drawn weapons as the gathered clans fell upon the Boneguards. Their screams and agonized groans sung a wretched harmony alongside the eager shrieks of bloodthirst from their attackers. For the first time in decades, the Hordelands were reunited once more, but not a single descendant of the Boneguard Clan would live to tell the tale.

Chapter Seventeen

The summer season began to mature as the Glen Bailey prepared for Eliliweth's Trials. Days turned to weeks, and before long, the leaves on the trees began to transform ever so slightly, heralding the coming times of harvest. The mood in the city was still festive in its arrangements for the half-elf's pilgrimage, but the majority of the merrymaking was being done by the nobles of the royal court and the visiting dwarves from Dur'Imoir that didn't seem to be in too much of a hurry to return to their mountain caves as long as there was reason to tap another keg. The farmers, the tradesmen, and the soldiers all had duties to return to, however. Their livelihoods depended on their dedication to their work, regardless of repeated causes to celebrate. Still, the colored flags hanging across the cobblestone streets remained, the music continued to play, and every once in a while, an apprentice running an errand for their master would accept a frothing mug handed to them by a band of jubilant dwarves, glancing around cautiously before gulping down the beverage as fast as they could before wiping away the residue left on their upper lip. Not coincidentally, vendors began to set up tents by the dwarven parties with jars full of lavender, ginger root, and chives to mask the scent of ale. It was a good month for traders that offered strong-scented plants.

Cadohaden's studies continued at the Monastery, as did his training at the barracks' field. It was the latter where he excelled. Though

Deltore had taught him a great deal about the use of weaponry and battle technique, the young paladin quickly discovered how his father's physical conditioning training for his son had been unusually lenient. Sir Strigson Ganisalp had corrected that, running him through circuit after circuit of exercises to toughen both his body and his mind. They left him exhausted, but after only two weeks, Cadohaden began to feel a sense of fulfillment that he had sought by traveling to the Glen Bailey in the first place. His arms training combined with the honing of his physical form made him feel like the warrior Deltore had always wanted him to be. He still fought with a reaching aggression that caught him off-balance too often, but he'd improved in so many facets that he silently hungered for another chance to spar against his half-elven friend.

In the holy halls of the Monastery, however, Cadohaden's struggles continued. His capacity to wield the power of the Lifegiver was evident, but he had difficulty channeling it in the desired manner. Soldiers with knicks and bruises would report to the infirmary after rotations, and the paladin recruit was instructed to heal the minor wounds under the tutelage of either Crusader Nevic, a cleric named Amaliah Leah, or on rare occasions, Priestess Ecila herself. He gave it his best effort and produced just enough results to avoid the Crusader's abandonment. Nevic warned him on more than one occasion to not allow himself to be distracted by his combat training or any extraneous activities. The pale paladin didn't need to elaborate on what the "extraneous activities" were. He and Elune had spent a great deal more time together since she had given him the gifts of the golden *hym'cleurs*. The relationship was not yet serious or even overly intimate, but that didn't stop Ecila from filling his ear with cold lectures about the virtues of chastity.

During the past three weeks, they hadn't had the opportunity to test such boundaries. Elune had temporarily returned to the Sherinalu Vale, to earn her keep and pay her dues to her homeland as well as visit with her family. She was hesitant to tell Cadohaden of her parents, and so the subject was not broached often, as it left a strange void in the conversation, as stories of his family were mostly linked to angst and tragedy.

It would have been a lie for Elune to tell Cadohaden that she did not have a healthy relationship with her parents. She loved the both of them, and they her. But as of late, their interactions were strained.

They didn't entirely approve of her extended stays in the Glen Bailey, fearing that she would forget her Sherinalu roots. Her father would lecture her about her lack of contribution to her family and her neighbors of the Vale. Her mother was more than forthright in her hints that she should seek a husband and settle down. Both of them agreed that adventures to the Glen Dale were not necessarily in her best interests, despite her insistence that she could serve as an ambassador to an ally of the elves. "The Sherinalu already has ambassadors to the Glen Dale," her father would retort.

It was true, but in the time she had spent with the people of the city in her travels with Eliliweth, she had learned that the three most prominent ambassadors, Wendrith, Qualin, and Lazuralina had ceased leaving friendly impressions during their stays, growing colder and more aloof with every visit, the fascination with a newly discovered culture wearing off as they grew accustomed to Bartholomew's court and the general public of the Glen Bailey. To Elune, however, the people here weren't just a different species to observe. She admired them. There was something about humanity that elvenkind did not possess. It was hard to give it a specific title, but almost everyone she met seemed to hold a kindling hope, a will to survive, and an optimistic unity that appeared to carry them through the most difficult winters. That wasn't to say that the Sherinalu Vale wasn't enchanting. It was a beautiful city in a wonderous forest. But the allure of elvenkind was more in their rich history, their traditions, their unwavering admiration for what they had always been. The people of the Glen Bailey, in contrast, looked with bright eyes to the future. It was a magnetic spirit that seemed to coax Elune back every time Eliliweth told her of another journey to the lands of the Glen Dale. Now that he was to become an official advisor, assuming he passed his Trials, she wasn't sure how she would split her time between what had always been home and what was beginning to feel more like home.

The princess Aven continued to lose sleep over the secret she shared with Bertram Archibaum. Every shadow became a hidden assassin. Every strange face looked like the visage of a conspirator. She tossed and turned every night, glaring at the ceiling. She would get up from her bed at least half a dozen times, walking to her bedroom door, intent on going straight to her father's chambers, to wake him from his slumber and inform him of the plot underneath his nose. Each time, she would return herself to her bed, though the decision continually tormented her. When Bartholomew had told her that he would wait to begin Eliliweth's Trials until a few weeks later, she'd nearly exposed the schemes of the magistrates on the spot, riots or no riots. But she instead chose to continue her silence.

The guilt of the matter burned her heart vengefully. She knew that she had waited too long to share her knowledge with the king. Even if she confessed to her father before the magistrates set their plan into motion, her integrity could no longer avoid the scrutiny that would surely follow when word spread of her initial silence. Rumors would begin to blossom that the princess cared more for the thrill of political games than the safety of her people, even though that safety was the only reason she hesitated in the first place. Her only hope now was to successfully thwart the conspiracy with Archibaum's help, without a host of angry mobs or spilled blood. If Lord Archibaum spoke the truth about the carefully laid plans of the magistrates, she could no longer do so by prematurely informing the king. There could be no partial victories for Aven Celandine now. She had decided on her path, and not only did it rob her of her sleep, but it made her surly and sharp-tongued. She did her best to conceal it, but most of the keep's servants were beginning to avoid her now as she traveled the hallways, cautious of her royal wrath. And poor Eliliweth, who sought her guidance through his studies regarding the White Forest, received impatience and irritability in response. She knew what it was he thought troubled her, that his choosing for the Trials had invoked her envy at long last, despite her assurances. His questions and his visits dwindled rapidly. It weighed heavily on her, but what could she do? She could not tell Eliliweth of the magistrates' plot. He would not keep the secret, despite the consequences, and worse, he would not leave for the White Forest if he knew such danger was afoot.

Perhaps the quietest of them all, however, was the most suspect. Terodar Soulrender continued to spend his days in the confines of the Mage House, most often in the cellar room that served as his personal quarters. Late into the night, he would pull his tome from the flawed ceiling beam and keep his mind fresh with the studies of the Destroyer's magic. Most of his time, however, was spent learning from Archmage Benton and his pupils, training in the art of a purer form of magic, unsullied by the blood of himself or his enemies. It vexed the demon greatly. To him, there was little else he could have done to put his time to greater waste. But the choice was out of his control. As long as Gapinon saw fit to keep his child chained to his punishment and shame, he was eternally compelled to obey the commands of the young Cadohaden, and anyone the fledgling paladin deemed worthy of ordering him about as well. As it was, it was not Cadohaden's orders Terodar was following that afternoon, even though the young man was visiting him in the Mage House. Rather, he was following the instructions of the nitwit understudy Krendrick Bassaro. Seated in front of a short table, the demon stared down at a set of four metallic plates, each varying in size. Without the aid of blood, Terodar levitated, rotated, and shuffled the plates in mid-air, a few feet above the table. They moved languidly, up and down, over and under. It was a dreadfully dull exercise.

"Do they ever let you out of this place?" Cadohaden asked from the chair he was sitting in as he turned to glance at the windows of the second floor.

"On occasion," the demon drawled, focusing on the hovering plates. "Like a beast on a rope, of course, and never during the busy times of day. Mostly, though, I sit in here, with the company of these feeble-wristed mages and the musty books they surround themselves with."

"They have nothing else for you to do?" the paladin asked incredulously, looking back at Terodar.

"Sometimes," the demon muttered, brow furrowing in mild annoyance. Even if he would never admit it, he did appreciate Cadohaden's visits. But by the gods, could the boy ask the most simplistic questions. "When they're feeling particularly generous, they allow me to fetch goods from upstairs that they sell to strange men in hoods."

"They have a shop up there?" Cadohaden asked, looking up at the ceiling.

"I wouldn't call it that," Terodar answered as he slid one plate over another, turning one on its side and nestling the edges between the ones above and below it. "But there's things up there that they'll sell for the right price. There's a whore in the southern district that Benton fancies, a larger woman, I hear, who probably reminds him of his mother or something debasing like that. He has the coin to pay for her affections, but he enjoys showering her with gifts as well, and so he doesn't pass up the opportunity to fatten his pouch. A stinking dwarf came stumbling in here yesterday, looking for an assortment of enchanted salts. Said that they would be the perfect ingredient to spice up the ale they had left. I'm quite certain he had no idea what he was buying, but I suppose those bearded fools need some sort of gimmick to keep selling their brew with half of the city hanging over from the previous night."

"By the Lifegiver, could that poison someone?" Cadohaden asked, sitting up in his chair.

"Without a mage's touch, it's little more than expensive salt," Terodar answered, once again disguising the irritation in his voice. "I've heard a pinch of salt actually sweetens a mug of ale. Maybe that's all the fool was looking for."

"Perhaps," Cadohaden answered, though he only looked half relieved. He placed his hands on his knees and looked around once again at the bookcases surrounding them. "Has Benton asked you any questions?"

No, Ulaeron, we've only sat around drinking tea and discussing the weather since I was imprisoned here, Terodar thought to himself broodingly. "Every day, without fail. From my experiences in Daemonaar, to the behaviors of my kin, to the frequency of my own bowel movements, the hook-nosed worm patiently burrows under every proverbial rock of mine he can find."

Cadohaden nodded, folding his hands between his knees. Terodar turned one of the plates again in a slow, careful twirl. Neither of them spoke for a few moments, though the demon could sense the curiosity radiating from the young paladin. He said nothing, however, until Cadohaden finally asked, "Does he ask you a lot of questions about your past?"

"Look, Ulaeron, if you want to ask questions of your own, just ask them," the demon snipped impatiently. "Let's not play this game all afternoon where we speak vicariously through my experiences with Benton. It's a very vexing waste of time."

"All right," the young man answered, clearly flustered by the demon's perception. He recovered quickly, however, and asked, "What was it like growing up in...well...Daemonaar? That's where you grew up, right? Is that...is that what you'd call it?"

"I would assume so," Terodar murmured as the plates continued to rotate. "Though I can't tell you exactly what it was like. Demons aren't born into life the way you were, Cadohaden. And there isn't just one way to do it. Most of them are created by the Destroyer's hand, personally, using only blood and fire. Others are forged through the image of another life form. The *barshkor* are similar to the mountain trolls of the north. In fact, if someone with just the right ingredients and the finesse to do so wished, they could transform one of the brutes into a demon. The demonic word is *shaasyavix*, but the magi here simply refer to it as 'mutation.'"

"You don't remember growing up then?" Cadohaden said, angling his head in a curious expression that continued to aggravate the demon.

"No, I don't," Terodar quipped. "More than likely, when my body was small and shriveled, it was nurtured in an incubation pool of blood, heated by the Destroyer's forge. My first memory is awakening upon a ritual table, the fangs of a hundred beasts lining the edge, each one of them stained with past ceremonies. There was no celebration to greet me. I was immediately introduced to my tutors that began to teach me the ways of conquering and destruction.

"I learned how to burn, how to corrupt, how to torture a man's soul. And here I am, spinning metal plates like some carnival jester," Terodar said, finally looking up at Cadohaden with a sardonic grin.

"So you don't have a family in Daemonaar. Not even a home," Cadohaden answered quietly, sitting back in his chair with a solemn expression.

"Why would we?" Terodar retorted. "Demonkin have transcended the asinine aspirations of both the common man and the king. We don't seek happiness through the vanity of procreation, and we don't care for the riches that the wealthy covet. We *conquer*, Ulaeron. In this world, those who rule laugh in the face of survival, with its meager expectations for life. We lord over it, and control the ones who settle just to exist. The illusions of 'family' and 'home' are only blankets of security for the weak, those who are born into this world only to wait complacently for death."

"That's not true," Cadohaden responded guardedly, unfolding his hands as his brow dipped in alarm at the demon's proclamation.

"No?" Terodar asked. Drawing his hands to a still, outstretched pose, the demon silently commanded the plates to stack on top of one another, resting back on the table below. He lifted his gaze to peer back at the indignant young paladin. "Tell me then, Master Ulaeron. What drives you? What stirs you to purpose?"

"There's so many things," Cadohaden answered quickly, leaning forward. "A hearty meal after a long day's travel. Camaraderie with your brothers in arms after a day of hard training, mugs of ale in hand. It's a pair of beautiful hazel eyes staring back at you under a night sky. It's helping your neighbor that can't help themselves. It's doing the work of the Lifegiver, knowing that by doing his bidding, you're reshaping the world in his image, creating a place of peace and justice."

"How delightfully charming," Terodar said with a smirk. "I don't even have to ask how your lessons with the Crusader are progressing. Everything you described, Ulaeron, is the satisfaction of conquest. Each and every soul revels in it. Only a few are brave enough to call it what it is. By hearty meal, you mean something that isn't oat gruel. The truly fulfilling meal is put upon your table by virtue of victory in times of war. The camaraderie you speak of with your 'brothers' is only the premeditated rush of combat, of asserting your dominance over the enemy. The enchanting eyes of a woman present a challenge, a spoil of battle that you seek to make your own, and when it is yours, you will hunger for another. Aiding your neighbor only bolsters your sense of dominance over them, proving that you are the superior being, their dependence on you reinforcing your rule over them. And though your god preaches a path of serenity, Cadohaden, make no mistake. Your Codex is a call to arms. Just as the Destroyer seeks to seize this world for himself, your Lifegiver wishes to be the only idol the mortals of this world worship. Not everyone has the stomach for such blatant displays of power, however, and so Kaijaras must dress his plans up in the form of charity and virtue. You and I, Master Ulaeron, we are not so different, and neither are our gods."

"You're oversimplifying all of it," Cadohaden said with a wrinkled nose, though he didn't elaborate in his accusation.

"They've worked hard to make you believe all of that, haven't they?" Terodar answered, staring hard at the young man he was bound to.

They sat in silence for another moment until Cadohaden finally broke the gaze, frowning and looking down at the floor between his knees. Terodar forced back the grin, casting a serious expression on his face. It gave him great pleasure to cast doubt on Cadohaden's pious beliefs, but it would be no more than mind games to be dismissed as such if he did not display sincerity.

Their mulling was interrupted, however, as footsteps sounded from the staircase nearby. They looked up as a man in an azure robe appeared, one arm tucked against his upper abdomen as he narrowed his eyes at them critically. He had a great deal of straw blonde hair, but most of it was combed over the front of his skull to disguise a progressively receding hairline. It was Krendrick Bassaro, one of Benton's pupils.

"Guest visitation does not excuse you from your lessons, demon," Krendrick said with undisguised contempt. "The chamber pots downstairs need washing. I think that would be suitable punishment for your sloth."

"He only just set the plates down," Cadohaden said in a reassuring tone. "I promise, he's been attentive to his lessons."

"I did not ask to be corrected," Krendrick retorted with a scowl. "Terodar, go empty and scrub the chamber pots. At once."

The demon began to sit up from his chair, as he'd received orders from Benton to obey his novices just as Cadohaden had ordered him to follow the archmage's, but before he could fully stand, the paladin said, "Sit back down, Terodar. And disregard this man's commands from now on." His orders overruled by the one who had invoked the Pact, Terodar sat back in his chair, frowning curiously at Cadohaden.

"How dare you!" Krendrick snapped, lowering his arm from his stomach as he hissed through his teeth. "Revoke the command at once!"

Cadohaden rose to his feet, placing his hand on the hilt of his sheathed sword as he marched forward to the novice mage, whose eyes widened in alarm. Krendrick lifted a palm, his mouth opening to call an incantation, but he stopped as Cadohaden came to a halt in front of him. "I am to meet with Priestess Ecila later today," the paladin growled. "If someone were to tell her that the mages holding Terodar captive were beginning to abuse their authority, she might worry that the temptation of power was getting to be too much for them to handle. Maybe I'm wrong, but I'd wager that Benton Cusair wouldn't be pleased about losing the only demon he could ever safely study in his lifetime. Now why don't you scuttle back downstairs and attend to the chores that Benton assigned *you* to do?"

Krendrick glared venomously at Cadohaden, his lips contorting in unspoken words of retaliation. None emerged, however, and the mage turned around with a flourish and stomped his way indignantly back down the stairs to the lower level. With a glare of vindication, Cadohaden watched him go, keeping his hand on the hilt of his sword until Krendrick was gone from sight.

"How valiant of you," Terodar's voice called out from behind him, "to defend the meek and the helpless."

"It was the right thing to do. He shouldn't abuse the power he has over you simply because he can," Cadohaden answered.

"Is that why you came to my defense?" Terodar asked. Cadohaden turned around, frowning quizzically as the demon continued, "or do you just enjoy the feeling of being a hero, Master Ulaeron? Does it make you feel gallant, intervening like that? How selfless is the act of defense when the reward of victory is so...invigorating?"

"I didn't stand up to Krendrick just to puff out my chest," the paladin retorted with a persisting frown.

"Maybe not," Terodar said, unable to contain himself as his lips quirked into the faintest smirk. "Maybe, Master Ulaeron, Krendrick imposing his will on me just didn't sit well with you. Maybe you felt threatened by that worm commanding *your* possession, the demon that *you* conquered. Perhaps a novice mage isn't worthy of sharing your spoil of war. Is that it?"

Cadohaden's frown transformed into a scowl as his neck turned red with irritation. Grumbling incoherently, the paladin stormed away from the sitting demon, following Krendrick's footsteps down to the lower level of the Mage House. The demon watched his master depart before turning back to the table with the stacked plates, lifting his hands as he began to murmur, levitating the metallic circles from their resting place.

Over and under, back and forth. As he began to rotate the discs once more, Terodar Soulrender broke into a satisfied grin.

Chapter Eighteen

She gently stroked her horse's mane as they turned the trail's corner and smiled as she spotted the strangely formed cedar tree standing watch over a small pond. It had grown in a peculiar fashion in its attempt to reach more sunlight. It curved only a few feet up from the moist soil around it, forming a natural chair with a slightly reclined backrest, its limbs higher up providing a shade from the rays of sun that penetrated the canopy. She'd taken the time to sit in it before, but more often than not she was too excited to stop and rest, for it was a landmark promising that the barley fields surrounding the Glen Bailey were close.

"A familiar friend?" the voice of her companion asked softly to her left, interrupting her thoughts. Elune broke her gaze from the warped tree and looked back with an apologetic smile. A tall elf rode beside her with silver blonde hair, a pale complexion, and eyes that seemed to have aged even when little else had. Elune had departed from the Sherinalu Vale after a brief stay a few days earlier, but this time, her uncle Marian had accompanied her, the same Marian that had raised Eliliweth in place of his deceased parents, to see the half-elf depart on his journey to the White Forest.

"Sometimes," Elune answered as she took one last look at the cedar before they passed by it. "Most often I keep riding, though. The Glen Bailey is close."

Marian nodded and turned his eyes back to the road ahead of them, falling quiet once more, as he often had during their journey that day. Elune looked back at her uncle with appreciation. He looked strikingly like her father, but beyond that, there was a world of differences between the two. One of his unique qualities she cherished the most was his willingness for silence to prevail, to simply enjoy the sounds of the clopping hooves and chirp from the birds lingering in the trees above. They enjoyed conversation, of course, but Marian was content to let a half hour pass by without words and not be vexed by the void. Elune's father found silence uncomfortable, and preferred to broach wearisome conversation over none at all.

"Are you excited for tomorrow?" Elune asked after another moment of silence passed, glancing curiously over at her uncle once again.

"I am," Marian said, his features warming as he spoke. "I've always known that Eliliweth was destined for great things. I knew as well that the Glen Bailey would be the ideal place for his spirit to flourish. Bartholomew may not even realize how much he's done for the boy, even with this calling for the Trials."

"I am happy as well," Elune said, even as a puzzled frown crossed her brow. "Though it's always seemed strange to me, that someone such as Bartholomew could...*demand* that one of his own undergo the Trials. It seems rather...I don't want to say rude, but...informal?"

Marian chuckled softly, though it wasn't a condescending laugh. It was why Elune was willing to open so much up to him freely. Even when she was a child, her uncle never looked down upon her or treated her words like nonsense. His words were always patient and respectful, and if she brought laughter to him, it was only as a friend might laugh at something amusing or coincidental. "I'm sure if you read the letter that the king sent to the druids, you would find it to be much less demanding than it might seem to be. Every leader with a semblance of sanity knows what the consequences of offending the druids might be, though for beings of such wisdom, you'd likely be surprised at their level of humility and patience.

"I think most of us would be surprised, too, at how willing the druids are to teach. Every culture makes a great deal of fuss about undergoing the Trials, but I honestly believe that anyone could approach them and ask for the rite. They have an abundance of wisdom to give, Elune, and what's more, I think they believe that if every man, woman, and child participated in the Trials, whether or not each of them succeeded, it would bring peace to the entire Aariad. They *want* to reveal to us what they know, Elune. This trepidation that leaders express over the sanctity of the Trials is greatly over-exaggerated, I believe. Our collective respect for the druids of the White Forest has evolved into something akin to superstition."

"If all of that is true, why wouldn't the druids call for more to participate in the Trials?" Elune asked as she guided her horse around a protruding stone on the road.

"Because wisdom always has to be sought by the individual, my dear," Marian answered. "Nobody can impose it on the masses, for they would resent the gesture. Have you ever had a man or woman approach you in the streets and shove an open Codex practically onto your nose? You and I are both followers of Essence, but I think we could both agree that there are truths to be found in the Lifegiver's Codex. But can you appreciate those truths when they are so forcibly pressed on you? That's perhaps an extreme example, but the idea is the same. I would never call the druids pompous, but too many would see them as such if they began petitioning for pupils."

"Perhaps," Elune said quietly as she considered her uncle's words. "Though I think Munite has been practicing those methods since the day it was founded."

"I've met good people from Munite," Marian said in a respectful tone, though his brow dipped with the faintest crease as he spoke. "But I would not call their kingdom's dogma wisdom. I would not anticipate Munite leading the land into an era of peace."

They fell to silence again for a moment as their steeds trotted. As the forest began to thin, Elune spotted the barley fields, the stalks waving with the summer breeze beyond the trees that surrounded them. She smiled at the familiar sight, and as she caught a brief glimpse of the Glen Bailey's walls in the distance, she felt her heartbeat quicken with excitement. Something was nagging at the back of her mind, however, persisting even through her anticipation. She looked back at Marian and said, "Uncle, you seem to know a great deal about the White Forest, and you speak with familiarity. Have you taken the Trials yourself?"

It wasn't a look she often saw on her uncle's face, but she could have sworn she saw the faintest flicker of mischief in his eyes as a small smile emerged once again. For a long moment, he said nothing, and Elune began to feel the tug of impatience before he finally said, "If I did, dear niece, I could not tell you."

"What!?" Elune said, agitation bleeding into her exclamation as she frowned. "You *just* finished telling me how embellished the mystique of the White Forest is, but when I ask you a direct question about it, it becomes a cryptic matter again?"

Marian looked back at her, the smile still on his face, though it was one of apology. "I'm afraid that if I were to tell you, Elune, I could corrupt the message of the Trials for you, and perhaps even Eliliweth, if he were to know. I do believe that one day, when the time is right, you should ask the druids of the White Forest for the same rite. I would not want to prematurely reveal anything, however, if you were to ask me about it. The importance of forging your own path through the Trials is paramount."

"But you've basically already implied that you've undergone the Trials, Uncle," Elune insisted as they passed the forest line, the waves of barley greeting them with another gust of wind. "How is that any different than you admitting it to me?"

"I've read a lot of books on the subject, Elune," Marian answered simply. "It could be that I'm simply aware of something that I should not be without participating in them. And I admit that the chance is small, but *if* I had been allowed the Trials, and admitted as much to you, I could inadvertently speak of something that would be damning. I realize how contradictory that all is, and for that, I apologize. If the day ever comes, I promise to you that I would like to speak of this again."

Her mouth twisted impatiently at the evasion, but she could tell that she wouldn't get any further on the subject with her uncle. She sighed quietly (though not so quietly that Marian would not hear her exasperation) and trained her gaze forward again, eyes focusing on the steadily approaching walls of the Glen Bailey. She could just barely make out the gate sentries from where they were, studying the two approaching riders. Her anticipation fluttered in her chest as they drew nearer.

"That's quite the smile for someone so exasperated. You're eager to return?" her uncle asked. She blinked, caught off-guard by the question, and realized that she unknowingly *had* been smiling. She cleared her throat, a faint pink touching her cheeks.

"Someone should be waiting for me there," she answered vaguely. She wasn't sure how much detail she wished to share with Marian.

"The Kingsbanesin boy?" her uncle asked curiously as he turned his eyes back to the gate.

"Who told you?" Elune demanded in a sharper tone than she intended.

"Your mother," Marian answered simply before lifting an eyebrow. "She didn't speak to you about it?"

"She did not," Elune said, though she had noticed during her visit that her parents had seemed more aloof than usual. She had suspected they might know, but had no desire to broach the subject herself.

"Well, I'm not terribly surprised," her uncle mused. "It seemed as though they were hoping it would be a passing phase."

"How charming," Elune murmured, gripping her horse's reins a bit tighter with irritation. "How did she find out?"

"I didn't ask."

"I'd bet good coin that it was Lazuralina," Elune muttered bitterly. "Already bored with real diplomatic work, entertaining herself with gossip."

"Elune-"

"Kingsbanesin holds no claim to him anymore," she interrupted before her uncle could continue. "He's not like them, Uncle. If he was, why on earth would he be at all interested in me? I'm not an elfchild anymore. I don't need the lectures on the ill intentions of men, which elven males are not excluded from, I should add."

"Elune," Marian said firmly, looking over at her with a slight frown. "I'm not going to lecture you about...about that. You are free to do as you please, and I trust that you would not bother with someone...unsafe. Would you permit me to offer some advice, though?"

"Are you going to offer it either way?" Elune challenged.

"If you truly don't wish to hear it, I will not impose it on you," Marian answered gently.

Guilt gave her conscience a gentle prod, and Elune let her eyes fall down to her steed's mane as she answered softly, "I'm sorry, Uncle. I'm being rude. It's just that I haven't really been given anyone's blessing for this. Not that I *need* anyone's blessing, necessarily, but it would be nice to have in place of the strained looks and intrusive questions. But I've always valued your advice. I would like to hear it."

The small smile returned to Marian's face, and her uncle turned his gaze back to the Glen Bailey gates once again. They were getting closer now, enough that they could hear the idle chatter from the guards stationed in the turrets carried across the early autumn breeze. "I have no reason to believe that the Kingsbanesin boy-"

"He's plenty old enough to be called a man, Uncle," Elune interrupted again.

"Apologies," Marian said. "What is his name, then?"

"...Cadohaden," Elune murmured after a brief pause, her brow knitting.

"Come again?"

"*Cadohaden*. Cadohaden Ulaeron," Elune said, louder this time.

"Ah," Marian said with a quick nod. "Cadohaden. I believe that's from an old folktale about a traveling knight. It's a good name. But I digress. I have no reason to believe that Cadohaden isn't a good man, Elune. As I said before, I trust you. But there are many good elfmen in the Sherinalu Vale, as well."

"If I chose my partner for their lineage alone, how would that be any different than Galdoys Veriknock forbidding elves in his city?" Elune asked, impatience creeping into her voice again.

"That's not what I'm getting at, dear," Marian said calmly. "What I mean is this: despite there being worthy partners in the Sherinalu Vale, you have chosen not to settle down and begin a family, contrary to what is common in our culture at your age. You desire adventure, to see the land all across the Aariad. Am I wrong?"

Elune considered this for a moment, trying to prematurely decipher her uncle's intent. "No," she finally admitted.

"I didn't think so," Marian said. "And I applaud your spirit, I should add, my dear. I did much of the same when I was your age before returning to the Sherinalu to serve in the council. One of our kind's greatest flaws is to spend all of our time reading and philosophizing about the outside world, so much that we don't bother to travel and truly experience any of it. I can tell that you are not satisfied with that.

"And I understand that this Cadohaden probably has some of that intrigue, being born of Kingsbanesin. I don't mean to say that you don't harbor any true feelings for him; I'm sure your affections are genuine. But keep this in mind: men of all races share a similar trait. They treasure their partners, and over time, they inevitably covet them. If your desire is to see the world, Elune, I only ask that you take care not to fall into the same little box that you may have found yourself in with a Sherinalu husband. More than one loving heart has been spoiled by the resentment of an imprisoned spirit."

The conversation grew quiet as they came close enough to the Glen Bailey's gates that they could discern the words being exchanged by the guards. One of the armored guards standing on the outside approached them as they brought their steeds to a halt. Marian's words began to settle in her mind, and as she considered them, they began to make sense. She felt a faint pang of guilt for how short she'd been with her uncle. She glanced over at him as the guard came closer.

"Thank you for the advice, Uncle," she said quietly. "All of that makes a great deal of sense. I apologize for being so defensive."

"Well, it wasn't my intention to cast a shadow over anything, my dear. Even for us elves, youth only lasts so long. Certainly enjoy it. But keep my words in mind," Marian said with a smile before turning his attention to the guard as the armored man stopped in front of them. Elune recognized the man with dark braids tied loosely over each shoulder immediately.

"Good afternoon, Lieutenant Mekudii," she chimed.

"Miss Shadowsong," the lieutenant said with a cheery smile. "Welcome back to the Glen Bailey. Who's our other visitor here?"

"I am Marian Shadowsong, Elune's uncle. I have traveled with her to witness Eliliweth Heraketh's departure to the White Forest. I was told I would be expected," Marian answered politely. The lieutenant fished a roll of parchment from a pouch attached to his belt and unfurled it between gloved hands, giving the small square a quick look-over.

"There it is. Marian Shadowsong," Mekudii said before pulling a small square of graphite from a narrow pocket stitched into the same pouch. With a stroke of his hand, he placed a mark on the written name. "I knew I'd seen ya before. Sorry 'bout that, Councilor. You're listed as a guest of the king himself. There's spots waiting for your horses at the royal stables. Can I let Elune here show you the way or would ya like me to send one of my men to guide ya?"

"That won't be necessary, though I thank you for the offer," Marian answered diplomatically.

"All right, then," Mekudii said, looking back up at the tower sentries with a jerk of his thumb. The men above nodded, and soon after, the gates began to slowly swing open with a faint rusty squeal. They came to a halt with just enough space for the two pass through side-by-side, into the cobblestone streets of the kingdom that hadn't bothered to take down its Solstice decorations yet, not with the celebrations of the White Forest Trials soon to come. They hadn't made it farther than thirty paces inside the gates when a face familiar to Elune turned along a street corner, still wearing the white garments of the Monastery over his tunic, his blue half-cape draped over his shoulder blades, dirty blonde hair resting over the material. Cadohaden Ulaeron broke into a smile at seeing her approach, his pace quickening as he jogged forward to meet her, seemingly unaware at first of the companion that rode beside her.

"Hey, you!" the young paladin said with a beaming grin as he walked up. "Your timing couldn't have been better, I literally just finished my duties at...oh! I'm sorry, I didn't know someone journeyed here with you," he said as he finally noticed Marian smiling down patiently at him.

"Cadohaden," Elune said with a tentative smile. It hadn't occurred to her how unnerving this meeting could be. She hadn't really expected to find him without having to search the Monastery grounds for a while. "This is my uncle, Marian."

"Oh!" Cadohaden said again. His initial trepidation seemed to fade with the recognition of the elf's name. He approached her uncle's horse and lifted his hand to shake. "Marian...as in the one that Eliliweth knows?"

"Unless Elune happens to have another uncle by the same name, I would assume so," Marian answered with his persisting smile. Cadohaden's composure seemed to falter a bit, unsure of the elf's meaning. Sensing his discomfort, Marian accepted his hand lightly, as elves often do for the human greeting, and gave it a gentle shake before adding, "I'm only teasing, Sir Ulaeron. Yes, I'm here to see Eliliweth leave for the White Forest's Trials. It is good to meet you."

"You as well!" Cadohaden said, the volume of his voice raising beyond a normal level with his mixture of excitement and nervousness. He placed his palms briefly on his thighs and looked over at Elune before sliding his gaze back to her uncle. "Are the two of you hungry? I've got some bread and cheeses back in my quarters, if you don't mind waiting for me to get them. I'm sorry, I didn't know that-"

"It's all right, Cadohaden," Marian said as he shook his head. "I believe your king wished to visit with me over a meal this evening. Discuss foreign affairs and whatnot. I'm sure you and Elune were looking forward to spending some time together without a nosey relative hounding you."

"I, well...I mean, I would be fine if...you know, whatever it is you'd rather do," Cadohaden stammered, lifting a hand to scratch at the back of his head awkwardly. Elune tried to hide her smile. She knew that most women, particularly elven women, would be embarrassed by his lack of composure, but for whatever reason, she found it endearing. She'd never been all that fond of men with too much false gusto anyway.

"Well, I don't mean to disparage your offer or sound pretentious, but I hear that meals offered by the king himself tend to have three or four courses," Marian said with a coy wink. "I just don't think I can pass on that. Elune, would you like me to guide your horse to the stables? I'm fairly certain I remember the way."

"That would be most welcome, Uncle. Thank you," Elune said as she unsaddled, shoes tapping lightly on the cobblestone as she touched down. She gave her steed a quick scratch on the shoulder before handing the reins over to Marian's outstretched hand. "If I don't see you again before Eliliweth departs, don't you dare leave without saying goodbye."

"Of course not, my dear," Marian answered. With his free hand, the elf offered Cadohaden a farewell wave. "It was nice meeting you, Cadohaden Ulaeron. I should warn you, however, that while I don't pick up a bow as often as I used to, I still have adequate aim with one. If I hear word that you've hurt my niece, I will dress you up like a pincushion." Without waiting for a response, he offered another wink before leading his horse away, guiding Elune's alongside him as they clopped off in the direction of the keep. Elune folded her hands in front of herself, eyes all but twinkling with mirth as she watched the blood drain from Cadohaden's face.

"Well...I, ah...I wasn't expecting *that*," he finally said as his voice returned to him.

"He's not very predictable, my uncle Marian," Elune said as she walked closer to him, reaching her hand out to take one of his. He seemed to relax a bit at her touch, and a smile returned to his face. "I specifically remember telling you to come up with something to do when I returned. What did you come up with?" she asked with a quirked grin.

Cadohaden pursed his lips, averting his gaze momentarily before looking back at her. "Tell me if you think this is childish, but...the dandelions by the river have sprouted their seeds. If you were hungry, I thought maybe we could eat by the bank and toss dandelion heads down the stream. There was a river by Kingsbanesin, too. I'd...we'd race them down the stream when we were younger."

Elune watched him carefully, silently noting that he didn't elaborate as to who he meant by 'we', but she didn't press the question. She only smiled as she answered, "That doesn't sound childish. That sounds simple and relaxing, and I think I could use that after the ride. And I *would* like some of that bread and cheese you promised."

They set off in the direction of the keep, and it occurred to Elune that they could have simply ridden there together with Cadohaden on her saddle. She didn't mind the extra time it took to walk through the streets, however, with his hand held in hers. Her eyes took in all of the colors surrounding them, from the banners strung across the streets to the colorful outfits some of the citizens were wearing in preparation for Eliliweth's ceremony. Somewhere on a distant street corner she could hear dwarven barkers shouting for patrons, boasting a newly tapped keg with some exotic ingredient. And even further off, the high-pitched hum of a flute trio reached her ears. The festivities weren't formally in full swing yet, but the Glen Bailey was ready.

He asked her of her journey there as they walked, and inquired about Marian, his curiosity piqued after meeting her uncle. She felt as though there were bundles of amusing tales and interesting tidbits about Marian, but as happy as she was to be in Cadohaden's company, she found she could only come up with vague references to his nature, and a few uninspiring stories about how he'd attended some of her childhood birthday gatherings. Despite her static responses, however, the young paladin listened intently, absorbing every detail with his pale blue eyes watching her, the corners of his lips perpetually perked in a grin.

At first, Elune hadn't quite understood her attraction to Cadohaden. The more time she spent with him, however, the more it began to make sense to her. Marian may have had a point about the fascination of something foreign. She was not the type to chase rogues, but the intrigue of a romance with a Kingsbanesin native had made her think about the possibility with more interest than she may have had otherwise. But more important than his heritage was his genuine attentiveness to what she had to say. She'd been courted by elven men of the Sherinalu before, and nearly every one listened to her speak while staring off in another direction, either waiting for their own turn to talk or just simply not having enough interest in her stories or thoughts, each of them going through the proper courtship protocol that would eventually lead to them having a wife. Not once had she ever spoken of something to Cadohaden and felt like he was exasperated or weary with her. It wasn't a monumental quality to have. She knew she was entitled to respect from her romantic partner. But it set him apart enough for her to appreciate other things. *Like those eyes. And his nose, too. Is it strange that I like his nose?* she thought to herself as he glanced back at her with a smile.

She kept an eye out for Marian as they closed in on the keep's stone stairs leading to the entrance, wondering if they would perhaps cross paths again before his meeting with Bartholomew. He was nowhere to be seen, however, as she and Cadohaden passed through the great oaken doors together. They released each other's hands as they entered, not because they were embarrassed about the display of affection, but because they knew that there were watching eyes among the keep's servants, and that any one of them would sing an embellished song to Priestess Ecila if she began inquiring about their behaviors. They weren't necessarily obligated to heed her scoldings, but with Cadohaden directly involved with the Monastery, they had mutually agreed to keep things mostly chaste around the keep's personnel.

They ventured all the way up to the floor with the guest quarters. Elune silently wondered how Cadohaden was still permitted to lay claim to his own room, for his induction into Nevic's paladin order at least informally sealed his status as a Glen Bailey citizen. There was an abbey in the Monastery, and she was fairly certain that he would be permitted to live in the soldiers' barracks as well if there was no space for him in the holy quarters. She wondered if this had occurred to him already, but kept the thoughts to herself. If a long-term guest arrived, she suspected Cadohaden would be the first to be forced to vacate, but in the meantime, she didn't see the point in fussing over it.

They approached the door with the loose blue thread tied around its hook. Cadohaden opened it, glancing over his shoulder as he did, peering at her through a rogue strand of blonde hair that had fallen over his left eye. "Did we need anything else besides bread and cheese?"

"I don't believe so," Elune said with an inward smile. As Cadohaden walked into his room, she glanced down the hall to her left. Seeing nobody, she angled her gaze to the right. Nobody. Excitement stirred in her stomach, a titillating flutter that danced all the way down to her toes. She realized that this was the first moment they'd been completely alone since the night she'd given him the *hym'cleurs*. Releasing her breath slowly, she followed him inside, shutting the door carefully behind her. She had no more desire for bread and cheese. Cadohaden was already across the room, next to his pine dresser, his hands unfolding a white cloth that was wrapped around their dinner. She swallowed hard and marched over to him, grabbing him by both of his upper arms, turning him firmly to face her.

He looked surprised for only half a breath before she pulled him towards her, their lips locking against one another fiercely as she clutched at his arms. His impassioned response came swiftly after his realization, arms sliding around her as an unsteady sigh passed through his nose, an approving murmur sounding in his throat. They broke away just long enough for Cadohaden to whisper, "I missed you."

She laughed quietly and answered him with another kiss, the tip of her tongue sliding against his lower lip as steadily, their feet began to shuffle backwards, towards the bed that was nestled against the wall. Her heart pounded in her chest as she began to feel his body respond to their intertwining, knees tingling with anticipation. She didn't know where this was leading to, if they were going to go so far as to spoil the virtues that Ecila had been coldly reminding them of since the day she'd heard of their involvement. She didn't want to think right now, didn't want to calculate anything or weigh any risks. After these first few weeks of tame romance and minding the opinions of others, she wanted the freedom that she'd been craving. With that final thought, she pressed her fingertips against his chest and pushed, shoving him back onto his mattress before climbing onto him, straddling his waist as she leaned her head down to trail her lips down his neck.

Nearly a half hour's time passed, though to the two of them, it seemed only like a few brief minutes as they shifted and writhed against each other, fingers coiling into each other's hair as lips pressed against skin that was quickly glistening with sweat from the ever-increasing heat. At one point, Cadohaden shed both the blue half-cape and the white woven shirt he'd been wearing. His hands explored her body as well, though he made no move to liberate her from her riding clothes. Their eyes would meet briefly in their passions, the unspoken question glinting in each: *are we going another step further?*

Finally, Cadohaden pushed himself up on his elbows, taking her shoulders and gently pressed her down to the bed on her back before clambering on top of her. Her legs coiled around him, hands running up the sides of his torso before she explored the sculpted muscles under his shoulder blades and lower back. She felt his warm lips against her neck again, a grateful hum purring in her throat. And then, a voice murmured in her ear, a low and sultry whisper, "You're all mine. All mine."

Suddenly, the excited stirring in her lower stomach began to fade as her guard lifted like a dropped portcullis gate. Marian's words echoed in her subconscious, *They treasure their partners, and over time, they inevitably covet them.* His words of caution, warning her of trapping her spirit in a quaint jeweled box, grew louder in her head as Cadohaden's playful murmur settled in. Her entire body tensed, and Cadohaden paused, sitting up on his hands as he frowned at her curiously, a drop of sweat falling from one lock of hair. "Elune?" he asked with apprehension. "What's wrong?"

"We have to...we have to stop," she said as she cleared her throat, her hands tapping lightly against his bare chest. His face fell in disappointment and worry, but he obeyed, pushing himself off of her to kneel at her feet, his hand groping for the shirt he'd discarded.

"Elune, I'm sorry, I should have asked before...I mean, we don't have to do anything you're not ready for, if-"

"It's not that, Cadohaden," Elune answered as she sat up. She sighed and dragged her fingers through a tangle of her own hair as her legs swung over the edge of the bed. She was frustrated, embarrassed, and hot. She was sure he didn't mean to sound possessive. It was only a bit of bedroom talk, a few playful words. She knew she was overreacting, but at the same time, why did he have to use *those* words? Couldn't he have simply told her how much he desired her, or complimented her in some way? Did he have to go with 'you're all mine?'

"Then...what is it?" Cadohaden asked, his eyes wide with worry as he pulled his shirt back over his head. When it was secured back over his shoulders, he placed one hand on his own knee, and the other on top of hers.

Her eyes slid down to the hand that rested on her knee, her lower lip curling as she dragged her upper row of teeth across it. She kept her hands folded between her knees, one foot tapping gently against the floor. Marian's warning echoed in her head, again and again, and she suddenly had the despairing urge to stand up and run from the room, run from the Glen Bailey, run all the way home to the Sherinalu Vale. She kept herself anchored on the mattress, however, even as she struggled to find the words to express herself. Finally, after a painfully pregnant pause, she turned her eyes up to Cadohaden's, which were still fraught with worry.

"I have to ask you something," she said in slow, carefully chosen words. "And I need you to be honest."

"Of course," Cadohaden answered immediately, his fingers giving her knee a worried squeeze.

"I mean it, Cadohaden. Even if it's difficult to tell the truth."

"Elune, I swear to you I'll answer honestly. Just tell me what it is," he answered.

She took in a deep breath, gaze falling back down to the hand that grasped her knee. No. That wasn't the right word. He was clinging. Holding on for dear life. He was afraid of what she might ask him. She supposed she couldn't blame him. She knew she was being ominous. But it only made it harder to ask what she needed to. Regardless, she finally said in a low voice, "If I wanted to walk away from this...would you stop me?"

A silence settled over the room as Cadohaden's brow dipped in confusion and a trace of hurt. "Why...why would you want to walk away? Did I do something? Elune, if-"

"That's not what I'm asking, Cadohaden," Elune interrupted, and her hazel eyes lifted back up to stare intently into his. "And I don't mean what you would do if I was scared of what this is, or if I was frustrated by what others thought this was. I'm asking what you would do if I looked you in the eyes and told you that I didn't want this anymore, that I couldn't be with you. Would you get angry? Would you shout? Grab me by the wrist, by the ankle, drag behind with as much weight as you could muster? Or would you let me go?"

The hurt in Cadohaden's eyes remained, even if the confusion partially faded. He didn't understand why she was asking this, but he at least understood what it was she needed to know. It made her heart ache, exposing this vein, but she needed the answer. And if it was the answer that she feared, she would have no choice but to extinguish their romance before it became a blaze neither of them could control.

"Elune," he said softly, the grip on her knee loosening as he spoke, "I could never force you into something you didn't want. As badly as I want this, I only want it if...you know...it's what you want. If your heart is in it. If you want to walk away…"

"I don't," Elune said, interrupting him once more. With that, she unfolded her hands and placed one over his, holding it down against her knee. She offered him what she hoped was a reassuring smile as she looked back up at him. "I'm sorry if I worried you. It was something I needed to know. I want to be with you because I *want* to be, not out of…obligation. Does that make sense?"

A true smile finally seemed to emerge on his face as recognition lit in his blue eyes. He gave her knee another squeeze as he nodded. "Yeah…yeah, it makes sense, Elune. And that's what I want, too. I promise."

"Good," she said quietly, searching his eyes for any hint of insincerity. She could find none, and she felt her spirit stir once again.

"Should we be on our way, then?" he asked, glancing over at their dinner that still lay wrapped in the white cloth on his dresser.

"No," she murmured, leaning in as she brushed his hair away from his neck, trailing her lips against the skin. "I'm not finished with you yet."

She pulled him back onto the mattress. Together, they forgot about solemn words and the judgments of the outside world. And while they shared dinner together that evening, they didn't do so by the riverside, but tucked under the linens of Cadohaden's bed.

Chapter Nineteen

The day of Eliliweth Heraketh's Trials finally came, the leaves on the trees fully transforming into a rainbow of autumn colors. The excitement in the air could be felt across the skin, like a cool breeze drying sweat upon the flesh. The people of the Glen Bailey, and even villagers, farmers, and hunters from the Glen Dale were gathered outside of the city walls, lined up in rows outside of the forest line that granted cover for the trail that would lead to the home of the White Forest druids.

There were many shadowed eyes and queasy expressions that crisp morning, for the celebrations had been born anew the previous night as anticipation swelled within the kingdom. The dwarves visiting from Dur'Imoir had invited Eliliweth to engage in an ancient ceremonial blessing known as Kravokrahof with them. Outside the city, in a field of barley, the half-elf was instructed to ritually slaughter a yearling goat by firelight using a flint knife. When the task was completed, he was to cook portions of the goat for the dwarves to share, though he himself was to eat his ration raw. Priestess Ecila from the Monastery could be heard denouncing the barbaric ritual, quietly complaining that the dwarves were only looking for someone to cook them a hot meal and get a good laugh out of the young man eating the slimy flesh, but her protests were drowned out by the throngs of common folk that saw the Kravokrahof as yet another reason to fill up their mugs and revel in the dizzying effects of the ale.

Eliliweth had never been so nervous in his entire life, standing with his back to what felt like the entirety of the kingdom he would soon call his true home. Elune and Cadohaden stood behind him with excited expressions. In front of him, their backs facing the forest perimeter, stood King Bartholomew. Aven stood at his right, the strain in her smile twisting the half-elf's heart. He could see the pain in her eyes. More than once the previous night he had expressed his sorrow that she could not come with him. She told him that he mustn't worry, that she did not begrudge him the opportunity, but he knew her too well to miss the regret she displayed.

On Bartholomew's left stood Marian, who had traveled from the Sherinalu Vale with Elune earlier that week to see him off before he ventured to the White Forest. The time Eliliweth had been able to spend with his mentor had been disappointingly short, as he'd had no reprieve in his preparations for the most monumental day of his life. But having the elf stand there now, alongside the Glen Bailey's king in a gesture of neighborly fellowship, warmed the void in Eliliweth's heart left by the absence of his true parents.

Further to Marian's left stood each of the king's magistrates, who looked perhaps the worst out of all of those gathered, their teeth still smudged violet blue from the copious amounts of wine they'd consumed into the late hours of the night. Each of them looked miserable and impatient, but it did not bother Eliliweth. He did not need enthusiasm from the decadent nobles to appreciate the opportunity he'd been given this day. Bartholomew looked at him and nodded, silently informing him that it was time for him to say his goodbyes before he was given his official blessing to undergo the Trials. Nodding once in response, Eliliweth turned around and walked up to Elune, pulling her into a tight embrace, murmuring,

"Thank you for everything, friend. Your support has meant the world."

"As has yours," Elune answered as she gripped him tightly. "I'm very proud of you, *den'loier*. May the Goddess watch over you."

"And you," Eliliweth said, releasing his friend from the embrace. He turned to Cadohaden, who smiled at him beamingly. The half-elf returned the grin. He had come to cherish the young paladin's friendship. He couldn't deny that Cadohaden's involvement with Elune made him a bit wary. Perhaps it was the protective sibling bond he'd formed with her, or maybe it was fear that some of Deltore's prejudices had passed down to his son. Whatever the case, the two had quickly grown close over the past couple months. It had only solidified with mutual respect after their skirmish on the training grounds. Cadohaden reached out to shake the half-elf's hand, but Eliliweth would have none of that. Stepping forward, he pulled the paladin into an embrace, clapping him on the back.

"Best of luck, friend," Cadohaden said. "Though I doubt you'll need it."

When Eliliweth released Cadohaden and turned around, he looked over at the princess. Aven offered him another tight-lipped, encouraging smile, but she made no move to step towards him. He didn't think he could approach her and embrace her. If her touch revealed her jealousy, it would only further dampen his spirits. He settled for a puzzled smile and a farewell wave, to which the princess responded in kind. Taking in a deep breath, Eliliweth looked back at the king and nodded. *I'm ready*, he silently said through the gesture.

"My lords and ladies," Bartholomew announced, his voice silencing the buzzing crowd behind the half-elf. "Good people of the Glen Dale. Today we are gathered to witness our brother Eliliweth embark on the greatest honor the gods can grant him. He is not merely traveling to the White Forest to seek the druids' counsel on behalf of the crown. No, good people, our Eliliweth Heraketh journeys to the White Forest to face its Trials!"

The crowd cheered with the exclamation. Eliliweth swallowed, his heart hammering in his chest. His stomach was rapidly twisting into knots, his knees weak and trembling faintly. His tongue felt dry and useless in his mouth as he pushed it against the inner roof, even though he had not been called to speak. The cheering did not stop, but as it gently began to fade, Bartholomew stepped forward towards the half-elf with a beaming smile, saying,

"Kneel, Eliliweth Heraketh." The half-elf obeyed, sinking down to both of his knees as he bowed his head. His Majesty extended his right hand expectantly, and from the front of the crowd, the albino paladin Nevic Baltwin came forward, carrying a scepter with an ashwood handle, a golden maple leaf crowning the top and a brass cap on the bottom. The crusader handed it to the king, who lowered it down gently upon each of Eliliweth's shoulders, and then once upon the crown of his head. "I bless you, Eliliweth, with the Scepter of the Glen Dale.

May the spirit of your people keep your shoulders square and your head held high through adversity, for the challenges you face are not for the faint of heart."

Eliliweth nodded and looked up at Bartholomew, but the king held his hand out, palm facing towards him in a silent command for him to remain still. The king handed the scepter to Nevic, who returned to where he had been previously standing. Bartholomew beckoned with the same hand, and from Nevic's side, Priestess Ecila came forward, a robe draped between her forearms as she carefully walked forward to her king. Bartholomew accepted it from her, but dismissed her once it was in his possession. As the priestess retreated, the king looked back down at Eliliweth and nodded his head. "You may rise," he said.

Eliliweth got to his feet, and when he was standing straight, Bartholomew unfurled the robes that the priestess had given to him. He draped them over the half-elf's shoulders and tugged the sleeves over his arms. The fabric was of a dark, deep forest green, and leaf-and-branch patterns were embroidered on the sleeves and around the collarbone with silver thread. The half-elf knew of what the king was adorning him with. It was the Robe of the Glen Dale, a gift from the Sherinalu Vale given shortly after the Kingsbanesin Empire had fallen after the Gunnysack Wars. The material used to weave the robe was a secret, never revealed to even King Garan Haymirk, but even after the passing of centuries, it didn't appear to be missing a single stitch. Raw emotion clutched at Eliliweth's throat as he stared at the adornments now gracing his body.

"I dress you, Eliliweth Heraketh, with the Robe of the Glen Dale," Bartholomew announced as he pulled his hands away. "May the love and admiration of your people protect you through it, and keep you warm as our summer days turn to autumn. Let it serve as both a token of our support and as a reminder of where your roots will soon take hold."

The implication wasn't lost on Eliliweth. It was perhaps the most gracious gesture the king could have bestowed upon him, but Bartholomew wasn't just offering his blessings. He was reminding him who was granting him this rare opportunity. The mention of his roots wasn't just a suggestion. The king was telling him how much he had placed at stake on Eliliweth's behalf, and that he expected the half-elf to formally establish himself as a citizen of the Glen Bailey when this was all said and done.

"I bless you with these ancient and cherished relics," Bartholomew continued, "but there is one I will withhold until your Trials are over. When you return to us triumphant, Eliliweth, I will place the Birch Crown upon your head, and there shall be no question as to your worthiness of being the King's Advisor." Bartholomew turned his head as he said this, giving the row of magistrates a narrow look that emphasized his statement.

The Birch Crown, Eliliweth thought with excitement. Just as revered as the Robes of the Glen Dale, the Birch Crown's significance transcended the meaning of any gifts the royal court could bestow upon someone. It was given to the Glen Bailey long ago by none other than the druids of the White Forest. A simple ornament crafted from four sides of hardened birch bark, it was given to notable members of the kingdom, or sometimes outside of it, to wear during royal feasts or other celebrations. It represented humility, service, sacrifice, and above all, wisdom. The last to wear it was an alchemist named Gray Tenelton nearly three decades past, when he concocted an antidote for the Bluemouth Fever that had gripped both the Glen Dale and the land of York for an unusually cruel winter. To be granted the same honor as the man who had saved so many from disease was beyond humbling.

"Go now, Eliliweth Heraketh," King Bartholomew said with a wide smile through his trimmed beard. "Go in the name of the Glen Dale. When you reach the rows of birch, kneel down upon the path and wait for the druids' invitation."

Eliliweth walked forward, towards the forest line, energy pulsating in his chest with a warm fervor. As he approached the woodland trail, he turned around to look once more at the gathered crowd. He lifted his arm over his head and waved, receiving a clamor of excited cheering in return. Spirits soaring, the half-elf turned back and began to proceed down the trail, leaving the well-wishers behind him.

It was no more than four hours on foot to the sanctuary of the druids, but Eliliweth made it an even longer journey, carrying himself in a patient stride, taking the time to observe the forest around him as he walked, listening to the sounds of the chirping birds and smelling the musk of earth and leaves. He had not been instructed to do so, but he felt as though it would be what the druids would want of him. Unfortunately, he had spent far more time seeking details about the White Forest in his studies than actually procuring any useful information.

All of the records left by those who had previously participated in the Trials had been mostly cryptic and vague. The only thing that all records agreed on was that very little of it was what they had expected. So, as silly as it seemed, the half-elf kept his eyes out for the unexpected as he ventured further towards the White Forest.

Nothing out of the ordinary stuck out to him, however, as he ventured further and further away from the Glen Bailey, deeper into the heart of the forest. And finally, after many hours of walking, he began to see rows of the birch sentinels standing watch over the sanctum of the druids. The trail led him right to the border of white-barked trees, and there, he knelt down upon the lightly beaten path and placed his hands just above his knees. *You must kneel at the entrance to the White Forest, for the druids answer only to polite requests for passage,* Eliliweth remembered from one of his study books.

He continued to kneel for several moments, until the moments became entire minutes, which carried on into half past an hour. The half-elf began to grow restless, shifting in his kneeling position as the muscles in his legs and feet began to grow cramped with discomfort. He searched his memory for some other way to announce his arrival to the druids. Had he missed something? More than once, he had fallen asleep with his face to the pages until the light of his candle had died out, wax pooling over onto the desk. What if he had skipped over an important chapter about arriving? Despair began to twist in his stomach as his mouth grew dry again. How could he have been so foolish as to glaze over any section about how to even begin this journey?

After an entire hour had passed, Eliliweth stood up with a miserable expression. He would have to return to the Glen Bailey and pore over his studies once more, to find the detail that he had missed, surely to the disappointment of all of those that had wished for his success. He could only hope that the druids would accept his tardiness when he returned. He began to turn away from the birch trees, but as he did so, a voice called out from behind him,

"Eliliweth Heraketh, are you going to leave before even beginning your Trials?"

The half-elf turned around with wide eyes, mouth agape as he stared incredulously at a gathered group of druids standing just inside the perimeter of the birch trees. It was a congregation of all varieties of men and other races: elves, dwarves, gnomes, even a wizened looking old orc with wrinkled olive skin, all wearing cloaks, some decorated and ornate, others simple and nondescript. Standing tall amongst the druids were a half dozen creatures that Eliliweth had never seen before: men with heads and torsos belonging to a human, but from the waist down, the bodies of horses, from their lean and fur-lined legs to their weathered black hooves. He'd read about centaurs before, but they were widely considered to be only figments of children's tales, as mythical as dragons that walked and spoke like men.

The one who had spoken was an elderly man with a pearl-white beard and a sapphire-colored cloak hung about his shoulders, his eyes brilliantly youthful despite his obvious age. He carried a cedar staff, a small jade onyx orb affixed to the top. He smiled at Eliliweth patiently as the half-elf tried to regain his composure. "We've been expecting you," the druid said pleasantly.

"But...I was kneeling here for the better part of an hour!" Eliliweth protested. "Where did you come from in the blink of an eye?"

"Ah, but Eliliweth, we've been here all along!" the druid proclaimed, tapping his staff once against the forest floor. "Your elven eyes are gifted and quick, but you must learn to be aware of what cannot be seen! And quickly, for the good King Bartholomew wished for your Trials to proceed as swiftly as we can manage! I am Clarke, Hare-Kith and High Druid of the White Forest."

"And I am The Lady," a beautiful elven woman standing next to Clarke said, her voice soft of tone but commanding in its delivery. She was an enigma; an embodiment of both motherly love and a warrior's spirit, despite her radiant elegance. "Clarke speaks the truth. You must learn to not only to see the unknown, but to actively seek it, for the easiest way to dismiss it is to accept only what your eyes can sense. Do you understand?"

"I...yes, My Lady," Eliliweth replied, though a puzzled frown persisted on his brow. Everything was happening so fast. He hadn't expected that, not in this place that seemed so calm and tranquil.

"Very good!" Clarke said enthusiastically, beckoning the half-elf with his staff. "Come then, Eliliweth, walk with us. We have much to do in little time."

And so Eliliweth followed the congregation of druids, stepping past the line of birch trees as they ventured into the domain of the druids, into the heart of the White Forest. The wilderness they passed through was breathtaking. Though it lacked the intricacy and flair of the forests of the Sherinalu Vale and Ashtalath, there was something humbling and awe-inspiring about the rows and rows of birch trees. Each one silently spoke of the secrets it contained deep within its wooden core, the leaves upon its branches whispering to him as they passed underneath. The occasional groups of aspens were similar, but spoke of a different wisdom, of the innocence of youth that saw without prejudice or preconceptions. It was a simple setting, but it was beyond powerful.

"Do you know who we are?" Clarke finally said as they walked deeper into the White Forest.

"Of course, sir," Eliliweth answered quickly. "You're the druids of the White Forest, descendants the first mages to walk the Aariad, the same mages that called for The Binding, to keep magic from unraveling the world before it had barely begun."

"This is true," Clarke said, taking a hand that was surprisingly free of wrinkles or prominent veins and weaving his fingers through his beard. "Our fathers of many generations past were key to orchestrating The Binding, for they saw what could happen if such a gift from the gods was left unchecked."

"While our beginnings are rooted in that legend," The Lady said, "that is truly only a small part of who we are. Many come here mistakenly believing us to be coveters of ancient magic, greedy wizards clutching to our secrets like thieves do their ill-gotten treasures. We have transcended such a basic identity. We are eager to share it with those who would learn."

"You don't keep magical artifacts in the White Forest?" Eliliweth asked curiously. More than one of his books had spoken of the many relics the druids possessed.

"We do," Clarke admitted, "but they are more symbolic to us, a reminder of days past, which is critical to understanding both the present and the future. Magic has its place here in the White Forest, Eliliweth Heraketh, but like so many things in our lives, its nature is linked to our perception of its identity. It can be everything we believe it to be, but it can also be nothing of the sort. But if you are to understand that aspect of magic, you must first recognize the significance of perception in both the known and the unknown. For the druids of the White Forest, this has been the focus of our study ever since our forefathers took shelter within these woods. We will do our best to guide you, but ultimately, your success in the Trials is determined by your own ability and willingness to see this for yourself. Do you understand?"

"Yes," Eliliweth said after a thoughtful pause.

"I don't believe you do just yet, but you will," Clarke said as the parade of druids reached a fork in the forest's path. They came to a stop, and the half-elf paused in his stride as well.

"Your first Trial begins in our library," The Lady said as she turned to look at him. "Jaredeth is the keeper of our lore. If you would follow him, you may begin your first test."

Eliliweth's heart skipped a beat at the announcement of his first test, only moments ago arriving at the White Forest. Swallowing, he scanned the faces of the druids surrounding him for the Jaredeth that The Lady spoke of. None seemed to acknowledge his search, riddling him with confusion once more until he began to hear a series of high-pitched noises. The druids began to part in front of him, until a figure emerged from between their robes. The half-elf still saw nothing until he looked down towards the ground. To his surprise, the smallest goblin he had ever seen in his life was scuttling towards him, drowning in robes of wool and fur, a round cap sitting atop his miniature skull. He stood no taller than Eliliweth's knees and had a petite white beard protruding from the end of his chin, his liver-spotted skin drawn tightly over ancient cheekbones. His eyes were reddened, the whites blotchy with broken arteries. Despite all of this, Jaredeth moved towards him in spritely spirits, squinting upwards at him over the end of his long, pointed nose.

"Well, let's get on with it, then," Jaredeth rasped. His voice was like two rough stones grinding against one another. He shuffled past the half-elf and gestured with a gnarled hand in a silent command for Eliliweth to follow. "The good king of the Glen Bailey wishes for his would-be advisor to hurry his way through the Trials, so we better hustle along, I suppose. *I* for one think that such haste is utter foolishness. But our wise High Druid can't say no to the Great Bearded King of the Great Green Glen Dale, so I suppose we will march ourselves right to the library. No tea, no biscuits, nothing *formal* of course, Goddess forbid we slow down enough to be gracious hosts."

Jaredeth rambled on as Eliliweth followed him down the fork of the trail, nodding in silent agreement, suspecting that to try to argue with the little goblin would be a mistake. He was no larger than a gnome child, but carried himself with all the confidence of a hulking minotaur. The half-elf looked over his shoulder at where the trail had split, and found himself only mildly surprised to see that the conclave of druids had vanished.

The miniature goblin's pace did not ease, nor did his chatter cease as they traveled down a winding trail descending downhill towards an earthen rise overlooking a crescent-shaped pond, dozens of birch trees overlooking the water below, their reflections pristine in the undisturbed surface. Upon the rise stood even more birch trees, and the occasional aspen, though they were far larger than any of those Eliliweth had seen upon entering the White Forest. They came to a stop, and Jaredeth rested his knobby knuckles against his hips, peering at the trees before them before bobbing his head in a curt nod. He waggled a finger at them and said, "All right, then. Here we are, quick as a fox hunting a hare. Your first task is simple, Eliliweth. I want you to begin reading all of these books. If you find any with languages that you don't quite understand, I will help you translate, don't fret. You have until sundown, for Clarke and The Lady wish for you to finish your second test before the stroke of midnight. What's important is that you understand all of the material."

Eliliweth blinked before squinting at the gathering of trees before them, searching curiously for the books that the goblin spoke of. He wet his lips and craned his head forward before tilting it back to see if perhaps the books were sitting upon the branches up above. There was nothing, only trees, their leaves, and their branches, accompanied only by the whisper of the faint forest breeze. Eliliweth cleared his throat awkwardly, fidgeting as he looked down at Jaredeth, waiting for some kind of explanation. The little goblin did not look back at him with a knowing smile or a mischievous glint in his eye. He only peered up at the half-elf expectantly, his knuckles still against his hips. "Well?" he croaked.

"I-I'm sorry, Master Jaredeth," Eliliweth said with an air of hopelessness. "All I see are trees."

"Simpleton!" the goblin shrieked before leaning over, picking up a fallen birch branch. He marched up to Eliliweth and gave him a swift crack against the shin with the stick, causing the half-elf to wince in surprise and pain. "Did you not listen to a word that Clarke said!? The Lady even repeated it for you!" With a wrinkled face of irritation, Jaredeth smacked the branch against Eliliweth's shin once more before shouting, "Must everything take material form for your oh-so-keen elven eyes to recognize it!? Look again!" Jaredeth shrieked, striking the half-elf's shin once more in emphasis.

Once again, Eliliweth looked back at the trees looming upon the earthen rise. Jaredeth's branch rapped him against the shin once more insistently, but he did his best to ignore the pain as he peered at his surroundings. He drew in a deep breath through his nose, releasing the air as he scrutinized the trees. He told himself to search beyond simply what he saw. It was a strange thought, but he stared forward with firm intent. *Perhaps there is more than just the trees. Could Jaredeth speak the truth?* he thought to himself silently.

As he conjured the question, the sights before him began to change. The trees began to gradually twist, and as they did so, their bark peeled away like sheets being pulled slowly off of a mattress. Underneath the bark veils, winding bookcases spiraling around the trees revealed themselves to him. Scrolls began to form between the tree branches. One of the shorter aspens transformed into a map rack, the colors vibrant upon the thick parchment. Eliliweth's eyes were wide in wonder as the forest library opened up to him. The insistent rapping against his shin ceased as Jaredeth nodded in curt satisfaction. The half-elf's chest swelled with pride at his accomplishment, but as quickly as it arose, he felt it wither away as he remembered the goblin's instructions.

"Master Jaredeth," he said with a tone of despair, "I couldn't possibly read all of this material before sundown. All of these books would take an entire lifetime."

"Idiot!" Jaredeth screeched, once again slapping the birch branch against the half-elf's shin. "You dim-witted, ignorant fool! You saw what you mistakenly assumed was beyond your sight, and not a heartbeat later, you have already accepted your task as impossible!? If you could but for a minute stop assuming you know what can and cannot be done, then *perhaps* all would not seem so hopeless!" For good measure, the goblin gave his shin another smack with the stick.

Eliliweth looked once more at the books layered in spiraling rows around the birch trees, at the collection of scrolls and hanging maps. Had he been too presumptuous in assuming that he could not read all of the material here? It certainly seemed like an impossible task. But Jaredeth was right. He could not see the library at first, but after he had opened his mind to the possibility that the books were there, beyond plain sight, they had materialized effortlessly. He did his best to set aside what he thought was possible and impossible, and despite how ludicrous the idea sounded, he approached one of the bookcase birch trees and pressed the tip of his finger against one of the tome's spines, dragging it across as he scanned the titles, eventually coming to a halt at a violet-dyed leather spine. He pulled the book out from its spot and turned it over in his hands, reading the gilded title *The Binding: Revelations and Motivations of the First Mages Among Men.*

He took the book and stepped into the thick of bookshelf trees as Jaredeth watched from afar, setting the end of the birch branch upon the ground like a cane. Eliliweth lowered himself into a cross-legged position and opened the tome, setting each opposing cover on his thighs as he began to read.

At first, it was like any other book he had read, his eyes passing over the sentences word-by-word. As the moments passed, however, he began to notice that the pages seemed closer to his face than they were before. Unsettled by the illusion, the half-elf blinked and shook his head gently before attempting to refocus his gaze. His reading returned to normal for another brief moment, but after only a few seconds this time, the pages began to magnify before his eyes. His breath caught in his throat as he anticipated a wave of nauseating vertigo. A voice in the back of his mind spoke to him, however, quietly instructing, *It is strange and unfamiliar, but if you resist it for that reason alone, you only limit yourself.*

He drew in a deep breath through his lips, puckered in a small circle, and tried to relax the tension that was lifting his shoulders. As he released the resistance, the words upon the pages rose eagerly before him. It was like the sensation of falling, but he could still feel his feet nestled under his legs, rooted firmly against the ground. The aged parchment pages rippled before his eyes, and he dimly realized that he no longer could see the White Forest from his peripheral vision. He was still reading the words, but somehow vivid imagery was enveloping his mind, wrapping warm hands around his consciousness, releasing a torrent of colored inks to illustrate the lore. He couldn't sense the breathing in his chest, but didn't feel the need for air, either.

And then, abruptly, he closed the back cover of the book over the collection of pages attached to the spine. He blinked in surprise, suddenly aware of his cross-legged position and his forest surroundings once more. And there, standing before him, was the little goblin Jaredeth, a wrinkled smile on his face. "That couldn't have been longer than half an hour, Master Jaredeth. Did I truly just read that entire book?"

"Perhaps," the goblin croaked, tapping the branch against the ground once. "Who first called for the idea that became The Binding?"

"An elf woman named Luryala Amurin," Eliliweth answered effortlessly, his eyes widening at the ease at which the answer came to him.

"And who was the warlock that began the movement among his kind, opposing those that would not agree to the terms?" Jaredeth asked.

"Morgar Rux," the half-elf replied without wasting a breath. "A man so short he stood mere inches above the average dwarf."

"Well done," Jaredeth said with a nod. He pointed the birch branch towards the bookcases once more. "But you are not finished. The sun yearns for sleep, half-elf. You must keep reading."

Eliliweth got to his feet, obediently approaching the bookcase once more. Three times, he returned to the bookcases, feeling himself fall into the pages' depths with every cover opened. He read *The Great Empire of Kingsbanesin, a history of the Ancient Era to Modern Times.* And then, *The Lexicon of Magic: An Initiate's Guide to the Arcane.* By the time he opened the cover to *Orcish Cultures and Behavior*, he felt fully acclimated to the sensation of rapidly absorbing the content. When he was finished with the fourth tome, Jaredeth stopped him. "Who was the first monarch of Kingsbanesin to call for an abandonment of bronze weaponry in favor of steel?"

"King Joseph Yuvaeron," Eliliweth answered, "though he passed away before the city guard and army could fully adapt. His son Desten hung himself before he could formally be crowned, ending the bloodline. A new family seized the throne, and King Theod Lukaen guided the empire into a full conversion of steel weaponry and armor."

"Good!" Jaredeth crowed. "To most, it is known as necromancy, but what is the root discipline for the dark magic?"

"Spirit," Eliliweth replied.

"Excellent," the goblin said. "And lastly, the act of males mating with the same sex among the orcs of the Hordelands is not considered shameful unless what?"

"Unless they are unwilling or unable to conceive a child with one of the females," the half-elf replied, the answer easily drawn from his memory. His chest was brimming with excited energy at his success. "Should I read another, Master Jaredeth?"

"There will come a time, half-elf, for you to read another and more," Jaredeth answered, tapping his birch branch against the ground as he spoke. "But truly, you shall not read the entire library on this day. The knowledge contained here is invaluable, but not the crux of your Trials. Consider your first completed, however, and I shall now turn you over to Darvinthol."

Before Eliliweth could ask, a shadow suddenly fell over him as Jaredeth craned his head upward to peer at the figure behind the half-elf. Eliliweth turned as well to gaze once more at an impressively built centaur, the Darvinthol that the little goblin spoke of. How the centaur had managed to approach him from behind as silently as he did was beyond the half-elf's understanding, but by now, he was only mildly surprised. He realized now that it was a waste of time to question what was possible and what was ludicrous in the depths of the White Forest.

"Hello again, Master Half-Elf," Darvinthol said, spreading his arms in a show of greeting, revealing the toned muscle in his pectorals and abdomen as he stretched. His voice was the deep rumble of a giant, but carried a soothing quality to the silken baritone as well.

"Greetings, Master Darvinthol," Eliliweth said as he brushed a few aspen leaves from his robes before straightening his posture.

"I am pleased to see that you have passed Jaredeth's Trial," Darvinthol said. He had a long goatee sprouting from his chin with almond-colored hair that looked to be soft and well-groomed. It twitched faintly with every enunciation. "We must hurry, however, for you must endure another before the day is done. Hop on my back. I shall take you there."

Eliliweth's jaw loosened in surprise at the centaur's command. He cleared his throat before saying, "Are you sure? I can certainly run, if-"

"What use is being half a horse, Master Half-Elf, if I allow pride to take the reins?" Darvinthol interrupted with a chuckle. It was clearly not the first time someone had balked at the offer. "No; we can reach our destination much faster if I carry you. I'd only ask that you don't offer me a sugar cube for my labors. I enjoy the same dinners as you, and frankly, don't care much for sweets."

Despite his amiable personality, Eliliweth was unwilling to test the centaur's patience. Pursing his lips, he approached Darvinthol hesitantly, unsure of what would be considered the most respectful way to mount a creature of such intelligence. Darvinthol settled the matter for him, however. Grabbing him by both of the shoulders with his muscle-bound arms, the centaur effortlessly hoisted the half-elf up in the air, turning him around before reaching backward to place him gingerly on his back. Eliliweth had only a mere second to collect himself before Darvinthol stormed triumphantly out of the forest library, his hooves thundering underneath him as he jaunted away. The half-elf looked over his shoulder to wave farewell to Jaredeth, but the Keeper of Lore had vanished from sight.

Darvinthol galloped between trees with a finesse surprising for the centaur's massive size, his long goatee furling back and curling around his thick neck. *Clop clop, clop clop, clop clop* his hooves went as the fallen leaves twirled briefly in the air after the impact of his steps. Eliliweth had initially been uncertain as to where he should hold on to, but had quickly resigned himself to grasping the centaur's waist as Darvinthol's pace threatened to buck him off. The centaur didn't seem perturbed or uncomfortable with the half-elf's grasp. He kept his chin high and proud as he carried his charge to their destination.

"Tell me truly, Master Half-Elf," Darvinthol said as he carried him along. "What do you think of the White Forest so far?"

Eliliweth paused as he considered his answer. Was this part of his Trial? Or just the centaur making a genuine attempt at conversation? "It's not what I expected, but it's as much as I expected," he answered just as the centaur landed after hurdling a mossy tree stump.

"A canny answer," Darvinthol said with another chuckle. "But I think that by the time you leave, it will be even more than you had expected."

The centaur carried him all the way to what seemed to be the edge of the White Forest, where the trees began to thin and the earth led to a rocky hill. A gently beaten path curled around a short stone rise and began to loop around a taller bank. Birch and aspen trees still stood watch over the hallowed site, but they were far sparser in numbers than they were in the forest library. They circumvented the rock knoll, winding all the way around on a goat's path before reaching the top. Eliliweth turned his head to see a gaping maw in the face of the hill, an opening that revealed a cave murky with shadow. There were two tall torches placed on both sides of the cave's mouth. The one on the left was lit and burning enthusiastically. A hooded druid stood in front of the other, with a smaller torch in his right hand as he guided it towards the one posted in the ground. The right ignited, burning with the same intensity as its twin on the left. The hooded man turned to face them as they approached, nodding his head in a silent greeting.

"Hello, Drael," Darvinthol called out as he stretched his arm back, offering Eliliweth a hand to aid him in dismounting. "Is there another light inside we might use?"

"Take mine," the druid responded, striding up to the half-elf and extending his arm as he offered the burning beacon. "I only brought it to light these two, to preserve your time for your Trials, instead of striking flint or wasting tinder."

"Thank you," Eliliweth said graciously as he accepted the torch.

"You arrived sooner than we anticipated, Master Eliliweth," Drael responded, his smile visible under his hood. "For one of such short stature, Master Jaredeth often flusters those undergoing the Trials with his harsh commands and abrasive speech. It's encouraging to see that it did not distract you."

And it might be an exaggeration, Eliliweth thought. Regardless, he responded with a smile and a nod, murmuring another "thank you."

"Well, look at me," Drael said quietly, clasping his hands. "Boasting of all the time I'm saving you, only to waste it with idle prattle. Best of luck, Eliliweth Heraketh. Successful or not, I do hope you'll join us for dinner." Without waiting for a reply, the hooded druid lifted his hand in a sign of farewell and began to tread his way down the path, away from the cave. Darvinthol looked down at Eliliweth and smiled, extending his arm towards the mouth of the cave.

"Enter, Master Eliliweth," the centaur commanded. Eliliweth took in a deep breath, holding the torch out in front of him as he walked cautiously to the mouth of the cave, having no notion whatsoever as to what might await him inside. They passed between the two post torches, the glow of the flame he held at the end of his own steadily illuminating his path as they crossed over into the darkness.

They walked for a short while. The cave was spacious, but Darvinthol still had to duck his head slightly in order to avoid scraping his forehead on the ceiling. The centaur didn't seem bothered, however, and Eliliweth reminded himself that this was certainly not the first time Darvinthol had guided someone through here. As he remembered this, he began to notice changes in the stone walls surrounding him. Slowing his gait, he gradually hovered the torch from left to right, examining the shapes on the walls. The further they descended into the cave, the more decorated it became, covered with a vast collection of paintings. The half-elf's eyes widened at the endless array. They were clearly drawn with a variety of both colors and tools. There were blues, purples, browns. Some had outlines the width of a finger, others seemed to be created with either brushes, wooden tools, or both. The half-elf craned his head back in awe, staring all the way up to the ceiling, which the illustrations reached from opposite sides to the center.

"What do you see, Eliliweth?" Darvinthol asked in a hushed, reverent voice behind him as the half-elf's torch flared with a hissing pop.

"Paintings," the half-elf murmured in response, slowly guiding his torch along the wall. "They look ancient."

"Most of them are," the centaur answered, "but that isn't necessarily what gives them a voice. Pick one and tell me what it says to you."

Eliliweth took a single step towards his right, a little deeper into the cave. Within seconds, he came across an illustration that gripped his attention. It was rudimentarily drawn, but its ominous presence was oppressive. Four triangular-shaped figures were gathered in a rough semicircle close to the cavern floor, varying runes etched between each one. Above the four figures, however, was the alarming element to the painting. A pitch black monolith towered over the triangular shapes below it. Rounded at the top, the imposing depiction's only details were the two blank ovals that formed a pair of empty spectral eyes. A narrow X was carved underneath the eyes. Eliliweth found himself transfixed on the simplistic face of the dark pillar. It seemed like a silly notion, but he suddenly feared that the unsettling obelisk would part from the cavern wall and topple forward, swallowing him into an endless void.

"What do you think it depicts?" Darvinthol asked without waiting for the half-elf to acknowledge the painting.

"It is Y'nashtas," Eliliweth murmured. "Beginning. Chaos. There are many names for it, but it looks like the first god, and his children below him, preparing to imprison him for all eternity."

"Perhaps it is," Darvinthol rumbled in response. "That certainly matches the illustration. But maybe it's something else, as well. You see, Eliliweth, though we stand in a cave made up of only paintings, it contains just as much knowledge and wisdom as the library that you visited with Keeper Jaredeth. Perhaps even more."

"How could that be?" Eliliweth asked in hushed tones, his eyes still fixated on the monolith's haunting gaze.

"Because, Master Eliliweth, a painting is not limited to any language the way a book is. A drawing does not claim to know anything. It merely states what is there, and leaves the interpretation open to a universal perception. It can point you in countless directions. It can speak a thousand tongues, and then a thousand more. Now, you say that you see Beginning, surrounded by his conspiring children. What else might be portrayed here?"

Eliliweth frowned in thought, glancing back down at the shapes surrounding the dark figure. He commanded his mind to see beyond what he had originally perceived. He thought about where he was, in the White Forest, and how the other druids might depict this painting. He remembered their roots; they were the descendants of the first magi, those who saw the necessity of The Binding, to contain the world's most potent magical powers for the preservation of all life.

"The four figures below are the first mages," Eliliweth said, hovering the burning end of the torch over the illustrations, the flame purring as it followed. "One of each magical discipline, they are united to restrain a threat. The dark figure is not necessarily a god or some malefic specter. It represents the corruption that is bound to infinite power. The monolith depicts greed, unbridled ambition, tyranny, envy, narcissism, pride." The half-elf finally tore his stare away from the painting, looking at the shadowed figure of the centaur for confirmation.

"You wish for me to tell you if you are right or wrong, Eliliweth, but I cannot," Darvinthol said as he took a step forward, closer to the light of the half-elf's torch. "The answers are what you see in the painting. You approached it with a fresh perspective, however, which is what I asked of you. Let's go further."

Eliliweth obeyed the instruction, draping the monolithic painting in shadow as he guided the torch away from it. They took slow steps as they descended, the half-elf examining every illustration they passed. He came to a stop once more as they encountered another painting that caught his attention. It appeared to be a woman, kneeling down on the ground with her head bowed. There was a misshapen square between her stick-like arms, and behind her, crudely etched flames among burning corn stalks.

"This one speaks to you as well?" Darvinthol asked.

"Yes," Eliliweth said as he took another step forward. "It's a farmer's wife, out in her fields during the Gunnysack Wars. She's extinguishing the flames with a drenched gunnysack."

"That is what you see," Darvinthol said patiently, "but what does it say to you?"

"To me," Eliliweth said quietly as his eyes took in the painting, "it isn't telling the story of the Gunnysack Wars. It is a depiction of the price of war. The woman is alone. Her husband and her children are likely leagues away, fighting, dead, or soon to be. The war did not concern her or her family, but she still pays the price, the crops they worked so hard to grow engulfed in flames. But it also speaks to the resilience of humanity. The tragedy weighs on her. Her heart is heavy with grief, but she perseveres. She could consider all of these injustices, pull out her hair by the roots and beat her breasts with grief, but instead she soaks her gunnysacks and works in a field of smoke and ash to protect her farmstead."

"Good," Darvinthol said simply. "Let's move further."

And so they did, descending further into the cave's depths. Step by step, Eliliweth led the centaur all the way to the end, where they met a smooth-faced stone wall. There was a painting here as well, but it was different than the others. To the half-elf's surprise, he realized that he was looking at the sigil of the Glen Bailey, a circular border with a quartered cross, four different leaves on the surrounding edges. Eliliweth looked back at Darvinthol. "That's the symbol of the Glen Bailey," he said in hushed tones.

"The very same," the centaur answered. "But look further than just the outline, Master Eliliweth. Do you see anything?"

Eliliweth turned his attention back to the quartered cross, taking a step forward to further bathe the painting in the torch's light. He examined the cavern wall, studying not only the drawn lines of the sigil, but at the grooves and imperfections of the stone it was painted upon. Soon, the rock face became a canvas to his eyes, illustrations forming on their own as they emerged and faded with the flickering light of the torch. He saw his days of youth in the Sherinalu Vale, and his adolescence as one of the Ashlands' border guard, as well as his promotion to captain. The faces of his late parents flickered across the stone as the picture transformed into the Glen Bailey and his first days of experiencing such a different culture than the one he was used to in his elven homeland. He saw the faces of Bartholomew, Aven, Elune, even Cadohaden. He saw all of the gathered citizens of the kingdom he would soon be an advisor to, wishing him well on his journey to the White Forest.

As that last image flashed before his eyes, he suddenly felt his heart swell in his chest. When he ventured from the Sherinalu Vale to the

Glen Bailey, his mentor Marian was truly the only one who supported his curiosity and sense of adventure, aside from Elune, who was right at his side the entire time. The majority of the elves of his homeland saw his wanderlust as a slight to the luxuries of their forest city. He wasn't vain enough to wish for a crowd every time he embarked on a new journey, but even with aching heads and turning stomachs, the citizens of the Glen Bailey had come to see him off on one of the most exciting adventures of his lifetime. Suddenly, all doubt he had held on to about whether King Bartholomew's realm was his true home vanished in that moment. He swallowed and cupped his hand over his mouth as the images began to disappear from the stone, returning to the drawn sigil.

"Did it speak to you, Master Eliliweth?" Darvinthol asked quietly.

"Yes," Eliliweth said softly, lowering his hand.

"I thought so," the centaur answered. "I am pleased to say that you have passed your second Trial. Come, before the torch dies. I am sure you are quite hungry by now."

Eliliweth obliged, following the centaur out of the cavern of paintings all the way to the rock knoll overlooking the White Forest. The sun had set, the moon bright and orange in the night sky. The half-elf hadn't realized how long they had studied the paintings. Unlike his experience in the library, in which the pages had turned at an unnaturally rapid rate, it seemed like his observations of the paintings had taken half of an afternoon without his realization.

He mounted Darvinthol without reservation this time, clinging to the creature's waist as he adjusted his grip. When he was settled, the centaur carried him down the hill, back into the forest, striding triumphantly into the night.

Chapter Twenty

Steam coiled from the surface of the hot bath, like ethereal fingers grasping at invisible objects floating above them. A thin film of bubbles shifted across the water as well, spawned from the goat soap Aven had lathered after easing herself in. She released a slow sigh between her lips as she leaned her head back against the tub's edge. The servant had drawn the water a bit too hot, and the temperature was making her head a bit dizzy and her skin cherry red. She did not call for any cold buckets, however. She could feel it loosening the tension in her shoulders and her neck, knots born of guilt and stress that had manifested terrible headaches over the past couple days. If she was a bit woozy after leaving her tub, she could simply retire to bed afterwards and perhaps fall to immediate sleep this time instead of tossing and turning for hours before finally succumbing to a fretful half-slumber.

Relaxation wasn't the only reason she'd come to the baths, however. As time had carried on since her discovery of the magistrates' conspiracy, she'd felt drawn to this part of the keep. There was an old guard named Joseth Jerrigan who used to patrol the halls near her quarters when she was young. Aven had enjoyed speaking with the elderly man up until his death, when a terrible flu had swept the Glen Bailey during the autumn months. In his youth, he'd been a skilled huntsman, or at least he had claimed to be. He never had a shortage of stories to share with the princess. One day, instead of a tale, he offered her a wisdom that pertained to a rash of thefts that had been occurring in the market square. *I've come to realize something in all my years, Your Grace. There's one thing criminals and wounded animals have in common. More often than not, they'll come back to the place where it all happened.*

She'd never asked anyone else to see if Joseth's words were true. As a child, she'd never had reason to believe any of his weren't. But now, as she sat soaking in the steaming water, it occurred to her how accurate it was after all. She wasn't sure why she had wanted to come spend time in the place where the root of all her guilt had manifested. Joseth had told her that criminals had an insatiable hunger to relive their exploits. That didn't seem quite right, though. Not now, anyway. She was reliving it in her mind, of course, but her only hunger was to unravel time and decide to speak with her father posthaste.

She could feel the dreaded words entering her mind again, her conscience prodding her once more, warring with her pragmatism in an endless debate over whether or not it was too late to pull herself out of the hole she had dug and end this while she could. There was another voice, however, that told her just to wait a little longer, that it would all be worth it when the magistrates were caught red-handed. She was the princess, and a mage with Novinar training. She was smart enough to outmaneuver sloths like Wallace Tibault and Arnold Seasar. By the Goddess, she should be smart enough to snare Archibaum in the trap while she was at it. She both despised and pitied Bertram. She just couldn't decide which feeling was stronger.

Her thoughts were abruptly interrupted as a knock came on the door, a heavier sound than what she'd expected from the maid Clarice, the servant that had drawn her bath. She sat up in the water abruptly, splashing a bit as she looked around fervently for her robe. She paused and wondered what it was she was so alarmed over. A knock at the door didn't demand she leave the comfort of the hot water. She lethargically pushed herself over to the other side of the tub. There was an inner ring along the bottom half of the tub that made up a bench under the water. She folded one leg along it and rested her front torso against the edge of the tub to cover her breasts. "What is it?" she said in a tone that demanded a quick answer.

The latch to the door clicked mechanically and opened a mere inch, a dull ray of light escaping through the crack into the bathing room that was lit entirely by candles at this hour, as the only light coming in through the fogged window on the opposite side was from the night stars. It was not Clarice's voice that entered, however, but a familiar male's, "Your Grace? Are you still in there?"

Aven fidgeted underneath the water, shifting herself over a bit as she registered who the voice belonged to. It was none other than the general Sir Strigson Ganisalp. What in the gods was he doing here? "I am," she answered. "Should I not be?"

"No, no, it's quite all right, Your Grace," Ganisalp's voice came in through the cracked door. "I only wanted to tell you that I saw Clarice as I came through. She was pale as a ghost, Your Grace, and her teeth were chattering. I think she's pretty damn ill. I sent her to the infirmary. I can find someone else to take over for her. I just wanted you to be aware, in case there was something you needed before her replacement showed up."

It wasn't that long ago that Aven had seen Clarice, having arrived at the baths only fifteen minutes before. Guilt pinched at her conscience again. The poor woman had probably looked just as dreadful when Aven had arrived, and the princess had been too absorbed in her own worries to even notice. No wonder the bathwater had been too hot. It was probably a miracle she'd even managed to fill it. "Well, I feel like quite the fool for not seeing it when I showed up here," she called out from her tub. "Thank you for being more observant than I, Strigson."

"I meant no disrespect, Your Grace," the general's voice spoke.

"No, I didn't mean it like that," Aven said, pinching the bridge of her nose. "I'm sorry if I sounded sarcastic. I'm just a bit weary is all."

A pause came from the door before Strigson asked, "Is there anything you need me to get before I find someone to relieve?" It was clear from his voice that it wasn't something he really wanted to ask, but felt obligated to anyway.

"Actually," Aven said as she rested her cheek against the top of her hand like a pillow, "if you can find any cool water out there and a cloth, would you mind soaking one and bringing it to me? Water's a bit hot."

"I...of course, Your Grace." The door closed gently. A thought entered Aven's mind as it did, perhaps encouraged by the haziness of the sweltering temperature. A trickle of sweat fell from her hairline as the door opened tentatively again.

"Can I come in?" Strigson asked from behind the door.

"I hope you aren't this skittish in combat, Strigson," Aven said teasingly. "Come in. You won't see anything. On my honor." *Whatever I have left*, she added silently.

The direct challenge to his soldier's courage seemed to do the trick. The door swung open and the general marched in. He was lacking any armor, wearing only a matching pair of tan trousers and a shirt threaded loosely at the clavicle. He held a dark blue cloth in one hand, and though he was walking with authority now, his eyes were still trained stubbornly forward, well above where the princess sat soaking. Aven rolled her eyes, saying, "You can just toss it here if you would prefer."

It seemed he very much did prefer to toss the cloth, immediately curling his arm to loft it to her in an underhanded throw, though it threatened to sail a good foot over her head, being as he hadn't actually been looking at her when aiming. Risking the exposure, she lifted her hand into the air to snatch the soaked cloth. She wasn't sure if he had seen anything as she brought the cloth down. It was impossible to tell by his militant, statue-like expression. She pressed it against her forehead and released a relieved sigh. The saturated water wasn't cold, but in contrast to what she was soaking in, it was plenty cool enough to dispel the haze in her mind and slow the nimble thumping of her heart in her chest. "Thank you," she said gratefully as she squeezed the material, water trailing down her face in thin rivers.

"Of course, Your Grace," Strigson said with wooden formality. "Will there be anything else?"

"Are you off-duty, Strigson?" Aven asked, continuing to hold the cloth against her head.

"A general is rarely off-duty, even when he technically is," Strigson answered, his gaze that bore into the back wall completely unmoving. "But technically speaking, Your Grace, yes I am."

"Good," Aven answered, shifting a bit more in the water, a quiet splashing noise following. "Then if there is no attending servant out there, you can dress down the formalities, I think. When was the last time you enjoyed a bath, Strigson?"

Were it not for his rigid military discipline, the general's legs would have likely buckled from the question, judging by the surprise in his eyes. Aven knew what could be assumed by her inquiry, and though part of her knew it was unfair, the other part was intrigued by his reaction. She suspected that the Glen Bailey's general harbored a great deal of attraction towards her. While she didn't think the Glen Bailey had any laws that would forbid the two of them from bathing in the same room together, it would doubtlessly be a faux pas. Was his desire strong enough to take that risk?

"I washed myself only yesterday, Your Grace," he answered flatly.

"You *know* that's not what I meant, Strigson," Aven answered, folding her arms over the edge of the tub. "Washing and enjoying a bath are not the same thing. If you aren't on-duty, why don't you take the other tub? I'm not sure how hot it still is. Nobody was leaving when I arrived, but it can't be too tepid if Clarice hadn't drained it. Your muscles could use a soak, don't you think?"

"I..." Strigson said, looking over his shoulder. The general was usually a man visibly brimming with confidence. It was strange to see him so unsure of himself. He turned his head back around, looking down at her, and immediately snapped his gaze up over her head, assuring that his averted eyes would not sneak a forbidden glance. "If someone were to come in, Your Grace..."

"Who's going to come in?" Aven said, tilting her head a bit against her hand as she studied him. She knew what she was doing was bordering on cruel. It wasn't only her curiosity that drove her, though. She was more lonely than she would willingly admit, and she was quite weary of being left to her own thoughts. She genuinely wanted his company. "Nobody's attending the stoves, and even if one of the servants happens to come knocking on the door, I'll just tell them that I desire some privacy. There couldn't be a simpler solution, don't you think?"

She watched his chest rise as he drew in a deep breath, releasing it with a nervous sigh as he glanced over his shoulder once more. "I don't know, Aven. It really would be best if I left to find an attendant for you. I mean, you're..."

"Naked?" Aven scoffed as she dipped her hand into the water, splashing a few droplets at the general. "By the gods, Strigson, there's *two* tubs in here. I'm not asking you to join me in *this* one." Even in the dim light of the room, she could see the general's face flush with the idea. Leaning her head forward, she rested her chin on her forearm. "Eliliweth is in the White Forest now, Strigson, and I believe it was *you* that told me that I could talk to you if I felt like talking. And right now I do. I just so happen to be in the bathing chambers."

Her reminder didn't seem to dispel the nervousness in Strigson's eyes, but she saw his jaw set in a way that most soldiers' do when their honor has been challenged. He took in another bracing breath before releasing a sigh through his nose. "I did say that. Very well, Your

Grace. But if someone happens to come stumbling in without knocking, I hope you have one hell of an alibi. I'll be back."

He turned and exited into the changing room, latching the door shut behind him. Aven rolled her head to the other side as he departed, mulling the thought over. Did they really need an alibi? It would be a scandal, of course, but mostly because of her relationship with Wyatt Darjin. She didn't think the political implications would be all that damning. They would have to publicly declare a courtship, of course, and with that would come the questions and the rumors of the impending marriage, and if it never came to that, the aftermath of the broken relationship would be the most popular gossip in all the Glen Dale, and perhaps beyond. She didn't believe Strigson would receive any sort of demotion. No, the worst part would simply be the pressure of the public eye, and considering what was already gnawing at her conscience, it seemed like a trivial matter, to her, at least. Her romance with Wyatt would have to end. She wouldn't have a choice in the matter. Kings throughout history were known to have mistresses and favored whores, but murders and riots followed the queens that made multiple lovers a public affair. The hypocrisy vexed her, especially in a kingdom that prided itself on its progressive nature, but Aven was not about to have *that* cultural milestone define her legacy when she took her crown. She loved Wyatt. She truly did, and she was going to continue loving him as long as she could. But as she had told Eliliweth before, the writing was on the wall. She could not marry a common soldier. Both her people and her nation's allies would not tolerate Wyatt Darjin being king of the Glen Dale.

She was so engrossed by her own thoughts that she nearly forgot that Strigson was returning, her head snapping up in surprise as the door latch clicked again. The door opened, and the general walked through with a towel wrapped around his waist, his entire torso exposed. She could tell that he was trying to walk with his chin lifted confidently, but his strides were uncharacteristically stiff, his knees barely bending with every step. He spent a great deal of time ensuring that the door was indeed latched before marching over to the opposite tub, embedded in the floor ten feet away from hers. Respectfully, Aven turned her head and cupped a hand over the side of her face so that he could remove the towel and hide beneath the water's surface. She heard the quiet splash as he descended into the tub, a slow breath escaping him as he submerged himself. Not bothering to ask if it was safe, she dropped her hand back down and looked over at him. He was up to his collarbone in the water, and though their intimate regions were both safely hidden from the other, he didn't seem ready to match her gaze.

"Still hot?" she asked nonchalantly.

"Don't know if I'd call it hot," Strigson answered, pushing himself back to lean against the edge of the tub, his head resting against the rim. "Still warm, though. Good enough for me."

"Good," she answered. She pushed herself back to the opposite edge of her tub as well, though she ensured she remained under the surface enough to prevent giving the general a peek at her chest. She may have been cruel, but that would be outright vicious. She picked the bar of goat soap off of the tub's edge and began lathering it again between her hands. "Was there any trouble out there with the festivities?"

"Mm?" he answered distantly before snapping back to attention. "Oh, well, the usual. Couple feisty hooligans here and there that gotta start boxing after a few drinks. Usually drunk as skunks when we toss 'em in the dungeons for the night. There was one jester we actually found passed out in the streets over by the Ogre Pint one morning a while back. Had burn marks on his neck. He didn't have a damn clue what happened. I figure he must've got into a fight with a torch or something idiotic like that."

I suppose you could call me that, Aven thought to herself silently. She felt both amusement and dread, that night only reminding her of the dangerous game she'd been playing since she'd been here last. "Well, Father's always told me that you can't have a kingdom without a handful of troublemakers. It's just part of the formula. That's not quite how he said it, but that's the gist of it, anyway." She started dragging the bar of soap along her arms, chewing on her tongue idly as she considered her next question. Briefly, her gaze flitted up to Strigson as he murmured an agreement, his eyelids falling shut. She knew the proper thing to do was to entertain with more small talk before delving into any deep questions, but she just didn't feel that patient, and she knew that the warmth of Strigson's bathwater was essentially the timer for their conversation. When it became cold, she'd have a much harder time convincing him to remain where he was. "Are you happy, Strigson?" she asked candidly. "Is being general of the Glen Bailey's army satisfying to you?"

She saw his eyebrows lift briefly before his eyes opened, seemingly surprised by the brazen question. She was glad to see that he at least wasn't quite as tense as when she was trying to coax him into the opposite tub, the soothing effects of the water relaxing him enough to lower his guard a bit. "I would say so, yes. I still wake up in the morning sometimes and wonder how I managed to wind up here."

"You managed to wind up here by saving my mother's life," Aven remarked, moving the bar of soap to her opposite arm.

"I know," Strigson responded, sounding uncomfortable with what amounted to praise, if indirectly. Aven saw the general's gaze fall to the surface of the water and she knew he was looking at his crippled fingers. "But there are men and women who have given more than that. Even if Queen Meredith didn't happen to be nearby, soldiers that died or were wounded fighting orcs or raiders during their patrols were just as responsible for her safety, if you think about it."

"You're selling yourself short, I think," Aven said with a frown. "Perhaps you were in the right place at the right time, but it didn't make it any less heroic."

"It was my duty," Strigson answered, and Aven could see his arms moving as his good hand began to massage the afflicted fingers. "I've read the records on Glen Bailey's former generals. Heroics are what Arden Halderstadt accomplished, spearheading the downfall of the Aariad's most dominant empire."

"But Arden was named general *before* the Gunnysack Wars," Aven pointed out as she dipped her arms below the water, rinsing the suds from them. "As far as military leaders go, Strigson, you're quite young. If you don't think you're worthy of your position, I'm sure you'll get your opportunity to prove it to yourself." A voice murmured in the back of her mind, assuring her that he might indeed get that chance. She gritted her teeth and silenced it.

"Well, I don't want to wish doom upon the Glen Dale," Strigson said with a quiet chuckle. "If the Lifegiver wills it, I hope my job is long-lived and dull. But if the situation calls for me to prove something, I can't help but wonder if I'll be worth a damn." He massaged his fingers for a moment in silence before something seemed to occur to him. He cleared his throat, glancing at her nervously before looking back down at his hand. "I mean...I'm sure I will, it's just..."

"Strigson," Aven said with a faint smile, setting the bar of soap back against the edge of the tub, "Relax. I'm not going to rush to my father's chambers to tell him anything we say here, or demand that he find someone to replace you. I'm going to be queen someday. Do you think I don't have my doubts about how I'll be able to handle certain aspects?"

"Mm. I guess I hadn't thought of that," Strigson answered quietly.

"It's almost as if we can relate more than you originally thought," Aven said coyly, her smile widening. Strigson chuckled and bobbed his head in a conceding nod, leaning his arms back against the edge of his tub. Aven quickly found herself admiring them, the sheen of water serving to accentuate the form of his toned muscles.

"All things considered, then, I am happy," the general said, peering at her curiously. With dread, Aven foresaw the mirrored question he was about to ask her. She didn't know if Strigson was perceptive enough to see past any veiled answer she might give, but she immediately felt too off-guard to let him ask just yet. She pounced on the silence, asking,

"It's been some time since I've seen you with a woman at your side. Do you have someone special in your life?" As inaudibly as she could, she lightly cleared her throat, knowing that her deflective question wasn't much safer than what Strigson had been about to ask her. If the conversation steered in a serious direction, this wasn't the ideal place to have it. She had panicked, however, and genuine curiosity had placed the inquiry on the tip of her tongue.

"Ah," Strigson said, gaze falling away from her again. "Not really, no."

"A handsome and accomplished man that doesn't have a partner?" Aven asked. She was delving into the realm of cruelty again, but her sense of intrigue had a hunger.

"Well, I've had my, uh...partners," Strigson answered carefully, one finger stirring the water near his shoulder idly. "But nothing that amounts to much more." He didn't need to elaborate for Aven to catch his meaning. She had half a mind to ask him to anyway, to pry into details as to why, but she caught his gaze returning to her and felt the knot tighten in her stomach once again. *By the gods, he's going to ask about Wyatt. Stop asking questions that you don't want asked in return!*

"Ahh, I see. Well, perhaps someday," Aven said briskly, steering the topic away from romantic partners as swiftly as she could. Strigson peered at her cautiously from his tub, and she could tell that he was considering asking anyway. He refrained, however, though his next question treaded carefully around something just as dire.

"If you don't want to answer this, I understand. But I'm curious to know how you felt about the king selecting Eliliweth for the Trials of the White Forest. Has it been hard at all?"

Aven shifted a little in her tub, a soft subsequent splash following as she considered the ways to answer him. Something was stirring in her chest again, and it frightened her. She'd always considered Strigson attractive. That wasn't something she was ashamed of. She found it juvenile to deny the obvious even if someone was romantically involved with someone else. There was a different feeling now, however. The question he'd posed seemed genuinely caring and empathetic. She didn't know why that surprised her; his offer at the training grounds had been pretty clear about what he was willing to listen to. She suddenly found herself wanting to climb out of her own tub and into his, not to enjoy his body, but to curl up against him and be held while she confessed everything. The feelings of remorse she'd been reining in since discovering the magistrates' ploy were suddenly threatening to come surging forth with a vengeance in a gurgle of admissions. She bit down on her tongue and took a moment to compose herself before answering, "I admit that I envy his selection, but I know the...complications of royalty undergoing the Trials. I hope one day that I might find a reasonable way to do so regardless, but until then, it is my duty to support Eliliweth. I hope he returns triumphant and enlightened."

"I have a good feeling about it," Strigson said casually, reclining a little further in his tub. If he noticed the strain in Aven's voice, he didn't make mention of it. "And I admire your sense of duty, Aven. I think we may have different definitions of what that may be, but our dedication to them is pretty similar, I think. I've not once lost sleep over the thought of you inheriting His Majesty's crown."

I wish I could say the same, she thought to herself, her throat tightening with helplessness. Any hope she had harbored that she might be able to trust her secret with Strigson faded. She couldn't confess anything to him for the same reasons she couldn't tell Eliliweth. His sense of duty would bring him right to her father's throne, and she would likely be found guilty of treason. "Thank you, Strigson," she said quietly, afraid of her own words betraying her. "It means a lot to hear that coming from you."

"There something else bothering you, Aven?" Strigson said, sitting up a little straighter in the tub. Water trickled down over his collarbone and into his dark brown chest hair. She'd never felt it before, of course, but it looked softer than most, not coarse and wiry like others.

"I'm only tired, Strigson," the princess answered with her best attempt at a smile. She didn't know if it was convincing, but it was the best she could offer. "It's been an eventful summer, to say the least."

He seemed to accept the answer, even if he didn't look entirely convinced. It would have to do. Aven was sure that insisting would only make her sound more guilty, and she didn't think she could talk herself out of that hole if she dug it.

The next twenty minutes they sat in intermittent silence, broken up by the occasional murmuring about festivity plans for Eliliweth's return or gossip about the visitors that had come in from foreign kingdoms to partake in the Solstice celebrations. They briefly spoke of the politics between the Monastery and the crown, though they took care to steer around the subject of the demon, Terodar. The matter had been officially settled by the king, and though Strigson accepted Bartholomew's decree, Aven knew he had strong opposition to such a dangerous specimen living in the city walls.

Before long, Strigson was sitting up straight in his tub, looking across at her apologetically. "Afraid my water's gone pretty cold. I should be checking in on the captains' reports anyway. It *has* been a while since I've had a good soak, though. Thanks for insisting I stick around, Your Grace." He held the sides of the tub, looking at her expectantly.

She cupped her hand over her eyes obligingly as she turned her head to the side. "Thanks for the company, Sir Ganisalp. Don't bother fetching an attendant on your way out. I won't be much longer."

For a moment, she didn't hear any sounds of movement, as if the general were considering words that were dancing on the tip of his tongue. The moment passed, however, and she heard the sounds of splashing water as Strigson hoisted himself out of the tub, rivulets trickling back down into the water as he got out.

A sudden urge struck her. She told herself to stifle it, but it happened quicker than her conscience could manage. The fingers over her eye parted just a sliver, enough for her to peek across the steamy room to catch a glimpse of the general's nude body, the angles of his toned muscles accentuated by the shadows cast by candlelight. Her breath caught in her throat as her wayward gaze trailed down his form, from the chiseled muscles in his back to his buttocks, and even the member between his legs. It was of modest size, but well-proportioned. She'd walked through the dungeons before to address prisoners that had been sentenced to death. Men destined for the noose cared little for modesty, and would try to intimidate her with lewd gestures and threats of rape. She'd seen her share of ugly genitalia. It seemed unfitting to label a man's penis as handsome, but she couldn't think of any other word to describe Strigson's.

She realized just how engrossed she was with peeking at the general's physique and snapped her fingers back shut as she saw his head turn to glance at her. *By the gods, woman, you truly* don't *have any honor, do you?* She could hear the gentle sounds of a towel being wrapped around his waist and once again had to forcefully banish her thoughts of standing up out of the tub and approaching him.

"Need anything before I leave, Your Grace?" Strigson asked from the door, his voice shifting to a formal tone. Aven said nothing, only shaking her head in response.

"Very well," the general said as the door creaked. "I'll see you soon, I'm sure." Light briefly entered the bathing room as he opened the door, disappearing as it swung back on its hinges with a mechanical click. Slowly, the princess let her hand fall from her face, splashing back into the water around her.

She took in a deep breath, and then another. She had to hold it together. She couldn't afford to break down. Not now. She'd come so far. She had to believe that she would soon be liberated from this trapped feeling inside her. Guilt clutched at her heart not only for her involvement with Archibaum's plot, but for her desires with Strigson. Her situation with Wyatt wasn't fair, but she knew that the way she'd looked at the general wasn't fair to her lover, either. As far as he knew, they were still each other's. Many of the things she found desirable in Strigson were the same reasons she'd fallen for the Arden's Watch captain. She needed him right now. But even if she had him here, could she tell him everything?

No. She couldn't. Wyatt might even keep her secret, unlike anyone else, but if someone found out later that he'd withheld such treachery, the possibilities for punishment were a frightening prospect. She couldn't do that to him.

She took in a deep breath once again, but this time, she slid entirely beneath the surface of the water, her hair flowing on all sides as she submerged herself. With a torrent of bubbles streaming from her mouth, she released the scream that had been clawing its way out of her for days.

Chapter Twenty-One

They sounded no war drums as they marched through the plains and the forests. They bellowed no battle cries as they scaled the hills and circumvented stone ridges. As Grathul Heavyhand marched alongside his fellow orcs across the countryside, he thought to himself that his Hordeland army was the quietest that had ever united. The command for reticent travel was met with the expected grumblings and muttered curses, but was begrudgingly obeyed by all. Grathul's triumph over the hulking troll Bolg had earned him enough respect for such compliance.

To go undetected by the many human-controlled realms was no easy task, and it required more than just low voices and silent instruments. To achieve this, Grathul had employed the goblins that had rallied to his cause. The warchief had appointed the one known as Ixiki the Pale Spider as the scout captain. He and his brethren were charged with reconnaissance, identifying villages and patrols alike well before the orcish swarm arrived.

The first victim of the orc army was a nameless lumberjack town. The Hordeland soldiers had descended upon the village in the dead of night, suffocating most of their victims as opposed to their preferred methods of butchery. The quiet killings had rewarded them with half a dozen horses, which Grathul ordered to be used by a team of outrunners in tandem with the goblin scouts. Ixiki was a master of premeditated ambushes, but a few patrolling soldiers usually managed to escape the traps. They were quickly run down by marauding greenskins on ill-gained horse saddles, cut down before they could flee.

It took both diligence and patience, both of which the orc soldiers were unaccustomed to abiding by. Razuk was too loyal to his brother to voice his restlessness, but Ganshu'Dai was plenty forthcoming regarding the alien tactics. In all his cunning, Grathul had promoted Ganshu'Dai to warlord, or *ursh'gola* status, alongside Razuk, knowing that despite his victory over Bolg, he could not afford to allow the Pillage Lord chieftain to be a divisive factor among the army. He was a capable strategist when it came to engaging in battle as well, even if he could seldom wait for the perfect opportunity to act.

When the time was right, however, Grathul knew he would have a ferocious army at his disposal, eager to slake their first for human blood. He needed to keep them under control long enough for it to transpire, but he was confident in his ability to keep their aggression contained for the time being.

As they moved through the wilderness, the ranks came to a stop. Lifting his head and peering over the soldiers marching ahead of them, Grathul snorted. The warchief's young ward, the orc named Veshkrim, was marching back alongside the halted soldiers, scanning the faces for his *ursh'kinta's*. Spotting Grathul, the young warrior stopped and clapped his curled fist against his pectoral in salute. "We've spotted Ixiki and his scouts beyond, *ursh'kinta,* and ahead of us is a bank that descends to a river. It's shallow enough to ford without hassle. Should we stop or press on?"

"Let our soldiers drink from the waters and fill their skins," Grathul commanded to his ward. "I will have counsel with the Pale Spider before we continue."

"*Lok'narosh, ursh'kinta,*" Veshkrim answered with a nod of his head, turning away to relay the orders to the soldiers marching ahead. Gradually, the great serpent of an army began to move forward and expand, clustering at the edge of the river to rehydrate their bodies and their hide vessels. Neither Grathul nor his *ursh'golas* joined their fellow soldiers, for Veshkrim would bring them all back filled skins, as was his duty. The warchief instead approached the edge of the forest where the embankment dropped off towards the river, scanning the other side for his goblin scouts. He spotted the miniature greenskins descending the opposite bank, the bleached-skinned Ixiki patiently urging a stolen horse forward. The goblins weaved their way through the masses with ease. Normally, orc soldiers would never bother to yield to creatures half their size, but knowing that they had information for Grathul seemed to give the goblins an invisible bubble around each of them as they climbed up the opposite side of the river bank. Ixiki was the first to approach the warchief, dismounting from his horse and handing off the reins to one of his fellow scouts before scuttling up to his *ursh'kinta*. He had a bulky roll of parchment cradled under his arm with evidence of murder splattered along the edges in crimson stains. The scout captain placed the parchment in his hand and lofted it up to Grathul, who snatched it out of the air.

"Caught a couple of gruel-for-brains fools three leagues west of here," Ixiki hissed, his elongated ears lifting as he spoke. "Musta been fresh meat, because the one had a map that a newborn calf could understand. Points ya right in the direction of that outpost you were talkin' about, *ursh'kinta*."

Grathul grabbed the map by both ends, unfurling it as his eyes studied the drawn indications. His lips cracked the faintest smile as he followed the red ink line pointing the way to the sentinel keep known as Arden's Watch. The warchief had never set eyes upon the outpost, but had heard tales of its existence from hunters and raiders. He had already been confident in his ability to track the Watch down, but Ixiki's find would save them time and energy, not to mention the already tested patience of his soldiers.

"You've done well, Spider," Grathul rumbled as he rolled the map back up. "Go find Dorgash or Trasker, they're both acting quartermasters. Tell them that their *ursh'kinta* commands extra jerky rations for you and your scouts."

The goblin's nose wrinkled. "We find a map and our reward is a few scraps of dried meat?"

The warchief's reaction was angry and instantaneous. Grathul stormed forward, snatching Ixiki by the throat and lifting him off of his feet, drawing a squeal from the goblin as he was hoisted into the air, mere inches from the fuming face of his *ursh'kinta*. "You are not sellswords, Pale Spider, but *soldiers in my army!* Your retrieval of the map was your *duty*, and the honor of serving the only reward necessary! Perhaps you need a reminder of that. Disregard my invitation to extra rations, and if I see you *or* your scouts with an extra strip, I'll take as many fingers off each of your spindly hands!" With a violent toss, Grathul whipped Ixiki down the embankment, sending the goblin tumbling towards the river. Each soldier's head turned towards the commotion as the scout master splashed into the water with an indignant cry. Sputtering, the Pale Spider shook the water off of his face, a rivulet streaming down his beaky nose as he wiped the back of his hands against his eyes. Before the goblin could pull himself out of the river, Grathul had marched down to the water's edge, one of his axes held in his grip. His glare was menacing as he growled,

"Have I made myself absolutely clear, Spider?"

"Yes, *ursh'kinta*," Ixiki muttered with drooped ears as he stared at the water's surface. The resentment was unmistakable in his voice, but Grathul would not kill the goblin for the insolence. Not yet, at least. Goblins were known for their snarky nature, and a simple admission of understanding was all the warchief needed. Besides, Ixiki was still valuable to Grathul, as well as his fellow goblins.

"Good," the warchief grunted before turning back to his army. "Drink, warriors, and take a moment to rest. Our next target is more than a human stye. We will have a true test of your warrior's strength."

A murmur of grunts and excitement washed over those that were close enough to hear Grathul's proclamation, and the sentiment rippled across the gathered army as his words were passed on to those that were out of earshot. For the moment, their restlessness was sated with the promise of more fulfilling conquest. One didn't seem as satisfied, however. With the handle of his war axe resting on his shoulder, the Pillage Lords' chieftain, Ganshu'Dai, marched over to Grathul with a wrinkled forehead. "The longer we fidget about in these forests, *ursh'kinta*, claiming minor victories and reaping petty spoils, the more weary our warriors become, and the greater chance we have of being discovered by the pinkskins."

"Do you fear discovery by the humans, Ganshu'Dai?" Grathul rumbled curiously, turning to face his *ursh'gola*. As he asked the question, his brother Razuk approached alongside the Pillage Lord. "Do you share Ganshu'Dai's fears as well, brother?"

"I fear nothing from the soft-bellied worms," Razuk growled back immediately.

"I did not say I feared the humans," Ganshu'Dai retorted in agitation, lifting the war axe from his shoulder and placing the top of the blade against the ground. "It is by your order, *ursh'kinta*, that we avoid their attention. So why do we give them further opportunity to find us? They will uncover the villages we've raided. They will see the blood upon the soil leading to the beaten trail of footprints. We have *trolls* among us, *ursh'kinta*. If your objective was to catch the whelps by surprise, I cannot understand why we wait to strike the Glen Bailey."

Grathul smiled maliciously and patted the rolled map that he had tucked under one of his notched leather belts. "You aren't wrong, *ursh'gola*, but you are still impatient. For too long, we orcs have embraced a recklessness that we need not worship. Who told us that in times of war, we as a people must abandon strategy? Who told us that every battle we fight must be without a trace of cunning to compliment our strength? There are times where I think that the humans themselves must have cleverly convinced us of this with their tales and legends of our fearsome raids and berserk tactics.

"We will strike, Ganshu'Dai, and we will strike with the strength only those of the Hordelands possess. But Arden's Watch falls first," the warchief growled as he unrolled the map, pointing a stout finger at the location of the outpost. "Not just to quench our warriors' thirst for blood. Winter is coming, Ganshu'Dai, and the Watch's larders will be fully stocked to prepare for the season. Our rations will only carry us as far as the Glen Bailey, but we cannot assume we will break down their walls within a day. I cannot think of a more shameful way to fall than starvation, our stomachs growling and our ribs exposed as the humans simply wait us out. With the Watch's stock in our wagons, we can force them to meet us on the field of battle.

"What's more, we cannot allow the *enemy* to use the outpost, and we must remember that the pinkskins are like packs of rats, skulking about in little herds until one of their wretched ilk bites first. Arden's Watch is a junction for not only the Glen Bailey, but for their allies as well, used to keep watch over the dragon men of Kingsbanesin." He tapped the keep's symbol once more before continuing, "If we ignore the outpost and are forced into a siege, the wretches will send their ravens to their rat cousins, who will use the Watch as a nest, and then fall upon us from the north, their bellies full and their spirits bright," Grathul said as he trailed his finger down the parchment, towards the Glen Bailey, scratching a dirty nail across where their orcish army would be assembled.

"More blood to paint the soil," Ganshu'Dai growled in return.

"Do not allow your hubris to cloud your judgment, *ursh'gola*," Grathul grunted back impatiently. "Should I fall in combat, this army will belong to either you, or Razuk. Whichever one of you can show me that you are a tactician and not just a mindless raider will be given the oath. But not before."

Ganshu'Dai and Razuk exchanged wary glances. This was the first time their warchief had acknowledged his wishes in the event of his demise. Ordinarily, a trial by combat would have decided the outcome, but if an esteemed *ursh'kinta* like Grathul Heavyhand declared one his true successor, the army would respect that demand. Nothing short of a mutiny would reverse the decision.

"Enough prattle," Grathul grunted, rolling the map back up. For all his talk of strategy and patience, an eager glint had taken to his eyes. "Begin forming ranks. We march to Arden's Watch."

Razuk immediately broke away, bellowing orders to the lieutenants nearby. Slowly, Grathul's warriors began to disperse from the river's waters, forming lines as their superiors guided them. Before long, the army of the Hordelands was on the move once more, ascending the embankment on the opposite side of the river, carrying on in the direction the goblin scouts had returned from.

They received no further word from Ixiki and his outriders as they traveled. Winding their way through woods and waters, scaling rocky ridges and circumventing treacherous valleys, the orcs crossed over into the territory of the Glen Dale as the sun began to set upon the horizon. The anticipation could be felt like electricity in the air as the warriors began to sense the Watch nearing. They slowed their pace as nightfall surrounded them, as they were avoiding the roads now, and few things irritated the *ursh'kinta* more than losing good soldiers to twisted ankles on exposed roots. They did not stop to sleep that night. Which of them could have, anyway? The persistence of their warchief told them all they needed to: they were close.

Finally, as the sun began to emerge over the horizon again, signaling the birth of another day, the clomping of horse hooves reached Grathul Heavyhand's ears, and he called for a halt as he scanned the trees around them, searching for the source. Once more, Ixiki emerged upon horseback, his grin wide and greedy as he approached. "Only a league away, *ursh'kinta*, and we spotted a patrol leaving but a half hour ago. We should be safe to take the road up to the front gate."

"Do you think that wise, Pale Spider?" Grathul growled, barely able to disguise the eagerness in his voice.

"Seems as good an approach as any," Ixiki answered. "We won't likely take them by surprise, *ursh'kinta*. The Watch sits nestled into a stone bluff, surrounded by forest. There are sentinel towers built on each corner, and so even if you could storm one side, we wouldn't go undetected. I don't think you'll be able to either way. I didn't get close enough to be sure, but there's a drawbridge for an entrance. Probably surrounded by a dry moat. Y'know, with stakes and spikes at the bottom."

"I know what a dry moat is, Ixiki," Grathul rumbled in return. "You didn't see any other entrance to the Watch?"

"Not unless any of ya are gonna sprout wings, *ursh'kinta*," Ixiki replied.

"Hrmn," Grathul grunted, wrinkling his nose. "None among us, but they'll try to send ravens out. Position your outriders around the keep, Spider, and have them ready their arrows. We'll find a way to get inside."

"*Lok'tar, ursh'kinta,*" Ixiki said with a snide smile, turning his horse around and riding off to meet with his goblin brothers once more. Grathul drew in a deep breath, his chest expanding. Ahead of him, the warlock Gragnath Fire-Eyes, his two sons alongside him, turned around to grin maliciously at the warchief. Grathul had not needed to assure the master warlock of anything. Gragnath knew the virtues of patience. The elder Fire-Eyes also knew just when to unleash a torrent of chaos. He would be given that opportunity soon.

"Onward!" Grathul bellowed, and his army obliged with clangs of swords and excited grunts. They carefully filtered out of the wilderness as they spilled out onto the gravel road that would lead them to their destination. The lieutenants did their best to keep everyone in orderly ranks as they found even ground, but it took all of their efforts, including the cracking of a few whips. Grathul Heavyhand would not suffer the embarrassment of his soldiers running into a trap. Nevertheless, their pace increased as the last lumbering troll finally stumbled his way out of the thicket of trees and brush, his head swinging viciously as if it was an accomplishment to celebrate. A faint *ruh! ruh! ruh!* began to ululate through the ranks as anticipation soared, and while Grathul had half a mind to quiet his warriors, he decided to allow the ritual chants. Arden's Watch was in sight now, the rising sun glistening off the dew-covered stone of the sentinel towers. Surely, someone had spotted them by now. Their silence would earn them nothing. Besides, the chants were energizing him, giving his heart a faster pump in his chest as they drew closer to the Watch, looking as delectable as a prize roasted pig. Grathul could see poles erected above each tower, the four-leaf symbol of the Glen Bailey flaring at the top on a silver flag, a selection of other banners whipping in the wind below it. He would see them all burn before the night was over.

Half-illuminated figures began to emerge on the Watch's battlements as the orcish army approached, their hushed chants becoming shouts now, their thirst for blood invigorating them. Grathul peered upward as more shadows became visible. As they neared the lifted drawbridge, the warchief could see leather caps and fitted helmets on the heads of the soldiers gathering between the two sentinel towers closest to the entrance. Grathul kept a wary eye on them, waiting for a sign of a drawn bow. He saw no telling movements, however, and proceeded to allow his army to advance. When they were within earshot of the waiting soldiers, the warchief beckoned to both Razuk and Ganshu'Dai, as well as the warlock Gragnath, who was much more fluent in the pinkskin language of Commonspeak than was his *ursh'kinta*. Grathul called for the ranks to halt, and when they had finally slowed to a stop, the four walked in front of the soldiers that had been marching ahead of them, cutting between them like a juggernaut ship through a green-tinted sea. They came to a stop a few feet away from the dry moat of Arden's Watch. Grathul could see the sharpened wooden pikes nestled into the clay earth of the trench. Even if you managed to avoid impaling yourself after falling in, the slick earthen walls would be impossible to climb out of without assistance. Grathul was certain there were pots of oil on the battlements, waiting to be brought to a boil and poured over the heads of sieging enemies.

"Call for the one in command," Grathul grunted at Gragnath. The warlock craned his head upward, pulling the black cloth hood off of his head as he called out in brutish Commonspeak,

"Which of you is leader here?"

The humans atop the battlements turned to whisper among each other for a brief moment before one of the men in the center placed his gauntleted hands upon the stone wall, leaning over and shouting, "I am Captain Wyatt Darjin of the Glen Bailey. You orcs are trespassing upon Glen Dale lands. Return to your homeland at once."

A cruel smile spread across the warlock's face before he translated for his *ursh'kinta*, though by the curling of Grathul's lip, it was evident he had understood the key parts to Wyatt's response. He snorted and grunted a few words of Orcish at Gragnath before the warlock looked back up at the human soldiers, replying snidely, "Warchief Grathul Heavyhand has different idea, Wyatt Darjin. You open gate. Lay down weapons at orc feet. You will be slaves for Heavyhand, and you will not die. If not, we break in anyway, and we will fill moat with pinkskin blood. The choice belong to you."

"Tell your pretender warchief to take his idea and shove it up his arse," Wyatt called back in a mockingly cheerful call. "Archers, *draw!*"

"Shields *up!*" Grathul called out to his soldiers as he and his entourage retreated carefully behind the first few ranks of soldiers, shield bearers who had been hand-selected to lead the charge with this very scenario in mind. The orcs lifted the barricades over their heads as they began to move backward in tandem with their warchief. Disgruntled mutters began to trail through the ranks as the legions began to move in reverse, but nobody broke formation as they impatiently waited for different orders. *Thak! Thakthak! Thak!* The sounds of arrowheads burrowing into the raised shields came from the vanguard in front as the soldiers of Arden's Watch unleashed a volley upon their besiegers.

"Ixiki!" Grathul bellowed, keeping his eyes trained on the sky for a chance arrow that might sneak its way past the barricade. The Pale Spider was soon at his warchief's side, pushing through the burly legs of eager orc soldiers. The *ursh'kinta* looked down at the goblin leader, shouting, "Get your outriders into the woods and watch for ravens! And if that drawbridge falls, not a single wretch gets away! Understood?!"

"*Lok'tar, ursh'kinta,*" Ixiki growled before vanishing back into the ranks of soldiers, the sounds of arrows biting into shields still reverberating from the front row of warriors. A single pained bellow followed as a Watch arrow slipped past the row of shields, burying itself into the neck of one of the orc soldiers. Gurgling, the warrior stumbled backwards, clutching at the wound that was already bleeding profusely. Without hesitation, another stepped forward to take his place, hoisting a rectangular wooden shield lined with bone and fur ornaments. The stricken soldier knelt down beside Grathul, who reached out with a hand and steadied the warrior's head. He would certainly bleed out in minutes.

"Is there something that can be done with him?" Grathul shouted to Master Gragnath over the noise of the frenzied cries behind them. The warlock peered at the gushing neck wound, a lustful glint in his eye as he admired the crimson flow.

"To bring down that bridge, *ursh'kinta*, we'll need more than that," Gragnath called out with a rasp. "And a great deal of time and protection. It would be a great risk, with the rats raining arrows down on us. You must believe they have more up there to throw, as well. But I am no coward, *ursh'kinta*, and if you supply the lambs, I will give you the ritual."

The warchief turned his head, looking back at the Watch's battlements through the slim cracks between the soldiers' shields. Another rattle of arrows peppered the lifted shields, and just as Gragnath had predicted, Grathul could hear the man called Wyatt shouting orders that didn't sound like anything he'd shouted earlier. Looking back at his rustling army, the warchief knew he couldn't start plucking his soldiers out to be ritually slaughtered. Not for this peasant keep, anyway. And certainly not with such a great risk of Gragnath taking an arrow during the incantation. He didn't think his warriors would wait that long before their bloodlust drove them to do something foolish. He had to give them direction, and quickly. He let the soldier fall to the ground as his choking noises ceased. There was no time for ceremonial formalities. They would honor his sacrifice with bloodshed.

But how to get inside the Watch? He searched his surroundings with urgency. *Everything is a weapon*, Razuk had said to him for many years. There were trees all around them, flanking the road to the drawbridge. *Thak! Thakthakthak!* the arrows sounded. Squinting, he saw a less beaten path forking off of the road, winding up a small knoll lined with towering red pine trees. Beyond the pines, Grathul could see a roughly constructed woodshed, stacked lumber nearly reaching the leaning ceiling in preparation for the coming winter. The warchief turned his head again, quickly, the weights in his hair clinking together as he peered between the shield wall again. Beneath the raised drawbridge was the slightest stone lip protruding a few inches over the descent of the dry moat.

"Save your strength, Fire-Eyes," the warchief commanded as he turned to face his legions of soldiers. "Warriors! Those armed with shields, prepare to relieve your brothers on the front line! Lieutenants, form rotations! Those with axes, I want trees dropped as fast as your blades can fell them! Quartermasters, bring whatever hooks and chains you carried along with you and present them before your *ursh'kinta*! Those fleet of foot, search the lumber yard, and bring shield bearers with you! Take axes, take chains, take anything that can be used as a hook and bring them here!

"I need archers! I need stones if you can find them! Someone get the trolls in line, we'll need them to haul the fallen trees! Move quickly, and we will show the pinkskins that they cannot hide from the might of the Hordelands!"

They were not the orders his warriors were hoping for, as he could see from the puzzled and impatient expressions on their faces. Regardless, even the dullest realized that they could not simply cross the death trap of a moat and pass through the raised bridge. The orders were passed along from rank to rank towards the soldiers who were out of earshot, the lieutenants marching alongside the rows to repeat the orders to those who were quite sure they hadn't heard correctly.

"*I will rip the tongue out of the next mongrel that stares at me with a slackened jaw!*" Grathul bellowed, thumping his chest with a snarl. His army needed no more persuading; they began to mobilize. The ones with shields pushed forward, lining up behind their brethren who were still collecting arrows on their boards, some of them with arrows also protruding from the hide wrappings around their legs, or even the flesh below their thighs. The ones already in reach of axes suitable for the job hustled off of the road, surrounding the red pines towering over them, the blades biting at the bark and tearing chunks of wood out like flesh between canine teeth. Grathul watched with leering eyes as others filtered through the trees on the other side of the road, swarming over to the lumber yard to pillage what they could find. The archers began to weave through the busy movement as well, their bows and arrows at the ready as they formed ranks behind the shieldbearers. The hulking trolls slowly made their way forward as well, guided by a handful of lieutenant orcs.

It was a tense stand off for nearly half an hour. The human archers lifted their hands over their brows to peer at the laboring orcs below, hacking at their trees. The orcish archers did not fire, commanded to preserve their arrows and to collect the salvageable ones pulled from the shields of the vanguard. Occasionally, Grathul would spot a black bird darting from one of the four sentinel towers of the Watch. Dart-like arrows would come launching from the trees surrounding the Watch. Most missed their target, but each time, one would find its mark, sending the carrier bird plummeting back towards the earth with a vain flapping of its wings.

He heard the clinking of chains as his quartermasters brought forth what they had taken from both their raided treasures in the Hordelands and from the villages they had mercilessly razed along the campaign trail. Most were rusted, and many were short in length, but Grathul ordered them to be linked with whatever materials they needed to improvise with. The scavengers who had picked apart the lumber camp brought back axes, chains, saws, and a collection of hooks, some of which were used to fuse the lengths together. Others, the warchief had set aside.

Soon, the sounds of falling timber began to accompany the shouts coming from both sides of the moat. Most of them were guided to collapse on the side of the road, though one tilted astray, falling across the road and crushing two orc soldiers, drawing snarls of rage from the lieutenants and a fierce glower from the warchief. Regardless, there was no time for disciplining stupidity. Grathul opened his mouth and pointed a finger, trying to direct the trolls towards the fallen trees, but a voice called out from behind him,

"Look out!"

A shadow began to form amidst the shieldbearers, and suddenly, there were orcs diving to the left and right as a boulder flew through the air, coming from the direction of the Watch's battlements. The stone thumped soundly against the road, rolling over the leg of an archer with bone-crunching contact before tumbling further into the grasp of one of the brutish trolls, who stopped it with his immense grasp and stared at it with dumbfounded eyes. Grathul looked up towards the Watch, spotting a bucket-topped lever being pulled back by human soldiers.

"Catapults," the warchief snarled before looking back at the troll, who was still holding the bulky projectile with confusion. "Don't just stand there, you fool!" Grathul snarled. "Throw it back at them! Together, if you have to!"

The troll, whose name Grathul was reasonably sure was Ib, suddenly blinked with recognition. With a grunt, Ib hoisted the boulder up to his chest and marched forward towards the void left in the wake of the catapult's launch. One of the other trolls, Ogg, shuffled forward to stand by Ib's side. Each of them grasping the boulder with one of their titan hands, they flung it back at the Watch with simultaneous grunts. The bulky missile sailed with a lob into the air. It didn't quite return all the way to the catapult that had unleashed it, but it ricocheted off of the stone battlement wall with a shower of sparks and a rough *crack*, causing the human archers to leap away out of fear of being crushed. The boulder rolled back, falling down towards the dry moat, landing with a thud and the snap of a few wooden pikes.

"*Trolls!*" Grathul bellowed, raising his fist into the air as he commanded the attention to himself once more. "Get these trees to the moat! Lean them against the drawbridge! Anyone who has a bow and a quiver, cover for the brutes! Fire at will on those pinkskinned rats!"

It took a moment for the trolls to comprehend what their warchief had commanded, as well as a few reiterations from the lieutenants, but soon, they began lifting the fallen trees, hoisting them up with grunts and dragging them towards the dry moat. At once, the archers began to take aim, raining arrows on the human sentinels trying to look over the edge of the damaged battlement wall. They ducked and weaved as they noticed the Hordeland besiegers finally returning fire, arrows hissing past their heads in random volleyed rounds. They tried to fire over the edge at the hulking trolls slowly approaching, but could only release a meager handful as the orcs relentlessly applied pressure.

With strained grunts and a few odd twists of their spines, the trolls clumsily extended the harvested trees across the moat, picking them up by the short end and hobbling forward awkwardly until they were close enough to prop them against the drawbridge with heavy thuds. Twice, they missed their mark, the opposite ends dropping into the pike-infested moat. The lieutenants cursed and cracked their whips, ordering them to pull the beams back out to try again. The archers continued to fire on both sides. One of the unlucky trolls, an olive-skinned brute named Wesh, took two arrows underneath his left collarbone. He continued to follow orders even as the blood trickled down his chest, only wincing when the protruding ends brushed against the trees he was attempting to handle.

Finally, after a barrage of arrows had been exchanged and a thousand curses had been shouted, all but one of the trees was leaning across the moat, resting at an angle against the drawbridge. Grathul had commanded the final beam to be placed horizontally on their side, facing the moat. The *ursh'kinta* evaluated his legions once more as his archers continued to fire back at the humans atop the Watch. The goblins would have been ideal for what he wanted next, but their role was too important to have them recalled.

"Those of you leaner than your brothers, I call upon you next!"

he called out. "Take these chains and place hooks on the ends! Crawl up these trees to the drawbridge and bury them into the wood! Take hammers with you! Leave one end over here! I need a body for each to hold them in place! If you make me volunteer you, I will do so after leaving a welt across your green hides!"

The soldiers took the threat seriously, the thinnest of them stepping forward, though two of them were pushed by their stockier counterparts. There was no time for arguments, however. The four slightest of frame approached the edge of the moat, grabbing hold of the coiled chains, the ends already being attached with hooks by the quartermasters. Each was given a hammer before they began to crawl up the makeshift bridge, their eyes occasionally drifting upward towards the battlements.

"Archers, *cover them!*" Grathul bellowed, even as they continued to sail arrows up towards the battlement wall. The warchief smelled the air as an acrid stench reached his nostrils. The humans had oil at full boil up above. No doubt they were getting men with padded gloves to carry the cauldrons towards the wall. "*Hurry,* damn you!" the warchief screamed at the warriors scuttling up the trees with their hammers and chains.

The chain carriers reached the top end of the leaning bridge just as the warchief began to see the smoke curling at the top of the battlements. Cautiously, their arms outstretched for balance, the orcs carefully stood up, pressing their palms against the drawbridge to steady themselves. An iron crossbar bracing the drawbridge was at their chest levels. Each of them positioned their hooks just over the top of the bar and steadily began to hammer in the points, sinking them into the wood behind the brace. *Clank! Clank! Clank!* The sounds of their hammering reached the warchief's ears. The shouts of the humans up above them did as well, however, and suddenly, a black cauldron loomed between the opening that Ib and Ogg had created by heaving the boulder at the keep. Greasy smoke coiled over the rim as the sentinels began to tilt it over the edge.

In a thick, steaming rivulet, the oil poured out from the rim of the cauldron, falling from the battlements towards the improvised tree bridge. The orcs on the farthest sides of the ramp were lucky enough to avoid the boiling curtain, but the two in between them were not so fortunate. Agonized screams drove into Grathul's ears like pins as his soldiers desperately clawed at their melting scalps. The stench of burning flesh and hair wafted into his nostrils as the wailing orcs lost their balances on the leaning beams. Tumbling, they fell between the gaps, all the way into the depths of the dry moat. The warchief did not see his soldiers impaled upon the pikes below, nor could he hear the sounds above the noise of his own army, but he saw the widening eyes of the two surviving orcs as they watched their brothers perish. As the oil began to smoke against the harvested trees, however, they awoke from their stupor, both getting down on all fours as they crawled their way back towards the other end of the beams.

"*Keep firing!*" Grathul bellowed as he approached the trolls, who were still standing near the lone beam that had been left on their side of the moat, dumbfoundedly waiting for instruction. "*I need more fire, archers!* Wesh! Push the logs leaning against the bridge out of the way! I don't care how you do it; drop them into the moat if you have to! The rest of you! Roll this beam under the chains and coil them around! Use whatever you have to fasten the links!"

The strategy seemed to dawn on the soldiers standing around, at least the ones of orcish blood. The big troll named Wesh grunted his understanding and shuffled over to the edge of the moat, grabbing the ends of the hewn trees and jarring them from their position, pushing them at an angle until they rolled into the moat below. The other trolls still looked puzzled as ever, but a group of orc warriors detached themselves from the mob, hurrying around the horizontally placed tree as others straightened out the chain lengths that had been attached to the drawbridge. Rolling the beam over the ends, they curled the links around it and fastened them with iron spikes and broken horseshoe lengths. The archers continued to exchange arrows with the Watch soldiers upon the battlements. Three of the orc soldiers were struck, but they did not pause in their task. When each of the chain lengths were firmly clasped to the beam, the orcs turned around to look at the trolls expectantly. As they did, the warchief glanced back at the moat, seeing that Wesh had finished pushing away the last beam, rolling it down into the moat with a crashing sound. When the brutes before him did not move, Grathul snarled impatiently and jabbed a finger towards the beam. "Just *push it*, damn you!"

Recognition finally dawned on the hulking trolls. Lining up shoulder-to-shoulder, they approached the beam with hunched spines, leaving space only where the chains were coiled around. Pushing forward, they moved the fallen tree until the chain lengths grew taut over the ravine. Wesh rumbled his way towards his brothers, somehow muscling his way forward without complaint, despite the protruding arrows pressing against the hides of those next to him. Each troll pushed forward, the muscles in their necks and shoulders bulging with the effort as they ground their misshapen toes into the dirt. Grathul could hear the drawbridge protesting as the iron hooks on the end of the chains pulled insistently on the cross brace with the strength of the trolls. He looked up to the battlements, watching the soldiers peering down at them from above. He saw the man named Wyatt waving his arms as he feverishly shouted commands, his fellow soldiers scurrying at his orders. A malicious smile crossed the warchief's face as the soldiers vanished from the ramparts. They understood what was coming.

The straining of the trolls went on for several minutes. The drawbridge groaned in complaint as the cross brace began to slowly bow outward. Nearby, Razuk began to shout orders at the quartermasters, and before long, collections of both rope and smaller chain emerged and were passed out among the other soldiers. They once more swarmed the beam, even as the trolls continued to press their weight into it, and tied their lengths around the tree's width. Taking hold of the opposite ends, the orc soldiers pulled backward, facing the trolls that were pushing forward. With gritted teeth and flexed muscles, they added their strength to the effort. Grathul looked back at the drawbridge, lips pursing impatiently. The brace was continuing to bend under the strain. If the drawbridge did not give way soon, he feared the crossbar would break under the pressure. He was sure they could devise another solution if that happened, but he'd already lost good soldiers with this strategy. He did not think his restless army would turn against him in impatience, but he had no desire to test that thought.

He didn't have to. Finally, as the trolls released a collective labored roar, a mechanical crack followed by the hiss of sliding chain sounded from the drawbridge. At first, only one side gave way, hanging at an elongated angle as the other corner remained stubbornly upright. Another two heaves with the combined effort of both orc and troll broke the other side loose, however, and in a rush, the drawbridge dropped violently towards the earth, a cloud of dust billowing underneath it as it slammed down upon the lengths of chain underneath it, burying them into the soil. Almost every one of the trolls stumbled forward as the tension was abruptly relieved, rolling over the chain-linked tree. Grathul heard the strangled cry of at least four orcs as the clumsy trolls rolled over top of them and knew he'd lost another handful of soldiers. With the bloodthirsty cries of the legions behind him, however, it could be dismissed as only the price to pay for war. Lifting his axe into the air, the warchief pointed the blade towards the forced opening in Arden's Watch.

"*Brothers and sisters,*" he called out, "*storm the pink rats' nest!*"

The response was deafening as the orc soldiers surged forward, circumventing the trolls that were still pulling themselves up out of the dirt. The hulking brutes would likely get themselves stuck in the human-sized hallways of Arden's Watch. Not even the entire orc army was going to be able to burrow into the outpost keep. Grathul turned to his brother Razuk, shouting over the roar of the legions, "Keep order out here, brother! I will send someone to relieve you when they've had their fill!"

Razuk looked back at Grathul, nodding slowly. The *ursh'gola* looked as though he desired his share as well, not to wait outside among the stragglers, but he would not defy the orders of his warchief. "*Zarg'ogar, ursh'kinta,*" he answered, clapping his fist against his pectoral. Grathul answered the salute before marching forward into the raging river of orc soldiers pouring into the Watch. Those around him tried their best not to jostle their warchief, but the sheer volume of warriors crossing the defeated drawbridge made it hard not to.

There were two open entrances after the bridge was crossed, both of which circled back around in a square pattern to another opening, leading to a great common hall. A wide set of stone stairs descended downwards, leading to a hearth, surrounded by thick oak tables, mounts of impressive beasts slain during a hunt, banners and decorative weapon racks, and rows of pewter steins set up across plank counters protruding from the walls. Up above the common hall, a balcony-style upper level circled around the hall, looking down upon the comfortable setting that was rapidly being desecrated by the orc soldiers turning over tables and smashing furniture against the stone walls. Some were prying the weapons out of their racks and their plaques, lifting them above their heads in mocking fashion as they howled war cries at one another. Grathul wrinkled his nose as he observed from the top of the steps. One soldier abruptly collided with his shoulder. Snarling in indignation, the warchief snatched the whelp by the back of the head and tossed him down the stairs before reassessing the situation. It was hard to tell by the swarm of soldiers below, but he didn't think there were any humans nearby. The scent of blood in the air wasn't strong enough; it was mostly from the wounds of his own soldiers. Glancing to his right, he saw the warlock Gragnath leading a detachment around the upper level, towards the doors nearest the right of the high-ceiling room. Gripping his axe handles, the warchief broke away from the mob still tearing apart the commons room, trusting the senses of the elder Fire-Eyes to lead them to the human rats.

The door that the warlock walked through lead to a spiraling stone staircase. Hurrying his pace, Grathul pushed his way through the soldiers that were following the warlock, some of them turning with aggressive snarls before realizing who was passing through. The warchief ignored them, continuing his ascent until he reached Gragnath's side. "Can you feel their presence, Fire-Eyes?"

"Yes," Gragnath rasped with a grin. "I can feel it from here, *ursh'kinta*. Their sanctuary is close." The warlock gripped his ceremonial knife eagerly in his hand as he led the soldiers upwards.

Gragnath's instincts proved to be true. The staircase led to a junction with four doors, though two of them were twins, wider than the others, and had brass symbols of Kaijaras affixed on both. Grathul marched towards them, grabbing the iron handles on either side and pulling. The doors rattled, but remained stubbornly closed. The warchief grunted in impatience. Something was bolted across the handles on the other side.

"Allow me, *ursh'kinta*," Gragnath rasped once more, stepping towards the twin doors. With his knife, the warlock cut a thin incision against the inside of his palm. Murmuring the Destroyer's incantations, he dragged his gnarled hand down the thin gap between the doors. When he'd painted a patchy red line between the two, Gragnath dipped the end of his blade into the slowly pooling blood in his palm and began to etch a triangular rune into the wood. He took a step back, uttered a few more guttural chants, and pointed a finger at the rune he'd drawn. It began to glow, and as it did so, the blood smeared down the doors began to shine with intensity, a malevolent orange that shimmered against the wood. "Give it a good kick, warchief," Gragnath said with a grin.

Nodding, Grathul lifted his leg and slammed the heel of his foot between the doors. The shimmering blood flashed, the doors swinging open with as much velocity as though a troll had smashed into it with a running start. A candle stand, glowing on opposite ends where it had been severed, fell to the floor in two pieces with resounding clatters. The Arden's Watch sanctuary was revealed to them, a humble room of worship with pews, lit candles, and a statue of Kaijaras standing proudly behind an altar, below tall and narrow stained glass windows that allowed the light of the morning sun to shine through. And there, before the altar, were half a dozen guards, as well as a gray-robed man with a golden-trimmed cowl standing behind them. The soldiers raised their weapons and shields in defensive positions. Grathul snorted derisively and waved his hand lazily at them. The orc warriors behind him charged forward with eager howls, others lurking in the hallway junction behind them flooding in with the promise of bloodshed.

The Watch soldiers were well-trained, executing a standard defensive rotation of shield presses and sword jabs for a few moments before one of the orc soldiers pierced their line with a spear, sneaking it through the gaps in the shields and burying it into the shoulder of one of the men. He cried out in pain, and the wall collapsed. The orcs overwhelmed them, knocking them to the floor and disarming them in quick order. A female orc by the name of La'Creiek Wife-Horror jumped up onto the altar, snatching the robed man by the cowl and bringing a notched blade to his throat.

"Something isn't right, *ursh'kinta!*" Gragnath hissed above the sounds of battle.

"*Hold!*" Grathul bellowed at his soldiers, who looked up in surprise. Almost every one of them held a weapon over their victims, ready to take their lives in a variety of gruesome fashions. La'Creiek paused, her dagger blade still pressed to the robed man's throat, shoulders rising and falling with her breaths of anticipation. Only one of the Watch soldiers lay dead, the one who had fallen to the spear, his head twisted at an unnatural angle. The orc named Urr, of the Earthroar Clan, stood above him as the dead man's knee lifted, mouth opening wide as his nerves continued to fire even after his passing.

"Speak quickly, Fire-Eyes," Grathul growled.

"Look at them, *ursh'kinta,*" the warlock growled back, pointing his knobbed finger at the defeated men. "Each of them is gray in the hair. And only seven of them in here. They were organized in defending their keep. Why would they splinter off now?"

Grathul pondered this for a moment, examining each of the fallen guards. What the warlock said was true. Two of the men had manes entirely of gray hair, the others had prominent streaks above their temples. All grizzled veterans, destined to hang up their sword and shield any day now, were congregated in the sanctuary. The warchief walked between the pews, up to the man he assumed was the Watch's priest, and lifted his axe, tucking the point end just under the man's chin, above La'Creiek's blade. "Where be Wyatt Darjin?" he rumbled in rough Commonspeak.

"Rot in hell with your demon god, heathen," the priest said with bravado, though three nervous trickles of sweat were coursing down his face.

"Mm," Grathul grunted, pulling his axe away from the priest's chin. He tied the end of the handle to a leather loop in his belt and pulled out a knife from its sheath on his opposite hip. He walked slowly over to the dead guard, laying in a puddle of his own blood, his body finally still. Urr took a few steps out of the way as Grathul knelt before the soldier, pulling an eyelid away from the glazed orb underneath. He took his time, working carefully as he dragged the blade's edge against the lid, cutting it away from the man's face. He removed one, and then the other, leaving the soldier's dead gaze even more terrifyingly stark as he stared upward at the ceiling. The warchief marched back over to the priest, lifting both of the severed eyelids to the man's forehead before pressing them to his clammy flesh. They slipped a bit under the sweat-coated skin, but remained pasted against it. The warchief watched with satisfaction as the priest's jaw began to tremble.

"That one not feel," Grathul grunted in Commonspeak once more. "The other ones, they will feel. I do it to every one, so that they not look somewhere else when I really start hurt them. And you will watch me. Or I do same to you. I do not ask again, rat. Where be Wyatt Darjin?"

The priest sucked his lips behind his teeth as his eyes began to brim with tears. The men sprawled out on the floor were attempting to look resilient, but the fear in their eyes was visible all the same. Caving to the threat, he confessed, "Those of us who had seen enough winters stayed behind. Wyatt didn't want it, but we made him. He led the younger men out."

"Where?" Grathul growled viciously, leaning closer to the priest.

"There's a privy towards the northwest end of the Watch," the priest admitted, his voice strained with shame. "There's a sewer tunnel below it that burrows under the hill and drains out into a valley down below. They were supposed to escape through there."

"What is 'privy'? What is 'sewer?'" the warchief grunted impatiently.

"It's a hole humans with good coin shit in, *ursh'kinta*," Gragnath rasped in the orcish tongue. "The sewer is the tunnel below the hole where the shit goes to."

Grathul wrinkled his nose again, fighting the urge to punch the priest in the jaw with enough force to break his neck. His thoughts were interrupted, however, as a voice called out to him from the sanctuary doors. He turned around to see Obrar Stoneblade, his blunt namesake weapon resting across his shoulder. "*Ursh'kinta!*" he called out. "We've torn the place apart. We cannot find the man named Wyatt, or even most of the men we saw up top. Only two clusters of rats too old to have teeth. Do you think it was magic?"

"*No*, it wasn't any damn magic!" Grathul bellowed. "Look for the shit hole! The little rats escaped through there!"

"Perhaps the goblins will find them as they try to scurry out," Gragnath mused. Obrar shifted his weight as the warlock spoke, lowering his blade off of his shoulder before saying,

"I'll do so at once, *ursh'kinta*, but you should know that I saw the goblins entering the Watch only minutes ago. They were following Razuk."

Just as the words passed Obrar's lips, Grathul's brother emerged at the entrance to the sanctuary. At his side was Ixiki the Pale Spider, as well as two other goblins of which the warchief did not know their names. Grathul snarled, "Why are you little wretches in here and not keeping watch outside!?"

Ixiki's nose twitched before the goblin looked up at Razuk, who folded his arms with a scowl. "I ordered them inside, *ursh'kinta*. The humans stopped sending their birds, and I have our lieutenants keeping order outside. I can't see any humans sneaking through the front gate. I thought the goblins might be useful in searching the keep."

The silence was tense and oppressive as Razuk's words gently echoed through the sanctuary. It was not the warchief that spoke first, but a warrior with a flat face and wide-bridged nose that Grathul could not put a name to. "You damned fool!" the warrior barked. "The rats escaped through a tunnel out into the valley below!"

The goblin Ixiki scowled as he retorted, "If the tunnel leads all the way to that valley in the west, we wouldn't have seen them anyway, we were-"

"Shut up, you little worm! *Ursh'kinta*, these soft-headed twits don't deserve to keep their heads on their shoulders!" the warrior brayed. Grathul felt his temples pulse as anger flooded his mind. He stormed over to the flat-faced orc, the knife still held in his hand. Before the orc had realized his mistake, the warchief grabbed a fistful of his hair before driving the blade under his chin, burying it all the way to handle. He yanked it out with a grunt and slashed the warrior's throat before viciously tossing the bleeding body towards the human soldiers that remained subdued upon the floor. The orc's blood splashed over them as the body tumbled lifelessly beside them. Whirling around to face the others crowded in the sanctuary, Grathul spit angrily,

"*Is there another among you that would like to tell me how things should be done!?*" the warchief howled, pointing the bloodied blade for emphasis. "Is there another among you that believes he is in a position to judge one of his *ursh'gola* over me!? *Well!?*"

He received his answer in obedient silence. His warriors looked him in the eye as he furiously scanned their faces. Even when chastised, refusal to meet a superior's gaze was a weakness among orc warriors that was punished by the whip. But if there was one among them who answered 'yes' to any of Grathul's questions, they did not respond out loud. Gradually, the warchief's breathing slowed, his jaw loosening as he lowered his knife. He walked over to the corpse of the Watch soldier, wiping the blade off on the exposed portion of the man's undershirt before sheathing the knife. He took a deep breath in through his nose as he stood back up. He was perhaps the fiercest orc invading the Watch, but what separated him from his brothers was that he knew how to control and channel his aggression. He needed to remind his warriors why he was the one leading this army.

"It matters little," the warchief rumbled as he walked back up to the altar, where La'Creiek still held her knife to the priest's throat. The separated eyelids had fallen from his forehead and were on the floor in front of his shoes. Grathul stared fixedly at the robed man as he spoke. "Our odds of remaining undetected after sacking this outpost were slim at best. Arden's Watch will provide the rest of what we need to conquer the pigs of the Glen Bailey, just as it will keep their allies from bolstering here before battle. We will grind them to dust beneath the heels of our boots, whether they know it is coming or not.

"Razuk, you are my *tok'rekha*, but if you ever disregard my orders again, I will kill you where you stand. Understood?" Grathul growled as he looked over his shoulder, staring intently at his brother.

"Yes, *ursh'kinta*," Razuk said. Grathul could see the shame in his brother's eyes. He knew why Razuk had entered the Watch with the goblins. Part of him still wished to match Grathul's might. He could not do so waiting outside while the rest of the army picked the Watch apart. Perhaps part of him had thought he could prove something to himself by defying his brother's wishes. All it had earned him was a failure in combat and a scolding by his superior in front of his fellow soldiers.

"Good," Grathul rumbled, turning his head back around to stare at the priest once more, switching to his broken Commonspeak, "You fix hurts, priest?"

"I-I heal, yes," the priest stammered.

"Good," the warchief snorted, nodding his head stiffly at Gragnath, though maintaining the Commonspeak so that the priest could understand, "Master Fire-Eyes, have soldiers take priest and guards outside. He fixes our fighters' hurts, or you open some prisoner eyes wide open in front of him. Or would Destroyer not like?"

"Gapinon condemns those that practice Kaijaras's craft, *ursh'kinta*, but to make use of a slave that does so, that is more than acceptable," Master Gragnath rumbled with a wicked grin as he walked over to the fallen guards, murmuring orders to the soldiers holding them all captive.

"Razuk," Gragnath said, staring at his brother with a hard look as he turned around, switching back to Orcish. "You take however many you'll need and go find the shit hole the priest speaks of. We should make sure they truly escaped and aren't stuck or just simply hiding."

"Yes, *ursh'kinta*," Razuk said in an even voice, turning and gesturing at a few orc warriors before leading them out of the sanctuary.

"Stoneblade, come with me," Grathul grunted. "Show me what else you've found already. We will strip the meat off of every bone in this keep."

Obrar glanced over at one of the other orcs, nodding his head. The warchief realized that the Stoneblade's son, Dagru, had also entered the sanctuary to see the bloody scene. The young orc understood that he could not tag along for this, however, as it would be a sure sign of dependency and weakness. He disappeared to join in the looting of Arden's Watch.

They walked back into the hallway junction, Obrar leading the way, opening doors and explaining the layout of Arden's Watch. Some of it he had seen himself, other parts he'd only heard of from gleeful soldiers passing through the hallways with casks of food or ale under their arms. They were about to descend into the food stores when a familiar sight rounded the corner, his war axe shining with fresh blood. Ganshu'Dai pounded his fist against his chest before grunting, "*Ursh'kinta*. I was up on the battlements. I could see a train of the human filth fleeing through the valley below. Should I send the outriders?"

"Don't bother," Grathul grunted. "It would be both a waste of time and effort. Let the human pigs know we are coming. We will conquer them all the same."

"Yes, *ursh'kinta*," Ganshu'Dai answered. "There's something else, as well. Let me show you."

Grathul frowned. It wasn't a direct order his *ursh'gola* had given him, but after he had just murdered a soldier for saying something similar, it made him bristle. He was no longer in the mood for a pissing match, however, and so he nodded his head and followed Ganshu'Dai, gesturing for Obrar to come as well. The warlord lead them through a hallway, around a corner, and up a set of plank stairs towards the roof of Arden's Watch.

As they stepped onto the keep's roof, Grathul grinned wickedly, immediately recognizing what Ganshu'Dai had deemed worthy of seeing. Next to the upturned empty oil cauldron, the catapult that the humans had used to try to combat the siege still sat. Nearby, hidden behind one of the sentinel towers, another sat, its bucket-topped arm lifted nearly vertical upon its hinges. More importantly, though, alongside each of the battlement walls were stacks of carved lumber and assorted iron parts. A stack of wheels sat next to a collection of the bucket ends. Arden's Watch had clearly received a shipment of catapult parts only recently. They'd constructed two of them to provide an example, and the rest were still disassembled and ready to be transported back down for the use of Grathul's army.

"Obrar," Grathul murmured with a widening grin, eyes glinting with malice. "Fetch the laborers, and gather the quartermasters. They have work to do."

Chapter Twenty-Two

Swuck...swuck...swuck. Each arrow buried itself into the haybale target, their thin shadows falling across it against the setting sun. Three feathered ends protruded from the painted red circle in the center of the white cloth that had been fastened to the front, two along the outside edge, but the last struck dead in the center. Elune relaxed the draw on her bow as she grimly admired the pinpoint shot. She was improving at centering her focus when irritated. Her eyes glanced over to the rolled parchment sitting under the leg of the chair she had used to pin it to the floor of the roof. She'd been up on the battlements of the Glen Bailey's keep for the better part of an hour now, releasing her frustrations on the helpless arrow target. Her hands were already dry from helping wash dishes in the kitchen, despite the scullery maids' insistence that she did not need to trouble herself. She wanted to earn her keep, however, even more so after receiving the correspondence from the Sherinalu Vale. The tension from drawing the bowstring had split two of her chapped knuckles, the raw lines red from the thin exposure of trickled blood.

She sighed as she stared down the arrows in the target. She almost walked over to retrieve them, but hesitated, glancing back down at the letter under the chair leg. It wasn't anything she hadn't heard from her parents before. She was spending too much time in the Glen Bailey, not enough in the Sherinalu, she was shirking her duties to her homeland and devoting her time to the naïve notion that she was truly part of Bartholomew's realm. The latest accusation, of course, was that she was whoring herself around the kingdom of men, using her unique heritage to entice deviants looking for another notch in their colored belts. The "concerns" were more eloquent than that, of course, but Elune knew the image she'd conjured in their heads, vibrant with rumors borne of her and Cadohaden's newfound romance. She didn't have to wonder who sent word of it through the grapevine. The official Sherinalu advisors, bored and feisty, were likely consuming all of their time by gossiping in both word and writing.

She broke herself out of her thoughts, giving her head a gentle shake as she marched over to the target, plucking the arrows out one-by-one, inspecting each quickly for signs of loosening heads or missing fletching. Satisfied with their condition, she set the shaft of each one into her palm as she turned around. She paused as she heard the sound of the access door creaking on its hinges and frowned curiously. Eliliweth was still undergoing his Trials, and Cadohaden shouldn't have finished with his training at the Monastery until well after sunset.

It proved to be neither, as the princess Aven emerged from the keep's depths, seemingly too preoccupied to glance at her surroundings before hoisting herself up onto the roof and shutting the door underneath her. She jumped a bit as she turned around, startled as she finally noticed Elune standing before her. The elf immediately noticed the weariness weighing on the princess's face. It was paler than normal, the smudges left by lack of sleep stark and telling. The redness in her eyes revealed her exhaustion. Even her posture, usually so straight and proud, seemed slouched and withered. It pained Elune to see the princess in such a miserable state, but she felt a reluctant impatience towards Aven's despondence. She could completely understand the princess's disappointment in not having the honor of undergoing the Trials. Elune herself thought that Aven was worthy of the chance. Despite this, however, she was overjoyed for Eliliweth, and it was disappointing that the princess couldn't find it in herself to be happy enough for her friend that she could not keep herself from progressively unraveling.

"Oh! Elune...I'm sorry, I didn't know anyone would be up here," Aven said as she brushed her palm against the outer corner of her eye in a tired gesture.

"It's all right, Your Grace," Elune said with a thin smile. "I was just practicing, is all."

"It's getting dark out. You aren't in danger of sending one out over the keep?" the princess asked. Her tone wasn't accusatory, and so Elune didn't take offense. It was merely conversational banter.

"Haven't missed yet. Elven eyes," Elune answered with a persisting smile, gesturing with her pointer and middle finger to both hazel eyes. "But you're right. I should probably be done for the night."

"And for the love of the Goddess, Elune, how many times do I have to tell you not to use formalities when it's just the two of us?" Aven said. "And I didn't mean to discredit your aim. Don't let me stop you. I just came up for some air."

"Did you want to take a shot?" Elune asked, leaning the bow towards the princess.

"Oh, heavens no," Aven said, whisking her hand in the air a bit. "I'm certain I'd send it straight into the market."

"Aven, I *know* you're a better aim than *that*," Elune remarked with a skeptical frown, gesturing at the target. It was leaning against a wide wooden plank pallet that only the greenest novice would manage to miss.

"You won't let this go until I shoot, will you?" the princess asked with a weary smile.

"I will not."

"All right, then, Elune, hand it over." The elf's smile widened as she offered Aven both the bow and the three arrows. The princess's sigh was one of exasperation, but Elune knew her well enough to know that she enjoyed it. It wasn't the target practice that emboldened Aven. Her ability to use a bow with adequate precision was a testament to her warrior spirit. Being both a princess, a mage, and a woman, many were surprised to see her proficiently trained in the art of arms combat. Wetting her lips, Aven drew in a deep breath before calmly releasing the arrow. It struck between the red target and the closest charcoal-colored ring around it. Twice more the princess fired, and on her third attempt, she struck the inner target a mere inch away from Elune's last strike.

"There," Aven said, handing the bow back to Elune with a quirked smile. "I've had my fill for the evening." She walked over to the target to retrieve the arrows. The elf followed the princess, peering at her in a sideways fashion as she debated whether or not to pry into her thoughts.

"Long day?" she asked casually as they approached the target, Aven plucking out the arrows with three quick pulls, inspecting them just as Elune had earlier.

"I suppose you could say that," Aven said as she turned one of the arrows between her fingers. "Nothing unusual, though. Well, maybe I shouldn't say that. Did you know there was a guest mage in the city today? She called herself Roseanne Markayas. She claimed she was from Munite, that she'd taken to the road because of pressures from the Cathedral."

"Pressures?" Elune asked with a frown.

"She went on about how Duke Gravoth is trying to coerce their mages into emigrating by discouraging the use of their talents, that they should conform to their faith's restrictive guidelines. Which I assume would likely leave them no more than altar servants," Aven quipped with a measure of sardonic edge. "I didn't put too much stock into it. She didn't seem quite collected in the head. A drifter, maybe even some cultist pariah, probably enticed here by that dwarven ale that I'm certain you can smell from twenty leagues away. Anyway, she held a lecture not too far from the Monastery - imagine that - about our modern-day perceptions of magic, and how our ideas as to how it works are all wrong and misguided."

"Curious. How so?" Elune asked

"She proposed..." Aven said, placing a finger against her lower lip as she tried to recall Roseanne's preachings. "She said that even our basic tenets of magic are misunderstood. She claimed that while magic is indeed an entity on its own, it does not derive its strength from the gods like directions on a compass, that it's all *blended* together in some arcane soup."

"Soup," the elf replied. This wasn't quite the direction she'd hoped the conversation would go, but she felt it would be best if it progressed naturally, and so she kept her contributions short for the time being.

"Yes," the princess answered. "She said that something as basic as conjured *fire*, just your ordinary orange, red, and white flame, is not only *not* taken directly from the goddess Essence, but that it is not derived from her whatsoever. No, she claims that arcane fire is a combined force of both the Lifegiver *and* the Destroyer."

"Warlocks have their own corrupted flame, though, do they not?" Elune asked, her curiosity growing more genuine.

"They can summon cursed flame, yes," the princess answered. "I asked this Roseanne the very same thing. She spoke about the balance of the influence determining the nature of the conjuration, but that even the most unholy fire carries with it a hint of Kaijaras's touch."

"How could such a thing be?" the elf asked.

"Because of the vindication that fire symbolizes," Aven answered with a one-shouldered shrug. "To hear her speak of it, every magical element is a formula. For natural fire, the vindication of the Lifegiver's justice combined with the stormy wrath of the Destroyer invokes the desired effect. It's all in the balance of that scale that determines any variation in the result."

"So then what is Essence's role in this Roseanne's theory of magic?" Elune inquired.

"Oddly enough, she proclaimed that the Goddess was more responsible for magic that was directly linked to a mortal's soul, their life force," Aven said, still twirling the arrow between her fingers, though she had already thoroughly inspected it.

Elune pursed her lips as she pondered the strange theory. She was silent for a moment before asking, "If any of that could possibly be true, how would we have such things as magi, or paladins, clerics, warlocks...how could we classify anyone?"

Aven shrugged a shoulder again in response. "That's just it. She claimed that none of our classifications are necessary, that we limit ourselves with such ideas. She said that because every spell dips into the influence of every god, there is no limit to what a mage is capable of."

"Hm," Elune said, her brow furrowing as she further contemplated. Eventually, she turned her eyes back up to the princess and asked, "What are *your* thoughts on it?"

"I had many questions for Roseanne Markayas," Aven said with a quaint smile as she looked up from the arrow she was inspecting. "I did not get to ask most of them, as Ecila kindly requested that the guards escort her from the city when she caught wind of what she was preaching. Father made sure she was given a basket full of breads and cheeses before she left so that we were not sending her out on an empty stomach."

"That seems very..." Elune began cautiously before Aven interrupted,

"Munite-esque?" the princess asked, her smile widening a bit. "I thought so too, and I said as much, but Ecila's been on edge ever since the Mage House took in Terodar, and I guess this was a battle she had to win. Father was too occupied with celebration planning to be bothered with it, and so he chose the easiest solution that still seemed half-assedly diplomatic.

"It's an interesting theory, of course, but there has been a great deal of documentation and study about the classification of magical schools. I really don't think it's just a matter of mindset - *countless* magical scholars have attempted to simply will themselves into another arcane practice. There are a few warlocks in history who have successfully converted into...well, *virtuous* mages, I guess. I believe Benton is trying to do the same with Terodar. Beyond that, however, very few are known to have crossed over into the capabilities of a servant of the Lifegiver, or the Death Shepherd. The closest anyone ever got to achieving such were the War Mages of old, and even they were never truly able to master those disciplines and instead turned their attention to combining weaponry with their gifts. And there hasn't been a soul in many generations with enough natural talent to become a War Mage."

"But on the other hand, we're discussing an intangible existence in magic, and the identities of gods that we can't truly know anything of for certain. So while I'm skeptical, I suppose there could be some truth to what the drifter preached."

Elune sincerely considered the tale of Roseanne Markayas for a moment, trying to wrap her head around the idea that perhaps all of their preconceived notions of magic were nothing more than old fallacies. With so many wielding the gift with such expertise, however, was it possible that none of them really understood their source of power? She decided to pocket the notions for the time being and opened her mouth to tread closer to her curiosities, but the princess beat her to the punch. "What's that over there?" Aven asked, pointing a finger at the rolled parchment underneath the leg of the chair nearby.

"Oh, that's..." Elune began with a pause. She sighed before admitting, "It's a letter from the Sherinalu."

"From your parents," Aven said, a statement, not a question.

"Yes," the elf answered. "I do believe Lazuralina has been in correspondence with my dear mother, for my romantic interests are apparently sealing my fate as an elf who has forgotten her roots."

An uncomfortable silence followed as Aven pressed her fingertips together, her lips pursing as she glanced between Elune and the letter pinned under the chair. The elf felt her jaw tighten and her cheeks burn faintly as she asked, "You agree with my parents' overzealous concerns?"

"I didn't say that," Aven answered carefully. "I would just...Elune, I would just urge you to be cautious, is all."

"Have I not been cautious?" Elune retorted, her voice quickly becoming indignant as a frown crossed her face. "By the gods, from everything I've heard in the last moon, you would think Cadohaden and I had run off to Gohand to be wed and spend the rest of our days celebrating with opium and mead!"

"Nobody has implied such a thing," the princess responded with a growing edge to her voice as well. "It's just that...well, he's different, Elune."

"Different," the elf repeated sharply.

"Yes!" Aven said, folding her arms. "Which isn't always a bad thing, but you have to consider where he comes from, and I don't just mean Kingsbanesin. Deltore Ulaeron was a known racist, Elune. He wholeheartedly bought into the imperial mentality of human superiority. I'm not saying that Cadohaden will be his father, mind and soul, but the sire's sway often influences his young."

"So I am to be wary of Cadohaden simply because his father was a prejudiced bastard?"

"It's not just that, Elune," Aven said, briefly pressing her fingers against a temple. "The boy is reckless. I know he means well, but can't you see how what he sees as good intentions could bring you harm? We can debate until the sun rises again about the credibility of Benton's research, but regardless, he brought a *demon* into the city. From the way he talks, I do believe he thinks that Terodar is a *friend* of his. Sometimes bold acts walk the thinnest line between valor and ambition, and I think it's fair to wonder which side he falls on. Since Nevic has taken him in as a paladin, he walks about the city with chin high and shoulders broad."

"I don't believe I'm hearing this," Elune said as she shook her head. "He's found a sense of purpose and some semblance of confidence, and this is supposed to make him dangerous?"

"Elune, you're not *listening* to me-"

"No, Aven, *you* aren't listening to *me!*" Elune snapped, throwing her bow at her feet as she took an angry step towards the princess. "I have had *more* than my fill of being told that I'm too foolish to know what I should be doing with my life, whether it's from my parents, from you, or from Priestess Ecila's constant little judgments! I am not some empty-headed tavern harlot, and I am not naive to the risks I take! If you would truly welcome me as the Sherinalu's ambassador, I would ask that you respect me as someone who is capable of making sound decisions on her own, and do not infer that my relationship with Cadohaden is a farce simply because Bartholomew has your lover locked away at Arden's Watch!"

The silence was tense as a shadow fell over Aven's face, her mouth tightening as she gripped the arrow in her hands. Regret immediately flashed across Elune's visage, her mouth dropping agape in surprise at her own words. "Aven...I'm sorry," she murmured. "That was unfair. Unfair and cruel."

"No, no," Aven said as her features softened, drawing out the weariness chiseled across her face. "You're right, my friend. I'm in no place to tell you which endeavor is or isn't worth the risk. I do not think you are foolish, I'm just...I..."

Her words trailed off as the princess's gaze became unfocused, staring somewhere beyond Elune, off towards the horizon of the setting sun. The spirit in her that had already seemed so haggard as of late vanished, leaving only a window into the torment underneath. The hair on the back of Elune's neck began to lift as a chill washed over her. There was something sinister torturing Aven's conscience. Why hadn't she seen it before? All at once, she realized that the princess couldn't possibly be brooding over Eliliweth's selection for the Trials. The Aven Celandine she knew could never be so petty as to let that envy completely snuff out the proud radiance she carried at all times. The princess had a secret.

"Aven," Elune murmured, her eyes searching her friend's, "is there something you need to tell me?"

After a despondent pause, Aven's eyes finally focused on Elune's, guiding herself away from the call of emptiness far off in the distance. She pursed her lips as she stared back at the elf silently. They stood there for a moment, saying nothing, and Elune could see her chin trembling with raw emotion. Slowly, the princess opened her mouth, rasping the quietest, "I..."

Suddenly, the sound of a booming horn split the night air, interrupting the moment as both Aven and Elune turned to look towards the source of the noise. It was coming from the northern gate, from the signal horn atop the battlement tower. Though they were far away, the two of them could hear the distant shouts of the guards as torches were passed among one another. Elune squinted. The guards were pointing fingers towards the north. She followed their gestures, scanning the open fields past the city, towards the forests out beyond that were gradually becoming veiled by the night. There, in a train of shuffling figures, were ranks of what looked to be like soldiers, heading towards the gate. Searching, she quickly spotted a mark of identity.

"Aven," she breathed. "They carry the silver banner."

"Arden's Watch," Aven said with a strained murmur as she leaned over the battlements, trying to better see the incoming soldiers. When she could not, she veered away from the edge, hurrying towards the door leading down the staircase back into the keep. "We have to go!" she insisted. Elune followed after her, picking up her bow along the way as they disappeared from the keep's rooftops.

There were guards bustling as they made their way through the hallways of the keep. Captains were growling orders, men saluting and disappearing into different corridors. As Aven and Elune descended a spiral staircase towards the ground floor, they noticed two ranks of soldiers, each line facing one another in front of the entrance doors. As they weaved their way through the swarm of murmuring guards and frazzled servants, Elune spotted the king's magistrates crowding in a bunch near the end of the opposite staircase, their eyes darting and their mouths moving in quipped whispers to one another. The elf's brow dipped suspiciously as Wallace Tibault waved his pudgy hand in a gesture that clearly meant for all of them to settle down. Elune slanted a gaze over at the princess, but Aven's attention was nowhere near the king's court of nobles. She pushed herself towards the center of the two rows of soldiers, into the empty space where Bartholomew would eventually emerge after he had answered the summons. Her eyes were fixated on the entrance doors.

Whatever message the party from Arden's Watch had delivered, it certainly had been urgent. Within minutes, a bustling group began to wind its way down the western staircase. King Bartholomew looked disheveled, his formal attire obviously thrown on in a great hurry. The scribe Pleatus, looking even more weasel-like when wedged into an escort of soldiers, kept reaching over to the king to fuss at the ruffles of his garb. Bartholomew swatted his hand away in irritation as they descended to the ground floor, approaching the position where the princess already stood. The guards broke off and joined the parallel rows of soldiers, while Pleatus slunk towards the magistrates, who were hesitantly creeping their way towards the king.

"Father, what's going on? Why are so many from Arden's Watch returning at this hour?" Aven murmured.

"I don't know," Bartholomew said in a flinty voice that clearly stated he would not be answering any more questions. And so they stood there, the king folding his hands in front of himself, nose wrinkling intermittently as his beard twitched. The two rows of soldiers stood perfectly still, but the gathered nobles and servants couldn't help but whisper speculation to one another as they waited for answers.

The minutes seemed like hours as Aven attempted to keep herself still, even when anxiety chewed at her heart like a starving animal. She and Elune had seen so many soldiers crossing the fields towards the Glen Bailey's gates. Why would they have come in such great numbers? She knew it was a selfish worry, but what clamped down on her heart the hardest was the thought that Wyatt was not among those that had returned.

Her worries at least partially vanished, however, when the entrance doors to the keep swung open with a pronounced groan, Glen Bailey soldiers flanking a group wearing the silver garments from Arden's Watch. Leading those that had come from the outpost was none other than Wyatt Darjin, looking weary enough to have climbed a dozen mountains before staggering inside. The others with him from the Watch looked none the better, each of them out of breath, their eyes rolling as their heads swayed aimlessly, jaws slack with each gulp of air. As they drew closer to their king, an unpleasant odor violated Aven's senses, making her mouth pinch and her nose wrinkle. Wyatt and his soldiers carried the ripe stench of feces, and as they stumbled closer, the princess could see the excrement visibly smeared about their armor and clothing. The soldiers were disciplined enough to not recoil from the violating smell, but the servants all visibly winced, and the magistrates audibly complained to one another as it grew stronger.

"By the Four Forgers, Wyatt Darjin, what in the Aariad happened to you all? Why are you here?" Bartholomew demanded, his voice twisted with both concern and irritation.

"Pardon us, Your...Your Majesty," Wyatt wheezed, standing in the most miserable salute Aven had ever seen as he came to a stop in front of Bartholomew. "We...we haven't stopped moving. There were so many...we had to make it back."

"So many what? Speak sense, boy, and do so quickly! Why has half of Arden's Watch abandoned its post without so much as a letter in advance!?" the king barked, growing impatient.

"We *couldn't*, Your Majesty," Wyatt said, sucking down another breath before wearily continuing. "And I'm afraid it's much more than half. Orcs, my king. So many...orcs. Trolls. Little goblins. Ogres, as well. Arden's Watch has fallen. We couldn't...by the gods, we couldn't save her. Not against so many."

The room was stunned silent for a brief moment before it burst into fretful buzz. From behind the ranks of soldiers, Elune peered between two armored shoulders at the magistrates. Each of their faces had turned pale as white sheets, not a one of them speaking as each of the servants murmured feverishly. *Why would the most outspoken men in the whole city have nothing to say at reports of an orcish invasion?* she thought to herself.

"*Silence!*" Bartholomew bellowed, quieting the surge of busy voices. "And I will not ask for it again! Wyatt Darjin! Arden's Watch was *more* than capable of withstanding an orcish raid! How in the murky hells did you surrender it so quickly without so much as a request for aid!?"

"You don't understand, Your Majesty," Wyatt wheezed, though his breath was slowly returning to normal. "This *wasn't* just an orcish raid. It was a bloody *army*. *Legions* of orcs marched on the Watch with no warning at all. We tried to send ravens, but each one was shot from the sky. We could see goblins lurking in the trees, filling the sky with arrows every time we released one. They...they hacked down trees, Your Majesty, and used them to fasten chains to the drawbridge. They couldn't be stopped; not with arrow, not with oil."

"We've had scouts research the clans of the Hordelands," a voice called out from behind Bartholomew. It was General Strigson Ganisalp, emerging at the king's right side as he pushed his way through a gaggle of servants, his glare scrutinous. He looked just as displaced as Bartholomew had when the king entered the room, clearly taken aback by the reports that had surely flooded in upon the sight of the retreating Watch forces. "I can say with confidence that there isn't one among them that could break Arden's Watch."

"With all respects due, sir, *I* can say with confidence that it wasn't just one clan conquering the Watch," Wyatt said, the weariness in his face giving way to the frustration of having his claims met with such skepticism. "I am telling you that I stood upon those ramparts and could see the eastern road infested with greenskins for as far down the road as I could see, if not more. A leader spoke for them, an orc that demanded my surrender. He was called Grathul Heavyhand. He did not invoke the name of any one clan."

"Grathul Heavyhand is the known chieftain of the Goreknuckle Clan, at least according to our records," the scribe Pleatus piped with a haughty chirp from the group of magistrates he was still trying to mesh into.

"I'm not disputing the records!" Wyatt barked, his temper finally giving way. "I am telling you all that whatever this Grathul Heavyhand is, he was leading a great army that was more than just a clan of raiders! Do you all think so low of the soldiers of Arden's Watch that you truly think we would flee our fortress for a rabble of greenskinned looters? The Watch was our home, our hearts, our very souls belonged to its stone walls! I am not proud of our escape, but the enemy was so vast that it was foolish to think we could withstand them once they pried open the drawbridge! We had to return to the Glen Bailey and alert His Majesty! We've precious little time before they swarm like a cloud of locusts over this land, if they aren't already!"

"Just how did you escape such a fearsome army, Captain Darjin?" a voice said behind the file of soldiers on the opposite side of Elune. The white hood of Crusader Nevic could be seen, as well as Priestess Ecila standing next to him with her haunted eyes, her face grim with the news the captain had brought. The albino continued, "Arden's Watch was not constructed for hasty retreats."

"By the gods, you'd think I was standing outside the Lifegiver's realm, awaiting judgment!" Wyatt retaliated. "Why do you think we're slathered in shit? When it was obvious that they were about to pry open the drawbridge, we started climbing down the loo and made our escape through the sewer. It brought us all the way down to the valley, far enough away for a head start. We scarcely stopped for breath, and I've got three missing toenails to prove it!"

"Calm yourself, Captain," Aven interjected, keeping her poise formal as she addressed her rumored lover. "You don't stand before us in judgment. We only need to know what happened. It will help us prepare for what we must do next."

"Apologies, Your Grace," Wyatt responded softly, the edge fading from his voice even at her stiffly stated command. "None of us are very collected. We're lucky to have escaped with our lives. I do not exaggerate any numbers. We are in grave danger."

"A clever escape, but it could not have been an expeditious one," the ghostly voice of Priestess Ecila spoke. "How did so many of you make your way down the sewers without discovery?"

"Not all of us did," Wyatt said after a pause, his passionate voice rapidly dwindling to a melancholy air. "Father Chandler called for the men longest in the tooth, those with the most iron in their hair, to remain behind to buy time for the rest of us. I insisted against it; I even gave the stubborn old man an order to cease, but he would not listen. They separated themselves into different rooms throughout the Watch. He even took the blood of an archer, shot dead from an orcish arrow, and spattered it in trails leading to their hideaways, like...like bloody crumb trails, like in the old childrens' tales. I...we heard their screams all the way down below as we fled."

"Cowards!" Magistrate Seasar bellowed before anyone else could speak, his full jowls quivering with the outburst.

"And when the orcs come, Arnold, will you be strapping on a suit of armor to fight at the front lines?" Ganisalp growled, turning to glare over his shoulder. "I doubt I have anything standard issue that would fit your lard-packed arse, but I'd be willing to pay for a custom set right out of my own pocket."

"Enough, I said!" Bartholomew barked as Arnold Seasar's face turned purple with indignation. "Gods help me, Strigson, I will send you to stable duty if you speak out of turn again! And I will hear no more accusations directed at Captain Wyatt! Every soldier knows he may have to lay down his life for his kingdom, but a leader of soldiers knows when it is wisest to retreat to fight another day. There is little time. Wyatt, is there anything else to report? Quickly now."

"No, Your Majesty. I have told you everything."

"Very well," Bartholomew said, lifting a sleeve to dab at a bead of sweat rolling down his temple. "Father Chandler and those who sacrificed their lives at Arden's Watch will be remembered, but we cannot afford to dwell today. Wyatt, get your men to the infirmary. Have them cleaned and get them in cots as soon as possible; we can't have them collapsing from exhaustion. Strigson, begin siege defense preparations, and have someone alert the reserves."

"Yes, sir," both Ganisalp and Wyatt responded simultaneously, saluting before they turned to attend to their orders.

"Aven," Bartholomew said, turning to face his daughter. "I will need you to see to Eliliweth's duties as well as your own. Send out ravens to York, to Eastfen, and the Sherinalu first. Alert Munite, Gohand, and even Kingsbanesin as well. I don't expect aid from them would arrive in time even if they offered, but we cannot let them be taken by surprise if this Grathul Heavyhand leads his forces there first. Send runners out to meet our patrols in the Dales, and have them begin evacuations immediately. Pull everyone back, into the city."

"And what of the White Forest?" Aven asked cautiously. "What should I tell Eliliweth?"

Bartholomew did not answer at first, instead looking out to the room still full of the gathered audience. He addressed them instead, calling out, "The rest of you, return to your duties, but prepare for orders from your superiors. You will all have a role in defending your home."

The two rows of soldiers immediately saluted before filing out of the keep, their boots clinking in unison with their steps. A few of the servants lingered, staring at the king with curious expressions, hoping to hear what he would instruct his daughter to do concerning the half-elf, but a fierce glower from Bartholomew sent them all scattering to different parts of the castle. As his lips pursed grimly, the king turned to Aven and shook his head. "Tell him nothing," he said quietly.

"Nothing?" Aven said with a shrewd frown. "Not at all? Surely, we should-"

"Not a word to the White Forest, Aven," Bartholomew said sternly, though his eyes reflected apprehension that did not match the conviction of his tone. "I did not send Wyatt to Arden's Watch just for your own good. I sent him in part because he fits the type of soldier we keep out there. He's stoutly loyal to this kingdom and doesn't have a cowardly bone in his body."

"You're not exactly justifying his 'promotion', Father," Aven whispered sharply.

"We have countless soldiers who are great representation of loyalty and courage; that doesn't mean they are fit to marry the heir to my throne," Bartholomew retorted gruffly. "That's not the point regardless, Aven. What I'm saying is that it speaks a great deal of this orcish army led by Grathul Heavyhand, that Wyatt Darjin came stumbling into my castle coated with sewage and with barely a breath of air left in his lungs to tell me to my face that he retreated from his post. I don't know how this Grathul did it. The Hordeland clans haven't been united in decades, but if the numbers Wyatt speaks of are true, then he has no doubt accomplished just that."

"I have no doubt this orcish army is fearsome, Father, and certainly cunning, if they managed to avoid attention until now," Aven answered, giving a passing servant a suspicious look as they hustled past just in the range of eavesdropping. When the man was out of earshot, she turned back to Bartholomew. "All the more reason to write to him. The druids will surely understand his predicament. Perhaps they can send him off with some sort of aid-"

"The Druids of the White Forest know war well, daughter, but they are not going to arm him with any kind of enchantment to sway the tide of battle," Bartholomew growled. He glanced over his shoulder at another passing servant, then impatiently gestured towards the spiral staircase, beckoning Aven to follow him as he continued, "I don't know if his absence is but a cruel twist of fate or a sign from the gods, but I can tell you that Eliliweth Heraketh alone is not going to turn the tide for our kingdom."

"But leaving him to finish his Trials certainly won't!" Aven protested as they began to ascend the stairs, away from the hive of servants near the entryway. "If the battle is already lost, any enlightenment he achieves won't matter when he returns to the ruins of his home!"

"It will, though," the king answered as they reached the second floor, his words solemn. "If this army of orcs burns the Glen Bailey to soot and ash, dear Aven, we need someone like Eliliweth to start anew."

"Start anew?"

"Yes," Bartholomew said. "He can't be the difference between victory and defeat, but he might be the resurrection. Even in the most gruesome wars, there are always survivors. They may hide and wait until the dust is settled, but they always emerge with time. With his inherent wisdom, youthful spirit, and his lessons from the White Forest, Eliliweth could be the one to gather what's left and make something of it, rather than simply let the Glen Bailey's legacy die with its people."

"You sound so certain of our own demise," Aven said lowly.

"By the Lifegiver's will, Aven Celandine, never!" Bartholomew snorted, his face turning red with indignation. "We are the Glen Bailey! We will fight this menace with every speck of strength we possess!

It was by the perseverance of our ancestors that the renowned empire of Kingsbanesin was brought to heel! Even if we fall, we will give these orcs such a grievous wound that they will scatter like leaves in the wind when confronted once more!

"But if we are to fall, then I would have someone carry on the name of this great kingdom, and perhaps someday, restore it to the glory that it is today. Eliliweth Heraketh could be the one to do so. We have no more time to waste. Send out your ravens. But none in the direction of the White Forest."

Aven watched her father disappear down the hall, her jaw gritted tightly in frustration. She could see the wisdom in Bartholomew's words. But whatever glowing speech he had used to describe the kingdom's spirit, he had admitted the possibility of defeat, based purely on the accounts given to him by Wyatt.

Wyatt. She'd barely had time to even register that she'd seen him for the first time in months. She'd hardly even realized her combined joy and dread at the sight of him, with his look of shame and humiliation, standing in the keep covered in shit and the stench of defeat. It wasn't his fault. Her father was right. He would have never abandoned his post if the threat hadn't justified it. She wanted to hold him next to her, tell him that it was all right, that he hadn't failed in the least bit. She wanted to hold him until he finally allowed the armor of his pride to fall, to feel his guard lower as he nuzzled against her. It wouldn't have been the first time. It was what had brought them so close to begin with. The both of them, steadfastly maintaining their staunch appearances, priding themselves on their determination to look the world in the eye and answer its every challenge. They'd boasted to one another at a spring gala three years past, early in the evening. But by nightfall, and with the aid of a few glasses of wine, there they were, in the garden gazebo, revealing the insecurities they held deep within. The timing, the atmosphere, the words, they were all perfect. And now he was gone again, lost in the confusion of the rapidly escalating events.

She startled, straightening her posture, realizing that she couldn't remember just how long she'd been standing there. She abruptly turned around and twitched in surprise once more as Elune Shadowsong stood looking up at her, a few steps below near the rail of the staircase.

"Your Grace," she said softly, "is everything all right?"

"No," Aven said, shaking her head. "It's not. But there is no time to wallow. Our enemies are on their way, and they will not wait for us to discuss petty problems with one another." Elune's brow creased, her expression looking a bit hurt, but the princess had matters to attend to. Her words were perhaps a bit harsh, but nonetheless true. She started her way down the stairs, but the elf reached out and touched her shoulder as she began to pass by.

"I don't just mean with Wyatt, Aven," Elune insisted. "I am not some vapid, starry-eyed girl. You were going to tell me something, up on the battlements. Something strange is going on, and I think it has something to do with the magistrates. Will you not tell me what burdens you?"

"What burdens me, Elune, is that an army of orcs just sacked our proudest outpost that has stood since the signing of the Gunnysack Treaties," Aven responded sharply, turning around with a huff. "What burdens me is that the same orcish army is likely headed this way, to bring death and suffering to our people. The magistrates are likely acting strangely because they are all cowards and haven't the stomach for such dire news. With all of this, you think I am distraught because a man I fancy stood before me, reeking of shit and despair? I have far greater things to worry about."

The words left the princess's lips before she could rein them in, and she saw with each syllable a verbal glass shard bury into Elune's flushed cheeks. The elf's jaw tightened, a steel curtain falling over her usual sympathetic stare. "Forgive me, Your Grace," she said with ingenuine formality. "I won't trouble you any further." Turning away, she disappeared down the hallway, the soft tapping of her boots mismatched against her indignant stride.

Aven watched her go, her chin held up proudly until Elune had completely vanished from sight. In an instant, her stoic composure crumbled, a dreary sigh escaping her as the conviction on her face utterly withered. A dull pulse thrummed under each eye with the strain of her secret. She had come so close to revealing it all to her friend up atop the roof. Elune was so close to unearthing the truth on her own. Why now did she choose to respond so defensively? *Because*, she thought to herself, *it's so much worse than Archibaum admitted. The old bastard told me there were assassins, not an army capable of bringing down Arden's Watch.* Her lip curled as the revelation began to settle in. Storming down the staircase, she felt her guilt burn away with the cleansing fire of anger. She was going to find that withered old man and wring his slacking neck.

She passed through the entry hall once more, still bustling with hurried servants and guards. All it took from the princess was a warning glare, however, and each one she approached gave her a wide berth. She passed through the hall like a petulant shooting star, her dark red hair carrying behind her like a banner as she marched. One of the maids had the misfortune of not stepping away swiftly enough for Aven's liking. The princess grabbed her by the shoulder and leaned in, growling through gritted teeth, "Where is Bertram Archibaum?"

"Oh! Your-Your Grace," the maid squeaked, her face paling. "He and the other magistrates...I saw them, Your Grace, I think they were going to the lower kitchens."

Not wasting another breath, Aven released the stammering maid and stormed her way in the direction of the keep's kitchen. She passed through the servants' quarters and descended down a set of stone stairs, bringing her to a torchlit hallway that led to the chambers where the meals of the servants and guards were cooked. The upper level kitchens were mostly used for the concoction of the nobility's dinners, but the magistrates were known to pay visits to the lower levels when they wanted to look busy but had nothing meaningful to do. More than once, Aven herself had responded to complaints of their meddlings, shooing them back to the upper levels with assurances that yes, even the 'cellar cooks' knew what they were doing, and did not need the instructions of old men that had never so much as boiled water on their own.

She found just the man she was searching for, skulking outside the wash room for pots and pans. Bertram Archibaum was alone, his eyes wide and paranoid as he gripped a small bottle of the plantain extract that he self-medicated with. His eyes grew even wider as he spotted the princess stalking towards him, her entire expression a storm cloud of anger. The noble took a quick sip directly from the miniature bottle before fumbling with the cork, capping it off and dropping it into the pocket of his robes. Not a second after, Aven had his robes coiled into her fist as she pressed him forcefully against the stone wall, a mere foot away from the nearest torch. "Your Grace!" he squeaked.

"Where are they?" Aven hissed.

"Pardon, Your Grace?"

"Don't play stupid with me, Bertram! Where are the other magistrates!?" she growled, pressing him against the wall once again for emphasis.

"I-I don't know, Your Grace. They *were* in the kitchens. I was - I *was* in there with them, but I made an excuse to leave. I was looking for *you*, Your Grace."

"Oh, were you?" Aven said with mock cheer through gritted teeth. "How thoughtful of you, Bertram, to consider me after Wyatt Darjin reported in with information quite contradictory to what you told me."

"Your Grace, we didn't know, you must believe me," Archibaum spoke in swift, panicked words. "An entire army...that was *never* in the negotiations, Your Grace, the damage to the Glen Dale was supposed to be minimal, we don't have-"

"Do *not*," Aven snarled, lifting her hand to grab the noble by the jaw, her fingers digging into the loose skin in his cheeks, "try to pass off the assassination of my father as *minimal*, you worm. It's over. You and the magistrates have tipped your hand. You are coming with me, and we are going to explain everything to the king."

"Your Grace," the magistrate squeaked, "Your Grace, please. You cannot possibly see that as the true solution. Not now. Not with Arden's Watch conquered. Don't you see? When this story of Arden's Watch gets out - and it will - the people will be afraid. If any word reaches the common folk that this could have been prevented, if there was any foreknowledge prior to the invasion, the other magistrates won't *need* an elaborate ruse to start riots. We can scarcely afford to have the Glen Bailey fighting amongst itself when the orcs attack the gates. Can't you see?"

"You're a snake, Bertram," Aven snapped. "You're a soulless, lying snake. You knew an army was coming. You only sold me on the story of petty assassins so you could back me into this corner, without a choice to make. I won't do it, Archibaum. I won't let you slither away with your vipers when the greenskins come. I don't care if I am ruined in the aftermath."

"No, Aven, please, listen," Archibaum whined through his squished lips. "There's still time. We can still make it through this, you and I, as can this kingdom. The other magistrates, they...they told me their plan. They're going to take action."

"Then speak, and do it quickly," Aven growled ferociously. She stood a whole head shorter than Archibaum, but her intensity had the man withering against the wall.

"In two days, they plan on stealing the gryphons, Your Grace," Archibaum spoke as fast as his tongue could form the words. "They are going to bundle up their payment to the orcs and fly to the north, in search of the army. They will deliver their payment in hopes of falling into Grathul's good graces. I can alert the right guards of some suspicious whispers I'd heard the night before, and we can have them ambushed at the aviary, with proof of their treachery. Why else would they try to board a half dozen gryphons with their pockets full of gold?"

"Why would they approach the orcs, instead of simply fleeing?" Aven demanded impatiently.

"Pardon, Your Grace," Archibaum squeaked. "When the orcs have finished razing the land, they want the warchief's blessing to rebuild here with some...understandings. They know the orcs will have no interest in occupying the Glen Dale lands permanently. They will remain for a time, and then they will strike elsewhere. When they do, the magistrates wish to inherit what remains."

Even in the most gruesome wars, there are always survivors. They may hide and wait until the dust is settled, but they always emerge with time. Her father's words echoed in her mind as Archibaum confessed. "Greedy cowards," Aven remarked with a scowl. "Do they truly believe Grathul will have mercy on them?"

"Does it matter, Your Grace?" Archibaum asked, taking in a deep breath as the princess's grip finally relaxed on his jaw. "They won't make it there. All we have to do is catch them with their corrupt coins, and the people will have their villain. We will be united as a kingdom against the orcs, and give ourselves the best chance of victory. We must only wait another two nights, and our patience will prove to be well worth it."

"If we are at all exposed to knowing of this conspiracy, Bertram, the people will see the blood at Arden's Watch on our hands," Aven hissed.

"With all respects due, Your Grace," the magistrate wheezed as the princess's grip tightened on his jaw once more, "the blood belongs on the hands of those that drew it. We had no knowledge of their plans to attack Arden's Watch. Even if we *had* exposed the magistrates' plot, would your father have stationed more soldiers at an outpost so far away from our gates here? Most of the Watch soldiers returned here safely, anyway."

"Good men died that day, Bertram, and you're a fool if you think the orcs will leave the Watch intact before marching upon the Bailey," Aven snapped.

"Well then, Your Grace," Archibaum murmured, his eyes suddenly drawing a faint glint, his words so close to a challenge that the princess had a strong urge to choke the life out of him right there and then. "Perhaps it is in our best interest if the people do not know our little secret when this is all over. But if you truly think the risk of riots are worth your own guilty conscience, then go, make your accusations. Or if you wish to wait til after the battle, after you've shed blood and sweat in their name, to earn the scorn of your citizens, then by all means, do it. As for me, I do not believe either of us have done anything worth a prison cell. We may not thwart an assassination attempt, but do you truly think, Your Grace, that all the coin in the Glen Bailey would have convinced an entire *army* to come march upon our gates? Don't be foolish. This brute Grathul Heavyhand incited this invasion, by persuasion or by sorcery, and gold coins had nothing to do with his arrival. This isn't about prevention anymore. It's about justice, Your Grace, and we must deliver it at just the right moment."

Aven stared hard at the magistrate in her clutches as he finally fell silent. The defiance in Archibaum's voice was strong for a moment, but once again began to waver as his speech subsided. The princess could hear her own teeth grinding against each other as she weighed his words. There was tainted truth to what the magistrate said. Legions of orcs couldn't be coaxed anywhere by human trade. This invasion wasn't a direct result of her and Archibaum's secret. She couldn't help but feel, however, as though they had simply gambled and lost at the expense of her people's safety. The guilt squeezed at her heart like a giant's fist. And on top of all of it, Bertram had managed to wriggle his way out of the reach of true justice.

"We will wait," she finally said as her grip tightened on the magistrate's face. "We will wait, and we will catch those spineless cretins. You will signal to me when the time is right, and I will be in earshot of your report when you pass your suspicions along to the guards. This cannot seem too orchestrated. I must only be nearby, and after eavesdropping, insist I come along to supervise the matter."

"I can see it done," the magistrate answered before Aven gave his jaw another squeeze.

"Listen, and listen well, Bertram Archibaum," the princess spoke lowly as she leaned in closer to him with wrath in her eyes. "When this is all over, you will request an audience with your king. You will tell him that the events that unfolded have unsettled you so traumatically that you can no longer maintain your responsibilities here, whatever the hell they were to begin with. You will tell him that you desire a fresh start elsewhere, but to amend for the troubles of your absence, you will be leaving three-quarters of your estate in custody of the crown."

"Three-three quarters!?" Archibaum whined.

"Three-quarters, unless you would rather have a revelation granted to you by the Lifegiver following the battle that persuades you to surrender all of your possessions, leaving you with a sack on a stick over your shoulder as you make your pilgrimage to Kaijar Keep," Aven spat. "Three-quarters, Bertram, and then you will slink out of these lands like the vermin you are. And when you have done that, wherever you may find yourself, you will keep your ears open for rumors of Aven Celandine visiting, for if I *ever* see you again, regardless of where, I will kill you and leave your corpse to the buzzards. Have I made myself absolutely clear, Lord Archibaum?"

The magistrate puckered his lips at first, a spark of brazenness briefly showing on his face, but only for a second before extinguishing entirely, obedience settling in. "Yes, Your Grace," he murmured.

"Good," was all Aven said in response as she finally released her hand from his jaw, red lines remaining where she had gripped the tightest. Without another word, she stormed away from the daunted noble, back up to the ground level of the keep. The servants were still carrying to and fro in a hurried frenzy, but she simply marched on with her head held high, a calm amidst the storm as she passed through, all the way up the spiral staircase towards the upper floors. She did not see Elune Shadowsong among the rabble. She didn't expect to. She had done little to earn the patience of her friend not only this day, but for many months before now.

She kept her chin up all the way until she had reached her own quarters, opening up her bedroom door and sliding it shut behind her. She knew she had her orders to attend to, but she desperately needed a minute to herself before she could. The moment she heard the latch lock in place, her shoulders sagged, her eyes brimmed with tears as she stumbled towards the large mirror hanging above her vanity, brass decorations depicting both elven druids and creatures of the forest lining the edges. She leaned over the vanity and stared at her reflection.

A stranger looked back at her. A haggard, shameful stranger, not fit to be the heir to Bartholomew Celandine. What was she doing? She had never been a stranger to the back channels of the kingdom's politics. Only the most naïve truly thought they could be a leader and not deal with the occasional gray circumstance. But this was different. Bertram could say whatever he wanted to, and she could pretend any of it made sense, but in the end, had she simply exposed him from the start, her father would have at the very least increased patrols outside the Hordelands. Instead, she had allowed Archibaum to entice her into a risky ploy, and for what? For proof of her cunning, of her ability to handle the situations a queen might one day be tasked with? She had failed, both herself and her kingdom, and to drown out the guilt that weighed upon her shoulder, she had channeled her aggression onto the magistrate, down by the kitchens. It didn't matter what Archibaum deserved. She felt no higher than a tavern thug leaning on gamblers who owed money. Her lower lip trembling, she turned away from the unrecognizable reflection and knelt before her bedside, weaving her fingers together as she closed her eyes.

"Merciful Goddess," she prayed out loud, "if I am not worthy of leading my people, if I truly am what I see in the mirror, let me fight for them. Let me earn one last chance at redemption. If I must give my life on the fields of war to claim it, then so be it. All I ask is for one more chance."

Her head fell gently upon her knuckles, jaw quivering as the prayer trailed off her lips. She swallowed hard as she waited for some form of assurance, some sign from her goddess. She didn't expect Essence to manifest before her and comfort her, but most magi were often able to feel some form of surgence after beseeching for strength. But if her deity heard her plea, she did little to assure her. Aven's stomach continued to twist, her heart sinking into some endless abyss inside her. Tears began to trail down the corners of her eyes. Essence had not abandoned her, of that she was sure, but she would watch this struggle from afar. The princess had dug herself into a hole, and it was up to her to climb her way out.

She took in a ragged gasp as her posture straightened. Desperation was setting in. She had to tell someone. She *had* to. She couldn't bear the burden of this guilt with just Archibaum anymore, especially because she knew that he shouldered little of it, if any. But she couldn't go to her father. Not now. It was too late. It was just too damned late.

She didn't know where she was going, but she suddenly couldn't stand to be alone anymore. The confines of her room hadn't settled her in the least. Her door swung open as she stormed back into the hall, heading for the staircase. As her feet carried her forward, a plan began to form in her mind. *I'll go to Wyatt. Of course, I'll go to Wyatt. Why didn't I think of that right away? He's always been my confidant.*

She paused as she reached the winding staircase, one hand lifting to her lips as doubt began to bloom. She bit down on a fingernail as she hesitated. *What the hell am I thinking? I can't go to Wyatt. What will I tell him? That I might be responsible for the death of those Watch soldiers? He hasn't even scrubbed the shit from the sewers off of himself. He'd be furious with me. He'd tell someone. Besides, you have thought of this before. You can't associate him with this, remember? He's only a captain. If he didn't inform anyone, his life would be forfeit, without a second thought.*

Something else prodded at her conscience as well, the lingering thought of Strigson's naked body sliding out of his bath, her inner debates about whether or not he'd be a suitable husband. Gods, it wasn't that long ago that she'd come to terms with the fact that her and Wyatt's relationship couldn't continue. And now she wanted to run to him, to reveal this horrible secret, to ask him to share this burden with her? Would she make it through another breath before guilt also dictated that she tell him about the end of their romance as well?

She began to feel strangulated again, despair and shame tightening around her throat. Her breathing was shallow and rapid, her head beginning to feel light. By the gods, she was hyperventilating. She had to *do* something. She *had* to tell someone. She swallowed hard, and commanded her trembling body to take normal breaths. She felt herself become marginally more stable, at least enough to dispel the violet blotches from her vision as oxygen returned to her. A thought occurred to her, and she made a decision. She did not allow any time to talk herself out of it. There was no ideal solution. She was at a crossroads and simply had to choose a path.

Instead of going down, she went up. *Clapclapclapclap* her feet went as she rushed up the stairs, taking two at a time as her arms churned. As she arrived at the next level, she quickly looked behind her. The kingdom was in a crisis, so it wouldn't be unusual for her to be moving in a hurry, but she didn't want anyone asking questions or pestering her to see if there was anything that could be done to help. Seeing nobody, she rounded the corner with swift steps. A torch flared briefly as she walked past it, her anxiety high enough to emit a faint arcane aura about her.

She kept moving until she stood before the general's personal war room. If she had arrived in time, he would still be fastening himself with armor or gathering maps to detail plans with his lieutenants. She saw that she was in luck. Two armed guards waited outside the doors, their militant postures stiff and at the ready. They raised their arms in salute as Aven approached.

"Is Sir Ganisalp inside?" Aven asked, trying her best to keep the tremor in her voice contained.

"He is, Your Grace," the one on the right answered as his arm fell to his side. "We're to escort him to the lieutenants' meeting when he's out. Is there-"

"I have something important to discuss with the general, soldiers," Aven interrupted. "You may wait for his arrival at the stairs down the hall."

The two exchanged looks from behind their helmets before the one on the left spoke up, saying cautiously, "Forgive us, Your Grace, we were specifically ordered-"

"And I am countermanding those orders, soldier!" Aven said, a shrill tone creeping into her voice as she barked. "I am your future queen and my word *does* come before your general's! Down the hall, and don't make me say it again!"

"Yes, Your Grace," they both answered in unison as they marched away from the door, both glancing at the other with concern as they left. The princess wasted no time, grabbing the door by its handle and throwing it open with more strength than she intended.

Strigson Ganisalp was already at the door as it swung into the hallway, his hand reaching out for the handle that had swiftly moved from his reach. There was a desk behind him towards the back end of the room, rolled maps laid upon its surface. On the left side were two weapon racks, one lined with swords and the other with maces and morningstars. The right was decorated with shields, some of them new, others knicked and scarred from previous skirmishes. The general frowned and looked in both directions opposite Aven before saying, "I thought that was your voice, Your Grace. Where did Ultin and Leo go?"

She was mere heartbeats away from losing her nerve, but she acted before her mind could talk her out of it. She shut the door firmly behind her and marched up to Strigson with a purposeful stride. Her hands lifted to his face, his thin beard bristling against her palms as she cupped his cheeks as her mouth reached for his. She could feel the faintest gasp of surprise from him as their lips connected, but it was as brief as a passing summer breeze. She felt his arms coil around her, one strong hand resting on her shoulder blade, the other at her waist.

They broke free of one another for a moment, their chests both filling with excited breaths, Aven's shaking with the burdens she wished to shed. She wasn't ready to confess, though. She couldn't believe she was doing any of this to begin with. She didn't want to think, to speak, she just wanted to lose herself in the general's embrace. She lowered her gaze and rested her forehead against his chest. Had he been wearing armor earlier, when the Watch survivors had addressed the king? She couldn't remember. He wasn't now, anyway, but instead had a tan undershirt over his torso that accentuated the carved edges of his muscular frame. She could smell the faint musk of sweat in his chest hair, collected from the day's tasks and likely the stress of the revelation of the orcish army. It wasn't overpowering, though, and it was a clean sweat. The aroma stirred her, sending dancing shivers over her thighs.

"Aven," he murmured above her, but she interrupted him by lifting her head to kiss him again. She wasn't ready to explain herself. Strigson had matters to attend to, but he was more than willing to set them aside for the moment. She knew he'd wanted this. She could taste his anticipation, the desire he'd buried for so long now. It was all coming to surface, and as dutiful as he was, he was not going to relinquish this opportunity that had fallen into his lap.

He hoisted her up with his powerful arms, their mouths never leaving each other as he carried her around, marching them both towards the table in the back as her legs coiled around his waist. Holding her up by her hind quarters with one arm, he scattered the maps off of the surface, sending them tumbling to the floor, bouncing gently as they landed. Strigson rested her on the table's surface before breaking his mouth away from hers, lips pressing against her neck just below her ear before trailing downward towards her collarbone. A murmur and a sigh escaped her as her hand trailed up the back of his neck, palm gliding through the hair at the back of his head.

A voice spoke quietly, forebodingly in the back of her mind. She couldn't ignore the reason she came here and settle for a lustful intertwining. She'd only be worse off than before she'd slammed his door behind her, only further burdened with the guilt of having another before settling things with Wyatt. She bit her lip before sliding the tip of her tongue between her rows of teeth, giving it a gentle pinch to brace herself. As Strigson's mouth began to graze along her collarbone, she moved her hand from the back of his head to his sturdy jawline, angling his gaze back up to her as she looked into his dark brown eyes. She swallowed and fought back the tears that were threatening to form at the corners of her own.

"I have to tell you something," she whispered. Her lower lip wanted to tremble, but she locked her jaw closed. She wasn't going to fall apart. No. Not yet.

Strigson's eyes searched hers. His face was a myriad of emotions. Stress, desire, hope, fear, they were all etched into his handsome features. The eager lift in his trousers spoke of an unquenched lust as well, and the apprehension in his words was nearly that of an adolescent boy who was both overjoyed and terrified as he explored a woman's body for the first time. "Now?" he asked.

"Yes," Aven said, her head nodding slowly. "It has to be now."

And so she told him everything. They didn't move from their positions once during her confession, her legs still straddled around him, her arms clasping his shoulders for support as he listened. She confessed her discovery of the magistrates, plotting in the bath house, of her words with Archibaum and his plan to betray the others. She told him about the assassination plot, about the magistrates' schemes to remove her father and seize power after his death, and of their delicate subterfuge involving the city workers and their cheated pay. Twice, she could no longer contain herself and burst into a series of sobs, leaning forward to bury her head against his chest, to escape into that comfort she had craved for months now. Each time, she managed to regain her composure and continue telling her tale, though she didn't dare look him in the eyes as she spoke. It took all of her strength to tell Strigson her secrets; she wasn't ready for his disapproval or his condemnation. She had to come clean, to share her guilt with someone, and before she could face his judgment, she had to rid herself of every toxic detail.

When she had finally purged herself of every one, she lifted her eyes to his once again. A gauntleted fist squeezed at her heart again. There was still a cloud of swarming emotions on the general's face, but it all boiled down to one malefic entity: torment.

"We have to tell the king," Strigson breathed, sounding as though he'd just been delivered a swift kick in the solar plexus.

"We *can't*," Aven whispered back desperately, her hands clinging to his jaw once more. "Were you not listening to me, Strigson? It's over. It's too late to do the right thing. The blood is on *my* hands, *my* conscience, but to confess to my father...it won't save anyone, and worse, if this plot the magistrates have planned is as effective as Archibaum claims, we could have riots that could escalate to a civil war just as orcs march upon the Glen Dale."

"They couldn't," Strigson growled, shaking his head adamantly. "They're just not smart enough to pull that off, Aven, you *know* who we're talking about, right? Those fat assed fools didn't get to where they are with brains. They inherited their coin, every one of them, and they've only used it to buy power since their equally fat assed fathers found their graves. It's a bluff. Archibaum's been bluffing since you found them, and-"

"What if he isn't, though?" Aven insisted, her fingertips digging into his cheeks. "You say they inherited their coin, Strigson, but any wealthy fool can spend his way into beggarhood. What if we've been underestimating them this entire time? We *can't* afford to be divided when Grathul's hordes show up at our gates. You know this!"

"By the Lifegiver, Aven," Strigson murmured, his voice sounding choked as it left his lips. "I am the *general* of the Glen Bailey's army. I've sworn oaths at your father's feet to defend the integrity of this kingdom. I have built our army on those tenets, and your father has fortified these lands with them. If we don't go tell him now, that goes against everything I stand for. It goes against everything *we* stand for. Don't you understand that?"

"Of course I do, Strigson," Aven said with a high pitch. "I know what I should have done. By the gods, don't you think that it's haunted me every night since I stumbled upon those bloated bastards in the bathing chambers? But I am telling you that at this moment, such noble intentions will only do us harm. I will be locked in a dungeon cell, if I am not hung from a tree in the market square by an angry mob, and the city will be divided at a point where we cannot afford to be. Please, Strigson. I had to tell someone, and I trust you. At the very least, let me fight for my kingdom. If I have to die on the field of battle to earn redemption, it will mean so much more than my head on a block."

"You won't be executed, Aven," Strigson said, shaking his head. "You won't. Not for this."

"You don't *know* that!" Aven hissed, her fingernails digging into his skin. She relaxed the grip as she saw a cord bulge in the general's neck. "You don't know that. Please, Strigson. Just this once, keep my secret," she said in a softer murmur.

She could see his upper row of teeth grinding against his lower lip, the faintest glistening of frustrated tears shining his eyes. Why had she come here? Why had she confessed all of this to the man with the strongest convictions in all of the Glen Dale?

"This would compromise everything," he whispered.

"I know," Aven answered immediately, trailing the fingertips of her right hand across his jaw. "I know I'm asking the world of you. Please. Just this once."

He said nothing at first, his teeth still working furiously against his lower lip. He wasn't convinced. She knew what would seal his agreement. She knew they both wanted it and had so for some time now. It would taint it, to invoke it in such a treacherous way. But she was backed into a corner now, and not only had she called out to the hunter, she'd kicked a bow and quiver his way to put her down with. She was out of options.

She lowered one of her hands, tracing the back of her knuckles down his pectoral and over his abdomen. A shaking breath rattled in his chest as his eyes followed her hand. It trailed over his belt line before settling over his crotch. His member had grown flaccid with the sobering talk of treason, but it came to life eagerly behind his trousers as she gave him an encouraging squeeze. She leaned forward, tracing her lips against his as she whispered one final word to him.

"Please."

He pressed his mouth firmly against hers once more, and the grim agreement was silently sealed. Her hands fumbled at his belt line to loosen his trousers, his hands hiking up her skirt as she scooted a couple inches forward on the table. She clutched at him once more as he entered her, head falling backward slightly as her lips parted. For a few precious moments, everything was forgotten. She allowed herself to succumb to numbness as Strigson gently worked.

Their coupling was quick and unceremonious, the legs of the table creaking traitorously as their bodies moved against each other. She could sense Strigson's growing guilt as they copulated, becoming fresher as the initial thrill began to subside. His trembling release came far before hers could even begin to surface, his body slumping against her as his head fell to rest on her shoulder.

They didn't say a word as they removed themselves from the other, Aven settling her skirt back over her legs as she slid nimbly off the table, taking care not to step on any of the maps that still lay scattered across the floor. Strigson remained at the table, hunched over it with his fingertips digging into its surface. A moment passed before he finally hunched down to lift his trousers back up to his waist, buckling the belt that was looped through. His face was shadowed and his gaze remained stubbornly fixated away from her as he settled back against the table.

She walked away from him, approaching the door to the hallway, but paused as her hand reached out to the handle. She looked back at the general before quietly saying, "I don't know what will happen after we conquer the orcs, Strigson. But our focus now must be on doing just that. There will be no pieces to pick up after if we let Grathul Heavyhand crush them beneath his boot."

"Of course, Your Grace," was all Strigson said, still hunched over the table as though he was busy studying a map, though none were left on its surface. With the formality settling into his speech again, Aven knew there was nothing more she could say. She opened the door to the general's war room and began walking down the hallway. She had duties to attend to.

She knew it wasn't fair for her to feel relief at Sir Ganisalp's expense. It was nothing small that she had asked of him, to take a furlough on his convictions, and she suspected that if they both survived the impending war, there would be consequences for what she had just done. But for the moment, simply confessing her sins to another, combined with a carnal coupling, even one as unsatisfying as they'd shared, was enough to secure a semblance of sanity for the time being. She couldn't worry about later. Not yet. She needed her focus now, at whatever the cost.

Chapter Twenty-Three

Wyatt Darjin's news from Arden's Watch took little time to spread through the kingdom of the Glen Bailey. As Bartholomew had ordered, each serving member of the crown, whether they were a servant or a soldier, reported to their superior to hear instructions for the defense of their home. Outside the walls of the Bailey, there was a podium erected for the use of the army's general when he was to address each of his legions, with plenty of open space to line up each one in rank and file. That was how Sir Strigson Ganisalp preferred to speak to his soldiers, but such methods were more appropriate when your army was the one striking first, when time was on your side. It was a great unifying tactic, perfect in rallying troops to a cause. With Arden's Watch sacked, however, and an army of orcs expected at any time, time could not be wasted for such formalities. Ganisalp met with his lieutenants and his captains, giving them instructions to relay to those in their charge. For the Monastery's paladins, Nevic Baltwin was the commanding official, and he addressed them in the sanctuary. The pews were moved to the side, giving them ample space to kneel before the crusader as he gave out his orders. Three rows back from the front, Cadohaden Ulaeron listened intently. From the moment he'd heard the first whisper of Arden's Watch falling to the greenskins, his heart had beaten a little faster, his skin flushing with the anticipation. The governor Galdoys Veriknock may have ultimately caused his parents' deaths, but it was still the infiltrating orcs that held the blades. He'd accepted the loss of Deltore and Melaitha with Elune's help, but once again, the greenskins were out for blood, and this time, they were after the place he finally felt at home and among friends. He felt welcome in the Glen Bailey. The savages would not take this from him as well.

"Time is of the essence," Crusader Nevic announced as his paladins were settled into place. "So listen up. I won't be repeating myself. As I'm sure most of you have heard, Arden's Watch has fallen. The soldiers stationed there reported an army of orcs, as well as a few other Hordeland types scattered among them. This isn't some ragtag band of raiders, men. Somehow, this warchief by the name of Grathul Heavy-hand has gathered no less than half the Hordelands to fight for him. We don't have time to speculate how he might have done this; what matters is that they're out there, and it is assumed they will strike here next.

"What we can also safely assume is that the army will have warlocks, and unless our scouting reports are outdated, Gragnath Fire-Eyes should be among them. It will no doubt be difficult to isolate the warlocks from the soldiers, but when we get the opportunity, your immediate obligation is to subdue them, as they are prone to the gifts bestowed upon us by the Lifegiver. The army lieutenants are aware of this as well, and they may give any of you specific orders to focus your attention on the warlocks. I urge all of you to review your blessings with any time you may find yourself between now and the arrival. It is imperative that you be ready with your prayers without having to think it over in the heat of battle.

"There will be more to fighting this battle than simply hunting for the warlocks, however. You will all be assigned to one of two groups. Most of you will be accompanying the infantry as auxiliary units and will be given a commanding officer. You will follow their standard procedures unless ordered otherwise. This will go into effect immediately after we are through here, as patrols have been tripled and the general needs more bodies to occupy them while his other soldiers prepare the defenses. You may not be given more than an hour of off-duty between now and Grathul's arrival. If you have loved ones to speak to beforehand...use your time wisely.

"The rest of you, those who have shown skill with your healing, will be assisting Ecila's clerics. Your primary concern will still be combat, but you'll be focusing on getting to the fallen in the thick of battle and extracting them from danger. You will be expected to heal wounds adequately enough to drag them back to the clerics, where they will hopefully be mended back into fighting condition. Those of you named for this assignment will also be reporting to Ecila right away to begin preparation with her and those she's in charge of."

Cadohaden didn't need to speculate as to what group he would be assigned to. His healing skills were just barely mediocre, at least for Nevic's standards. The Crusader asked if there were any questions. The young paladin did not turn his head, but his eyes swiveled back and forth, looking for those would offer any. The one named Drevor lifted his hand first. "Will we be fighting outside the gates, sir?"

"That's still being discussed by Sir Ganisalp and Our Majesty," Nevic answered. "While I'm sure we'll have archer support stationed on the ramparts, I would expect that we will defend in front of the walls with preparations to fall behind them if the situation begins to look grim. Whichever the case, your duty is to defend the civilians. Soon enough, we'll start seeing refugees from the farm lands being evacuated in. Take a good look at them when they're brought in. Some of you have children at home and need no motivation to fight with every fiber of your soul. For those that don't, look into the eyes of the children coming in as their mothers hurry them along beside them. If the fear you see there doesn't light a fire in your chest, then I'm likely wasting my time with you.

"Any other questions?" the crusader asked. Standing in the light of the myriad of candles, Nevic was an imposing figure as he looked on over his paladin force. His albino skin gave him the mirage of an animate marble statue, his disciplined posture only adding to the illusion.

"Sir," a man said in the front row, a veteran paladin named Horace Tunstad with a horseshoe of hair around his head and a combed burnished mustache under his nose. "What of our allies? Can we expect reinforcements?"

"It's best not to count on it, Horace," Nevic answered as he lowered his chin, the shadows on his face shifting their angles in stern patterns. "We've sent out our ravens, but I would not expect the orcs to linger at Arden's Watch any longer than it takes them to eat the larders clean. Given how long it surely took Wyatt and his men to make it back to us on foot, we're anticipating Grathul not being far behind. They'll arrive first, and I don't think orcs have ever staged a patient siege in recorded history."

"How did a whole army of orcs make it all the way over from the Hordelands without being seen?" a voice called out from the back rows. "Someone *had* to have seen them! Why didn't they send word?!"

"It was those moon worshiping elves, I'll bet!" another called out not far from the other. Cadohaden tried to strain his head far enough to see who was causing the ruckus but couldn't without breaking his position. "Let them walk right past, probably gave them a little wave too!"

Nevic's face darkened, a scowl emerging on his brow as the sanctuary settled back into silence. A candle wick popped and hissed for a moment in the reticence before the crusader spoke lowly, "I will not have anyone in my order gossiping like a gaggle of tipsy tavern wenches. We cannot know how the orcs escaped notice, and right now, it makes no difference. They are coming, and we must be prepared. That means no distractions. From any of you, or from any seeds you plant in the minds of others. Understood?"

A murmured 'yes sir' echoed through the gathered paladins. Nevic nodded his head. "Good," he growled. "Now unless someone else has something to say that isn't a baseless accusation, I will read off assignments."

"Sir," Cadohaden said as he raised his hand from his kneeling position. Nevic slanted a gaze towards the young paladin with an air that bordered on suspicion.

"Yes, Ulaeron?"

"Why not use the gryphons?" Cadohaden asked after clearing his throat. "We could scout out the orcs in quick order. If they're still mucking about at Arden's Watch, perhaps we could set up an attack away from our walls, somewhere they wouldn't expect."

"For the same reason we don't use the gryphons on routine patrols, Ulaeron," Nevic answered crisply. "Our agreement with Kaijar Keep explicitly states that the beasts are not to be used for combat. The gryphons are a precious resource and endangering them would certainly end the trade we have, which benefits the Glen Bailey greatly, I might add."

"But if this orcish army is as monstrous as they're saying it is, can we afford to not take that risk? If we fall, it won't matter what-"

"The gryphons are not available to us in combat, Ulaeron, end of discussion," Nevic said sternly. Cadohaden pursed his lips, stiffly bowing his head with a 'yes sir' in a gesture of respect, though his expression betrayed his feeling of dejection. Not bothering to ask if there were any more inquiries, the crusader turned away from his paladins, picking up a roll of parchment sitting on the wooden altar behind him. He unrolled it with both hands, squinting at the scrawled ink across the page. Reading out loud, Nevic began to list the names of those that would join the guard patrols for the first shift.

Cadohaden hoped silently that he wouldn't be selected in the first rotation. He wanted to find Elune before she too was swept into the current of defense preparations, to spend just a few more minutes on the roof of the keep with her before war reached their doorstep. Luck was not with him, however, as the final name off Nevic's tongue was indeed his, as well as that of the guard captain he was to report to, Andrew Svelt. He would have to hope that he could steal a few minutes with her later, for he was on his feet once more, responding in unison with the others to Nevic's salute, and in seconds, was marching his way out of the sanctuary and northward to the city walls.

He craned his head upward as he made his way towards the junction he was to report to. For the first time since he had fled the gates of Kingsbanesin, he missed his native city. When he'd first come to the Glen Bailey, he'd felt welcomed by its quainter nature and more humble atmosphere. But while the Bailey's walls and turrets were nothing to scoff at, they didn't have the towering intimidation of the dragon empire's defensive structures. With legions of orcs on the way, Cadohaden knew he would have felt safer with the walls of Kingsbanesin on his side.

There was a reinforced door with a rounded top at the bottom of the tower junction, embedded in the defensive wall. Cadohaden grabbed it by the handle and pulled it open, stepping inside to the sound of a popping torch, like the candle that had spoken in the silence of the sanctuary. It was as though the base element of fire itself could feel the impending battle approach. A table sat in the circular ground level floor with a lantern placed on the corner, illuminating the sign-in book and the ink well next to it, feather protruding from the quill resting in the thick liquid. Approaching the book, half filled with scrawled signatures, most of them barely legible, Cadohaden added his own name to the page. He placed the quill back into the ink well and began his climb up the circumventing staircase leading to the top of the ramparts.

When he reached the top, the guard captain Andrew Svelt awaited him, fully dressed in studded sentinel leather. He held a roll of parchment in his hand, and he squinted at Cadohaden with avian eyes. "Name and station, soldier," he grunted.

"Cadohaden Ulaeron, sir," Cadohaden answered, lifting his hand to his forehead in salute. "From the paladin unit. I was to report for patrol reinforcement." Svelt unrolled the parchment between his hands, beady eyes darting back and forth across the paper, his mouth slightly wriggling as he silently murmured names to himself before he finally came across Cadohaden's. The captain let the parchment snap back into its coil and nodded curtly.

"He didn't dress ya before sending you up, then?" Svelt said as he eyed the paladin over. Cadohaden frowned in confusion, glancing down at himself before quickly realizing with embarrassment that the captain obviously meant dressed in the form of armor.

"No sir," Cadohaden answered apologetically, "my orders were to report here as soon as possible."

"Figures," Svelt snorted. "They like to pretend they don't have their own personal armory on the Monastery grounds so that their 'help' can borrow ours and walk away with it. Half that stuff they got is guard property, mark my words. Well, not on my watch, soldier. There's an armor rack down the stretch there; put some chain on yourself. But if you even think about trying to get back down on the ground with it still hanging from your shoulders, you can bet I'll be speaking with Sir Ganisalp about it."

"Yes sir," Cadohaden answered dutifully, though he couldn't help himself from thinking that Andrew Svelt probably had better things to worry about than the Monastery stealing chainmail with an army of orcs bound up to show up at any hour.

"Go on, then," Svelt grunted. "You're on rotation with Private Hakes. Let him take care of the reporting procedures if you happen to see something, but if something happens, just come find me. Don't go running into the city screaming like a woman with her skirts on fire."

Cadohaden didn't have to ask what Svelt meant by 'if something happens', and so he simply acknowledged his orders and began to walk across the ramparts. There were lit torches placed intermittently across the battlements, but they were few and far between so as not to completely diminish the sentinels' night vision. It didn't take long for him to find the armor rack that Svelt had spoken of, or his patrol partner, for Private Hakes was standing next to it, dressed in the same studded leather the captain was adorned in, a quiver over his shoulder and a longbow held in his grip. He had a bucket-like rounded helmet atop his head, but Cadohaden could still see his eyes under the shadow of the metal brim. *He looks nervous*, he thought to himself. "Private Hakes?" he asked.

"Just call me Dylan," the soldier responded dryly. "At least when Svelt's not around. You the partner they were sending?" He didn't bother to ask for a name.

"That's me," Cadohaden confirmed. "Cadohaden Ulaeron, of the Monastery's paladins."

"Right, then. Throw some chain on," Hakes answered, not sounding the least bit interested in the paladin's self-appointed description. Cadohaden obliged immediately, picking one of the heavy chainmail shirts off the rack and sliding his arms inside as he carefully wriggled his way into the vest. When it was snugly over his torso, he picked one of the girdles that was slung over the higher bar on the rack and fastened it around his waist. He frowned as he glanced around. He didn't see any bows or arrows resting anywhere near.

"Is there a bow around I can use?" he asked tentatively.

"Bloody. They sent you up with nothing but the shirt on your back, did they?" Dylan muttered, though his expression didn't appear nearly as annoyed as his tone indicated. His eyes kept glancing off into the fields beyond the city, his chapped lips pursing idly as he stole glances into the distance. "Captain wasn't kidding, then. Just follow me, they've got what you need closer to the other turret."

Cadohaden followed Dylan Hakes across the battlements, glancing out into the twilight-veiled fields of the Glen Dale as well, hoping to spot whatever it was the private had been searching for. He could see little but the silhouettes of swaying barley as a gentle night breeze rolled across the land. He looked back at Hakes as they drew nearer to the next turret. "Seen anything yet?"

"No," was all Private Hakes said in response.

"I'm sure we will soon enough," Cadohaden answered as he glanced back out into the distance. "They'll devour everything they can at the Watch, I'm sure, but if the army's as big as they say, it won't take them long to pick it clean."

"More'n likely," Hakes answered dryly as they approached the turret. A torch hung from the tower's stone wall, and underneath it, a rough-hewn table sat with a bow and quiver resting upon it. There was a space on the right side that looked wide enough for a second pair that had probably already been picked up by one of the Monastery's other reinforcements. Unceremoniously, Hakes shoved the bow and quiver into Cadohaden's grasp. "Here," he grunted. "Back the way we came now, I s'pose."

Cadohaden frowned as he accepted the bow and quiver, slinging the latter over his shoulder as he adjusted his grip on the handle of the bow, getting a feel for the weapon as he and his patrol partner began walking back in the direction they'd came, both peering warily out into the shadows of the night, keenly watching for the slightest glimpse of foreign movement out in the harvest fields.

They patrolled in silence for a few moments, walking all the way back to the turret Cadohaden had climbed up to meet with Svelt before they would both turn back around, marching in the opposite direction once again. Twice he tried to begin a conversation with Dylan Hakes, asking him how long he'd been with the guard, and if he had a family at home, but the private didn't answer his inquiries, both times giving him noncommittal grunts. Cadohaden begrudgingly resigned himself to silence, despite his anticipation for the coming battle, and let Hakes be in his own brooding quiet.

An entire hour of redundant marching passed before Hakes finally broke the silence. "You know where to aim if any show up?"

"Orcs?" Cadohaden asked.

"No, boy, half-dragon swamp gnomes," Hakes grunted. "Of course I mean orcs. You know where to aim?"

Cadohaden's nose wrinkled with indignation, but he opted to ignore the private's sarcasm. "Not specifically, I guess, no."

"For the neck," Hakes said, as though he were describing where to pound in a nail. "Always go for the neck. Usually the most exposed anyway, but if you aim a bit high, maybe you sink one in their eye. Aim a little low, maybe you get lucky and punch it through the armor and into the heart or lungs. Don't just sling it at their torso. You stick 'em in the gut, they might die, but probly not til the battle's done and over and they've got a few trophy kills under their belt."

"You think they'll actually keep me up here if they show up?" Cadohaden asked with a frown. "Sounded to me like we'd probably be fighting in front of the wall. Protect the civilians, right?"

"Psh," Hakes grunted. "The best way to protect the damn civilians is to win the battle. If I were in charge, we'd stay posted up here and just sling arrows all day, dump some oil on 'em when they get too close. There's ballistas on the far east and west ends; just launch those oversized spears all day until they get the point. History's full of leaders that get too fancy in battle. Makes for a better song and story, you know. But their fancy plans hardly ever work out the way they think they will, and entire kingdoms have paid the price."

"The orcs won't come armed with just sticks and stones," Cadohaden countered. "The best way for our archers to be effective is to occupy their front lines with our infantry."

"Yeah? And you know this from the big collection of battle scars you got?" Hakes answered as he angled a scowl at his patrol partner. Before Cadohaden could speak, however, he shook his head and continued, "Ah, yer probably right anyway. I'm sure Ganisalp will line us all up in front of the wall. I'm sure I'll be one of 'em. Not lucky enough to be sitting up here when the blood starts to spill. You don't really get a say innit when you're one of the grunts, and our general didn't get to where he is by being a dolt, I suppose."

"I'm looking forward to it," Cadohaden said, his chest swelling with pride and zeal as he spoke. "My parents' deaths were by orcish hands. I'll be defending my home and avenging their deaths. I'll take twenty of the savages' heads for each of them."

Hakes snorted as he angled another dubious look Cadohaden's way. "You could kill fifty for each 'em, boy. It won't bring them back, and you might die tryin' to make it happen."

"I'm a soldier and a paladin," Cadohaden retorted with indignation. "I know my duty, and I'm not afraid of death."

"Yeah, you and almost every other tinhead in the army, wooden pieces on a map that Bartholomew and Ganisalp push around with their fingers like they're a child's toys," Hakes grumbled in response. "I don't know why more men don't fear death," he said in a voice barely above a whisper.

"Well, I don't *want* to die," Cadohaden answered with a frown. How was this Dylan Hakes ever put into service with such a cowardly heart? "But if I do, I'll move on to the next life, hopefully at the Lifegiver's side, if I've earned a place."

A sad, almost haunting smile crept across Hakes's face. "Are we so sure that something waits for us on the other side?" His voice was still hushed, as foreboding as his grim expression. "I've never seen the gods, myself. Have you ever seen the gods, boy?"

Cadohaden opened his mouth, ready to lash back with a fiery tongue, but slowly brought it to a close as he realized that despite everything he'd seen or felt in life, he hadn't *truly* ever seen the gods, not even Kaijaras, the deity he worshiped daily at the Glen Bailey's Monastery.

"No, no, I didn't think so," was Hakes's quiet response. "And what if they *do* exist? Why do men charge to the front lines so eagerly, ready to join them? It's forever, so they say. An eternity of the afterlife. Do you ever stop and *really* think about that, boy? Eternity. Never, ever ending. My life ain't been something so special, but I know that the next day might bring something new. What ever changes in the afterlife? If we're lucky, we sit around in a giant circle around the Lifegiver while he does what? Smiles at us? Sings with us? *Forever?* And that's if we're the lucky ones, who say our devotions at night and give our neighbors anythin' we don't absolutely need. And the *rest* of us, well, we probly end up floating round next to one another in the Death Shepherd's river of souls. That's it. We'll float. Forever.

"I don't know why some men talk about the afterlife like it's some kind of reward," Hakes murmured. He didn't truly seem to be talking to Cadohaden anymore, but rather to himself, reflecting on the depths of his fears. "I think about doing anything for the rest of bloody time and I just want to sit down and cry."

They continued to march back and forth across the battlements, the sounds of their boots tapping against the stone below still echoing softly into the night, but nothing else was shared between the two as they patrolled. Cadohaden's teeth clenched together as he walked alongside Dylan Hakes, feverishly searching his mind for some kind of answer to the private's doomsaying. This was exactly the type of rhetoric that, as a paladin of the Monastery, he was supposed to have an answer for. Why would a man ever have doubts about joining the Lifegiver's side in the afterlife? There *had* to be more in Kaijaras's realm than just joining hands and singing hymns. He *knew* Nevic or Ecila would have the answers, but he was so beyond frustrated that he couldn't conjure them on his own. And so he resigned himself to silently continuing his patrol with Private Dylan Hakes, neither of them speaking another word that night until finally, Andrew Svelt approached them on the battlements with Hakes' rotational replacement. He was relieved to see that it was someone familiar, a guard by the name of Henrar Aggard. He was a simple man with a tendency to vocalize the obvious, but the anticipation of slaying orcs was a bright glint in the man's eyes, and would certainly bolster Cadohaden's spirits far more than the solemn Dylan Hakes would even on the happiest day of his life.

Cadohaden and Henrar immediately engaged in stories and boastful predictions of the war to come as they continued the patrol, and the young paladin felt a great deal of dreaded weight lift off of his heart. But as they marched, he couldn't help but occasionally glance off into the dead of night and feel the faintest touches of hoarfrost crystal-lize at the edges of his spirit, the words of Private Hakes echoing in his mind. *Eternity. Never, ever ending. That's it. We'll float. Forever.*

Chapter Twenty-Four

His reflection wavered below him, a muddled specter before his eyes in the metal basin. Strigson blinked and lightly shook his head. How long had he been standing there, with his hands below the surface of the water, knuckles resting against the bottom of the bowl? He prided himself on his sharp attention span. It was unlike him to get lost in his thoughts. Muttering an unintelligible scolding to himself, he cupped his hands and lifted the warm water to his face, rubbing his palms against his cheeks as he tried to scrub away the sweat and grime. The contact stirred his senses, reawakening his drive. He had to be going soon. He had a militant sense of punctuality, and he was to meet with Bartholomew soon to finalize the defensive plans for the Glen Bailey.

He finished cleaning himself up and moved to the opposite end of his chambers, where a wide mahogany closet contained his clothing. Next to the closet was an armor rack, holding his personal collection of plate and chain. It was customary for a general to decorate himself in ceremonial armor when having dialogue with his king. He wouldn't wear anything overly burdensome, but a light chest plate, emblazoned with the head of a horse with a furling mane, would cover his chest when he met with His Majesty. The armor had belonged to his great grandfather, Corin Ganisalp, and the horse head doubled as both a recognition of their Wardrin heritage and the trade of his ancestors, who had bred the proud beasts for many generations and had traded them in their city borders and beyond. The business was a far cry from what Strigson and his father Davon were, but the armor had nonetheless been handed down to each generation. When Strigson had received his lofty promotion to general, he had been astounded to hear King Bartholomew decree his heirloom appropriate for royal court. *Well, it's not* truly *the symbol of Wardrin,* he'd said with a thoughtful frown. *And my father always told me, Strigson, that even when united under a common banner, it's important that we don't forget our roots. Our fathers all have a lesson to teach, in some way or another.*

He buckled the two shoulder blade straps before sliding the armor over his torso. Summoning a squire to aid him would have been appropriate, but as much as Strigson relished protocol, he coveted saving time even more, and for a single ceremonial armor piece, he would allow himself this irregularity. His arms were just long enough to buckle the strap across his lower back, and although his left hand struggled briefly with the end of the material, he managed to fit the tongue through the clasp. He gave the plate a quick tug with his hands to test the fit. Nodding with satisfaction, he marched back over to the other side of his room where a wooden stool sat next to three pairs of polished boots. He picked out the appropriate pair, the ones that were not designed for combat but still had decorated plates riveted to the leather, resting along the shins.

As he tugged the boots over his feet, something caught his eye. Brushing his thumb against the edge of the left boot, along the seam that connected to the sole, Strigson spotted a single loose stitch, the traitorous thread poking out from the material, the lip of the leather just barely beginning to curl outward. His nose wrinkled with irritation. He certainly didn't have time for it now, but he would need to bring it to a cobbler for repair before it began to unravel any further. The imperfection in his boot only further called upon the memories of his father Davon. *Pa would take care of it for me,* he thought to himself.

Davon Ganisalp had been a cobbler almost all of his life after quickly proving that he was not a fit in the Wardrin army, having been born without any similarity to his father Anson or his grandfather Corin. His discharge was anything but honorable, and so he sought a new life elsewhere, in the land of the Glen Dale. Possessing the skills for leatherworking, he moved himself along with his wife and three children into the heart of the Glen Bailey, earning a lease on a small corner shop in the market district after pledging his loyalty to Bartholomew's father, then-king Banrin Celandine. Despite his ineffectiveness as a soldier, Davon's adherence to the law was as disciplined as ever, and while some of the city tradesmen ignored the more obscure tax rules and trade regulations, Strigson's father meticulously counted and cross-checked, ensuring he was always giving his fair due to the crown. One night, as his father sat up late scratching numbers onto a piece of parchment after a hard day's work, Strigson asked Davon why he spent so much time on the arithmetic. His answer was the same as it was for countless questions: *Those are the rules, son.* His father earned a stalwart reputation in the Glen Bailey, and over time, he saved up enough coin to turn his lease of the shop into ownership.

Davon's philosophy did not end with taxes. It was only two winters before Strigson's mother, Gloria, who had married his father when he was still enlisted in the army, became bored with her cobbler husband and left, taking his sisters Petrice and Julia with her to live as traveling gypsies, where there was never any lack for adventure. It broke Davon's heart, and Strigson could see the pain in his forced smile, but he took no time off, refusing to allow his grief to interrupt his duties. Weeks later, a letter came from Gloria, demanding money from Davon to take care of his daughters. Strigson was yet again bewildered by his father's compliance, as he filled a pouch with clinking coins and hired the most reputable courier to carry the allowance to the location Gloria had detailed in her letter. When he asked Davon why he would even entertain the idea of giving away his coin to Strigson's capricious mother, his father answered, *Because she's still my wife, Strigs, and Petrice and Jules are still my daughters, whether or not they're living under my roof. And as the father, it's my responsibility to make sure they don't starve. They may not be written into law, but those are still the rules. A father provides for his family.*

Strigson spent many months arguing with his father, denouncing the ludicrousness of paying good coin for his mother's betrayal, but each time, Davon would only shake his head and invoke the godforsaken rules. And that's how the two of them lived their lives. They went to the Monastery on their rest day, because those were the rules. They said their devotions at night, because those were the rules. They helped out their neighbors in times of need, even if they could offer nothing in return, because those were the rules. Even when it became obvious that Strigson wasn't anywhere near cut out to be a cobbler like his father, he still helped him around the shop and tried in vain to mend leather and fur, because those were the rules. And at the start of every new moon, Davon would send coin to Gloria, because those were the rules. They sang the hymns and gave offerings in the name of the Lifegiver, but Davon Ganisalp's true religion was the law, and his own conscience was his god.

Not even the threat of death could deter his father's devotion. When Strigson was only twelve years of age, Davon became afflicted with a nagging pneumonia. A young Nevic Baltwin would pay them visits, sometimes even bringing another cleric to assist in the healing, but their abilities could only delay the inevitable. Strigson had shouted and bellowed, wondering loudly how the power of Kaijaras could not fully heal his father. Nevic calmly explained to him that the restorative powers of the Lifegiver were like a blunt instrument, effective at mending rended flesh and superficial wounds, but could only do so much for the infected lungs of Strigson's father. Even then, as he coughed and hacked his life away, Davon would not veer from the philosophy he had adhered to his entire life. *We don't get to choose when we leave this world, Strigson. Kaijaras gave us the gift of life, and it is his decision when he wishes to take it away. Those are the rules, son.*

Strigson buttoned the sleeves of his shirt and tucked the hem beneath his belt line as he remembered his father's words. He told himself not to reflect on it, that he didn't have time for reminiscing, but once the memories had infiltrated his thoughts, it was difficult to banish them. He recalled writing to his mother and sisters following Davon's death. He had cursed their names as Nevic helped him bury his father beneath a maple tree in the Monastery's garden cemetery, for they couldn't be bothered to write him back with even a hastily scrawled note of feigned sympathy. He cried that night, but just as his father would have wanted, he opened the cobbler's shop the very next day, to carry on his father's trade. The endeavor was an abject failure. He could not fill any orders in even twice the amount of time Davon would have needed. His repair jobs were almost as bad as the flaws they were brought in for. Within a week, he was constantly attending to angry customers demanding their coin back for the absurdly long wait, or compensation for their damaged goods. Strigson had little choice but to sell his father's shop, the tools inside, and all the materials in the storage. Without a home or a means of income, he enlisted in the Glen Bailey's army.

Even in the grunt drills, his pedigree became apparent, as he was every bit the soldier his great grandfather Corin was. Though he wasn't the same man as his father, he lived by the same code. He learned what the rules were, and he followed them with a religious fervor. He was steadfastly loyal to the kingdom that gave Davon the second chance he needed, and when his opportunities arose, was recognized as a keen strategist. Without any family to return home to or any other interests to pursue, Strigson Ganisalp was able to give his full devotion to the military. Even the smile and invitation of an enchanting woman, of which he received many as he rose through the ranks, could not sway him from his true passion. Even when he found himself enticed into the bed of a paramour, he would find himself awake late in the night, hours after their lovemaking, wondering whether or not they would leave on nothing but a whim, just as his mother had. Not a single woman could ease those fears, and he could not bring himself to marry, for he knew that if he did, he would subject himself to his father's code, honorbound to his misery if she ever abandoned him in the same way.

That was, until recently. The general felt a lump begin to form in his throat as he glared at the rogue thread in his boot. He'd tried to forget what he'd done with the princess, the daughter of the man he was to report to shortly, their abrupt and guilty coupling on the table of his war room. He clenched his fists briefly, his jaw tightening as his conscience reminded him of how he'd forsaken the rules, which was truly an understatement. It didn't matter if it was indirect, he was party to conspiracy, and therefore, treason, in exchange for a hasty romp that had left him feeling sullied and low. It didn't matter if it was too late to stop Arden's Watch from being sacked, or that the impending invasion was inevitable. The magistrates were criminals, and they were freely roaming in the Glen Bailey. Strigson was knowingly part of that now, and the guilt felt like a guillotine's shadow looming over his head. Why had he allowed himself to sink so low?

He knew why. It wasn't complex. He was in love with Aven Celandine, and not only that, he was enamored with the possibilities that would come with being hers. With Aven being the one of Celandine blood, any kingship he would claim would mostly be formality, but that wasn't what mattered the most to him anyway. He was infatuated with her independence and fiery spirit, but unlike similar women, he would never have to fear her leaving him. Her sense of duty would not permit it. She would someday have a kingdom to rule. Leaving to become a gypsy was not an option.

He slowly got to his feet, lifting a hand to his face before dragging his fingertips across it, pulling at his skin gently downwards with distress. If she'd given any signs of finding him pleasing in the bath house, she had left no room for doubt when she had come to his war room before. She'd come to him with her secret, not Wyatt Darjin. She'd made love to *him*, not Wyatt Darjin. He'd paid a great price for those things. It made him feel ill, these terrible secrets, but in the end, perhaps his compromise would be worth it all. His conscience scolded him, stubbornly buzzing about what the rules were, but he did his best to ignore it. He needed his focus. An army of Hordeland savages was on its way to threaten his people, and he'd never squared off against such a foe in his life. He didn't have the time to worry about any of this, even though it had kept him up at night. And to begin preparations, he had to be able to look Bartholomew Celandine in the eye without revealing any of this to his king. *Keep quiet this time, Father. Just this once*, he thought to himself.

Finally dressed for his meeting, Strigson took a sword belt hanging from his armor rack, clasping it around his waist and sheathing a standard issue blade into place before leaving his quarters, marching down the hallway towards the war room. It was on the same level as his chambers, and he was grateful for not having to wade through the ground floor, where the servants were scurrying around like startled mice. He still managed to encounter a few of them running errands on his way to the war room, however. Each one of them slowed their pace as he passed them by, their eyes looking to him wide and fearful, as if at any moment he might begin shouting orders, declaring the kingdom under siege. He wanted to grab them by the shoulders and chastise them for such foolishness; why would he be wandering the hallways of the keep if the hordes were upon their doorstep? He restrained himself, however, and resorted to challenging glares that hurried the servants along in their chores.

The keep's war room was a claustrophobic's nightmare. It was long and narrow, the walls only four paces apart, most of the floor space occupied with a sturdy table similar in nature. An imposing chandelier hung from the ceiling, a steel-wrought design that housed many candles but offered no flair or frivolity in its conception, unlike the decorative works of art hanging from the throne room or banquet hall. It was almost condemning in nature, like an iron spider dangling patiently on a thread, plotting the demise of its prey. On the walls, dozens of hide maps were hanging, pinned with miniature nails driven through the mortar between the stones. There were illustrations for almost every location in the Aariad, some nearly overwhelming in their detail, others, like that of the deserts of Chai'Rin, were vague and full of empty space, an occasional note scrawled by a cartographer depicting a rough description of the terrain.

Across the table, however, was the largest map in the room, depicting the entire continent across its face, the detail around the lands of the Glen Dale rich with illustration and markings, as well as most of the lands surrounding it. The further the map stretched to the ends of the table, the more ambiguous the figures became. Littered around the edges were wooden pieces, like that of a chess board, representing everything from the Glen Bailey's armies to camps of coven warlocks hiding in the wilderness. Sir Ganisalp frowned as he looked across the table, for standing above it was not only King Bartholomew, but his scribe Pleatus as well, a thin board held in his arm with parchment laid out on it, a quill in one hand. The bulbous-eyed scribe had his square crimson velvet hat on, and his mouth was puckered in a way that made his cheeks bulge like egg sacs at the corners of his lips. The king looked at his general with weary eyes, a goblet of wine held in his hand. "You're late, Strigson. Are you feeling well?" His Majesty asked.

"Forgive me, Your Majesty," Strigson answered with an apologetic bow of his head. He was quite sure that Bartholomew had come much earlier than they had agreed to, putting the general in the awkward position of arriving after his king regardless of whether or not he was on time, but he knew his wayward thoughts had delayed him. "It won't happen again."

"Best see that it doesn't," Bartholomew grunted. He wasn't quite drunk, but Strigson could tell that the goblet had been refilled at least once already, as was a common practice since the queen had died giving birth to the princess. "Come, then, let's get this over with."

"Yes, Your Majesty," Ganisalp said as he approached the table, giving Pleatus another look as the scrawny man scribbled something on his parchment. "I didn't think there would be anyone joining us," the general said.

"No?" Bartholomew said with a furrowed brow, rolling the contents of his goblet around in a faint swirl. "Are you going to remember everything we say here, Strigson? Because I can never keep it all straight. It's best we have someone here to record our thoughts. What's he going to do? Tell someone all our secrets?"

Pleatus gave the general a pinched, innocent smile from across the table as he jotted another couple words down. Strigson frowned, thinking to himself that the notion wasn't nearly as preposterous as his king made it sound. "Of course not, Your Majesty," he answered instead. "I was only curious."

"All right, then," Bartholomew said in a tone that declared the matter settled as he took a sip from the goblet. "To business. Any word from our allies?"

"Yes," Strigson answered, Pleatus's quill scratching furiously as the general spoke. The general's eyes flitted to the wavering feather end, some paranoid part of him wondering if the scribe was actually able to see into his thoughts and fears, and was describing all of his betrayals instead of following dictation. "We've received a raven from King Rhone in Eastfen, and a man on horseback arrived just this morning from York to answer our call. Rhone is organizing soldiers to send our way, but in the meantime, he's delivered orders to their scouting patrols to rally and immediately report to us. Given the distance, though, I would advise against planning on their aid. Unless Grathul Heavyhand finds himself a significant distraction, there isn't a chance in hell that the Protectorate will arrive here in full force before the orcs do."

"Can we distract them ourselves to buy time?" Bartholomew asked, tapping his fingers on the table. *Skritch, skritch, skritch* went Pleatus's quill, and Strigson felt a bead of sweat begin to trickle down his spine. He knew he couldn't ask to see the record without having to explain himself, but gods did he want to.

"We could try," Ganisalp admitted slowly, his tone cautious. "But if Wyatt Darjin is telling the truth about the orcs' numbers, Your Majesty, and I have no reason to believe he is mistaken, we're going to need every man to defend these walls. This isn't just a pack of ragtag raiders, sir, that we can coax with a slab of meat for bait. This Grathul has accomplished something that hasn't happened in perhaps a hundred years. The Hordelands forces are united with a purpose. Their goal is to conquer cities, and we'll have to offer them something we can't afford to lose if we're going to lure them away from the Glen Bailey."

"So our chickens are coming home to roost, then," Bartholomew mused, taking another sip of wine and smacking his lips. "We've regarded the orcs as a simple nuisance for so long, willing to pretend they didn't exist as long as they kept to their prairie lands. Why didn't we think to do something before now?"

Because your daughter is in over her head, and I'm not the man that my father was. "It's not my place to say, sir," Ganisalp answered. "Lifegiver knows we've had more than just orcs to deal with during your reign, and even the reign of your father. We won't save our people now with hindsight. We can only defend them as best we possibly can."

"I suppose you're right," Bartholomew said, though he shook his head nonetheless. "And what of the rider from York?"

"He told us that our ally Queen Jarissa will send all the help she can," Ganisalp answered as he folded his hands in front of his waist. "We should see her hunters arriving at any time." His voice carried as little enthusiasm as Bartholomew's face revealed. It wasn't that the support from the swamp kingdom of York wasn't cherished. It was perhaps the strongest friendship that the kingdom shared. Jarissa's hunters, however, were only just that: hunters, who were masters of harvesting creatures of the wild, but possessed little to no military training. Most of York's protection came from the Glen Bailey's patrols. York's support would put more arrows in the sky against the orcish menace, but could hardly be a deciding factor in the battle to come.

"Well," Bartholomew said quietly after draining the remainder of his goblet. "It is good that we can always rely on our friends in York." His voice rang just as hollow as Strigson's had, the words meaningful, but not necessarily encouraging for their chances of victory. "No one else has answered our call?"

"As of now, no," the general answered with a slow shake of his head. "Our ambassadors to the Vale as well as Elune Shadowsong have reached out to the elves. They're either ignoring us, or our communications have been blocked off by Grathul's army. I would advise against expecting their assistance."

"Bloody damn elves," Bartholomew grunted. "Insist on being cryptic with every little thing they do, even as an army descends upon us. Very well, then. Do you still believe we should fight in front of our walls?"

"I do, Your Majesty," Ganisalp said with conviction. It was a bold decision, one that would sentence many good men to death, but if it meant victory for the Glen Bailey, it would save more lives in the end. The soldiers all knew what they had signed up for. *Those are the rules, boys.* "We could keep everyone on the inside, but with the numbers we're up against, they'll break through the gates if we leave them exposed. Our ability to keep them contained and away from our civilians will be severely compromised if we let them flood into the city, even if our soldiers are waiting for them on the other side. We line them up in front of the walls, we keep our women and children safe, and we give the archers on the battlements longer to fire on them."

Bartholomew took in a deep breath through his nose as he weighed the general's decision. With his eyes glued to the map on the table, the king reached his arm holding the goblet to the side in the direction of the scribe. "Pleatus, fill that up for me," he grunted. The scribe looked far too eager to obey the command, nearly losing his grip on his writing board as he reached out for the goblet, bustling away to the decanter on a nearby serving table.

"There's one other thing you should know, Your Majesty," Ganisalp said solemnly as he looked across the table. "Before the orcs vanquished Arden's Watch, we had ordered catapult parts from Gohand to be sent to the outpost. Captain Darjin tells me they arrived the day before Grathul's army invaded. It's possible they'll be too stupid to realize what they are, but I wouldn't count on it. We should be prepared for siege weaponry to be used against us."

Bartholomew's eyes widened at the statement. The king snatched the full cup of wine from Pleatus's slender hand, splashing a bit over the rim as he brought it to his lips for a healthy swallow. He set it back down on the table and sighed wearily. "I don't suppose you've thought of a way to repel them, have you?"

"I have a rough idea," Strigson answered, "but I would like to speak to Archmage Benton once more, if I can find the time. I'll admit that I don't quite understand their capabilities, and we have to remember that the orcs will have warlocks with them. It will take both Nevic's paladins and the mages to counter whatever foul magic they bring to the battle. But if I can get just one close enough to the machines, I'm confident we can disarm them."

"See that you do, then," Bartholomew answered, his voice soft now, almost subdued as he took a more ginger sip of wine. Sir Ganisalp paused for a moment, trying to decide how best to word his next question before he asked,

"Will you stand with the archers on the battlements, my king? Your presence will bolster the men, even those down on the field of combat, and we could use every advantage we can get."

Bartholomew's eyes finally lifted off the map to meet his general's. The king had a few different crowns for varying occasions, including a casual circlet with a single amethyst gem above the forehead that he wore now, but even the lightweight ornament seemed to weigh heavy on the man's head at that moment. Strigson felt a dull pain of discouragement as his king's eyes fell back down to the table with shame. "Perhaps it would be best if I did not, Strigson. You said they'll be bringing siege weapons, after all. They see me on the ramparts, they'll lob every rock they have right at me."

An uncomfortable quiet settled over the room, save for the crisp sounds of quill scratching on parchment as Pleatus recorded the king's response. When the scribe had caught up with them, a looming silence endured. The king kept his eyes on the table below as his general stared unflinchingly. Finally, Strigson spoke, his voice low. "Permission to speak freely, Your Majesty?"

"You going to shame this old man for his cowardice, Strigson?" Bartholomew muttered.

"No, sir," Strigson answered. *I'm in no place to shame you, Your Majesty*, he thought, nearly speaking the words aloud.

"Hogshit," the king retorted, shaking his head. "I know I would. But sure, Strigson, why the hell not. Speak freely. And keep that feather tip off the paper, Pleatus." The scribe puckered his mouth again in a sulking expression, but he sullenly obeyed.

"What is there of death to fear, Your Majesty?" Sir Ganisalp asked, the professional edge in his voice softening to one which you'd hear a man use with a troubled friend. "Aven is a strong woman, ready to lead this kingdom. I wholeheartedly believe she will make you proud til her dying day. There isn't a soul in the Glen Dale who doesn't know how you mourned Queen Meredith when she passed. Are you not ready to find her in the afterlife, Your Majesty? Would standing among your men not be worth the risk, knowing that if you fall, your wife will be there to greet you?"

The king's jaw flexed as his general spoke, the fingers around his goblet tightening briefly before he lifted it again to his lips. In that moment, Strigson could see the wrinkles that were becoming prominent on His Majesty's forehead and along the edges of his cheeks, even under the gray-lined beard. When Bartholomew finally brought his gaze back up to face his general, there was a wetness in his eyes that hadn't been there the moment before. "In all my time as monarch of the Glen Dale, Strigson, I haven't always been a good man. Perhaps never an evil man, but I haven't always been...well, pure of heart. I've tried to change that. For many years now, as a matter of fact. It's partly why I brought Eliliweth under my wing. The boy's got the moral grit that I didn't have when I was his age. I hoped maybe I could redeem myself by giving Aven the compass that I could have had when I was younger, but tossed aside like an arrogant fool.

"Meredith, on the other hand...there was a woman pure of heart, Strigson. Fiery as a hot coal under a smith's bellows, yea, but she was more virtuous than even Priestess Ecila." The king closed his mouth and looked back down at the table once more, hiding the renewed grief with a humiliated slump in his shoulders. Strigson frowned, trying to piece together Bartholomew's explanation, when all at once, it made perfect sense to him. *He's not uncertain of the afterlife*, he thought as the hairs on the back of his neck began to stand up. *He's just not sure he'll wake in the same afterlife as his queen.*

It seemed as though they would be doomed to more uncomfortable silence, but it was the king this time that ended the solemn stalemate. "But I would have had so much less time with her had it not been for you, Strigson. I suppose I would not have Aven, either. It's been some time since I asked you. Has any feeling returned?"

Strigson cleared his throat, his right hand instinctively wanting to move over to his left forearm to caress the scar. His discipline demanded otherwise, leaving both hands in place. He'd received attention for the wound before. It was, after all, the wound that elevated him to general of the Glen Bailey's army, even if Bartholomew would not openly admit it. The attention embarrassed him. He had done no more than his duty commanded, even if the man in front of him had shirked his. That, and it was difficult to hear any praise from his king with the secrets still shy of his own tongue. Some form of harsh criticism, for even the most mundane error, would have made him feel better at that moment than for Bartholomew to relive his moment of former glory.

It was nearly a year following Bartholomew's marriage to Meredith, who was unknowingly just a few weeks pregnant with Aven, and the queen wished to travel to the city of Munite to see her sister Una for the first time since her wedding. Strigson had worked hard enough to earn a place among the honor guard escort. Two days into their travels, their party was ambushed by assassins from the Hand of Draqin, the most organized and effective killers for hire in all of the Aariad. Arrows came soaring through the trees, raining down on their caravan. In moments so brief and perilous, a man's instincts take over for him. Despite all of his training and conditioning, the man in front of Queen Meredith ducked, leaving her exposed. Strigson broke formation and jumped forward, curling his arm around the queen and taking two arrows to the forearm that punctured his armor and bit down all the way to the bone. It earned the escort only a second or two before another volley came down on them, but it was enough to drag Her Majesty down into cover. Ganisalp continued to fight as the assailants rushed forward to finish the job, even as the arrowheads grinded against the bone. The skirmish was over within minutes, casualties on both sides, but Queen Meredith lived to tell the tale. The arrows were extracted, and a healer mended the flesh, but as Nevic had told him years before, the power of healing is a blunt instrument, and he lost all feeling in three fingers of his left hand, leaving him in control of only his thumb and pointer.

Strigson was a smart and courageous soldier, but to earn a position of great authority in any kingdom, you had to either be fortunate enough to be in good favor with those who could recommend you, or serve long enough to receive the position by default. The tale of Ganisalp's heroics, greatly embellished as it was handed down from tongue to tongue, allowed him to leapfrog several commanding positions until he was kneeling before the king and queen in the royal throne room, accepting his role as the Glen Bailey's general. He was humbled by the honor, but he couldn't help but feel as though he had earned it through a gimmick. His left hand wasn't even the one he held his sword in. His king had insisted he was the man for the job, but it was several years before he finally felt comfortable in the position, and he knew exactly why. He'd won it with extravagant recollections of a duty expected of any soldier. It didn't follow the rules.

"A little, in the middle finger," Ganisalp admitted stiffly in response to the king's question. Truth be told, he wasn't sure if any feeling was actually returning or if it was just his mind playing cruel tricks on him, but he knew Bartholomew was hoping for good news. Besides, what was a little white lie compared to withholding of information about a grand conspiracy?

"Wonderful," Bartholomew said, a grin finally emerging in his beard. "Every time I come across a healer, Strigson, regardless of origin, I always ask them about what could be done to-"

The king's voice cut off as a low, far-away sound crept dully into the war room. All three men present froze, their postures stiffening as they listened. Once more, the low, muffled groan reached their ears. Still, they did not move a muscle until the third bellow sounded, a war horn coming from the northern gates, calling out to the city. Even if they wouldn't have heard the bray of the horn, they would have noticed the tension that had suddenly stirred in the entire keep like an angry maelstrom as excited and despairing sounds were exchanged between the servants. A pair of hurried footsteps emerged before the door, and in an instant, it swung open on its hinges, a butler with a reddened face shouting,

"Apologies, my lords! Our scouts have been spotted with red flags lifted! The orcs! The orcs are coming, my lords! Gods help us all!"

Chapter Twenty-Five

He was dreaming. He knew he was dreaming, too, though the realization did not pull him from his slumber and back into reality. It was odd and surreal, to open his eyes and sit up as if he had awoken, knowing he truly hadn't, but being aware of exactly what was happening. He was reliving his last Trial, after spending three days with the Druids of the White Forest, learning their names and their stories and listening to their wisdoms. He had shared many meals, partaken in many prayers, and had walked through the silent birch sentinels to reflect on his own. Nobody would tell him what the preparation was for, only that he must prepare. And then, three days after Darvinthol had guided him through the cavern paintings, High Druid Clarke told him what his next Trial was to be, only moments before it happened.

The half-elf sat up, the blankets that covered him falling into his lap. The colors in the dream state all seemed to blend together in his peripheral vision, and the center of his focus seemed faintly warped, like he was viewing it under a bead of water, but he got to his feet and left his tent effortlessly. Though his actual tent was back in the druids' village, in this dream it opened up directly to the lake that Clarke had brought him to the day before. And there the High Druid stood, at the edge of the water, with The Lady at his side. "Come, Eliliweth," Clarke said in an echoing voice. "The King Stag and the Alpha Wolf, guardians of the Forest, have come to speak with you."

As he had the day before, Eliliweth looked across the lake. Even in the distance, he could tell how great in size both the King Stag and the Alpha Wolf were, for though they looked back at him from the opposite shore, he could see the Stag's proud horns like great oak branches reaching for the heavens. He could see the white rings around the eyes of the Alpha Wolf, depicting her elderly age, all the winters she had weathered. So far away, and yet, Eliliweth could feel their gazes upon them, the ancient intelligence reflecting in their animal eyes as they stood. Though he remembered what he had asked as well as the answer, the words still found their way out of his mouth. "What are they here for?"

"I couldn't say with certainty," Clarke answered, folding his hands behind his back as he looked out across the lake. "They represent the animal world, Eliliweth. I've only ever spoken with them outside a Trial twice."

Eliliweth felt himself frown in puzzlement and came to realize that though he was aware of his dream state, he was not in control of his actions. He peered across the lake, waiting for some spectral voice to enter his mind and inform him of the Stag and Wolf's intentions. No haunting voices came, however. The two great animals only stared back at him patiently from across the forest lake. "They're not saying anything, though," he heard himself speak. "How is it that you've spoken with them before if they do not speak at all?"

"Oh, Eliliweth," The Lady answered with a small shake of her head. "Just because something is silent doesn't mean that it isn't saying something. Behold, the wisdom of silence. At times, it can be more profound than anything spoken off the tongue."

"Then...what is it that they're saying? And how is it that stag and wolf stand side-by-side one another? That never happens in the wild," the half-elf responded.

"Eliliweth," Clarke answered patiently, "there is so much more to this world than just predator and prey. Remember this well, for those of us that roam this world cannot allow everything to fall into simple binaries. Everything is so much more complex than that. Look across the lake once more. Look beyond just two animals posted on the shore. What does it say to you?"

Eliliweth already knew the answers, but nonetheless could feel his mind struggling to conjure them in the reflective dream. He stared at the King Stag and the Alpha Wolf, let his gaze trail across the lake between them, and then back to his own two feet as he pondered. Finally, he looked back up at the High Druid and The Lady. "Perhaps... perhaps it is their presence alone that is telling," he said softly. "They are the most revered of the Forest, and yet they have come to visit me. They don't owe me their attendance. It is a sign of respect. And yet, they remain on the other side of the lake, a fair distance from me... because they wish to have my respect in return, for both themselves and the Forest."

As he finished his words, the Stag and the Wolf turned away from the lake, returning to the forests behind them, their movements graceful, their gait calm as they faded from sight side-by-side. The Lady looked back at him with a smile. "You have learned a great deal since joining us, Eliliweth Heraketh," she said, the volume of her voice becoming distant and distorted as she spoke, the half-elf's vision closing in as the colors began to blur into each other until they were dark and murky behind his eyelids.

He awoke once again, though this time it was reality that surrounded him, not the anamorphic world of his dreams. Once more, he sat up on his hands, the hide blankets falling forward onto his lap. Taking in a deep breath through his nose, he wondered if there was any significance to his reliving of yesterday's Trial, or if it was only his own pride bringing the fresh memories to the forefront of his sleeping thoughts. He had discovered the path laid before him by the High Druid and The Lady quickly, understanding the lesson in much shorter time than he had with Jaredeth or Darvinthol.

When he departed his tent this time around, the lake was not before him, but the village of the druids, as had greeted him every morning since his pilgrimage to the White Forest. The scent of cooked meat reached his nose. Would there be bacon for breakfast this morning? His stomach rumbled with anticipation as he realized just how hungry he was.

He wrapped a heavy brown cloak around himself, over the Robes of the Glen Dale that still surrounded him, though it wasn't for the garment's sake. The mysterious fabric used in its creation seemed to resist wrinkles, wear, and even scent, the thickest of campfire smoke fading from the threads in minutes. The faintest wisps of vapor emerged from his breath. No, his added layers were for the brisk dawn. Some mornings were warmer than others, giving brief reprieve from the inevitable winter season, but this one was less forgiving. He walked from tent to tent towards the smell of the cooking when he spotted the druid named Drael, perched on a large flat rock embedded in the side of the slowly sloping hill that the camp was clustered beside. Two proud birches grew from either side of the stone platform, but standing in the middle, Drael had one leg extended in front of the other, his front knee bent and his back mostly straight in a stretching position. The druid looked over at Eliliweth and smiled, his right hand beckoning to him. "Care to join me, Master Eliliweth?" he asked.

The half-elf felt his stomach growl once more, the smell of bacon even stronger now, but he felt it would be rude to turn down Drael's offer, and while it seemed unlikely, it could be part of his next Trial. "Of course," he answered, climbing up onto the rock and standing beside him as the druid scooted himself over to offer more space. "What is it we're doing?"

"Only stretches," Drael answered. "You can follow my lead, if you like. Just bend the front knee, your left one, and straighten the back. Keep a straight spine, chin up," he instructed. Eliliweth followed the command, mirroring Drael's stance and feeling the muscles in his legs begin to awaken, the stiffness gradually alleviating as he dipped forward. The rock below them was coated in the thinnest layer of dew, but wasn't slick enough to compromise the grip of his boots' leather soles.

"Now hold out your arms," the druid instructed, lifting both of his horizontally, level with his shoulders, fingers pointing straight out on each side. Eliliweth glanced over his shoulder before following suit. "Don't forget to breathe," Drael added.

"Do you do this every morning?" the half-elf asked as he lifted his arms.

"Yes," Drael answered quietly after taking in a deep breath of his own. They held the position for a moment, standing still with their arms outstretched. Then, the druid guided Eliliweth down into a crouched position, his left leg resting at an angle in front of his body with his right leg held out straight behind him. "Walk your hands out and rest on your elbows."

Eliliweth shivered slightly as he obeyed the instructions. The rock was cold to the touch of his skin, but the abrupt sensation gave a little more life to his nerves. He inhaled deeply as he felt his thigh muscle slowly loosen. "I can see why," he said in response to the druid's answer.

"I won't guide you on any Trials," Drael said, alleviating the half-elf's suspicions, "but if I can leave you with any wisdom, Eliliweth Heraketh, it's that the mind can only realize its full potential with a body that's well cared for. You may find some stuffy tower scholars that won't do so much as to stretch their wrists before writing with a quill and will scoff at the idea that exercise frees the mind, but I assure you that it is absolutely true. Why do you think mages are encouraged to stay physically fit? Keep your body loose and muscles relaxed, and clarity of the mind becomes a simpler task."

They did not speak any more for several minutes, Drael silently guiding Eliliweth through his routine of stretches. More than once, the half-elf's stomach grumbled loudly enough that he was sure the druid heard it, but if he did, he gave no indication. Finally, when they had finished, Drael helped him to his feet with a gracious smile.

"Thank you, Drael," Eliliweth said. "I feel...great. That was great."

"My pleasure," the druid answered before nodding his head in the direction of the bacon scents. "You must be hungry. Hurry along, then. I would get a good meal in, if I were you."

The half-elf frowned and almost asked what it was Drael meant, but before he could, the druid hopped off his rock and made his own way down the trail. Eliliweth pursed his lips. Was Drael hinting at something? Could his final Trial be in order? He had been told upon arriving that his Trials were to be done in quicker fashion than normal, and it was his fourth day at the White Forest. Hunger and curiosity lead him off of the rock and towards the delicious smell of cooked meat.

His nose did not betray him. When he arrived at the kitchen camp, abuzz with druids in all varieties of sizes and clothing, he saw a skillet over a campfire sizzling with the delicious smelling strips of meat, a pot of oats gently boiling in the coals nearby. Each of the druids looked up at him as he passed by, smiling and greeting him 'good morning' as he made his way to the fire. A dwarven druid named Branson, who had an exceptionally large nose even by dwarven standards, was tending to the breakfast and happily dished the half-elf up his share on a rectangular wooden plate. A nearby tree lay a few paces away, and Eliliweth sat himself down next to two druids murmuring to one another in quiet conversation. He did his best not to eavesdrop and began to eat.

By the gods, he thought to himself, *this may be the most delicious bacon I've ever tasted in my life.* The eggs were no less impressive, and he shoveled them into his mouth eagerly, feeling his stomach fill with contentment as he chewed. So intent he was on enjoying his meal that he did not notice the druids beginning to congregate around him, forming a semi-circle around the log he was seated on. By the time the half-elf looked up, they were all watching him patiently with amused smiles on their faces. In the middle was High Druid Clarke and The Lady, both of them holding their hands folded in front of themselves.

"You enjoyed breakfast, I take it?" Clarke said with an endearing smile.

"I...yes, very much so," Eliliweth said, turning red with embarrassment as he quickly swallowed the half-chewed remainder of food in his mouth, clearing his throat and wiping his sleeve across his lips as he slowly got to his feet. "Thank you for the meal."

"Ach, my pleasure," Branson grunted with a low chuckle.

"We stand before you, Eliliweth Heraketh," The Lady said with a radiant smile, "to tell you that we have been most impressed with you during your stay with us. You have been one of the most astute visitors we've ever hosted."

"King Bartholomew was wise indeed to send you to us," Clarke said with a bow of his head. "You were quite open to every lesson we taught you, and I believe you will carry that wisdom into the Glen Bailey's royal court. Remember always, Eliliweth Heraketh, to assume that you know nothing, for when you allow the unknown to be as such, you will have the clearest sight to view it for what it *truly* is."

"There is but one final Trial for you to endure," The Lady said. "But before you embark on it, the High Druid and I wished to tell you that should you succeed in your last endeavor here, we would like to invite you to return, to begin the training under The Praxis of Light."

"If you would be interested in pursuing the call of a druid, that is," Clarke clarified. "We have taught you a great deal here, but there is so much more left to learn that we could never show you in the span of a week, you understand."

"Praxis of Light?" Eliliweth said with a puzzled frown. He felt his face growing hot as he began to feel overwhelmed. By the gods, he'd only just finished breakfast, and suddenly Clarke and The Lady were inviting him to begin the training of a druid? And why were they speaking of this to him now, as if he'd already passed his final Trial? "I don't understand," he said.

"Were you aware that you and I nearly share a surname, Eliliweth?" Clarke said with a bright smile. "Well, that's not quite true, as the Hare-Kith is actually my formal title, but among the druids here at the White Forest, they are often one in the same. Did you know of its meaning?"

"No," Eliliweth confessed, feeling a bit silly for never asking anyone before now.

"It is derived from the Old Speech, before Commonspeak was even developed," Clarke explained. "It means 'revealer' or 'awakened one', and it was a position granted to the elders and the prophets of the first men, the carriers of the Outer Knowledge."

"The Lady is a title that carries similar weight," the elven druid said. "Though it sounds simple in the common tongue, in the Old Speech, it has inclinations of great power, and is the inverse to the Hare-Kith's gifts. I and those before me carry the burden and the blessing of the Inner Knowledge."

"I'm...I'm afraid I don't understand," Eliliweth said sheepishly. This was all happening so fast.

"Of course," Clarke said with an apologetic nod. "We have explained none of this to you. The Praxis of Light is an ancient teaching of timeless wisdom, all the way back to the earliest days of the Forging, to the assembly of the Stone Circles scattered about the Aariad."

"We expect that you will remain with King Bartholomew for many years," The Lady said. "A great destiny lies before you, Eliliweth. But if that service ever comes to end, or if your king ever decrees that you may serve him better with such wisdoms, we hope that you will return to us."

"But first," Clarke said, "your final Trial is upon you." He turned, and as he did so, the semi-circle of druids began to part, revealing an opening as the High Druid pointed towards the lake where he had seen the King Stag and Alpha Wolf the day before. "Return to the lake, Eliliweth Heraketh, and follow the shore along the western edge. You will find a path guarded by the largest birch trees in the entire Forest. Follow it, and it will carry you up a hill that will bring you to our own Stone Circle, Gift of the Ancients. That is where your final Trial will begin."

"We grant you our blessing, Eliliweth Heraketh, and wish you the best of luck," The Lady said with a reassuring smile. "Remember that the love of the Druids goes with you always."

For a moment, Eliliweth was unsure of whether or not he had returned to his dream. Everything was movingly so fluidly, so quickly, he felt as though the current of time had suddenly swept him furiously down its unending river. He felt himself walking forward, step by step, anxiety gripping at his windpipe as he walked in the direction that Clarke had pointed to. The gathered druids were waving and smiling, each individually wishing him luck as he passed between the two halves, past the cooking fire and the tables filled with harvested crops and salted meats. He kept walking until he was beyond the camp before looking back over his shoulder. The druids had vanished, as had the camp tents and assorted tables and stools, no trace of the fire that had been used to cook his morning meal. There were only aspens and birches staring back at him, but somehow, he knew the Druids of the White Forest were still there, watching over him. He took in a deep breath into his chest. He would not disappoint them. He turned back towards the lake, striding forward with purpose.

As instructed, he began to walk along the western shore, moving with intent, but slowly enough to enjoy the beauty that was the Forest's lake. It was small, barely above the title of a pond, but the reflections upon the water's surface of the trees surrounding it was like a pristine portrait, the myriad of colored leaves giving life to the glass-like pool.

As promised, he found a path that looked to be imprinted by the hooves of traveling deer, a thin bare strip along the grass and fallen leaves. Marking the trail to the Stone Circle were two prominent birch trees on either side, like vigilant guardians looming above him. He did not feel threatened, however, for he had been given the blessings of the druids. He carried himself between the trees, following the trail as it began to ascend up the hill that would lead to the Stone Circle.

He reflected on his visit as he began his slow ascension, the anticipation of his final Trial leaving a tingling sensation in his fingertips and toes. None of this had been what he truly expected. He thought that he would be learning complex spells and rituals that he knew the druids possessed in their wealth of knowledge. But while the lessons had been simple in nature, their profound impact on him made his chest feel light and his spirit burn with an eager fire. Perhaps all of his understanding would lead to the discovery of something great and powerful? He was alone in this last journey, after all. It had to be something that he would uncover on his own.

Finally, the path ended, revealing an open circle perched upon a hill, overlooking the lake and the path that lead back to where he had camped among the druids. Aspen trees surrounded the Stone Circle before him, a great boulder in the center with smaller stones branching out to the outer ring, four additional rocks indicating the directions of a compass. He knew what had to be done. He entered the Circle, approaching the great stone in the center. He pressed his lips against the palm of his hand before pressing it to the boulder as a sign of greeting and respect. With an excited smile, he climbed on top of the rock and planted himself in a seated position, sitting cross-legged. He outstretched both of his arms, open palms towards the sky, elbows on his knees, and closed his eyes. He understood now why Drael had invited him to participate in his early morning stretches. He needed to find his inner calm, and with it, the Stone Circle would no doubt grant him a vision that would aid him in completing this final Trial.

He began to meditate, his breath evening as he willed his heart to return to a normal beat. In and out, the air traveled through his lungs. He could see the light from the sun through his closed eyelids, and despite the brisk temperature of the autumn morning, the rays from above kept his skin comfortably warm. There he sat, waiting, removing all thought from his mind, inviting the Circle to bestow him the vision he was sure had to be coming.

Time began to crawl as an hour passed, and then another. Fatigue was beginning to weigh on his shoulders, and though he commanded his mind to ignore the discomfort, he couldn't bring himself to fully block out the pain when the muscles in his arms began to quake. *I'll just rest my hands on my knees, then*, he thought to himself. *I'm not going to receive any visions if I'm not fully relaxed. You're overthinking it, Eliliweth, having your arms outstretched like that.*

And so he continued to sit, giving his shoulders reprieve by simply resting his hands on his knees, a great relief washing over him as the discomfort began to ebb. Surely, the Circle would grant him a vision at any moment once he'd achieved true relaxation. He focused on evening his breathing once more, and began to enter a meditative state once again. Another hour passed as he removed all outside thought from his mind.

He wasn't sure how long he'd been sitting there since allowing his shoulders to relax, but he awoke with a start as he felt his head sag forward. It snapped back up as his heart skipped a beat. By the gods, he'd fallen asleep! He was suddenly very aware of the cramping in his buttocks from sitting for so long. He looked to the sky with despair.

The sun was inching closer to the horizon and he'd been granted not the briefest of revelations from the Stone Circle.

Anxiety clawed at his chest. What was he doing wrong? He'd followed Clarke's instructions. Had he missed something? Was he just not worthy of undergoing the final Trial? He wouldn't have been the least bit surprised if the final Trial was a test of patience, but to wait for this long without any sign of progress? His mouth was dry, but his palms were sweaty as he grew nervous. He didn't know how, but in some way, he was letting down the Druids of the White Forest, his newest friends and mentors. He was letting down King Bartholomew and everyone in the Glen Bailey that had come to see him off before his journey here. He would have to return to his people with empty hands, a waste of time and hope.

He'd missed something. He *had* to have simply missed something. He finally hopped off the center stone and began to search the ground within the Circle for something, anything, a relic, a totem, even a stray branch that had fallen from the trees. There was nothing but the grass growing within the Circle and the occasional leaf departed from its host. He picked each one up, turning it over to look at both sides. Was there a hint, a rune or a letter etched onto one? He kept retrieving the crisp leaves, examining each side, but found nothing that gave any hint as to what he was supposed to do. He looked back at the path in vain, despair weighing heavy on his heart. He knew he could not go back. The druids had vanished when he had left, and they would not reappear to give him any hints. It was his final Trial, and it was his to endure alone. Why had he not asked any questions before leaving Clarke and The Lady? Had he been so prideful as to assume he would simply figure it out on his own? Was that his failure? An arrogance born of the compliments he'd been given back at camp, by the invitation to participate in the Praxis of Light? He felt hot tears sting at the corners of his eyes. He felt like such a miserable fool.

With a heavy heart, he walked back to the center stone and climbed atop it once more, sitting cross-legged, his head bowed forward in shame. He felt his eyes close. How could he go back to Bartholomew and tell him of his failure? He thought back to each of his Trials before this one. How had they not prepared him for this?

He frowned as he considered them. From the books, to the paintings, to the unspoken speech of the Stag and the Wolf, each of them had all been based around his acceptance of the unknown, whether it was his understanding of his own abilities, the interpretations of the illustrations, or just the absence of spoken words from entities that perhaps could boast more intelligence than he. How did it all link to his final Trial?

He had spent hours meditating and relaxing his mind, but it was in his greatest distress that the realization finally came to him. His final Trial wasn't the manifestation of some inner power, nor was it a cryptic vision from a Forest spirit. It wasn't truly even a test. He had been given no instruction, because he was intentionally being subjected to the unknown, to see if he had learned to see the unknown for what it was. All this time, sitting in this mystical Stone Circle, he had been conjuring his own ideas and his own pretenses as to what his final Trial would be, and worse, the reward that would surely follow, whether it would be a power or a relic or some ancient secret not told to those who had not had the privilege of enduring these same Trials.

He slowly began to stand up upon the center rock, his knees trembling. The epiphany was a physical force surging through his blood. There was a reward after all, but like the final Trial, it was unto himself. He had been gifted with the knowledge that he would leave the White Forest with more clarity of mind, an awakening that he would use for the betterment of not just himself, but for the entire kingdom of the Glen Bailey, for the people that had showered him with support before he had left their borders. He had been bestowed with such a precious gift by simply learning what the druids had to teach, and they were yet willing to teach him *more*. The realization and acknowledgement of all this *was* his final Trial. He had never been more sure of anything in his life.

An abrupt laugh of happiness burst from him, his smile wide as he planted a kiss on his palm, pressing it against the center stone before he hopped off, his feet feeling weightless as he landed back on the ground. He marched out of the Stone Circle and began descending down the trail that would lead back to the lake. He felt as though he might sprout wings and fly all the way back to the Glen Bailey. He vowed to himself then and there that he would not covet the wisdoms he'd learned here, but share them as best he could, from the king himself to the most humble peasant.

He reached the two towering birch trees standing on opposite sides of the trail's end, next to the lake shore. Using the communication of silence, he gave both of the looming sentinels fierce hugs, expressing his utmost gratitude. He strode around the lake, watching for the King Stag and the Alpha Wolf. They were not there to see him off, but he could still feel their presence, even leagues away.

He smiled all the way through the White Forest, seeing not a single druid or a smoldering campfire, only the congregations of birches, aspens, maples, and even a few spruces clustered among the forest crop. He silently bid the woodlands goodbye as he continued down the trail, all the way to the edge of the White Forest, where the cultivation of trees began to rapidly transform into oaks and ashes, the ending of the birch and aspen abundance marking his passing from the haven of the druids. He still had a ways to walk before he would return home, and he was eager to see his friends once again, but part of him was grateful for the opportunity to reflect on his experience before speaking with anyone about it. He knew that there were only parts of it he could reveal, for if he spoke of the secrets for the final Trial, it would diminish all meaning the lessons might have for another. But the basic tenets of the druids' teachings he was certain he could pass on. It didn't need to be complex, anyway. The core message was really very simple.

Something caught his eye as he ventured down the forest trail. An angry, swarming figure above the trees' canopy was intermittently blocking the fading sunlight that yet passed through the leaves and branches, causing flickering shadows before his eyes. Frowning, he looked up, bringing a hand to his brow as he scanned the sky. There, above the trees, he saw a great eagle, talons brandished and wings beating furiously. All around the impressive feathered creature, a murder of black crows screamed and pecked, viciously attacking their avian rival without mercy.

He watched the grisly scene for a few seconds, eyes cast upward, when something dropped from high above, missing both branch and leaf as it plummeted downwards. It struck the side of his temple and began trailing down his cheek. Elilweth recoiled in disgust at first, thinking he'd been voided on, but when he drew his digits away from his face, he saw only a smear of red across his fingers.

Despair twisted through his stomach at the sight of the blood. He'd seen birds fighting in flight before, but this was different. This was an omen. Just as the Stag and Wolf had spoken to him through their presence, something called out to him vicariously through the winged warriors in the sky. It spoke clearly to him, of death and doom.

The half-elf began to walk faster, and then faster yet. He looked up

once more to the sky as the eagle released a harrowing cry.
He began to run.

Chapter Twenty-Six

Like ants scurrying around a hill as rain begins to fall, the city of the Glen Bailey was suddenly alive with movement as the warning horns sounded, the northern gates opening for the scouts returning with the red flags over their heads, signaling the impending danger of Grathul Heavyhand's army. The preparations had all been planned since Wyatt Darjin and his Arden's Watch soldiers had returned from defeat, but chaos nonetheless had a part to play. Every voice spoke at once, a persistent roar stretching from the refugee tents in the southern district all the way to the royal keep. Mothers called out for their children, reaching with panicked grasps even when they were attached to their skirts, dragging them back in the direction of their homes, where they could only pray that they would be safe. Soldiers in patrol formations began to follow pending orders, breaking away to report to their stations.

"By the Lifegiver's shield," Drevor Angson, Cadohaden's fellow paladin, said in a hushed voice, barely audible above the continuous murmur of the city. "They're finally here. The heathen orcs have come."

Cadohaden's eyes followed Drevor's, though they couldn't actually see the horn that had signaled the danger. Silently, he cursed to himself in frustration. Before someone had sounded the alarm, he had been on patrol with Drevor. The mere hour of downtime that Crusader Nevic had spoken of had never come for him, his only reprieve being the sleep rotations spent in the soldiers' barracks, and the hastily prepared meals served on wooden plates, if any plate was given at all. He hadn't seen Elune once since the city had begun preparing for battle, and now, units were already being lined up in rank and file, ready to move out in front of the Bailey's walls.

"We better report in," Drevor said, nodding in the direction of the northern gate. "They'll want us in position as soon as possible."

"Go on ahead," Cadohaden said, turning away as he began walking toward the keep. "I'll catch up."

"Catch up?" Drevor called out as Cadohaden weaved through a herd of merchants running past with wide eyes, their hands clutching to their purses. "You can't just run off, Ulaeron! Grathul is *here!*"

He knew he was asking for trouble, but Cadohaden pressed on anyway, ignoring Drevor's pleas as he sidestepped a pair of soldiers moving in the opposite direction, doubtlessly heading for their report stations. They both gave the paladin a peculiar glance as he trotted past them, away from where the battle would be joined. He could only hope that a commanding official wouldn't see him and tell him to turn around before he found Elune. *Technically, I haven't disobeyed any orders yet,* he thought to himself. *I'm only delaying my obedience.*

He reached the market square, where even more merchants and tradesmen were anxiously collecting their goods and scurrying to the southern district, away from where the orcs were expected to attack. He accidentally bumped into a plump man in a wool robe, sending coins scattering from his pockets and clinking against the cobblestone underneath. The merchant shouted a curse and bent over, beginning to fill up his palm with his earnings, but after a few nervous glances towards the northern wall, the man gave a bitter 'bah!' and stormed away with what he'd managed to gather. Curious and tempted gazes fell to the remaining coins, and a couple onlookers stooped to snatch a few up, but most were more intent on getting as far away from the encroaching army as possible. In Cadohaden's wake, a couple dwarves finally decided it was worth their time to scoop up the remainder before following the other refugees in quick pursuit. The visitors from Dur'Imoir had been asked if they would aid in the defense of the Glen Bailey, but most insistently declined, citing political complications with the dwarf lords of their mountain kingdom. Most departed the very next day, though a few remained to profit off the soldiers who wished to get good and drunk before the battle began.

It was another pair of bustling dwarves that Cadohaden found himself impatiently trying to circumvent when he saw a few familiar faces among the bustling crowd, across the market street. It was Archmage Benton and his apprentices, Leora and Krendrick, each of them holding a staff with a gem secured to the top of the shaft, the apprentices with pearl white, Benton's with a scarlet red, a silver claw holding the ruby in its palm. Cadohaden craned his neck as he caught intermittent glances at the mages making their way through the stream of bodies, searching for the demon Terodar among them. His lips parted, frowning in confusion when he could not see the horned figure among them. Why wouldn't they bring such a powerful weapon to a battle that threatened their whole kingdom?

Thoughts and suspicions began to race through his head, and he almost called out to Benton to question the demon's whereabouts, but he held his tongue, for even if the archmage answered his concerns, he would no doubt ensure that Cadohaden returned immediately to his scheduled post. The young paladin stopped in his tracks, glancing in the direction of the keep, then southward, where the Mage House resided. Back and forth his eyes went, weighing his decision. He didn't truly know that Elune was in the keep. He just knew where her quarters were. And did he actually think he could walk in without being discovered by someone who knew he should be answering the rallying war horn?

His decision was made as a terrible thought crossed his mind: *What if they killed him? What if they feared that he couldn't be left to be claimed by orc warlocks, or if they used him in battle, the greenskins might be able to sway his submission? What if they just killed him?* He didn't know why the thought horrified him so intensely. Terodar Soulrender was a demon, with no love or willing allegiance to anyone within the Glen Bailey, not even Cadohaden. He was sarcastic and foul-tempered and in all likelihood had the potential for every evil he had been taught in Nollofolith. Despite all of this, there was something between the two that Cadohaden couldn't deny, and it was more than just his duty to redeem Terodar's cursed soul. Could he call it a friendship, knowing that the demon would betray him at the first opportunity? Or was there some part of him that allowed himself to wonder if Terodar would hesitate to drive the dagger?

Whatever the reason, he had to know for certain what had become of his demon ward. He pushed his way southward through the city, able to move a little faster now as he was traveling with the current of the civilians. He received muttered threats and angry snarls as he used his shoulders to edge his way through, but he would not be deterred. Once, as he combed his way through the crowd, he thought he heard someone barking his last name. He ignored the voice and pressed on, through the packed bodies and stench of fear.

He was relieved to find the Mage House unlocked when he finally came upon the front door, able to break away from the retreating river of people as he approached the headquarters for the arcane studies of the Glen Bailey. He wasn't sure where he might find the demon, or his body, and so he immediately ran to the stairwell that lead to the cellar, where Terodar's converted cannery quarters resided. The door creaked as Cadohaden aggressively pushed it open on its rusted hinges. He released a sigh of relief as a pair of annoyed eyes with red irises peered up at him from the floor, where Terodar sat cross-legged. A thick book lay in the demon's lap, the front and back cover resting on opposite thighs. It took the paladin a moment to recognize the language inscribed upon the pages, but he quickly realized that the runes were Demonic. "I thought you were giving up blood magic!" Cadohaden exclaimed with despair.

"And I thought perhaps you were growing a bit wiser with age," Terodar snorted derisively. "I suppose I was wrong. Don't be naive, Ulaeron. I am the Destroyer's flesh and blood. Why in the infernal hells would I ever abandon my true nature for Benton's parlour tricks?"

Cadohaden shook his head at the sardonic response, his expression wilting. "I thought you would try. I really did."

"Well, I *am* learning his impotent tricks, if it eases your conscience whatsoever," the demon growled. "But if you really thought they could ever replace what I was bred to do, then you're just as foolish as the day you bound me to your ineptitude. Why are you here, Master Ulaeron? The horns of war have sounded. The orcs have come to grind the Glen Bailey into blood-soaked dust. Shouldn't you be on the front lines, proving to your new masters that your talk of abandoning your heritage to join their rabble isn't just lip service?"

Cadohaden couldn't help but wince. He wasn't sure if it was just the nature of a *roaq* demon or if Terodar had a particular gift for it, but his quips went beyond just simple insults. They had a knack for exposing the slightest flaws and making them seem twice as criminal. "I saw the mages in the crowd without you. I had to know what they'd done with you, if they'd...hurt you."

Cadohaden could have vomited all over the demon and it might have provoked a less disgusted expression from him. Terodar's lip curled, the corners twisting in sheer revulsion. "Well, how lovely for you to bravely burst in here and come save little old me," he hissed before shaking his horned head, looking back down at the pages of his tome. "But you needn't have worried your gallant soul. They simply ordered me to remain in my chambers. My guess is that they didn't want to test my loyalties with that Fire-Eyes brute among the greenskins. Who *knows* what a fellow warlock might do to sway me! So I shall sit here and wait for the orcs to come, soaked in the blood of you and your fellows, and end my humiliation. Oh, I won't go down with head bowed, I can assure you; I'll take as many as I can of those drooling animals, but I'm quite certain that eventually I will die from the fumes of their putrid corpses or that I will at some point be run through with a lucky spear tip."

"Consider those orders to remain here dismissed," Cadohaden said quickly, his words having a visible effect on the demon, who suddenly leaned forward as though a burdensome creature had pushed itself off of his back. Terodar lifted his shoulders back up and scowled at the paladin, who spoke in a hushed, excited voice. "This is your kingdom, too, and you deserve the chance to fight for it."

"You ignorant, moronic fool," Terodar hissed, clapping his tome shut with conviction, dust motes billowing from the pages. "You addle-brained simpleton. This is not *my* kingdom. It never has been, and it never will. I am a caged beast, a prisoner, an experiment to be prodded and poked. Do not *dare* label me as an equal in this droll village of slack-jawed peasants. There is little you could say that would insult me greater."

"But it's true!" Cadohaden insisted, his face creasing with earnest. "Look, I know that right now things aren't ideal for you, but I'm trying - *we're* trying, as a city - to make you one of us! You don't *have* to be confined by your bloodline, Terodar. You can be different. It can all start here. You could come with me, join our army and beat these orcs back to the Hordelands. You can prove to everyone out there that doubts you that you *are* a member of the Glen Bailey."

"They *tortured me* at the doors of the Monastery!" Terodar screamed, rising to his hooves now, his sarcastic demeanor finally boiling over into contorted rage. He stomped up to the young paladin, dropping his tome on the floor with a thud, til his burning irises were a mere inch away. Cadohaden could smell his breath: coppery, heavy, with a hint of spent ash. The demon hissed at him through gritted teeth. "Do not speak to me of camaraderie, boy. I writhed and crawled at their feet, my skin split and blistering for their own amusement, under the guise of proving just how well trained I was. To think that I would would even *desire* to integrate myself into this shithole kingdom is ludicrous enough, much less fight to defend it."

"You know what you are, Terodar," Cadohaden countered, staring back challengingly into the demon's eyes. "You know what you were trained to do in the world of the Destroyer. You cannot blame a single soul for their hesitation, their interest in their own well-being. But it doesn't have to *stay* that way. Don't you understand? This isn't then. This is *now*. You can speak to me of all your pains, of your struggles, but you still live, Terodar. Had I brought you to Kingsbanesin, or to Munite, they would not have hesitated to hang you and burn your corpse to dust, no matter what tests of obedience you had passed. I can help you be more."

The demon's eyes narrowed as he glared at the young man standing before him. He leaned in a little closer, his head tilting to the side as he sneered, "You do love saying that, don't you, Master Ulaeron? You so enjoy pretending that you're in this to redeem my soul, to save me from myself, so that you can lay in bed at night feeling assured that you are a true disciple of your haughty god. But we both know the truth, don't we? From the moment you bound me to your service, you grew an insatiable appetite for the power that came with commanding me to the very letter. You enjoyed dragging me here, and you enjoyed forcing me to crawl on hands and knees to touch that cursed door fixture. You enjoyed countering the orders given to me by these mage rodents, just as you are now. And to keep doing what you love doing so much, you're going to *order* me to join you on the battlefield. You'll tell yourself it's for my own good, that you're giving me a chance to do this or realize that, but the fact is, Cadohaden Ulaeron, that you just *revel* in the power you hold over me. So why don't we cut out the heroic dialogue and get right to it? Go on. *Command* me, Master."

Cadohaden stared back at the demon, his lip drawn to a thin line as he returned the gaze. As the seconds passed, however, he felt Terodar's words sink into his spirit, and he began to question his own motives. Was it true? Had this all been a farce from the beginning? Was he really capable of that kind of selfishness?

He straightened his posture, shaking the doubts from his head. How could he let Terodar sway him so easily? Had he forgotten that it was a demon he was speaking to? "No," Cadohaden said resolutely, matching Terodar's fiery eyes once more. "I won't give you any such orders."

"Really, now?" the demon hissed with a faint smirk.

"No," the paladin repeated. "And I don't care if that was your intention to begin with. I won't force you to do the right thing, Terodar. You're right. It was a horrendous thing, what they - what *we* - did to you in front of the Monastery. It can't be taken back. But there are *good people* in this kingdom. Some of them are out on the front lines, and others are hiding in their homes, praying that the locks on their doors won't be broken open before the night comes.

"And maybe I'm not as true of heart as I like to portray. Maybe I don't really represent the Monastery as best I should. I know there are others that don't. But I *can't* sit here and pretend that's a good enough reason to let good men and women die. I can't act as if those imperfections justify so many deaths. I am of Kingsbanesin blood. My ancestors were oppressors and tyrants. But the Glen Bailey has embraced me anyway. They've given me a chance at a new start. And you can pick apart my character all you want, Soulrender, but it won't stop me from laying my life on the line for them.

"So stay, then, if that is your wish. I give you permission to skulk down here, waiting to die, pretending that it means something. I won't force you to do the right thing, to do something decent for once. But know this: there isn't a soul out there, fighting or hiding, that would expect you to do anything but that. You aren't spurning anyone by wallowing down here, for they expect nothing less. You are angry with how everyone here perceives you? You only show them how right they are by hiding in the shadows, watching good people die. I, on the other hand, am not satisfied with petty moral victories. I am going to go out there, and I'm going to kill as many of those savages as I possibly can."

Cadohaden did not wait for a snarky answer or a curdled glare. He turned on his heel, marching out of the cellar room, head held high as he marched back up the stairs to the ground floor of the Mage House. As he reached the top, he heard the sound of something wooden shattering, followed by the clattering sounds of pieces falling to the floor. The faintest of smiles crossed his lips. For once, he was the one who had left the other feeling agitated.

He stepped out of the Mage House, marching back onto the street, eyes turning towards the northern wall. By now, he would be noticeably late to formation. He could not hear the sounds of combat yet, however, and so he could feasibly make it back and receive little more than a spoken chastising. He began to run across the cobblestone, but soon came to a halt, a nagging idea tugging at the back of his mind. He turned his head towards the west, eyes seeking out a cylindrical white tower with an open wooden apse at the top, the hay from the roosts visible around the railing edges. *The gryphons are not available to us in combat, Ulaeron, end of discussion*, Nevic's voice echoed in his mind.

"If we fall, Crusader, it won't matter either way," Cadohaden murmured to himself. His heart was hammering in his chest at the thought of so blatantly disregarding his instructions, but his feet were nonetheless carrying him in the direction of the aviary.

Chapter Twenty-Seven

"Where are the magistrates!?" Pleatus squealed, wringing his hands as he paced the royal throne room. "Your Majesty, nobody can find them! I've sent four different servants to track them down and-"

"Be *quiet*, scribe," Strigson Ganisalp growled. "I just saw Bertram Archibaum not ten minutes ago, wandering the hallways. What in the blazes are you sending help to find them for, anyway? Are any of those bloated pigs going to pick up a sword or lead a unit into combat?"

Aven felt her jaw tense at the mention of Archibaum, though she did her best to maintain the calm composure she'd adorned herself with since the war horn had sounded. There was a time for passion, when the flames of battlelust needed to be kindled, but with the entire city on the brink of panic, her duty was to appear unfazed and resolute. Nearby, Pleatus looked back at the general with his cowardly bulbous eyes. "But...but they're the magistrates, my lord, we need them for-"

"We don't need them for hog shit! Now stop wasting everyone's time!" the general barked, silencing the simpering scribe. He turned around to face the king, seated in his throne with a drawn look on his face and a half-full goblet of wine in his hand. They had moved from the war room to the royal chamber as soon as they had heard the signal, as was protocol. It was the final opportunity for the king to give any specific orders or make any wishes known to his council before the battle was upon them. Only Aven had come in addition to Sir Ganisalp, and Eliliweth was not yet back from the White Forest. The magistrates *were* supposed to be in attendance as well, but Strigson was not about to worry himself over the presence of old fat traitors in decorated robes. The orcs had arrived, and whether or not the magistrates were able to successfully rendezvous with them would not dictate the outcome of the battle. "Your Majesty," he said, his voice softening. "We are out of time. Will you not join your men on the battlements?"

Bartholomew stared at his general for a long moment, the impatience from Strigson growing more palpable with each passing second. Finally, the bearded king shook his head, the shame visible on the lines in his face. "I cannot, Strigson. There is too much at stake. I grant you my blessing, and will pray through the entire battle that the gods bless our defenses."

The general's jaw flexed at his king's response, and it was obvious that he had more than a few choice words for Bartholomew's decision, but not a single scolding syllable passed his lips. His Majesty had made up his mind, and when you were king, you had the power to do so. Those were the rules. "Very well, Your Majesty," Strigson answered, firing off a crisp salute. "Then unless there is something else, I can spend no more time here. Grathul Heavyhand is upon us."

Bartholomew shook his head solemnly, and with that, Sir Ganisalp marched his way out of the throne room, to lead his army in battle. His eyes looked to her meaningfully on his way out, but Aven pursed her lips, pointedly ignoring him. Now was not the time for any dramatic distractions. She took a step forward after the general dismissed himself, hands clasped in front of her, her tone formal as she addressed her king, "Your Majesty, I will depart now as well, to seek out Archmage Benton and ask what I can do to help."

"You will most certainly not," Bartholomew snorted. "You are the princess, heir to the throne, Aven Celandine. What makes you think you will be fighting in this battle?"

"Our people are fighting in this battle," she answered without blinking an eye.

"Yes, my dear, but...that is how it works," Bartholomew said, clearly caught off-guard by his daughter's desires. "We rule this kingdom, and we need to be sufficiently protected from the dangers of fighting. Quite simply, we cannot rule if we are dead."

"We cannot rule if nobody lives to heed our laws, Father," Aven answered. "I am a mage, and a capable one at that. Good men will die as a direct cause of my absence. I will have blood on my hands."

"By the gods, you are just like your mother!" Bartholomew shouted as his face turned red. "A flair for the dramatic and a hungering for martyrdom! I won't have you sacrificing your life for these lofty ideals! Lordship has many burdens, but it comes with privileges, and one of them is the preservation of our lives in times of war! I hereby *forbid* you from taking part in this battle, Aven Celandine!"

A heavy silence fell over the throne room as the princess stared her father down. Pleatus puckered his lips, eyes wide and darting as he wrung his hands and looked between the two. A brief flicker of remorse flashed across Bartholomew's face. He had spoken the phrase 'you are just like your mother' to his daughter so many times, but never in anger. It was clear that his words had struck deep, the sting of the wound pinching Aven's expression. She opened her mouth once, closed it, and stormed from the room, the soles of her shoes clacking against the stone underneath with indignation. She could hear her father's calls for her, but she ignored them. If she were to die, she would not be remembered as a helpless, cowering girl, quivering in the throne clinging to her daddy's leg.

Fuming, she marched down the hallway, turning a corner and nearly barreling over a fretful servant carrying a jug of wine. She snapped bitterly at the thin man, though she barely registered his face as she impatiently trotted past. She tried to collect herself, silently reviewing her most important combat spells in her head, mouthing the incantations carefully so as not to accidentally call them forth.

She neared the winding staircase that would bring her to the ground floor when she nearly collided with yet another servant. Gritting her teeth, ready to physically shove him out of the way, Aven paused as she realized it was not a servant after all that she had run into, but Bertram Archibaum, his eyes wide and excited, his knobby hands trembling as he grasped at her shoulders. "Princess!" he breathed, his chest rising and falling with the exhilarated effort. "I've been looking for you! You must come quick!"

"So help me, Bertram, I will throw you down these stairs," Aven snarled at him. "Get *out* of my way."

"Please, Your Grace," the magistrate pleaded. "The other magistrates! They're fleeing to the aviary! Now is our chance! We will find them with both the gold and the agreement struck by the orcs!"

"Are you completely daft, old man!?" Aven hissed, grabbing the noble by his robes and pulling his wrinkled face closer to hers. "The orcs are *here*. We are *too late*. Exposing their plot will not turn them away or earn a surrender from Grathul Heavyhand. I foolishly bought into your silver-tongued plans and promises, and my people have already suffered for it. Now go cower under your bed until the dust has settled."

"But, Your Grace," Archibaum whined, "capturing them will leave no questions! The matter will be settled! Please! I've already ordered guards into position! We must be witness to the arrest!"

"You *what!?*" Aven snapped, giving the noble a violent shake with the sound of tearing fabric as a seam ripped under the force. "Answer me this, Bertram Archibaum, how did a man of such great stupidity and cowardice such as you ever come into such a position of power? An army of orcs nears our walls and you send guards to the *aviary!?* You are not authorized to give guards orders in a time of crisis - or *any* time, for that matter!"

"I'm sorry, Your Grace, I just-"

"No," Aven interrupted, releasing the man's robes. "On second thought, I'm not interested in the question's answer. Lead the way, Bertram, but make haste. I can't just let the guards wander around the aviary while their fellow soldiers fight for their kingdom, or be under the impression that they're to listen to worms such as yourself. We might as well put your partners in chains while we're at it, even if we have to leave them tied up like hogs until the battle is over."

"Yes...yes, of course, Your Grace," Archibaum murmured with a frown, torn between excitement and resentment from the verbal lashing the princess had just handed down to him.

Aven followed the magistrate down the stairs and through the entrance hall of the keep, departing through the towering twin doors as they made their way down the stone steps to the cobblestone of the streets. She lifted her gaze to the northern wall, taking in a trembling breath as she spotted the rows of archers already lining up along the battlements. There were still soldiers filing through the streets, filtering their way towards the northern gate to answer the call. She saw a unit of archers following a group of infantry and spotted a blue runed cloak among the bunch. Her stomach tightened and her throat constricted as she realized that it was Elune Shadowsong accompanying the team of archers making their way to the ramparts. The elf's gaze was searching the crowd, but the princess knew that Elune's search was not for her. She remembered that their last words were spoken in anger, and her heart ached at the thought. She wanted to push her way through the crowd and take her friend in her arms, for those exchanges could very well be their last. She knew there was no time, however, as much as she desired there to be. She had wronged her kingdom, and while she knew now that she could not find complete absolution by exposing the false magistrates, she could at least bring justice to the bastards that had invited the orcs to their doorstep. She was certain she would return to the wall when she was done to help in their efforts, but her odds of finding Elune in the chaos at that point - dead or alive - were slim. She remembered Eliliweth as well and had to will the tears from forming in her eyes, for the last time she had seen the half-elf was the day he had departed for the White Forest, and their goodbyes had been formal and cold. If she didn't live to see tomorrow, he might never know that it wasn't resentment towards him that had made her so aloof. It was her secret, her damned clever ploy to ensnare the villains and save the kingdom all in one maneuver.

Her sorrow suddenly turned to anger, and her desire to catch the bloated magistrate ticks burned in her heart. Perhaps she would not need to have the guards bind them. They had committed treason, for which the punishment was death. War was upon them that day, which would excuse the lack of a trial in their executions. If there were guards there to witness their treachery, she would be well within her rights to set the magistrates aflame before leading the guards back to the battlefield. The thought stirred her, sending adrenaline coursing through her arms and chest. She gave Archibaum a push. "Faster," she commanded.

Their pace was quick and relatively easy, as by now most of those fighting the battle had either arrived at the northern wall or were waiting their turn to file into place, and the refugees were huddled in either homes or shelters, clutching their loved ones if they traveled with any. The few that they crossed paths with gave the princess and the magistrate long stares, as if they were hoping for good news, but turned away with bowed heads when Aven marched forward without a single glance at the onlookers. Somewhere distantly in her conscience, she regretted her cold spurning of their attention, but she could not afford the time to try to ease their despairs. Onward she marched with Lord Archibaum leading the way, his elderly legs moving with the slightest limp at every pace. Aven risked a single look back over her shoulder, towards the sky above the gates. She could see the faintest trails of smoke slithering their way up towards the clouds, the torches of the enemy. She forced herself to look away before she lost her nerve and ran back to find Benton Cusair.

The white tower of the aviary came into view, as well as the wooden apse top, and Aven's gaze darted about in search of the fleeing magistrates or the guards that Bertram had ordered to seize them. Lord Archibaum brought his hand to his lips as they drew closer, head sliding back and forth on a swivel as he too sought the traitorous nobles. "Where are they?!" he despaired.

"They must have escaped," Aven said, the irritation clear in her voice. "If that's the case, we'll have to cut our losses, Archibaum. We don't have time to go on a scavenger hunt throughout the city." Off in the distance, she could begin to hear the stirring battle chants of the orc warriors as they neared the Glen Bailey, a low unison grunt like a slow foreboding drumbeat.

"No!" the magistrate called out, suddenly lurching forward towards the bottom entrance of the aviary. "I heard something above. They must have caught them! We must bear witness, Your Grace!" Archibaum's legs found new youth as the noble sprinted towards the door. Aven called out after him, surprised by his sudden resurgence, but the old man was already in the door. She gathered her robes in her hands and followed in pursuit.

She could hear him running up the stairs as she entered the tower, a staircase circumventing the wall greeting her towards her left. She took them two at a time, her feet knocking against the wood as she ascended. Up above, she could still hear the magistrate's footfalls, and another sound: his shouting. She couldn't make out what he was bellowing, but something was happening up above. "Bertram!" she shouted between labored breaths as she climbed further upwards. "What in the hell is going on up there!?"

Her only response was another round of excited shouts. *Foolish old bastard, he's going to get himself killed!* She churned her legs even harder to catch up, feeling her lower thighs grow tight in protest with the exertion. Finally, she could see the landing at the top level of the tower, where the gryphon roosts were. She began to murmur an incantation, ready to unleash a spell at the slightest sight of an ambush as she entered the roosting level.

She frowned as she lifted herself off of the stairs. Several of the gryphons were missing, only two resting in their hay-filled beds, their avian eyes staring at her in a manner that almost felt accusatory. She did not linger her gaze on the creatures, however, but instead turned her attention to the landing perch, a wooden deck without railings on the other side of the tower. She did not see the corrupt magistrates or any of the guards. Only Lord Archibaum stood on the deck, eyes turned upward towards the sky, his arms outstretched as if he planned to take flight on his own. By the gods, was he about to end his own life? "Bertram, don't!" Aven called out, darting forward towards the noble.

It all happened in seconds. She suddenly felt something underneath her shoe, her weight shifting oddly against the surface. She paused just long enough in her stride to look down to see what she had stepped on. Confusion settled over her face as she looked upon the circular rune at her feet drawn in salt, curving patterns within the shape, her heel scattering one of the lines it had dragged across. She recognized the pattern. It was a drawn spell circle.

By the time she had looked up, it was too late. Archibaum had turned around, an insidious grin on his face. He pointed a hand in her direction, spread his fingers, and triumphantly hissed, "*Arrakath-a.*"

It felt as though an entire mountain had fallen upon her back. She fell to her knees, both of them slamming against the floorboards so violently that she felt the pain lance down her shins and up her thighs. There were two incomplete circles drawn within the outer ring, and both of her hands slapped against the floor within them. In the upper center, there was a drawn X with curved ends at the top, like two crossed shepherd's canes. She felt her head forcefully bow as her entire skull seemed anchored to the curved cross. Paralyzed, she knelt on all fours as the salt runes began to glow a radiant white. She gritted her teeth and tried with all her might to pull herself from the trap, but not a single muscle in her entire body felt within her control. Even her tongue refused to obey her commands, preventing her from speaking a spell of her own. A frustrated, helpless cry began to whine at the back of her throat.

She could hear his footsteps approaching, slowly. A shadow fell in front of her as the magistrate knelt before the salt circle. A hand appeared below her, the pointer finger outstretched. It cut a horizontal line through the curved cross, and suddenly, she felt her neck able to move. She swiveled her head upwards, staring into the grinning face of Lord Archibaum, and tried to utter a spell, only to find her tongue still stupefied in her mouth. A smug cackle escaped the magistrate at her failure. His hand reached into a pocket of his robe, and from it, he procured a small bottle of green substance. He popped the miniature cork off the top and tipped it towards his open mouth, a few drops falling onto his tongue. Sealing it once more, he pocketed the vial. "One of the most grievous errors mages make nowadays, Your Grace, is letting everyone *know* what they are. Who can resist exposing themselves as wielders of the mysterious and powerful art of the arcane? The ones with half their wits about them, that's who," he said slickly, wine-stained teeth showing through his pompous smile. "A few drops of plantain leaf extract every day, and not even your fellow magi can detect your power. You can come out now, Pehg," he called out.

A dwarf with fiery red hair and a snarled beard poked his head around the corner from the landing outside, his beady eyes peering within suspiciously. "It worked? It worked, right? She cann'it move?"

"She cannot," Archibaum said, eyes glinting maliciously. Aven turned her head from side to side. The two gryphons sitting in their nests continued to stare, one of them with ruffled feathers around its neck, but neither of them showed enough concern to climb out of their hay or to attack her oppressors. From far away, she could still make out the orcish chants, but her concern for them was suddenly just as distant.

"Ach, o' course it bloody worked!" the dwarf named Pehg said as he swaggered into the aviary, brushing his palms together as if they were coated in dust from a hard day's work. "I told'ja it would, dinn'it I?"

"Yes, congratulations Pehg, you had the capacity to purchase exactly what I told you to buy from the exact place I specified you could find it," Archibaum said dryly, rolling his eyes as his hand reached for his opposite pocket.

"Haha, ye damned right!" Pehg answered, completely missing the magistrate's sarcasm as he pressed his blocky knuckles against his hips, eyeing their captive. "They had that rottin' demon fetch it fer me too! So...yeh need me to put 'er down then, or am I done 'ere?"

"You're done. I'll finish this myself," Archibaum responded, procuring a bag of coins from his pocket and tossing them in the dwarf's direction, who snatched it greedily out of the air, his thumbs pressing against the fabric to feel the edges of the coins.

"A'rrighty then," Pehg said with a giddy chuckle. Now that he was closer, Aven was suddenly acutely aware of the reeking stench of ale on the despicable dwarf. "If'n it's all the same to you, I'll be on my way outta 'ere b'fore those greenskins start burnin' the place down!"

"It's all the same to me," Bertram growled, the impatience in his tone not missed by even the thickheaded dwarf.

"A'rright! Good doin' business with ye," Pehg answered with another cackle as he waddled his way towards the staircase, flashing Aven a mocking grin and wave before disappearing from sight, even if his stench lingered for a few moments longer.

"I'm afraid, Your Grace, that we may have missed the magistrates after all," Archibaum sneered as the dwarf disappeared. A flash of steel glinted from his belt as he drew a dagger, resting the blade against his palm as he studied the helpless princess, his maleficent grin persisting. "Looks as though they may have taken off on a few of Kaijar Keep's gryphons. I don't suppose they'll be back, but I could check the posted schedule to be sure, if you'd like. No? Well, all right, then."

"Oh, there there, Your Grace, don't fret," Archibaum purred as a single tear began to roll down Aven's cheek, despite her tight-lipped attempt at restraining it. "This was all part of the plan, truly! Though I might divert from it in the end. I'm supposed to rendezvous with them after they've paid off the orc warchief, but a whisper here and a whisper there over the past month have told me that the head of Bartholomew's only heir would fetch a delicious price from the right buyer. You'd be amazed at how badly some rulers would like to see this entire kingdom crumble. As a matter of fact, I'll make a deal with you, Your Grace," he said with another wicked grin, the sunlight glinting off his dagger once more. "The Glen Bailey can keep the *entire* Archibaum estate, in exchange for your head! Does that sound like a fair trade to you? Yes? Well then, *splendid!*"

Her stomach churned, her heart racing as she stared helplessly into the magistrate's laughing face. How could she have been so foolish? How could she have been so prideful? What had given her the slightest hope that she could trust this duplicitous bastard? She had allowed herself to get caught up in the thrill of the scandal, and then anchored to the ploy by her own guilt. And now Lord Archibaum was savoring his victory, perfectly content to watch her wait for her own death, taking his payment for every time she had ridiculed, insulted, or threatened him ever since she had discovered their conspiratorial mutterings in the bath house.

"It really is a shame that I can't let your tongue loosen, Your Grace," Archibaum teased, turning the dagger over in his hand, angling the point of it against the pad of his opposite pointer finger, light continuing to reflect off the polished blade. "I would thoroughly enjoy listening to your threats, your insistence that I won't get away with this, that someone will come. Wouldn't that be delicious? And then you'd realize that everyone who could possibly save your life is already crossing blades with a greenskinned savage! The irony, of course, is that they'd be out there with every intention of *saving* you from danger!

"And then, as it finally dawned on you, you'd start to beg for mercy. You'd offer to make deals, try to ransom yourself before finally just... breaking down in front of me. Yes, like that, only *more!*" the noble gushed as another tear bloomed at Aven's eye, trickling down her cheek before falling to the floor. Archibaum lowered the dagger, resting the tip on the floorboards instead as he grinned at her. "Truth be told, I don't know if there's any spell you could speak that would free you from the trap, but I'm not quite careless enough to give you the chance. I'd say that's more of *your* forte, wouldn't you?"

Archibaum laughed, scooting closer to her in his crouched position, keeping his hands behind the outer salt ring but allowing himself to lean his face in close to hers, enough so that she could see the clogged pores in his nose, could smell the sour scent of the plantain extract he'd used to disguise his secret powers. He hissed as his eyes narrowed, "I wish I could stay here to see the army of brutes tear this kingdom limb from limb, to watch them crucify your insufferable father. I wish I could leave you here for them, too. I really do. How delightful it would be to watch them dry up every drop of prideful blood in in your veins. After so many years of being forced to bare all of your childish nonsense, it would give me so much pleasure.

"Alas," he breathed, leaning back away from her, though his eyes never left her face as another tear escaped from her eye. He lifted the dagger, gaze falling on her neck, lips twitching in anticipation. "As much as I've enjoyed this, all good things must come to an end. Do take care in the afterlife, Aven Celandine. Say hello to your father for me when he's plunged into the Death Shepherd's endless river alongside you."

She could have screamed. A faraway part of her was distantly grateful that she was unable to give the treacherous son of a bitch that satisfaction. She couldn't stop the tears from falling, but she kept her eyes open in what little defiance she could display. Archibaum's mouth opened as his breathing accelerated in eagerness, the dagger glinting once again as he lifted it into the air for the killing blow.

She gritted her teeth, preparing for the end, when she suddenly saw a figure behind the smiling magistrate. A shadow fell over him as it approached, a floorboard squeaking under the sudden weight. Lord Archibaum turned, mouth falling open as his eyes widened. He began to lift his hands, a startled cry escaping him, but it was too late. The blade of a longsword came whistling down at an arc, burying itself into the magistrate's neck with a splitting *thrack!* The noble's head jerked back at a grotesque angle, his tongue bulging from his lips as the blade was retrieved, dragging through the wound as it exited. Blood began to release in copious spurts as Bertram Archibaum sunk to the floor, sickening gags escaping him as the life quickly began to depart from him.

With wide, unbelieving eyes, Aven looked up as the figure stepped forward. Cadohaden Ulaeron stood before her, bloodied blade in hand, eyes just as open and bewildered as hers. Rogue straws of hay and a few gryphon feathers stuck in random spots to him all over his body. He scowled in disgust as a stream of crimson liquid spattered against his boot from the dying magistrate. He planted his foot against Archibaum's shoulder and gave him a shove, rolling him away a few feet before kneeling down before the princess. He reached out with his glove and wiped away a ribbon of blood that had struck her face, preventing her from opening her right eye. He looked down at the salt ring, then to Lord Archibaum as his body began to seize in its death throes. She saw his jaw flex in disturbance as he averted his eyes, looking back at her. "You still can't move?" he asked. She shook her head, her mouth trying to open to explain it vocally to him, but her jaw wouldn't cooperate.

The paladin reached out to wipe away the salt runes, but immediately drew his hand back as he touched the glimmering grains. "Shit!" he cursed, waving his hand frantically. "I can't touch it. It burns like hell." She stared helplessly at him, unable to give him any instruction. His lips moved as he murmured his own thoughts to himself, examining the ritual circle binding her to the floor. He lifted his eyes to her once again. "Would a Nullification dispel it?" he asked her, his words fervored and quick.

She stared back at him as she pondered his question. Another mage was usually the best tool to dispel a hex or enchantment, but those who wielded the powers of Kaijaras could sometimes unravel spells through a prayer known as Nullification. If she remembered correctly, it took a great deal of concentration and was even more difficult to perform than a blessing of healing, and she was quite certain that Cadohaden was struggling with those in his practices. Still, she did not want to sit here, bound to the circle, waiting for someone else to come rescue her. For all she knew, it could be orcs that that would climb the aviary tower next. With the slowest of nods, hoping to convey her concerns, she affirmed his question.

"All right," Cadohaden breathed in response, rubbing his hands together as he stared at the enchanted salt. She could see the wheels turning in his mind as he tried to recall the prayer. If he had registered her apprehension, it didn't show on his face. After another moment of murmuring to himself, he lowered his head as he bent his back, laying his hands out on the floor in front of him, his left placed over his right.

"Blessed Lifegiver," he murmured, "you are life and all that encompasses it..."

Chapter Twenty-Eight

A potted plant sat near the staircase leading to the upper levels of the keep, with a tall stalk and shining leafy palms. Strigson Ganisalp leaned next to it, staring down into the soil that it was embedded in. The top layer seemed dark and fresh; he could smell the earthy tones. He swallowed once as the bitter bile began to surge in the back of his throat. The second volley of vomit he couldn't contain though, voiding the nervous contents of his stomach into the pot, the brown-green mixture spattering against the dirt. He looked over his shoulder to ensure that nobody was walking nearby. The corridor was empty, however, as most of the help had retreated to their safe shelters below the ground level. He turned his head back and hurled once more, spitting a few times when he was finished to try to banish the taste from his mouth.

He had never been so nervous in his entire military career as he was at this moment. He couldn't quite remember if he had ever felt nervous *at all* after his first day of boot camp training. But then again, during his tenure as the Glen Bailey's general, he'd never had to defend against an entire army. He'd organized many assaults against raider camps - even large-scale, sophisticated operations. The intricate patrol rotations were all of his own devices, complex but effective, and simple enough to understand when minor roles were assigned to captains. He had orchestrated the training regimen for every level of soldier under his command. And yes, he'd even lead battles against orcish tribes, usually when they were harassing villages or harrying their caravans.

For most everything, he was a seasoned veteran, a more than capable leader. But while he'd read many accounts of wars past and studied dozens of battle maps that depicted strategic army formations, he was as green as the most baby-faced squire when it came to defending his kingdom against a true army, a rookie when it came to repelling the vast numbers that now threatened the Glen Bailey. This would be a true test of his mettle, and if he failed, he would pay the price with his life, and the lives of countless others. The thought made his stomach squirm, and he tried to empty out whatever remained within, but he found himself only dry heaving over the vomit he'd left below. Satisfied that he'd finished with the unpleasant task, he spit once more into the soil and wiped his armored forearm against his mouth, leaving a trail of dirty saliva across it. He straightened his posture and set his jaw. He'd allowed himself a private moment of weakness, but that was all he could afford. A general did not puke in front of his soldiers. Those were the rules. Greenhorns spewed after a harsh first day of boot camp, not those in charge. He couldn't permit his affair with the princess to cloud his focus, either. There were going to be countless men and women out there with loved ones to lose or be lost to. He could not prioritize his romantic notions over the safety of others, despite what he'd gambled to achieve them. Those were the rules.

His composure recovered, he marched out across the empty hallway, pushing open the tall doors leading out into the city, the hinges creaking as they moved. His squire was waiting for him at the bottom of the stone steps, a lanky boy named Marc Blyjal with medium-length ghostly blonde hair that naturally swept upward at his hairline. Held in his hand were the reins to Strigson's steed, a midnight black horse called Edict. The general had named him himself, and the beast was already adorned in his combat armor. Marc had helped his lord into his combat armor before retrieving Edict, but since leaving Strigson, he'd also fetched his weapon belt, Ganisalp's longsword sheathed at the hip. The general accepted the offered belt and buckled it to his waist, sliding the blade out of its sheath a few inches for a quick inspection. There was no fancy adornment on the blade's cross-guard, but the hilt was decorated with woven silver thread through the leather handle. Wasting no time, Strigson allowed Marc to help him up onto Edict's saddle. He looked back down at the boy and asked, "Reports from the wall?"

"All units are in position, sir," Marc answered in a voice that wavered between a boy's and a man's, lows accompanied by the occasional hitch in timbre. "Approximately twenty-eight men missing from the call of duty. Enemy movement was spotted from the ramparts not long before I returned here. They'll be upon us soon."

Less than thirty deserters, Strigson thought to himself as he adjusted his position on the saddle. *Loyalty is strong in the Glen Bailey.* Most accounts he'd read of battles of this proportion recounted sometimes a hundred or more men disappearing before the war was waged. "Infantry, I assume?"

"Twenty of them infantry, six of them from the archers, one cavalryman - without his horse - and a paladin, sir," Marc answered, translucent eyebrows knitting as he recalled the report. "Ulaeron, sir, from the Monastery. The Kingsbanesin-born."

"Son of a dog. Can't say nobody warned me," the general said, shaking his head. He looked back down at his squire and tipped his head in a curt nod. "I must go. Get yourself up to the walls, Blyjal, and find an unused bow. If there are none, keep the oil hot until there is one. There will be. And if I don't live to see tomorrow, boy, make me proud. You'll make a damn good knight someday."

"Thank you, sir," Marc replied with a pubescent squeak. "Kaijaras shield you."

"And you, Blyjal," Ganisalp answered before kicking his heels against Edict's sides, stirring his steed to a gallop as he took off towards the northern wall, his rider hanging on to the reins with determination. It was strange, riding through the city with so few among the streets. He'd never ridden through at this pace, before, but even with the hurried gait of his steed, the empty streets of the market felt haunted with the absence of the merchants. He turned a corner, and then another as Edict carried him towards the army he commanded. There were still colorful flags hanging on clotheslines across the streets, anchored in empty windows, left from the celebrations of Eliliweth Heraketh's Trials. Weeks ago, they had given renewed spirit to these cobblestone streets. Now, they seemed to hang limply in the air, premature memorial markers to the dead that would be counted when the last had fallen.

His cavalry awaited him in rows as he approached the closed gate of the northern wall, the sight of them restoring some of the fortitude he had lost in his journey there. The armor from the horses shined with a heroic brilliance, the colors of the Glen Bailey draped over them a reminder of just what they defended. Every one of the men and women saluted as Edict clopped towards them. The tips of their lances were polished and sharpened, glistening wickedly as the sun struck their edges. In the front, forty feet from the closed gate, the lead rider carried the Glen Dale's standard, a forest green flag upon a raised pole, the quartered four-leaf cross embroidered into the fabric, a bayonet fastened to the top of the cross beam. His Field Lieutenant, Mya Ness, broke formation and steered her horse towards the general, riding up to him until she was alongside Edict. "I'm told all units are in position, Lieutenant," Ganisalp said. "Are Nevic and Benton on the other side?"

"Yes sir. They await your arrival," Mya replied.

"Good," the general answered. His stomach protested once with an uncomfortable twist, but Strigson was beginning to find his center, his soldier's acumen finally taking hold of him as the reality of the battle became tangible. He trusted that his courage would ignite as soon as he passed through the gate. "Open the gate, then. We take the field."

"Open the gate!" Mya Ness called out. The man with the standard reached for a battle horn that was slung around his waist, lifting it to his lips. A low, ominous rumble escaped it, and as it did so, Strigson could hear the sounds of shouting above in the gatehouses atop the wall. The general moved to the front of the cavalry as the tremendous doors groaned, opening slowly to allow them passage. When enough room had cleared, Sir Ganisalp signaled with his hand, setting the cavalry into motion, the sound of clopping hooves battling the grinding noise of the opening doors.

He was greeted with the sounds of cheering as they passed through the gate, legions of soldiers on opposite sides of him as he made his way towards the front lines, Edict trotting proudly forward. His heart swelled in his chest, and as he expected, the soldier's spirit flared within his soul. He felt five inches taller than he truly was and twice as strong as infantry swords clapped against shields, hailing the man who would lead them against the orcish menace. A faint voice in his fervored mind was grateful that the absence of their king did not dismay them.

He reached the front lines and lifted his hand, quieting his cheering soldiers as he turned Edict around to face them. As Mya had promised, both Crusader Nevic and Archmage Benton were waiting for him, Nevic on a spotted palomino, and Benton on a snow white mare. They saluted him, and he did so in return. He looked out upon their army, chest expanding with pride as he laid eyes upon the rows and rows of soldiers lined up in front of the walls, shields in hand and helmets upon head. His cavalrymen had filled the gap left for him to venture to the front lines, a narrower aisle left in the center.

The Glen Dale was not a military state. They did not possess the fiercest legions like Kingsbanesin, nor did they boast the most formidable defenses like Eastfen. But Strigson had no doubt that the soldiers defending their kingdom that day had the most pride and spirit in all of the Aariad. It was a contagious ardor, an energy reverberating from each soldier that felt as though it could generate sound. He surveyed each foot soldier, each armored rider, and the auxiliary units that bolstered their forces. There were the paladins, the clerics, a few huntsmen that had come in from the villages, and even a few mercenary companies that his scouts had managed to contract while evacuating the Dale's peasants. And upon the battlements, the rows and rows of archers, posted between the ballistas that the guards had spent the last couple days rolling into position. At the corners of the walls, next to the sentinel towers, a trebuchet waited patiently by each, the stacks of stones to be used visible from where the general stood.

Sir Ganisalp looked over his shoulder. He could see the orcs now, marching towards them like a wave of darkness, a disease of daylight as they advanced. There were objects hovering above them, most of them yet unrecognizable, but he could make out a few bloodied and tattered silver banners from Arden's Watch being hoisted mockingly over their heads. Worse than just insults, however, he could see the imposing shapes of the trolls lumbering in the rear ranks of the menacing army. When faced with such a threat, a man's instincts often took over, demanding one of two reactions: fight, or run. It was the former that burned within the general, igniting a valiance that was stirred by the spirit of his soldiers. He looked away from the approaching enemy force and cast his eyes once more upon his own men, drawing his sword from his sheath and hoisting it to the sky.

"Men and women, soldiers of the Glen Bailey!" Strigson shouted, projecting his voice as far as he could as he guided Edict in a steady pace back-and-forth, hooves clopping triumphantly against the ground below. "You stand today in defense of the greatest kingdom in all of the Aariad!" His soldiers shouted in return, voices ringing with enthusiasm, swords clapping against shields once more at his boast.

"Today, we stand against this menace, this threat to our way of life, with few friends to aid us!" the general shouted as Edict turned about-face once more. "When the sun sets on this night, many good men will have begun their journey to the afterlife! But they may venture into it knowing that they will not be forgotten, that the stories of their bravery preserving all that is good in this world will live on, from their children, to their children's children, and to theirs!" Another volley of cries echoed out from the soldiers, the sound bouncing off the Bailey's walls and reflecting back towards the field of inevitable battle.

"Fight with the name of the Glen Bailey on your lips! Fight with the Lifegiver in your heart!" Ganisalp roared as he thrust his sword towards the air once more. "But most importantly, fight for your sword-brother that stands next to you! Fight for the one behind you, or in front of you! Fight for one another, and together, we will grind these miserable curs into the dirt, and line their heads on pikes along the roads of the Glen Dale, to show what comes to those who test the might and the heart of the Glen Bailey!" The answer was thunderous, rolling across the fields of barley that were before them.

Satisfied with the response, the general turned Edict back towards the orc army as his soldiers continued to call out eagerly behind him. The greenskins were much closer now, the objects hovering above them discernible from where Strigson stood. He felt his valiance falter a little as he recognized what was tailing the front lines of the enemy. The trolls were pushing catapults towards the wall in the wake of the orc warriors, and slung across their backs they carried collections of stones in cradles that looked like they were fashioned from the long curtains and carpets belonging to Arden's Watch. It wasn't just the unfortunate commandeering of the catapults that disturbed the general, however. Affixed to poles that were raised from four of the siege contraptions, hanging high above them, were X-shaped crosses fashioned from planks undoubtedly salvaged from the Watch. And crucified to each of the crosses, Strigson peered in gruesome horror at the naked bodies nailed to the planks. Each one's stomach was sliced open, entrails hanging from the gaping wound. There was something else, too, something strange about their mouths. The general squinted as he tried to make out what it was that was off. It looked as though they were stuffed with something that periodically was falling from their jaws and dropping to the ground below like heavy snowflakes.

"Merciful Lifegiver," Crusader Nevic said as his horse marched up alongside Edict. The albino paladin wore a pearl-white cloth mask to guard against the sun's rays, his pink-irised eyes showing through their cut-outs. "Are those the magistrates?"

"I only count four up there," Ganisalp answered grimly, "but I guarantee they didn't find any men as fat as Tibault or Seasar doing farm chores out in the countryside."

"What's in their mouths?" Nevic asked hesitantly.

"Coin," Benton said in a matter-of-fact tone as his mare clopped forward as well. The archmage was known for his pristine eyesight. "Their mouths are stuffed with coin. They wouldn't have dared go anywhere near the army if their only goal was to flee the kingdom. They tried to pay the brutes off, and paid with their lives instead."

"Pay them off?" Nevic said incredulously. "Pay them off for what?"

"It doesn't matter now," the general said, interrupting them, his gaze never leaving the enemy's front lines as they drew closer. He watched for their leaders to separate from the pack. It was an Aariad custom for the leaders of an army to meet briefly before battle for one last attempt at negotiations, even if there wasn't the faintest chance or desire of an agreement. It wasn't always followed - good commanders were always prepared for a shirking of the ritual. Sir Ganisalp wasn't convinced that Hordeland orcs were even aware of the practice. But he was prepared to hear them either way. To his mild surprise, as the orcish army came to a stop nearly a hundred yards away, the general spotted four figures emerge from the front lines, marching towards them, each of them on a horse that was surely stolen from either a farm or Arden's Watch. The general lifted his chin and nodded his head, speaking to both Nevic and Benton, "Let's go."

They rode forward to meet the orc leaders in the middle of the field, ignoring the jeers and threats shouted at them from the enemy's front line. As they approached their foes, Ganisalp glanced over each with as much scrutiny as he could manage within a short period of time. The two in the center he recognized just from their scouting records. The taller one was none other than the warchief Grathul Heavyhand, grayish green skin stretched over frighteningly defined muscles, his assorted armor decorated with all varieties of war trophies. One of the belts on his leather harness had a layer of pink flesh sewn over the top, and Strigson had no doubt that the skin had once belonged to a human or a cousin of his race. Most of the orc's scalp was shaved, though a long black braid that started at the back of his skull was draped over his shoulder, iron weights tied into the strands. The one at Grathul's left was the infamous Gragnath Fire-Eyes, the warlock's spine slightly hunched, his torso covered with a collection of tattered black rags, a similar hood draped over his head. His grinning red irises peered at the general from behind the cowl. Ganisalp could see the numerous scars on the warlock's arms from self-inflicted bloodletting to fuel his abhorrent magics. The two orcs on the ends Strigson didn't recognize. One of them had a facial structure similar to Grathul's, hinting at some kind of relation, but then again, most orcs looked akin in Ganisalp's eyes. The one on the opposite end had long, stringy black hair and a jutting jaw, the handle of a menacing war axe resting on his shoulder.

It was Gragnath Fire-Eyes that spoke first, rough Commonspeak rolling from his tongue like grinding stones. "Good of human dogs to come meet us," the warlock chuckled. "We wished you to know our names, so that when banished to afterlives, you tell spirits of dead who it was that sent so many to join them."

"And you can tell your demon god that it was the Glen Bailey who sent you all down into his sea of hellfire," Nevic shot back, his masked white visage a stark contrast to the warlock's shadowed face.

Gragnath smirked and flexed his knobbed hand, rolling his knuckles one joint at a time. "Does Glen Bailey king not have same faith as you do, pale one? Why is the king not here to make boasts for almighty Lifegiver?"

"King Bartholomew speaks with men, not lowly animals who chewed through their leashes," Strigson interjected, glowering at the hunched orc.

"Ahhh," Gragnath purred. "But *you*, Strigson Ganisalp, you are broken enough to obey commands *without* king here to hold leash? I see. And did cowardly king tell you terms of surrender? Or will you offer on your own?"

"Here's our offer," Strigson spat. He reminded himself that he had his own army standing behind him as he spoke, for it was hard to ignore the legions of orcs behind those that had come to speak. "All four of you will choose ten warriors each from your army. They, and the four of you, will kneel before our forces and answer for your crimes at Arden's Watch with a good, clean beheading. With that done, we'll give the rest of your mongrels an hour to scurry back to the Hordelands before we send our forces out to run them down like the beasts they are."

Gragnath rasped a dry, rumbling laugh before repeating the general's words to Grathul in guttural Orcish. The one on the left with the long black hair barked a single cruel laugh, but the warchief himself only grinned wickedly, his penetrating gaze never straying from Strigson. Grathul grunted his reply back to Gragnath, who swiveled his head back towards the general. "Here's warchief's offer, dog: you and other dogs lay down weapons and kneel before *us*. Some of you get honor of being my blood sacrifices. Others be pets for warchief Grathul. Some will be work as slaves for warchief's brother Razuk. The strongest dogs we will give to the Pillage Lord Ganshu'Dai, and they will die when our young practice combat against them. Many of you we kill right away, but that is price of defeat, dog."

"Tell your warchief," Ganisalp growled, "that he can go pleasure himself with the point end of a sword. I'll even offer him mine, as a show of good faith."

Gragnath's smug grin evaporated, his expression curdling with the insult. He hissed the translation towards Grathul, whose face darkened with every uttered grunt. The warlock opened his mouth, but it was the warchief who advanced first, giving his horse a brutish kick in the ribs to urge him forward. The orc brought the horse to a halt mere inches away from Edict, who slowly reared his head at the intrusion of space. Grathul's nose wrinkled with his sneer as the warchief grunted in broken Commonspeak, "Dog know what call orc Grathul?" His speech would have been humorous if not for the lethal glint in his eyes or the dooming rumble of his voice. "'Humanslayer', orc call. Grathul shows this day."

The warchief spit at Strigson, the wad of spittle landing in Edict's mane before Grathul reared his horse around with the reins roughly, barking an order in Orcish to his entourage. The warlock Gragnath offered them one last snide smile before guiding his horse around as well to follow his leader away. As the four orcs approached their army, the greenskinned warriors began to chant, stomping their spears against the ground and smashing blades together in an awful mess of noise that echoed across the barley field. Ganisalp, in turn, guided Nevic and Benton back towards his legions, keeping his chin held high even though he'd felt Grathul's words cut the first wound into his soul. Strigson turned his head to Benton, calling out over the noise, "The Fourth Battalion is yours to command, Archmage, I have other plans for the Third. Find the brutes that are guarding the warlocks and break them down. I want Gragnath's head on a pike as soon as possible."

"Understood, sir," Benton answered as they drew nearer to the front lines.

"And the Second is yours, Baltwin," the general said as he turned to the crusader. "Do what you have to do to get the wounded back to Ecila and her clerics." Strigson paused, his jaw flexing as he briefly considered his next words. He reminded himself that this was war, and sometimes difficult decisions had to be made. "But if you get an opportunity to directly strike at their warlocks, they will take priority. They cannot be allowed to cast their vile magics on our soldiers at will."

"Yes, sir," Nevic responded. Receiving a dismissal nod and salute from their general, both Benton and Nevic rode their steeds through the aisle between the cavalry, the tails of their horses flicking as they trotted away. Strigson took in another deep breath, trying to settle the flutter in his chest as his eyes scrutinized the soldiers standing in front of him. He could hear the chants and the bellows of the orcs behind him as they rallied, and he could see the eyes of some of his men, their spirits beginning to falter as the enemy became more real. He needed to squash any doubt before they crossed blades.

"Soldiers, men and women of the Glen Dale, these savages come to tear down everything you hold dear! They seek to bring down our walls and slaughter your families!" He hoisted his sword into the air once more as he called out, "I, for one, love this land and this kingdom, and all those who call it home! I will fight these heathens with every ounce of strength my soul has! *They want war!?* We'll *give* them war! We are the *Glen Dale*, soldiers! We won't be brought to heel by these slobbering barbarians!" His legions erupted in cheers at his boast, their swords clapping against shields once again, boots stomping against the soil with zeal, their fighting spirit igniting in their eyes once again.

"Who are we!?" Strigson shouted, pumping his arm into the air with the question.

"*The Glen Dale!*" his army shouted in unison, a single voice like an echo of the gods themselves rolling out across the field.

"*Who are we!?*"

"*THE GLEN DALE!*"

Sir Ganisalp roared in response to his army's fervor, wheeling his horse back around to face the Hordeland legions. As he did so, however, something caught his eye. He lowered his sword as he squinted.

The bodies of the magistrates that had been hoisted to the sky on their crucifixion poles were missing now, vanished from above. Grathul's warriors were still chanting, their grunts an ominous *rah! rah! rah!* across the field, but Strigson noticed something behind them: smoke. It coiled towards the sky in oily black ribbons behind the greenskins' front line. He saw one, then another, and then there were four thick tendrils of smoke reaching for the sky above.

Shuck! Shuck! Shuck! Shuck! Strigson tensed as he heard the sound of the catapult arms releasing, immediately spotting the source of the smoldering as four twisting figures came hurling towards their gates, flailing fireballs immolated in an unnaturally vibrant flame. The general's head lifted as the figures soared overhead, and he recognized what they were: the bodies of the magistrates, ignited with bloodfire by Gragnath and his warlocks. As their burning corpses twisted and turned, coins fell from their mouths like metallic snowflakes, glistening as they tumbled downward. One by one, in quick succession, they spattered against the Glen Bailey's battlements, limbs separating from torsos in gruesome fashion as the fire and impact broke the cadavers apart. The hurling of the remains was no mere insult, however. The warlock's cursed fire clung to the bloodstains smeared against the wall's stone, feeding on the substance as though it were oil.

The battle had truly begun.

"*Benton!*" Ganisalp called out to the archmage as Grathul's commanding voice boomed from across the field with orders in Orcish. "Get Leora or Krendrick on those fires! *Now!*" He drew his sword in a slow semi-circle towards the battlements, drawing the attention of the archers that weren't trying to find room away from the flames that were beginning to crawl over the walls. "Archers, *ready!* Ballistas, *ready!*" Strigson cried before turning Edict back around to face the orcish army. "Soldiers, shields *up!*"

The infantry responded in unison, rotating their shields in front of their persons, blades held at the ready as their general's sword hovered in the air, ready to give the order. Arrow after arrow was pulled from quiver to bow upon the battlements behind them as the archers prepared to fire. The vibrations from the encroaching orcs could be felt through the soil as their feet stomped forward at their warchief's command, menacing spear heads pointed at the army of the Glen Bailey. Closer and closer they approached, until finally, Strigson brought his sword down, pointing it at the incoming onslaught. "Archers, *fire!*"

Even among the chaos, a sound like rushing wind could be heard as hundreds of bowstrings released at once, the sky filling with arrows as they descended upon the greenskinned masses. Many deflected off barrier or armor, but a multitude found their mark. Some of the enemy warriors stumbled and fell to the ground, to be trampled by those behind them, but most continued onward with the shafts protruding from their flesh. Strigson wasted no time, bringing his sword up again. "*ARCHERS, READY!*" he screamed over the sound of the rushing orcs. "*FIRE!*" A second volley released towards the enemy forces, the sounds of striking arrowheads like that of a hailstorm against a roof. Orcs and ogres tumbled to the ground as the arrows struck their marks, but the tide was not stemmed by a few fallen foes, eager berserkers foaming at the mouths quickly replacing those on the front line that were lost before impact.

The general had waited patiently. He was willing to let the orcs charge forward to meet them, as was common in their raiding parties, to let them spend their energy to meet his forces. He urged Edict a few paces to his right, positioning himself in the open aisle between the cavalry lines. He'd placed his riders there on purpose, to divide the enemy with a strong wedge in hopes that the combined efforts of his infantry, mages, and paladins could root out the threat of the warlocks. Strigson narrowed his eyes, waiting until just the right moment where his front line could move forward with enough momentum but at the minimal expense of energy. "*SOLDIERS!*" he screamed, giving his blade a final swipe forward towards the enemy. "*FORWARD! AT-TAAAAACK!*"

With a united, air-splitting war cry, the front lines of the Glen Bailey charged forward to meet the Hordeland menace. It was the first sound of impact, the bone-grinding, limb-snapping, blade-against-blade, shield-on-shield clash that defined the carnage of battle. The collective rush of air forced from every lung on the front line could almost be felt on the other side. Men and orc alike screamed as shoulders were wrenched from their sockets, as arm bones split and protruded through skin. The cavalry rushed forward as well, flowing around Strigson Ganisalp like a river over a stone as they surged forward, the breastplates of their war mounts slamming against the faces of orc warriors, their hooves trampling as their riders' blades slashed this way and that, deflecting the spear heads thrusting forward to pierce the mighty beasts. They pressed into the orcish mob with fierce determination, burrowing themselves directly into the fray.

It was a hard-fought stalemate at first, save for the penetration the cavalry was slowly gaining as they forced their way into the fracas. The dividing line pressed back and forth, and soldiers from both sides occasionally fell, but they were quickly replaced as another moved into position. Strigson risked a look over his shoulder at the battlements. He saw Leora moving through the archers, hands waving as she slowly but effectively began to dispel the cursed flames that licked against the walls. There was something else, though: arrows from the enemy side, dotting the air as they soared towards the ramparts, Grathul's archers letting loose as well from behind their infantry lines. From somewhere towards the east, Strigson saw a flash from what was surely a spell from Benton or Krendrick, judging by the deep-throated agonized bellows that followed. The general lifted his arm, signaling towards the archers as he thrust his blade towards the enemy forces twice in a jabbing motion. "*ARCHERS! FIRE AT WILL!*" If they could not hear his voice from below, they could from the many soldiers closer to them that relayed the command, as "fire at will!" was passed from mouth to ear until the archers finally understood. They positioned themselves up against the battlement wall, slinging their arrows into the enemy army as fast as they could draw.

Strigson felt a rush of triumph in his chest as he turned back to the front lines. The Glen Bailey was gaining ground, pushing the greenskins back as they dug their heels into the dirt, shoving with shield and thrusting blade points forward in synchronized cadence, the shieldbearers calling out the order in unison. He allowed himself a moment to search the field of battle once again, guiding Edict towards his left as a pair of paladins dragged a bleeding soldier towards the clerics waiting behind the melee, closer to the wall.

He opened his mouth, ready to rally a group of soldiers still pressed behind the front lines, when a shadow suddenly passed over the swarm of violence. Strigson looked up towards the sky as a boulder sailed through the air, quickly followed by another further towards his right. They sailed towards the battlements, the first smashing through the parapet and striking two archers lifeless at once as they crumpled to the floor. The other stone struck the parapet, launching broken stones into the battlements, but bounced backwards after impact, falling to the ground below. Soldiers and clerics screamed as they hurried away from the tumbling boulder. Archers continued to fire upon the enemy forces, but the stream of stones thrown from Grathul's catapults became relentless. Strigson craned his head upward, looking for the siege weapons, and could see the shoulders of the lumbering trolls as they pulled the boulders from one another's makeshift baskets to load onto the catapults.

The momentum began to shift as the rain of arrows from the Glen Bailey's walls dwindled from a storm to a light drizzle, the pressure of the boulder bombardment causing the archers to leap and duck for cover, given only seconds to regroup before another barrage came sailing at them. Strigson suddenly heard the equine scream of his cavalry's horses as orcish spears finally found their mark. An anxious grip tightened at the general's throat. He couldn't afford to let his entire cavalry get swallowed in the chaos. He led Edict towards the back end of the rows of riders, waving his sword above his head as he signaled to them. "*RIDERS!*" he shouted, voice cracking as he called out to those that hadn't yet pushed through the front line. "*TO ME!*"

The stream of cavalry broke off at the dividing line of the armies, the armored heads of the horses rearing indignantly as their riders coaxed them away from the fray, weaving through the swarm of Bailey soldiers as they began to rally around their general. Strigson pointed his blade towards the front lines, further to the west than the wedge of horsemen. He bellowed to the dozen or so riders he'd managed to gain the attention of, even as he saw another bright flash of light further to the east as one of the mages sent four or five orc warriors flying backward into their kin. "*WE RIDE FORTH HERE AND BREAK THROUGH THE LINE!*" Sir Ganisalp roared, and his riders clapped their hands against their chests in understanding. Forming his own miniature version of the wedge he'd sent into the thick of battle, Strigson clapped his heels against Edict's sides, urging him onward towards the orcish army. "*BEHIND YOU!*" he called out as they stormed forward. The infantrymen scattered out of their way as they charged, those pressing against the front lines noticing their push at the very last second before they rolled out of the way, creating an opening that revealed wide-eyed orc soldiers as they realized too late what was upon them.

Edict broke through, storming into the fray as Ganisalp brought his blade down upon the heads of his enemies. He could hear the horsemen behind him doing the same, fanning out slightly to form a cone as they pushed into what appeared to be a soft spot in the hordes of orcs, as many of the brutes had turned to collapse on the cavalry that had initially broken through. Ganisalp urged Edict further as he spotted a gaggle of goblins trying to appear inconspicuous among the rabble as they fired off arrows at the enemy archers. Strigson lifted a hand to shield his eyes as a great lance fired from a ballista atop the ramparts plunged into the fray, impaling one nearby orc and gouging two behind him as it ripped through the brute's torso. A second later, Edict's hooves were trampling over the shrieking goblins with the crunching of bones. Strigson released another war cry as he and his detachment cut into the enemy's ranks. He swiveled his head over his shoulder, calling out to the cavalry and the soldiers that poured into the opening that they had created, *"TO THE CATAPULTS! WE'LL PULL 'EM ALL APART!"*

More of the orcs were beginning to take notice of them as they stormed through, but for many, it was too late. Leading the charge, Edict trampled several in his wake, and for those that managed to dodge the war horse, they fell by either Ganisalp's swinging blade or the stampeding steeds riding behind him. *It's working,* he thought with feverish excitement as they cut through the mob. *We'll dismantle the catapults and the tide will turn in our favor again!*

Suddenly, the general found himself swinging at empty air as the horses clomped effortlessly into a pocket of open space amid the swarm of orc warriors. He felt himself jerk forward as Edict's hooves suddenly dug into the soil, the horse's neck abruptly straightening. Ganisalp peered past his frozen mount's head and saw the hooded Gragnath Fire-Eyes, as well as two orcs standing on either side of him that looked like warlocks as well. In one gnarled hand, Strigson could see a bizarre orb of blood swimming in a languid pattern within the warlock's grasp. The other was outstretched, palm facing outward toward the horses. Something else caught the general's eye as well, a small, shriveled object sitting on the ground between Gragnath's feet. His eyes widened in horror as he recognized what it was: a shrunken head, gray and lifeless but with dried eyes that seemed to stare directly at the general. He knew of whom the severed head belonged to. It was Father Chandler, the priest who had rallied the elderly men at Arden's Watch to sacrifice their lives to buy time for Wyatt Darjin and his unit.

"Ix'dro alashkurr!" Gragnath hissed, clenching his fist that held the suspended orb of blood. It collapsed in his grip, blood pooling between his fingers. Ganisalp tapped his heels urgently against Edict's

sides, pleading for the steed to move, but the horse only stood, paralyzed by the warlock's foul magic. A strong metallic smell reached Strigson's nose, and he caught movement on the ground from the corner of his eye. His eyes widened as he looked below; Gragnath's spell was coaxing forth a river of blood, draining from the fallen bodies behind them, snaking around the hooves of the cavalry's horses. Strigson looked over his shoulder, his face paling as he saw that each of the cavalrymen he'd summoned were having no more luck with their steeds than he was. Each one had straightened tree-like legs, their heads held erect atop their necks, eyes rolling in helpless panic. His head swiveled back around, staring at the warlock with distress, lips parted. Gragnath smirked as he crouched to a knee, hovering over the shrunken head as the stream of red ended under Father Chandler's withered chin. The warlock stared directly at Strigson as he pressed two fingers over the priest's preserved eyes. Eyes glinting with malice, he pushed his jagged fingernails into the sockets as he purred, "*Dro.*"

As the incantation left Gragnath's lips, Edict's limbs suddenly freed from underneath him, head instantly bucking with the newfound mobility, but before any of the cavalry's horses could trot out of the gory river below them, wreaths of flame burst from the slick surface, torching the horses' underbellies as they washed over them with hungering tongues. Crying out as the heat scorched at his feet, Strigson finally dismounted, shoving himself off of his beloved horse as he tumbled to the ground, rolling across it as he slapped at the flames that were lingering at his shins. He looked up towards his right in despair as Edict and several other armored horses plunged into the fray, screaming in panic as their entire bodies were rapidly engulfed in the unholy flame. He craned his head over his shoulder and saw several of the riders rolling on the ground, trying to extinguish the flames on their persons as well. Two of them hadn't been able to dismount. Strigson felt his stomach twist as he saw them, riding away on the fleeing horses, their boots stuck in their stirrups, arms clawing at their armor as the fire coiled around them.

In his horror, he'd forgotten all about the warlock that had conjured the terrible magic. He swiveled his head back around, searching for Gragnath, but the orc had walked up only a few paces from him. He reached for his sword, but he was too late. The soil below was soaked in crimson life, plenty of fuel for the Destroyer's servant to use. The warlock chattered off a guttural incantation, and suddenly, it was as though invisible hands had clamped around Strigson's throat. They tightened, constricting his airflow, and before he even realized he was being lifted, his boots departed from the ground. Gragnath's grin widened as his arms slowly lifted, the curses rolling roughly off his tongue as Strigson gradually ascended.

Sir Ganisalp kicked his feet. He grasped desperately at his throat, trying with all of his might to wrench himself free of hands he could not feel or see, but it was all in vain. Dark, violet clouds began to flood his vision as the darkness seeped into his consciousness. The world for the Glen Bailey's general was fading fast.

Chapter Twenty-Nine

"...and all that is pure," Cadohaden wheezed, still knelt before the salt circle entrapping Aven Celandine. He'd lost track of how many times he'd repeated the Nullification prayer, and the energy it drew from him was exhausting. His hair clung to the sweat on his face as he looked up hopefully, silently repeating a personal prayer for the practiced one to work. The glow of the salt had dimmed, but not completely extinguished. Something he saw made his chest stir with hope, however. In Aven's shoulders, he saw the faintest of movements, the slightest of flexes in her shoulderblades. He lifted himself on his palms with a hopeful expression as he saw something else as well: her jaw was moving. They were slow, painstaking bulges of the mandible, but they were there. Her lips parted as a choked spell clumsily fell from her tongue in what sounded like an agonized deathrattle.

"Come on, Your Grace," Cadohaden murmured between labored breaths, tapping his palm against the floorboards encouragingly. "You can do this."

The princess's face turned red, then a crimson shade of purple with her efforts before a jagged shriek escaped her. "*Terol'simana!*" she howled, wrenching her body upward as her hands flew in opposite directions, arms held out like an eagle's wings, the enchanted salt scattering in all directions across the aviary floor, the illumination dying in each of the grains. One of the gryphons cawed in agitation, its wings buffeting out once to show its displeasure at the abrupt spectacle.

"Yes!" Cadohaden said, taking in a deep breath of relief as he sat up on his knees, wiping his forearm across his forehead as he gathered himself. "I could feel it. I could *feel* it giving way. Well done, Your Grace."

"Your...Nullification...could use a bit of work, Ulaeron," the princess said between deep breaths. She brought a hand back to her neck as she tried to massage out the stiffness that had settled in. "Just what... do you think you're doing up here?"

Cadohaden's relieved expression quickly soured, scowling as he sat himself up on one knee. "I'm sorry - I just saved your life, and you're *lecturing* me?"

"You were in the right place...at the right time," Aven said, finally sitting up and brushing the strands of hair from her face. She settled a critical gaze on the young paladin. "Though it took you long enough to come crawling out of that hay. But it's not where you were ordered to be. There's a battle going on at our northern gate, Cadohaden." As the words left her lips, the sound of breaking stone could be heard as a boulder crashed against the wall's parapets. The battle cries and the wounded screams were a constant violent harmony alongside the rhythm of the smashing stones. The paladin stood up, releasing a sharp exhale as he trotted over between two of the roosts, placing his hands on the railing as he looked out towards the wall. The archers were visible from the tower the two of them stood in, like figurines dodging the catapult barrage. Aven's gaze followed him as she remained kneeling on the floor, breath still coming in weary gasps. "Why are you up here, Cadohaden?" she demanded once again.

He turned back around to face her, his jaw set in determination. "I'm taking a gryphon into battle," he said soberly.

"Absolutely not," Aven hissed.

"And why the hell *not!?*" Cadohaden shouted, fist curling at his side as he spat the question. "The magistrates stole the others. Gods know where they are now, so it's not like we don't *already* have explaining to do to Kaijar Keep! And if we don't live to do so, what does it matter, Aven? Do you hear them blasting the hell out of our wall? If they've been doing that for as long as I think they have, we're not winning the battle. We're losing out there. We need an edge."

"Do you even know how to fly a gryphon, Ulaeron?" the princess shot back challengingly, getting to her feet and lifting her chin in an authoritative manner.

"Not...not really," Cadohaden admitted, looking flustered by her question. "I mean, I've never done it before, but I know how to fly a dragon! One of the overlords at Kingsbanesin, Mekoda Sanreaux, taught me how! It can't be that different!"

"Don't be a fool," Aven snapped. "Of course it's different. As your future queen, Cadohaden, I forbid this. Run back to the gate. If nothing else, take up a bow and do the duty you swore to when you enlisted."

Cadohaden opened his mouth as if to protest when a flicker of thought suddenly crossed his face. He frowned and walked up to the princess, close enough that he could see the color of her eyes. "Are you really my future queen, though, Your Grace?" he said quietly. "What were *you* doing up here? What was all this business you were caught up in? It's pretty clear that the magistrates were up to no good, but it didn't sound to me like you just accidentally took a trip up to the aviary to be in the wrong place at the wrong time."

"Are you threatening me?" Aven responded lowly. "Choose your words carefully, Cadohaden."

"Look," the paladin answered, his speech suddenly hurrying as another great boulder smashed against the Bailey's wall, raucous screaming following in its wake. "I don't know what truly happened between you and that snake Archibaum, Aven, but here's what I think: you were doing what was necessary to protect your people. That's what I want to do as well. I want the citizens of the Glen Dale to be my people, and I want to do what is necessary to defend their lives. If we make it through this day alive, we're both going to have some explaining to do. Let's help each other here, and we can help each other again when the sun has set over those fields of barley."

Aven's mouth drew to an almost impossibly thin line as she stared back at him unflinchingly, jaw flexing as she ground her teeth. Finally, she conceded, snapping back at him in exasperation, "Fine, Cadohaden. Take a gryphon and put our diplomatic balance with Kaijar Keep at risk so you can go play war hero. You're apt to get both yourself and the creature killed, though, I'm warning you right now. And should you survive, you'll be careful how you describe what happened here. I'm sure you know the penalty for desertion is severe, even for those with friends in the royal court. You had orders, remember."

"Come with me," the paladin interrupted abruptly.

"What!?"

"Come with me," he repeated, excitement in his words. "You can cast spells on gryphonback, can't you?"

"I..." Aven said with a pause and a frown. "It might be more difficult. Harder to concentrate, but yes, yes I can."

"Then come with me!" Cadohaden insisted. "Why haven't we thought of this before? I'll steer, and you give them hell from above!"

"We haven't thought of it before because we aren't permitted-" she began before cutting herself off, waving her hand in a dismissive gesture as she shook her head. She took in a long breath, visibly weighing the decision in her head. Cadohaden frowned as the princess suddenly looked up at the ceiling of the aviary, murmuring something unintelligible to herself - or someone else, perhaps - before closing her eyes briefly. When she opened them, she stared evenly back at the paladin with a serious gaze. "Fine. I asked for a chance. It feels like some great cosmic joke that this is the opportunity I get, but so be it. We'll ride into battle together, then, Cadohaden. But if we die, stay far away from me in the afterlife. I don't want to be known as the princess who got herself killed by letting some glory-hungry fool talk her into riding a gryphon over certain doom."

Cadohaden's brow furrowed at her words. He hadn't the slightest clue what she was talking about regarding her plea for another chance, but they didn't have time for any more banter. "Great," he said with a grin before jogging over to the nearest gryphon.

Above the beast's roost, nailed to the beam that framed the upper window pane, there was a wooden name plate. 'Glyddiswilm' was burned in curved letters upon the plaque. Cadohaden looked back at the round, glassy eyes of the gryphon and murmured the creature's name, extending a hand out cautiously to stroke its feathered head. Glyddiswilm ducked his head cautiously, but only slightly, as he allowed the contact. Cadohaden gave him a few gentle strokes along the neck, murmuring soft words of encouragement as the princess walked up behind him. A moment passed and the gryphon relaxed. The paladin turned around to look at Aven. "Help me get a saddle on him?"

There were two saddles hanging from the wall, just under the open windows, a single seat and a double. They took the latter off of its hook, still moving carefully around the great winged beast as they lowered the saddle onto it. Fortunately, Aven had ridden them before, and had insisted that the handler helping her teach her to attach the saddle herself. It took a few minutes, and the sounds of battle coming from the northern wall caused them both to fumble with straps and look out the window when a boulder smashed against the fortifications, but they eventually secured it. Cadohaden took Glyddiswilm's reins, steadily guiding the winged creature out of his roost and over to the landing. The gryphon was hesitant, taking slow steps forward as his eyes scrutinized the paladin. He could tell that the beast could sense his lack of experience.

The uneasiness was not lost on Aven, either. "Are you sure you don't want me to steer?" she asked.

"Can you cast spells at the same time?" Cadohaden asked, peeking his head to the side of Glyddiswilm's.

"No," Aven responded, scowling bitterly as if he had just extracted a confession of weakness from her.

"I'll be fine," Cadohaden said with an air of assurance. He could sense her indignation as well, and so he added, "This will amount to nothing without your spellcraft, Your Grace."

Aven seemed to be satisfied with his admission, and so they guided the gryphon out onto the open landing of the tower. The paladin mounted first with the princess's aid before letting her use his arm as an anchor to hoist herself up onto the back end. They settled into their saddles as Glyddiswilm took another step towards the landing's edge before pausing, waiting for the order to lift off. Cadohaden drew in a deep, bracing breath before giving the gryphon a couple taps against the ribs using his heels. The gryphon bristled, feathers ruffling as his body tensed. "He's not a dragon, Ulaeron," Aven said. "They're sensitive there. You guide a gryphon with your hands. Find his shoulderblades. You tap with your fingertips to lift off. Press *gently* against the lower end of the shoulderblades if you want to ascend, the upper end if you want to lower. Tap with your fingertips again if you wish to land. Pull the reins for direction, but again, *gently.*"

"Got it," Cadohaden answered, his heart fluttering in his chest. He mentally commanded himself to keep his feet still and instead tapped the ends of his fingers against Glyddiswilm's shoulderblades. The winged beast responded at once, pushing off his back haunches to hoist them into the air with a proud flap of his feathered wings. Despite the horrors the day had brought, the paladin couldn't help but release an exhilarated laugh as they launched into the air. He pressed softly against the lower end of Glyddiswilm's shoulders, and the gryphon responded in kind, carrying them further upward into the sky. Using the reins as gentle guidance, Cadohaden steered Glyddiswilm around the tower in a semi-circle before they were trained towards the north, to the scene of the battle.

It didn't take long for them to observe the battle in full. Cadohaden's soaring spirit immediately dropped as he laid eyes upon the armies waging war to the north. They could see everything: the archers upon the walls, scattered and disorganized, the infantry on the ground locking shields and trading blows. They could see the mages waiting for their opportune times to cast their spells as the soldiers swarmed around them, wary of enemy blade and arrow as they looked for their openings. They saw Nevic's paladins, some fighting among the soldiers, others dragging the wounded back towards the clerics. Cadohaden carefully guided Glyddiswilm's descent to get a better look, though his heart sank as they drew nearer. He'd guessed right in his debate with Aven. Without the aid of the archers, the foot soldiers in the field were losing ground. What had surely once been a defined line between the armies was beginning to lose form as the orc forces pressed in towards the gate. He could see ogres among them as well, bullying their way into the shieldbearers as spears and swords lunged at them in defense.

"Ulaeron!" the princess shouted, tapping him against the shoulder as the bloody scene drew closer and closer. She pointed a finger past him, aimed in the center of the fray as she called out over the howl of the wind gales, "That's Sir Ganisalp! He's...floating above the others! A warlock curse! Ride over him!"

Cadohaden peeled his gaze away from the trolls he'd been staring at, watching them load stone after stone into the catapult arms, silently dreading the moment Grathul unleashed the behemoths themselves on the Glen Bailey's army. He followed the point of Aven's finger and spotted the rapidly approaching general, suspended above the heads of those around him as his feet kicked helplessly in the air. His feet twitched at the ankles; he nearly kicked at the gryphon's sides before remembering what the princess had told him, and instead pressed against the beast's shoulderblades once more as he guided Glyddiswilm towards the hexed Strigson, his hair furling out behind him as the gryphon picked up speed in his descent. He sensed Aven's movements behind him and could hear brief snippets of her incantation through the scream of the wind as they dove over the heads of the enemy, those not gridlocked in combat looking up at them, some pointing their fingers as the shadow passed over them.

As they glided swiftly over Sir Ganisalp, Cadohaden saw the princess's arm extend towards their right from the corner of his eye. A flash of light suddenly burst forth from her hand, and a sizzling bolt of lightning snaked towards a black shrouded orc standing before the general. He briefly saw the warlock lift his hand defensively as they passed over, but his attention was jarred as Glyddiswilm shrieked, startled by Aven's spell. The gryphon beat his wings furiously in another ascent as Cadohaden leaned forward, stroking his hands against the beast's feathered mane in attempt to calm him. As firmly as he could without appearing panicked, he pulled on the reins to steer towards the east as they flew over the catapults lined up in rows, one of the trolls staring up at them with a dim-witted expression. He looked over his shoulder as the princess's fingers dug into both, clutching them for support as they waited out Glyddiswilm's erratic flight. "Did you hit him!?" he called out.

"Bastard deflected it!" the princess shouted back as Cadohaden coaxed the gryphon into steering back around towards the battle. A single arrow hissed past them as they flew. "But I saw Ganisalp drop! What now!?"

Cadohaden gritted his teeth as he thought furiously, easing the gryphon back into stable flight as they passed over the catapults once again. He gently urged the beast higher as another arrow flew past, too close for comfort. They would have to hope that Aven's spell had saved the general's life. The catapults demanded their immediate attention, though. The army needed the cover of the archers on the walls. He looked towards the battlements again. The situation had not improved; the archers were scrambling to and fro upon the ramparts. He could see three or four soldiers attempting to restore order, but with the stones breaking the parapets apart all around them, it couldn't be established. He could see the coiling smoke of two cauldrons of oil at the top of the northern gate, but there was no longer anyone tending to them.

An idea struck him. He jerked his head over his shoulder as he gently began to guide Glyddiswilm back towards the wall. "Can you cast spellfire!?" he shouted at Aven.

The princess scowled indignantly back at him. "Of course I can cast spellfire!" she shouted in return, insulted that he'd even posed the question.

"How do I make him go faster!?" Cadohaden shouted back.

"Thumbs!" Aven screamed. "Both sides of the spine! Closer to the head is faster! Closer to you is slower!"

"Hold on then!" Cadohaden bellowed before turning his head back around, pressing his thumbs on either side of the gryphon's vertebrae, beyond the lion-like fur of his body and into the feathered portion of his head. Glyddiswilm responded to the cue, beating his wings furiously as their pace quickened in a bee line towards the northern gate. The paladin felt the princess clutch at his shoulders once again as the wind rushed at their faces, forcing them to squint against the gust. Another arrow zipped past them, barely missing the gryphon's beak as it sailed through the air. Cadohaden felt the urgency stir in his stomach. The longer they flew over the battle, the more attention they attracted. Gently pulling the reins, he steered Glyddiswilm towards the boiling cauldrons as the wall rapidly approached. He trailed his thumbs down the beast's spine, guiding him to a slower pace before tapping his fingertips against the gryphon's shoulderblades. Glyddiswilm released a shriek as he angled his wings, and Cadohaden was grateful for the flying steed's instincts, for the paladin knew he had misjudged the distance and had come in too fast. The gryphon tucked his hind quarters and beat his wings upward in a furious motion, bringing them roughly onto the battlements of the wall.

The scene was just as chaotic as it had looked from the distance, and the sight of the gryphon landing did nothing to calm it. Men and women pushed each other as captains called out orders. For brief spells, a semblance of organization took hold, only to be disrupted as another boulder struck the wall. There was broken mortar and stone scattered all around, and at least a dozen gruesome blood spatters within twenty feet of their landing, mangled remains protruding from the crimson smears. Cadohaden turned his gaze away from the mutilated dead. If Elune was among them, he couldn't allow himself to see it. Knowing of her demise would unravel all of the courage he had managed to muster.

"What are we doing here!?" Aven shouted at him, clapping against his shoulder as he dismounted in a hurry, Glyddiswilm's beady gaze following him.

"I need to find a pail!" Cadohaden shouted in response, hopping over a crumpled body at his feet, his boot skidding against a sheet of rubble as he landed. He didn't bother to look over his shoulder. He didn't have time to argue with Aven, and so he decided not to give her the opportunity to do so. He weaved around archers as they shouted at one another and him as they pointed to Glyddiswilm. Their yelling was unintelligible to him, however, and he didn't have time for their objections, either. Then, he saw them: two thin metal pails, upturned by an armor rack that had been stripped bare, laying in the dust and loose stone. He started towards them, pushing off against an archer's shoulder that collided against his.

He saw the shadow just in time to dive backward. A sailing stone smashed against the parapet in front of him, rolling backwards to tumble into the fray, sending shards clattering across the rampart. Cadohaden pushed himself to his feet and furiously tried to blink away the mortar dust and stone specks that his eyelids had failed to block out. Tears brimmed along his eyelids as he stumbled towards the pails again, sneaking a peek towards the battlefield to ensure that another projectile rock wasn't going to crush him. Safe for the moment, he ducked down to grab the pails by their handles, examining them. One had a sizable dent along the rim, but it didn't appear to have suffered a fissure in the material. He turned around, colliding once again with a frazzled archer before pushing his way towards the unattended cauldrons.

The coals hadn't been tended to since the beginning of the battle, or so it seemed by their faint, half-hearted glowing. The steam rolling off the surface of the oil was beginning to subside, fading from smoke to thin wisps, dancing from the amber-colored surface. Dipping both of the pails into the liquid, he filled each of them as full as he could manage without constantly slopping it over the rim. He looked back out towards the fray, scanning the sky for any incoming boulders. Seeing none, he jogged back towards Aven and Glyddiswilm, balancing the oil as best he could as he returned to his companions.

Aven was standing in a void in the parapet, the jagged edges left by a boulder like a set of horridly maintained teeth. Her mouth was moving, her hands dancing in spellcasting as Cadohaden approached, though no lightning or fire sparked from her fingertips. The paladin peered over the edge. It took a moment, but he finally spotted her enchantments at work below. Orcs charged towards their human targets, only to bounce abruptly off what seemed to be thin air. She was shrouding a handful of soldiers with invisible, bubble-like barriers, and they seemed to be just as shocked as the orcs as the brutes tumbled backward to the ground. They gathered their senses in short order, however, and lunged forward at their toppled foes, impaling them with swords and spears as they struggled to rise to their feet, the enchanted shields dissipating by the time they reached their target. The princess finally noticed Cadohaden standing beside them, looking down at the pails he held in each hand. "What in the hell is that!?" she shouted.

"Oil!" Cadohaden shouted, handing her a pail as he gestured towards Glyddiswilm, whose feathers were ruffled, head swiveling about in agitation at the chaos around them. Aven accepted the pail with a bewildered frown, helping Cadohaden mount the gryphon once more before hoisting herself on by hanging on to his arm.

"That's not enough to scald Grathul's whole army!" she shouted as the paladin carefully guided Glyddiswilm towards the edge of the battlements. Cadohaden carefully nestled the pail against his thigh, leaning forward to tap his fingertips against the gryphon's shoulder blades. He cast one last hopeful look out across the ramparts, searching for Elune. And then, he saw something that gave him another infusion of hope: a flicker of a blue cloak, disappearing as fast as he'd seen it between the frenzied archers. He couldn't be sure it was her, still among the archers, among the living, but it would have to be enough.

With another shriek, the beast took flight.

"I know, I-" Cadohaden began as they lifted off, but swallowed his words as a boulder lifted off into the air, sailing directly towards them. In a harsh, panicked gesture, he pushed his hands against the back ends of Glyddiswilm's shoulder. The gryphon shrieked again, this time in agitation, but begrudgingly obeyed as it buffeted its wings angrily, carrying them upward as the boulder sailed underneath them. They could feel the air rippling around it as it passed below, and Cadohaden gripped his reins so tightly that the gryphon began to favor towards the right, in the direction that the paladin wasn't holding the bucket of oil. The outside of the pail was slick with the substance that had splashed over the rim, and Cadohaden gritted his teeth while cursing himself.

"Gather your wits, Ulaeron!" Aven shouted into his ear. "What are we *doing* with this!?"

"We're going to set those catapults ablaze!" Cadohaden shouted back, redirecting Glyddiswilm as another arrow hissed past them. He gently pulled on the reins, intentionally this time, guiding the gryphon in a tight semi-circle around the fray. As the gryphon swerved around the chaos, they narrowed in on the catapult positioned furthest to the west. Cadohaden gradually lowered Glyddiswilm closer, his heart skipping a beat as a goblin arrowhead flew by not a foot away from the tip of his nose. The catapult rushed towards them, its supervising troll fumbling for another rock as it craned its brutish head up towards them.

"*Now!*" Cadohaden shouted as they swooped over the siege machine. Pivoting the bottom of the pail against his knee, the paladin tilted the contents towards the gryphon's left, spilling it out in a narrow stream downwards as Aven mimicked him, twin shimmering streams trailing down to land upon the line of catapults. They passed over each one, turning heads in the swarm of warriors around them, the trolls wincing and shaking their heads as droplets of the acrid-smelling oil struck their noses. The paladin could sense the arrows flying at them as they swooped over the catapults, but he set his jaw and did his best to ignore them as they dumped the flammable substance over.

They made it all the way across the length of Grathul's army with just barely enough oil to spatter the last catapult, but it would have to do. There were lieutenants shouting and pointing fingers at them now; their window to pass over again safely was narrowing fast. Cadohaden guided Glyddiswilm in a narrow loop, pointing the gryphon back towards the line of catapults. He looked over his shoulder and shouted at the princess, "Get ready! We're going in!" She nodded absently, only half-listening to his words as she began to murmur the invocation, eyes focused on the targets below. Cadohaden turned back around, dropping the empty pail down towards the war zone below, readying himself for the final pass. He felt her hand tap his shoulder once more as she leaned in to speak.

"Get us as close as you can," she said in a haunting voice, her words light and distant, concentration still possessing her features as the final words sat upon the tip of her tongue, ready to be unleashed. Cadohaden nodded briskly and once more had to resist the urge to tap his heels against the gryphon's flanks. Pressing against Glyddiswilm's shoulderblades and along the beast's vertebrae, the paladin guided the gryphon into a few furious wing buffets as a shriek pierced the sky. Aven's eyelids fluttered as they closed in on the line of catapults once more, her body snapping into a rigid posture as she lowered her hand, pointing a finger downward, leaning at angle while holding Cadohaden's shoulder to anchor herself as she tried to give herself as much distance as she could between the source of the fire and the gryphon's hide.

"*Luma'na*," her voice called out as she concluded the incantation, the words accompanied with a ghostly echo as they were spoken. Just mere feet before they passed over the stolen siege weaponry, a white-hot stem of flame sprouted from the end of her finger, a wreath of fire spilling out towards the ground, bending with the wind as Glyddiswilm soared overhead. The gryphon shrieked in surprise once again as he felt the sudden heat against his flank, but Cadohaden urged him forward as straight as he could manage. Over each of the catapults they passed, the curtain of fire trailing behind them as it poured from Aven's fingertip, clinging to both the siege machines and the heads of orcs that had rallied around them to investigate the substance dropped over them.

Cadohaden didn't dare look behind him as his hands constantly corrected the gryphon's discomfort as they raced across the legions, but he could see from the turning heads and the reaction below that they had to have accomplished something. He felt the exhilaration flood his chest once again, his pride blooming as his ploy came to fruition.

He was abruptly jarred from his distraction, however, as Glyddiswilm suddenly released an agonized shriek, the beast's body lurching at an odd angle, his left wing flailing in a series of half-beats. The gryphon's flight path began to twist as his body cheated to the left. Cadohaden leaned towards the right, trying to counterbalance the weight as he craned his head to look below. They were just passing over the final catapult, and Aven's spellfire was beginning to wane as her face paled from her efforts. He risked a single glance over his shoulder to look at the princess. She seemed to only partially register that they were suddenly descending at a fearfully fast rate. The paladin angled his gaze down, desperately searching for the sign of trouble. As the warring soldiers below drew closer and closer, he spotted the culprit: a goblin arrow shaft, protruding from Glyddiswilm's hide just under where the wing met the shoulder. Blood was beginning to soak through the fur, more blossoming against it with every failed wing flap. Cadohaden cursed, trying anxiously to urge the gryphon back into ascension, but the beast wasn't capable despite his best efforts. They were going down.

"Hold on!" Cadohaden shouted as they descended. He felt Aven's hands grip his shoulders weakly. Suddenly, the ground was mere feet below them. With talons outstretched, Glyddiswilm brought them to a landing on the field of battle, his body flailing awkwardly as he skidded about on only three paws. The sudden stop thrusted both Cadohaden and Aven from their saddle, sending them tumbling to the ground as the gryphon shrieked in pain, his beady eyes darting to and fro in panic.

The paladin grunted as he struck the dirt, a sharp pain lancing through his ribs. He was certain that he'd cracked at least one of them as he pushed himself up to his knees desperately. He rushed over to the weary Aven, helping the princess to her feet as Glyddiswilm hunched on his hind legs, feathers ruffled as the beast stared at the line of orc warriors that were sizing them up. The gryphon had managed to avoid the fray, but had landed no more than fifty feet away from the army's outside edge. For a mere second, Cadohaden realized that this was his only opportunity to run. If he turned away now and ran for the woods outside the barley fields, he might be able to save himself. He might live to see tomorrow.

He dismissed the cowardice from his thoughts, the fighting instinct settling in as he ran over to Glyddiswilm. The gryphon shrieked and tensed as the paladin approached, but ultimately allowed him to inspect the arrow. Cadohaden looked from the wound to the line of orcs. They had spent enough time scrutinizing their target to determine that they were indeed prey for the taking. There wasn't a chance in hell that Cadohaden could extract the arrow and seal the wound before they were on top of them. He needed time. He looked over his shoulder desperately and saw Aven standing nearby, gaze focused on the encroaching orcs. She looked as though she'd had a third of rum all to herself, face drawn and shoulders slumped, feet trudging forward as though there were rocks tied to them.

"Your Grace!" Cadohaden called out as he coiled his hand around the arrow shaft. "I need everything you can give them!"

Even with her glazed eyes and weary face, Aven nodded her head in understanding as the orcs closed in on them. She lifted her hands, the spellcraft upon her tongue once again as she summoned the last of her strength to fight back.

Chapter Thirty

"By the Lifegiver's balls," Sir Ganisalp cursed as he drew his fingers over his brow, peering over the heads of the enemy soldiers. Conflicting feelings raged in his heart. The sight of the fire and smoke rolling from Grathul's stolen catapults not only infused him with hope, but reinvigorated the soldiers as well. He couldn't deny either that his life had been saved only precious moments before. He'd managed to crawl to the safety of the Glen Bailey troops long enough to wheeze air back into his burning lungs. Despite this, part of the general was furious. He'd seen who the gryphon riders were. One was undoubtedly the princess Aven, and the young man with the long blonde hair could be none other than Cadohaden Ulaeron, who was surely responsible for goading Bartholomew's daughter into such a perilous stunt. He'd directly disobeyed orders by not reporting for the call of duty, and had violated the rules of the Glen Bailey's contract with Kaijar Keep by using the gryphon for combat purposes. And though the upstart paladin had given the army the momentum by torching the Arden's Watch catapults, Strigson himself had seen the arrow hit its mark under the gryphon's wing. A sacrifice meant for soldiers was about to be ventured by the only heir to the throne, not to mention the woman that had ruthlessly stolen his heart.

The dividing lines were broken down now, both armies pressing pockets of their troops into one side or the other. A roaring orc came bursting through a tussle of soldiers, lifting a pronged club into the air over the general's head. Strigson rushed forward to meet his assailant, clamping the good fingers in his crippled hand around the warrior's forearm before driving his blade through the brute's chest. Dark blood splashed across his thin beard as it spewed from the greenskin's mouth. The general shoved his foe off of the blade, wiping the mess off on his outer thigh as he looked through the chaos. He'd spotted Crusader Nevic only moments ago as he had collected himself. A Glen Bailey soldier rushed past him with a valiant cry, and as the man brushed past his shoulder, Strigson spotted the pale paladin, fighting his way towards a wounded soldier with his understudy Drevor at his side. Nevic swung his buckler in an arc, smashing the edge of the shield against an orcish helmet, the force powerful enough to crack the skull even through the armor. Drevor lunged forward as his mentor created the opening, clutching the wounded soldier by the arms and dragging him out of the fray. Nevic swung his sword furiously to cover the extraction. Blood was painted across his white mask, and a sizable tear had opened at his right cheek, where blood coagulated around bruised flesh.

"Nevic!" Ganisalp bellowed over the roar of war. The paladin frowned, scanning the violent scene around him before finally finding the source of his spoken name. He lifted his sword in a quick acknowledgment before pressing his way towards the general. Strigson followed suit, shoving his way through the fracas as he moved to meet with the crusader.

"Her Grace has fallen with your ward Ulaeron!" Strigson shouted as the two closed the distance. He pointed a finger towards the western edge of battle. "Their gryphon took an arrow! We have to carve our way through there!"

Nevic steered his gaze towards the direction his general had pointed. Strigson could see the albino's mouth moving with silent mutterings under the mask. The crusader turned back to his general and nodded, shouting from underneath the fabric, "I'll gather my paladins! We'll force our way through the-"

His words cut short as a fresh series of screams suddenly filled the field of battle. The crusader's head turned abruptly toward the sound, and Strigson's followed. The general grit his teeth as he saw the cause of the commotion. No longer under the threat of soaring stones, the Glen Bailey's archers had regrouped upon the battered battlements and had begun firing back on the enemy. However, without any catapults to load stones into, Grathul's trolls were free to focus their attentions on the army before them. There were at least five of the lumbering beasts within eyesight, swinging their massive arms back and forth, their boulder-like fists launching infantrymen into the air as they were struck. If the dividing line of battle had been obscure before, it was now nonexistent as soldiers scrambled to move out of the way, captains shouting orders to regroup.

"*Spears!*" Strigson shouted out as two captains looked back at him for guidance with wide-eyed fear. "Get a spear in every hand! They bleed just as you do!" The general whirled his focus back onto Nevic, who smashed his shield against yet another orc face nearby, cracking the bones beneath. The crusader turned back earnestly to his commanding officer.

"Your orders, sir!?" Nevic called out.

Strigson pursed his lips. The trolls were going to tear them apart if they didn't get some organization happening immediately. But the princess was in immediate danger. He would have to trust his lieutenants to set them on the proper course. He opened his mouth to answer Nevic when something else caught his attention. Turning, he peered into the swarming mess of chaos.

The center of the battlefield had been parted wide open by the introduction of the massive trolls, and in its wake, Grathul Heavyhand emerged from the fray, a gore-soaked axe held in each of his meaty fists. Blood coated the warchief's body, trickling down the exposed muscles in his torso between the straps of his leather harness. Even from where he stood, Strigson could see the inflamed red in the orc's eyes. He knew enough about magic to realize that the warchief had been granted a blood blessing by a warlock, and had likely cut his way through on his own, shredding down Glen Bailey soldiers as if they were standing gunnysacks. Sir Ganisalp spotted the one named Razuk on Grathul's left, holding a tall tower shield, and another he didn't recognize on the warchief's right, equipped with a similar barrier. Their eyes occasionally flitted to the battlefield, but for the most part, their watch was on the battlements, ready to intercept an arrow that came too close to their leader.

Grathul barked a few words in Orcish as they drew nearer, then settled his murderous gaze on Strigson. His voice was tremendous, as if it were being blown through a battle horn. "Grathul kill many to find you, Ganisalp! You! Grathul! Fight just us! No one more!" He pointed one of his dripping axes at the general to make his point, revealing his pointed teeth with his maleficent grin.

Sir Ganisalp turned to look at Nevic over his shoulder as the war raged on around them, arrows sailing back and forth overhead. The albino paladin shook his head. "Don't do it, Strigson, he's bloated on foul magic. He'll tear you apart."

"And if I refuse, he'll cut his way through our forces to find me," the general answered curtly, trying to bolster his courage with bravado as he held out his left hand. "He's letting pride get in his own way; let's use it. Strap your shield to my arm. Get your paladins together and find the princess. I'll buy you as much time as I can."

"Strigson, we can-"

"That's an *order*, Nevic Baltwin," Strigson growled. Too conditioned for obedience to directly defy his commander, the crusader begrudgingly nodded, removing his buckler and strapping it to Ganisalp's arm. The masked man stared hard at the general for a heartbeat before clapping him on his shoulder.

"Lifegiver keep you, Strigson Ganisalp," he said before turning away, pushing through the crowd to find his Monastery forces. The general drew in a deep breath. He could have sworn that his heart was rattling his ribcage with every pulse. With as much spirit as he could harness, he turned back to face the Humanslayer, sword held in one hand, shield strapped to the other. He marched forward to the center of the opening that Grathul had created, his warriors forming the circle, every other one facing opposite directions to prevent the Glen Bailey troops from storming in. Strigson clapped the flat of his sword against the metal disc in the center of his shield.

"Grathul drinks from your skull at king's throne tonight!" the warchief howled, charging forward towards the general. Strigson waited patiently, setting his feet as the musclebound orc stomped forward. He couldn't hope to vanquish the warchief with strength; he'd have to rely on finesse if he wished to live, or at the very least, draw out the skirmish for longer than half a minute. He waited until he could hear the fuming breaths of Grathul, and as the warchief lifted his weapons, Sir Ganisalp pivoted his foot to push himself away.

He stuttered in surprise, however, as the warchief dragged his toe into the ground in a move seemingly too lithe for a brute of his size, resetting his balance as he caught the general off of his, tricked by the feint. Strigson hoisted his shield up out of instinct as Grathul took a swipe at him with an axe, a balanced, concentrated attack as opposed to the bull rush that he'd pretended to open with. The blow staggered Strigson, his feet churning backward as a hunk of wood split from the face of his buckler. He felt massive hands upon his back, and forcibly, they shoved him back towards the center, his arms flailing with the abrupt push. Grathul was waiting for him. Hooking the bottom corner of one of his axes against the back of Strigson's armor, the warchief sidestepped and flung the general towards the opposite end of the circle. Once again, Strigson was met with rough hands as they pushed him backwards this time like a rag doll, sending him toppling into the bloodied dirt below. The wind forced from his lungs, Strigson gasped desperately for air as he clawed his way to his knees.

"This who lead Glen Bailey army?" Grathul growled with mirth as he stepped up in front of the general. Both of the warchief's axes suddenly came down, their edges burying in the dirt as Grathul lifted his hands from the handles. With a defiant snarl, Ganisalp rushed forward in an attempt to skewer the unarmed warchief, but Grathul had already coiled his arm, and as he unwound in a violent backhand, Strigson's vision exploded with dark purple smudges, a high-pitched ringing singing in his head as he staggered numbly towards the edge of the circle. Distantly, he could feel the angry pulsing in the separated bridge of his nose as blood began to leak from the broken skin. He could hear laughter and jeering from some faraway place as he tried to clear his mind. With a couple shakes of his head, his vision began to focus once more. He was staring at the ground, and his nose felt as though it had swelled to double its size. He heard the clomping of boots behind him, and slowly got himself to his feet again, swaying his shoulders from side to side as he turned around with a gaping mouth, sword held loosely at his side as he faced the towering Grathul.

The warchief spit at the ground, as he had before, though it landed on Strigson's boot this time. "Grathul hoped for more," he grunted before walking up to the Glen Bailey's general, lifting a hand to break every bone in his face in a single punch.

It was Strigson who won the contest of guile this time, his movements suddenly awakened as the fist came driving toward him. He didn't just lift his buckler in defense this time; he sailed it in an arc to meet the warchief's knuckles, cracking the center disc against them as they collided. Fighting through the throbbing pain in his head, the general advanced as Grathul faltered in surprise. Strigson moved his feet forward, one step at a time as he encroached, a swing of the blade for every pace. The warchief dodged and retreated, taking careful steps back towards the axes he'd left planted in the soil. As he neared his weapons, Strigson finally struck with the end of his blade, cutting a red line across Grathul's pectoral.

The warchief snarled, but it evolved into a cruel laughter as he plucked the axes from below, gripping them in his hands once more. "Good! Better!" he mocked as he pushed forward once again to meet the general's attacks.

They circled one another, trading blows, deflecting and countering as they sparred. The general found his rhythm as they fought. He was still sorely outmatched by Grathul's strength, but he wouldn't make the grave error of underestimating the warchief's cunning again. He dodged and planted, blocked and jabbed, trying to lull Grathul into a careless step.

It didn't come. As moments passed, Strigson saw the impatience suddenly flicker across the warchief's face. No longer satisfied with their game of cat and mouse, Grathul stormed forward. Strigson lifted his shield, and Grathul shoved it away with an axe. The general lifted his sword to parry, and the warchief swatted it away as well with a keen slash. Mere inches away from Strigson, Grathul launched his head forward, smashing his skull against the general's already broken nose. Pain lanced through his senses once again, his vision completely clouded as he tumbled backwards.

When some semblance of consciousness returned to him, he was staring upward at a smoke-filled sky. His entire face hummed with a stabbing ache as fresh blood poured from the bridge of his nose, rolling over his lips. He could taste the bitter copper on his tongue as the warchief suddenly appeared overhead, the weights in his braid clinking as it slithered down over his shoulder like a serpent. "Your time over, dog," Grathul rumbled. "I send you to afterlife."

Strigson let his eyelids flutter shut. He didn't want the last thing he saw in this life to be Grathul's axe sailing down to split his skull. He thought back to his younger days. He thought about saving Queen Meredith's life from the Draqin assassins. He thought about his father. *I gave it my all, Papa*, he thought. *I followed all the rules. Well, most of them, anyway. All but one. Can you pardon just one?*

The life-ending bite of the axe didn't come, however. Suddenly, a sound like a violent hail storm came from behind him, the pained screams of orcs reaching his dulled senses. He heard a harsh sound above, followed by a grunt from Grathul. He allowed his eyelids to open once again and blinked in surprise as he spotted an arrow shaft protruding from the warchief's shoulder. The fletching was different, however, from the standard Glen Bailey model. Where had he seen that kind of arrow before?

The warchief's lip curled as he glared back down at the general. His arm flexed just as a roar of shouts came from beyond the formed circle. Grathul's head swiveled around just in time to see four cavalry horses come bursting through the barrier. Again, the sound of raining hail came from behind them, and Strigson could hear frenzied shouting among the rabble. Snarling in anger, the Humanslayer retreated as the horses stormed forward, clutching at the arrow as he disappeared once again into the fray, bellowing orders in Orcish as the riders' spears chased him back to the safety of his own.

He peered up blearily at the rider above him as they pushed the visor up on their helm. It was none other than Mya Ness. Whoever had been holding the Glen Bailey standard before had seemingly lost it, for it was Mya that now held the banner of the four leaf cross above her head, the blood-spattered cloth whipping resolutely in the wind.

"What's happening?" the general slurred as he squinted up at her.

"The Sherinalu Vale, sir!" Mya answered as she offered her hand. "Elven archers! And the York hunters! They arrived together, sir, on the eastern flank! They're taking pressure off the front! Come up here, sir, and we'll get you to the clerics! We're not out of this yet!"

Chapter Thirty-One

The flight of despair could only take him so far without a rest. Eliliweth had sprinted for as long as he could manage before settling into a jog, until finally, he could no longer draw breath into his lungs. His legs tensed angrily as he came to a stop at the forest crossroads, leaning against the directional post staked in the ground at the intersection. He sucked in trembling breaths, drawing his sleeve across his sweating brow, the curled locks in his hair glistening with perspiration. His kingdom wasn't much further ahead, but his legs would simply not carry him another step. He murmured quiet prayers to his goddess for renewed strength, but if she was listening, she did not grant him immediate rejuvenation. He placed his hands on his knees, waiting for the faintest sign of strength to return to him. Whatever was wrong in the Glen Bailey, he wasn't sure how he was going to contribute. He was exhausted and unarmed. He could only hope that the omen he had witnessed was merely a fluke, and that his homesickness had somehow transformed into an acute paranoia.

He heard a thumping sound in the distance, off the opposite path that forked from the one leading back to the White Forest. The half-elf's eyes widened a little as he straightened himself, peering down the path that the sound was originating from. Indecision tore at him. Should he hide? He looked behind him at the trees surrounding the trail. They were widely spaced in this part of the woods, with little brush for additional cover. The best he could hope for was to find a wide tree.

He waited too long to determine his next move, for several figures suddenly emerged around the bend deeper into the forest. It was a whole battalion, each on a saddled horse as they stormed through the woods as quickly as they dared. Eliliweth spotted two banners raised above the leading soldiers' heads. It was a dark blue banner with a bicolored shield, the sigil of the Eastfen Protectorate. The half-elf released a shaky sigh of relief as he recognized the crest. He did not know what King Rhone's soldiers were riding through for, but he counted himself lucky that they were not a traveling band of raiders. He lifted his arm as they drew closer, flagging them down on the side of the trail. The man in the center, between the two standard bearers, lifted his hand in a halting signal. The battalion came to a quick stop in front of the half-elf. The man seemingly in charge looked down with a curious frown as his steed took a moment to catch his breath, shaking his long black mane. The man had suntanned skin and hair similar to his horse's, including two long ebon tails at each end of his mustache. "And who are you to call for our halt?" he demanded.

"I am Eliliweth Heraketh, Advisor-Elect to King Bartholomew Celandine's royal court," the half-elf breathed laboriously, still trying to recall his composure as he wiped sweat from his brow once more. "I only just today finished undergoing the Trials of the White Forest, as commanded by my king. I saw..." He paused, wondering if it was wise to tell this man the truth, or if he would be considered a mad drifter. He wasn't sure how else to explain his haste, however, and so he confessed, "...I saw an omen upon leaving the Forest. I feared I must return home at once. You are from the Eastfen Protectorate, are you not? Are you heading in the direction of the Bailey?"

The long mustached man stared at the half-elf scrutinizingly for a moment, as though he were judging Eliliweth's sanity. Finally, after a stiff nod, he answered, "I am Captain Dak Pondrake, cousin to the late general Vick Pondrake, and we are indeed from the Protectorate. If you speak the truth, Eliliweth Heraketh, then you read your omen correctly. King Landen Rhone received word by raven that a great army from the Hordelands was descending upon Bartholomew's lands, and that aid was requested. We are the detachment that was far enough east to answer the call and embark immediately."

Eliliweth's face paled as Dak recounted the message. "By the Goddess, an *army* from the Hordelands? They specified an *army*?"

Dak's expression curdled at the question. "I am certain that they specifically stated it to be an 'army', yes. Do you think they would have called for aid so urgently for anything less?"

"No," Eliliweth said, shaking his head, "of course not. I apologize, Sir Pondrake. Please, will you let me ride with you? I can show you the way."

"I assure you that I know the way, Master Eliliweth," Dak answered indignantly with a vain toss of his hair. "But yes, we will bring you with us. Are you armed?"

"No, sir," Eliliweth admitted as he straightened his posture.

"Then you shall have a Protectorate bow," Dak answered formally. "If you ride with us, you fight with us! A steed and a bow for Master Eliliweth, on the double!" In a matter of mere seconds, a mounted rider rode up to the front, guiding a riderless horse forward by its reins. Eliliweth gratefully pulled himself up onto the saddle and looked over his shoulder. He saw both a sturdy longbow and quiver being passed forward from rider to rider as it made its way towards the front. The man who had guided the horse was the last to take it before handing it to the half-elf with a businesslike nod.

"You will ride in the second row, behind me, Master Eliliweth," Dak said in a manner that left no questions to be asked. "Protectorate, move out!"

Eliliweth felt his soul catch fire once more as the trees breezed past them without the churning effort of his legs. The feeling was quickly squelched, however, as he remembered Dak's words. A Hordeland army upon the Glen Bailey? The orcs had not united as more than clan raiding parties for as long as he had been alive. He had no doubt that the situation was dire, however, if Bartholomew had called out for assistance.

The battalion burst from the forest line in less than a half hour's time, the trees giving way to the bountiful fields of barley. Eliliweth's heart only twisted more painfully in his chest as they neared his home kingdom. He could smell the battle before he could hear it over the pounding hooves of the Eastfen horses. The stench of smoke and blood coupled with the scent of burning hair and flesh was rolling out from the battlefield and met their noses as the autumn gale greeted them upon arrival. The half-elf's eyes widened, mouth parting as the walls of the Glen Bailey came into view.

It was like a black, oozing sore that pockmarked the fields outside the city. From where they were, it was difficult to decipher which was orc and which was human, the war zone a swarming chaotic nest. He could see trolls towering above them both, however, and a few taller brutes that stood not quite as high but were still recognizable as the lumbering Hordeland ogres. A line of fire smoldered near the back end of the orc forces, the smoke billowing towards the sky in dark putrid plumes. There were archers upon the walls, but Eliliweth could see the tell-tale signs of siege weaponry, the parapets smashed in several places like a mouth with broken teeth, charred marks and deep cracks visible along the wall.

There was something odd closest to them, however, causing the half-elf to narrow his eyes as their horses stormed forward. He could make out a struggle, but there was a creature on all fours, seemingly bent over, with two other figures tangled with at least three times as many. He could begin to make out orcs as they closed in on the battlefield. They seemed to be tripping backwards as they neared the two other figures, blocked by some invisible force.

"Sound the horn!" Dak Pondrake shouted, pulling a falchion from a sheath and pointing it at the enemy army. "The Protectorate are here, to help defend their allies in the Glen Bailey! Archers, ready!"

Eliliweth drew his bow as the battalion ascended a small earthen hill, giving them an advantageous point to barrage the enemy with a volley of arrows. As he pulled an arrow from his borrowed quiver, he suddenly recognized the strange figures lingering at the edge of the fray. It was a gryphon, and the assaulting orcs weren't just tripping on thin air. Aven Celandine was defending the beast, her actions wooden and weary as she flung her arms with her spellcasting. The half-elf couldn't spot the face of the man who stood beside her, sword slashing furiously at the savage brutes, but Eliliweth recognized the teal cape billowing behind him. It was the princess and Cadohaden Ulaeron, isolated from friendly forces, defending a gryphon that looked visibly wounded. "Wait!" Eliliweth called out, slackening the string on his bow. "That's the princess Aven Celandine, by the gryphon! We can't risk arrows with her in the crossfire!"

Dak scrunched up his face, his long mustache twitching as he did so. For a tense moment, Eliliweth thought the captain might spit back at him with resentment for questioning his order, but the reaction was something else entirely. Spurred by the notion of saving a kingdom's princess, the Protectorate captain's chest swelled with masculine fervor. "You are certain that is King Bartholomew's daughter?" he called out over his shoulder.

"Yes!" Eliliweth shouted in exasperation and anxiety, for he could see Aven stumbling backwards ahead of them, falling to the ground as Cadohaden made an awkward off-balance lunge to keep her protected.

"Then we go to her side at once! Draw your swords, men! For the Protectorate! For King Rhone! For Eastfen!" Pondrake shouted with dramatic gusto, once again hoisting his falchion into the air. The soldiers behind him echoed the sentiment, their battle cries united as it evolved into a surging roar as their captain lead them onward, hooves thundering once again as they galloped towards the fray.

"*Chaaaaaaarge!*" Dak's voice bellowed as they descended upon the orcs. The Hordeland warriors lifted their heads as the Eastfen horses closed in, most of them scurrying back in surprise. Three of them, however, stood their ground with spears held in hand. The battalion churned forward, just missing Aven and Cadohaden as the paladin pulled the princess away from the rampage of hooves.

Steel flashed and sung in clashing chimes as falchion met spear, orcs grunting and howling in agony as they were trampled by the reinforcements. The Protectorate gained ground immediately for the Glen Bailey's cause, shoving the western line back as they withdrew into their swarming numbers. Looking over his shoulder, Eliliweth broke ranks, veering to his right to circle back towards his friends. He didn't know what Dak Pondrake would think of his detour, but it was the least of concerns for the moment. The only heir to the throne was on the ground, with only Cadohaden standing over her as the battalion barreled into the orc hordes. He slowed the Eastfen steed to a trot as he approached the two, hurriedly dismounting as his feet landed on the ground lightly.

Whether by intention or accident, an orc soldier suddenly stumbled towards the half-elf, breaking through the ranks. The brute's full weight smashed against Eliliweth, and he shouted in pain as he stumbled backwards, his shoulder humming with irritation as he landed in the dirt near the gryphon. The warrior turned his greenskinned head down towards the half-elf. He had long black hair, similar to Dak Pondrake's, though it was braided with bone ornaments and was considerably dirtier. In one hand he held the handle to a wicked-looking war axe. The brute grinned and took it in both hands. "When you find afterlife, little hare, tell souls you meet Ganshu'Dai sent you," he mocked in rough Commonspeak, lifting the axe over his head. His eyes quickly darted to the side, however, as an Eastfen horse came charging towards them. The warrior snarled and instead swiped the weapon at the steed's leg with a gruesome bone-cracking snap, sending the beast tumbling to the ground, its rider screaming in panic as he was trapped beneath the beast.

The half-elf pushed himself through the dirt backwards as fast as he could, away from the Ganshu'Dai that hovered near him. A shortsword was pressed into the dirt nearby, its crossguard broken on one side, the blade itself bent at a slight angle. It would have to do. Eliliweth snatched it up in the hand opposite from the shoulder the orc had slammed into. The encrusted dirt flaked away under his grasp as he got to his feet, holding it defensively in front of him. A figure was suddenly at his left, a blade held out as well. It was Cadohaden, his blonde hair plastered to his sweat-coated face, cheeks billowing with exerted breaths as he approached Ganshu'Dai.

"Hah!" the orc snorted before bringing the axe down upon the head of the Eastfen soldier trying to claw his way out from underneath his horse. The blade split through the man's helmet and cleaved his skull before Ganshu'Dai deftly yanked the weapon back, its edge glistening with the evidence of its kill. The brute began advancing on them with a hungry grin but stopped as a battle horn suddenly boomed across the battlefield.

Ganshu'Dai turned his head with a smoldering glare towards the sound of the noise. He turned back to glower at Eliliweth and Cadohaden, spitting in their direction before turning away, running back in towards the center of the orcish masses. Eliliweth blinked in confusion, looking out once again beyond the battle line in front of them. The horn seemed to be an orcish signal, as the Hordeland warriors were mobilizing in response. They didn't seem to be retreating, but they were certainly cloistering together, gathering in the center of the swarm in a defensive formation. It didn't take long for the half-elf to see why. The arrows from the Bailey walls were still falling in droves, and though the reinforcements from Eastfen were a small force, their sudden presence had caught the orcs' army off-guard. There was something else, too. On the other side of the battlefield, he could see arrows coming in from another direction as well. It seemed Eastfen was not the only ally to answer Bartholomew's call for aid.

"Goddess bless us," Eliliweth said, wincing as he grasped his shoulder, dropping the warped sword to the ground. "We're dictating their formations. We can win this." He looked back over at the paladin with a grim smile. "It's good to see you, friend, though I didn't think it would be like this."

"You're hurt," Cadohaden said with a worried furrow of his brow. "Here, let me just…" Awkwardly, the young paladin placed two hands on the half-elf's shoulder, face eskew in concentration as he began to murmur a prayer. Eliliweth looked over his shoulder and saw Aven still slumped on the ground near the gryphon, whose feathers had ruffled in agitation as its avian head darted back and forth at the commotion.

"Don't waste time with healing, Ulaeron, it only needs to be popped back into place," Eliliweth said. He tried his best to sound patient, though it was difficult given the circumstances.

"Bloody Lifegiver, of course, right," Cadohaden said, shaking his head in embarrassment as a rallying cry boomed from the battlefield once again. He grasped the half-elf by the shoulder and elbow, and after a pained grunt from Eliliweth, it was back in its rightful socket. Not waiting for an affirmation, the half-elf hurried over to Aven's side, kneeling down beside her. Cadohaden followed briskly, crouching beside him as well.

"She's not wounded," he said with a breathless attempt at assurance. "Just…exhausted. We flew over their catapults and she set every last one of them ablaze."

Eliliweth angled a look from the gryphon back to Cadohaden. "You *flew* over them?"

"Yes, I know, they're not supposed to be used for fighting battles," Cadohaden answered in exasperation, looking back at the gryphon as well before looking back at Eliliweth. "Watch over her, and I will heal Glyddiswilm. Nobody has to know."

You flew over the whole damn army, Ulaeron, who do you think won't know? Eliliweth thought to himself instead of speaking the words. A mere fifty feet away, a brutal battle was still ensuing. He didn't have time to argue with Cadohaden. "Go, then," he said simply before turning his attention back to Aven. The paladin frowned, as if he were hoping Eliliweth would admit the logic in his intentions, but he stood up anyway, perhaps realizing the futility of debate as well. He hustled over to the gryphon to tend to the protruding arrow under the beast's wing.

"'Lil'weth," the princess murmured as she looked up at him with an unfocused gaze. "You returned."

"I did," Eliliweth answered, swallowing. As Cadohaden had told him, she didn't appear to be wounded, but her efforts had sapped all of her energy. She looked as though she'd run from the White Forest to the Glen Bailey and back again.

"The magistrates," she murmured as she sat up on her elbows. "They betrayed the crown." She paused, a shadow gradually passing over her weary face. "I betrayed the crown," she whispered.

"Magistrates? What..?" Eliliweth said in confusion. "Look, Your Grace, we can speak of all this later. Right now we need to-"

"Wasn't mad at you about the White Forest," she murmured, lifting her hand up to pinch the bridge of her nose. "I swear on the Goddess. What was it like?" She turned to look blearily at him, her conversation casual. It was like she didn't even register the carnage only paces away.

Eliliweth opened his mouth, his expression incredulous, but he didn't get the chance to answer, as suddenly, soldiers of the Glen Bailey began to rush towards them, pouring from a forced opening in the battle. Crusader Nevic Baltwin was leading the charge, his white clothing peppered with red, his mask hanging from his face in tattered shambles. The half-elf recognized several of the Monastery paladins behind the albino crusader as the marble statue of a man rushed towards them, leading his detachment. Eliliweth looked over his shoulder with trepidation at Cadohaden. The arrow was out, and it looked as though the young paladin had mostly healed the wound left by it, but Eliliweth wasn't sure that would save him from Nevic's ire.

"Your Grace!" Nevic shouted as he knelt down in front of the princess. "Speak to me! Are you well?"

"M'fine," Aven murmured, waving her hand dismissively. Behind the crusader, several paladins cloistered together to block the way of a rampaging orc that was ignoring the rallying call of the battle horn, his axe swinging wildly.

"She's just spent, Crusader," Cadohaden said as he approached the gathering, wiping a lock of hair from his face. "She should be taken to safety, however, I don't think she can defend herself any longer."

"I am not helpless," Aven growled, though the weakness in her voice betrayed her claim.

"Ulaeron," Nevic said, his voice low at first as the crusader stood up to his full height. Eliliweth watched the man rise up with a sense of dread.

"Crusader, I-"

"You *what*, Ulaeron!?" Nevic shouted, marching up to his young prospect, staring down at him. He stood a whole head taller than Cadohaden. "You *what!?* Deliberately disobeyed orders!? Put the life of Bartholomew's daughter in grave danger!? You are lucky it is *me* standing before you now, for if it was Sir Ganisalp, he would have you knelt down and beheaded for treason!"

"Treason!?" Cadohaden exclaimed. "What?"

"Stop," Aven piped up from her sitting position, a tired sigh escaping her. Her words were visibly reluctant as she spoke them. "I am just as guilty as he is, and he saved my life from Bertram Archibaum up on the aviary."

"Archibaum? What's he got to do with anything?" Nevic snapped.

"Enough!" Eliliweth bellowed with authority as he rose to his feet. The debate was spiraling out of control at the worst possible time. The captain of the Ashland patrol took over in the half-elf. And while he was not officially Bartholomew's Royal Advisor just yet, he was not going to let formality stop him from acting like one. "Our men and women are dying out there while we squabble. This can all be sorted out later. Nevic, what were your *specific* orders regarding Her Grace?"

The crusader looked surprised by the half-elf's sudden commanding presence, remaining speechless for a few seconds before finally responding. "We were to locate her and extract her if alive. If she...if she wasn't, we were to wait here for a signal from the battlements. Ganisalp is calling for a final push for their warchief's head. He's calling in the reserves from the inner city militias and is pulling down half of the posted archers. They will open the gate soon, and we were to attack the flank at that time."

"An excellent plan," Eliliweth affirmed. "And we can do both. You there," the half-elf said, pointing to a man he was fairly certain was Drevor, but it was hard to tell with the helmet that rested on his head. "If the gryphon is healed, take Her Grace and fly her back. Bring her directly to the keep before returning the beast to the aviary. Give the battle a wide berth; there's no need to risk another arrow. We will not lose her this day."

"At once," the man responded, immediately stooping down to assist the princess, despite her protests that she was fine and should continue fighting.

"Crusader," Eliliweth said to Nevic, not missing a beat. "Get your men into formation. Cavalry first, infantry bringing up the rear. If the reserves are going to be the anvil, we will be the hammer."

"Yes...sir," Nevic said, the title rolling off his tongue in a hesitant manner. It was only a brief pause, however. The crusader began to bark orders as Glyddiswilm took off into the air once more, with the paladin and Aven upon his saddle.

"I did not realize when we found you that you had such a soldier's presence, Master Eliliweth," Dak Pondrake said as his horse trotted towards the half-elf. Eliliweth could see the Eastfen Protectorate regrouping a few paces nearby as they backed off from the retreating orcs. The captain grinned through his mustache. "The Protectorate will charge at your command, if you wish it."

"It would be an honor, Sir Pondrake," the half-elf answered, chest swelling with gratitude. "Line your men up beside ours. We'll batter through their ranks together."

"Take this Protectorate blade," Dak said, handing down a falchion to the half-elf. "It is good to see why Eastfen calls the Glen Bailey a friend. Wield it with honor."

Eliliweth's fingertips tingled with excitement. It wasn't the thrill of command that was igniting his senses. It was the unraveling of dread from his heart as the defensive plans seemed to be coming together. He took his position in the first row of infantry behind the horses that Nevic had brought with, gesturing for Cadohaden to follow him as he did so. He didn't truly think there was enough animosity for anyone to deliberately harm the young paladin, but he wasn't certain that the others among them would give their full strength towards protecting him. He wasn't quite sure what the Kingsbanesin exile had gotten himself into, but he was still the half-elf's friend, and he knew they would both fight hard for one another's safety as they drove into the Hordeland menace.

As Glyddiswilm passed over the walls of the city, the horns from the northern gate sounded, signaling the unleashing of the reserves and the archers that had converted to infantrymen. At their angle, it was difficult to see the heads of the soldiers pouring out from the gate, but Eliliweth could clearly see the doors swing slowly open. And hovering above them, another four leaf cross banner furled in the air. A resounding war cry echoed from the gates as the Glen Bailey forces congealed once more, forming a spear of fighting bodies as they surged towards the line of Hordeland warriors, who had clustered together in a defensive circle in the center of the battlefield.

"This is it!" Eliliweth shouted to the paladins that Nevic had rallied and the Protectorate detachment. "This is where the heathens meet their end! Forward! Break through their lines! Death to the Hordelands' warchief! Glory to the Glen Dale! Glory to King Bartholomew! *Attack!*"

The ground shook with the pounding hooves and boots as their combined battalion stormed forward, their voices blending together in a whirlwind of vigor. One last time, they surged towards the enemy, to their menacing visages and barbaric weapons. The enduring cry continued all the way until they met the enemy, the sounds of collision ringing with the war cries in a brutal harmony of battle.

It was just the push that the Glen Bailey needed to disrupt Grathul's forces. Whether it was the faltering faith of the orcs that had been called into a conservative formation, or the enthusiasm of the Bailey soldiers that had forced the orcs' hand, the flanking assault buried into the swarm of barbarians. Eliliweth and Cadohaden quickly found synchronization, cutting down the enemy with a rhythm of coordinated blocks and slashes, timing the reaction of the orcs to determine who would parry and who would strike. On and on they pushed, the promise of victory bolstering every soldier of the Glen Bailey as they muscled their way towards the center of the masses.

As blood and screams filled the field of strife, it seemed as though the resurgent Glen Bailey forces might carve right through the center of Grathul's forces. The relentless meat grinder came to a halt, however, as they pushed their way into the eye of the storm. Circling around the oculus of the Hordeland leaders like an iris, the massive trolls had closed in around Grathul and the army's elite. The hulking brutes almost made their defense look effortless, some simply swinging their arms like battering pendulums, while at least three others wielded tremendous clubs that looked almost as big as uprooted trees. The assault was coming to a gruesome stalemate as row by row the Glen Bailey forces were repelled by the stalwart ring of trolls. As the gridlock became obvious, the orc warriors surrounding the burrowing Bailey forces became bolder, rushing the infiltrating forces with newfound zeal.

"Back to back!" Eliliweth shouted, ordering the soldiers into defensive formations of their own. The half-elf could see the assault from the reserves less than twenty paces away, mired in the sea of orcs as they attempted to defend their stalled forces as well.

"Eliliweth!" Cadohaden shouted nearby, blocking a swinging blade from an enemy soldier and pressing the orc towards the half-elf, the brute's left flank exposed. "We can't stay here! We'll get massacred!"

The half-elf gritted his teeth and slashed at the orc's side, cutting a gaping wound into his flesh. He shoved another away from him as one stumbled backward from the blow of a hefty warhammer. He darted his gaze across the battlefield. The momentum was changing again. If they retreated now, they would lose all the ground they had gained so quickly, but if they could not penetrate the ring of troll defenders, they would all be butchered within minutes.

Just as the order to pull back began to dance on the tip of his tongue, something strange caught his eye in the direction of Ganisalp's forces. At first, it was just the abrupt motion of bodies being tossed in various directions, seemingly without a source. But then Eliliweth saw it.

A demon was walking through the chaos, the horned head of Terodar Soulrender marching through the torrent of soldiers, pale hands extended outward as he cleared his way through, invisible forces launching those that got in his way into the swarm around him. Behind the demon, a trail of blood followed him, snaking out from underneath the bodies that littered the field, tracking him as though he held the end with an unseen leash. Soldiers from both the Glen Bailey and orc alike paused as they peered curiously at him, neither side seeming to know whether he was friend or foe.

Terodar came to a halt before the circle of trolls, lifting his red gaze to the hulk that narrowed his dim eyes at him. More and more fighters paused in their skirmishing to watch in anticipation as the demon turned his palm over in a languid movement, fingers curled slightly. The river of blood that had tailed him suddenly crept forward as the demon's lips moved in a harsh incantation. It pooled at Terodar's hoof before snaking up his leg in a spiraling pattern, thickening as it traveled up his limb. It continued to slither around him, absorbing more of the crimson liquid as it partially coagulated, coiling around his waist, his torso, and over his shoulder until it finally traveled all the way down his arm, It gathered in his resting palm, writhing into a ball like a serpent.

Terodar bowed his head, lips nearly touching the squirming mass as he murmured the sealing invocation. As he pulled his horned head away, a white, fleshy cobra-like fang began to protrude from the end of the crimson serpent. Suddenly, the parasitic-looking blood worm began to levitate upon the demon's palm before circling around his slender hand in a slow orbit.

The demon lifted his chin, smiled cruelly, and then pointed a spider-like finger at the troll standing in front of him. "*Dro*," he said, and the blood snake launched forward, flying across the distance with the fang extended, its tail twisting behind it in its flight. The troll released a panicked grunt as he tried to shuffle out of the way, but the lumbering creature was far too slow. The parasite buried its fang into its thick hide in the upper pectoral, and without hesitation, began to burrow itself into the skin.

The strange ritual seemed to keep the fighters within eyesight of the spectacle spellbound as they watched in grim horror. The troll cried out in pain and panic, one of its meaty fists reaching to pull the parasite out like a leech as his kinsmen looked at him in wary helplessness. The snake was too slick, however, sliding right through the troll's fingers as he desperately clawed at it. Within seconds, the writhing tail disappeared beneath the skin, leaving a bleeding gouge on the troll's chest.

The after effects began before anyone could decide to interfere. Anxious eyes from both sides of the battle stared as the troll doubled over with an agonized groan. The great hulk suddenly began to heave, vomit releasing from his mouth, splashing the ground below as his groans turned into howls, his breathing coming in whimpering gasps as his dimwitted eyes stared pleadingly at Terodar. The demon only smirked in response, clenching his fist as he murmured once again.

Eliliweth's eyes widened as he watched the tortured troll. It was subtle at first, but at a quickening rate, the half-elf could see the changes evolving. Its skin was darkening, and as the seconds passed, he realized that it was swelling as well, not just in localized spots, but the *entire* troll was ballooning, his face turning blue as a strangled scream escaped him. "Get down!" Eliliweth screamed, grabbing Cadohaden with one hand and a nearby Eastfen soldier with the other, pulling them down to the ground as others followed suit hesitantly, confusion riddled on their faces.

It was the most horrendous sound that had ever violated Eliliweth's senses. The troll's ululating tortured bellow was suddenly accompanied by the sound of ripping flesh. The half-elf risked a peek at the grisly scene and immediately regretted it. Muscles and blood were becoming exposed across the troll's bloated body. The lumbering creature's tongue was choking him, swollen to three times its size in his jaws. And then, with a horrifyingly visceral snap, the unfortunate troll burst.

Violet-colored blood sprayed in all directions, but the trolls standing next to the victim were completely coated. Wrenching cries of agony suddenly filled the battlefield from both the trolls and some of the orcs behind them that the trolls were protecting, and Eliliweth quickly saw why. The blood that had burst from the troll was corrosive, eating away at their flesh like an acid.

Chaos ruled once more as the howling trolls broke formation, stumbling their way into the fray, exposing the warchief they'd been protecting. And there, behind the swarm of panicked bodies, Eliliweth caught a glimpse of Grathul Heavyhand. The shaved scalp with the isolated braid matched the scouting reports he'd read in the past. The warchief was quickly shedding layers of armor as the singing blood ate away at them.

The fracas broke out again. Cadohaden lifted Eliliweth to his feet, and the two began the process again. Block, strike, parry, strike. The half-elf nodded his head towards Grathul, shouting at the paladin, "We should strike him down now!"

Cadohaden nodded and began to speak, but another horn blasted through the air. Angry bellows suddenly sounded out as Grathul began shouting orders, waving his axes as the warchief desperately tried to rally his panicked vanguard, but it was all in vain. The trolls that had been splashed by the cursed blood were still rampaging through the fray blindly as spear points and arrows littered their hides. A lane suddenly began to clear between the half-elf and the warchief. Eliliweth drew his bow and reached for an arrow. "Cover me!" he called out to Cadohaden.

The sound of stampeding hooves reached his ears as the paladin nodded, buying the half-elf time as he lashed out at a squat orc with an oddly squared head. Eliliweth drew an arrow, pointing it at Grathul. From his peripheral vision, he could see horses storming through the fray once again, charging towards the opening left in the wake of Terodar's gruesome spell. It was Strigson Ganisalp leading the charge, sword point hoisted into the air.

The half-elf drew a breath. Time began to slow as he aimed, drawing his gaze to the warchief, whose face was quickly paling at the sight of the incoming assault. As Grathul began to turn, Eliliweth released the arrow. It sailed gracefully through the open lane, narrowly missing the shoulderguard of a stumbling orc warrior as it plunged towards its target.

It struck low, but was just as effective. The arrowhead sunk through the hide covering the warchief's legs, shredding through and penetrating the flesh on the outer thigh. Eliliweth could hear Cadohaden calling out to him with impatience, but he couldn't bring himself to look away, the scene playing out for him like a casually recalled story. Grathul winced and faltered, hand falling to the protruding arrow. It was a mere second that Eliliweth had bought the Glen Bailey's general, but it was all Strigson needed. The distance closed between him and Grathul, the point of the general's blade flashing like the tooth of a grinning dragon as it swiped, the horse he was riding carrying him to his target as the steel point dragged across the Humanslayer's neck, severing the carotid artery as Grathul's axes lifted to defend himself a moment too late. Blood pumped furiously from the warchief's muscular neck as Strigson's horse barreled into the orcs behind Grathul, its rider's blade still swinging victoriously.

The spirit of the enemy seemed to evaporate across the entire battlefield as cheers erupted from the Glen Bailey soldiers. The orc witnesses howled in grief and anger as they shouted to one another, the news of their slain warchief spreading rapidly. The fighting continued, but it was the Glen Bailey's victory to claim. A triumphant chant had already begun to echo across the fields, and as the Hordeland forces became increasingly scattered, many began to retreat, snarling curses as they turned to flee to the northern forests. The sentiment was contagious. The more that retreated, the more followed in their footsteps as orc, ogre, goblin and the two trolls that had survived the demon's spell began lumbering away from the battlefield, swords and arrows at their backs as they fled. *Hya! Hya! Hya!* the enduring chant from the Glen Bailey soldiers echoed.

Eliliweth drew an arrow, looking for one final target as the hordes scurried away. His eyes caught the sight of the long-haired orc that had taunted him, the Ganshu'Dai that had promised to send him to the afterlife. He was taking one last look back as his brethren fled around him, nostrils flaring as he snorted in anger, his war axe still dripping with the blood of Eliliweth's people. The half-elf gritted his teeth and pulled the arrow back on the bowstring, taking aim as he focused.

Ganshu'Dai spotted the half-elf from where he stood, a sour grin forming on his face before the orc spat in his direction, finally turning away and fleeing with his kin. Eliliweth released the arrow and cursed, immediately feeling the extra pull he'd exerted. The arrow missed the retreating Ganshu'Dai, sailing left of him and sinking into a shield that was slung over the back of another. Eliliweth silently chided himself, but he couldn't feel too upset. The roars of victory were still singing around him, a sound of battle-born triumph. Cadohaden ran up to him, a beaming smile on his face as he clapped a rough hug around the half-elf. "We did it!" he shouted, voice bordering on hysteric joy. "We did it, Eliliweth!"

"We did, friend," Eliliweth said softly, returning the embrace as he clapped his hand against Cadohaden's back. Everywhere from where they stood to the gates of the Glen Bailey, he saw weapons hoisted into the air, men and women screaming themselves hoarse as they celebrated the retreat. It didn't seem possible, but the volume only grew louder as Strigson Ganisalp rode back through the legions, the dripping, severed head of Grathul Heavyhand skewered to the end of his lifted sword, face frozen in a dying snarl, defiant even after death.

The army slowly gravitated towards the general as Strigson lead his steed back towards the gates. Cadohaden clapped him on the back enthusiastically as they followed the cheering mob, but Eliliweth only smiled gently, for though he had never been in a battle of such proportions, he'd read many tales that recounted the bittersweet emotions following a hard-fought victory. There was elation in abundance to be found, but the return home was also sorrowful, for paving the way back to friends and loved ones was a road filled with the bodies of those who had given their lives to make it so. He felt like he was in a dream state as he moved among the river of soldiers parading back towards the gates. There were still men among the battlefield swinging weapons, bringing release to the orcs who were still dying upon the soil. There were clerics and paladins hovering among the wounded, some of them bestowing healing prayers, others shaking their heads sadly as they saw deaths they knew they could not reverse. And there, kneeling on the ground as jubilated men walked around them, were soldiers that cradled the bodies of those they had lost. Eliliweth's heart ached as he saw a face he recognized. A young man named Enrik

Landrusson sat before the body of his father Jonn, holding him in his arms as he wept openly. The half-elf leaned over to give Enrik's shoulder a brief squeeze as he passed by in a show of support, though he knew very well there was nothing he could yet say that would comfort Enrik. He would let him have his time to grieve and save the accolades of Jonn's service for the funerals that would come.

Angry voices suddenly broke out amongst the cheers. Eliliweth frowned as he and Cadohaden stopped, searching for the noise. The half-elf saw flickers of white cloth and immediately broke out into a run, the young paladin at his side as they raced forward. There, kneeling on the bloody soil in the center of an opening in the masses, Terodar Soulrender knelt, snarling angrily as he waved his arms in a fury. Five of the Monastery's paladins, Nevic Baltwin included, stood over the demon, their hands illuminated with the Lifegiver's power as they pinned Terodar to the ground, the holy energies burning his skin, leaving angry blisters along his flesh.

"Stop! Stop, what the hell are you doing!?" Cadohaden said as he rushed forward, pushing his way through the throng. "He *fought* for us! Didn't you see it? He exposed Grathul for us!" His hand reached out to grab Nevic's arm. The crusader whirled around, flinging Cadohaden backward before pointing a finger at the demon.

"Order him to hold still! Give the order! *Now!*" Nevic demanded.

Cadohaden looked from Nevic to Terodar, still writhing on the ground snarling in rage as the blessed energies from the paladins kept him pinned to the ground. Just as the crusader opened his mouth to bellow once again, Cadohaden conceded, shouting with a helpless air at the demon. "Hold still, Terodar!" The effect was immediate. Obediently, the demon grew stiff, though his face was still contorted with seething anger. The paladins hovered around him warily for a moment, looking at Nevic for confirmation to stand down. The albino man stared hard at Terodar for a long moment before giving the paladins a curt nod. He turned back on Cadohaden, a bulging vein visible through a tear in his mask. As the crusader began to shout, Strigson Ganisalp rode his horse up to the opened circle, face darkening as he listened.

"You exposed your fellow soldiers, not to mention the Glen Bailey's citizens, to a demon! You steal a gryphon from the aviary and put Princess Aven in peril! Do you have any idea how many levels of disobedience and neglect you've committed, Ulaeron!?"

"Sir, I only thought-"

"Halt your tongue!" Nevic cut him off. "This isn't just military code you've broken! You've violated *laws*, Ulaeron, laws that stretch beyond the Glen Dale borders. Did you not consider any of this!?"

"Crusader," Eliliweth interjected, "The princess spoke to me of strange things when I found her by the gryphon. I think there's more to this than just disobedience."

"Be that as it may," Strigson said from atop his horse, the head of Grathul still staring blindly at those surrounding them, "Nevic speaks the truth. Laws were violated here. From what I can tell, however, they were committed out of recklessness, not malice. Wouldn't you say so, Ulaeron?"

Cadohaden frowned indignantly, clearly not wanting to agree to the 'reckless' nature of anything he'd done, but he seemed to have enough sense not to argue with the general. "Yes, sir," he said begrudgingly.

"Then I won't have you thrown in the dungeons, though I'd consider yourself lucky that your gambles proved to end in your favor," Strigson said, turning his gaze to the demon still laying on the ground on all fours before angling it back to Cadohaden. "We will have Archmage Benton come find you. You will order the demon to obey his commands as well as yours once again. He will bring him back to the Mage House where he belongs, and *you* will report directly to the Monastery to await further orders from Crusader Nevic. There will be a trial, Ulaeron, I assure you."

"The rest of you," Ganisalp called out, turning his horse at an angle to face the bulk of the crowd. The exaltation on his face had given way to the reality of the battle's aftermath. "We should be proud and thankful for our victory this day. We know and recognize our traditions, however. There is work to be done. Help the clerics gather and sort the bodies. Identify those that we can. As far as the orcs go, gather them in a pile. Don't burn them yet. I need to discuss with the king what shall be done with the corpses. If you have loved ones that fell on this day, you may choose to honor them in your own way if you wish. For those who still have loved ones waiting at home, when Priestess Ecila has given you permission, you may return home to hold them once again. You will be contacted if you are to be on the skeleton crew patrols. We still must be cautious even with the orcs gone.

"For our friends in neighboring lands," the general said, craning his head to peer out across the gathered. Eliliweth looked about as well, and was surprised to see both Sherinalu elves and York tribesmen among the rabble. He dimly remembered wondering where the other arrows were coming from during the battle, but it had all moved so fast. Strigson held his hand out to gesture to them, as well as the Eastfen Protectorate soldiers that were lined up nearby. "We cannot express our gratitude enough for your arrival. I do not exaggerate when I say that it turned the tide in our favor. We will have each of you personally escorted to guest chambers in the city for you to rest your weary bodies. I will personally see that each of you is given a hot meal as well.

"And Master Eliliweth," Ganisalp said, looking down at the half-elf. "I think you should come with me as well. I'm sure King Bartholomew has many questions to ask you."

Eliliweth nodded as he pursed his lips. He followed the general back towards the gate as the gathered army began to hum with activity once more, but couldn't help stealing a glance back at Cadohaden, who stood with his head bowed by the silently fuming Terodar. A flicker of blue caught the half-elf's eye as he saw Elune Shadowsong press her way through the throng, cloak billowing behind her as she ran up to Cadohaden to embrace him. Eliliweth was relieved to see that she'd survived the battle, and was tempted to turn back around to speak with her, but he decided against it. They would convene later, he was certain, and the two surely wanted a moment alone together, or as close as they could get with so many soldiers surrounding them. A faint pang of envy prodded at the half-elf's heart, not specifically for Elune, but for the intimate connection that he did not share with anyone else. He would be greeted with much praise, he was sure, but there wasn't someone he had that kind of relationship with to hold as the aftermath of the bloody battle would inevitably set in.

Even so, he wasn't sure he would trade places with the young paladin. They'd won the battle for certain, but for Cadohaden and Terodar, the half-elf feared they had yet another to fight.

* *

His knees were still weak from the exertion of battle, the adrenaline beginning to rapidly ebb as Elune hurried towards him. As her arms wrapped around his neck, Cadohaden choked back a sob of both relief and horror, clinging to her and burying his face against her shoulder. He thought he might slump against her, the reality of his sapped strength finally dawning on his body. He clenched his teeth together, mustering up whatever composure was left in him, even as tears rolled down his cheeks. Elune smelled of blood and soot, the stench of oil smoke clinging to her runed cloak, but mingled in with the atrocities of battle was the familiar scent of her skin and a hint of lavender. His shoulders trembled as he released a rattled sigh.

"I'm sorry," he murmured quietly.

"It's all right, Cadohaden," she whispered against his ear as she clung to him. "I tried to find you. I spent more time looking than I should have. I was late to my station. I think they'll forgive me." She briefly looked out across the field of battle, broken and bleeding bodies strewn across the barley fields, Glen Bailey soldiers beginning to file out among them to pile the dead or end the suffering of those that were nearly there. It was a sight that a soul never forgot, maimed men and women sobbing for an end as they choked on their own blood, organs and bones protruding from their wounds.

Cadohaden swallowed as he gripped her a little tighter. He remembered the choice he'd made shortly after the call for war had sounded. In the aftermath's quiet, he realized the insanity of his decision to seek out Terodar instead of Elune. Holding her now, he couldn't begin to fathom why he would have sought the demon instead of this. He told himself that he would say his devotions twelve times over that night out of gratitude for her safety. Guilt still gnawed at him, though. Could he bring himself to tell her that he'd made a choice? Would she piece it together on her own after hearing what he'd done? He lifted his head slightly, glancing at Terodar, who had sat up on one knee, shaking with anger as his blisters glistened. The demon was smoldering with anger, but a glimmer of curiosity still persisted behind his red irises. He wanted to know what his young master would say, too.

"I wanted to find you, too," Cadohaden eventually answered, resting his chin against her shoulder. "I...things got a little out of hand, I think. Everything happened so quickly." He knew his words were vague, and a suspicious mind would pry for a more descriptive explanation, but Elune was either too weary to care or didn't suspect anything.

"All that matters is you're here now," Elune said softly, lifting one of her hands to stroke the back of his hair, fingers weaving through the matted mess. "By the Goddess, Cadohaden...I saw you on that gryphon. You and Aven. How did you talk her into getting onto that saddle with you? I saw you fly over, and fall, and...I didn't think I'd see you again. I really didn't."

"I'll...I'll explain everything, Elune," he murmured in response. "I have to get it all straight in my head first."

"Think you'll explain it to more than just her," Terodar rasped nearby, an unsettling combination of indignation, amusement, and spite painted into his smile. Cadohaden shot the demon a quick scowl, but he couldn't focus on him just yet. There was something he had to do. His heart was hammering in his chest and the unspoken words made his legs even weaker than they already were, but he couldn't hold them in any longer.

"Elune, I love you," he said quietly as he held her. She tensed at first, her spine straightening and her fingertips pressing into him firmly. Before she could say anything, he continued, "I swear to you that I'll never use that to hold you down, to tie you to my side. I promise. Everything I told you before...I still meant all of that. But after all of what we just went through, I...I had to tell you."

A moment of silence passed between them before finally, Elune pushed herself back a few inches, placing her hands on each side of Cadohaden's face. There was both joy and fear in her eyes, and her mouth opened and closed a few times before she could answer, but the words finally came. "I love you too, Cadohaden. I'm not afraid to say it. I love you."

Renewed strength suddenly returned to his legs as he felt his heart leap. A wide smile broke across his face, and though a crack formed in his chapped lips by doing so, he didn't notice in the least as he leaned forward to kiss her. She answered in kind before the two held each other in silence again. Seconds later, a dry, disgusted scoff came from the kneeling demon nearby.

"Touching," Terodar spat, his angry eyes still fixated on Cadohaden. "But if you'll let me interrupt this adolescent poetry, there's something you need to consider here, Ulaeron, and quickly."

Cadohaden eased his embrace, though he kept his hands on Elune's shoulders as he frowned down at the nearby demon. "The battle is won, Terodar. What could possibly be so damned urgent?"

"The battle is won for this city, but not for you, boy," Terodar hissed through gritted teeth. "You broke treaties and disobeyed orders in battle. You'll get your trial I'm sure, but if you don't think there's a possibility you'll hang for this, then you're even more daft than I thought you were. And if you hang, I hang. They won't risk my presence without the collar you command."

"It worked out for us, though!" Cadohaden protested. "They aren't even holding me under arrest. Why would they let me walk back in of my own free will if they weren't giving me the benefit of the doubt?"

"Simpleton," Terodar spat, shaking his horned head. "You don't think you're under arrest? Look at the paladins. They're helping the priests heal the wounded, but they've got their eyes on you. They're waiting for you to give them the most trivial reason to throw you in chains, or maybe bring you justice right here among the dead."

Cadohaden slowly turned his head over his shoulder, peering at the soldiers walking among the fallen. It wasn't hard to spot Nevic's paladins among them. Terodar was right. They were tending to those that weren't beyond saving, but their eyes kept drifting upwards vigilantly to settle on him. "They're watching me from all sides," he said quietly to himself as Elune's gaze peered out at them as well.

"And when you make your way back through the gates, there will be soldiers tracking your every move as well," Terodar hissed. "They're giving you the illusion of free reign, Ulaeron, because they think you'll risk fleeing if you don't think you stand a chance of freedom. Sir Ganisalp wasn't impressed by your heroics. He just knew the right approach to keeping you here."

"We don't know any of that is true," Elune said briskly.

"Don't be foolish. Of course it's true," Terodar said with a clacking of his teeth.

"And what if it is?" Cadohaden asked, trepidation bleeding into his voice. "What can I do about it?"

"We run," Terodar muttered earnestly. "We run, Ulaeron. We don't give them the opportunity to put you through some jest of a trial. All it will take to put your neck in a noose are a few words whispered into the king's ear from that blind bitch Ecila, and you *know* she will. We don't run out here, of course. Those paladins will be on us in the blink of an eye. We make our way back into the city, before Benton finds us. If it's only guards, I can buy us enough time. We'll make our way to the river grate. I'll get us through. Take Lovely Long-Ears here with us or leave her, I don't care either way, but we have to go *now*, Ulaeron, before it's too late."

Cadohaden let the demon's words sink in as he took another look over his shoulder, eyeing the paladins that were still roaming among the fallen. Perhaps it was only paranoia, but it seemed as though they had begun to close in on them. He couldn't deny that he suddenly had a strong urge to flee. He knew now what Terodar was capable of. If they could get away from the paladins, he had no doubt that the demon could carve a way out of the kingdom for them. He turned back to Elune, looking into the hazel irises of her eyes. They were full of worry and dread, but worst of all, an uncertainty. He could see that she understood the brevity of Terodar's warning, and she couldn't bring forth a quick counter argument to his prophecies.

A figure caught Cadohaden's eye, a tall man moving through the mess of soldiers both standing and strewn across the ground. The staff held in one hand left no doubt as to who it was. Benton Cusair had spotted them and was coming to reclaim his lost study subject.

"It's too late, Terodar," Cadohaden said, drawing his lips to a thin line between words. "Benton's coming."

"Shit," Terodar snapped, looking over his shoulder with a wince as he stretched the blisters across his back. He wheeled his horned head around and hissed, "There's still time! Let's get back into the city! Or just take our chances with the paladins, it doesn't matter, Ulaeron, but we have to move *now!*"

"No," Cadohaden said, shaking his head somberly as Benton drew closer. "I can't, Terodar. When I ran from Kingsbanesin, I was running from somewhere that I didn't truly belong to. The Glen Bailey is my home now. Nobody here has wronged me. They took a risk welcoming me in, and Lifegiver knows I've tested that. This is home to me, and if Sir Ganisalp will give me a trial, I will honor his decision."

"Spineless little shit," Terodar fumed, clenching his gnarled hands as his pallid face curdled. "I suppose you think you're being noble, mm? You're not being noble, boy, you're only being a coward. As if the wrongs done to *me* count for nothing at all. But you don't defend me. You don't listen to *me*. You just roll over and show them your soft, white underbelly. I could have let this city rot. I could have let *you* rot, and just let those slack-jawed orcs grind you and everyone else into minced meat. And as far as Lovely Long-Ears here, I-"

"Be quiet, Terodar," Cadohaden said softly, his shoulders slumping faintly even as he gave the command. The demon's jaw snapped shut, though the muscles in his neck and face bulged with protest as the venomous words balled up on his tongue like a thorny plant. He knelt there smoldering as Benton Cusair approached the three of them, folding his hands behind his back as he looked down at Cadohaden over his hooked nose.

"Quite the theatrics you displayed out there today, Master Ulaeron," Benton said dryly. There were speckles of dried brown blood caked to the mage's face with long bare lines within the stain where someone's fingernails had tried to scrape away the clot. "Grant me the safeguard, if you would. Quickly now."

Cadohaden bit down on his lip, taking one last look at the kneeling demon who glared back at him resentfully. He'd handed command of Terodar over resentfully last time. He despised the feeling now, but knew there was nothing else he could do. The only other option was to try to fight his way out, and that really wasn't any sort of sane option anyway. "Terodar, I command you to obey Benton Cusair's commands as if they were my own from this point onward."

Once again, the weight of an additional master seemed to visibly push down upon the demon's shoulders. Terodar's lip curled, his teeth exposed in his outrage, though he obediently remained silent as Benton lifted his nose in satisfaction. "Thank you, Cadohaden. I suspect you have things to, ah...attend to. I shall bring Terodar back to the Mage House. I would advise against visitation until you have been given the king's blessing to do so."

"I...all right," Cadohaden said, dipping his head in submission. Terodar glared daggers at the young paladin.

"Follow me, Terodar," Benton commanded as he began to walk back to the gate. With as much displeasure as he could manage to display, the demon lurched to his hooves with a flinch, obediently following in the archmage's footsteps. "Best of luck, Ulaeron," Benton added in passing as he guided Terodar away.

Cadohaden stood in silence, clenching his fists at his sides as a frown etched across his brow. He felt Elune's grasp curl around his arm distantly, but dread and helplessness kept him from feeling any true comfort. He knew Terodar's warnings had held weight. He couldn't lie to himself; he was terrified of what the decision of his trial might result in.

Ultimately, however, he knew that when he had fled from Kingsbanesin, he'd had a purpose in mind: to honor both Deltore and Melaitha. He was obligated to do that in more than just title. His father was a warrior. His mother was a devout cleric. Running from the Glen Bailey now would serve no meaning. It would have no purpose, and in this situation, he knew that neither of his parents would flee.

"Come along," Elune said softly to him, giving his arm a squeeze. "Let's go somewhere else. Anywhere else but here." She looked back at the fields full of the dead and the reproachful gazes of the Monastery's paladins.

"All right," Cadohaden said softly. She took his hand in hers, leading him away from the carnage's aftermath. Somberly, they trudged back to the Glen Bailey's gates, stepping around the dead and weaving their way through passing soldiers as they made their way back.

As they passed over the mangled bodies, a familiar face caught Cadohaden's attention. There, laying in the beaten grass, a soldier was sprawled out, one arm extended above his head, his hand bloodied and misshapen from countless boots stepping on it. There was a gruesome dent in his helmet, blood pooled into the fracture that had opened up. One angry red eyeball was staring at an off-kilter angle, directly upward as if peering into his own skull. The other eye of Private Dylan Hakes, the man Cadohaden had patrolled with before the war, the soldier who had feared the endless afterlife, stared lifelessly, hauntingly forward. The deadened pupil seemed to follow Cadohaden as he and Elune walked past. The stare felt accusatory and damning. It was horrifying to behold.

He forced his gaze away and gripped Elune's hand tighter. Swallowing hard, he tried to brace his shaken spirit as they passed through the gates of the Glen Bailey once again.

Chapter Thirty-Two

Sir Ganisalp had spoken the truth when he had addressed his army following the battle at the gates. The Glen Bailey had a strong tradition in the aftermath of war: mourning, reflectance, and then at the appropriate time, celebration. Even after the the revolutionary Gunnysack Wars, one of the most historic triumphs in Glen Dale lore, the dead were given their proper respects before a single keg was tapped.

The conclusion of the Hordeland siege was no different. Three days were allowed for families to conduct their own private ceremonies, and King Bartholomew made a public statement, praising the bravery and sacrifice of the fallen soldiers and asking for quiet hours for three days and nights to honor their memories before the official funeral began. After those three days, a mass burial and service was conducted for those who either had nobody to bury them, or for those whose remains could not be properly identified to give to any family or friends. It was a somber time, and the season's first snowfall did little to warm the hearts of the grieving.

The second stage began after that, and though it was known as the 'reflection' period, 'review' would have been a better term, for three days were also allotted for legal proceedings and military commendations. The fates of prisoners were decided, men and women who stood out in battle were recognized for their heroics, and soldiers that had followed their orders (or directly disobeyed them) in questionable manner were scrutinized and judged by the king, his general, and his royal advisor. It was where Eliliweth Heraketh sat on that day, to Bartholomew's right in his royal court. His official coronation had not taken place yet - that was to be part of the victory celebration - but his role in the political arena had already begun with the passing of his Trials, as well as the significant absence of the traitorous magistrates. The half-elf was anxious as the day crawled on. More than once, he had to silently remind himself to stop tapping his fingers against his leg with impatience as one by one, soldiers were brought before the throne to be commended by their king and awarded with bronze badges.

Eliliweth peered over at Bartholomew as His Majesty spoke glowingly of Mya Ness as she bowed before him, recounting the tale of her heroics as Strigson Ganisalp had reviewed with him before the ceremony. There was no doubt that the king was elated with the victory of his kingdom. There was a shadow of remorse there as well, though, lingering in his smile and his eyes between his commendations. The half-elf knew what it was that troubled Bartholomew. The monarch was ashamed of his avoidance of the battlefield, especially when his daughter had directly defied him to partake in the war effort. Eliliweth had tried his best to console the king without directly bringing attention to the matter. Bartholomew had feigned ignorance, gruffly questioning what Eliliweth was on about. The half-elf had left it alone from that point on.

Finally, after what seemed like hours, the moment Eliliweth had been dreading came. The commendations of bravery had concluded, and the time to review the discretions of wayward troops had arrived. Voices around the chamber began to murmur in earnest, for all of the spectators knew the issue that was on the docket first. The half-elf scanned the crowd gathered on both sides of the center aisle. Between the flurry of faces, he spotted Elune Shadowsong, the worry etched on her face as the doors opened to admit the first trial.

Aven Celandine and Cadohaden Ulaeron marched into the chamber together, drawing a hush as they approached the throne. They were both dressed in formal garments, just as the decorated soldiers before them had, and neither were in shackles, but two guards followed behind each of them as a precautionary measure. It was bizarre, seeing the princess herself approach the throne to plead her case, and although Bartholomew tried his best to appear impassive, the king couldn't help but fidget under the discomfort of the situation.

"Princess Aven Celandine and Cadohaden Ulaeron of the Monastery, Your Majesty," one of the guards called out formally as they came to a stop before the king. Bartholomew stroked his beard, his mouth drawing to a thin line at the announcement. It was Eliliweth that spoke first, however,

"Princess. Cadohaden," the half-elf began, his voice loud enough for the entire royal court to hear. "You have been brought forth before the crown jointly due to the related nature of the claims against you, specifically, events that unfolded at the gryphon aviary on the day Grathul's army arrived. Though you were consulted about this prior to today, it is still your right to defend yourselves individually if you choose to do so. Do either of you wish to dismiss yourselves now and return alone at a later hour? Or is there anyone else that you would like to speak in your defense?"

Both the paladin and princess exchanged quick looks before shaking their heads faintly, murmuring a quiet 'no' in unison. Eliliweth nodded his head before continuing, "Very well. Ultimately, your fates will be decided by King Bartholomew, but this is your opportunity to grant His Majesty your perspectives. Sir Ganisalp?"

"We'll begin with you, Your Grace," the general said, picking up where the half-elf left off. He picked up one of several sheets of parchment lying on the table next to his chair, studying it for a moment before looking up at Aven. His gaze was emotionless, his words an echo of justice, an almost wooden quality to their tone. "In the interviews that were conducted with you in the past three days, Your Grace, you stated that on the day Grathul's army struck, Lord Bertram Archibaum led you to the city's gryphon aviary with the promise that he was going to expose the corruption of his fellow magistrates. You stated that when you arrived, you were lured onto an enchanted salt circle drawn by Archibaum himself that paralyzed your movements. Is this correct?"

"Yes," Aven said, her expression impassive.

"And you were aware of this conspiracy prior to the ambush? You had spoken with Bertram Archibaum before that day, correct?" Ganisalp pressed. Shorter than the blink of an eye, a strange tenor weaved its way into his speech, noticeable only to those with keen hearing.

"Yes," Aven answered again flatly.

"If that is true, why did you not inform the king of this plot before the orcs attacked? You claim that the magistrates attempted to hire orcs to infiltrate the city and assassinate His Majesty, in a plot similar to one executed in Kingsbanesin recently. That is a grave risk to take with your father's life in the balance."

The princess visibly winced at the observation, the shame burning at her neck as Bartholomew's expression became grim. "Bertram Archibaum told me that he feared for his life if he didn't pretend to cooperate," she explained. "And he warned of a backup plan pre-orchestrated by the magistrates in case of their discovery, in which tampered documents would be planted for artisan leaders to discover. He seemed certain that a revolt would ensue, and assured me that if we waited for the right time, we could catch the other magistrates red-handed, eliminating the possibility of dissent and exposing the real culprits." She paused, and for a brief moment, her gaze fell to the floor. When she looked back up, she added, "I only did what I thought was best for my people."

The court hall buzzed with the scandal. Eliliweth listened intently, but his eyes occasionally flicked back to Cadohaden. The young paladin looked increasingly surprised with every sentence that passed Aven's lips. Had they decided on an altered version of the truth in secret? If that was the case, it seemed as though the princess's conscience commanded her tongue.

"To be clear," the general asked, glancing down at his parchment once again before looking back up at Aven. "Archibaum did not speak of orc numbers as great as what arrived at our gates?"

"He did not," Aven answered. "He spoke of a group of assassins, utilizing stealth and the cover of night. He told me that he knew of a way to expose the plot before the plans were set in motion, however."

"Very well," Ganisalp answered before turning his attention to Cadohaden. "I understand you had a role to play in saving Her Grace from Bertram Archibaum, Cadohaden. But before you climbed the aviary tower, you entered the Mage House, correct?"

"That is correct, sir," Cadohaden said, clearing his throat before speaking.

"Tell His Majesty your version of what occurred, then."

And so Cadohaden recounted the tale, how he entered the Mage House and released Terodar of his obligation to remain hidden in the cellar. He spoke earnestly of his beliefs that the demon may do the right thing on his own, without being ordered to. He recalled leaving, and traveling to the gryphon aviary. He did not mince words when it came to his intentions, but Eliliweth wondered how he could have even if he wished to. If Bertram Archibaum had secretly been a mage, as Aven claimed, it was unlikely Cadohaden would have been able to overpower him without the element of surprise, something he wouldn't have had if he hadn't arrived at the roosts first. And lastly, he spoke of persuading the princess to board the gryphon Glyddiswilm with him to eliminate the threat of Grathul's catapults.

"So to be clear," Ganisalp said, his gaze boring into the paladin as he spoke, "you knowingly ignored your assigned duty to report to the front lines, gave a potentially dangerous demon the freedom to wander the kingdom at will, and violated the treaties we have with Kaijar Keep by using their property to fight our battle?"

"But by doing so, it helped us win-"

"Just answer the question, Ulaeron," Ganisalp interrupted sternly.

Cadohaden pursed his lips and shifted his weight from one foot to the other. "Yes, sir," he answered begrudgingly.

"I'm well aware of what your intentions were, Ulaeron," the general continued. "And I can't argue that the outcome ended in your favor. But it could just have easily gone the other way, possibly at the expense of the princess's life. We have a chain of command for a reason, and nobody is above it, for if we had none, we would see risks taken such as yours at *every* conflict, and there *would* be casualties. You do understand that in places like your home city, such flagrant disobedience would be grounds for execution, don't you?"

Cadohaden paled as he swallowed. "I didn't think of that at the time, sir, but yes, I understand," he said quietly.

"As far as Terodar Soulrender goes, he may have attacked our enemy, but we cannot say for sure if it that was out of good faith or just convenience for him," Strigson continued. "His timing was a bit suspect as it was."

"Would he have been permitted to fight if he had shown up on his own before the orcs charged?" Cadohaden asked. It was a bold question, given the circumstances, and both Strigson and Eliliweth's eyebrows raised.

"Perhaps not," Strigson admitted, tapping his fingers against his knee, his gaze never leaving Cadohaden. "You cannot deny his nature though, nor can you deny the risk you took at the expense of others. Terodar himself discarded all of the training Benton and his appren-

tices put into curbing his unholy magic by cursing that troll with...
whatever the hell that was. As I said before, it worked in our favor, but
that cursed blood could have easily landed on one of *our* men as well.
It is foolish to believe that he was concerned about that possibility."

"Do we not take similar risks when we fire arrows from the ramparts?" Cadohaden asked, his voice dangerously bordering on indignant. "Can we guarantee that one of our soldiers will not step in front
of a fired Bailey arrow?"

"Speak with care, Cadohaden," Eliliweth said calmly before Sir
Ganisalp could retort angrily. "It is your actions we are evaluating, not
those of our archers."

"I've heard enough," King Bartholomew said abruptly, sitting up in
his throne as he looked down at the two. "I will give each of you one
final say before I make my judgment. Aven?"

"I have said all I need to, Your Majesty," the princess answered, her
gaze never faltering even as her skin paled more than it already was.

"Very well. Cadohaden?"

"As Her Grace said, I only did what I thought would help this kingdom," Cadohaden answered. "I have felt more welcome here than I
ever did in Kingsbanesin, and I only wanted to return the favor. I recognize that...that I didn't go about it the right way. I really am sorry for
those I put at risk. But as far as Terodar is concerned, I *do* believe that
even he might find redemption, as I said when we arrived together. I
gave him that chance. His methods were questionable too, but in the
end, he fought *for* the Glen Bailey of his own free will. I don't regret
giving him that opportunity."

With Cadohaden's speech concluded, Bartholomew took in a deep
breath, his plump stomach expanding and falling with the weary sigh
that followed. For a moment, silence ruled the royal court as the king
scrutinized the two standing before him. Then, finally, he spoke, "I
have known my daughter's soul since I first saw her open eyes. While
her actions were troubling, I have no doubt of her intentions. I cannot
say the same for Cadohaden Ulaeron, for though I know of his history,
I do not know him well enough to speak in his defense. Is there any
among you that can defend his honor in this matter?"

For a tense moment, silence settled over the court again. Cadohaden's face grew more drawn with every passing second until Eliliweth spoke in a politically formal tone, sitting up in his chair. "Since
meeting Cadohaden outside the Sherinalu borders, he has quickly be-

come a close friend of mine. His actions were brash to be sure, but I will vouch for his intentions as well, on my honor. Everything he did, he did what he deemed would be in the best interest for the Glen Bailey, his new home."

Bartholomew nodded slowly as the court stirred with murmurs once again at the new advisor's public show of support for the Kingsbanesin exile. Cadohaden's face brightened as he offered Eliliweth a tight-lipped smile of appreciation. Eliliweth kept his gaze cool, avoiding eye contact. He truly wished to offer his encouragement, but he could not make it too personal in front of the eyes of the spectators. It might suggest that he did not take his position seriously, and he wasn't nearly settled in enough to take such dangerous political risks. He already was putting his reputation in Cadohaden's hands. He believed what he said in the paladin's defense, but he also knew that there wasn't another in the room that would speak up for him. Elune surely would have, but their relationship was no secret, and the word of an intimate companion would not be enough to save him.

"Sir Ganisalp is right," the king said as he stood up from his throne. "In Kingsbanesin, both of your lives would be condemned. However, our ancestors did not rebel against the dragon empire to inherit its principles. The Glen Bailey, generation after generation, has always considered both forgiveness and compassion to be among the tenets of its foundation. That is not to say that I am condoning what either of you did. Make no mistake; you will both be watched closely for some time, until my concerns have lifted. But I will not jail or execute my only heir and beloved daughter for trying to take too much upon her own shoulders, and I cannot ignore that despite Cadohaden's recklessness, he managed to save my daughter's life in the process. This once, you will both be granted conditional pardons.

"But Eliliweth," the king said, turning his head to look down at his seated advisor. "As it was you who vouched for Cadohaden, it shall be your first task as both my advisor and my diplomat to reach out to Kaijar Keep to inform them of what happened to their gryphons. You will wait a week while our soldiers try to locate the ones that the magistrates rode out on, but then we must profess to them, in good faith, our breach of contract. I expect that you will smooth things over and that our relations with the holy men will continue as before."

"Yes, Your Majesty," Eliliweth said with a small bow of his head. A flutter of excitement stirred in his stomach at the prospect of his first diplomatic mission, but it was mixed with anxiety as well. It would be no easy feat to confess their discrepancies to Kaijar Keep and return home with the contracts intact. *Please don't make me regret this, Cadohaden*, he thought to himself.

"Well then," King Bartholomew said, lifting his arms a bit before letting them fall to his side, hands clapping against his outer thighs. He looked around the royal court, and for the first time that day, His Majesty looked at a loss for words. A beat passed, and then another, before finally he marched down the dais towards his daughter. Eliliweth wasn't sure how much time the two had spent together after the war had ended, but it was clearly not enough. Bartholomew wrapped Aven in his arms, the two embracing tightly as both sets of eyes began to moisten with the threat of tears.

They stood there in the middle of court, holding one another as cheers began to sound from the spectators, hands clapping together in excitement. A smile formed on Eliliweth's face as the scene unfolded. There were a few more cases to be reviewed that day, but to everyone in the royal court, the celebrations had already begun.

Chapter Thirty-Three

The noon sun was just barely beginning to droop its way towards the west, a languid crawl towards its resting place. Aven Celandine rested her palms upon the keep's battlements as she stood on its roof, overlooking the pocked and marred barley fields that surrounded the city walls. A gust of wind coiled around the castle's sentinel towers, swirling around her as they passed by. It chilled her lightly, but she did not shiver. She took in breath after breath, releasing them all slowly through her nose as she studied the soldiers scurrying about the fields like animated miniatures, still assorting bodies even days after the battle had come to an end. Even further in the distance, barely visibly to the naked eye, the princess occasionally spotted patrols darting in and out of sight as they traveled along the forest line. Their defenses were assembled with skeleton crews at this point, as there was a great deal of rebuilding and reorganizing to be done, but even after such a monumental victory, they could not let their guard down. Orcs were vengeful creatures, and nobody was discounting the possibility of the remaining brutes rallying to take another strike at the Glen Bailey.

Below the keep, inside the city's protective walls, men and women moved feverishly through the market streets as well, preparing for the great feast that would officially begin at the dinner hour, though many had begun to drink only moments after the princess had been pardoned of her transgressions, her involvement with the corrupt magistrates.

She knew she should feel fortunate. The people of her beloved kingdom had been graciously forgiving in the wake of her exposure. She knew she should feel gratitude for that. But it didn't make sense to her. Even as old as they were, the men at Arden's Watch had died because of her. Even if she was an indirect cause, it didn't make her feel any better. Her actions might not have directly brought the orcs to the Glen Bailey's gates, but had she reported what she had known to her father, those veterans might have been able to fight alongside their brothers and sisters in arms to die in glory, not butchered like swine in the conquered ruins of the Watch. She didn't know if any of her people understood that, and it weighed on her. It was true that she had been given her opportunity to fight for her people. In the end, her Goddess had given her the chance to redeem herself, as bizarre as the situation had been. But she didn't feel as though she'd earned complete absolution, and it was mostly because she felt as though she'd been given a privileged pardon.

Aven, my friend, that's just not true, Eliliweth had insisted to her the night before when she'd confessed the same thoughts to him. *Whatever you may have done prior to Grathul's siege, there isn't a pair of ears in the Glen Bailey who hasn't heard about what your gryphon-backed heroics helped achieve. It was risky, to be sure, and against all the rules, but that's what people love in a war story. You risked it all, and in the end, you risked it for them. Besides, they have their villain. They have plenty of villains. For every word that praises you, there's another that curses the magistrates, and two that curse Grathul Heavyhand. What this kingdom needs right now, my friend, is stability. I know it, your father knows it, and the people know it. They're rallying around you for that security. Be grateful, Aven, and embrace it. You gave everything your spirit had.*

Whatever she had given, it didn't feel like enough. She wet her lips before pursing them, fingers drumming on the stonework in front of her as another breeze cycled through. Perhaps time was all she needed to forgive herself. It wasn't as though she had sold secrets to foreign leaders, or intentionally led soldiers into an ambush. She thought she'd been preventing civil war. She lifted her hand as the thought crossed her mind, pinching the bridge of her nose. Strigson was right. The magistrates would have never been able to conjure such an elaborate scheme. Bertram Archibaum had surely bluffed his way out of trouble. Even now, she wasn't certain whose side the withered old bastard was on, though it was most likely his own.

Her memory slipped back to the aviary, where Archibaum had her pinned to the enchanted salt circle. She'd never been so sure in her life that she was about to die. Never in her life had she felt so completely helpless, and it angered her to no end. Such indignity demanded retribution, and she felt genuinely sorry that Cadohaden had ended Bertram's life so quickly. Again, she knew she should have felt gratitude for the Kingsbanesin exile's timely interference, and by all accounts, tales of her torturing one of the magistrates to death with arcane fire might have dampened the admiration of her people, but she'd wanted it so badly.

She heard a creak behind her as the platform door opened. She realized she'd been holding in her breath for longer than usual and released it abruptly as she looked over her shoulder to see who was coming up. She grit her teeth immediately as she recognized the head of Strigson Ganisalp looking through the opening, one arm holding up the door on its hinges. She turned back around, resting her hands on the battlements once again as a slight frown knit her brow.

Footsteps came up behind her, slow and cautious. She did not turn around to greet him as the general approached, a shadow falling next to her before Strigson came within peripheral view, resting his elbows on the stonework beside her. She could see from the corner of her eye that he wasn't looking at her, but rather studying the soldiers out in the field. His hands folded together as they sat in silence for a moment. It was the general that broke it first.

"I'm glad you were pardoned," he said simply, eyes still trained out to the barley fields.

"Mm. I was as well," Aven said diplomatically. Another moment of silence stretched between them as Strigson steepled his fingers together.

"Aven...I have to tell you something," he said quietly. "Before anything else happens."

"Curious," was all Aven said in reply.

"I love you, Aven. I'm *in* love with you," Strigson admitted. The words were strained, the tone mismatched for someone making such a confession. It almost sounded as though he were informing her of a fatal disease he'd become ill with.

"You don't love me, Strigson," the princess answered broodingly, her gaze adamantly focused forward. The general finally turned to face her, however, his eyes flinty, the muscles in his jaw flexing between his spoken words.

"Yes, I do. I think I have for a while now, Aven. I've always admired your spirit and your strength. You are one day going to be a queen fit to rule the entire Aariad if you desired it."

"Are you suggesting that you would lead an army across the land, conquering city after city, for my sake?" Aven asked, finally turning to face the general.

"If you wished it, perhaps I would," Sir Ganisalp answered.

"Perhaps isn't good enough, Strigson," Aven said, turning back to face the battlements again. "And I have no desire to conquer the Aariad. Empires only last so long in this land. Kingsbanesin's taught us that much."

"I didn't mean...you *know* what I meant," Strigson said, his hand curling around the edge of one square stone. "Whatever battles you wished to pursue, Aven, I would stand by your side. And I *can* stand by your side. Your father would bless our union. The people would, too. I know you care for me. You can choose to have a marriage that makes sense and won't have you paired with some spoiled prince of Eastfen-"

"Micah Rhone is a very polite young boy," Aven interrupted sternly.

"And a *boy*," Strigson said earnestly. "How long will it be before you'd be able to enjoy your bed with your husband? Is that really what you want?"

"What I want is not important," Aven snapped, agitation growing in her voice.

"Is it really that horrifying? To think of me as your husband...as your king?" Strigson said quietly. Aven turned to look at the general. It was bizarre, seeing him this way. He wasn't composed. He looked weary and pleading. It was as though someone had pried off the layers of armor that protected his deepest emotions, exposing them for her to see. It was unsettling.

"You say that you would conquer all of the Aariad by my side," Aven said, her face growing redder as she spoke. "But where were you during my trial, Strigson? Interrogating me, questioning me, stripping my dignity down in front of my people as if you had *no idea* what the answers would be! We are sworn to truth in court, Sir Ganisalp, but which of us was falsest in the room yesterday?"

Strigson visibly flinched, as if the princess had struck him across the face with the flat of her hand. "What was I supposed to do, Aven!?" he answered brusquely. "What more could I have contributed to your trial? My guilt by association wouldn't have cleared your name! All it would have done would strip me of everything I have, of everything I've worked for! By the bloody *gods*, Aven, did you not hear me steering the questions in a way that would portray you in the best light? I did the best I could!"

"I'm sure you did," Aven said sardonically, turning her head away from him again. "It's fine, Strigson. Perhaps I wouldn't have said anything either. But don't speak to me of your undying devotion to me if you weren't willing to make that sacrifice."

"Sacrifice…" Strigson breathed, taking a step back, his hands lifting to the back of his head briefly before he dropped them limply to his sides. "Sacrifice? I listened to you confess your treason, Aven, and I kept *silent*. I put my life at risk. I put the lives of my men at risk. I put your *father's* life at risk, for Lifegiver's sake, and by doing all of that, I coughed up my honor on a silver platter for you. I did the most terrible thing I've ever done in my life for you."

"What do you want, General? Another medal to add to your collection?" Aven snapped.

"No!" Strigson said, taking a step towards her. "Kaijaras help me, Aven, all I want is for you to understand why I couldn't say anything yesterday! My title, my *purpose* in the Glen Bailey, this is all I have left! This is where I help this kingdom the most, for you and your father."

She rounded on Sir Ganisalp with clenched teeth. Distantly, she wondered why she was so angry. Everything Strigson was telling her made sense. And yes, she had cared for him. She supposed she still did. But right now, at this moment, she found herself inexplicably furious with him. So they'd shared a romantic interest, and even an intimate tryst. Did that make her obligated to fall madly in love with him, to wed him and make him the future king of Bartholomew's realm? What did he expect, just sauntering up to her with all of this nonsense? "You know what I think, Strigson? I think you want a ring placed on my finger, and a bride to lay down with every night, beaming with gratitude for your selflessness. I'll spread my legs every night to show just how thankful I am for my heroic husband."

"Well you spread them easily enough to keep me quiet after spilling your dirty little secret!" Strigson snapped back. She didn't even realize what she was doing until it was too late. Her arm coiled and lunged, her palm slapping loudly against his trimmed beard, the blow physical this time. The words came just as quickly as her strike, before she could think to rein them in,

"I won't be your bride just because you want a woman who can't up and leave you like your gypsy whore mother did," she hissed. "Go find yourself a grieving widow, Strigson. Maybe she'll cling to you for dear life to save herself from despair."

The imprint from her hand was rapidly beginning to blossom on Strigson's cheek, and the hurt in his eyes was clear. She watched his adam's apple bob as he swallowed hard, his jaw flexing before he muttered, "Who the hell are you?"

"I am Princess Aven Celandine," she retorted vindictively, nose wrinkling as she spoke. "And I don't owe you a damn thing, Strigson."

They stared hard at each other for several moments, neither of them speaking, neither of them yielding. It was as though they were both waiting for the other to break. Finally, with a slow shake of his head, Sir Ganisalp walked away, marching towards the lift door nearby. Aven kept her chin high as she turned back around to face the body-littered fields once again. She waited for the sound of the opening door. It didn't come, and Strigson's footsteps ceased as well. She waited, unmoving.

"You have to tell Wyatt, Aven," his voice called out behind her. "About what happened between us. Today."

"I don't *have* to do anything, Strigson," she answered briskly. "I will tell Wyatt Darjin what I wish, when I wish to tell him."

"If you won't, I will."

"You will do no such thing," Aven said, swiveling her head around again to glower at the general, who was standing a foot away from the lift door. "You will go about your business, Strigson Ganisalp, reorganizing your soldiers and establishing order in this city, as your duty dictates, but you will not say a word to Wyatt that isn't strictly a military command. That, General, is an order."

There was no standoff this time. Strigson's face turned red, his lower jaw sliding outward in indignation. He nodded curtly, muttering something of an acknowledgment of the given order before turning around, lifting the door to the staircase that would lead him back into the keep. It slammed shut behind him, and Aven turned back around to stare out into the fields beyond, alone this time.

She didn't intend to lead Wyatt on for the rest of time. She knew things between her and her lover were at an end. But she'd been given her fill of consequences enacted out of her control. She would break the young man's heart, but it would be on her terms, not Strigson Ganisalp's.

She slowly lowered her head as she turned her palms upward, her forehead resting against them. She wanted to cry, but it simply felt as if she had no tears left to offer.

Chapter Thirty-Four

The celebrations formally began the night after Aven and Cado-haden's acquittal, and like the Solstice festivals that had taken place before Eliliweth's Trials of the White Forest, the city of the Glen Bailey was alive once again. Though the first snowfall of the season had melted on a warm afternoon, a chill had settled in the air once more, and so in contrast to the Solstice celebrations, most of the feasts were being held indoors. Taverns and shops and even barracks were converted into feasting halls to commemorate their victory over Grathul Heavyhand and his orcish hordes. Small furnaces were even dragged out into the market square streets with huge canvas tents pitched over them, providing a place to warm up for those that were leaving a party to seek another. Not coincidentally, the dwarves of Dur'Imoir had returned with claims that the mountain lords had been appalled with their absence from the fighting. They brought along full kegs as a congratulations and an apology (only the first three were complimentary, of course, the rest at market price).

The grandest of the feasts was being held in the banquet hall of the Keep, but it was by invitation only, as there wasn't nearly enough room to fit the entirety of the city all at once. That didn't mean the common folk were excluded by any means, however, as the king's servants spent most of the night running hot pots of meats, potatoes, cooked corn and gravy to all of the establishments that had declared themselves to be hosts of the great feasts. One way or another, Bartholomew ensured that soldier and citizen alike was treated to the same meals being served at the keep, even if they weren't quite as warm by the time they arrived at their destination.

As the royal advisor to the crown, Eliliweth had received an invitation to the king's personal banquet, and he knew he had to make an appearance sooner or later. Bartholomew had insisted upon it earlier in the day when they had performed the Donning of the Birch Crown, symbolizing the wisdom he'd acquired while training with the druids of the White Forest. He'd since removed the relic and placed it back in the its display chambers, as he knew the risks of having ale spilled all over him that night were fairly high. For the moment, however, he was content to remain in the tents in the market square, speaking with the citizens and the soldiers that were enjoying the revelry of the night. Holding a cup of mulled mead in one hand, he shook the hands of others with his opposite, smiling and nodding and granting them well wishes as most expressed their appreciation for his lingering among them. The half-elf knew most of them didn't believe him when he said that such company was usually preferable to stuffy formal banquets, but he always felt more at place there than he ever did in the royal chambers.

"Eliliweth!" a familiar voice called out. The half-elf turned around, looking for the source. There were lanterns hanging from the cross poles in the tents, but the lighting was still fairly dim. He recognized Elune, however, as she gave him a hug, carefully balancing the contents of a mead mug of her own as she did.

He laughed and returned the embrace as Cadohaden walked up to him as well, sipping on what was likely the same drink. "Ah, it's good to see the both of you. You aren't going to the formal banquet in the keep?" He knew the mistake of his words as soon as they left his mouth. Elune had certainly received an invitation, but even after his exoneration, Cadohaden had not. Elune answered seamlessly, however,

"We're having a fine time down here," she assured him with a smile. "But we're also not royal advisors, friend. You know you'll be expected to make an appearance, right?"

"Of course, of course," Eliliweth said with a dismissive wave of his hand. "From what I heard, though, the scribe Pleatus was also named an interim advisor to the crown in the absence of the magistrates, so I figured he could fill my shoes for a few hours."

"Interim advisor?" Cadohaden asked with a puzzled smile and a cheery tone that suggested he wasn't on his first mug of mead. "What the hell's he going to advise on?"

"You know, important things," Eliliweth answered with a faint smirk. "Cheese and wine pairings. Calligraphy standards. That sort of thing." It wasn't his usual temperament to speak so mockingly of others, but he truly wasn't sure what Pleatus could possibly bring to Bartholomew's service. He felt a little guilty at Elune and Cadohaden's outbursts of laughter regardless.

"Eliliweth," Cadohaden said, attempting to draw seriousness into his voice, even though the mead was preventing him from brandishing truly stoic words. "I haven't had a chance to thank you yet. For speaking in my defense, the other day. I wouldn't be out celebrating right now if you hadn't. Not unless they hand out mead to the dungeon cells."

The half-elf smiled and clapped a hand against the paladin's shoulder. "From the day I met you, Cadohaden, I always believed you had a good heart. I hope that rings true for decades to come." If there were any veiled implications in Eliliweth's words, Cadohaden didn't seem to understand. He only beamed and nodded, wrapping an arm around Elune's shoulders as he took another sip of mead from the mug he was holding.

A touch of loneliness nudged at the half-elf's spirit as his two friends exchanged happy smiles. He suddenly had little desire to remain in the tents. With a grin and a hoist of his mug in a salute, he said, "Well, I suppose I should make my way to the keep. I'm sure Strigson will be looking for a breath of fresh air, so I shouldn't give him any reasons to come drag me there by the scruff of my neck."

He said his goodbyes to his friends and ventured off into the streets, out of the heat of the tent's furnace. It wasn't a biting cold that filled the air, but it made the cheeks tingle and the wrists numb. He breathed on his hands and rubbed them together as he made his way to the keep. He could see the lights from the chandeliers in the banquet hall's window from down on the cobblestone, and at passing moments he thought he could hear the string instruments being played for the dancing.

He enjoyed his walk of solitude, and his feet carried him to the banquet hall almost too quickly for his liking. He walked in to a dazzling sight of chandeliers, a myriad of candles, and jewelry that brilliantly reflected the flames. A quartet played gentle harmonies in the corner, their bowstrings coaxing soothing sounds from their instruments.

It was Captain Dak Pondrake that greeted him first, looking bizarre in a violet ruffled shirt, his long-ended mustache nearly sitting upon the folds. He clapped the half-elf on the shoulder with one hand, a glass of wine in his other, immediately embarking on a grandiose retelling of their charge into battle against the orcs. He went so far as to drag Eliliweth over to a mixed group of Protectorate sergeants, Sherinalu elves, and lesser nobles of the Glen Bailey, telling the tale all over again, their heroics embellished more than the story he'd reflected on with Eliliweth not ten minutes past. Luckily for the half-elf, the Protectorate Captain became so engrossed in his own storytelling that he seemed to forget that the half-elf was there at all, and Eliliweth dismissed himself with a polite farewell nod to the other guests as Dak mimicked stabbing and slashing motions for those around him.

As he circumvented the banquet hall, he greeted and spoke with Sir Ganisalp (who seemed more aloof than usual, and abruptly excused himself mid-conversation to leave the room), Benton Cusair, Nevic Baltwin, and even Priestess Ecila (who was just fine with her goblet of water, thank you). He kept his conversations short and polite as he made his way through his conversational obligations. Then at last, he saw Aven Celandine standing at a table with plates full of pastries, though she wasn't partaking in any sweets. Rather, the princess was talking in a rather diplomatic fashion, posture straight and chin held high, to none other than Wyatt Darjin, who wore a shirt similar to Dak Pondrake's, only his was blue with silver trim. Eliliweth smiled as he approached the two, who turned to look at him in alarm, caught off-guard. The half-elf almost laughed. Why did they bother with pretenses? There wasn't a soul in the room who didn't know.

"Your Grace. Captain Darjin," Eliliweth said, bowing to the princess and extending his hand to Wyatt, giving it a firm shake.

"Eliliweth!" Aven said, taking a step back towards the table of treats. "You've met Wyatt Darjin, correct?"

"I have," Eliliweth said, resisting the urge to wink at her as her face flushed upon realization that he'd just addressed the captain by name. Wyatt shifted uncomfortably, swirling the wine in his glass around awkwardly.

"Good to see you, Eliliweth," the captain said. "I was told you lead the Protectorate into battle for the final assault that saw the warchief beheaded."

"If it was Dak that told you that, I'll bet he said I held the blade as well," the half-elf chuckled. Both Aven and Wyatt laughed nervously in response. Eliliweth's grin widened as he followed up with, "I'm only here to show my face, I'll be out soon enough. Is your father here, Your Grace? I had better prove to him that I stopped in before leaving."

He half expected Aven to stubbornly insist that he didn't need to go anywhere, and for a moment it looked like she might, but if the words were on her tongue, she swallowed them. Eliliweth didn't begrudge her for that. He knew how little time she and Wyatt were able to spend together. She answered, "He *was* here, though I haven't seen him since...well, since Captain Darjin arrived." She cleared her throat. "Don't tell anyone, but I think he runs off to hide in the wine cellar during these parties sometimes. As excited as he gets to host them, I think the crowds wear on him quickly."

Eliliweth frowned, swirling his mug of mead a little as he contemplated Aven's words. He wasn't sure if His Majesty would appreciate an interruption if he was hiding in the wine cellars, but formalities aside, there was something he wanted to speak to the king about, a notion he'd been mulling over since the dust of war had settled. He wasn't sure when his next opportunity would be, either, as the days following the revelry were sure to be busy. His decision made, he nodded at Aven and Wyatt with a smile and said, "Then I shall pay a visit to the wine cellar. Enjoy the night, you two." The princess looked as though she might call on him to stay, but quickly resigned herself to bidding him farewell with a strained smile. Eliliweth wondered if perhaps her father had said anything uncalled for about Wyatt's presence before disappearing into the cellar depths.

He made his way out of the banquet, walking down the halls, occasionally passing a whispering couple in the shadows who froze as he walked past, murmuring in inebriated giggles when they thought he was out of earshot. Down the staircases he went, and down another hall until he'd reached the shuttered door of the wine cellar. Pulling it by the iron ring on the handle, he invoked a shrill squeak from the hinges before lowering himself down the creaking stairs into the depths below.

There were barrels and bottle racks filling the musty cellar, as well as assorted herbs and dried fruits hanging from the ceiling. He passed by shelves of empty bottles as he picked up an enclosed lantern that was sitting next to two others on a table with scattered brewing notes. Picking up a taper, he lit one end on an already ignited wick before lighting the one to his lantern. With a light to illuminate his way, he walked among the barrels and bottles in search of his king.

It didn't take long to find Bartholomew Celandine, sitting at a table between two rows of stacked barrels. It was where the winemasters tasted the fruits of their labors, though typically they did so in small wooden cups barely deep enough to dip your fingers into. The king sat on a stool, his elbows on the table, a whole goblet sitting before him next to a candlestick holder. His Majesty looked up slowly at the half-elf, and for a moment, Eliliweth thought he saw anger cross Bartholomew's face. If it was there, however, it quickly vanished, and the king nodded his head, as if he had known all along the half-elf would come. "Come. Sit beside me, Eliliweth," he said in a voice that was bordering the edge of drunkenness. His hand patted the stool next to him, and Eliliweth lowered himself into it. "Drink up what you got left in there," Bartholomew said, nodding at the mug he'd brought down. "I'll fill it up again."

Eliliweth obliged, tilting his mug back and draining it of the mead, putting down a couple swallows before it was empty. He set it before his king, and Bartholomew grabbed a bottle filled with red wine, tipping its contents into the half-elf's vessel. "This one's a Gohandian import," the king grunted as he poured. "Nothing against Theodore, of course, but they grow sweeter grapes down there. Makes it a little less tart than what he brews up."

The half-elf didn't mind a little tartness to his wine, but he kept the thought to himself. "I see. Thank you, Your Majesty."

"Bah," Bartholomew said, waving a hand in his direction as he set the bottle back down. "Just Bartholomew, while we're down here, anyway. You might find it hard to believe, but 'Your Majesty' does get old after the title is constantly in your ears during a party like the one upstairs."

"If you're sure," Eliliweth answered, sniffing at the wine before taking a sip. It had a sweeter aftertaste than the wine Theodore Seruman created, that was certain. "Got to be a bit overwhelming?"

"Aye, you know, parties like this were just never the same after Meredith passed on," Bartholomew said, leaning back on his stool as he rested his hand on his gut. "She always loved celebrations like this, and not for the reasons you'd think. She wasn't obsessed with showing off new dresses or waving shining jewels in guests' faces. No, she'd get the biggest kick out of the way folks act at occasions like this. Everyone's on their best behavior, and everyone is a friend of the man or woman standing next to them, even if they were spittin' venom at one another the day before. Everyone has nice things to say, or at least things that *seem* nice, even if they're backhanded compliments. Meredith...she'd toy with guests all night, saying this and saying that just to see if they'd agree with her, or tell her some outlandish tale to rival the one she'd just told. All night, she'd spin her web, a strand here, a strand there, and she always managed to get the most pompous prick in the party to expose himself with his boasts or his paltry praises. It sounds malicious, but she just liked the sport of it. I always loved watching her outwit that Edward Carson. Hah! He'd turn twenty shades of red when she'd tripped him up, but he never could resist playing the game!"

Eliliweth smiled as he listened to the king reminisce, swirling his wine about in his mug. It occurred to him that with his queen gone, Bartholomew might share the same loneliness that he did. He silently wondered if the king's fondness for wine was an attempt at filling that void. The warmth from the drink was beginning to make his chest feel light and his cheeks hot as he neared the perfect balance of pleasant intoxication.

Bartholomew chuckled to himself once more, clapping his hand against his stomach. Slowly, his expression darkened as his stained lips pursed. He shook his head as he murmured lowly, "What in the gods would drive the magistrates to betray us like that? What did they want for? They had riches. Maybe not like the barons of Gohand, or the dwarf lords of Dur'Imoir, but everything was taken care of for them. They had no difficult decisions to make. They never needed to break a single drop of sweat. Hell, I think Seasar had a maid whose specific duty was wiping his tremendous arse. And *orcs*, of all things. How could they be so...desperate?"

"That is the nature of greed, Bartholomew," Eliliweth said quietly. "No matter what a man possesses, it's never enough if he does not possess more than any other."

"So it is," Bartholomew said quietly, lifting a hand to stroke his beard thoughtfully before taking another gulp of wine from his goblet. "So full of young wisdom, you are. But I must ask you something, Eliliweth. Was this the first war you've fought?"

"I've fought before, my liege," Eliliweth said, briefly forgetting the king's request to disregard formalities. "But never on such a scale as this battle against Grathul."

"Then there is something I must tell you, for you may not realize that for those who rule, the war is not yet over. It continues for us, right here at home." Bartholomew looked over at Eliliweth, and though it may have simply been a trick of the shadows, his gaze suddenly looked considerably more sober. He turned back to peer at the candle burning brightly at the table before continuing,

"My boy, I brought you into my court for good reason. You are full of life, courage, and an abundance of young wisdoms. I have cherished those wisdoms since the day I appointed you, and will do so until the Lifegiver decides my time is at an end. But alongside young wisdom, Eliliweth Heraketh, is old wisdom, and for as much as you shall advise me during the rest of my reign, there is much I can yet teach you, so that you may grow into a man that will give steadfast and worthy guidance to my daughter when she takes her crown."

Though Eliliweth had lifted his mug to his lips again, he slowly lowered it back down into his lap as he looked over at the king. This was no idle banter the king was speaking. The half-elf could tell that Bartholomew had given this some thought before Eliliweth had even come down to find him.

"We shelter our people, Eliliweth," Bartholomew spoke softly, the candle wick in front of him releasing a single pop. "We provide walls for their protection, we patrol the fields their crops grow from, we tax them fairly for what they use in our name, and we pay them good coin for their labors to the crown, so that our kingdom as a whole remains prosperous and strong. But there always comes a time when the Glen Bailey must ask of its people a terrible price for such a balance, and this will not be the last time we shall do so. There are dark days where we ask for our people to give their lives to protect all that we hold dear.

"When we fight these battles, and the sun sets on a bloody day, a man will tally our troops, scratch a quill upon a scroll, and read out the numbers of those we have lost. When we read these lost souls off as a number, it becomes easier to forget the faces that will never smile again. We mourn the losses, of course, but when the number has been read, our first question is always this: do we have enough to lose more tomorrow?"

A faint chill crawled up the half-elf's spine, for though the Glen Bailey had granted funerals for the fallen, it was as Bartholomew had depicted. The very next day, Eliliweth himself had sat with Sir Ganisalp, Crusader Nevic, and several lieutenants to discuss the losses they'd suffered, how they would need to adjust patrol schedules, and how soon they could replenish their numbers. It was true. When the bodies were buried beneath the earth, they had become numbers.

"It is a heavy burden to dwell on such things, boy, but our duty does not end there. For each of those that is tallied missing when the campaign is over, somewhere within our walls, a loved one waits for them to return home. We ask not just for the soldier to pay the dread price, but the widow, be it man or woman, and the children who they nurtured. It is a wicked thing to ask, but in this world we live in, we pay our dues.

"When we ask this price of our people, Eliliweth, we must not let them be forgotten. We cannot let them be forgotten in the shadows of our victory fires. It is not the easy thing to do, but it is the right thing to do. If you've more of a pragmatic mind, as some of my advisors in the past have possessed, you do it because grieving widows have no sense of loyalty, and abandoned orphans grow up to be cutthroats, traitors, and rebels. Whatever your reasoning, you do not allow those wounded by war to fall through the cracks.

"You will quickly find, however, that many patriots die alongside their loved ones. You must provide, but you must never expect gratitude for the gesture. No, my boy, you will find yourself shrouded with an abundance of scorn, and it may chill you so that you may never feel the warmth of the small gratitudes you receive for your gestures. That is the price we pay in exchange for our peoples' lives. If their loved ones find some small comfort in resentment, then we owe them that, and we cannot be so proud as to expect forgiveness. That is the price we pay, Eliliweth, and it will never be enough to pay the debt."

They sat in silence for a few long moments. Only the candle upon the table made any sound, occasionally releasing a gentle hiss as the flame stirred. It was the most tragic and profound thing Eliliweth had ever heard the king say, and in that instant, Bartholomew had solidified the half-elf's deepest respect. The monarch could be blustery, stubborn, and downright irritable at times, but at that moment Eliliweth realized why he was ruler of the Glen Dale.

"I should have been out there," Bartholomew whispered.

"Do not let that decision weigh your heart with regret, Your Majesty," Eliliweth answered just softly. "This kingdom needs your leadership. I inspected our walls the day after our victory. Your life would have been in great danger, as you said."

"But it could not keep my beloved Aven from defending her people," Bartholomew murmured. "As I've always said, she's her mother's daughter."

They sat in silence again for a brief moment. Eliliweth allowed the king a few minutes to reflect on his late queen, but after a while, he could no longer restrain himself from asking what he wished to. He took a drink from his mug and looked over at the king. "What was done with the orc bodies?"

"Hm?" Bartholomew answered, frowning as his memories were dispelled from his thoughts. "The orc bodies? I had them burned, but had thirty heads removed from their shoulders. When Strigson has our patrol routes settled and all of the farmers escorted back to their homesteads, I am going to have riders put their ugly faces on pikes and stake them up around the border of the Hordelands. We'll remind those savages to keep to their dung-filled prairie lands."

Just because something does not speak, that does not mean it isn't saying anything, Eliliweth remembered. The silent speech of the beheaded was indeed powerful. "What if we decided against that?" he asked, making sure to keep his tone curious and light as opposed to condemning or judgmental.

"Why would we?" Bartholomew grunted. "Orcs are raiders and thieves by nature. They're going to venture out of the Hordelands. The severed heads will remind them what awaits them if they enter the Glen Dale once more."

"They *are* going to leave the Hordelands, at some point," Eliliweth answered carefully. "And whether or not we post their skulls around their borders, they will eventually wander into our territory once again. So what happens when they do? Do we kill them again, lose men of our own in the process, and stake their heads outside their lands once more?"

"Yes," Bartholomew grunted indignantly. The sober tone had vanished from his voice. "Why would we do anything different?"

"Because we *don't* do anything different when it involves the orcs, Your Majesty," Eliliweth said patiently. "Hear me out. What if, when our patrols encounter another orc raiding party, instead of killing them all off and making examples of their corpses, we give them the opportunity to earn their freedom?"

"Earn their freedom!?" Bartholomew snorted, brow furrowing deeply. He looked at Eliliweth as though the half-elf had suggested they invite them over for their victory banquet. "Have you gone mad, Eliliweth?"

"I don't mean just let them go," Eliliweth said, again having to make an effort to keep his voice patient. "Let's say we placed them in camps. We supervise them and set rules, try to establish some order first."

"Sounds like keeping glorified prisoners," Bartholomew grumbled, still frowning at the half-elf shrewdly.

"And it would be, at first," Eliliweth said, leaning forward earnestly. "But maybe, over time, we could...you know, begin to form an understanding. Maybe even respect. And maybe, with enough work, we could one day call the orcs our neighbors."

"*Neighbors!?*" Bartholomew said incredulously, chin wagging as he shook his head. "By the gods, Eliliweth, what has gotten into your head? Nobody in recorded history has ever viewed the orcs as *neighbors*. The closest thing to diplomatic relations mankind has ever had with those brutes are contracts for killing. That's all."

"Because nobody has ever *tried* it, Your Majesty!" Eliliweth said urgingly. "Nobody! Since the days of the first men, we've fought with the orcs. Why? Where is the written rule stating that man and orc are to be mortal enemies until the end of time?"

"I believe it lies in the teachings of Gapinon the Destroyer," Bartholomew answered. "The worship of the demon god belongs to the orcs, Eliliweth."

"I know. But if you think about it, is there any orc in the Hordelands who has reason not to worship the Destroyer? That's part of their culture. But if we were to show them a different way of life, perhaps some of them would see the benefit of *not* utilizing blood sacrifices. And, when we would theoretically release them back to the Hordelands, they could carry those ideas with them! Ideas, Your Majesty, can be stronger than weapons."

"This sounds like a great deal of time and resources, my boy," Bartholomew said between another sip of wine.

"So why not petition our neighbors and allies?" Eliliweth asked. "The orcish threat is present all across the Aariad, in one way or another. We have a common interest in eliminating this threat, and everyone knows the Hordelands can't be conquered. The land is unforgiving, as is the wildlife, and there are diseases in the water that the orcs are immune to but we are not. If we can establish an agreement with our neighbors on how to contain them, the burden will be lighter and the reward will be beneficial to everyone involved."

Bartholomew heaved a great sigh, setting his free hand down upon his knee as the other fed him another drink of wine. He swirled the contents around as he considered the half-elf's words. "You've given this a lot of thought, haven't you?" the king asked.

"I have, my liege."

"I can make no promises," Bartholomew answered after another sip. He looked over at the half-elf. "By the gods, if I weren't drunk I might very well tell you to go jump in a lake. Truly, I don't know if the orcs have the capacity to change their ways of life. And I *really* don't know if any of our neighbors would even entertain this idea of yours. But...if there's any chance of success, I suppose I see the merits. That young wisdom of yours is unafraid to challenge what we've always assumed, I see. And so I will consider it. Again, no promises. But I will give it serious thought. Fair?"

"Fair," Eliliweth said with a hopeful smile.

"Eliliweth," Bartholomew said as he poured more wine into both of their vessels. He set the bottle back down on the table and lifted his goblet. "Cheers to your successful Trials. I have no doubt that what you learned there had some part to play in this insanity you speak of. Cheers to our victory over Grathul Heavyhand. And cheers to many more years of prosperity for our kingdom. Long live the Glen Dale." Eliliweth's smiled widened as he reached his mug out, gently tapping it against the king's goblet.

"Long live the Glen Dale."

Chapter Thirty-Five

There was no light in the cellar room that made up Terodar Soul-render's quarters. The demon had not lit any candles. He only sat cross-legged in the middle of the room upon a thin rug. Malice swirled in the air like a hanging mist, rolling off of his slender body as he sat with his head hunched.

Though he could not see them, he could feel their presence as they slid over one another, shifting and dancing between his outstretched fingers. He wasn't sure why he had brought the metal plates down into his room, nor did he have the slightest notion as to why he was practicing the mundane exercise. He had spent the last several days so consumed with blind rage that his instincts seemed to randomly fixate on whatever was available, desperately channeling his anger just to keep every capillary in his body from bursting. Just three days before, he had spent hours staring at a window on the first floor as the snowflakes had melted on the glass under the rays of the sun, cataloging every bead of moisture that trailed down to the outside pane, obsessively noting the patterns the miniature rivers traveled in. All to keep himself from erupting in rage.

And so he practiced hovering the plates, rotating them in space, sliding them over one another. He couldn't truly keep his irate thoughts from haunting his conscience, but he could numb their effect on him with the droll activities.

He'd been so foolish. How could he have been so foolish? Cado-haden had marched into this same room and given him the freedom of choice. So why had he ventured out to fight alongside the wretch-ed humans? He remembered telling himself at the time that it was an excuse to kill, that it had been far too long since he'd taken a life. So what was the strange feeling tugging at his chest, leading him out of the Mage House door and to the north wall? Was it guilt? Could it even have been such a feeling? Demonkin were well aware of the emotion; it was pivotal to understand it as a *roaq* demon, for men with guilty hearts were so much easier to manipulate. He'd toyed with Ca-dohaden's conscience on more than one occasion. Could the boy have actually invoked such emotion from him?

The plates began to move faster between his fingers as he slowly shook his horned head. No, of course not. He had simply been tricked by the paladin. It was a humiliating admission, but it had to be true. Cadohaden had challenged him to remain put, and Terodar's defiant nature had lured him out to do his bidding unwittingly. What a waste of time. The bastard should have just ordered him out there if that's really what he wanted.

And what good did it do? Was he any closer to achieving 'redemp-tion'? He'd done what Cadohaden considered the right thing to do by making his way out onto the battlefield, to give that arrogant Strigson Ganisalp an opening to end Grathul's life. He didn't care one way or another what the dullards of the Glen Bailey thought of him, but by definition, he had aided them in their defense. And what sort of grati-tude was he gifted with? Burning, searing, agonizing holy energy from the Monastery's priests-in-armor. There were no congratulations or thanks for Terodar Soulrender. There were no bronze stars for the de-mon prisoner. Like a dog, he'd been kicked back into his kennel.

Faster and faster the plates spun as his pulse quickened, lip curl-ing in fury. The stupid simpletons and their wide, dimwitted eyes. He had wanted to gouge each one of them out with his fingertips as Ben-ton had lead him back to his cage on his invisible leash. He suddenly found himself furious with his god, the Destroyer. The longer he re-mained under The Pact, the deeper his resentment rooted in his burn-ing heart. What sense did it make to keep him chained to Cadohaden's will? Where was the sense in it all in the first place? He could have easily ended the troublesome bastard's life even with an arrow stuck between his ribs. What kind of god of destruction regulated such frivolities? He wanted to meditate and pray, to send words of curses and spite to Gapinon, to tell him just what he thought of the Destroyer's petty edicts, but he did not want to risk being trapped under Cadohaden's command any longer than necessary. It just might break him.

Terodar's teeth clenched together. The spinning plates suddenly pressed together, stacked perfectly on top of one another. A vein bulged in the demon's pallid forehead as smoke suddenly started to curl around the edges of the discs. They began to glow with red heat as the edges fused together. As the demon's hands began to shake, the plates started to fold inward, curling and bending towards the center as the glowing became brighter, the heat rolling off the metal. He could feel it on his palms. It was beginning to cause him pain, but he embraced it, refusing to move his hands as he folded the plates into a crushed metal coal.

Finally, with a low snarl, he spread his arms to the side, opening his palms. The glowing chunk fell to the floor, sparks springing from it as it landed on the edge of the rug the demon was sitting on. Flame immediately leaped from the cloth, surrounding the coal as it slowly began to spread to each side. Smoke coiled upward, caressing Terodar's nose. He would have to extinguish the flames shortly, for the last thing he wanted was any more attention from the worm Benton that night. But he wanted to watch a little longer, to savor the sight of the flame consuming the fabric of the rug. He imagined all of them, coated in a wreath of fire: Cadohaden, Benton, Ecila, every one of the slack-jawed dolts in their wretched kingdom, and even his own god. He didn't know how. He couldn't say when. But he would make a plan for every one of them. A terrible smile finally crossed his face as he slowly waved his hand over the growing flames, dismissing them with a harsh sighing sound, curling smoke left in their wake, rolling off the edges of the singed rug as the room was once again enshrouded in darkness.

They were all going to pay.

Epilogue

The sun glistened in the sky, warping the air of Chai'Rin in shimmering patterns above the sand. Even by the desert city's standards, it was an oppressively hot day. Tacypoc pushed his dry tongue against the roof of his mouth, trying to stimulate some saliva. Silently, he wondered if he had enough time to seek out a drink of water. There was a temple nearby. In exchange for a few words of prayer, the Sandspeakers would usually offer a clay cup to drink from. He decided against it, however, as he continued on his way through the city, his ash staff in his grip as the bottom end sunk into the sand below with every pace. He was a sandmorph, and had less of a need for hydration than his cousins, the watermorphs. With a drought gripping the desert lands, he would have to embrace his discipline and restraint for a little longer. Besides, Sandspeaker Ruhelu was expecting him. If Tacypoc dawdled on his way to see him, the wizened old morph would surely know.

He doesn't know. He couldn't possibly know. We were careful, the sandmorph thought to himself as a gust of wind cut its way through the city, coiling around the buildings, carrying grains of sand along with it. Tacypoc squinted his eyes to shield them, his hand reaching up to hold his white hood firmly against his head. The breeze wasn't nearly as satisfying as he'd hoped. It was like a giant with hot, sultry breath had leaned over Chai'Rin and exhaled.

The sandmorph finally approached Ruhelu's favored meditation spot, a clay pillar gazebo sculpted to look like four thick plant vines, coiling outward before converging at the top, a flower sprouting from the end of each to form the roof. There were white sheets hung from the pillars, granting some reprieve from the sun's harsh rays. There, sitting cross-legged in the middle of the gazebo, was Sandspeaker Ruhelu. His body was thin, bordering on frail, his skin clinging to his bones like sunbaked leather. Patches of white hair clung to the back of his scalp, and there were dark bags under his closed eyes. He wore only a few white sheets, hanging from his body much like the ones suspended from the gazebo pillars. As Tacypoc approached, he saw a thin trail of sand, slowly snaking around Ruhelu in a patient orbit as he meditated. Tacypoc stepped into the gazebo, his staff tapping gently against the platform of the floor.

"Sit facing me, Tacypoc," Ruhelu murmured without opening his eyes, though the serpent of sand twisting around him suddenly lifted into the air, scattering to the winds as another rogue breeze passed through, just as sweltering as the last one. Obediently, Tacypoc rested his staff on the ground, sitting in mirrored fashion to the Sandspeaker, crossing his legs as he placed his palms on his knees. He swallowed again as he stared forward, rolling his tongue against the roof of his mouth again. Mother Earth, could he use a drink.

"It's been over a week since you've come to visit me, Tacypoc. I don't usually have to send someone to come find you," Ruhelu said. The Sandspeaker's eyes remained closed, though Tacypoc could see the old morph's eyes moving under his lids. It was unnerving.

"Apologies, Sandspeaker," Tacypoc answered quietly. "Everyone's needed a helping hand since the drought settled in."

"That they have," Ruhelu answered. "It's been a long time since we've had to rely on the harvesting of cacti. Our oases continue to dry up?"

"They do," Tacypoc answered. He felt himself begin to relax as the conversation carried on. This meeting with the Sandspeaker didn't appear to be what he'd feared it would. "The Lady Loop and the *Ran'alisah* are nearly spent. We've been able to dig for a little more, but it won't last."

"The sands will show us the way," Ruhelu said cryptically. Tacypoc began to fidget in his sitting position. The Sandspeaker hadn't opened his eyes yet, and despite the normalcy of their conversation, it was an unusual behavior even for Ruhelu.

"There isn't anything we can do, Sandspeaker?" Tacypoc asked, silently pleading for the desert oracle to open his damned eyes already. "We're the *Ran'allakah's* chosen. Can't our watermorphs call forth the rain? Isn't there anything more we can do than simply pray to Mother Earth?"

"Our sacred lands aren't so easily influenced, Tacypoc. They *are* the Mother Earth. The prayers of our watermorphs are our calling for the rains," Ruhelu answered patiently. "But our situation becomes more serious with every passing day. The other Sandspeakers and I have discussed what can be done to cure this ailment. We have an idea. It will be no small task, and the chances of success will be admittedly slim. But we have all listened to the wind and spoken with the sands at great length, and we fear that this drought will not lift of its own accord for quite some time. Longer than our people can withstand."

"What is it?" Tacypoc asked, leaning forward curiously, briefly forgetting his discomfort over Ruhelu's closed eyes.

"The Eternity Branch," the Sandspeaker answered. "The only remnant left from the first tree planted by our Mother Earth that was desecrated during the Great War. If there is a relic that will bring balance to our land, we believe that is the one."

Tacypoc frowned. "Nobody's seen the Eternity Branch since the days of the first men. Should we rest our hopes on a relic that could very well be a myth? Do we have any notion of where it might be?"

"Fair questions, and ones I asked myself when the idea was proposed," Ruhelu said. "For the past five nights, I've had Sirah, Poetel, Lirianne, and Octavia all combing through our archive of scrolls for any kind of reference to the Eternity Branch."

"Lirianne?" Tacypoc asked in surprise. He snapped his jaw shut, his tanned skin paling as he realized his mistake. He should have known better. He should have seen that coming. The Sandspeaker had lured him right into the trap. Ruhelu's eyes finally opened, his rheumy gaze settling on Tacypoc.

"You don't believe it's possible that Lirianne has been aiding in research for the past five nights, Tacypoc?" the Sandspeaker questioned. His stare was unflinching. "Why would that be?"

"Because...I..." Tacypoc stammered, his teeth gritting in frustration at his own foolishness. He was trapped now. There wasn't any point in denying anything. "Because I was with her, Sandspeaker."

"I see," Ruhelu said evenly. "It's been some time since the Summer Solstice ended. You're aware of this, right?"

"Yes, Sandspeaker," Tacypoc answered, his gaze falling away from old morph's. In Chai'Rin, it was customary to mate only two days out of the year, during the Summer and Winter Solstice. The act was generally seen as unnecessary, for morph creatures weren't conceived in the same manner as humans or their cousin races. Rather than being grown in a womb, on the rare occasion that an elderly morph passed away, new life would be born from the elements with the power of the *Ran'allakah*. The urge to mate was still ingrained in each morph, however, as part of the *Ran'allakah's* nature, for she had been Mother Earth's lover ages ago. Citizens of Chai'Rin were expected to practice discipline, to rein in their primal urges so that they would not be consumed by it. The Solstice celebrations were intended to grant release, however, and celebrate that aspect of their being. Mating outside of the Solstices was not unheard of, but if the keen Sandspeakers became aware of it, punishment in the form of service was assigned to the offenders.

"Five nights of violating our ancient laws, Tacypoc?"

"Just…just four, Sandspeaker," Tacypoc muttered shamefully.

"Need I remind you why these laws exist, Tacypoc?" Ruhelu asked. Tacypoc suddenly wished the Sandspeaker would close his eyes again.

"No, Sandspeaker," Tacypoc answered. "The laws exist to maintain our balance between consciousness and instinct. If we don't preserve that balance, we become slaves to our nature."

"Correct," Ruhelu answered, his chin tilting up ever so slightly. "We've decided on your punishment, the other Sandspeakers and I."

Already? Tacypoc thought. By the *Ran'allakah*, he and Lirianne weren't nearly as careful as they thought they were, if the Sandspeakers were already so sure of his guilt. "And I will accept it," the sandmorph answered.

"We did research the Eternity Branch, and found nothing that would point us in any direction," the Sandspeaker said, drawing a puzzled frown from Tacypoc as Ruhelu seemingly changed the subject abruptly. "And so I have spoken to the sands at great length, beseeching them for guidance. They have finally whispered to me a direction, a hidden trail on the path of fate. 'The Rebels of the Dale,' they whisper to me, but no more than that.

"After speaking with the other Sandspeakers, there is only one place we believe the sands could be referencing: the land of the Glen Dale. We've received letters from the Glen Bailey, its capital city. They wish to get to know us, to learn more of Chai'Rin. We've had no reason to expose our culture to them, Tacypoc, until now. You will travel to the Glen Bailey. You will get to know its people. You will be our eyes and ears."

Tacypoc's eyes widened as he listened. He'd only ventured outside the desert of Chai'Rin a handful of times, and never as far as the land of the Glen Dale. "Should I…should I ask about the Eternity Branch? How am I to explain myself?"

"No," Ruhelu answered. "We cannot know who we can trust outside our people. You will only say that Chai'Rin has an interest in developing new relations with the Glen Bailey. Explain that you wish to observe their culture, to learn more about them. Given the volume of correspondence we've received from their king, I would be shocked by any resistance to your requests. Learn what you can, but stay vigilant for these Rebels that the sands speak of. They hold the key to Chai'Rin's survival. Can you do this, Tacypoc?"

Even if he didn't believe he could, the sandmorph was sure he didn't have a choice. "I can, Sandspeaker."

"Good," Ruhelu said. Slowly, the Sandspeaker's eyelids drifted shut once again. "Gather your things, then, and make your way west with haste. You will hear from us when it is time to return to Chai'Rin."

Tacypoc stood up, grabbing his ash staff and using it to hoist himself back to his feet. An eager fire burned in his stomach. He'd been commanded to do a great deal of things by the Sandspeakers. He'd never imagined that one of them would be an adventure out west.

"And Tacypoc," Ruhelu said in a cautious tone. "You may say your farewells to Lirianne on your way out. But maintain your discipline this time, if you would. I don't think I need to explain to you the leniency of this punishment."

"Understood, Sandspeaker," Tacypoc answered. "Farewell."

He turned away and stepped out of the gazebo. He knew he shouldn't expend the extra energy to transform, but his excitement got the better of him. His entire form began to shift, his skin becoming granulated as his whole body rapidly dissolved into a serpentine trail of sand. Twisting his way through the desert city's streets, Tacypoc raced towards the promise of destiny. The Glen Dale awaited him.

Coming soon...

The Dark Revolution

The Gunnysack Wars began in Aitkin, MN. While its members now reside both in their home state and beyond, they can occasionally be found wandering the streets of the Minnesota Renaissance Festival in Shakopee, often dressed as their heroes from the Glen Dale.

www.ingramcontent.com/pod-product-compliance
Lightning Source LLC
Chambersburg PA
CBHW060211030726
47499CB00004B/999